Mrs. Bundle's Dog Days of Summer:

A Case of Artful Arson

Allison Cesario Paton

P-3-14

The secret is in *journey!*

Allison C. Paton

Other books in the Mrs. Bundle Mystery Series:

Mrs. Bundle Takes a Hike:
The Case of the Singing Swans (#1)

Mrs. Bundle's Maine Vacation:
Subterfuge at the Seashore (#3)

Mrs. Bundle's Hair-Raising Adventures:
Peril on Skitchewaug Mountain
and other Tales of Mystery (#4)

Mrs. Bundle's Midnight Mystery:
The Case of the Springfield Shock Jock (#5)

© 2007 by Bundle Publishing. All rights reserved.
Design: Univoice, Portland, Maine
Illustrations: Donna Stackhouse Illustration and Design
ISBN 10: 0-9790270-1-2ISBN 13: 978-0-9790270-1-7

The author is a member of
Sisters in Crime, Mystery Writers of America

*for more information about the
Mrs. Bundle series, please contact*

Bundle Publishing
bundlepublishing@yahoo.com
bundlepublishing@gmail.com
www.mrsbundle.com

This book is dedicated
to the art of love and the love of art;
to loving life in its simplest and purest state
and to the active pursuit of
ageless, requited love.

GRASSHOPPER

DOC DOTS

NORTH

TATTLE RIDGE

← TO LUDLOW

TUSOM

NORTH PILLSON CORNERS

ANDERSEN FARM

"OKEMO"

20 MILE STREAM

OLD GRANITE SWIMMING HOLE

CORNERS

CASCADING WATERFALL

PILLSON PUBLIC LIBRARY

← TO PERKINSVILLE

HARPER'S FEED STORE

GREEN HOUSE

THE ART CO-OP

PILLSON ELEMENTARY SCHOOL

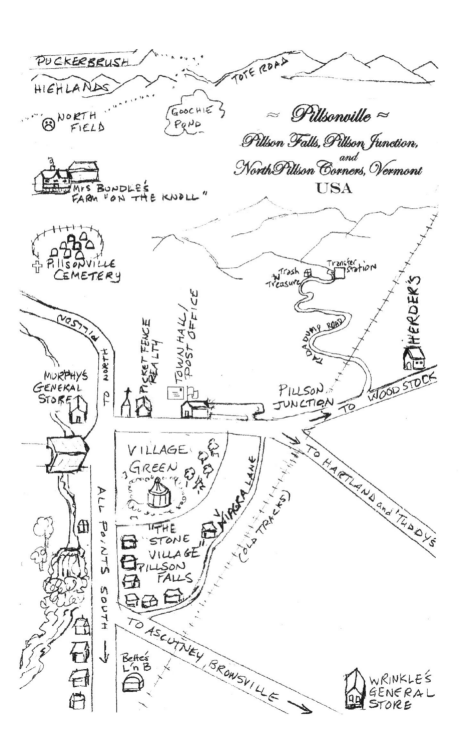

Acknowledgements

To Janice Parkinson Tucker, whose invaluable advice and guidance have been instrumental in my success in not just one career, but two.

To Sam Benoit, neighbor and friend, talented in many ways whose zest for life and expertise in one unusual area were helpful in shaping a section of the storyline.

To Kevin Forrest, intelligent and witty individual whose unique style as Editor of the *Vermont Standard* sets that newspaper well above most and whose affection for his native state (and its people) is apparent to all who admire him.

To Mary Cesario: mother, friend for life, and avid reader, whose ongoing encouragement, affection, and keen insight are always of great value to me.

"And think not, you can direct the course of love,
   for love, if it finds you worthy, directs
   your course...
Love has no other desire but to fulfill itself...
To melt and be like a running brook
   that sings its melody to the night...
To wake at dawn with a winged heart and give
   thanks for another day of loving."

— KAHLIL GIBRAN
The Prophet, 1923

Part I:
JULY

Chapter One

Hot, Hot, Hot

Mrs. Bundle was livid.

Patience was not her strong suit, and she had waited, good-naturedly at first, then with ever-growing agitation, for well over an hour.

An hour!

"Where *on earth* could he be?" she fumed. She blew out her breath, making a huffing sound of disgust. Her usually calm, unruffled disposition had been pushed to the limit.

She thought to herself, *This isn't like me at all! Snap out of it!*

She fidgeted uneasily, blaming it on in the incredible heat that engulfed every room like the slippery tentacles of an octopus, heat that seemed to be reaching in and suffocating every square inch of her home, heat which was, she acknowledged with vexation, near intolerable!

She blew out air again, this time straight upward past her barely-moist top lip, cooling her brow and gently lifting the damp tendrils of hair that escaped from the crown of her heavily braided head. The stiflingly muggy summer air surrounded her like a blistering torture chamber. *Was there ever going to be any relief*, she wondered? The knowledge that everyone in Pillson was in the same boat—like it or lump it at this point—didn't give her one scintilla of comfort.

Cracker languished on the chair beside her, motionless, his body a dead weight—a sweltering, drooping feline carcass.

Nope, Cracker cat-thought, throwing in his two cents for what it was worth, *not one flaming iota of relief.*

Mrs. Bundle fanned her face, the nostrils of her elegant nose flaring as she took another halfhearted sip of the now-lukewarm lemonade. "Oh, Lord, help me!" She drew in the sultry atmosphere in a measured breath and, like an exhausted set of bagpipes, let loose the contents of her lungs with a pathetic, "Hooo-ooo..."

In rhythmic measured breaths, she counted, "One, *one-thousand*...whew! *Two*-one-thousand, *oh-I-just-don't-know-how-I'm-going-to-get-everything done...Three*-one-thousand, *but-I'm-not-going-to-think-about-it...Fou—rrr* one-thou-ou-ou-sand...UGH!" She quit abruptly, realizing her noble attempt wasn't worth the effort in this heat.

With all patience having finally taken leave like a fugitive in the night, she raised her voice in an ear-splitting curse. "Ohh! Cat's *granny!*"

Cracker's supine body twitched, his mistress' shriek cutting through the dead air like a knife. He burrowed his head deeper into the soft cushion and, as inconspicuously as possible, covered his feathery, pointed ears with his paws.

"*Hmmphh!*" A sound rumbled from Mrs. Bundle's throat, a strong pronouncement, though wordless, resonating with full force, gaining momentum as it rolled out into the empty back yard, past the garden and beyond, into the apple orchard. "*HMMPHHH!* I suspect he's not coming!"

Oh, yes! Cracker agreed, cat-thinking, *if anyone had an axe to grind, she was entitled, to be sure. Certainly, her patience had been tried on a number of occasions with this individual, no doubt about it!*

"All summer long!" she cried, hands outstretched.

Who wouldn't be frustrated? he cat-empathized, *with your 'tolerance meter' maxed to the limit?*

Thoughts swirling, she tapped her fingers on the table, "And, on top of it all, it doesn't appear to matter to him, *and* with so very little time left!" Her eyes searched past the kitchen curtain out the window and she massaged her hands together in exasperation, kneading her fingers vigorously.

Some...men! Cracker cat-thought with disdain, knowing most women would be ready, at this point, to throw in the towel—but they weren't his companion, were they?

"Dang! That's it!" Her mind, somewhat clouded with frustration, sent her into motion. The snap decision—an action not uncommon to her impetuous nature—propelled her as she scribbled a quick note on the small pad of paper on the kitchen counter, tore off the page (a bit over-dramatically, Cracker thought) and hastily attached it to the back screen door with a pushpin.

"*Waited for an hour,*" she read aloud, "*back soon as I cool off!*"

She pushed the pin in extra hard for final emphasis and huffed once again, "There! So much for *your...* 'very important meeting,' Mr..." she struggled to find some good name-calling relief, "...Pain-in-the-neck!"

She sniffed, distinctly piqued and fully indulging herself in this rare opportunity for venting. *So inconsiderate!* Couldn't he have at least made the obligatory, "*I'm-sorry-I-can't make-it*" or "*I'm-going-to-be-late*" phone call? She sniffed once more, attempting to shrug it off, then paused as a small scrap of doubt entered her mind.

It was *quite* possible he'd had an emergency of some sort, or, she conjectured with growing concern, he might even have been taken ill at the last minute...

Oh, Heavens!

She trotted back inside the house, picked up the hall phone, and tried his line once more, this time more worried than vexed.

*Ring...ring...ring....*no answer! At that moment, all the angst and worry that she had internalized the last month seized up inside her and stayed caught in her throat; tears of frustration welled up in her eyes. She hung up the phone. She had to admit it. At this point, "overwhelmed" didn't even half-describe the emotion she was feeling.

She snatched her battered straw hat from the back shed wall hook and dashed out of the farmhouse, barely noticing her loyal best mate following behind as best he could. She moved silently and briskly out into the back yard, past the limp gardens which only still held the heartiest of the perennials, through the maze of gnarled apple trees, and up the sloping hill toward the expansive backland of her property.

The late afternoon sun beat down relentlessly. She plopped the large-brimmed hat squarely on her generously plaited head of hair and tied the frayed ribbed under her chin, squinting into the distance.

The sun was so bright she could just barely distinguish the faraway tree line — a good quarter mile away as the crow flies — and where the forest's deep shade would be a welcome respite. Quickly changing direction, she turned away from the blinding sun. She hiked downward from the knoll resolutely, heading north toward the Andersen's, then traversed upward again into the open field, tramping through the high, parched grass.

"*Ooooh!* This intolerable heat!" It was hotter than she'd ever remembered it to be in Vermont. Free to say whatever she wanted in this vast field, she let loose, fussing and declaring her woes in mumbles and spurts to the empty pasture. "Gaw! I haven't been this upset…in a dog's age!"

Cracker, knowing when to give her space, followed safely to her rear. He jumped and wiggled his way through the warm, dry meadow grass, grasshoppers and crickets flying every which way as his soft feet invaded their miniature personal space. The late-July grass was so high now that he had trouble seeing where his companion was. He jumped up frenetically, his eyes searching, finally finding her in the distance. *Hey, there,* he cat-thought, *Hang on! Would you wait up, please?*

Totally distracted, Mrs. Bundle trudged forward in private thought. No doubt, she realized, she had hit her limit. Weeks of worry and hard work had taken its toll. Yes, it was true. Even *she*, finally, had had enough!

The past weeks of planning, frustration, and anticipation had finally caught up with her — and this blasted endless heat wave surely didn't help things. *The Dog Days of Summer! Hah!* she thought, harrumphing again cynically.

Head down and slogging along rhythmically to the sound of the distant whirring of farm machinery, her pent-up anger gradually dissipated to minor annoyance and, after a few minutes, she stopped to catch her breath. In the meantime, Cracker hopped, slithered, and fairly leapt through the tall grass, straining to reach her but ever watchful (in a marvelous dramatization as a fearless African safari hunter) of the many pretend lions, tigers, and dangerous jungle beasts.

Finally, the heat consumed him, too, and he slowed to a snail's pace. Mrs. Bundle was, by now, a fair distance ahead of him, but she was no longer in motion. The sides of his body heaved as he pushed through the tall grass and eventually came within a few feet of her. Mustering all his cat-thinking abilities and wanting his mistress to notice him, he cat-thought loudly, *Hey! Dear lady, **atencion!** Remember me? (Puff, puff...) Might you possibly...be inclined...to kindly...(puff, puff, pant)... slow...(huff, puff, puff)...down?* He stopped, drew in another parched, yet indignant, cat breath, and meowed loudly, but she didn't hear him.

Still enmeshed in her quiet world, Mrs. Bundle sputtered, "Well, now!" She blew out a large breath. "*Whew!*" Looking skyward, she cleared her throat briskly. It was still a beautiful, bright day, even with the heat; every natural thing around her was in its glory.

"*Oka-ay...*" she sighed, inhaled, and then, pushing her palms downward and raising her shoulders, she blew the air from her swelled lungs. "Let's all *calmmmm... dow-nnn...*" The low, slow tones seemed to soothe her.

By then, Cracker had reached her side, his small ebony body twisting uncomfortably in the overly long grass whose dry stalks scratched relentlessly at his body.

Blasted itchy stuff! He sneezed delicately...*Ah-choo!* His nose gave an involuntary twitch and he sneezed once more, clearing the fog of ragweed dust in his princely cat head. Issuing an emphatic "*Ph-Ph-Phffffttt!*" he gave a vigorous shake to his head and sneezed once again.

Mrs. Bundle looked down at Cracker in surprise. "Why, C-C! Hi there, old friend! Dear, dear, cat-buddy, was I going too fast for you?"

He wriggled his body nearer toward hers, his elegant coal-black head giving a slight nod, a forgiving, knowing look in his lozenge-shaped eyes.

"I'm *so* sorry. I've been in my own world, a bit of a 'pity party', that's what I've been having!" She smiled kindly down at him. "But I'm better now, Cracker."

Okay, good, cool down, he cat-thought, *it'll be all right, I guarantee!* Everyone knew what a trial the last month had been; he didn't need to remind *her,* that was for sure. *Dear lady, you can't let things get to you; it's just not worth getting this upset. I say keep doing what you're doing. Why, look at that beautiful world out there!*

She watched as he scratched at his smooth, sable brow and pushed his face downward, rubbing his furry head into the ground, thus brushing away the bits of straw and fluff that had accumulated. He sneezed one more time (longer and a tad less delicately than before) *Ahhhchoooo—pppppppphhhhhhhtttt!* and then, with his signature dramatic aplomb, shook his little solid body violently from head-to-toe—and then back again the other way for good measure!

Mrs. Bundle couldn't help but give a hoot of amusement. She laughed at her little partner, bending down and giving his sleek body a few light, affectionate pats. "I ask you, Cracker! What the heck have I been doing, getting so upset? Especially about things I cannot change! Crackerjax, I love you! Why sweat the small stuff? That's what we always say, right?"

His body wiggled under her tickling touch, and he rubbed affectionately against her ankle. *Right! Now, c'mon, let's have some fun!*

Thereupon, together, as a team, they hiked along at a much more leisurely pace and slowly entered what everyone called "Andersen's Meadow." They both loved this field, especially today; the open space was breathtakingly pristine and natural, with a plethora of butterflies, birds, and colorful wildflowers interspersed amidst fresh grass. In the distance was a dramatic backdrop; to the far north loomed Tattle Ridge, daunting in winter, but harmless and beautiful during this summer season, and unseen beyond, in the Highlands, was "Old Man Boulder."

Mrs. Bundle took in more long, soothing breaths of the clean Vermont air.

Before she knew it, she was humming to herself, lost in the beauty of a summer afternoon's beauty.

As they tramped through the meadow and across the large expanse of the Andersen back farmland, they changed direction once more, heading toward the welcoming dark forest and its cool shade at the far field perimeter. Further beyond, past the tree line and deeper into the woods, were the winding woodland trails that traversed in a southerly direction toward Goochie Pond and further still, acres and acres of beautifully untouched land containing hundreds of remote back lanes and winding, countrified, Class IV dirt roads that comprised their little world.

It felt good to walk through this lovely vastness of wild flowers, and her humming became louder, and merry lyrics were added; her voice became downright cheerful! No matter that she was a bit off-key; this childhood ditty was a particular favorite and she sang every word, surprised that she could remember, *"The year's at the spring, and day's at the morn, morning's at seven, the hillside's dew pearled, The lark's on his wing, the snail's on the thorn, God's in his heaven, All's right…all's right with the world!"* Trilling like a warbler, she became lost in her song. How lucky she was to live in her world! She hiked along for a time, oblivious to anything other than the surrounding peace and beauty.

After awhile, she looked up from her reverie. In the distant meadow acreage, visible to the naked eye, sat Walter Andersen's old John Deere tractor; to that was hooked the large, old, hay baler. Hefty circular buns of golden hay dotted the field like butterscotch bonbons against the background of a large swathe of neatly cut meadow grass.

Hmm, she surmised, *Walter and the boys must be around somewhere.* She searched for them expectantly, squinting once more through the incredibly bright sunlight. Even at mid-afternoon light now, the sun was still overwhelmingly dazzling, and she shielded her eyes with the back of her hand. They were nowhere in sight, but a voice rang through the air.

"Hey, Mrs. B! *Mrs. B*!"

She turned and searched the lower pasture for the familiar female voice until she spotted Angie a good measure away, climbing up the valley from the farmhouse in the hollow.

"Angie!" she yelled, "Hi!"

She waved her hand, waiting for the teenager to reach her.

"Hey!" Angie said amiably, "What's up?"

"Oh…we're just getting our exercise, needed a bit of a break, don't you know—me and Cracker, that is to say…," she fumbled a bit with her words, and then said resignedly, "Angie, the honest truth is, I'm getting over a little hissy fit, that's all!" She gave her young friend a slightly embarrassed grin.

"*You*? A hissy fit?" Angie smiled back, incredulous. She pushed the sweat from her brow, sending the golden chestnut-brown wisps that had escaped from her long ponytail up, past her smooth forehead, and behind her ears. A worried look spread over her classic Italian-Scandinavian features, her comely face slightly frowning. "You *never* get upset, Mrs. B! What's going on?"

"Oh, just frustrated! And hot, too! Lots happening with the upcoming plans, you know. *And* all the rest that's going on," she sighed and rolled her eyes in exasperation, "I feel like I'm working for Barnham and Bailey's, you know?" She extended her hands outward and mimed a juggling action, "It's a regular three-ring circus trying to keep everything up in the air and running smoothly!"

Angie gave her an understanding nod. "I hate to say it, but…we told you, didn't we? It's too much work—even for you! You've got a lot on your plate, that's for sure! Jack and I were just discussing it last night. We'll help you more—"

"More than what you're already doing? Why, you and Jack are a godsend to me, dear! No, no!" she waved off Angie's protestations, "Really, dear, that's not necessary. It's all organized, and we're on track. Really, it was just a combination of a lot of little things today, last minute stuff to be readied, calls from committees with lots of questions, and then this afternoon it all came to a head. I'll be fine."

"Well, you just let me know what you need, and I'll be glad to help. Oh, by the way! Are we still on for the LiMB Society tomorrow night? I've checked with everyone. They've all been working their butts off—between summer jobs and having fun, that is! Nothing really like we hoped for—yet! But, we've got a few irons in the fire...I know everyone's looking forward to showing you what they've come up with so far." She looked at Mrs. Bundle with genuine concern. "Are you sure you're up for it? Cuz, if you're too stressed..."

"No, no, we'll get together, for sure. It's just that I got discombobulated by this blasted appointment today that was supposed to happen and didn't. Quite...unsettling. It threw me for a loop, that's all."

"An appointment?"

"Yes—really, it was a no show. Waited for an hour, mind you—and I could have been getting other things done. I've got the proofs ready to go, just have to run them over to Madge before tomorrow. And then I was going over to find out how the show was shaping up and ...well, listen!" She chuckled, "You don't need to hear about all of this detail, now, do you? I've got about a million and one things to get done in the next two weeks and waiting around today just set me off for some strange reason! And then, there's Vincent, too!" Angie nodded sympathetically. "I'm so disappointed—I must admit all that mess is really distressing to me. I just wish—!"

Mrs. Bundle caught herself up, her diatribe halting abruptly as her eyes scanned the field. Distracted for a second, she looked past Angie, out over the expanse.

Angie turned, her eyes following Mrs. Bundle's gaze. "Mrs. B?"

"What—on earth? Angie, move a bit so I can see." She stared around and past Angie, squinting in the direction of the tractor and hay baler.

"What? What is it?" Angie asked cautiously, sensing Mrs. Bundle's change in tone and demeanor. She peered over her shoulder, directly past Mrs. Bundle, into the open, blazing sun; it was blinding. She shaded her eyes, trying to get a better view of the field and woods beyond.

Seconds passed; when Mrs. Bundle finally spoke, her tone was flat and low. "Some-thing's...not right." She took a tentative step toward the big farm rig in the distance. "Look...do you see? Look at the back...the hay baler."

Mrs. Bundle couldn't make out the full image entirely, but the shape on the back of the baler was unusual: larger, darker, and unlike anything remotely resembling hay.

They both edged tentatively a few feet closer, the baler still a good seventy-odd feet away, and Mrs. Bundle stared intently. "I think it's...wait!" First disbelieving, she confirmed with a detached, clinical manner that her eyes and the hot sun weren't playing tricks on her.

There was something unnatural, something totally inconsistent in front of her. *Yes,* she validated, *it was...*she saw...something—other than hay—in the baler. *Something* incongruent was sticking out of the baler's large, swollen mouth, *something* that was abnormally large and terribly real.

"Oh, Lord!" Her voice was barely a whisper.

She moved closer still, never taking her eyes from the scene, and murmured quietly and intensely, "Angie, dear. Don't look."

Their mood, now somber, was like an ominous premonition; the field momentarily darkened as a huge cloud passed over, blocking the sun.

Cracker leapt up in agitation, straining to see from his low position in the high, dry grass. *What, pray,* **was** *it?*

Angie stood motionless. Her attractive mouth had formed a large "O," her well-shaped eyebrows were arched in a cartoon-like question mark and her large, dark brown eyes morphed into even larger flat circles as big as teacup saucers.

She stared around Mrs. Bundle's body, her feet glued to the ground as she finally caught a fleeting peek at the undeniably grotesque scene—and just before Mrs. Bundle turned and placed her own body in front of the teenager, shielding her from viewing any more.

Angie asked in disbelief, "What the—? What is it? *Oooooh!* Ohmigosh—is that a b-b-body? Oh! Oh-mig-gosh! It *is!* Someone's caught up! Daddy? *Dad?*" Staring obliquely, she exclaimed, "Mrs. B! What the h-heck is going o-on?" Stuttering in a mix of bewilderment and horror, her young eyes had taken in the snapshot picture in staccato-like frames.

"Angie!" Pulling her own self together as best she could, Mrs. Bundle declared, "Hold on, Angie. Here—take a deep breath. It's *not* your dad. I can tell you that for certain! Look—look at the shoes! Not work boots, honey, *shoes*! Not your dad's, or your uncle's, and surely not Gumpy's!"

Angie covered her face, nodding.

"Okay?" Mrs. Bundle urged, "I need you to keep your senses. Listen!" She blocked the view further and Angie lowered her head instinctively. "Angie, look at me! Look here," Angie raised her eyes to look deeply into Mrs. Bundle's, "Please girl. Quick! I want you to go find your father! Tell him to bring Uncle Carl up here, too!"

Angie stood as though her feet were bolted to the spot, staring blankly at Mrs. Bundle, and then turned her eyes once again downward to the detail of grass and insect life below.

Mrs. Bundle tugged at the girl to gain her attention. "Angie! Listen! You're…it's a shock, I know. I'm saying, now, though, Angie, run down and get your dad, and tell Gumpy to call Sheriff O'Malley and tell him he better get out here quick! Post haste, mind you! I'll stay right here and wait for them."

Angie blinked, trying to take it all in, her usually golden-olive skin now pale hues of chalky white. She dragged her eyes toward Mrs. Bundle and then reluctantly shook her head, her eyes shifting uncontrollably back at the grisly scene. "No. Nuh-uh. No way! You can't stay here alone!" She pointed, "There's someone…o-over there! I…I *can't* leave you here alone, Mrs. B."

"Yes, you can. It's all right, girl. Really! I'll be fine, I've got Cracker right here, you see?" Ready for anything, Cracker stood at attention beside Mrs. Bundle, who continued gently, "Go on, now. I'll be waiting right here. You run down, now. Time's a-wastin'! Run and get your Dad."

She gave her a push lightly, but firmly, but the girl didn't budge. Mrs. Bundle grabbed her by the shoulders and stared into the girl's intense, dilated eyes, finally catching her full attention and, though the older woman's voice shook slightly, she nodded encouragingly, "You've got to go! It's all right, luv. I'll be okay, right? Go! Now!"

Angie turned and sped off down the hill like a nimble gazelle, her long legs barely touching the ground.

Chapter Two

Death Comes to North Pillson Corners

The gruesome truth set in. Mrs. Bundle's whole being was shaken; her senses were on overload as the horrible scene became too real for her. Scared to death though she was, she was riveted in that one spot, just yards away from the body.

The lifeless man's legs stuck out of the baler. On his feet hung worn, sienna-brown loafers with little whimsical tassels, she noticed, the shoes somehow magically staying on as though super-glued, even though upside down and strangely twisted. His head and upper body were stuffed into the baler like so much lifeless hay. Looking at what was more accurately called the shredder section of the round hay baler (a device meant to effectively shred hay, corn stalks or stubble and built to discharge the shredded stubble into the baler to form a round bale), it was apparent, by all appearances, that the baler's primary function had clinically mutilated his upper frame to shreds, severing all remnants of recognition.

She was repulsed and bit her lip to keep from screaming. It was ghastly; blood had oozed and spurted everywhere, most having dried quickly in the hot sun; flies were swarming and buzzing sluggishly around the gory area. She had a flashing mental image of miniature planes circling King Kong and the Empire State Building in that ancient black-and-white motion picture. Horror and helplessness swept through her, and sadness, too.

Who…?

She wanted to run, to turn tail and let the authorities handle it from this moment on. But she didn't—couldn't, in fact. *I must stay…until they get here. I must. He shouldn't…be abandoned.*

Mrs. Bundle knew he must be dead.

Quite by instinct, she moved closer, stepping carefully, intent on getting a better look. Gingerly, she studied the scene; the interior sharp tines of the baler sadistically encircled the upper torso and his extended arms. The closely-space steel pickup teeth clutched greedily at the man's head, so irreversibly imprisoned as it was in the bloody death grip that it left no doubt. Little bits of leftover straw stuck to the sides of the chamber; their usually pale-yellow shade was tinged with striated bright reds and murky pinks.

Cracker stepped lightly beside her and sniffed at the base of the baler, then delicately moved around the general area, his keen nasal inspection tentative, yet very thorough.

Mrs. Bundle's head was spinning, the torrid sun beating down mercilessly as wild thoughts bounced around in her mind. Feeling somewhat lightheaded, she leaned on the tractor's front fender for support.

Uncontrollably, she slid to the sun-baked ground. She sat back on her haunches, unsteady and in shock, taking in huge breaths as she began to hyperventilate in her agitated state.

The realization had hit her like a ton of bricks.

Good God! She knew those shoes—and those dark pants, too! Usually impeccably pressed but now sadly rumpled, they covered the man's distended legs like two stubby, broken cigars, limbs that were bent unnaturally, awkwardly.

She dared not look again, couldn't bring herself to look any deeper into the baler. *It could surely wait*, she thought, *at least until help arrived. Oh, how he must have suffered*; she shuddered, trying to put the picture out of her mind.

She was cognizant of one cruel fact.

This was no accident.

15

This was murder.

She shivered unnaturally in the sweltering air and the snippet of an old saying popped vicariously into Mrs. Bundle's head. It went something like, *"He who has a thousand friends has not a friend to spare, but he who has one enemy will meet him everywhere."* Whimsically sing-song and incongruent to the scene, the words bounded and bounced back and forth in her busy mind like the old Mitch Miller white dancing ball.

The annoying verse reverberated in her brain like an echo in a cavern, repeating itself over and over, *"…everywhere…not a friend to spare…"* Finally, it stopped abruptly and she was left with the eerie silence of the muted buzzing in the big field.

She felt as though she was going mad. Truth be told, she was scared to death, for the first time worried now about her own safety. *Murder!*

Yes, she acknowledged resignedly, even here it can happen. She looked around her.

Here, in *our little world.*

Detached from her emotions, yet somehow strangely sharpened by the over-stimulation of the present moment, her brain was moving quickly, racing at mach speed, as she fearfully looked past the baler into the distant woods. Something irregular nagged at her mind, facts and questions she couldn't get just yet, overridden by the jumbled mass of jagged nerves and the feverish pitch of her thoughts.

Calm down, she urged herself, *you need to calm down.*

Cracker's body slid neatly, soothingly, against her bare ankles.

Hold on, he cat-thought with as much assurance as he could muster, *hold on, old girl, help is coming.*

What was it? What is it, she asked uneasily. The teasing itch at the back of her mind's eye was as persistent as an irksome, unrelenting gnat as she tried desperately to control and organize her thoughts.

With lost discipline and total abandon, Mrs. Bundle suddenly surrendered to an uncontrollable giggle! Holding her shaking and shivering sides, she giggled again and again. *You're in shock*, she tried to tell herself, but it didn't help. She heard the unhealthy giggles from some faraway, detached place in her mind.

More uncontainable twitters and ludicrous gulps burst forth, born from the comically tragic and one conclusive, undeniable thought that had instantly jumped into her mind.

Delayed consequences of trauma? *Yes,* she assured herself clinically, *a delayed reaction.* Her mind tried to reason, to take over these impulses; she fought to gain control. An anxious Cracker stood by protectively, concerned at his dear mistress's apparent hysteria, but in a flash, the contrary, fickle half-laughs were choked out, stifled, drying to a stop.

She came to terms with her realization.

Oh, Lord help us, it's true! It's really true. It's him. *He's dead.*

Well, her shocked mind numbly expressed the truth, *now you know why he was late.*

The fact of the matter was, she knew it could only have been a brief minute or two, but it seemed an eternity had passed. She collected herself by degrees, methodically inhaling, and then exhaling, and began to calm down. She stroked Cracker's smooth ebony back and drew in quiet, deeply comforting breaths.

There, there, he cat-thought, and waited patiently as she slowly recovered.

And so, as she and Cracker stood watch at the murder scene in those brief minutes before everyone's arrival, her mind couldn't help but wander back to numerous episodes that had taken place the last month. All the controversy, the misfortune: events that had ultimately led to today.

Why, she asked herself, *why?*

First jumpstarting her traumatized mind, then step by step going over the chain of events—so began her recollection of the summer's wild journey, commencing with the first defining incident...

Part II:
LATE JUNE
INTO
JULY

Chapter One

Our Little World

Sitting at the kitchen table with Cracker at her feet, Mrs. Bundle unfolded the *Rutland Daily News*, focused, and reviewed the morning headlines.

"Hmmm….'*Mom Told to Take Down Ribbons*'…" she read aloud, and then looked up at Cracker over her rainbow-colored reading glasses. He licked his already-sleek paws fastidiously.

She made a few quick clicking noises with her tongue.

"Can you believe it, C.C.? What is this world coming to?" (More clicking sounds of obvious disapproval.) She explained, "There's this town in Maine, see? Well, '*they*'—the officials in the town, that is— have told a mother she's in violation for putting up yellow ribbons on telephone poles and the like, on city property! She's supporting her son who's fighting in Iraq, and why not, I ask you! Some bureaucrats believe it's against the city ordinance to," she quoted, "'*display any personal message on public property*.'"

Accentuating her mild disapproval again with more brisk tongue-clicking sounds, she tapped her slippered feet against the rung of the chair for even more emphasis.

Finding no palpable reaction from her breakfast partner, she bent over and stared down at the impassive furry heap and restated with emphasis, "She's got a *son* in *Iraq*."

Cracker yawned, his mouth elegant and long, and stretched his body full-length on the braided rug, the regular post he claimed as "his" in the morning. That was, of course, unless he was curled up in the rocking chair next to the woodstove, a position he preferred during the cold winter months. The thin, dapper line of his prim whiskers neatly framed his pristine wide mouth, accentuated by his delicate ebony ears and his perfectly shaped triangular nose; everything about Cracker seemed to state categorically: *"panache."*

*Yuh. Uh-huh...Oka-ay...*he cat-thought, his half-closed, topaz eyes thin slits, glassy with boredom. *What else have you got there?*

A loud shriek erupted from Mrs. Bundle. *"Oh, no!"*

His head jerked up, eyes immediately alert as the involuntary action made his furred neck sting with pain. Mee-*owwwww!!!*

"Oh, goodness, Cracker! *Tuddy's* is gone!"

Tuddy's? Our Tuddy's? Now fully engaged, Cracker jumped into her lap as she read the bold headline aloud. *"'Hartland's Historic Restaurant Burns Down.'* I—I can't believe it!" She stared intently.

Oh Lord, he cat-thought, *not Tuddy's! A fire, too?* Distractedly, he licked at the buttery toasted crumb morsels that had gathered and stuck on the side edge of the hanging floral tablecloth, and then looked up at her expectantly. *So, what happened?*

She continued on, reading the article aloud:

> The landmark Tuddy's Diner at Hartland Corners burned down late Monday night in a blaze that drew seven area fire departments and also destroyed an attached gas station and floral shop. The building was engulfed in flames when firemen arrived. "Firefighters arrived on the scene at about 10:30 p.m. Monday evening," said Gerard Tudhope, who owns the restaurant, a gas station, and a floral business run by his daughter Viola.
>
> Tuddy's, with the welcome addition of the gas station and florist shop, was a well-known family diner that attracted generations of patrons from southern and central Vermont, along with tourists who came back every year for the distinctive, home-style cooking and atmosphere.

As this edition went to print, only the remnants of dining room walls remained standing, including an original brick wall dating back to the late 1800's. Flames leveled the building; the heat was so intense firemen could only get within 100 feet of the blaze. The roof of the diner and attached building that housed the floral shop had collapsed, along with the small structure that contained the gas station. Luckily, underground gas tanks at the gas station did not erupt in the blaze.

No injuries were reported, although it appears there may be a dog whose life was lost in the fire. He has been missing since the fire was discovered but has yet to be found under the still-smoldering rubble, according to the authorities. A local celebrity of sorts, "Tuddsley" the Golden Retriever, was the official greeter of Tuddy's, meeting patrons at the door. Decked out in his customary red neckerchief, he would customarily arise from his favorite spot beside the entrance and lead patrons to the next available table. Speculation is that the dog perished in the fire and is presumed dead.

"Ger" Tudhope said, "Tuddsley's been with me as long as I can remember. He's always been a favorite with the kids. Hell's bells! Everybody loved him. We're hoping he's in the woods out back somewhere, you know, that maybe the fire spooked him and he ran off. This is a huge loss for our family."

The cause of the fire is, as yet, undetermined, a Hartland firefighter said. The state's fire examiner was expected to begin investigating the blaze later today.

Ger's wife Phoebe told the *Daily News*, "We went home as usual, right up the road there, Monday night, after closing at 8. Got home around 8:30, per usual. Ger let Tuddsley out around 9:30 to do his business. That dog always does the same thing; traveled down to the corners, makes a wide sweep checking on things, and then come home when he pleases. We leave the screen door ajar for him sometimes, just like we did last night, and we went to bed. Now we're wondering what happened. We're sick about the fire, but if our poor dog lost his life there…it's a tragedy."

The fire was called in when a nearby farmer, Axel Conroy, headed out to his barn to check on an ailing heifer, said he heard a loud boom and then saw the flames light up the valley below his hilltop farm.

Towns sending firefighters included Hartland, Woodstock, Pillsonville, Windsor, Quechee, Brownsville, and Ascutney, according to Fire Chief Sandy Simpson.

Phoebe said she was still in shock over the fire, "It just hasn't hit me yet."

Ger Tudhope said he wasn't sure what his plans were at this point. "Hopefully the insurance will kick in. We'll be looking into a temporary trailer to put on site if need be. My daughter's devastated! Just started her floral business less than a year ago and has been going great guns. That diner's been in my family for four generations." Tudhope's great-great grandparents started the restaurant, "right here on this spot with their home cooking fare. Just a little farm stand became a one-room eatery, then a small diner, Gaw! It's all just sinking in! Everything in the restaurant, all lost! Lord! It was irreplaceable."

"Well!" Mrs. Bundle sat back and sighed, "What a shame! Imagine that! Tuddy's, of all places. Burned to the ground! Those poor people."

She pulled her lightweight cotton housecoat around her, its lacy vintage collar tugging at her neck. Accentuating her compassion with more sympathetic clucking tongue sounds, she reached over to the abundant fruit basket and selected a plum, rubbing it on her sleeve. She took a juicy bite.

Yes, Cracker cat-thought, *most unfortunate, very sad. No more succulent leftovers, at least not for while, to be sure.* He closed his yellow eyes and daydreamed. *Doggie bags…*such a pitifully unsophisticated term, he cat-postulated. *Oh, well.* He licked at his already shining coal-black coat absentmindedly. Further cat-postulations made him wonder about the state and current condition—dead or alive—of poor Tuddsley. In the animal world, Tuddsley was held with deeply high regard: friendly, courteous, and known for his deep reddish-golden coat, which was always brushed to an impeccable sheen. Sounded like it was not the best of news for the aging pooch—that is, if the newspaper was accurate, Cracker reasoned.

Mrs. Bundle munched distractedly, daintily wiping the juices from her lips, while she read through the news story once more, trying to grasp the story as real. "Yes, poor Tuddsley, too! I just really can't believe it. You just never know, do you C.C.?"

Sucking in the last luscious remnants of the tasty fruit, she set the paper down and reminisced. Hartland Corners—and Tuddy's Diner—was a fifteen-minute ride through the back roads from her home here in North Pillson Corners. She and her family had visited the hospitable local establishment numerous times over many years, especially when the kids were younger. Back then, it had been a real treat when she and Arthur could afford to take the children out to eat, and Tuddy's had fit the bill on a number of levels. Most of all, because it was easy, quick, and tasted like home.

She and her husband Arthur had shared many unpretentiously prepared, modestly priced, family-fare meals at Tuddy's after the kids had left home, too. The memories flooded back, giving her a warm rush of pleasure. Tuddy's was famous for butter-topped rolls, their special fried chicken, and the "great-great-grandma's recipes" which included the best meatloaf she'd ever tasted and a Sunday Special to die for. Every Sunday fifty-two weeks a year, never fail, their menu always offered a "Roasted Turkey" dinner special, served family-style with all the fixings for only $7.55 per adult, the price calculated to total an even $8.00 when the tax was added in, all served with a complimentary Grammy's Hot Chocolate "on the house" during the winter months.

An old-fashioned dining establishment that never seemed to change, Tuddy's was one of the remaining constants in the area;

throughout the decades it had always been there to serve the most discriminating tastebuds. In a world of fast food mediocrity, it had been a pleasure visiting the traditional diner where everything, from the checkered tablecloths to the old family photographs on the aged walls, stayed the same.

And now, it was gone. *At least, hopefully, only for awhile*, Mrs. Bundle thought, *until they could rebuild.*

She drew her attention back to the paper, flipping the thin newspaper pages crisply so that they made a sharp snapping noise.

"Well, it's official! We've got a heat wave on our hands, according to the paper. One solid week with no rain and stifling, dry air makes it the real deal, or so they say. Don't think we need the experts to tell us *that*, do we C.C.?" She fanned the papers at her comely, mature face, "Whoo-*eee!*" Lighter, cooler air sent the tiny wisps escaping from her loose chignon hairstyle, flying every which-way. "Here it is only…" she looked up at the Bakelite clock on the kitchen wall, "…uh-huh! My Lord! Nigh on seven-thirty a.m.! And it's already getting too danged hot!"

Doing his best proverbial 'straight-man' imitation, Cracker cat-thought dryly, *so, how hot is it?*

Eyeballing the nearby thermometer on the outside window frame, she cried, "Holy Mackerel-Andy! It'll to be another scorcher today! It's pushing seventy already!" She wiped her brow delicately, pushing back the wisps of lovely silver-brown hair, then deftly secured the errant strands once again within the loosely gathered bun, and sighed, her attractive face already exhibiting the faintest signs of a dewy sheen.

She peered at the heading of the newspaper, then confirmed, "Tuesday, June 24th! Yuh-huh."

Her thoughts wandered for a bit, as they usually did nowadays, to other past Junes in her sleepy little North Pillson Corners as Cracker, watching her from his distinct vantagepoint, noted proudly how beautiful a woman she still was. Her hearty face was softly outlined, healthy and warm lines defining full, vibrant past chapters of her life. Her dancing, ever-youthful dark brown eyes were still sharp and bright—lovely almond eyes dressed with long, coffee-colored lashes. A solid, reliable chin, classic Roman nose (long and straight), and high, uncomplicated forehead completed the picture. Even in these early morning hours without a touch of makeup, she was a natural, mature beauty. And when she gathered her long hair up into the brilliantly long, braids and wrapped them neatly around her head like an intricate pillbox, it appeared to crown her extraordinary features like a regal headdress. *Shoulders square and straight, no sign of weakness there*, he continued his critique. In fact, she was still incredibly strong despite her age (he tread here delicately) and, of more importance, despite all she'd gone through the last year.

Yes, she was a real gem, no doubt about it, he cat-thought. Realist that he was (and not unlike most of his aristocrat feline contemporaries), he was sure his opinion counted for a great deal.

He watched her in her pondering state, her intensely-dark eyes now turned dreamy and introspective. *Extraordinary!* She defied the average description of someone of her era, she who was now retired but not content to rest on her laurels. She exuded confidence and vitality which, he observed without prejudice, was pleasantly accentuated by her still trim, well-built frame.

A *no-nonsense, straight shooter*, he cat-thought, *just like me!* Never lacking in overconfidence, he was sleek and to the point, from the tips of his well-groomed ears to his impeccably groomed silky tail. And how she often *did* rely on his honest assessment of situations and crisis, especially after Arthur's death. The wonder of their unique relationship was that even when they disagreed they always came back together as one with unequivocal mutual respect, to work as a team.

She sighed again and picked up the nearby deserted coffee cup, saturated grains of coffee swirling in its murky bottom. Using the palm of her hand, she wiped the still damp ring of coffee (or "*caife*," as the Irish lad called it) stain left by the cup from the surface of the shiny fruits-and-flowers vinyl tablecloth.

"I'll have to show Jack where the sink is…," she said, tongue-in-cheek, smiling to herself. Turning to Cracker, she quipped, "Well,

I guess we can give him a break," both of them knowing well the habits of the young man she had willingly taken into her home.

Cracker cat-thought, *Yes, dear girl, cut the chap some slack; he is a very busy fellow!*

No doubt about that, to be sure. Jack Corrigan, the boy from Ireland that they now considered to be part of their extended family was, in fact, like a son to her.

They had a special bond, she and Jack, particularly in view of the hardships they had endured together the previous year.

And now, sharing his younger sisters with the Andersens was a wonderful testament to their friendship, determination, and collaborative effort to, as Walter put it, "jist make it work." The girls were settled into their everyday life, Jack was going to college and working, and everyone's life was the better for having incorporated the Corrigan clan into their lives.

Mrs. Bundle looked at the clock once more. Jack was long gone, having already risen at 5 a.m. for his busy day. First, he helped the Andersen men with their early farm chores, then returned home and quicker than a duck's wink got himself cleaned up, ate a quick breakfast, and was on the road by 7:15 for a long day of back-to-back summer session community college classes in nearby Springfield.

Back around 2:30 p.m. or so, he would hustle over to Hudson's Garage in Pillsonville to his part-time job. The unflappable proprietor, Royal Hudson, Jr., was thrilled with Jack. "Best nose for mechanic-ing I ever seen! Brightest tool in the shed—between you, me, and that fencepost over there!"

Jack did everything from pumping gas, to changing tires, to being a humble "gofer," and the extra money he made went toward his sisters' care and his education. Even though Mrs. Bundle and the Andersen men had said this was not necessary, Jack's Irish pride prevailed and he insisted he must contribute, and so they honored his wish.

Around 5:30 p.m., he would return to help with the evening farm chores and spend time with his sisters. Dinner was usually around 7 (either down at the farm or at Mrs. Bundle's, depending on what else was going on in each respective family's schedule or more often than not, who had planned the most savory meal).

As complicated and busy as Jack's life was, Mrs. Bundle marveled at how well everything worked. Everyday life between the two farmhouses was like a well-oiled treadle happily clacking away with Jack and the girls happy, well-adjusted, and square in the middle of the two families; it was as if they'd all been together their whole lives.

She reread the note on the table that Jack had left her early this morning:

Top of the morning to you, Mrs. B—Should be home at the usual time... have a grand day—
'Slán go fóil!
Jack

His standard Celtic "good-bye for now" always tickled her, and she smiled good-naturedly and looked outside at the early perennials in full bloom. Peeking over the windowsill by her elbow were luscious deep scarlet peonies. Oh, she cherished her lovely peonies, the rich reds, the intense pinks, and the cool white clusters of the various verdant-dense bushes throughout her expansive yard. They gave her such pleasure; not just their look, but the aroma! The bloom period was brief, which made it even more of a special event when they finally blossomed after the long Vermont winter and an even more dismal typically cold, drab, ever-long spring. Mrs. Bundle often dried the peonies, their creamy centers blush pink with hints of yellow and white, and made them into wreaths or arrangements.

Drinking in the wonderfully sweet morning fragrance through the open window, she daydreamed, her mind wandering like a winding, miles-long river as she soaked up the sun and nature's glory. Beautiful! She loved her gardens—and the poppies especially! The reedy, spindly stalks strained under the weight of the gorgeous, gargantuan flowers. Looking like bright bobbing bonnets in the wind, the flapping lobular orange petals enveloped the smudgy black centers, resembling gushy licorice gumdrops. How exquisite! Mrs. Bundle admired the whimsical look the grounds took on as the wild flowers and perennials mixed together in a happy summer union, most of which all flourished without much tending to.

Further out back, behind the farmhouse, she always put in a small vegetable garden each summer, where her favorite legumes (string beans, peas, and the like) stood in ambitious rows beside tomatoes, peppers, corn, summer squash and zucchini. Off to the side, by the leach field, she planted a patch of pumpkins and squash every year for fall harvest. Without fail, the pumpkins and various winter squash flourished in that spot; no wonder, she thought, with such fertile soil all around! She always relished the final booty; the growing season's last vestiges in October decorated her house in the late Fall with festive and colorful dried gourds and pumpkins.

A wild plum tree and a couple of pear trees stood further back on the property next to the 100-year-old apple orchard which consisted of about twenty knarled-branch fruit trees, all of which bore round, luscious MacIntosh apples in late August through mid-September.

The remainder of Mrs. Bundle's acreage was open fields and woods, which she often tramped on a daily basis, regardless of the changeable Vermont weather. She and Cracker would head out for their customary hike, sometimes over the backland, but more often, up past the Old Stone Church to Grasshopper Lane and into the woods.

But, today, the heat was going to be intense, or so the paper said. Best to save their hike for later in the afternoon—especially as she had quite a number of important things on her "to-do" list this morning.

Coming back to the real world, she plaintively forewarned in her best soothsayer voice to Cracker, "Oh, the *dog days of summer* are coming…" and then chuckled.

She knew her cat so well! At her words, Cracker had hunched his sleek ebony back upward, arched high, stood his cat paws on tiptoe (an outward sign that he always exhibited when was slightly perturbed), and meowed loudly!

"Well, it's true! Cracker, those '*dog* days of summer'! The hottest days of the year!"

He meowed again, beseeching her to stop—Cracker had a personal anathema to any English language references that used the word "dog" (which happened on a fairly regular basis) and he *knew* his mistress knew that!

"Pshaw!" She crinkled her nose. "P-cat, c'mon now, don't get yourself into a snit just because I use the 'd' word to describe a summer phenomenon!"

The persnickety cat sniffed at the air, his dainty nose high and noble. His eyes became bright yellow almonds as he viewed her imperiously from his post. *Two can play at this game*, he cat-thought.

As though reciting from a textbook, Cracker cat-thought with exactitude from his gifted memory, *Yes-s-s, The Dog Days of Summer.* **Ahem!** *The ancient Romans observed Sirius, the brightest star in the night sky, which appeared annually at the onset of hot, sultry weather. Sirius, whose Greek origin means "scorcher," became known as the Dog Star* (he meowed loudly for dramatic effect, and then continued) *and the proceeding hot weather was called 'dog days.' The ancient Romans believed that the star caused the overly hot weather, so they sacrificed brown dogs to appease the rage of Sirius. That is why today, each year, around the first week of July, the earth's Northern Hemisphere reaches its farthest point from the sun, approximately 94,510,000 miles. That point - the aphelion - ironically begins the hottest and stickiest days of the year, ending sometime in mid to late August.*

As he concluded this spurt of canine-related knowledge (his feline oration wasn't *quite* finished), he eyeballed a very impressed Mrs. Bundle with complete satisfaction; she waited patiently for his finale.

Hence, he added as a postscript, **DOG** *days*, (he elevated his imperious nose even higher), *refers literally to the demise of dogs, a practice I will not editorialize further on due to my own justified prejudice!*

He gracefully licked his velvety paws and tried his best not to appear *too* pretentious.

"Well, I never!" Mrs. Bundle shook her head, "Honestly!" She chuckled, "Cracker, you are a wealth of invaluable knowledge. On the matter of dogs, though, C.C., everybody—even me—occasionally spatters their vocabulary with canine sayings. It's just part of our vernacular." She chattered on good-naturedly. "Uh-huh! You know… like, '*dog-eat-dog world*,'" she raised her fingers in quote marks, "or, emm.., '*dog-tired*,' '*the tail wagging the dog*,' etcetera, etcetera…," she paused, "shall I go on?"

Cracker raised his hind end energetically toward Mrs. Bundle and gave a quick, expert flick to his long black tail.

"Oh, same to you, you most remarkable and *favorite* feline of mine. If you really think about it, dear Cracker, there happen to be *just* as many *fabulous* cat phrases floating around. Let's see…there's, '*cat and mouse game*'…" she cajoled, giving him an affectionate pat, "and '*curiosity killed the cat*'…," a chuckle escaped from her lips, "oh, yes, and don't forget '*Cat got your tongue*'? Or, '*cat calls*,' or '*cat burglar*' for that matter!"

Cracker's sleek back skyrocketed once more.

"Oh, wait! *Cat's granny*! That's my own personal favorite!" Cracker sauntered away, thoroughly bored, and she gently joked, "My, my, aren't we a very sensitive cat today?"

She gazed over at her latest "reads," piled high on the table beside her; she didn't have much time anymore for reading all the mystery novels she loved so well. Time was at a premium now, between tending to Jack's needs, her volunteering duties at the Good Neighbor Food Shelf and the Library Board, and, of course, *B and C Detectives*.

She leaned into the sunny vista, peering out the window for one final look at her little world, and sighed again. She called over her shoulder to Cracker, "We'll get the watering done first and then head down to the Library. Everything's coming to an ugly head, and I need to check in with Louis."

Mrs. Bundle had been on the Pillsonville Library Board for almost twenty years—that is, up until her near-fatal injury last November which had precluded her from any activity for two months. She had sorely missed her directorship seat during that time, mostly because over the many decades of its existence, the Pillson Library was Pillson's pride and joy, a grand structure that heralded a past era. When she had returned to her post, though, she found things had changed considerably.

She furrowed her brow in frustration.

Truth be told, the most recent Trustees meeting she had attended in May had been a rough one. The old building was in major disrepair, especially the roof and its substructure which had leaked significantly during the last heavy rain; it appeared a crisis was imminent. The town's coffers could not provide the relief in funds needed to make the necessary repairs to the building. Hence, the Library Board had been charged with the responsibility of a life-changing decision: whether to close the Library down or come up with a solution that would provide funds to handle the necessary large repairs with the intention to ultimately restore the Library to its original grandeur.

Louis Montembeau, Head Librarian, was the institution's strongest advocate, an ever-faithful employee who worked for meager wages. Many were of the mind that, if the Library were to close down due to lack of funds, it would never reopen, a vacant building fading into further dilapidation and final ruin. Louis agreed.

There was a faction, a small but very vocal group of Pillsonville residents, whose mantra of "too high taxes, too many free services" seemed to be gaining momentum, and this group was spearheading the move to close the Library. Sadly, this solution would be an unfortunate, albeit successful, means to accomplish the village's fiscal dilemma. Mrs. Bundle, always one to advocate education and progress, was not one of these naysayers of gloom and doom. In fact, she was working with Louis to come up with a proactive plan to save the Library. Additionally, (and as bad luck would have it), one of the biggest (and most vocal) supporters of shutting down the library actually sat on the Board with her. His name struck a painful nerve with many people, including Mrs. Bundle.

That name was *Armand Limpert*.

Shaking all unpleasant thoughts from her mind, she resumed her chat with Cracker. "*And,* we've got to take care of the errands and be back here in time for tea and a quick nap before dinner."

Cracker meowed loudly.

She turned back to her daily paper, occupied once more.

"Okay, let's not get off track...we'll finish the paper and then move on. Let's see...what's all the news that's fit to print on the global front?" She cleared her throat importantly, chuckling in a most satisfactory fashion and giving a nod toward her captive audience of one. "Ahem! Really, Cracker, I do amuse myself!"

Cracker blinked impassively.

She actively searched, scanning the world headlines for something that would stimulate their combined interest.

"Yes...yes...say! Here's something with some intrigue." She glanced at Cracker who, as yet, had refused to acknowledge his curiosity in the world's current affairs.

"Listen to this!" She read the bold headline. "'*Art Thief Absconds With Rare Painting*'." Picking out the article's salient points, she shared the literary tidbits with her mate. "Genoa Italy, Cracker! Here, listen—'*In a bold and unprecedented caper last Thursday a thief, posing as a security guard at the National Museum of Italian Sciences*'...ahhh, yes, yes..." she read to herself, "right! '...*a dramatic robbery estimated at a half of a million dollars.*' My, my! '*The imposter removed a Bernardo Strozzi painting right under the noses of the gallery staff at closing time. As yet, the painting has not been recovered, and the trail appears to be cold.*' Uh-huh! '*Strozzi is notable for rekindling the spirit of great painting in Venice in the 1600s.*'..." she paused in thought. "Ahhh, Venice!"

Her eyes looked dreamily at the vacant wall, imagining a younger and even more impetuous Vermont girl reclining lazily in a handsome Gondolier's boat after an afternoon of wandering from one fabulous art museum to another. *Ah, youth!*

There was a resounding, "*PPFFFF-TTT!*" as Cracker cleared his cat sinuses.

Startled out of her private reverie, Mrs. Bundle cleared her throat and postured, "Art is so…very interesting. Wouldn't you agree, *il mio amore Crackissimo?*"

Her *gatto nero bello* issued a colossal cat yawn and wriggled impatiently. *Wishful thinking, it sounds like to me*, he cat-thought.

"I ask you, C.C.…,"she implored in wide-eyed sincerity to her quiescent partner, "Why can't we have something as exciting and—" she searched for the right word, "—*intriguing* as *that* happen in our neck of the woods? Right here," she motioned expansively, "in our little world?" Her eyes turned dreamy once more.

Uh-oh, Cracker cat-thought with trepidation, *I've heard those words before. 'Our Little World' makes me think trouble with a capital 'T'!* Oval, luminescent eyes watched her as she sat totally oblivious, so deep in imaginative thought.

In this flight of fancy, she could have been anywhere, and…he couldn't help but join her. Was she totally involved in international intrigue on a bleached white beach in the Greek island of Corfu, he wondered, or on a camel's back in Morocco chasing a jewel thief?

He wiggled his pointed ears, studying her with rapt attention, wishing fantasies of exciting escapades, near-death brushes, and much more fun than they were having here in their little world of North Pillson Corners.

In the darker recesses of a world consumed with evil, an old saying lurked like a greedy troll raising a twisted, far-reaching finger…"Be careful what you wish for…"

Chapter Two

The Mind is a
Terrible Thing to Waste

Minutes later, the dreamers still sat in their respective same places, bored to tears.

Mrs. Bundle put down the newspaper and sighed, then sighed again, longing for…*what?*

All things considered, Mrs. Bundle had somewhat altered her perspective and expectations of *B and C Detectives*. Her preconceived notion of excitement and suspense surrounding detective work had been tempered with the truelife, everyday activities of the newly-chosen vocation.

Undeniably, her business had started with a bang and she preferred to view her first case as a lucky and exhilarating event, rather than the harrowing and life-threatening incident that had transpired. Truth be told, detective work involved long hours, sometimes boring and not as glamorous as portrayed in film and TV.

Cracker's views on this matter were the same. *I suppose*, he had noted regretfully, *all our cases can not be as invigorating as that first case last Thanksgiving…*

He watched as Mrs. Bundle reached over to the seasoned maple butcherblock countertop beside her and, stretching her long fingers past the ancient coffee grinder, retrieved her old recipe file box chock full of her collection of favorite dishes, breads, desserts, etc.

The rectangular tin canister with hinged top, originally belonging to her grandmother, now doubled as her informal filing system for her crime-related cases.

Opening the cover, she found the "C" section quickly and pulled out the card titled *Children*, (between the recipe cards *Chicken Cacciatore* and *Clam Chowder*) and read the notes, facts, and details she had scribed during their momentous first case.

Yes, it had all begun with this case, the Corrigan children and the Children of Lir Necklace—her entry into the unlikely field of detective work. In the short months since then, she had fully recovered from her chest injury, the result of a gunshot wound at the hands of that madman Terrington Askew Whitewick. A combination of luck (good and bad) and some skill had carried her through the dangerous episode. However, after her brush with death came the full realization that she honestly didn't know a blessed thing about detective work.

First things first, she thought logically as she tapped the card absentmindedly on the table.

So, when she was finally up and around—healthy and fully mobile—she had decided to begin taking courses offered by the PPIAV—the Professional Private Investigators Association of Vermont. An avid learner, she now knew how to set up an office and interview clients, something she could have used in her dealings as a novice in her earliest case. Suffice it to say, she felt much more qualified now and welcomed the few jobs that had come to her.

Let's see, she ticked off in her mind all the recent activities. *So far, not too bad.*

The media coverage she'd received after her brush with death had been good publicity for her fledgling business; her notoriety had preceded her and she had received various incidental offers of employment.

The first job that had come through the pipeline had been from Reichart's Clothing Company in Rutland. She placed the *Children* card back into the file and drew out this next case's card under the "D" section—snugly placed in between *Delicious Roasted Duck*

Breast and *Devil's Food Cake* and read the card aloud, *"Department Store."*

The hundred-year-old bustling department store was a mainstay for anyone visiting downtown's historic Merchant's Row. She had been hired to do a short-term surveillance job, primarily to go undercover for one week as an average shopper with the ultimate intention of ferreting out a small, but organized, shoplifting ring that had been wreaking havoc on the store's monthly sales numbers.

She had enjoyed this first assignment—especially dressing for the part as an average, unnoticed shopper who melded into the woodwork each day, and had quickly put the matter to rest; four transients, (ultimately also wanted in Portsmouth, New Hampshire for writing back checks) were caught red-handed with stolen garments, watches, and electronic equipment. Mrs. Bundle had been paid handsomely, along with a $300 bonus for bringing the case so quickly to a close.

Since then, she'd had only two other detecting jobs—both minor in scope and use of brain cells—helping two parties in Pillson: first, a local couple named Richey who were robbed during their wedding reception and second, an elderly woman named Hazel Balshemnik whose expensive jewelry seemed to have disappeared into thin air.

Ahh, she thought as she took out the next card, *this one was right up our alley, wasn't it Cracker?*

Under "R" (sandwiched between *Raspberry Trifle* and *Roasted Chestnut Soup*) were Mrs. Bundle's notes on *The Richey Case.*

The wedding celebration of Hiram Richey and Cynthia Combs, two well-known locals, had been a huge event for Pillsonville. The reception had been held at the Pillson Town Hall first floor dining hall, often used by residents for various public events. Attended by most of the village, the gala affair had turned near-disastrous when it was discovered that the whole table of gifts, wedding cards chock full of checks, and the fully-replete money tree had all disappeared without the notice of those celebrating inside the dining hall.

It seemed Weezy Bunton, Wedding Planner for the event, had left her place of duty at the gift table at the Town Hall's front door entrance for "just a few minutes" while she went upstairs to the ladies' room to freshen up. Upon her return, she was mortified to find all the celebratory booty had vanished without a trace; the table had been picked clean. Hoping perchance the four groomsmen had loaded the items into the wedding couple's 1968 Dodge Charger pacer car without her knowledge, she'd tentatively checked with each one individually. The tuxedo-attired quartet were well into their third or fourth Pabst Blue Ribbon; each man, solidly plunked at the makeshift bar, knew zilch about any wedding presents having been moved anywhere. With anxiety gaining a chokehold on her, Weezy had made the rounds alone once more, searching for anything remotely looking like a wedding present, her tour including the upstairs bathrooms, all four corners of the upstairs community hall (commonly known as the Great Hall inclusive of the back stage area), then back down to the building's service kitchen off the dining room, into the back hallway to the coat room and utility closet, and finally reconnoitering back to the wedding gift table in the Hall's front foyer. For good measure, she had even tried the door to the small room housing the local Postal Office, which of course, being after hours, was locked up tighter than a pig's patootie.

Then and only then, Weezy had panicked; somebody had stolen all the gifts! It was then she'd found Mrs. Bundle (who happened to be a guest at the wedding), Weezy had urgently motioned to her across the dining hall expanse and then rushed her into the empty, soundproof coat room and utility space.

"What's up?" Mrs. Bundle had asked, alarmed at the stout woman's agitated state.

"I swear, I wasn't gone but a minute. Had to go tinkle really bad! Somebody's taken all the gifts—and the money, too!" Weezy whispered raggedly, her tremendous bosom heaving with panic under the tight constraints of her favorite party outfit, a black-and-white herringbone polyester jumpsuit. "*Gaw!* Hiram and Cynthia ain't never goin' to forgive me. Oh, Lettie! You gotta help me!" Her chest heaved, causing each breath to come in deep drags of oxygen. "There was over *five hundred dollars* in checks in all them envelopes! And the cash! 'Bout three-hundred-and-fifty! I know, I put it all on the money tree and counted it whilst I was standin' there! What'll I do if we can't find them things? It'll be devastatin', truly devastatin' to that couple!"

Taking stock within the small confined space, Mrs. Bundle noticed that the heavy gold buttons from Weezy's neck to waist were pushed to their limit. Surely this ensemble had been a very smart number when Weezy had purchased it twenty years earlier at JC Penney's, but truth be told, she had also been three sizes smaller back then. Now the bold outfit barely fit Weezy's blossomed, mature figure and she resembled a queer combination of King's Jester and the agitated egg boy, Tweedledum.

"Now, now, Weezy, calm yourself." Unconsciously erring on the side of caution, Mrs. Bundle stepped to the side of Weezy *just* a hair, fearing the projectile force of the one of the most gravity-challenged brass buttons on the northernmost tip of Weezy's vast wasteland of chest area *might* give way—quite rightly perceiving that just one more of Weezy's overwrought heaves could possibly catapult the orb at any given moment.

Comforting her as best she could, Mrs. Bundle had determined that the theft had occurred sometime between the best man's toast and the garter toss. Assuring her that she would take care of everything and urging Weezy to go get herself a Moxie and calm down, Mrs. Bundle had put a quick call in to her old friend, Sheriff Will O'Malley and asked a favor. While the festivities continued, she was like an undercover hound dog in hot pursuit.

First, she found the evidence of the well wishers' cards having been opened and then tossed aside underneath the makeshift plywood bulkhead of the building three doors down from Town Hall. Of course, the gift certificates, personal checks, and cash had been removed from the cards; additionally, the forlorn, now-empty money tree had been tossed aside carelessly underneath a nearby rhododendron bush. Knowing that the parking lot had been very active with the comings and goings of the wedding guests, she had then deduced that the culprits could not have gone very far without notice with all the contraband, and concluded that they would have either stashed it in one of the vehicles or hidden the presents somewhere nearby to be retrieved later.

It didn't take her long to conclude that the culprits were of younger age and rather inexperienced—probably kids—who had left a significant paper trail in their wake. She paid a visit to Murphy's General Store (located within a short walk up Main Street). Her suspicions were affirmed when she discovered that a local boy, Harold Snargle (whose parents happened to be attending the wedding) and Tommy Moyer, his alleged partner-in-crime, had, not a half-hour earlier, been in and dropped a bundle of cash on candy, bubblegum, skateboard magazines, and other sundries. Both boys lived two streets over on Maple Avenue, and were not only next-door neighbors but best friends.

"They were pretty cocky!" young Betsy Murphy, the owner's daughter and afternoon clerk, confirmed. "They even asked me for cigarettes!," which she was adamant to proclaim she had flatly refused to sell them. "And they were acting really goofy when they left the store."

Within minutes, Mrs. Bundle had returned to Town Hall, having solved the case. Stashed underneath a large lot of cardboard boxes and other refuse in the Town Hall dumpster were two shiny, oversized, heavyweight trash bags. Inside were all the presents. She surmised the boys had taken the bags from that same utility/coat closet she had shared with Weezy, located conveniently next to the gift table.

The bags were too heavy for Mrs. Bundle to pull out, so she fetched Weezy who, without hesitation, jumped headfirst into the dumpster and retrieved the treasure (all of which were still in their original boxes).

"I'm ever grateful!" Weezy had gushed as she and Mrs. Bundle brought everything back to the coat room without drawing undue notice.

"We need to play this out if we're going to get the money back, too." She apprised Weezy of the alleged culprits' identity and urged her to keep mum about this discovery until she could find the rest of the takings.

Harold and Tommy were in the dining hall. They sat angelically—under their respective parents' noses—both chewing away with gusto while they watched the festivities. Mrs. Bundle watched as Harold created a very large pink bubble which Tommy then reached over and, with lightning quickness, proceeded to pop. Harold snuck his hand covertly into his pants pocket and boldly showed Tommy the tip of a crisp twenty dollar bill. Both snarked and chortled with cagey delight.

Hmmm, Mrs. Bundle nodded with certainty, *guilty as sin!*

With the party still going full-boat, Mrs. Bundle inconspicuously approached Cynthia and Hiram. Making the newly married couple aware of the crisis, she assured them she had a good idea who the guilty parties were and they implored her to find their wedding proceeds as discreetly as possible and, at Mrs. Bundle's suggestion, agreed that they continue to enjoy their reception as best they could. She promised the Richeys that she would be back with the cash later on and not to worry; between her and Sheriff Will-O, things would be resolved within the next couple hours, to be sure.

After the party (and in darkness) when the misbehaving juveniles returned to the dumpster for their contraband, the jig was up and they were caught red-handed. As the two young men sorted through the refuse looking for their treasures, Mrs. Bundle and Sheriff Will O' sat undiscovered, yards away, within her trusty, harmless VW Junebug. With the element of surprise in their favor, they confronted the thieves, who were scared to death at the sight of Will's massive and imposing uniformed frame and immediately confessed their transgressions.

"I told him not to take it!" Harold cried.

"You *lie*! It was your idea!" Tommy had hollered back. They both passed the blame back and forth, giving up the ghost quicker than a striped jaybird. It turned out the kids had taken the rest of the cash and personal checks and stashed everything—where else? Just up the street at their respective homes underneath their mattresses.

Ultimately, all of the gifts and money were returned, save for $10.51, which Harold and Tommy would end up paying back in a modified work release program overseen by the village Constable Zack Benois and which would involve cleaning the Town Hall weekly until their debt to society was paid in full fivefold.

Hiram and Cynthia had been thrilled with Mrs. Bundle's handling of the case and went away on their honeymoon to the Embassy Suites in Burlington happy and content. They left behind a letter thanking Mrs. Bundle, along with a year's worth of cinema tickets (including mention of all the free popcorn she could eat) from the White River Junction Playhouse where Cynthia worked as the manager. In addition, Hiram, a chef at the five-star Jackson House Inn in Woodstock, wrote that he and Cynthia were in the process of opening a small catering business "on the side" and that she should plan on their services "for free" the next time she needed a catered event.

Mrs. Bundle smiled as she recalled that promise. "Detective barters sleuthing skills for catered event," she proclaimed, carefully placing the card back into the box.

The second job was the case of Mrs. Balshemnik's missing jewelry: somewhat intriguing, though short-lived in its intensity.

"What a hoot that was, wasn't it Cracker?"

He purred softly, thoroughly enjoying this trip down memory lane.

She read the last card she had removed from the slim pickings under "W" entitled *Wedding Ring Case* and began deliciously reviewing the details and clues that had lead to this case's successful resolution.

"And don't we just love that Hazel?"

He jumped into her lap, purring even louder, and they reminisced together. This one case was especially poignant for Cracker because, as he was inclined to point out, he had played a major role in solving this challenging "crime" steeped in mystery and intrigue.

Hazel Balshemnik had contacted Mrs. Bundle, distraught over a series of puzzling in-home robberies, and in dire hopes that Mrs. Bundle would be able to solve the mystery of her missing jewelry. It seemed that over a period of weeks, Hazel had noticed her jewelry disappearing from her bedroom jewelry case, in particular, her precious wedding band. The elderly lady's bedroom was on the second floor of her modest cape-style dwelling and she maintained unequivocally she had been at home each time the robberies occurred. On this detail she did not waver.

In point of fact, the burglaries took place consistently on Wednesdays and in broad daylight; coincidentally, this was the same day Hazel performed her weekly house cleaning chores. Furthermore, in between her domestic duties, Hazel did her baking.

Mrs. Balshemnik was known throughout Pillsonville for her baked delicacies: European breads, desserts and pastries, and the like. She supplemented her meager Social Security income with a very small baking business; products were picked up by customers on Wednesdays only, and only after noontime.

Added to the mysterious disappearance of jewelry was the fact that, later in the day, anyone visiting or picking up their bread or pastry order always remained on the first floor level, either in the kitchen or the parlor, which was where she entertained customers, guests, and family.

Invariably, later in the day, she would check her jewelry dish on her tall bureau and, thoroughly frustrated, would find that another ring, earring, or precious bauble was missing.

Mrs. Balshemnik was beside herself wondering whom she could trust. Totally at a loss, she had called Mrs. Bundle to help her solve the mystery. And so, *B and C Detectives* had arrived on the scene, fully galvanized and ready to unravel the mystery at hand.

Hazel had met them at the door in an anxious state. "Come in, come in, you let dat cold in and ve freeze! *Ach!* Ist that Cracka vit you, the little tink?" She leaned over and gave him a nervous pat on his head. "Vant some milk, *bubbee*? And, you, Lettie, a cookie you vould like, yes?"

"No, no, we're fine, really, Mrs. Balshemnik. Both of us just ate before we came over, thank you very much."

Mrs. Balshemnik led them into the darkened living room, shades pulled shut, laced doilies everywhere—on the dark mahogany tables, on the ornate, marble fireplace mantel, under all the antique Banquet lamps and fancy jardinières, the Majolica pottery, and other *chatchkes* sprinkled throughout the room—and even a large star-shaped one on the old hassock that doubled as a coffee table in front of her favorite recliner.

Noting with an experienced eye all of the expensive antiques in plain view, Mrs. Bundle asked, "So, tell us, Mrs. Balshemnik, exactly what jewelry is missing?"

She threw her hands in the air. "Oy, gevald, my vedding rink! Can you believe it, Lettie? My Manny—vhat a *hitsik* he vas, Gott rest his sool—he has that rink—vhat you say—*inscribet*, yes, inscribet for me for our veddink day," she recited with emotion, "'H—ICH HAB DU LIEB—M 12/1/1952.' Ach! I couldn't stand to be losing it from all these years! *Halevei*—if only ve vould find who teks it! *Nishtgutnich!*" She twisted her fingers, pulling in distress at a disintegrating tissue. "A *kappore!* Yes, it's, vhat you say? Catastrophe! Each veek I look, vone more pisse gone! Vhy, oh *vhy*," she wailed, kneading the tissue, "vould anyone vant to tek my veddink rink? End my beautiful seffire earrinks! End, Gott knows, my ruby stickink-pin, too!" She raised her eyes skyward. "From my dearest *Memeleh!* End the rest of my tinks! Vhat, I esk you? Vhat else vill dey tek from me! *Oi, vay iz mir!*"

The stringbean-bodied widow daubed the flimsy Kleenex gently at her moist gray eyes and then tucked it safely away into her apron pocket, guardedly saving it for future use.

Tapping the distressed lady's worn hand, Mrs. Bundle murmured, "Now, now, dear, if it's meant to be, we'll discover what's become of your cherished wedding band, and the ruby stickpin, too—and all the rest, earrings, everything! Don't worry yourself so!"

Mrs. Bundle soothed her while Cracker engaged in some serious sniffing at the base of the stand that held the cage of Hazel's pet canary, Sadie.

"Ach, ve shoult be so lucky!" the woman sobbed.

Mrs. Bundle had spent time going over Mrs. Balshemnik's recollections in detail, recording the dates of the thefts, along with the people and tradesmen who had visited the elderly woman. Each hypothesis seemingly ran into a dead-end. At the end of the first day, Mrs. Bundle wondered if there was a viable explanation for the missing jewelry.

So, she and Cracker had decided to return on the following Wednesday to quietly observe Hazel's routine, hoping that that might shed some light on the matter at hand.

It was at that point that Providence seemed to intervene.

In point of the previously-stated fact, Cracker had been the driving force in cracking the case, as his keen cat skills allowed him to quickly determine *exactly* what had taken place. As it turned out, the crux of the case centered on a small, but very significant, discovery: a family of crows that had found a new home late that winter in the immense oak tree on Hazel's property. Cracker first picked up the nearby relentless "cawing," and then the dark outline of their feathered bodies, all observed from Mrs. Balshemnik's bedroom window sill.

When Cracker skipped downstairs and outside, climbed the large tree, and then looked into their lofty nest he discovered the wedding ring, the brilliant ruby stickpin, both of Hazel's coveted sapphire earrings, two shiny bottle caps, a cigarette butt, a Star of David tie tack, and a small pile of ragged aluminum foil gum wrappers.

Crows, famous for being uncommonly smart birds, have a penchant for indiscriminately collecting anything bright-colored, small, and shiny. But how did they get inside the bedroom? Remarkably, the savvy birds had systematically removed the lustrous gold jewelry pieces from Hazel's bureau top whenever she left her bedroom window wide open. This event occurred only on Wednesdays, rain or shine, as Hazel routinely aired out the bedroom during her weekly cleanings.

The clever crows' cache was quickly confiscated (with the help of the Pillson Fire Department ladder truck) and the case was closed.

Mrs. Balshemnik had been elated. *"Azoy gich?* Ahh, my tinks—so soon? Tank Gott! Oy, dat Cracka, such a cutie-pie! Mazel tov!"

As she covered the fastidious cat with affectionate, wet kisses, he tried not to squirm, concluding that this deeply passionate woman had emotions in two ranges: either deep doldrum lows or very lofty highs. This was definitely one of her most elated peaks as she hugged him to her as tightly as a bear clutching a prized trout before devouring it whole.

Mrs. Balshemnik, ever-so-grateful but unable to pay the going rate, had sent Mrs. Bundle and Cracker home that day with a huge batch of chopped chicken liver pate and fresh-baked *bialys* (scrumptiously chewy round yeast rolls), which they both, without question, had thoroughly enjoyed.

"That's one case we won't forget, right C.C.? *Hah!*" Mrs. Bundle held her sides, laughing aloud at the memory of her and Cracker arriving home with a shopping bag filled with Jewish goodies. She wiped her wet eyes. "Chopped liver! *Oy, gevald!* Do you think someone's trying to tell us something, 'cutie-pie'?"

Oy, gevald indeed, Cracker cat-thought.

Mrs. Bundle snorted good-naturedly as she snapped the top of the tin box shut. "Anyway, that's *that* for our detecting! Say, aren't we a grand pair, Cracker?"

The singular cat jumped laterally from her lap into the empty chair next to her and meowed loudly.

Well, I must admit...yes, we are, he cat-thought proudly.

Curling up into a ball on the braided seat cover, Cracker delved into his own memories now, pausing to relive his own detecting prowess. Why, hadn't he *himself* experienced perils personally as Mrs. Bundle's sleuthing assistant? And didn't he proudly wear the scars proving it? During their autumn escapade, he had suffered greatly under the cruel, heavy boot of a very mean man. His body still ached at times, but really, the adventure had been worth it.

Yes, he cat-thought, *but here we are now, with no prospects in sight.*

Their recent short-lived cases had been resolved quickly for not a lot of remuneration.

"Of course, money isn't everything..." she said, both knowing money was not the main reason for *B and C Detectives.*

Mrs. Bundle gave one last long, drawn-out sigh. Bored just as much as she was the autumn before with her everyday mundane activities, she had come to the decision that light crimes and domestic surveillance were not as much her cup of tea. She was ashamed to acknowledge what she really liked: the limelight and intrigue of a hard-core crime. Give her murder and international intrigue any day of the week—Adventure with a capital "A"!

Her first case had spoiled her—in fact, ruined her to a certain extent; becoming involved right off the bat in a crime involving kidnapping, fraud, aggravated assault, and attempted murder was right up her alley. The icing on the cake was aiding in the apprehension of an intercontinental criminal.

"And he's right where he belongs—Allenwood Federal Prison, thank you very much! With no chance of parole until the year 2034!"

Cracker meowed in agreement.

After the whole ordeal, she knew how precious life was and how important it was to not just *live* but fully seize the day with gusto.

So, as she sat here in this glorious sunshine looking out on the absolutely pristine vista, she asked herself: *what exactly do you want? What more could you want?* She absentmindedly reached over and stroked Cracker's velvety soft back, trying to define what she would be happy with, something totally alien from their everyday existence. *Something…*she thought, *like the Strozzi painting caper, something….with allure. Yes, that was it!*

"*Allure.*" She said the word deliciously aloud, letting the word flow from her lips as though it was tempting, golden elixir.

A long purr came from the sleek black body she caressed.

*Allure…*Cracker rumbled contently, his torso totally relaxed, *ye-e-sssss…allure.*

Mrs. Bundle could just feel it in her bones; something WONDERFUL was going to happen. Yes, she was ready, *really* ready for an Adventure. What intriguing mysterious voyage would come their way? *Time would only tell*, she thought, patting her partner.

She gave a gentle push and Cracker slid down from the braided round on the comfortable chair and stretched his long body in anticipation. He, for one, was ready for their travels today.

Mrs. Bundle expertly hand brushed the last crumbs from the kitchen table to the floor, where Cracker deftly polished off every last bit of the tiny, flavorful morsels for good measure.

Securing the leftover bag of Mrs. Balshemnik's magnificent homemade swirled cinnamon bread and placing it inside the vintage green tin breadbox, she said brightly, "The mind is a terrible thing to waste, Cracker-jacks! No time to dilly-dally, time's awastin'! Let's get a move on!"

Chapter Three

Althea and the Artists Guild

The phone rang just as she and Cracker were walking out the door, he, dressed in his favorite bowtie, she in her comfortable sundress.

She grabbed the receiver on the last ring before the machine automatically picked up.

A familiar voice said, "Hey, L! What's cookin'?"

"Allie!" Mrs. Bundle returned the familiar hello. "We were just headed out the door!"

"Good grief! You're in full gear already?" Her best friend Althea (or as Mrs. Bundle had fondly called her since middle school, "Allie") Swain had recently purchased a little brick cape cottage in Pillson Falls and now, to Mrs. Bundle's great delight, lived not three thousand miles away in California but, wonder of all wonders, "just down the road a piece." In fact, Althea's new abode was four houses down from the original Swain family homestead where she had been raised and which had been sold and resold long since Althea's exodus from Pillson Falls many years before.

Returning to her roots in Vermont from the West Coast last year had, at first, been in the form of a surprise visit for Mrs. Bundle. However, after months of continuing her "visit," Althea quite simply had decided to stay.

Everything about Althea Swain was rounded off, friendly and comforting. A perpetual optimist about most everything in life,

Althea's body shape was what a fashion image consultant would call "plentiful" in all the right places—definitely not fat. She was pure *"zaftig,"* pleasantly curvy and pretty and still sensual-looking. Having been her best friend for decades, Mrs. Bundle knew Althea had been the prettiest girl in their high school (whose mature figure had been a hit and dreamed about by all pubescent-aged boys). But, Althea's best quality was her cheerful, open personality. She had always been just plain friendly, one of the few people in school that had liked and been liked by everybody.

Her rich oval face and accentuating bright, welcoming smile were fringed by dirty-blond streaked hair with golden highlights, layered short for ease of care; all of this gave one a sense that she was an open book whose pages were filled with comfort, encouragement, and support. But it was her eyes that captivated most men: large, opalescent-green, as round and perfect as a doll's with long, long golden ash-colored lashes curling just at the end. When Althea looked at you, it was as though you could see exactly what she was thinking, so frank and clear was the brilliant green. Perpetual laugh lines crinkled at the corners of her eyes and her incredibly optimistic approach to life had taken her through some very rough assignments, namely nursing during wartime and a political activism-based second career. She was the epitome of altruistic support and Mrs. Bundle had sorely needed her friendship and assistance after her own brush with death. So, Althea had stayed until Mrs. Bundle was well.

As fate and luck would have it, the "For Sale" sign had gone up on the Pillson Falls brick cottage that same February day that Althea had driven by on her way to the podiatrist's in Springfield. Instead of tending to her sore bunion, she called their old friend and astute realtor, Maisy Tuttle.

Before she knew it, Althea was the new owner of the sweet cottage—*she* was moving back to "The Falls"! Of course, Mrs. Bundle was thrilled that her lifelong friend had decided to remain in Pillson and Althea, never looking back, had settled her affairs in California, moved in March, and was now comfortably settled into her new digs.

Moving to Vermont had provided her the means to spend more time on her favorite pastime: painting with watercolors. Although not replacing her ardent advocacy for the underdog (she would be the first to admit there hadn't been much money in a life of nursing service and human rights activism), Althea's fervor for the watercolor medium had begun to take up her spare time to the point that now it had become her vocation and it was a much-needed respite from the life she had led previously working "for the people."

She had taken up painting as a hobby, but the love of color, the way the paint hit the paper, the graded nuances of the medium—all these elements overwhelmed her imaginative spirit and gave her great joy; so, Pillson Falls was a perfect fit for her burgeoning artist career.

Over the last three decades, Pillson Falls had become somewhat of a sanctuary for artists and fine craftsmen, all of whom reveled in the positive atmosphere of the peaceful, introspective hamlet's setting and the camaraderie of other artisans to canoodle with.

Pillson Falls' setting was an understated place of beauty and tranquility with all of fifteen homes unique in their presentation. These Vermont cottages, made of rough stone whose building techniques were brought to the area by Scottish craftsmen in the early 1800s, were the epitome of quaintness in a scene that could only be described as quintessential Vermont beauty with the cascading water of "The Falls" providing a backdrop and reaching upward toward the majestic mountain views.

Artists took refuge in the quiet setting and their imaginations were challenged to soar without boundaries as they created studios of creativity within. Pillson Falls had become a popular stopping place for tourists and art lovers alike, an afternoon (or morning) of fun for the avid shopper looking for something unique and interesting to bring home from Vermont. Each stone dwelling's exterior and grounds had its individual personality, created by the owner-occupied artisan whose private studio was conveniently accessed either by a path to a side entrance, back shed, or front walkway typically leading to the converted parlor room or porch.

Over the years, this growing Pillson Falls artist community formed a cooperative marketing venue to support their painting habit called "The Guild," eventually becoming a viable commercial entity offering original artwork and exquisite original handicrafts. As luck would have it, the local Pillson Greenhouse also owned a small building fronting on the main thoroughfare, and the owners, art aficionados of sorts, had donated that prime commercial space to be used by The Guild as a cooperative store called "The Falls Artisans Guild." Owners Ellen and Ralph Tarbox felt that it would enhance their expanding business and bring people into the greenhouses to buy their plants and shrubs.

Each Co-Op artist worked his or her few days a month in the modest 15' x 15' retail space. In addition, special workshops, seminars, and open houses were held at different artisan's houses periodically, fostering the arts for area residents.

"The Falls" (as the locals called it) was just south of Pillsonville, past the covered bridge over Twenty Mile Stream and center Pillsonville. Heading northward, a five-minute drive brought Althea right to her friend's driveway in North Pillson Corners.

"Yup! Full gear and rarin' to go," Mrs. Bundle returned the familiar hello. "How are you *today*?" She placed the slightest of emphasis on the last word.

"I'm totally discombobulated! You?" Agitation filled Althea's voice and she didn't wait for a response. "I can't believe it! I was just reading the *Daily*! Did you see the story? About Tuddy's?"

"Yes, I did! What a shame!" They both clucked in sympathetic unison.

"And *just* terrible about poor Tuddsley, too!" Althea said.

"Hopefully, they'll find him alive."

"Could have been scared off by all the commotion…what do you think?"

"Highly likely. Wonder how the fire started…maybe the fryolator?"

"You always hear about the *fryolator* being left on, don't you now, with a restaurant fire? But it sounds like the whole shebang went up fast, even Viola Tudhope's darlin' little shop. What a shame, just a total crying shame! Good *grief*!" Althea sighed deeply. "I loved stopping in there for flowers and the like. It was a real pick-me-up." Her voice dragged a bit and Mrs. Bundle noticed the faint shift downward. Quickly, though, Althea's voice became bright again as she gushed, "Oh, and her arrangements! Oh *Gawdy*! They were truly a work of art, weren't they! I *really* hope she can keep the business going, I've grown to depend on her and *it*. She's the sweetest *girl*, so quiet and unpretentious."

Mrs. Bundle knew that Althea, as usual, was being her typical kind self in her description of the girl. Truth be told, Viola Tudhope was just about the shyest, most gawky person Mrs. Bundle had ever encountered, an odd duck of a girl who rarely, if ever, left the Hartland Four Corners. Pudgy and sweet-looking, Viola kept to herself, rarely spending much time even at the diner next door. Devoid of specific features, she was a brown, drab wallflower amidst all her beautiful shop's blossoms, a sad girl who had never married (with no apparent suitor on the horizon): unassuming and clearly in love with only one thing—the peaceful, private world of growing plants and rendering exquisite floral arrangements. With a personality like a thorny and reclusive little badger, she fairly blushed crimson from head to toe every time a potential customer entered her modest shop, stammering her stock greeting with lowered, heavily lidded eyes, "Hi—*err*... um...hep you?"

Before the patron could respond, Viola would turn tail with the quickly mumbled rush of, "*Okay-let-me-know!*" and then scurry to the back recesses of the shop, an antisocial mass of nerves of the greatest proportions. As she hid behind the shop's back half-wall, she could be observed working feverishly, her pasty features hidden behind a halo of magnificent floral color. Like a line cook plating the daily special, she entered into a new magical world where one could (if one reached their necks to the longest degree) observe Viola's lively, beautifully-shaped hands working on her latest creation, her homely head down, flowers and stems haphazardly flying into the air along with the frenetic sounds of clipping and snipping.

Her lack of sociability skills and embarrassingly bashful nature would naturally make one assume that surely, on the surface, she did not come off as the best retail businesswoman. However, this anomaly was marvelously, gloriously and incredibly superseded by her innate artistry with flowers. Each creation was a true work of art. The phenomenon that occurred was that her business had literally—and figuratively—flourished in the short span of time of less than a year, its success due solely to her tasteful, decorative window displays which brought people through the door and her unbelievably imaginative arrangements, for which she was becoming renowned.

Her wares, without the aid of any salesmanship on the wretchedly shy Ms. Tudhope's behalf, almost walked themselves out the door on their own legs. In fact, customers felt compelled to beseech her to take their money. Her introversion precluded any small talk as she would quickly take their payment (without regard, inspection, or confirmation that it was the right amount), hustling back to her comfortable badger hole.

"Yes," Mrs. Bundle agreed, "quiet and unpretentious is an understatement, to be sure. And *sweet*, too if you can get her to stay and converse at any length. I'm not sure '*girl*' would be an apt description, though. You know, Allie, Viola's got to be *at least* in her thirties now, wouldn't you say? I'm pretty sure she was in Karen's class."

(Karen, Mrs. Bundle's 33-year-old daughter, had attended Woodstock Regional High School around the same time as the quiet artisan whose maiden vs. old maid status was in question.)

"Yes, you're right—not really a 'girl' anymore, the bloom is off the rose, so to speak." With a snort of pessimism, Althea said, "I guess one should say…'young woman'? Isn't that the politically correct term by today's standard?" A sardonic huffing sound was followed by, "Good grief! What does that make us, L?" She made that same sound again, much more cynically.

"Uh…let me think, Allie. Got it! How 'bout 'Mature Babes'?"

"That's us, for sure! *The mature babes*…uh-huh! Of little Pillsonville, Vermont, USA."

"Say, we'll form our own society, call ourselves the 'MB's' for short!"

"'MB's'? I can think of another 'M' word...how 'bout menopausal?"

Mrs. Bundle could see this conversation going downhill fast; recently, she'd noticed that the way Althea framed her normally-positive thoughts seemed sometimes jaded. She changed the topic quickly. "So, what else is new, Allie?"

"Oh, nothing of any significance. Nothing much happening really. 'Bout as boring as...boring can be. By the way, before I forget," Althea's voice had turned to an even duller gray, "that *new guy* moved in."

Flat, solid tone—Mrs. Bundle thought she also heard distinct displeasure in Allie's voice. "Oh, ye-e-es! The *new guy*...," She waited for Althea to continue; however, when no further information came, she said expectantly, "*Well?*"

"Uh-huh! Moved in, huge boxes and all. Very mysterious, if you ask me...he's only leased the house for two months, or so I hear. Well, that is if you can believe what you hear—all this according to that *buffoon* Tim Scott." She emitted a huge "*Hmmph!*", then went silent, clearly miffed about something.

"Is that right?" Stalling with the best of them, Mrs. Bundle knew that sound. It was Althea's "taking umbrage" sound; before today (and in all the years of their friendship) she'd only heard it a few times. Definitely, that was disdain in Allie's voice and she was going to get to the bottom of it. Deciding to jump in with both feet, she asked, "What on *earth* is bothering you, Allie?"

She waited patiently, in silence, for only a second, until the other line exploded like a firecracker.

"*Good grief!* I mean, *really!* Much ado about nothing, that's what I say! Why all the hoopla? *Gaw-dy!*"

"Oh, right, I see." Mrs. Bundle empathized, knowing somewhat Althea was referring to.

The house that backed up directly behind Allie's and whose frontage was on narrow Niagra Lane had been vacant for quite some time while the owners traveled throughout Europe. However, all that had changed recently as the agent managing their property had rented the little cottage to a Flatlander, someone from "away," and the slow-moving village, always ripe for some local gossip, had speculated with great interest while awaiting the new tenant's arrival.

To date, Tim Scott (also known as Pillson's U.S. Post Office employee) was the only one in the village who seemed to know what was going on with the outsider. Having met this unknown somebody when "he" had come in earlier that month to apply for a post office box, Tim was more than smug, holding all the cards surrounding the delicious details of who the stranger was, what he did, and when he would be arriving.

Consequently, a bit of a busybody, Scott had proceeded to relentlessly tease each and every single Pillson woman of marrying age who entered the post office, kidding that "a debonair bachelor" was moving into the Elliot house for the summer and that "someone better be quick and land him before he headed back to the big city in the fall." Tim particularly enjoyed kidding the most mature women in Pillson and Althea had been his particular target, bearing the brunt of his joking because she was lucky enough to share the back property line.

"You just wait, Miz Swain, 'til you meet this handsome devil! He'll knock your socks off, I daresay, or I'll be a monkey's uncle. Better be quick, though…I'll wager there'll be a line waiting outside his door!" From what Tim implied, *everyone* was dying to meet him but, as yet, this mysterious playboy from afar hadn't shown up at the property.

Hence, today was quite a momentous occasion for Pillsonville (especially if one listened to Tim Scott). A true "Red Letter Day" for all available spinsters, especially Althea, because she seemed to be the only one, as yet, that had now seen *him*. The recommendation appeared to be that if she moved fast, she could pounce on *him* quick as lightening, lasso him, throw him to the ground, and get a wedding ring through his nose before anyone else eyeballed him.

With some marginal curiosity, Mrs. Bundle asked, "So? What's he like? Did you actually meet him?"

Althea sniffed, her manner that of having one's nose *slightly* out of joint. "Sssssst! No, not in so many words. I met his *dog*, though." She sniffed again. "Good *grief!*"

"What?"

"Most unpleasant! As it happens, when I went out this morning to get the paper, I stepped in something very *disagreeable*."

"Oooh…not good."

"No, not at all, not by a long shot! And I mean to let Mr. New-Neighbor-Fancy-Pants know—when I see him—that it wasn't something I desired or intended to experience on a regular basis!" Althea proceeded to go into a lengthy, animated diatribe about people who couldn't control their dogs, especially the Flatlanders, ad infinitum while Mrs. Bundle did what best friends do in this circumstance. The friend's manual clearly stated: *patiently tap foot, nod head, smile, add a well-placed,* "You're *so* right, Allie," *and* "Uh-huh, I so agree, know what you mean, uh-huh!" *until "friend" winds down.*

Finally, when there appeared to be a window of opportunity, Mrs. Bundle jumped in with more interest than she wanted to own up to, "But you say you haven't seen *HIM*."

"Well, no, *ah-hh,* I take that back—actually yes—well, kind of. I did catch a glimpse of him, but he darted—like a snake in the grass, mind you—back into the house. Probably afraid to face the music, the…big *nincompoop!* At any rate, what I did see wasn't so special, if you ask me. Looked kind of lanky, a tall drink of water, and *old* to boot! Well, older than us, I'd say." She sniffed once more, this time in resignation. "Suits *me* just fine. As long as he keeps his distance, that's all I care about! I don't need to meet this," she spat out, "*Lothario,* especially until the rest of the town gets their own good gander at him. Let the dust settle. Doesn't interest me *in the least*. Personally, I like my privacy just fine, thank you very much!"

"Well, you know," Mrs. Bundle said encouragingly, "he might be a very nice gentleman..?"

"Good grief! Are you kidding? I don't think so!" Althea's answer sounded as though she had crinkled her nose into a very sharp point, a point so needlelike it could very well have made a serious puncture, and she eked out one more, well-emphasized knifelike grunt of derision. "*Gaw!!!*"

Aware she had already ventured way too far out onto the thinnest of ice, Mrs. Bundle lightened the subject matter once again. "Well, think about it, Althea…" and modulated the tone of her voice to replicate Tim Scott's boisterously squeaky, gossipy tone, "'Althea Swain, how on earth are you ever going to find a MAN—capital 'M,' capital 'A', capital 'N'—with that there attitude?'"

Feigning helplessness, Althea replied, "*Man?* You say, man? Oh, my, Tim! You're so right, you...*man,* you!" Althea went with it, her voice a bundle of twittering girlish nervousness, "Oh, Tim, you're so…*incredibly*…fascinating! Show me this new 'Wonder Guy,' please, *please* I'm desperate to meet him! Where is he? Oh, help me, please, won't you?" She shrieked through the receiver, "I need a man!"

They both roared at her female caricature of total male dependency. The suggestion that Althea Swain *needed* a man in her life, or for that matter, would *ever* actively search for a man, was as absurd as Mother Theresa dating James Bond. She was, and always had been, the epitome of the independent woman; her middle name—"Self-reliant"—might as well have been emblazoned on her forehead.

Mrs. Bundle sighed deeply; it might be best to change the subject to something more palatable and with larger scope. "And so goes life in our little world…so it goes!"

"Well put!" Althea chuckled. "So, what's up for you today, 'L'?"

"Oh, the usual same stuff. As I said, we were just headed out the door. I've got my 'to do' list and I'll just keep going till it's done. How 'bout you?"

"Well, I'm working at the Co-Op today. Stop in if you have time."

"Would love to but can't today, sorry! I've got to get in to the Library and check in with Louis."

"Oh? Do you need me there, too?"

"No, just want to make sure we're ready for the next meeting, trying to prepare. You know, it's going to be a big one. I do have a couple thoughts I want to run by you. Nothing spectacular yet, though…" Mrs. Bundle didn't need to tell Althea what was going down at the next meeting; an item addressing the creation of some type of fundraising event on their motion had been placed on the agenda; this appeared to be the only way of saving the library.

"We've got to figure something out, that's for sure!"

"A good brainstorming session between us might help!" (Mrs. Bundle had yet to come up with a solid, viable idea that would put thousands of dollars into the Library coffers—a small problem, she acknowledged to herself, but one she determinedly would solve.) The library had always been free to the public and subsidized by the Town. The decision to either stay open or close the library's doors *"until further notice"* would be made at this week's Board meeting, the results of which would then be passed along to be sanctioned by the Town Select Board at their subsequent meeting scheduled to occur in a matter of days.

"Right! But L, what about…our other big problem?"

"Armand?"

"Uh-huh." Both women immediately felt squeamish.

Armand Limpert had moved to Pillson as a well-to-do transplant from New York City. No one knew when he first arrived on the scene that he would be so much trouble. When Armand had first been asked to join the Board, snippets around the village portrayed him as "as a previously influential literary and art critic of independent means," and a "flatlander" who had migrated a year-and-a-half earlier to purchase a gentleman's farm on North Puckerbrush Road. Initially keeping his flashy and overbearing side "on the down-low," he had settled quietly into their little community with no indication that he needed to work for a living. In the first few months of his arrival in Pillson, he had reached out to every village official, endearing himself and offering his expertise and services for whatever public event or position he could volunteer for. Seemingly benign, extremely helpful, and with plenty of time on his hands, Armand had been welcomed by the village, his reputation ostensibly preceded by his wide experience and knowledge in many subject areas.

"Right. And don't forget Archie, too, for that matter." said Mrs. Bundle, "What on earth has gotten into him? His *father* wouldn't want this, to be sure."

Archie Plummer was the other thorn in their side. Archie, a native Pillsonite, was considered a major player in the area, well-liked and well-heeled, someone who always, it seemed, had his hands in every pot, wheeling and dealing everything from retail to real estate. With natural ease, Archie had taken over his father's well-established real estate company, along with Bud Plummer's antique auctioneer side business, a half dozen years earlier when Bud had retired to the Florida Keys. Archie was known by most, albeit begrudgingly, as a "go-getter." Coming from a bit of money, he was what some called an opportunist and others called a show boater. So, as new resident Armand Limpert had made himself known in the village, forming a quick union with the Pillson "powers-that-be," he cleverly fostered one relationship in particular—with longtime member of the Selectmen's Board, Archie Plummer. And when Archie contacted Mrs. Bundle (then Pillson's Public Library Board Chairperson), gently suggesting Armand Limpert for the newest director chair opening (vacated by Sam Parkinson's job transfer to Burlington), she had been amenable and Armand had quietly slid into place.

"Well, Bud's probably happy just golfing and enjoying life in the Sunshine State." Althea said, "He doesn't want to hear about our problems, I'm sure."

"Really, I've never had any issues with Archie but I do remember him more as he was when he was a young boy growing up with Leslie. They played sports together through every grade until they graduated high school and went their separate ways. He had quite a competitive edge, you know, even as a youngster."

"Hasn't changed much, has he?"

"Nope. I can just see that eager face...him standing on the basketball free-throw line for a foul shot, right? There's Archie, wiggling his little body from head to toe, waiting for complete silence—savoring the drama, don't you know! *Slowly*...he finally shoots the ball, everyone watching...it goes around the rim once, twice, three times and finally—in it goes! The crowd went crazy and that look on his face! Didn't he love all that attention! He was a true grandstander, even then."

"Well," Althea said, "he loves the limelight like a rat loves cheese, that's for sure. And it's uncanny how he always seems to be in the right place at the right time when it comes to finding a good deal. Seems like he's got his fingers in every pie—he's making quite a name for himself. I've never seen anything like it."

"I just wish he hadn't been so *helpful* with Armand." Mrs. Bundle sighed.

"Bushwhacked, that's what I'd call it!"

Yes, they had all been fooled; the first couple months on the Board with Armand had been delightful as he integrated his wealth of metropolitan knowledge and experience into the small community's soul.

The beginning signs of discord only became evident around September, when word came in writing from the state-mandated building evaluation report that there were some major updates and repairs that would need to be done to bring the library up to code. There was no turning the clock back; these things had to be done. Armand had implied at that time that he *might* not be in favor of any significant expenditure relative to the library's upkeep and so began his systematic, calculating mission to close the Library.

Incapacitated in late November and unable to fulfill her chairperson duties, Mrs. Bundle's absence allowed opportunity for Armand, who adroitly volunteered and was unanimously voted into her Chairperson's seat. Althea had subsequently volunteered to attend in Mrs. Bundle's stead until she was well enough to rejoin the Board. Then, Zack Benois' wife, Betty, had taken ill and suddenly passed away that winter. In May, Mrs. Bundle had returned to find the Board in chaos. Althea had then volunteered to take Betty's empty position. Even for the locals, it was a merry-go-round of musical chairs that was hard to follow, to be sure, but by then, it was too late to undo the damage that had been done by the crafty Armand; an enemy was embedded deeply within the Friends of the Pillson Library Board and, at this point, the damage might never be repaired. Although a feeble attempt had been made to raise some local money by setting up a donation box at the front desk, Armand Limpert, Head of the Library Board, had remained adamant in his assertion that the Library should be closed.

The instability within the board because of all the changes had fostered an underlying sense of disorganization, which led to disagreements (primarily generated by Armand Limpert) about exactly how the code issues should or could be handled. Nothing seemed to get resolved under his leadership and a couple of the board members had threatened to quit. He continued to run the board without much open resistance, doing so with an iron fist and his loud, New York-pushy accent.

"I just don't want to have to listen to him hammer away at us like he did at our last board meeting. It's really hard to take!" Althea said.

That meeting had become very heated as various trustees (including Mrs. Bundle and Althea) tried to reason with the verbose and abrasive man—who offered no proactive solutions, only rhetoric, to the library closing issue.

Mrs. Bundle shuddered at the memory of Armand's scathing words. "Those books should all be moved out before any further damage is done! Everyone's taxes will go sky high if we continue subsidizing this monstrosity of a building! The taxpayers just won't stand for it. It's an old relic that has seen better days, a dangerous albatross, and we are just prolonging the agony by keeping it open. The building is worthless, at this point, and its days are numbered. And we've already been told that the elementary school building's *basement* would house the public library just fine!"

"L? Are you still there?" Althea's question brought Mrs. Bundle back to the here and now.

"Yes, Allie, yes. Right! We *need* a plan. We've *got* to come up with something! How 'bout if you and I meet for lunch tomorrow at Herder's?" Located just outside of Pillson Junction on the way to

Woodstock, Herder's was the local country café, known for its casual environment, modest prices, and great food.

"Great idea! We'll put on our thinking caps and dream up a way to beat this problem. Don't worry, L. Maybe after lunch we can take a ride over to Hartland Four Corners and see what's left of poor Tuddy's Diner."

"Sure, why not! It's not that far from Herder's. And, Allie?"

"Yuh?"

"Wear your sneakers so we can get in a hike, too, maybe right there on the Hartland Green around the Square, or something."

"Good grief, L! In this hot weather?"

"Yes, in this hot weather. It'll be good exercise."

"You're twisting my arm. Ouch! God knows I could use it."

"Oh, it'll be fun. Noon at Herder's?"

"Perfect. See you then!"

"Have a good one!"

Chapter Four

Time to Get a Move on… Maybe?

As she reached the end of her gravel driveway, Mrs. Bundle stopped Junebug (her automotive pride and joy) to get out and place two letters in the massive, drab green mailbox. The little emerald-green 1963 Volkswagen's engine awaited her return, idling joyously. "Junie," as Mrs. Bundle called her, was happy to be out of the musty old barn and on the road once again. This was the diminutive Beetle's favorite time of year, when her sporty sunroof could be thrown wide open to let in the glorious sun while Mrs. Bundle and Cracker burned up the roads of Pillson. Royal Hudson of Hudson's Garage made sure Junie's engine hummed contentedly, continuing to service the Bug since the first day Mrs. Bundle had acquired her. The music from the original 8-track stereo cassette player blared through the steaming summer air, the strains of Petula Clark's "Downtown" melodiously stroking and massaging the dewy morning.

One of the posted letters was to her daughter Karen, who was an environmentalist in Alaska, and the other letter was to her son Leslie, a diplomat in Japan. Both of her children were very independent and had been high achievers with goals far exceeding anything their parents had ever desired for them. In fact, Mrs. Bundle often wondered where they had gotten their ambitious energy and drive. She loved them dearly, wishing nothing but the best for her two children, and the world had quickly taken them into its large arms.

Leslie and his wife Donna had talked about sending Leslie, Junior (Mrs. Bundle's only grandchild) to Vermont for a visit this summer, and those happy plans were in the works for a visit in July and possibly into August if all went well. Mrs. Bundle hadn't seen Les (as he liked to be called now that he was ten) since before they'd left for Japan when he was seven. The photos they'd sent recently revealed a tall, very slender, but healthy-looking boy with a huge, toothy smile dressed in a baseball outfit; she hardly recognized him now that he had grown so. Naturally, she was elated that he might be coming for a stay this summer. *How fast they grow up*, she thought regretfully.

She was sending them the most recent pictures of the splendorous garden, along with pictures of the Memorial Day get-together with the Corrigan clan and the Andersens.

As she opened the VW sedan door, she heard a distinct rumbling sound, its resonance growing greater, and turned, not at all surprised at the distinctly uncommon sight before her.

It was Lonnie Macomber, her local mail carrier, coming up the road. The clamorous noises came from his alternative to the traditional postal truck: a Harley Davidson Servi-car, which to all motorcycle buffs is also known as a "three-wheeler." Crafted in true American tradition, these "Servi-car 45ci" trikes were sold between 1932 and 1972; Lonnie's 1945, with its large, square back box behind the comfortable seat, efficiently carried each mail run's heavy load. In their day, many of these unique utility motorcycles were used by police forces, a favorite of police parking-enforcement divisions. Commercial retail vendors also discovered them as a unique way to sell their wares (many were used as ice cream or hot dog wagons in seaside settings or city parks). Nowadays, companies sold conversion kits to fit the most popular touring bikes so that the nostalgic look of the Servi-Car would not be lost to future generations. At any rate, Lonnie's coveted machine was the real deal, and he was known throughout the county; the added benefit was hearing his distinctive approach, which allowed for proper notice of their mail's arrival.

Postal service was in the Macomber blood. On the rare day that Lonnie was under the weather, Arletta, his 75-year-old mother, would take the trike out and do the mail delivery herself. Arletta had been Postmistress from 1950-1980, and her mother Esther, the same before her. Esther had first kept the post office in her husband's ironmonger shop, then later in her home for twenty-five years before the post office was moved officially into the Town Hall. Lonnie had taken over delivery duties fresh out of high school in 1986. Granted, it was a blessed sight to see Arletta Macomber on the rugged trike, putt-putting along, cycle goggles over her dainty spectacles, leather jacket flapping over the postmaster delivery outfit, determined to get Lonnie's mail run done on time.

Lonnie's forty-ish sister, Bessie May Macomber-Scott, and his brother-in-law, Tim, (the afore-mentioned needling buffoon) completed the family US dispatch dynasty. Bessie May, the elder, had deftly slid into the postmistress position by birthright when her mother retired. Tim worked unobtrusively in the mailroom, occasionally filling in for Bessie May at the front desk when things got hectic or he could escape his back room prison. The fact of the matter was, everyone knew that if there was a ten-story building and Bessie May, who towered over her husband by a good ten inches, said, "Jump!" he would break both legs trying to complete her directive. Tim was, unfortunately, a man of many words *only* when his wife wasn't around to hear him. Conversely, when she was within hearing distance, he was as timid as a rabbit and twice as skitterish. (As Althea would say often, "Bessie's got him wrapped up tighter than Tupperware!")

All in all, the Macombers had held the corner on the U.S. Postal market in Pillson since 1939. They all took the United States Postal Service's motto "The mail must go through" very seriously. Indeed, their service and commitment were so fanatical that not one Pillsonite would ever dream of interrupting the smooth flow of the Macombers' superb handling of their mail.

Located in two tiny rooms off the first floor entrance of Town Hall since 1976, the Post Office was a mainstay, a meeting place for many of the locals and a constant hub of activity. Residents who lived in the outlying areas, like Mrs. Bundle in North Pillson Corners, had their mail ceremoniously and diligently hand-delivered by Lonnie, now here in front of her in full regalia and ready to serve without fail.

"Hi Lonnie, you're early today!"

"Hey there, Mrs. Bundle! Hey there, Cracker!" He cut the engine and jumped off the motorcycle, unwinding his spindly frame, then propped his U.S. Postal hat farther back on his head, and reached for the letters Mrs. Bundle had just placed in the box. His wide grin flashed brightly and eager eyes gobbled up her envelopes with great interest. "Yuh, I sure am! Early, that is! We got an overload of mail today, so I'm 'bout an hour ahead of schedule *due to the fact* that I left about an hour earlier than usual. Pretty clever, ain't I?"

He peered with greatly unbridled interest at the posted letters in his hand. "So, where are *our friends* headed today?"

The term *"our friends"* was one that Lonnie used on a regular basis. It was an endearing term meant not for her and Cracker, but for the actual letters in his hand. Lonnie, purely and simply, just loved letters: big, small, plainly wrapped or colorful, thick or thin, it didn't matter. The power each communication held over him was within each of their contents; *where* they had come from (or where they were going), *whom* they were from, *what* valuable and exciting information they held—for him, it was like holding precious gold bullion in his hands. Above all, most dear to him was that he loved talking in imaginative detail about "his friends" and their relationship to his world to anyone who would stop long enough to listen.

A quirky fellow he was—but everyone knew he truly loved his job. One could say, unequivocally, that postal service was his life and there wasn't much (as it appeared to the naked eye anyway) outside of that life. He was unceasingly intrigued with the comings and goings of his precious letters and packages. His interest knew no bounds and, as he read off the names and addresses, he would freely offer any remote knowledge or experience he had, connecting the dots in an excrutiatingly unremarkable way.

"Kalamazoo, Michigan...," he would begin his lecture, reading the postmark on the envelope, "Oh, yes, uh-huh! A bunkmate of mine in the Guard—*National* Guard—had a great aunt from Kala-

ma-zoo…I think her name was Mary. Yes…called 'May' for short—
that's the abbreviated version for Mary, don't you know. Now, give
me a minute…what was her last name? Kinda funny, rhymed with
sneezer—I'll get it, you just hold on… yes, began with 'W'—I know
it was a 'W' 'cuz I remember Ma and me looked her up when we
went down to Niagara Falls—we made a big U-turn, don't you know,
just to see her. Mmm…'twasn't Geezer, it was…Weezer! There, just
like I said! Weezer….what the *hake* was the rest of it? I know it had a
'bissell' or something *odd* like that at the end, funny-like, you know? I
like to make a connection with something real when I'm rememberin'
things…you know, like '*crow*' would mean 'blackbird', which would
be '*Black*', right? Anyhoo, bissell rhymes with…yes, that was it!" He'd
snap his fingers in success. "*Weezer-wissell*!" (By now, even the most
polite listener's interest would have been tested to the limit.) "May
Weezerwissell! That was her name! Oh, *what* a nice lady. *Real* nice
lady." Eyes glazed over, the listener would nod encouragingly for
closure as Lonnie wrapped up with, 'And if you ever get to Kalamazoo,
I'll give you the address and you can look her up!"

Today was no different as he curiously looked over the two letters.
His reaction to the Anchorage address was a heartfelt, "*Yessir*, would
you look at that!"

Eyebrows raised, he looked toward the wide blue sky in deep,
deep thought and then rattled off his well-stored trivia knowledge in
staccato-like fashion. "Anchorage, located in Alaska. Alaska: 'the last
frontier', stretches 1955 miles, the size of Delaware."

He stopped and beamed; his benevolent smile focused on Mrs.
Bundle. Hawk-nosed, with an overly large Adam's apple (which
wobbled wildly when he was excited), he exclaimed, "*Love that
place*! Hey now, how *is* Karen? Why, I remember when she was this
high!" He held his gawky hand up to his thigh and then raised it
slowly while his eyebrows rose simultaneously, till he reached above
his six-foot-two frame.

He gave a huge guffaw. "*Hah*—gotcha! Just kiddin'! *Gawd*! Ain't
that somethin'! Is she still workin' for that outfit? Them treehuggers?
Greenpeace, it is, right?"

Mrs. Bundle smiled graciously and nodded (in likewise-friendly fashion).

He placed the letter carefully in his letterbag, and then looked with interest at the postmark on the other letter. "Don't tell me, I can pronounce this one on my own! It's Shan-na-*gaw*-wa! That's how they'd say it over there, wouldn't they now, Mrs. Bundle?" He laughed good-naturedly. "Shinagawa, Japan! Good ol' Leslie! What a guy! Who'd a thunk that quiet little kid with them buckteeth woulda ended up way the heck over there!" Mrs. Bundle cringed at his description of poor Leslie at the awkward age of ten-through- twelve, just before his now-handsome face grew into that toothsome smile. "Just goes to show you, don't judge a book by its cover—it'll come back and bite you every time! Shinagawa, Japan, don't that beat all?" he repeated, his lopsided grin counterbalanced by the lopsided blue worsted jersey postal cap he wore so proudly. "Say! Danged if I don't have one right here for you from the *exact* same locale!" He reached into his bag and handed her the letter. "From here to there, from there to here! Back and forth across the wide blue ocean. Just like that. Unbe-*liev*able! All the way across the world that letter came! Mrs. Bundle, I daresay, if I had to wager—and mind you, I ain't a betting man, but..." he looked at her with complete adulation, "...I'd bet my eyeteeth you got some of the best mail around these parts!"

Mrs. Bundle placed the letter in her pocket. "Why, thank you Lonnie!"

"You're welcome! You truly are!" He turned back to the trike. "Hey, now! Before I forget, I got a letter here for Jack, too."

He reached into the back compartment on the Servi-car and pulled out a large, thin manila envelope, neatly sealed and quite official looking. "Pretty tight seal on the back! Take a look at that, would ya? I declare!" He peered longingly at the prize, "Looks pretty important. *And* they want confirmation of delivery—usually means it must be special! Love those! We can let you sign for Jack, right here."

She took the outstretched pen and signed, and he held the ocher envelope away from his failing eyes and squinted. "Yup. Says it's from 'Barlow, Reed, Fish, McDougall and Dolan'—Holy Moley, that's a long name! *Very* official-like. That's a law firm, ain't it? Postmark's somewhere in New York, I think…if I remember correctly."

Mrs. Bundle took hold of the envelope and tugged lightly as Lonnie stretched his long neck even longer to get a good look at the postmark.

He tugged back, grinning from ear-to-ear, but Mrs. Bundle gently, but firmly, removed it from his grasp. He looked at Mrs. Bundle expectantly, innocently hoping to gain just a bit more information.

She glanced at the postmark and shrugged, then adroitly propelled the envelope, like a miniature missile, into the back seat of the VW. "Huh! No idea, Lonnie…" she said, smiling nonchalantly. "We'll let Jack discover that. Goodness knows—could be just about anything!"

"Right you are! Could be just about anything! Jack being a foreigner and all. Probably some more of that 'green card' stuff. As you say, could be about anything. Well, you usually are, Mrs. Bundle! Right, that is!" He shuffled, rambling amiably, feathers unruffled, and turned his attention to the movement inside Junie, where Cracker had jumped from the back seat into the front.

"Hey, Cracker! How's the world treatin' ya?" Lonnie turned, shielded his mouth and whispered to Mrs. Bundle, "He looks kinda antsy, don't he, Mrs. Bundle?"

Meeoow! Excuse the interruption, Cracker cat-thought impatiently, *but do you think we could just get going? We've got places to go and people to see!*

Mrs. Bundle reached down and stroked his shiny back, chuckling, "Gracious me, yes! Cracker just loves visiting with all his friends downtown."

Truth be told, Cracker was always anxious to get down to the village—especially now that he was a celebrity. He was often the center of attention while Mrs. Bundle did her errands. Having gained a certain amount of notoriety during the Children of Lir pendant mystery, he had (with complete cat condescension mixed with a dash of aplomb) acquiesced to the fact that it was incumbent upon him to maintain a certain level of privilege with his peers and patrons. Wasn't he 'The Bundle Cat,' after all, the one who had saved the day? Children loved him, women showered him with praise and treats, and men, well… men accepted him into their manly fraternity, the private arena when they all sat around and parleyed *their* own heroic exploits.

He would be the first to acknowledge that he basked in the glory of his recent celebrity. So, on the occasions when he accompanied Mrs. Bundle, he always wore one of his many natty bow-tie collars, all fashioned with care by his mistress.

In addition to Cracker's penchant for natty attire, he was ever-conscious of maintaining his pristine toilette. Mrs. Bundle, more than willing to accommodate her cat's proclivity for individuality and elegance, created outfits for Cracker that suited the occasional outing or social event. Young and old alike noticed and often commented favorably on his snappy *accoutrements* and dapper appearance.

Today was no exception; Mrs. Bundle had snapped on a particularly bright and festive number: his ocean blue, catfish-patterned bow tie, which was his current favorite. He strained his neck toward the open window and meowed loudly, then hopped into the back seat again.

"Well, I can take a hint, *doggone* it!" Lonnie happily jumped back on the rumbling motorcycle seat; his scrawny frame, positioned on the bike, reminded Mrs. Bundle of an emaciated praying mantis perched with a purpose on the large metal monster.

As Cracker despairingly squeezed his cat eyes shut at this most recent canine reference, Lonnie exclaimed, "Time's awasting! Gotta keep on my schedule; people depend on me! Time to get a *move* on!"

"Yes, we must fly, too, Lonnie!" Mrs. Bundle agreed, waving.

"As you know, Mrs. Bundle," he sat up straight in his seat, raised his right hand in a saluting motion to his head, and proclaimed officially, "*the mail must go through!*"

He rotated the clutch handle and fired up the old engine. It was an ungodly commotion.

Lonnie yelled over the loud machine and noxious fumes, "See ya, Mrs. Bundle! See ya, Cracker! Don't take any wooden nickels!" Above the noise of the ancient muffler, he gave one last heartfelt bellow over his shoulder, "*Have a good one!*"

He drove off in a blaze, pea gravel flying every which way, down the country road.

Chapter Five

Walter and Aineen

Mrs. Bundle got back inside the uncomplaining Junebug, primly adjusted her sundress and pressed her foot lightly on the gas pedal, gently revving up the ever-steady engine. She smiled coaxingly into the rearview mirror at Cracker.

"Hold on, Cracker. I promise you we're going! By the way, thanks *ever so* for being so patient. I'd say we're ready to roll now."

His tiny teeth glistened into the semblance of a cat smile. *Not a bit of trouble*, he cat-thought graciously.

Alas, the best-laid plans are often sidetracked; their quick escape was not to be.

As she shifted into first gear, she stopped again, looking up the main road. "Why, look, Cracker, there's Walter!"

She waved merrily at Walter Andersen's old panel truck which had just entered the main road and was headed their way.

Walter spied them and deftly pulled the beat-up pickup beside Junebug. In the back seat of the extra-cab truck was a small curly head bobbing frenetically. Aineen Corrigan, the Andersen's tiny ward, was secured but straining in her car seat. Her little wispy mop swayed back and forth, bright eyes struggling to peer up over the passenger window, anxious not to miss a thing. Clear little spit bubbles flowed like animated balloon expressions from her cute rosebud mouth.

She giggled gleefully when she spied Mrs. Bundle, then craned her neck even higher, straining upward in the car seat.

"B! Bee! *BEEEE!*" She cried out her name for Mrs. Bundle and then, seeing Cracker, quickly turned her affections toward her favorite little friend. "Kack-a! Kitt-eeeee! K-K-Kacka!" she shouted from her imprisoned perch. 'Kith! *Kith!!* *Br-r-r-rurrrrppp!*" she spluttered, "Kith Kitty!" She formed her adorable lips into a big, wet smooch, reaching out in vain to make contact across the void of the two vehicles.

Cracker, despite usual decorum and his persnickety nature, was excited to see his little friend and he strained to climb out the passenger window but the opening was too small.

Hey, Neeney, Cracker cat-thought, *how goes it, little one?*

"*Blllurrrrrrr*…kith, kith!!" She held her arms out and gave a fair imitation of purring. "*Blllluuurrrrr!*"

Truth be told, Cracker was exceedingly fond of both the diminutive Aineen and her sister Erin. *Hugs and kisses later, little one,* he assured her in precise cat-thought. *I'll be down to play later this afternoon!*

Mrs. Bundle said. "Walter, how goes the day so far on this fine morning?"

"So far, so good. Nothin' major yet," he joked, " 'ceptin' this little one here." He pointed a large thumb in the direction of Aineen. "Holy Mackerel-Andy, don't she got a mind of her own and then some! Hey!" he chided the baby, "Stop *scrumplin'* your *brandy-new* dress, you little goose! See what I mean, Mrs. B? She's like a nonstop *locomotion* at the farm! Hell's bells, it's a train wreck and a half, and then some! There ain't nothin' like a two-year-old to make a mess in a heartbeat! I got her out with me—captive like she is in that there car seat—to give the boys a break, don't you know."

Removing his John Deere hat, he shook his head back and forth 'til his ears waggled of their own accord. Most of his hair was gone, but one long wispy strand of straw-colored hair stretched far and long around his forehead. Although Walter would never attempt the "comb-over" look many men of his age desired, this one long piece just naturally wended itself around and around like a long, unruly ribbon of saffron hay.

"*Ha!*" He laughed heartily and scratched at the baby fine tawny wisps protruding from the crown of his knobby head.

"Indeed!" Mrs. Bundle smiled, knowing that his real motivation for having the baby with him was self-seeking—in a good way—because what he loved was spending quality time alone with the rambunctious, but totally loveable, toddler. Little Aineen had Walter wrapped around her little finger as tightly as a springloaded hinge.

"Gumpy! *Fay-fie*! Fay-fie, Gumpy, *Mmmm*, good! Fay-*fie*!"

"No, you little moppet, Gumpy cain't get you no french fries. Jumpin' jee *hozafats*!" He wiped his brow, and yelled over his shoulder, teasing, "What the *heck* are you thinkin'? Goldarn, it's way too early for french fries—it ain't even lunchtime yet!"

"No! No, *no*!" Aineen shook her wild wispy curls and, pursing her fat lips together, she blew hard. A plethora of bubbles and foam emerged as she gave "Gumpy" a wet, drooling raspberry from her confinement. "S*pppllllluuuuhhhhd*!"

The challenging "terrible two's" had been firmly planted in Aineen's little being. Stretching her chubby little arms out toward Mrs. Bundle, she pleaded shamelessly, "Gug! *Bee-ee*! Me, gug!"

Mrs. Bundle reached in through the back window, un-"scrumpled" the bright bodice of Aineen's little sundress, and gave her a big embrace. "Beee," knew from her own mothering experience all about the "terrible two's"; she knowingly reached into her pocket and, after unwrapping it from its plastic wrapping, handed Aineen an anise biscotti. The hard, crunchy cookie was a favorite of the little girl who squealed with delight and immediately began munching.

Walter gulped, motioning emphatically towards Mrs. Bundle's pocket. "Snatch me baldheaded if you ain't always got some kind of vittle in that dang pocket of yours!" He watched Aineen chomp away with gusto, her tiny teeth enclosed around the cookie. "Cat's granny! Ain't she just like a little hurricane twister though!"

Cracker raised his tail in total agreement as Walter continued, "Gettin' into everythin'! Yessa! You heard Angie found her trying to put on her lipstick a week back, right? By crikey, she had it in her mouth right ready to take a bite out of it! *Jumping gee hozafrats*!" (Aineen ceaselessly babbled and fussed in the back seat.) "And, she scared the *bejeesuz* out of us yesterday mornin'. You cain't take your eyes off her even for a mini-second! She was sittin' in the rocking chair in the parlor, big as life, when we all got up. She got out of the dang crib all by herself, went downstairs, and *toodled* around for God knows how long all by her lonesome. Don't know how she did it, but she sure made herself t'home. Got out her own food, didn't you," he yelled over his shoulder as she ignored him, "you little pipsqueak? Cereal all over the floor! She got into the lower cupboard, poured herself a bowl of crispies in a bowl, then poured the sugar bowl all over it. Couldn't get the milk out of the fridge, though," he huffed, "otherwise, we'd still be cleaning up the mess!"

Aineen, really, little one, Cracker cat-thought to his little friend, *must I be over there all the time keeping you from trouble?*

Aineen spit out a longer, fuller raspberry infused with cookie matter this time.

Cracker was getting jumpy from his confinement in the small VW and nervously hopped from one fidgety paw to another.

"Gumpy, *wa-wa!*" Aineen yelled.

Walter handed the baby's water bottle to her. "And the other one!" he motioned with his superhuge thumb toward his farm, "she's got more brass than Carter's got liver pills!"

Mrs. Bundle chuckled, "Well, I won't disagree with you. Our Erin certainly knows her mind, no doubt about that. She's got spunk, pure and simple." Erin was a charmingly sweet "eight-going-on-thirteen-year-old." "How'd she fare with Chester yesterday?"

"That dang bird! They're thicker 'n *fleas*, the two of them! He follows her around crowin' and cocka-doodlin' to beat the band! What a hooter he's got on 'im! Hey, and she's learning herself that…" he took a deep breath and tried to pronounce it as best he could, "*euka-layleehoo,*" (he'd gulped it out in one breath) "pretty good at it, ain't she now?"

My! Cracker cat-thought, *Now, that was a doozy Walterism!*

Mrs. Bundle threw back her neatly braided head and laughed aloud. For years, she and Cracker had enjoyed Walter's ongoing war with the English language. He brutalized pronunciations and word meanings as no one person legally should or could, rearranging words into fanciful, and often amusing, double meanings which Mrs. Bundle and Cracker had fondly come to describe as "Walterisms."

Regaining momentum and thoroughly undaunted, Walter pushed on, wiggling his long fingers in the breeze, "She's a-strummin' to beat all, like a real pro doin' *quadribble*-time! By the by, she's got a surprise song to strum for you, she's been a-practicin' and a-practicin'—wait'll you hear it! Don't you know she's got Chester eating Cheerios for tricks, training him like a blasted circus animal to '*company* her! *Geez Lou—eeez!*"

Walter was on a roll. Mrs. Bundle did not attempt to interrupt him; she merely nodded and smiled. *Proud he is of the little urchin,* she thought, *there's no doubt of that!*

He continued, "I ain't never seen the likes of it. That Erin's aimin' for the stars, that one. Well, at any rate," he tempered his boasting and became serious, "she's a *dite* too headstrong; we all know that! From my way of thinkin', I tell you what! She can be trouble—capital T! This habit of sneakin' off without tellin' anyone where she's at has gotta go. If she didn't have that cockeyed rooster with her, we wouldn't know where she is! Jack and me had us a powwow about it last night and she's on *probationary restrictions*! She ain't allowed out of the yard or anywhere else, mind you, unless she's got the okey-dokey from either me, the boys, or Jack! That's it! No excuses!"

Mrs. Bundle nodded, "Yes, I think that's wise for now. She just seems to love to wander, doesn't she? I don't think it's intentional. It's more her impetuous nature, combined with that little inquisitive mind! And now that she's got the bicycle...well! She's Pillson's goodwill ambassador. Frankly, I'm not sure how some people take her, as forward and friendly as she is!"

"Oh, they just love her, just like the rest of us." He guffawed loudly. "*Hah!* You cain't help it! Right you are, that's what she is...our *goodwills* ambassador! We gotta keep her busy, that's for danged sure! Othertwise, she's prone to gettin' herself in a heap of trouble."

"She has an inquisitive mind..."

"Inquisitive! She'll likely put the touch on you as plain as day! Don't you know, she tol' me this mornin' she wants to be famous someday and 'make lotsa *moola!*' Yessa! It's exactly how she said it. '*Moola*'. Ha!"

He slapped the side of the truck with the flat of his worn work hand and Aineen gave a loud squeal.

Mrs. Bundle agreed, "Yes, we chatted last night and she said she has a 'super special idea' about how she's going to make some spending money this summer."

"Yup, she done run that idea by me this mornin'. She's got some *hare-brainy* scheme about sellin' rocks. Right there on the farm—out front over there." he pointed. "She knows she ain't supposed to leave the yard now, so she's come up with that. Don't that beat all?" He slapped the truck door harder this time and roared. "Jumpin' lizards! I says, 'Sellin' rocks', I says? 'Why, Erin you're a regular *entrapree*—'" he paused, struggling with *just* the right pronunciation, then spewed out, "—*manure!*"

A yowl erupted from Cracker; his tail went skyward. *Oh, holy cat's eye! This*, Cracker cat-thought in total resignation, *was today's crowning glory of Walterisms.*

Walter, true to form (and never one to rest on his linguistic laurels), swiftly changed gears and exclaimed, "Hey now, before we get a move on, I gotta ask you...how 'bout that Tuddy's!"

"Yes—*and* it made the front page of the *Rutland Daily!*"

"Who needs the *Rutland Daily News*? I heerd it right from the horse's mouth! 'Burned right to the ground' is what Axel Conroy says, 'ceptin' one original brick wall,' so he says."

"Is that so?"

His chest puffed slightly as he drew in a deep breath in an attempt to exhibit modest aplomb. He repeated, "Yessa! 'Course, I known him for years from the Ag Fair, don't you know. He said that there blaze were quite a sight to see!" He shook his head sadly. "A *fine* place, Tuddy's was. Just plain fine. Hope they can rebuild—wouldn't like t' see it gone for good."

"Yes, I would think the insurance will take care of it, wouldn't you? So that they could start it up again? Althea and I are going over tomorrow to take a look-see."

"Uh-huh! We might take a jaunt over there today, me and the little one, if she don't get too wound up and need a nap afore then." He turned his thumb backwards toward the angel behind him who promptly lunged forward and tried to bite it; failing, she grabbed at the thumb, giggled, and flailed her little legs, making as much noise as she could muster.

"Have they got any idea how the fire started?" Mrs. Bundle asked.

"Well, according to Axel, they ain't found anythin' yet, but they're talkin' arson. Nothin' official though..." He leaned forward and lowered his voice, "Axel over*heerd* the Sheriff on his two-way while he was at the scene."

"You don't say!"

"Yes I do! Axel mentioned they found old Tuddsley's *necker-thingamabob* this morning. You know, that dang red hankie he always wore round his neck? Cryin' shame it is! Said they found it lyin' way out back in the brook—in those back woods out behind the business. You know, over by—what the hay do they call it? Mary's Stream, I think, ain't it? Don't look too good for poor Tuddsley at this *junction*..." he trailed off, removing his John Deere cap and holding it lightly to his chest. "May he rest in peace in dog heaven," adding quickly, with respect, "*if* that's the case, mind you."

He scratched his nearly bald head and the slight patch of sandy-white fluffy hair split every which-way.

The noises in the back seat grew louder.

Cracker roamed across the back seat, straining, now, to get out of the car. A small "*Pf-pftt!*" of exasperation escaped from his tiny cat mouth. His feline patience had been worn to a nub and, pacing like a caged lion, his immediate cat-thoughts would not be printable for the faint of heart. More to the point, the update on Tuddsley's unknown whereabouts was truly disconcerting to him.

"Really?" Mrs. Bundle said with interest, "They found just the neckerchief? By Maggie's Stream?"

"*Mary*, Maggie—you know where I'm talkin' about?"

"Sure, I do! And all the way back there in the woods? Isn't that rather odd?" Mrs. Bundle asked.

"Yup. No sign of Tuddsley—yet. *Very odd*, I'd say." He jerked his head toward the back seat. "*Jeesum crowbars*, child! What is all that wailin' about? My ears is ringin' with pain! Come now!" He squinted over his shoulder at the fussing toddler, then reached back and affectionately patted her on her curly head. Feigning a scolding demeanor, he said gruffly, "Stop that *cat*-er-wailin' and cut out that *jibber-jabberin'*, you silly *goose!*"

Cracker hissed with frustration. *Heavens, it's no use*, he cat-thought as he slid his rough tongue over his sleek coat for the hundredth time.

Aineen stopped squawking and squealed with glee.

"Yes, you!" Walter pointed at her in mock scolding. "You be quiet now, *Petunia!*"

"*No!* No, no-no-no-no!" Aineen giggled and shook her head back and forth, becoming increasingly intrigued with the sound of her banging feet on the hard carseat base which was intermingled in joyful unison with her own voluminous echoes.

Walter shook his head, grabbed the steering wheel like a man with a purpose, and restarted the truck, chuckling. "*Gaw!* Don't she just beat all? Yup, she's a pip, all right!" He motioned to Mrs. Bundle. "Watch this." Once again, he changed his voice: this time to mimic a comical cross between Mr. Rogers and Sesame Street's Oscar. "You're quite a riggin', yes you are, little one!"

She chortled and yelled at the top of her lungs, "*Wiggin'!* Me wiggin'! *Big girl* wiggin'!" She raised her chubby arms wide and pushed at the truck's ceiling. This was a game they had played before!

Hurriedly, he said, "Like I say, Mrs. B, we cain't stop to chitchat! I gotta get down to Harper's Feed and see what they got for baler parts. Keep your fingers *kitty-crisscrossed* they got what we need. Otherwise, we're up a *crick* without a *piddle!*"

"What's wrong with the baler now?" Mrs. Bundle asked.

"Oh, that dang tying mechanism's broke down—the blasted thing keeps catchin' and she won't engage without stickin'!"

Mrs. Bundle nodded, knowing enough farm lingo to interpret that this meant the ancient John Deere hay baler wasn't working properly; the rest could be filed under *Too Much Information*.

"We ain't gonna get nothin' done this summer 'til we get it fixed! I'm sick of fiddlin' with it—too dangerous for anyone but the boys and me the way it is! Everyone down at Harper's is got their own opinion about how to git it fixed. All I know is, someone's gonna get their dang *hoozimagigger* cut off if they fiddle with it!" His brow furrowed and he looked piqued. "Ain't there always somethin'?"

"Seems that's so, Walter."

Shaking his head, he quipped, "C'mon, Aineen, let's *skedaddle*!"

He squinted at Mrs. Bundle; the sun beat down mercilessly. "See you both down at the house for suppa? Steak on the barbie per usual and a dite of my *curious lemonadey* on the back porch. Mixed it up special this mornin'—secret ingredient and all." He winked. "Oh! And I'll be jiggered but didn't Carl say he's been workin' out a new tune for Jack and Erin! Something snappy by the sounds of it! Maybe he'll bring it forth tonight."

"You bet. Remember, only a week or so 'til Angie gets home!"

"Uh-huh, you better believe it! July the second—but her bus won't get in 'til late-—around ten or so. Clay'll pick her and Natalie up."

"I can't wait to see that girl!"

"Shoot, things have been too quiet around here what with her gone to sport camp! We all miss our Miss Bossy-boss Angie, that's for dang sure!" He called over his shoulder, "Don't we now, Petunia?"

Aineen clapped her hands loudly, happy again as she blew out more juicy bubbles and gurgled, "Jeee!"

"So, she'll be here for the burnin'." Mrs. Bundle said.

"Yup! Just in time for the big ol' *bomb-fire* up at Doc Dot's, to be sure!"

The big engine rumbled and revolved noisily as Walter put the truck into gear. He yelled over the clamor in the backseat, "Say bye-bye, 'Neeney!"

"Bye-bye, Beee! *Bye-bye, Kacka!* Bye-bye, bye-bye, *Gumpy*!"

"Gumpy?" Walter yelped, "No, *I* ain't goin' bye-bye, you silly poop! You and *me's* together!"

She chortled and waved, "Bye-*bye*! Bye-bye, Kack-a! Bye-bye, *Beeeeeee*!"

The "bye-byes" continued, trailing off into the summer air like joyful butterflies in flight as the truck lumbered down the road.

Wonder of wonders! Mrs. Bundle and Cracker were also, it appeared *at last*, on their merry way, too.

Cracker wedged his body into the leather cushion and closed his weary eyes. *For the love of Catdom*, he cat- thought as he checked the side view mirror to make sure the catfish bowtie was perfectly straight. Assured that his appearance was flawless, he couldn't help but burst forth with a very wide, magnanimous cat grin.

And we're off, he cat-thought gaily!

Chapter Six

The Center of Controversy

The Pillson Public Library, once the pride of Pillson's municipal buildings, was like a miniature version of the grand public structures built during the mid-1800s in the large industrial northern cities. As was often the case, these loftier grander structures, emulated by visitors to those big cities, were then replicated on a smaller scale in their tiny towns and villages; this had been a major wonder for its day in such a small village as Pillsonville. A marble commemorative inscription above the front entrance commemorated the date of its construction: 1849. Wide granite front steps with four large columns commanded the entrance along with two heavy, large oak front doors, which opened inward to reveal the Library's rich interior, seen through the custom-built, ten-foot-high, summer screen doors. The brass fixtures and knobs on these doors were old, ornate, and had seen many years of the repeated activity of its patrons coming and going.

The hanging sign swayed gently in the summer breeze, the black, distinctively elegant lettering identifying the municipal building and its hours of operation:

𝔓𝔦𝔩𝔩𝔰𝔬𝔫 𝔓𝔲𝔟𝔩𝔦𝔠 𝔏𝔦𝔟𝔯𝔞𝔯𝔶

HOURS:

SATURDAY: 10 A.M.-2 P.M.

TUESDAY AND THURSDAY: 9:30 A.M. TO 7 P.M.

(CLOSED 3:30-4)

Those hours of operation had been the same for as long as Mrs. Bundle could remember, with the library closing during the late afternoon mid-week so that the sole paid employee, Louis Montembeau, could partake in a light meal before going back to work.

Mrs. Bundle and Cracker came up the brick walkway, past the hand-painted second sign, only recently installed. At the top, bold letters spelled out "Donations—Library Renovation Fund." Below that, a hand-drawn barometer with incremental dollar markings showed the sad state of the library's coffers, now miserably near-empty.

"Thank God for Hattie!" Mrs. Bundle said, shaking her head.

The sad truth was told in the bright white, blank space within the arrow pointing upward indicating the Library's discouraging attempts thus far to solicit donations from the community. The arrow's base was barely filled with red; a benevolent but nominal two-hundred dollar gesture (to start the ball rolling) had been contributed by the aged (and purportedly very rich) philanthropist, Miss Hattie Underwood, a local legend of sorts.

Every bit of ninety-nine years old, Hattie still scribed the weekly "Pillson Goings On" news column in the local *State Standard* newspaper. A job she had acquired in 1973 when Cloris Felch married her second cousin and moved to Minnesota, Hattie's practice over the last three decades had been to ferret out and provide the column with tidbit-sized morsels of gossip the likes of, *"Sophie Crocker needs new glasses and has to wear an eye patch, which makes it exceedingly difficult for her to read but she is getting by quite well, all things considered,"* to *"Esther Watkins just put up a fresh batch of her award-winning bread and butter pickles, totaling twenty-one jars—the best in the county. She calls them 'sweetness with a punch'! And don't ask her for the recipe, she keeps it secret, says she's never even written it down."* (a particularly newsworthy item as Esther had won the blue ribbon three years in a row at the Windsor County Agriculture Fair). Over the years, her entries might describe new arrivals to Pillson, like, *"LouEllen Rigby's granddaughter Katie and her fiancé Stu Hillington, (who proposed in May and is originally from Cincinnati), are visiting from Valparaiso, California. Both are enjoying the changeable Vermont weather, which they say is much more interesting than their regular dose of daily sunshine."*

Hattie loved to get the scoop; truth be told, she could find a story better than a bloodhound on a scent. Chauffeured around on her daily beat by the local cemetery keeper, Buster Benham, she would strike like a cobra, bedecked in her signature purple brimmed couture hat (regardless of the season), pen and writing tablet ready. She had the uncanny ability to be able to arrive earliest on the scene to interview the newest arrivals in the Pillson area. Hell-bent to get the inside track, she would send Buster to the door to beckon the unsuspecting victim to her interview chamber: the back seat of the ancient 1951 "200 Deluxe" model Packard sedan. In her reign as the Hedda Hopper of Pillson, she always seemed able to elicit all the news fit to print, and more. Simply put, she was an institution of mammoth proportions in the tiny village. Now retired and living comfortably in a nearby nursing home, she still liked to be included in all the charity events, women's teas, and town business.

At any rate, thanks to Hattie, the fund had been started, albeit not with a "bang," but barely a blip.

Mrs. Bundle sadly observed that arrow hadn't moved at all, not since the previous Tuesday when she was last here.

She and Cracker walked briskly up the walkway, lined with multi-colored hues of freshly planted annuals; Cracker pranced merrily around the impressive marble-inlaid sunburst, an intricate medallion design of mosaic pieces located at the bottom of the Library steps.

The solid brick reproduction Georgian structure had a whimsical round-stone foundation, hand-fashioned by local craftsmen from the smooth riverbed stones found locally. Inside was all original: high ceilings, hanging lights with frosted glass, lots of mahogany, all of which gave one a sense of fading grandeur surrounded by the rich comfort of heavy library tables and oversized chairs; even the most casual observer could see everything about the place was tired and needed a new coat of paint.

The annual expenses for the Library's general maintenance were costly, and the building now needed a new roof and some exterior brick work, including the repointing of the chimney and the cornerstones. There was asbestos on the basement heating pipes which needed to be removed, and that was just the beginning. The most glaring issues were the major cosmetics needed inside. The high, plaster ceilings were dark and peeling in places and the mahogany wall panels had lost the lion's share of their original luster, now taking on a dull hue. The dated electrical service still had some knob and tube wiring so that lights flickered slightly each time someone turned on the fan in the public bathroom. The general overall appearance in modern day terms could only be described as *very* shabby "shabby chic" and all agreed that a new facelift was in order.

Additionally, the State had now stepped in with a new challenge: the Library must comply with their State Code within the next two years and install a handicapped-accessible wheelchair ramp and lift, both of which would cost much more than the cooperative villages of Pillsonville, Pillson Falls, and North Pillson Corners could afford.

Every inch of space in the Library was used, from the basement to the rafters. The first and second floor of the stately structure housed many shelves chock full of books. There was also a good-sized conference room on the second floor. The full basement under the front half the building had been converted to a cozy children's reading and game area; the remaining back area of the basement behind a locked door housed the old boiler and some huge, unmovable boulders in the earthen floor that the building had been built around.

On the third floor, there was a large landing leading to a long, narrow hallway which, like a long hedgerow, connected three tiny rooms to the left no bigger than today's modern-sized walk-in closets. All three rooms (whose low ceilings precluded any use other than storage) were jam-packed with boxes, unused old furniture, and old library paraphernalia. A yellowed, handwritten sign of unknown age met any curious patron before the third floor stairway. It read, "Third floor off limits! *Employees only, please.*"

Apart from the cherished but somewhat shabby interior, the most divine part of the library was its location. Situated on over two acres in the middle of the village, the building in itself was an impressive historical treasure, but the mature perennial gardens in the rear yard behind the small parking lot were impressive. Considered a hidden jewel by all who came to the library, the gardens beckoned patrons to sit on the old benches scattered in happenstance throughout the grounds. These secluded pockets provided a quiet place to reflect or read during the warmer Vermont months. Marginally maintained, this rear grounds area seemed almost to take care of itself, offering a quiet sanctuary that stood timeless, taking on an enduring life of its own. In years past, Book Club luncheons, charity book sales with long tables laden with used books, and the children's story hour had periodically taken over the pleasant back garden area.

The Pillson Public Library's *piece de resistance* was the dramatic distant view (even better from the upstairs back windows of the library) of an offshoot of Twenty Mile Stream, which began with a spectacular five-tiered waterfall upstream and ended with the winding, peaceful rivulet that passed through the Library's back property line. Although large, ancient oak and maple trees now obstructed the sight to a large extent, the crashing water could still be heard after heavy rains; but more often than not, the stream could be heard as a pleasant, calming melody rippling in the background during reading.

Mrs. Bundle walked slowly up the steps, as she often did, and took the time to read the brass letters. Like twin borders flanking the large, thick entry doors, two full-length verdigris-colored plaques of approximately twelve feet in height detailed in formal, old-fashioned script: "Sons of Pillson." These massive double plaques looked like stalwart and silent soldiers themselves: tall, straight, and quiet, the militia personified, reading:

SOLDIERS OF PILLSONVILLE, VERMONT
THE UNION ARMY 1861-65
VERMONT REGIMENTS
NATIVES AND RESIDENTS

It had always intrigued Mrs. Bundle to read the long list of Civil War soldier's names, their ranks, and companys, along with the numbered Vermont Regiments. Dedicated in 1868, the memorial plaque names read like a "Who's who" of the Pillson area.

Beginning with the *Second Regiment*, the alphabetically listed names ran by regiment, ending on the second plaque with the *Seventeenth Regiment*, the *First Battery*, the *Second USSS*, the *1st Vermont Calvary*, and finally, the small *Miscellaneous* section. Alone in her thoughts, Mrs. Bundle began to read the names:

SECOND REGIMENT	CO.
ALLEN, HENRY	H
EMERY, ELMER A, SGT. CORP.	I
GILSON, CURTIS H.	A

THIRD REGIMENT	
BAULLAS, ALPHONSO	A
JENNESS, ORZO A.	A
MESSENGER, WM. O.	A
PILLSON, GEORGE W.	A

FOURTH REGIMENT	
BIXBY, MARTIN J., COR. SGT.	C
WAIT, HENRY O., 1ST SGT.	C

FIFTH REGIMENT	
HAGAR, HENRY D.	A
PARKER, GEORGE G. , CORP.	A

She scanned the *Sixth Regiment*, then the *Seventh Regiment*, then her eyes jumped to the *Ninth*. The names seemed to continue on and on; so many gone to war! Her eyes rested on the last section's *Miscellaneous* headings. Yes, so many *boys* off to war, some never to return again.

She felt a connection to her dear husband Arthur, who had always been a rabid historical buff, and remembering how he talked about the Civil War's key battles and the generals who fought them was a comfort to her now. Sighing, Mrs. Bundle stepped through the oversized double screen doors into the cool, quiet space. She walked into the foyer, past the familiar oil paintings on the wall. Stern founding fathers faces looked down at her, and she smiled at an 18th-century likeness of George Hartland Pillson, painted sometime around 1775 and in whose memory the Library had been built.

As she walked into the Great room, she acknowledged that, by all appearances, it could still be the 1800s. Truly, the Library's basic soul, its infrastructure of mahogany, inlaid parquet floors, and antique brass lighting had not been altered for many, many generations; most of the Library's interior retained its original, albeit aged, beauty.

She sauntered up to the main desk (a huge oak counter anchoring the large room) to address the young man whose back was to her.

"Good morning, Louis," she whispered loudly. "How goes your day?"

The young Head Librarian sprung up from his computer, long legs as spry as a most agile grasshopper, and, with a *boing!*, landed neatly, feet positioned perfectly behind the front desk.

"Mrs. Bundle! How lovely to see you this fine morning!" Louis Montembeau was impeccably attired, his ensemble faultlessly matched, as usual. His button-down collar was starched to perfection, his striped shirtsleeves fastidiously rolled up within a quarter inch of each other to just above his forearms, dark tan shimmering deeply through the pale blonde hair on his arms. His handsome features were framed by flaxen hair (almost white), gelled and lightly spiked into the current trendy style and his clean-shaven face was scrubbed red and squeaky clean; he exuded youthful innocence and goodwill. A transplanted Flatlander of four years from Minneota, Minnesota (according to Louis, well-known for the song *"Minneota, Minnesota, It's the place I wanna go ta"*), Louis had chosen Pillson Falls as his home, conveniently residing just minutes away from his job. Louis' natural friendliness and witticisms, along with his extensive librarian expertise, had made him quick friends. Now fully ensconced into Pillson life, it was evident to all that he loved his job in this rural community so similar to his homeland.

Mondays and Fridays he worked at the Chester Public Library; Wednesdays was his official day off, the day Louis gave private vocal singing lessons "on the side." He also volunteered with a local drama group in Springfield, where he designed all the sets for the Young Players' Theatre.

"And how is our dear Cracker this wonderful day?" Louis's natural, lofty voice was light but distinctively penetrating. The spring-heeled gentleman's possession of two very attractive traits — genuine attentiveness *and* an unbridled zest for life — were launched in kind with exactitude.

Salutations, Louis, Cracker cat-thought as he flicked a hello and made a beeline to the periodical section, in search of the magazine, *Cat Fancy*, anxious to read the latest article on "litter box rejection." This was often how he passed the time during Mrs. Bundle's many visits and meetings at the institution; he enjoyed catching up on all the latest "cutting edge" feline practices, not to mention, how much he loved the *"Ask the Experts"* column. Frankly, he believed *he* could do a much more professional job authoring the question-and-answer feature. All the same, he always found the magazine's contents amusing and fresh.

"Hello, friend!" Mrs. Bundle responded to Louis' happy greeting.

A wonderful aroma instantly filled her senses, and she realized the scent was emanating from the Librarian.

Louis' cologne was enchanting, like a breath of spring hyacinth in the flat humid air.

Leaning forward, her eyes sparkled lightheartedly and she whispered in pure delight, "You smell *wonderful!*"

He smiled, rolled his eyes loftily, and whispered back, dramatically *sotto voce*, "Oh! You like? It's Italian!"

She grinned. Inasmuch as both Mrs. Bundle and Louis were conspirators in the enjoyment of the finer things in life (and good enough friends so that she could be so bold as to ask) she went ahead and asked, completely enthralled. "What *is* it?" She drew in another long, dramatic sniff. Her sensitive nose drank in the lovely, delicious fragrance. "It's heavenly!"

She waited expectantly; he smiled in mock coyness and his long eyelashes fluttered imperceptibly. A split second pause passed, after which he replied in jocular repartee, "*I'll* never tell."

Louis was always so quick with his usual witty comebacks and snappy replies—so clever and theatrical—that Mrs. Bundle expected nothing less from him at any given time and today was no exception.

Their light laughter broke uncontrollably at their affected exchange, causing the stoic, elderly man sitting erect as a wooden totem pole at the farthest corner table to raise his wooly white eyebrows derisively above his newspaper at them both and give an opinionative, "*Ahemmm!* I say! Har-*umphh!*"

Mrs. Bundle waved gaily, "Oh, good morning, Hector! How goes the day?" Her friendly greeting carved the essence of a smile out of the old man's shriveled expression. He grumbled good-naturedly and went back to his newspaper.

Reverting to a slightly more professional demeanor in deference to Hector Humbolt, Mrs. Bundle leaned forward on the counter and asked gently, "So, how goes the battle with you, Louis? Are we all set for our next meeting?"

"Well, the roof hasn't caved in yet," he said, raising his eyebrows and chuckling; they gave each other a knowing glance.

Although his statement referred to the old building, she knew the dual meaning of his words. His reference to the building's precarious fiscal status was also apparent.

He whispered, "Oh, Lord! I just can't believe we've come to this low point." He shook his head sadly. "Do you know, this morning I went back into the archives and looked at this library's grand history—it was quite remarkable. The Pillson Public Library has been open *to the public* since 1849! Can you imagine! All those years, taking care of the public's needs—beginning in an era, mind you, when reading was pretty much all that was all there was to do! No TV, no movies! When reading was the only way you found out about the world! I don't think people realize what a huge thing it was at that time to have a library brought to an out-of-the-way, little place like this."

"It must have been remarkable," Mrs. Bundle said.

"Right! And, get this—I came across an interesting fact. Without fail, library's always been available to the public free of charge, week in, week out, year in, year out, same hours, same everything! I couldn't believe it. All those many decades, generations of families coming here. Their kids, and theirs, and on and on, no doubt, to the present. It's mind-boggling!" He paused for a second, "Of course, it was open all that time *except* for a short time in the late 1800s, according to the old ledgers." He nodded at Mrs. Bundle's questioning look and continued, "Yes! Evidently, it closed when the operating funds went toward the war effort. I guess that was common practice back then," he smiled. "Point being—other than that, never fail, this library has been open to the public as a completely free service for the community!"

"That's fascinating! And quite noteworthy, too, that the library provided this community such a service for over a century-and-a-half! I mean, I knew that, but I hadn't really thought about it in, you know, real terms. Maybe we could use that information…"

"People might find it very interesting! There's a really old record from the first decade the Library opened, a journal of library information written in each librarian's own penmanship. The records are spotty, to be sure, but you can kind of read between the lines." He crinkled his nose and smiled. "You know what I mean. Mostly pretty boring stuff just documenting what books were ordered, budgets, what took place during each's term of employment. But it kind of shows what life was like during that time."

"I'd love to take a look at it sometime."

He pointed at the huge desk behind him. "Got it right down here in the bottom drawer."

She looked around and smiled. "Good ol' Georgie Pillson's descendents really wanted Pillson to shine when they planned this building."

"Yeah, even though some people in the village were against it because they thought it would be too grand and too rich for their Yankee tastes! It was almost unheard of to have a public library in those days! Quite a feather in the Pillson town fathers' caps, it was, when that first patron walked through those exact same double doors—right there—and withdrew books for the first time for *free*. It must have been huge! To actually be able to take a book home and read about the world outside of Pillsonville!" He sighed and his eyes took on a dreamy look. "Such a long time ago." Picking up some loose library cards, he began to shuffle them, his long fingers moving like a magician's. "At any rate, my point is that *nothing* has changed in this building in all those years Same lighting, same built-in wood shelving," he gestured to the ten-foot high wall shelves, "even all those free-standing bookcases upstairs, everything the same, all top notch quality in its day. All original! It's a diamond in the rough, that's what it is." He thumped the cards down on the counter. "I don't need to preach to the choir, do I, Mrs. Bundle? Sorry if I go on too much ."

"No, not at all, Louis. I love to hear you talk about the Library. I'm your biggest fan."

He bend toward her and whispered even lower, somewhat unabashedly, "You know, sometimes when I'm here alone," he leaned even further forward and, with a dramatic flair, paused, breathed in and said, "I can *feel* their presence."

Mrs. Bundle looked askance at her melodramatic friend. "Their presence? You mean, the people who've been here *before* us?"

He nodded emphatically.

"Really?"

His thin face bobbled up and down with even more enthusiasm. "Yes, truly!" he whispered. "It's like…I can almost *feel* the history, all around me! It gives me the shivers!" Beneath his shirt, his slender shoulders shuddered. "Just *imagine* all the different people that have come through that door! It's quite.." he paused theatrically once more, this time closing his eyes so tightly that they trembled and, reaching out blindly to grab her hands resting on the counter between them, he exclaimed, "*exhilarating*!" He popped one eye open wide and gave her a spirited wink.

"Oh, Louis!" she chided, laughing.

"I mean it! And I just hope we can keep it going! Such a shame if we can't!"

Amused and thoroughly entertained by his superb performance, she said, "You know, Louis, I don't know many people that get as excited as you do about libraries! It's very refreshing to see someone that really loves his job! My, oh my! And, even though you may not think so, I guarantee there are a lot of people who love this Library and feel the same way that you do. Personally, I, for one, can't imagine it any other way."

"Yes, well, one can only hope." The youthful skin on his forehead creased uncomfortably, all of a sudden giving him the look of someone decades older. "Of course, if some *other* people have their way…" he shook his head and pointed at the front doors, "those will be locked forever—I'm afraid, frankly, before we know what hits us!"

"Well, as far as I'm concerned, this Library should remain open for the good of the whole community to enjoy long after we're gone—no matter what!"

Just then, two young girls came up the stairs from the "Children's Nook" chattering away, their slender arms heavily laden with colorful books. One girl was taller, with dark, long hair and heavy bangs. The other was petite and giggly. Mrs. Bundle stepped aside.

Louis smiled down at them, giving them his full attention. "Hi Sissy!" The older girl with the straight bangs smiled shyly. He turned his gaze on the younger girl. "And how's Tricia today?" She giggled and they both blushed, completely captivated with his charm. "Step right up! I can help you two young ladies right here!" His smile was dazzling, his voice filled with enthusiasm. As they dropped their books on the library counter, he leaned away from them toward Mrs. Bundle and whispered, "Don't worry! As long as I'm on the job, you know I'll do everything I can to help. Anything short of murder, that is!" he quipped with a vibrant smile.

Turning his attention, he said brightly, "Now ladies, let's see what new and exciting books you've chosen this week!"

As Mrs. Bundle waited patiently for Louis to finish his business, her mind wandered, ruminating over the library's existing dilemma. *Why, even Louis, usually the sunniest, most positive person around, is feeling the stress*, she thought with dismay as Armand's face loomed into view in her mind's eye.

Armand Limpert had fostered the gossip of tearing down the library and incorporating the library into a separate area in the Pillson Elementary School Building to the extent that now, it appeared, he had everyone up in arms. Mrs. Bundle knew that she, Louis, and the other Board members had their work cut out for them.

Something needed to happen fast to allay the demise of their little building!

Louis was just finishing up with his young patrons. As they left the library, their books happily secured in their knapsacks, she asked quietly, "Has…you-know-who…been in yet today?"

"Oh, yes!" Louis pointed toward the stairs and whispered, "Armand! Oh, I should have said right away! Of course, he's already here, came in first thing, on the dot! I hadn't turned the key in the lock and he was at my elbow. Sometimes I think he comes in just to make my life miserable. Sorry, Mrs. Bundle, but it's the truth."

She nodded and he continued his lament, motioning above him, in an undertone, "He's up there as we speak… going through the boxes up on the third floor. Why? I don't know. I think what he said exactly was, 'I'm checking to see what rubbish is up here!' I gathered he had some other hidden agenda—God knows what and I wasn't about to ask," Louis said, rolling his eyes toward the ceiling in utter frustration.

"My Lord! It's a mess up there! What on earth could he be looking for?"

"No idea. Earlier, he was complaining about the kids making too much noise—that was before he went upstairs, so I was glad to see him go, frankly." He shook his head, the golden spikes of hair unmoving, gelled neatly to a perfect state of stiffness. "If he had his way, no one would be allowed in here except the 'high society' folk. I think he wants to make this into a private club, like one of those old-fashioned men's clubs! Do you think?"

Mrs. Bundle shrugged. "I really couldn't say what his intention is, Louis. Other than to intimidate, or make waves."

"Personally—sorry again, Mrs. Bundle—but…he gives me the *willies*!" He shivered once more, and Mrs. Bundle thought she could see the fine hairs on his forearms standing on end.

"That's okay, Louis. Don't worry yourself. I'll go up and talk to him."

He smiled and whispered mischievously, "Are you sure you want to be alone with him? You're taking your life in your hands…" he backed away and sat down in his computer chair.

She smiled. "Oh, Cracker and I like to live dangerously," she bantered and turned round quickly toward the stairway, moving with a purposeful resolve in her step.

Just at that point and without warning, a teenage boy, gangly and all feet, emerged like a bursting volcano from behind the floor-to-ceiling bookcase, his view obscured by a heaping mound of books he was attempting to control. He nearly collided with Mrs. Bundle.

His thick, dark hair, rumpled and coarse as a tawny owl, complete with widow's peak, was sticking out every which-way (as was his long-sleeved, disheveled shirt) and if he had a dollar in his pocket for every freckle on his face, he'd have been a millionaire. He carried a large stack of heavy hardback books, hands tightly clenched around them, obviously in a war of strength versus stamina, bound and determined not to buckle under their weight. His round-rimmed glasses were set precariously halfway down his sloping nose as he negotiated his balance, teetering on his cigarette boat-sized shoes following his near miss with Mrs. Bundle. Beads of sweat rested on his forehead as he valiantly maintained (with amazing ability) his equilibrium.

Finally, like the most agile plate-twirler's circus act, he gained control of the pile. Scrunching his dampened nose in self-exasperation, the boy's glasses helplessly slid further down from the bridge to just above his flaring nostrils.

He muttered shyly, "Oops, sorry!" Then, he looked up above the top rim of his glasses. His desperate face changed into friendly recognition of his near target, obviously pleasantly surprised to see who it was he had almost crashed into. He said, "Hey, Mrs. Bundle! Uh! Sorry!" His words came in spurts, the glasses roosting dangerously at the end of his slippery nose.

"No problem, Anthony! How are you?"

Mrs. Bundle was familiar with this boy. Anthony Clancy, the third oldest of the five Clancy boys, worked part-time at the Library. Quiet and studious, Anthony was the scholar of the Clancy bunch, often spending hours at the Library exploring, researching, and reading about everything under the sun.

"Good." He stood, moving from one foot to the other, still holding his load of tomes. Anthony was short on words; that is, unless you asked him about his one passion—books—at which point he opened up like a budding gladiola and could talk your ear off.

Anthony was a veritable encyclopedia when it came to most subjects. Mrs. Bundle found his knowledge of trivia quite remarkable for a boy his age. His area of expertise, though, was history, for which he had an astounding acuity, and Mrs. Bundle always liked to hear about which book or subject was fascinating him at present. She loved these discussions and always looked forward to seeing him.

Arthur's favorite pastime had been reading about history, too, and Anthony's keen interest in historical events fondly reminded her of pleasant past discussions with her husband.

The last time she had visited with Anthony, she had asked him the same question she always started with: "What are you reading now?"

That time, he had just finished the memoir *I Am Alive*, written by an American World War II prisoner-of-war in Japan. She recalled the time before that, it had been a book about a famous Vermont Civil War general, George Stannard.

Realizing that today he appeared to literally have his hands full, she simply asked, as she reached out to help him, "How's your mother and father?"

"Great! Dad really likes workin' for the State. He's doin' really good now." His pinched nose gave his voice a nasal, strained tone indicating he might be lacking sufficient oxygen.

He expertly moved the large pile of books to his hip, evidently used to negotiating a stack that high, but Mrs. Bundle grabbed at and caught the top book just before it slipped away from him. They gave each other victorious smiles and he continued without a hitch. "So now Mom's not working three jobs, only one." He cleared his throat and his lips opened wider (the better to breathe with), then added, "And that's only part-time, too!"

The family had fallen on bad times in the past, what with their father's arrest for bear-poaching; the boys (Anthony and his four brothers) had often been left to fend for themselves while their mother worked to support them all. Anthony's father, Jesse Clancy, had been released from prison last year with the expectation that his new job as a wilderness guide with the State Parks Division would become permanent after his probation period.

Mrs. Bundle found this boy of limited means and opportunity to be a very interesting study. She liked Anthony's droll, Vermont wit, his intellectual aptitude, and his survivalist spirit. He was like a thriving cactus living in a desert of challenging natural resources, soaking up every bit of cerebral water and nourishment he could put his hands on.

She glowed at him. "Wonderful! As they say, all's well that ends well!" Noticing his growing discomfort under the strain of all those books, she said, "Would you…like to put those down, Anthony?"

Cracker, newly arrived from his reading, snuffled at Anthony's feet.

Anthony nodded gratefully, smiling with more confidence, his glasses teetering near the end of the precipice, and he finally plopped the myriad of books with their eclectic titles down (overly noisily by library standards) onto the table next to him. Then, in one adroit action, he pushed his glasses back up on the bridge of his nose in triumph.

Old Hector visibly jumped at the sound of the books smacking the table and executed his own private protest by boisterously rustling his newspaper once more in resigned exasperation.

Anthony shrugged bashfully in his direction and repeated again to anyone within hearing distance, "Sorry! Sorry, Mr. Humboldt!" At his age, an apology was often the first word out of a teenage boy's mouth, usually covering every occasion or possible scenario of awkward social happenstance. He reached down and absentmindedly patted Cracker for support, who stretched his sleek backside upward and purred loudly. Anthony repeated to anyone within hearing distance, "Sorry."

Mrs. Bundle placed a light hand at his elbow and gave him an encouraging, warm smile. "Not to worry, dear." She leaned in closer and whispered loudly, "Cracker and I have a saying—'*Sometimes people need a little shaking up!*'"

She could hear Louis' strangled snigger from behind the desk.

"Really?" Anthony asked.

She winked conspiratorially at Anthony, who returned a relieved smile back at her; then she turned, knowing a hornet's nest was awaiting her up on the third floor.

Chapter Seven
Then...And Now

THE YOUNG GIRL RAN UP THE SECOND FLIGHT *of stairs swiftly and silently, trying with all her might not to let her foot sounds alert the stalwart, ironfisted Miss Bromley, who sat like a prison guard at the large front desk below. Her kidskin boots, laced up along the inside of the ankle, made sharp, tiny pinging sounds against the shiny, hard, oak treads, the slight weight of her toes barely imperceptible in the cavernous hallway.*

When she reached the top landing, she loosened the worsted wool shawl that hung heavily on her slight shoulders and gently smoothed her long dress and petticoats. She tried without success to tame her windblown curly long tresses, straightening the large silk blue bow atop her head, its long double ribbon cascading loosely down her back. Then she promptly pinched her already-flushed cheeks just for good measure.

She looked at her image in the massive, dust-covered, ornate mirror leaning dejectedly nearby against the plaster wall.

Yes, *she assured herself unwaveringly,* ready or not!

Slipping between the long, heavy tables shoved up against the hallway wall as tight as jammed river logs, she squeaked through the small opening left between the tables, then scooted past the wooden crates piled one atop the other; crates that held new, richly bound books as yet unread, stored along the dark corridor walls. She peeked around the corner of the doorway of the last room...

Mrs. Bundle walked briskly up the stairs, asking herself. what was it about this man upstairs that was so distasteful? It seemed he had affected almost everyone in Pillson since his arrival last year. As she took each step, she became more resolute. *If I have to listen to another diatribe about the merits of closing this Library*, she thought to herself, *I'm not sure I'll be able to keep my cool.*

For two decades Mrs. Bundle had been on the Library Board of Trustees and it had always been a friendly, loosely managed but very committed group of interested citizens dedicated to keeping the Public Library a viable entity in their rural community. As she walked up the second floor stairs, she wondered how things had become so volatile in such a short amount of time. Was it really true—that old saying "One bad apple can spoil the whole barrel"?

She knew the situation was coming to a head. The last board meeting in May had set the whole town on its ear; the library issue appeared to be dividing the town, setting one villager against another and it was the unofficial consensus that Armand Limpert's contentious behavior had steadily aggravated the growing controversy, subtly fueling the fire.

Oh, she thought as she forced each foot up the stairs, *that man makes my blood boil!* What else did they really know about this prematurely-retired art collector before he came to Pillson to wreak havoc? Nowadays, he was the self-proclaimed pillar of Pillson community: an active member of the affluent garden club—he owned his own greenhouse and grew delicate orchids—and very inclined to rub elbows with the more posh community of nearby Woodstock. In fact, he claimed to be one of the Sons of the American Revolution, maintaining he was a lineal descendant of George Pillson, the village's illustrious namesake and who, Mrs. Bundle couldn't help but note, had also had the reputation for being a pompous and domineering male chauvinist in the 1760's.

It was rumored that the gentleman's farm Armand had purchased on North Puckerbrush Road had been entirely rehabbed—and that a great deal of money had been spent. Local contractors who had been allowed inside this inner sanctum had gossiped that Armand's property had all the latest gadgets and finery, including an extensive security system intended to protect the fine art collection he had brought with him from New York City.

After Armand had been asked to sit on the Board, the dispositions of at least two other board members besides Mrs. Bundle and Althea had been set on edge and later, tempers had flared as he bullied and cajoled his way into his present position of power.

There were six total board members including Armand: besides Althea, the other three Board members were, like Mrs. Bundle, long-standing Pillson citizens who had a strong interest in the literary arts. Unfortunately, the personality and dynamics of the board had changed markedly with the addition of Armand Limpert to the extent that the docile, easygoing group had become strained and troubled.

Firstly, there was Sarah Church, a former Museum of Modern Art employee who was as civilized and reserved as a tabernacle mouse. Authentic to her given name, she had turned to ministry in midlife, and now conducted the small weekly Sunday service at the Old Stone Church in North Pillson Corners. Dull gray, lifeless hair, bespectacled, thin and wan, she would be the first one to acknowledge that the Library Board was the highlight of her existence. Not much else happened in poor Miss Church's ecclesiastic world of sparseness and self-deprivation; most of her extra earnings went to tithing. She had always been reserved, helpful, and very private.

All that changed when Armand joined the board. At first, Sarah Church had submissively stood by, not daring to interrupt or disagree with Limpert's strong opinions. Then, as he began to pay attention to her—leaning over and whispering in her ear, asking her questions, fawning over her—she became transformed, her priggish color deepening and her breath visibly quickening every time Armand spoke to her. Over time, Miss Church appeared to be putty in his hands; she was his willing slave by all appearances. She silently sat by nodding, perpetually acquiescent, making sidelong, lovesick calf eyes at him from across the meeting table as he seemed to manage and mold her opinions before their eyes.

Director Ellie Waterhouse was a local part-time freelance writer for *Mothers Unite* and a full-time, stay-at-home mom; she had been a welcome addition to the board. She usually arrived at their monthly meeting late and out of breath from her busy, already-stretched schedule. Attractive and articulate with windblown good looks, her presence was always refreshing to Mrs. Bundle because she exuded a youthful energy and free spirit that seemed to galvanize the group. Although her book knowledge was extensive, her time resources were limited. Quietly astute, Ellie's style was efficient and non-judgmental, primarily because she was time-challenged. Often under the gun, her interaction with Armand was pleasant but strained, especially when he became verbose and overbearing and she frequently leaned heavily in the opposite direction of his dogma.

Lastly, there was Professor Watson DeVille, a quiet and unassuming retired educator from Dartmouth College who had lived in Pillson for four decades. Sadly, he was the member who appeared to be most affected by Armand's forceful manipulation and anger.

Watson was…well, *Watson*. A scholar and tutor, he had worked *pro bono* for the last few years helping young students with special needs. During his spare time, he delighted in arcane historical research and could share, *ad infinitum*, factual details specific to the history of Pillson and its region to anyone willing to listen.

With no family to speak of, he was an educational fixture in Pillson, a library trustee with twenty years of service under his belt. He was also a solid, never-changing reminder to all of the formality of yesteryear's academic world—one which Watson had yet to extricate himself from.

Slight in stature and round like an egg, Watson still wore a freshly starched white shirt and meticulous ensemble suit (usually tweed or gabardine) with matching plaid sweater vest underneath, every day—work day or not. He completed this outfit with his understated signature bowtie, always looped and hand-tied neatly in place. He rarely deviated from this self-imposed rigidity and formal demeanor, preferring stiff to relaxed, and stood firmly on the side of politeness and order. He also absolutely abhorred any type of confrontation, viewing it as a mortifying *faux pas*. Life, he believed, should be stable and uniform, without glitches, snags, or any type of unpleasantness.

Although he was very learned and well-traveled, he was not even close to the type of individual that could embrace strife or controversy. Timid as a koala bear (and nearly as chubby as one, too), he was prone to fits of sneezing at the slightest hint of anything stressful or problematic.

"I fear it's some sort of allergy reaction—or my asthma kicking up," he would apologize after one of his traumatic bouts (eyes watering and breath labored), and haul out an exceedingly large, immaculately white handkerchief and blow very loudly.

Accordingly, as one could imagine, the erudite but timid Watson had not fared well on the Board the last few months; more often than not he had erred on the proverbial side of cautious silence through most of the dispute, choosing to sit quietly, yet firmly, "on the fence" throughout the discussion of the Pillson Library's volatile issues.

Adding insult to injury, there was also a *personal* vendetta interwoven within the relationship of Watson and Armand. As bad luck would have it, Watson's property happened to abut Armand Limpert's, and their houses were situated so that each was visible to the other through their contiguous fields.

The controversy began when Armand moved in and centered chiefly upon Watson's only companion, his apricot-colored female Bichon Frise named Twinkles, and to whom Watson was very much attached. Twinkles was the perfect complement to Watson's needs because, besides being very sweet and harmless like him, she had low dander, Bichons often being the ideal pet for people who suffer from allergies and asthma. Although she was five years old, she tended to act like a baby, and Watson treated her as such, showering limitless love and affection on his little companion.

Watson's daily retirement routine was carved in stone; he was as much a creature of habit as one could be. His first order of business in his early dawn schedule was to put Twinkles out for her morning tinkle. This was a ritual that had occurred since Twinkles was a small pup and the consequent reaction to her morning tinkle was a predictable occurrence, and like as not, happened daily, without fail. Invariably, as she was executing her task, a squirrel or other small woodland creature would entice and then excite Twinkles (herself no larger than ten or eleven inches from the top of her shoulder to the ground). Initially intent on doing her business, the slightest sound would make the poor pup freeze in place, unable to complete her mission. Truth be told, Twinkles was afraid of her own shadow and even more afraid of anything else that moved; so, at that juncture, she would proceed to yelp, yip, and yap helplessly until Watson (who at the same time fussed, consoled, and cooed loudly) brought her inside. The occurrence usually lasted all of sixty seconds and was one that the neighbors on North Puckerbrush were all accustomed to. Unfortunately, it was sixty seconds too long for the new, unpleasant neighbor next door.

At the first yelp, Armand Limpert had been at his back patio door with a roar, and his booming, obnoxious voice could be heard across their adjoining meadow as he shouted like a foghorn blasting at the top of his lungs, *"Put a sock in it!"* What followed were numerous profanities too off-color and vivid to mention in this account.

Mortified and completely embarrassed by the attention drawn to Twinkles and him, Watson tried his best to quiet the miniature mutt while encouraging her to quickly do her business and come inside. Armand's shouting, along with Twinkle's yelping, meant more time outside for the agonized pooch and thus created a chain reaction for all the other dogs on North Puckerbrush, who joined in with more commotion, all of which induced Armand's prized stud horse, Jockular, to commence his own frantic recitation, whinnying and bleating as he banged his body against his stall, straining to get out.

The next level to the drama was the inevitably-unpleasant phone call Watson would received within minutes thereafter from Armand, threatening the poor scholar with untold violence and a hefty lawsuit if his high-priced, high-strung horse died from heart failure or anything caused under the duress of the miniature Twinkles' uncontrollable anxiety.

"I will guarantee that *you* will be the first one my insurance company contacts if my horse is injured in his stall or dies!" Armand's fuming would go on uninterrupted for many minutes as he added insults laced with, "you and your pipsqueak dog, "mealy-mouthed egghead," and the like.

Armand would yell so loudly that Watson's ears would hurt, but all Watson would dare reply was a submissive, "Yes, yes, I know. I'm so sorry. I'm so very sorry. Yes, you're right, Armand, I will try to control her," until his burning ears were pardoned from further injury as Armand, in utter disgust, would slam the phone down. Poor Watson. Like most people his age, Watson lived a simple, ritualistic life where peace and tranquility reigned, avoiding confrontation at all costs. From these confrontations, Watson had developed a terrible case of shingles, and his nerves were constantly on edge.

Thus began the first of many stressful days for Professor DeVille and Twinkles. It didn't matter that they had lived there many years, or that they had been on North Puckerbrush long before Mr. Limpert. All that mattered was that the pressure of this ongoing tension was taking its toll on the both of them.

Twinkles, who weighed in at a paltry ten pounds, had developed a tic, an uncontrollable spasm, it seemed, in her right front paw, and now took daily calming medication. In addition, she could not be left alone, primarily due to her latest habit of chewing on the windowsill directly opposite Armand's farm, leaving tiny teeth marks of distress if Watson left, even for a few minutes.

As a result, she accompanied Watson everywhere—even to Library Board meetings. Quiescent as a Carmelite nun and confined to her petite leash, she would lie at Watson's feet, contemplating nothing other than the distance between her body and Armand's large shoe.

She knew how much he hated her.

Truth be told, it was clear there was no love lost on either side betwixt Armand Limpert and Twinkles. She shivered pathetically every time the intimidating man even looked at her or shuffled his feet. Periodically, a small whimper could be heard from under the table; Twinkles knew better than to yap in his presence and was comforted in the knowledge that her Professor would protect her as best he could.

Mrs. Bundle and everyone else on the Board knew that Watson was a wild card in the voting structure of the Board. His sense of logic and vast research of any given subject made for longwinded explanations or theoretical questions; however, his unassuming nature precluded him from exhibiting any sense of assertiveness toward anyone, much less the verbose Limpert. Mrs. Bundle sensed that Professor DeVille was not interested in becoming the conduit for any retaliation from the unpleasant Armand and so, in the interest of survival, did everything in his power to steer clear of disagreeing with him. Mrs. Bundle was very surprised that Watson had not resigned his board position long before now and wondered where his allegiance would be in the final showdown.

The one sliver of hope that Mrs. Bundle held onto was that Louis Montembeau also sat with the Board as a non-voting member; that is, unless there was a tie and they needed a deciding vote to carry a motion. His primary role was to provide the board with resource services and working knowledge about the library, along with updated statistical and financial information, in addition to scribing the minutes at each monthly meeting into the official library log.

"What a mess we've made!" Mrs. Bundle muttered to herself, pausing on the second landing. She eyeballed the second flight of stairs, listening for sounds of Armand. Hearing nothing, she walked quietly up the stairs, not relishing what she would be faced with on the third level. *One bad apple*, she thought, *is all it takes…*

Systematically, Armand Limpert had attempted to alienate every board member with his senseless bickering and constant disagreement, ostensibly without logic or reasoning. He seemed to have acquired a lot of clout (or at least his bold demeanor terrified the other board members enough to get whatever he wanted); so much so that in the last few months the Board had gone from a happy group of concerned citizens to an autocracy headed by Limpert, whose bullying ways pitted board member against board member.

Mrs. Bundle had discovered Mr. Limpert was not the benign, gentle philanthropist he had purported to be. In her absence while she was convalescing, Mrs. Bundle had been kept enough up to pdate by Althea to sense there was a huge storm brewing. Still though, she was shocked when she saw the transformation that had occurred in her absence.

Everyone now sat by meekly — broken down and resigned to acquiescence while Armand wielded his gavel like a huge nightstick, slashing and carving his words as everyone sat by and mutely watched. Watson DeVille had tried in the nicest of ways to sway Armand's opinion to a more user-friendly approach with the Board but Limpert had swiftly and efficiently put him in his place with his constant and cunningly-phrased inferences to the early morning Twinkles issue.

His sly references to DeVille's dog drew a look of fear. When Watson turned away, Mrs. Bundle was sure she had seen an unadulterated look of loathing clouding the poor man's face. Armand's bullying tone appeared more than Watson could bear and hence, he chose silence over protest.

In that first meeting, Mrs. Bundle had also mentally bookmarked two very bizarre events involving Armand, strange occurrences that had caused her to wonder what was really going on in the wicked man's mind.

First of all, as the meeting opened, Armand had benevolently welcomed her back to the Board. Like a condescending minister receiving a wayward sinner, he'd raised his hand (as if in absolution) while everyone lightly clapped their approval that their preceding, beloved chairperson had finally returned. What occurred next was the bizarre event that had left Mrs. Bundle in shock for, as he lauded her with one hand, Armand had simultaneously reached his other beefy hand under the table and very irreverently (and with surprising gusto) squeezed her knee!

Certainly mildly alarmed and surprised — but not entirely thrown for a loop — Mrs. Bundle had been amazed at his pure cheek. She could remember all too well (from her younger days, mind you) what it felt like to be *involuntarily* propositioned, and she didn't like it at any age, not one bit.

Showing amazing restraint at this impertinence, she had looked Armand square in the eye and, while the others innocently looked on clapping and smiling, *she* smiled sweetly as she dug her pen deeply into the lecherous, groping hand under the table.

His muffled cry came amidst the applause, weakly disguised to a sharp, "*Ow—weeee—Y-yes!* Yes! *We* welcome you back!" He quickly recovered from his deed, smiled brightly and continued on with the business at hand, although his sidelong scowl at her seemed to pledge some future retribution for this embarrassment.

Upon reflection after the meeting, it occurred to her that this groping technique was likely not a new practice for him, more a grotesquely aberrant mating strategy that was probably common practice for the egocentric Don Juan. Her further consideration concluded it was also probably not the first time that he had made advances toward an unsuspecting matron or widow like herself and she wondered about Sarah Church. She had a sense that Armand liked to be in charge, that he liked to prey on others less fortunate or less secure than her. Because she had spurned his advances, she speculated whether she would now be added to his mentally tortured "hit list" and her defense system went into place. She was no longer on his good side and she made a note to watch her back whenever dealing with Mr. Limpert.

The second occurrence in that same meeting had left Mrs. Bundle almost speechless. During a discussion of the possibility of fee charging for any patron wanting to use the library services, Armand's offhanded comments had alarmed Mrs. Bundle. It was a remark made in passing—seemingly harmless—but she had copied it down verbatim because she truly could not believe that she had heard what she had heard.

Surprised that this was an agenda item, she had asked the group why it would ever be the combined position of the Library Board to privatize the library's services by charging fees, indicating the thought had never been explored as long as she had been on the board.

Armand's velvety smooth but imperious reply had been, "An

annual fee would not be unrealistic in these times. Why, look at what people spend for those wretched 'Playstations' for their kids! Or, to go to the movies! They can certainly afford those luxuries, can't they? The fact of the matter is, we don't necessarily want to discriminate with the fee structure. We simply need to exclude *certain* types of people so that a more...enhanced, intellectual patron will come to use the services."

Appalled, she'd responded, "Well, it's a *public* library, utilized by many families who could not afford to buy books and tapes."

Althea had jumped in with, "And, people who could not afford the tremendous historical and resource materials that the library offers."

"Or families that don't have computers and audio visual equipment at their disposal," Ellie Waterhouse had added.

"Frankly, Armand, to discriminate by charging fees would be unfair." Mrs. Bundle had said.

"I never said the word *'discriminate'!*" he had shouted, "Did *I* ever say we should discriminate?"

The matter had been put to bed quickly with a solid "no" vote, but she had remembered his contentious words, his insinuation for a better quality of patronage. Not to discriminate, yet exclude! She had been dumbfounded by this extremism, this quietly treacherous prejudice; she had never experienced anything like this in all her years in Pillsonville.

Ultimately, Mrs. Bundle had walked away from that meeting realizing the full scope of this man's negative impact. After that, she was very concerned about the future of the library. More urgently, she knew that as long as people like Armand Limpert were involved in any of the decision-making process for the village, they all had cause to worry.

Chapter Eight

Come Ye Forthe and Show Your True Colours

At the top step, Mrs. Bundle called out, "Armand, are you up here?"

The slightly podgy figure of a man prone to excess appeared from nowhere, exiting from the third doorway of the hallway's last room, his dark fleshy face and wide Roman nose flushed from the heat, his bushy full head of overly dark black hair appearing *en vogue* mussed and spritzed, as usual. Too-perfect, too-bright, white teeth flashed a counterfeit smile; his perpetually tanned face looking somewhat offset by the rosy, apple-shaped cheeks. Some might consider him good-looking in a dandified, overdone way. Mrs. Bundle did not.

He was dressed in a trendy outfit that looked outrageous on his large figure: a massively-flowered, tropical Ralph Lauren shirt, too-tight tennis shorts, and dark brown, heavy thong sandals. Today, in this heat, he had forgone his usual attire of exquisite, cosmopolitan Italian suits or casual, yet pricey, designer golf apparel. This was apparently what he wore "roughing it." He stuck out like a sore thumb in Pillson; whatever he wore was for pure impact.

Everything was pushed to the limit with this man: colossal toes popped out of the expensive thong sandals; fleshy, hairy legs were exposed like mottled pork sausage; lots and lots of chunky gold jewelry sprouted like vegetation from his burly hands and wrists. His strong French ancestry overrode the pasty English Pillson genes that he claimed coursed through his body.

Atop his luxuriant head of hair sat his signature attempt at trendy fashionableness: designer sunglasses, secured around his large neck by an expensive leather strap (with a very visible "Vittadini" icon). He wore these sunglasses all the time; it mattered not what time of day or season or what the weather was. Today, Mrs. Bundle couldn't help but think that he looked like a brownish, cream-centered éclair, overloaded with saccharine and packed into his foppish clothes with no room to spare.

Of course, she thought wryly, *that annoying, mean-spirited smile is pasted on his face, too.*

He spoke with the smoothness of silk. "Why, my dear *Le-titia,* surprise, surprise."

His words slipped and slithered out like an oily stream of the most toxic, cinema popcorn butter—*the kind that you know is very bad for you but that you can't help but take in by the cupful,* she thought. The slickly polished, pompous voice grated on her like no one else's as she winced at his use of her formal first name. He gushed, "What, pray tell, brings *you* up here?"

"Armand." She restrained herself from reacting, choosing not to tell this aging dilettante where to get off. *He was so irritating.* She put a smile on her face and said, "Greetings! Finding anything useful to our patrons up here?"

Her straightforwardness seemed to throw him off a bit and he laughed, his obnoxious guffaw blasting loudly as he pointed a large, imperious digit in her face. "Ha, ha! Oh, you *are* a piece of work, Le-*titia.* You can't mean up *here?* In all these old boxes? Good Lord! We both know it's all *junk*! If I had my way, we'd get rid of the lot of it! Just have someone come in with a huge dumpster and throw it all right out the window!"

As he spoke, he moved in closer to her and stared directly into her eyes, invading her personal space, and she involuntarily stepped back. This was a practice of Armand's that was particularly obnoxious to Mrs. Bundle, an offensive intimidation that he liked to use often.

With all the feistiness she could muster, she said, "Who was the wise woman who said one man's junk is another man's treasure?"

"You are always one for a good joke, aren't you, *Letitia*?" Again, the slippery words fell on her like gumpy Karo syrup, and she felt the way she always did after one of these encounters with this man: as though she needed a long shower. She flinched slightly at the familiar use of her formal first name but bravely stood her ground.

Somehow, Armand had an uncanny ability to find one's sorest spot. He must know how deeply affected she was at being called "Letitia." Truth be told, there was only one person in her life that had called her by that name, lovingly, and in the privacy of their union; that man was her dear husband, Arthur.

Magically, Cracker appeared from behind Mrs. Bundle and meowed loudly at the large man. *Enough already, you big buffoon,* he cat-thought, *back off!*

When Armand didn't step back, Cracker purred, expertly moving in. *Two can play at this game,* he cat-thought, slinking between the man's feet and, taking a deep cat breath whilst trying not to breathe through his cat nose, he licked Armand's exposed toes. Armand jumped in surprise at the feeling of the rough, dry tongue against the bare—and very ticklish—toes, and Cracker smiled in triumph. He sat back on his haunches and purred. Mission accomplished!

"Must that cat accompany you everywhere, Letitia dear? Why, it's almost as unbearable as having that pest Bichon around!" groaned Armand.

Again, he knew the right hot buttons to push—her dear Cracker meant the world to her.

Don't do it, Cracker cat-thought, *don't bite!*

Mrs. Bundle had purposefully resolved not to get upset or have any kind of volatile exchange with Armand at this point. *Save all your strength for the meeting,* she told herself. She smiled dully and asked, "So, what *are* you doing up here?"

He leaned casually against the doorjamb, towering over her. "Oh, you know, just poking around! Those boxes in the back room need to be reviewed, in my estimation. And they're in the way! After going over the building inspection recommendations, I wanted to see for myself the full extent of the roof's interior leakage. I could barely squeeze in there because of all the boxes!" A phony smirk appeared again and he exclaimed, "Conclusively and unequivocally, I have to agree with the report; it's all really quite deplorable! Just terrible!" With greater importance, he said, "Likely *unsalvageable* at this juncture, should be destroyed is the way I interpret it."

He leered at her like the most devil-possessed French Cheshire cat, his grin wide and menacing as he leaned into her personal space once again, taunting her to respond.

Standing her ground, Mrs. Bundle said quietly, "It is a matter of interpretation, to be sure. I read the report, too. And nowhere in the inspection does it say the building should be destroyed. Certainly something we can debate in a much more formal setting than here."

"C'mon…" he cajoled, "you and I both know it's inevitable, Letitia."

"I'm sorry, but I cannot agree with you, Armand." Although his exaggerations annoyed her, she kept her emotions in check.

Returning his gaze with a solid, unflinching look, she said, "I'm looking forward to finding solutions that will work for everyone." She paused, "Aren't you, Armand?"

He gazed as though trying to dazzle her with his smile and good looks; she continued to stare back at him. The Cheshire cat smile slowly faded until it was not so bright, not so cheery.

Fleeting moments passed as he stared her down, but she did not flinch. Inside, she was seething at his flip, arrogant demeanor. *Oh, you groper, what I'd really like to say to you! You'll not get the best of me*, she thought distastefully as their eyes locked in silent battle. She heard Cracker meow loudly.

In utter disdain, Armand drawled, "Oh yes…no doubt…" The viscous words stuck to her like nasty glue, "We *all* want what's *best* for the community."

He laughed lightly, his lip curled into a sinister, charitably indulgent grin. "By the way, Letitia, have you and our *dear* Althea met the new man in town? Our chatty postman seems to think he's *quite* the catch." His words floated out like a spider spinning his web, slowly, deliberately. "I hear he's an artist from Manhattan. I happened to see them moving his paintings into the Elliot house. Large, expansive, canvases, very Jackson Pollack-style. Of course, if he's *anyone* with any credentials, famous or not, I should know him — or at the very least know *of* him — having been so involved as I was in so many fine arts and endowments boards for *so* many years in Manhattan."

"Really? Why, Armand, that is *truly* fascinating."

"Well, I like to keep my eye on the competition, as it were. That is, *me* being the only *other* eligible bachelor in town." He opened his wide donkey mouth and brayed loudly.

Mrs. Bundle's head spun and she wanted to giggle at his ludicrous comments but she said gaily, "Hmm, you *do* amuse yourself so, Armand!" She leaned in, "I, on the other hand, am most interested in finding only…solutions, as I said before, to our library's crisis. Not in finding eligible bachelors."

Cracker thought he was going to cough up a hairball. *Oh, you're good, my dear!*

"I see!" His response was as sugary sweet as a bowl of Count Chocula cereal. He threw his large head backward and heehawed again. "Say! Do you have a minute? I'd like to show you the roof's interior damage. I can show you exactly where…" he stepped aside and bowed, one arm making a grand gesturing motion toward the crowded third room.

Coincidence or not, his hand imperceptibly brushed hers in passing as he straightened. Her body went completely rigid as she looked at his large frame. His tongue caressed his full lips and she could have sworn she saw wolf fangs peeking through at her, reminiscent of the famously salacious animal licking his chops just before a delicious meal.

Oohh! Ugh! Recoiling at the thought, Mrs. Bundle shivered. She knew better than to be confined in a room (especially with only one way out) with this trifling, odious figure.

Then *she* laughed out loud. She couldn't help it; the laughter just bubbled out of her. Her fertile imagination had created an image of her kicking Armand very precisely in an undisclosed private area. Without one iota of shame or fear, she laughed again, ascertaining the faintest hint of darkness cloud his face.

"What's so funny?" he asked.

She composed herself. "Gosh! Nothing. Really. Thanks for the offer to look but," she said lightly, "I've already seen it!" She reached into her pocket and nonchalantly pulled out a pen, clicking the pen's head repeatedly as she gave him a cold stone look, just for good measure.

The further exercise of tapping the pen ever-so-daintily against her hand seemed to do the trick. He backed away slightly. *Why, he's just a big bully*, she thought.

His face had turned a queer, pasty, pea-green shade at being gently but firmly reminded of his impropriety. Armand was obsessive about his own social standing and power in the community; of that there was no doubt. She knew he would never want any sort of allegation surfacing concerning his improper behavior under the boardroom table.

Mrs. Bundle continued, smiling sweetly, gaining steam, "Really, Armand, you must have better things to do with your time than hanging around up here in this heat! Louis reminded me—and I should remind you—that everything up here should be left alone and untouched—unaltered in any way—until the Board can explore it as a group." She looked around, hands outstretched. "Everything appears to be fine. Why don't you just leave things as they are until our next meeting, at which point we can *all* make a decision about how we, as a board, are going to handle things?"

"Yes, well…as you say…" he cleared his throat and his pasted-on smile was back. Attempting to regain ground and impart an air of pretentiousness, he looked at his watch, as though short on time. Huffing with imperious grandeur, he blared, "Whew! Ahem! Would you look at the time? I've got a tennis match momentarily with Archie Plummer—gotta run, as they say. Much more of a priority than this…" he looked down the hallway with distaste, "…drivel."

She chuckled. "Good ol' Archie Plummer? He went to school with my Leslie, you know! You seem to have become the *best* of friends, haven't you?"

"Well, not really…he has been very helpful, though."

"Yes, he seems to have his hands in everything."

He blanched and turned as though ready to leave her standing there, but she smiled and added sweetly, "Well, Armand, Cracker and I must get on with the rest of our errands! You have a *good* day. And, give Archie my regards, would you?" She was glad to be done with him; the attic space was already stiflingly hot and she had things to do. There was no victory here, only an unpleasant feeling in her stomach reminding her that, by no means, was this the end of her troubles with Armand Limpert.

Leaving a glowering Armand standing there, she turned smartly with Cracker at her heels, little knowing she would return to that same hot spot in less than twenty-four hours for even more dreadful reasons.

Chapter Nine

Jack...and Junior

That evening around dusk Mrs. Bundle said her good-byes to the Andersens and the little Corrigan girls and she and Jack sauntered up the hill to her farmhouse. They had spent a lovely time dining and afterward, singing. Jack had tucked both the girls into bed and promised to take them swimming on Saturday before he and Nick Clancy went fishing on a well-deserved day off. As they strolled along, Cracker at her side, Jack gently guided her up the driveway in the darkening nightfall by holding her arm as they discussed their long day.

"Sure and I'm just about as tired and dead as that there post!" Jack said, his Irish accent now tinged with the Yankee slang he had absorbed in the last few months of being amidst Vermont's rich culture. He rubbed his tired eyes; the cerulean blue brilliance set against his ruddy Irish-looking good looks could have stopped Central Square traffic, his features striking with a strong cleft in his chin, thin nose, and dark, untamed eyebrows. Jet-black curly hair, cropped short for the summer heat, framed his face.

They reached the front porch and sat down; she in the rocking chair, he in the old porch glider couch whose worn vinyl cushions were ever so comfy. The sun was going down and the horizon was lit like a bright orange cantaloupe. Thus began their end-of-the-day ritual—starting with the long hike up the hill, then sitting down to rocking and talking, enjoying a good chinwag before going inside.

"Some sight!" Jack admired, the glider's springs gently creaking as he sent it back and forth in a soothing rhythm with his feet.

"Some sight." She repeated, never jaded by the beautiful sunset vista before her. "Ah, Vermont!" They both rocked away in silence.

Suddenly, the quiet was broken as she exclaimed, "Oh, Jack! I forgot—a large envelope came for you today! I had to sign for you, in fact."

"For me, you say? Where?"

"Yes, where did I—? Oh, dang! I *left* it in the back seat of Junie."

She started to get up but he put out his hand, motioning her to stay. "I'll get it, Mrs. B. You sit tight, now."

He jogged to the barn and came back, slightly out of breath and holding the large envelope limply in his hand.

She asked genially, "Who's it from?"

He flopped back onto the glider. "Oh, well now, I don't know! Advertising likely, some solicitor's office—not from around here. Likely trying to get me to buy something, aye." His voice held an unreal quality of disinterest and he slipped the large envelope in between the chair's side panel and his body. He leaned forward intensely, his eyes spanning the distant horizon.

She watched the young man, surprised, and asked, "Aren't you going to open it?"

"Ach, no!" He exhaled, feigning aloofness. "That's okay, *emm*…I'll open it later." He sat back, sullen and quiet, his demeanor completely changed as he looked out over the now-darkened field.

They sat quietly for awhile, both deep in their thoughts in a somewhat uncomfortable silence.

It was the first time Mrs. Bundle had *ever* seen Jack act evasive— why, it was almost as though he was hiding something.

Time ticked by as they sat silently, his face an emotionless mask, somber and half-hidden in the dim shadows of the roof's overhang.

Finally she asked gently, "Do you want to tell me what's going on?"

He sighed, staring out blankly at the scene, then uttered miserably, "Right, and it's probably just like the other two packets I received before this one."

"The *other two* packets? When?"

"Last month and the month before."

Suddenly, Cracker appeared from underneath the porch; he wedged his sleek body between the young man's fidgeting feet and admonished in cat-thought, *time to spill the beans, Jack.*

"Jack, what are you talking about?" She was concerned. This wasn't the Jack she knew; no, it wasn't like him to keep things from her.

He sat, quite sullen, then proclaimed resolutely, "Right, mum, those that went into the bin—and this one, too, will follow!"

She looked at him in complete surprise. What, she wondered, was bothering him about this correspondence?

Resignedly, Jack took the large envelope back out from its hiding place and shoved it toward Mrs. Bundle. "Here, mum, *you* open it, would you now?"

He held it out to her and she peered at it through the fading light. Reaching over without comment, she turned on the porch lamp beside her. Peering at Jack through the dusk and noting his apprehension, she slowly tore off the flap and reached inside.

It was a very official-looking letter.

"Aye. Read it." he said morosely.

She read aloud: "'*Dear Mr. Corrigan, This is our third attempt to reach you and we are in hopes that you will respond. Our client, who, at this point, continues to choose to remain anonymous, has asked that we make contact with you. This correspondence is written solely for one reason: to inform you that you have a distant relation that desires a meeting with you at your convenience.*'" She stopped and looked up in surprise—he gave a slight nod to his head, and she continued on, "'*Our client is aware that you have two younger siblings, sisters named Erin and Aineen. After aiding the client's search with our own extensive research, it is our combined belief that all other family (i.e., relatives) are deceased. Our client does not want anything from you monetarily; he hopes only to establish contact with the intention, at your choice, to build a relationship. Please contact us at your earliest convenience and we will be happy to make arrangements for you to meet this relative in a neutral setting of your choosing, after which, it will be your decision to proceed further.'* It's signed 'Steven Fitzgerald Barlow, III, Esquire. Attorney at law, Barlow, Reed, Fish, McDougall..' — etc. etc!"

She set down the paperwork in her lap. "My *Lord*! Why, Jack, that's unbelievable! Do you realize what all this means? You have family! Real family — not just the Travellers! Isn't that wonderful?"

His words cut hers like a machete, "*Wonderful?*" He fairly choked out the word as though it was putrid bile. "Wonderful, you say?" He scoffed, "Blimey! Not likely, Mrs. B!" His intense eyes were wild sapphires; he was as angry as a hornet ready to sting. "Why, I ask you, would *anyone* come out of the bloody woodwork *now*? And, for what reason? Other than skullduggery, to be sure. Aye, I'll not be taken advantage of again!"

Mrs. Bundle could see that same wounded look she had seen the first time she had ever laid eyes on him. Then, he had been freezing cold, alone and starving, trying to save him and his sisters, barely surviving in a new country where he didn't know or trust one soul.

With the security provided the last few months, along with good food and lots of love, Mrs. Bundle had seen those worry lines slowly disappear. It pained her now to see some residual hurt still lurking there behind those brilliant eyes. *What was hurting him so much at this moment?* She certainly didn't want to see anything or anyone ruin that contentment.

She waited for him to calm down. As she watched him, his head down, shoulders hunched, it came to her. "Oh Jack, I think I understand!" She spoke softly. "You're afraid, aren't you?"

He wiped his eyes disgustedly. "Right, I'm *scared* to death if you need to know!" he confessed. "I'll not have anyone messing with my family. Just as when we first arrived from Ireland, and I won't have it ever again, will I!"

"But Jack, this might be someone who can help you, a relative! Someone who probably knew your parents or your other kin!" Mrs. Bundle tried to reason with him.

"There's *no* one that we need to hear from now, I tell you! I've thought about this long and hard, haven't I now? *Where* was this relative when me dear Ma was sick, her, lying in her bed and dyin' of the cancer? Aye, with no one to care for the wee ones but me? Or, helping us when we were starving orphans in Dublin? Aye, coming to take us away from the miserable Travellers way of life and bringing us to a new life in America? *No one!* We did it all on our own, didn't we, without someone trying to be a 'mate,' someone horning in!" He stood up, agitated, turning his back to her and walking the length of the porch floor. When he reached the end, he turned around and walked back. His said passionately, "Sure and there's *no one* that I want to hear from now letting on to be me long lost relative!"

Jack wiped his eyes, all of the years of hardship and distrust bubbling over as he stared fixedly far away, toward the mountains.

With a purpose, she replaced the paperwork inside the large envelope and folded it neatly in half. She had made a decision. She said softly, "I understand, Jack. Really, I think I do. And we'll table this; we can talk about it another day."

He turned around, looking at her.

She said, "There's no decision that's so important it can't wait. And, mind you, I understand—this is a life-changing choice for you! So, don't you worry about a thing, we'll face it together, as a family. Right? As we have done from the day you came into our little world. Okay?" She sounded confident and strong in the growing darkness and his head gave a barely perceptible nod.

He sat down again, this time less agitated.

They sat quietly together in silence and, in time, the glider began its customary creaking once more. Jack asked in a low, calm voice, "The lass is back next Wednesday, right, mum?"

Mrs. Bundle smiled to herself.

Cracker, who lay nearby, would have liked to remind Jack that the answer would still be the same, even after his having asked that same question now for (Cracker counted on his paws) the *fourth* time in the last few days.

Try as he might to be nonchalant, it was evident to Mrs. Bundle and Cracker that Jack missed Angie as much as everyone else did; the two had a kindred spirit than transcended ordinary friendship. Since their ordeal at Thanksgiving, Angie's kindness toward him—and his gentle return of brotherly concern toward her—had been wonderful to watch over the last few months.

"Yes, dear. She'll be back the second. That's what Walter said— they'll pick her up late in the evening."

Jack stood up quickly, as though renewed, and stretched. Through a large yawn he said, "Right! I'm knackered! Sure, and it's time to hit the hay!" His native Irish accent and the burgeoning Vermont twang were pleasantly incongruent and Mrs. Bundle smiled again to herself.

"I'll be in in a minute. Goodnight, dear boy."

"*Oíche mhaith*, Mrs. B—a pleasant sleep to you."

As Jack headed inside, Mrs. Bundle was left alone with her thoughts. Today had been a jam-packed day and she, too, had to admit she was bushed. The current events melded with many past summers' memories and she daydreamed a bit as she and Cracker sat there alone, together.

Mrs. Bundle fumbled absentmindedly in her sundress pocket and felt the bit of small folded paper. Removing a crumpled white envelope, she realized she had been so busy that she had forgotten to open her letter from Japan; it would be a pleasurable way to end the day!

She strained to read the contorted block letters that formed words written in the ten-year-old penmanship of her grandson, Les, Jr:

Dear Grandma,

How are you? I'm fine and I'm having loads of fun this summer. I hope you won't get mad when I tell you this. I can't come to see you this summer because I'm playing baseball. We have a good team—well, really a great team! And I'm the pitcher! So, I can't leave. I'm sorry and I miss you a lot. A real lot! Can you come and see me sometime instead? I could show you my

new salamanders and take you to the ballpark, too.
 Our team is called Shinagawa Sushi.
 I miss you and love you! Say hi to Cracker!
 hugs, Les

A second page, in her son Leslie's handwriting, apologized for his and his wife's decision to allow Les to play ball that summer rather than make the planned trip to Vermont. Happy that his son had found a sport he not only loved but excelled at, Leslie anticipated the team would make the playoffs. Ultimately, it was just too hard to pull the boy away from his commitment at this point.

Mrs. Bundle wiped a stray tear from her eye, so very disappointed she would not be seeing her only grandchild this summer.

Cracker rose slowly from the porch floor and rubbed his sleek ebony fur against her leg, then went to the screen door and scratched his long talons against the mesh. The sound jarred her from her thoughts.

Tomorrow is another day, he cat-thought, *mind—that is what you always say, dear partner.*

She shivered, despite the humid night air. "Cracker, will you look at that sky!"

Almost instantly, the air pressure had changed and the sky was looking particularly angry and dark. There was a rushing, rhythmic "whoosh" as the tops of the trees swirled amidst the muggy atmosphere.

She sighed, "Well! No use crying over spilled milk. Better head inside. It looks like we've got a good storm brewing!"

She shivered again, strangely unsettled, distracted by the wind and her own thoughts that hinted that something…ominous…was lurking behind those dark clouds.

———◆·◆·◆———

It was midnight.

Junior sat alone in the damp darkness. His sad, slight man-body leaned forward, dejected and forlorn. The loneliness was insidious, stealing confidence from him like the stealthiest of bandits until it became a strange, comforting silent partner. This ready friend never judged him, never laughed or jeered at him. He had learned the hard way, over time and through a multitude of sordid experiences, that this isolation was his only true best friend, his only judge and jury.

Who cared if he was alone? Who noticed him? Sad to say, he knew, far too well, the dismal answer. Long ago, he had resigned himself to a world of one. A world of one, until...he pushed the misty, blissful image from his mind, anxious to revel for a little while longer in the sorry, sad pit of gross injustices that were his cumulative life experiences.

Sequestered from his peers at an early age, his disability had tethered him further from the everyday world of communication, placing him sometimes on the brink of frustration and madness, restraining his enjoyment of any group interaction. He saw the looks on *their* faces, the impatience and loathing whenever he had tried. So, he just stopped trying. He had given up.

Here, in the quiet darkness, he could be himself. He could vocalize without the looks, without the judgment; he could be as loud as he wanted without repercussions.

His voice rang out in dejected anger.

"*E-e-eeeeee!* O-o-oh!" Opening his mouth wide, larger than normal, he thrust the two vowels forth, slowly and deliberately.

Then, with even more anger, he shouted, "I *h-h-hate* y-y-you!" He paused and slammed his fist down on the hard surface, utterly frustrated and alone in his painful loudness. Forming his lips in a pursed circle, he pushed and pushed his vocal wind from the back of his throat, straining his gullet muscles to the maximum to form the consonants he so despised.

He struggled again, and finally, in a rush of syllables, blurted out, "h-h-hate y-y-you all!"

He spit disgustedly, sending the glob of saliva arcing up and out into the gloomy, dank air and watching it disappear into the detached darkness.

He shook his head severely, pushing away the bad thoughts. Creating a blank palette, he wiped the nasty cobwebs from his brain and a soft smile came to his lips as he thought of his one ray of hope, his passion…his Muse, his Mona Lisa.

Ah, love!

To love and be loved was to feel the sun from both sides. He didn't know where that quote originated, but the words gave him comfort and a sense of calmness in the midst of his cruel inward existence.

Her sweetness and innocence had enveloped his affliction and, opposing his wall of silence and loneliness for once, he had let…*her* in. She, his beautiful inspiration, had only seen his soul, nothing else, and he adored her, to be sure. She was his only love, now and forever; her beauty his only motivation.

But…a well of emotion caught in his throat, sticking there as uncomfortably as though he'd swallowed a golf ball, and he sighed forlornly, acknowledging with complete, devastatingly final resignation, that that wondrous part was to be no more.

He stared at the nothingness through the thick wraparound lenses. His cry of anguish broke the lonely silence.

Argggghhhhh!

He sat back and closed his weary eyes in total surrender. Of course, it couldn't be; he knew it could never be. He should have known that from the beginning. He, better than anyone, realized that nothing good or right ever, ever, came into his sphere of hapless existence.

Hadn't his father warned him? "Stay away! Don't never trust no one!"

A menacing, fatalistic chortle escaped from his raw throat and he chided himself, beating himself up further: *you should have known what would happen*! You should have known…and he slumped further into his hard seat.

He sighed deeply. Tenderly, as though choosing a lacy, fragile valentine, he picked up his tool of choice from the nearby counter. He held it high, the steel end pointed menacingly into the low-lit, clammy air.

Here was his power. In his quivering hands, he held the instrument that caused good and evil, its intent resting solely on the executor.

Beauty is not in the face. Beauty is a light in the heart. Another quote. How he wished she had believed him when he spoke those words to her. Now, it was too late.

The huge crash and subsequent bang startled him into complete darkness. The thunder before the storm, he observed.

He knew what his purpose in life was, even as he held the appliance ever so lightly. At that instant, his tool could be lethal, even deadly. His mouth contorted slightly.

More thunder crashed and growled, dry rumblings in anticipation of the deluge about to descend.

He hit the piezo electric button.

With one stroke, the auto-ignition butane gas blowtorch came to life, the power of its intense fire and light illuminating the darkness. Sparks flew everywhere, creating small, broken branches of bright blues and orange in the darkness. He sat quietly transfixed by the magical light. As many times as he had performed these beginning steps of his ritual, the power of *fire* never ceased to impress him. Fire that was sapphire blue, then passionate red-orange as he aimed the hottest center of heat toward his purpose. Simultaneously, the noise came softly from his throat as though foreign, manifested in a low growl, then amplified, doubling in bestial crazed intensity until, as he threw his head back and opened his mouth wide, it changed, reverberating into an eerily high-pitched and frenzied, staccato-ridden laugh!

"GRrr-rr-gr!" he yelled, laughing. "Hah!! H-h-haaa-hee-hee! H-haa!"

He would show them. He would show everyone. *Just you wait and see, my love.*

The blowtorch spit violent fire and sparks, the adjustable flame temperature reaching 1300 degrees, crimson-hot and deadly serious, ready at any moment to weld, to fuse, or to maim *whatever* was placed in its path.

Ahhh, he sighed in total gratification, *didn't he love a good fire!*

He went to work.

Chapter Ten

A Big Problem

The skies were crazy that night; loud crashes and serious lightning illuminating the sky with combustible fanfare. Finally, with a vengeance normally seen in tropical climates, it rained intensely for all of five minutes, so hard it was as though heaven's lakes overflowed into all of Pillson.

Then, as quickly as it began, the rain stopped abruptly—except the sky's loud clamoring continued on, rumbling and burping like the inside of a huge belly undergoing a bout of uncomfortable indigestion.

Lying in her bed wide awake and alternating between staring out the window at the illuminated sky's lightshow and then tightly closing her eyes in frustration, Mrs. Bundle tried desperately to fall asleep. This state of insomnia was rare; she usually slept like a log. But not tonight. She flipped and flopped, restless and unsettled throughout the long night as each round of thunder and lightning crashed and resounded through the large house. She tried everything from putting her pillow over her head, to counting sheep, to watching one of her very long, very dry, British Masterpiece Theatre drama videos.

It was hopeless, and the muggy humidity didn't help one bit. Sleep just would not come. Fretting as the morning hours loomed nearer, she resigned herself to the situation and lay back in complete exhaustion.

At last, all was quiet around two-thirty and, as she listened to the gentle rhythm of the drip, drip of the roof gutter outside her bedroom window, she finally fell into a deep, heavy sleep.

She was ten years old. She knew that for sure because she had just celebrated her birthday and Mrs. Torp was her favorite teacher. She could hear the distant school bell ringing. She closed her book and jumped up from her desk. Yeah!!! It was recess time and she wanted to get outside quickly to play with the new baseball ball and glove her father had picked up especially for her on his way back from his business trip in Burlington.

She raced toward the coatroom.

Hammond Lovelace (known as "Hammer" for short and the biggest bully in the school) stepped in front of her; his two, huge boxcar-feet firmly planted themselves with a thud directly in front of her at the coatroom entrance. He smiled, blocking the door so that she couldn't leave the classroom. She gritted her teeth, summing up her thoughts with one word of exasperation—boys! They were the bane of her existence.

Standing her ground, she clenched her fists and, with quiet, measured determination, said, "Kindly get out of my way, Hammer. I want to get my things." (She always tried to be nice first, especially because her mother always said, "Lettie, always put your best foot forward and meet each challenge with a smile.")

However, the oversized, mastodon-toothed lunk's mother had not taught him the same axiom, and he guffawed loudly and then, taunting her, leaned even closer, disgustedly, into her personal space.

"Ahh, c'mon, Lettie," he cajoled, "can't I have a little kiss? I like you. How 'bout it?" His wide freckles leapt out from his face as his dirty hands groped for her like greasy leeches in a pond.

More than being repelled, this made her mad. Dang mad, in fact!

"*Yuckkk!*" *she shuddered and, without giving it a second thought, kicked him squarely and with keen precision in the right shin—just below the knee—where she knew, from previous experience, it would really count.*

Her mark was true and, as he doubled over screeching in agony; she ran around him, deftly avoiding the jumping, hysterically-hopping mass of minced machismo.

"*Owwww!*" *he yelled wildly.*

In reluctant triumph (because she wished girls didn't have to resort to that kind of violence), she told herself with conviction, that will teach him!

The recess bell still rung incessantly in the distance and she ran, grabbed her ball and bat, and made a dash for the playground!

The bell still rung, and rung. Was there time to play? Shucks! Am I too late, she wondered?...

Mrs. Bundle stirred fitfully, hazily realizing it was all a dream and there was no school, and thankfully, no Hammer Lovelace in the room with her. Yes...she *was* sleeping, and it *wasn't* recess time, and no, she wasn't ten years old. She was...she pulled her tired mind together.

What on earth was that ringing? She stirred again, stretching her tired body. What the heck was that clamor? The school bell...

She reached out groggily, gaining her bearings, grasping that the bell was actually the sharp ring of her bedside phone. Glimpsing with one heavy eye at the bedside clock, she could vaguely make out the time. Was that 6:28 a.m.?

"*Ohhhh*, no...," she groaned. Her body felt as though it had been run through a washing machine's wringer.

The lump at the bottom of her bed twitched, and she gently pushed at it with her feet. It twitched again, this time more spasmodically.

Ring, ring! Ri-i-i-nnng!

She drew herself up on one elbow, inadvertently jarring the soft mound once again with her foot as Cracker's carcass moved lazily, slumberously, from beneath the deep recesses of the rumpled quilt.

She finally captured the phone from its cradle.

"Hel-lo?" Her voice sounded two octaves deeper.

"Mrs. Bundle, it's me! *Louis!*" Louis Montembeau's voice was highly charged (even more than usual), emotion clutching at the edges of his throat like a vice squeezed tightly onto his vocal cords.

"Louis. Yes…oh, hello..Louis!" Her reflexive thinking was on empty.

"Oh, Mrs. Bundle, what a mess we're in!" he bemoaned, his voice shrill and undeniably panic-filled. "I think…you'd better get down here *right away!*"

"Louis? Louis, what's wrong? *Where are you?*"

He screeched into the phone, "*Here*, of course! At the Library!"

She raised her head and shook it, desperately trying to clear the entanglement inside. Her long hair tumbled onto her shoulders and she pushed it back out of the way of the phone's receiver. "Wait a sec…it's Wednesday, isn't it?" Raising herself onto her elbows, she sneezed loudly. "*Ahhh-cchoooo!*" Her whole body shuddered. Wet with sweat, she threw the light sheet back, her body yearning for some cool morning air.

Meee—*owwww!* First long, dainty whiskers, then a round ebony face with very brilliant almond-shaped eyes appeared from beneath the lightweight satin quilt.

I give up, Cracker cat-thought in exasperation—*what's going on?*

"God bless you!" Vocal chords bursting with hysteria, Louis cried, "Oh, I'm so sorry I have to wake you, but…we have an emergency!"

Mrs. Bundle tried to put her confused thoughts together in *tout de suite* fashion. "What on earth are you doing there *today*? It's… Wednesday. And why this early?"

His words ran together like the most talented speed talker ever, in quicksilver fashion (faster than his usual clever banter), "Right! I know! It's my day off, yes, it is! Oh, *Gosh!* But, you see, I had some cataloging left, work I didn't finish up yesterday, so I decided to come in for just a couple hours this morning, real early, to finish up. Heavens to Myrgatroyd! It's a good thing I *did* come in!" He stopped, clicking his tongue impatiently in total frustration, and then, becoming even more agitated, he cried out, "Oh, dear God!"

Mrs. Bundle held the phone slightly away from her poor ear, fearing the combination of decibels and frequency too much for her to handle at this early hour.

He rushed on, "I think I spoke too quickly yesterday, you know about... Oh, me and my big mouth!" He hesitated, then lowered his shaking voice to barely a whisper. "I'm on the *portable* phone... upstairs. Best if I don't...we'd better not—not on this phone anyway." He seemed incoherent and she opened her mouth to speak but he interrupted first with, "Okay, so," his voice barely squeaked, "Can you come down here? We've got trouble and I need you here, right away! Can you come? *Now?*"

Lord, what now? Louis' panicked state and his measured use of discretion told her something serious was up, to be sure. He was clearly in a state.

"Yes. I can," she said, "Please, take a deep breath." She heard a gasp of pure desperation. "Hold on, Louis. Just sit tight. Give me fifteen minutes and I'll be down the hill as fast as a race horse in full trot!"

"Thank you, thank you! I'll be at the back door to let you in!"

She hung up, then sat up and grabbed the first garment nearest her—the faded old farmer blue jean overalls she wore when she gardened. Rushing into the bathroom, she splashed water on her face, deftly and strategically placed bobbie pins here and there in her hair until she had fashioned a loosely braided chignon, then brushed her teeth—all in two minutes flat. Leaving on her sleeveless, black-and-white-cow-figured, pink pajama nightshift, she jumped into her overalls and tucked it all in helter-skelter, snatched her ever-faithful fanny pack (containing her detecting tools and items necessary for most any emergency) from its customary place by the piled-high rocking chair, found her sneakers under the bed, threw them on, and rushed downstairs. She found her keys and she and Cracker were off, like a shot, out the door.

Louis Montembeau met her at the back library service door located off the small parking lot and out of sight from the main road.

He had been standing there with the door opened just a hair, anxiously awaiting her arrival. As she stepped out of her car, he opened the heavy wooden door very cautiously another six inches—just enough for her and Cracker to enter.

She was shocked to see that his normally meticulous deportment had been completely ravaged, his appearance downright messy. Yes, Mrs. Bundle observed with increasing alarm, things must be pretty awful, because here was Louis looking, well…disheveled! Louis! Always the gentleman, always impeccably pulled together, he now depicted the opposite.

He was an absolute jumble of nerves, his whole body a virtual frenzy of quivering flesh, his flushed, crimson face damp with sweat. He wrung his hands anxiously as he tried to talk as she stepped into the Library's main section, "Okay! I came in this morning, as usual, and everything was fine! Oh, heavens!" He was perspiring to beat the band. The muggy summer morning air had already taken its toll on his usual cool demeanor.

Looking so disturbed that she feared he might be in shock, Mrs. Bundle said gently, "Louis, *calm* down." She patted his shoulder protectively and pointed to the comfy Queen Anne chair nearby. "It's all right…here, sit down for a minute and get your breath."

He sank heavily into the oversized leather arm chair, his chest heaving like overworked bellows. Mrs. Bundle guided him gently to put his head between his knees and he sat this way for a time, his breathing labored and deliberate.

"There, there, now. My, Louis, you're about as nervous as a long-tailed cat in a roomful of rocking chairs!" She heard the makings of a titter erupt from him and sighed with relief. "Are you calm down?" He looked up and nodded. "Okay. Now, what on earth is going on?"

Louis took a couple long, deep breaths. "Okay! I was here--at the computer, see? Just doing my thing, you know, in my own world when all of a sudden, I heard a huge crash upstairs! It scared the stuffing right out of me! I ran up to the second floor—saw nothing unusual—so, I went flying up to the third floor, thinking it's one of those big storage bookcases or something like that, that's collapsed, right?"

She nodded, "Yes?"

"Oh, it's *terrible!* Just terrible," he wailed, running his dirty hands through the straight stalks of light blonde hair and then down across his face, giving him an even more electrically-charged, wild appearance.

He lowered his voice to a bare whisper, "It's a mess up there! One of the low eaves and a portion of the ceiling have totally collapsed! Caved right in, from what I could see. It's one of the rafters, I think, Mrs. Bundle. In that far back corner room at the end of the hall! Water, dirt, old shingles everywhere! That rainstorm last night must have been too much for that section of the roof! Or, something could have hit it from outside. Did you hear the thunder? Oh, God, Mrs. Bundle, what a mess!"

"How bad is it? Do we need to call the fire department?"

"Well, there's no evidence of fire." Cracker had hopped up into his lap and he stroked the sleek fur in a comforting rhythm. "Well, I couldn't be sure. I could see the early morning sky peeking through where the roof opened up. I panicked and tried to pick up some things, but I realized it was pretty serious. I came right down and called you." He ended his story and gave her a fishy stare, finally taking her in from head-to-toe. "My *Gawd!* What on earth have you got on? You look... a sight, Mrs. B!" He focused on her get-up, mortified to see her disheveled appearance.

"I'm glad we don't have a mirror here, Louis—for your sake *and* mine." She gave a wry glance at his grimy hands and he looked down in horror. She added, "Yes, well, there wasn't time for *me* to get spruced up, was there? You called and I came—straight out of bed! And with only a few hours' sleep, mind you!"

"Oh, I'm so sorry! You've rushed down here and—"

"It's okay! You sounded so panicked; I just threw on my overalls and flew down as fast as Junie could go!"

Louis wailed. "Oh, my! I'm so sorry! Thank you for coming. What are we going to do? I thought you should be the first one to know, before…"

"Louis, really, don't worry. I know. Whatever's happened, it's not the end of the world, really it isn't. You know the Board will take care of it."

"Oh, Mrs. Bundle, I know only too well. That's exactly what has me scared to death. This is just what Mr. Uppity has been waiting for! This will be the frosting on the cake for him and you know it! Our dear Mr. Limpert will have me out the door in a heartbeat, and the Library will be closed down for good!"

She clamped her lips firmly into a thin line. It was a very serious situation, to be sure. "Let's not get ahead of ourselves. We can't worry about that now, Louis. Let's go up, assess the damage, and then we'll go from there."

Chapter Eleven

The Damage

After picking their way cautiously through the rubble in the back room, Mrs. Bundle stood back and looked at the mess.

"It's hotter than Hades up here already!" she said, wiping the sweat from her brow.

The previous night's five-minute deluge clearly had been the last straw for the back section of the already-impaired roof. The old oak floor was slippery with leaves and grime, still slightly damp from the unwelcome rainwater. Cardboard boxes were dark brown and water-stained, having received the bulk of the drenching. In the corner of the room, where the kneewall met the roofline, the appearance was disastrous. Peeking through the now-opened knee wall area was the bright morning sun.

Upon closer inspection, it looked as though a branch had crashed through the already fragile roof membrane; the offending piece of hardwood woefully piercing the opening like a bare thumb sticking out of a ripped-apart glove.

A large chunk of old, wooden, wide board paneling (used in the 1800s as lathe overlayment and approximately 5' by 6' feet in size) lay dejectedly on its side, the force of the caving roof causing the resultant dislodgment of the panel. She knelt down tentatively on one knee and looked inside under the eaves to see the damage.

Louis stood fearfully behind her, "Mrs. Bundle, please! The rest of that ceiling could go any minute!"

"No, Louis, I think it's fine. Look! The branch caused the bulk of the damage—mostly on the outside. It looks like rain came in from the gutter after the tree branch fell, causing the rest of the ceiling and the knee wall panel to give way. That's all, I think." She made a sweeping motion with her hand and then wiped her brow. "It looks worse than it is. With this heat, this will all be dry by noon!" She peered further into the gap. "The basic structure is sturdy...it's just right there at the roof line," she turned to him and gave a shrug, "consequently, there's just a *little* opening here under the eaves now."

Louis pointed an accusing finger at the area. "That's not a *little* opening, Mrs. Bundle. That's what I'd call a gaping hole, or my name isn't Louis Montembeau! I'm as optimistic as the next person, but I think you're pushing the envelope on this one."

"Yes, well, it *is* better to look at the half-full cup, isn't it? See there, that whole section is fine." Abruptly, she stopped her assessment and bent over, eyeballing the darkened interior of the knee wall, further along under the covered eaves. "Hey, what's this? Wait a minute, here!"

She stood up, opened the zipper of her fanny pack, and retrieved her high-intensity penlight and her penknife. Then she placed experienced fingers into her braided chignon, carefully extracting a large bobby pin. She knelt down on one knee and shone the light into the small area behind the fallen panel.

"What is it?" The crease lines were back on Louis' forehead. "What are you after?"

"Hold on, Louis. I'll be back in a jiffy." Gingerly, she moved deeper into the small dark recess, edging her knees forward inch by inch until only her blue-jeaned backside was visible.

"Wait! Where are you going? *Don't* go in there for God's sake..." She ignored his uneasy warning. "Mrs .*Bundle*...what on earth are you doing?"

Louis could hear a rustling sound, and when first her upper torso reappeared, and then her flushed face, he saw that she was clutching something in her hand. She had used the bobby pin as a clip of sorts to secure a fragile, flimsy material. She showed him two dusty, cobweb-like pieces of crushed, waxen-like paper squares, approximately 2" x 2" in size; both appeared to have fancy old lettering festooned with lots of curlicues adorning one side of each paper.

"What have you got there?" Louis inquired, leaning down to her level to see what she held in her hand. "They look like wrappers of some kind…is it trash?"

She held one up to the illuminated penlight. "No! It says '*Fry and Fils*'. Fancy that, Louis! Don't they look old?"

He shook his head; his concerned expression made her smile. "*Louis*, don't worry! I'm going to take care of this, so don't worry."

He attempted a tired-out smile. "Ok-ay. If you say so…"

"Louis, look here," she held out the wrappers and asked, "Why on earth would these be all the way up here, way under the eaves like that?" She looked around, wondering. "Look," she pointed down into the corner molding near the floor where he was standing, "there! There's another one! And another!"

He reached down and pulled about a half dozen or so more of the same small papers from the small space under the eaves. With some interest, he said, "It's like a little cubby hole there, isn't it?"

From all appearances, the small area of about 3' by 5' had been a repository, a cache area of sorts, for some unknown creature. Littered on the floor were more of the same finely etched, old paper wrappers, all of which had the identical general appearance of a discarded covering or wrapping of some sort.

"Interesting…" Louis said, becoming intrigued, attempting to forget the daunting hole in the ceiling for a minute. "Hey! They're written in French!" In his best French accent, he read, "*Fry & Fils*,'—that would be Fry and Sons, Mrs. Bundle—'*Chocolat Delicieux a Manger*'—'Delicious Chocolates to Eat'—that's the translation."

"Why…it must be an old candy wrapper—judging by that fancy writing!" Mrs. Bundle exclaimed. She shone her light further into the space. "Look, there are a whole bunch more of them! If I were to theorize, I would say someone or something—an animal or the like—stashed them there!"

Cracker, who had appeared from nowhere, began sniffing the area with the zeal of a bloodhound. *Yes, quite some time ago, too,* he cat-conjectured.

"*Very* long ago, wouldn't you suppose, Louis?" Mrs. Bundle turned to him.

Louis drew the faintly-etched paper closely to his eyes and continued reading, "It says, '*Bonbons Chocolatier*'—I can't make out the rest. It's in French and it's old. I think there's more writing at the bottom here…wait a minute…" He squinted and held the paper closer to the natural light of the open roof area. "Yes, here it is. '*Présenté à l'Exposition de Prince Albert*'." He scratched his head. "Hmm, that would be 'Presented at Prince Albert's Exposition'—yes, that's what it means! Let's see, Prince Albert, wasn't he the one…that would have been Victorian England…right? Uh—what are you doing?"

Mrs. Bundle, fascinated and back on the scent, was already focused on what else the small space might be hiding. She knelt again, scrunching down on all fours so that she resembled a turtle of sorts and poked her long-necked head back in further to see what else she could find. As he watched her lowered backside go deeper into the dark hole, Louis could hear her rummaging around in the semi-darkness, her bare ankles and the soles of her sneakers the only visible part of her body.

Concerned for her safety, he kept a running commentary, more to set his own mind at rest. "Well? What are you seeing? You wouldn't get *me* to go in there. I'm sure it's *ab-so-lute-ly* filthy! Seriously, Mrs. Bundle, are you listening to me? You're crawling around in mouse droppings, probably—and who knows *what* else, I'm sure. You're going to pick up some dreadful illness! Oh, gosh! I'd never forgive myself if you got hurt. Watch out for nails, would you? Can you *hear* me?"

After a good thirty seconds of silence, he leaned down on his haunches and begged exasperatedly, "I *must* insist, *please*, Mrs. Bundle! You're too.." he stopped himself just in time from using the word "old," then "mature" came to mind and he rejected that, hastily managing to come up with, "too…*dignified* to be mucking around in there! Come out of there, now, would you?"

With only silence to keep him company, he finally gave up and waited. *What was it about this fine lady?* He had to admire her; she just didn't give up, not even when things got dirty or unpleasant. When she was on to something, whether it was solving the library problems or one of her mysteries, he knew there just was no stopping her! *Heavens*, he thought as he listened to her rustling movements, *she reminds me of a dainty female root hog foraging around in the darkness. Really*, he thought, more amused now than exasperated, *like the most ardent pig searching for truffles!*

He laughed aloud! Cracker just purred from his vantage point outside the wall opening.

Just then, all the rustling stopped and they could hear a light tapping.

Inside the darkened area, she had carefully reached under the eaves and was delicately picking away with her penknife at the surrounding wood in one specific area. She had spied something as the daylight's sunbursts streamed through the cracks in the roof.

The focus of her attention was a rather large, hard object. *It's been jammed in here somehow*, she observed. *What is it?*

She stuck the penknife under the item and, using the knife as a fulcrum, hinging it *just so* under the object, she pushed upward. All of a sudden she heard a "pop" and it moved slightly. *There!* She wiggled it again with the knife point, moving it back and forth, and it was almost free. She pushed up again and was able to dislodge it! The size of a small knapsack, it was hard and four-sided. As it fell the six or so inches to the rough wooden floorboards, it made a loud, bumping sound, followed by a reverberating *clunk*! She reached out a long hand and secured it firmly, pulling it toward her in one broad stretch. She inhaled quietly and whispered breathlessly, "*Got it!*"

Her breath caught, distracting her, as she felt two strong hands pulling on the only part of her body sticking outside the cubby—her feet!

Louis was grabbing her—quite unceremoniously—by the ankles and was pulling rather hard. "Mrs. Bundle! I mean, *really*! What was that bang? Are you all right? You need to come out of there right now! Do you hear me?"

She snuffled a loud, "Wow!" That exclamation was followed quickly by a garbled, "Yuh-huh, *okay!* Yes, I'm fine, *Louis, please let go!* I'm coming out. *Oh, mercy!*" Still on all fours, she slowly backed out into the attic room, pulling her treasure with her.

Cracker, observing the activity with much interest, sat impatiently beside the knee wall opening, his sleek body straight and tall as he watched his tousled partner emerge.

He meowed vociferously—*Lord, was she a mess!*

Louis implored, "What happened in there? What on earth have you got now?"

She slowly righted herself and came up for air.

Short-winded, hands full, and with a big dark smudge of grime on her perspiring brow, she paused and took in gulps of fresh air. "Hoo—*eeee!*" she cried, the loose chignon at the nape of her neck (albeit, swiftly pulled together earlier) now listing considerably to the right with bits and pieces of the long silvery-brown strands stuck to her face like cooked spaghetti to an empty pot. The black-and-white cows on her pink pajama shift were now a splotchy dirt-brown.

Although disheveled, filthy, hot, and out of breath, there was no mistaking the glow of excitement on her face as she looked up at Louis and smiled, a broad, voluminously proud smile, her dark brown eyes radiant.

"*Look!* Look what I've found! It's…hidden treasure!"

Chapter Twelve

A Big Discovery

Kneeling, she held out the object with quivering hands. Her fingers, dusty and soiled, were tightly wrapped around a hard, rectangular object that appeared to be solidly wrapped in an old oilskin and then firmly tied off with a frayed, jute-like twine.

"It was *behind* that wall panel! Right there! Kind of shoved in, wedged inside the back wall area, you know? Isn't it...*fantastical?*" Mrs. Bundle's face shone with wet enthusiasm.

Cracker sniffed at the package, his interest clearly heightened.

"What is it?" Louis asked, gently taking her elbow and helping her to her feet.

"I haven't the foggiest! But see, it's hard and square, actually, more rectangular..." She palpated it gingerly and exclaimed, "It feels like a picture frame! Yes, I can feel the edges. This wrapping's very fragile, very old. I think it's old oilskin, for goodness sakes!" She looked back at the small space under the eaves. "Who knows how long it's been in there...?"

"Oilskin is waterproof, isn't it? Probably a good thing that whatever's inside is covered in that material. Doesn't look at all damaged, at least from the outside, anyway. Say, who do you think would have put that inside *there?*" Louis pointed into the knee wall, his forehead scrunched tighter than usual as he pondered this question.

Mrs. Bundle shrugged, "Don't know. Let's open it, shall we?"

"Do you think we should?"

Mrs. Bundle nodded. "Definitely! But very carefully, Louis."

She wiped her hands on her overalls. With great care, they first turned the package over and inspected it. She said, "No unusual markings on the outside, *umm*..it appears relatively tightly wrapped."

"Yes, the string is really old and fragile, too." Louis added, testing the string gently.

Cracker jumped from one paw to the other, weaving back and forth with anticipation as he wedged his way in beside Mrs. Bundle to get a better view.

Open it up, he cat-thought eagerly.

Mrs. Bundle held the edges of the package while Louis slowly and ever-so-gently undid the tied bow and the string. Then, they removed the oilskin wrapping. As they slowly uncovered it together, an ornate, gilded frame, tinged with bursts of hued and aged coppery gold and sized about 17" by 19", peeked through. They laid the wrapping abstractly to the side, both dazzled by the frame's distinctiveness.

"Ooohhh…" Mrs. Bundle sighed, "it's lovely."

Even more remarkable was the brightly colored scene painted inside the frame, measuring approximately 12" by 14".

"It's an oil painting! Original, too, if I'm not mistaken! Oh…My… Gosh!" Louis exclaimed.

It was a tranquil nature scene, its colors so beautiful and intense as to catch one's breath. There was a small boulder-laced waterfall cascading into a small river or stream, an illusion it seemed—or someone's vision—of a calm, deep, watering hole. There was a strange sense of harmony about the scene, stillness interspersed with the intensity of the active water cascading spontaneously throughout the tiers of many progressively larger, unusually formed rock formations. The artist's expertise of color and perception was evident even to a layman's eyes. Leafy trees shaded the small river scene, by all appearances motioning, beckoning the beholder to come and sit on the rocks awhile, to spend some quiet time. There was one larger tree that stood out—an aberration of sorts, enormous and welcoming but with a massive branch hanging low over the water; the tree's arm reached out like a crooked finger, bidding all to climb out and over the water, to hang from its branches, to enjoy the view, to swing above the cool, deep pools. One was immediately tempted by the coolness of the water, wondering could this magical scene be real, and if so, where was it? Color and beauty came together with such intensity—where was this beautiful grotto? Was it just the product of the artist's fertile, imaginative mind, or did it really exist?

Well, there's your painting, Cracker cat-thought. *It may not be a Strozzi, but…it has all the elements…*

"Holy Moley," Louis gave a low whistle, "look at that water! It looks real, the colors are so brilliant! The blues, and the greens—they're incredible! I sure could use that cool stream right now!" he exclaimed, his eyes mesmerized by the rippling pools before him.

"Isn't it *beautiful?*" Mrs. Bundle held the painting up closer to the light streaming through the jagged opening in the roof. "Cats granny! The shades are so vibrant! I love the greens and teals and that saffron-yellow on the banking. Oh, *look!* There's just a hint of a rainbow over that distant field, as though it must be just after a summer shower! And, that thing the size of a quarter…is that a building in the far back corner?"

"Yes, I believe so! Looks like a farm."

"Beautiful! Just look at that water! Emerald green here, deep cobalt blue shadowing right there, and look at that incredible deep purple in places! It's absolutely stunning!"

"And doesn't it look just like a scene right out of Vermont—somewhere pleasant and private, don't you suppose?"

"Absolutely!" she agreed.

"It takes your breath away, for sure! A lot of *detail* for such a modestly-sized painting. Even the leaves on the trees—look there—just like they're swaying in the summer breeze. This sure beats *anything* I've seen lately—not that I'm a connoisseur of fine art, or anything as grand as that, but I do like to dabble." He turned to her and nodded, "However, I know enough to tell you it's really quite good." Mrs. Bundle nodded, and his artistic eyes continued to critique the painting; his face was serious. "You know, you're *right,* there's something about the water! It's so peaceful, so…serene. I love that big tree with that branch hanging over the stream." He smiled at her. "The only thing missing is seeing someone enjoying that cool water! It really reminds me of one of those *'dog days of summer'* afternoons, do you know what I mean?"

"Yes, I do! Cracker and I were just discussing those *'dog days'* yesterday…isn't that odd?" She paused and gave Cracker a playful wink and he meowed. She said, "This scene gives you such a…" she hesitated, trying to find the right words, "a sense of …*intimacy*— almost as though you've been made privy to a very secret, very special place."

They both were silent for a few moments, each going over the painting's finer details, their eyes drinking in the simple beauty of the piece.

"It's really…quite exquisite," she concluded.

Louis chuckled, "Especially with this heat we've been having! I want to go for a swim!"

"I think I can make out the artist's signature. Wait!" She reached for the fanny pack and drew out the small magnifying glass, then held it close over the painting and peered through it. She drew in an excited breath, "*Ah-hah*! It says…*Corny*. Corny? What kind of name is—no, wait, that's not an 'R.' It's an 'N'! *'Conny'*, that's it! Conny, it says, and there's a date under it, too!" Mrs. Bundle's words rushed out; she could barely contain her excitement. "'*1861*'. Oh, my Lord, Louis, look! Do you see? *1861*!" She grabbed his arm and they looked at each other in astonishment.

He gasped. "I've got shivers!"

"Imagine that!" Mrs. Bundle's face was luminous with this discovery.

She carefully rotated the painting over, cautious to handle only the frame, and peered at the brown paper backing that was still like-new. She could barely discern some faint pencil markings. "Look here, Louis, there's more!"

"What is it? Something written?" He peered over her shoulder. "What does it say?"

She handed it to him to read (admitting to herself that his eyes were younger and didn't require the machinations of adjusting cumbersome reading glasses, getting the light to fall on the paper just right, and then looking through a magnifying glass).

"Let me see...okay...yes, I've got it!" He hesitated, squinting through the glass at the lettering, and read slowly, " 'To my'– jeez, some of the pencil markings are so faint and there's a bit of a water stain—or something—right here—okay, yes! That's exactly what it says: *'To my Sweetness, May our love endure forever,'* and it's signed 'C',—just 'C.'"

He looked at Mrs. Bundle expectantly.

They both were speechless, their words choked back by the excitement of this huge find. *Huge!*

Cracker rubbed against Mrs. Bundle's leg, then looked up with anticipation.

Here it comes, he cat-thought. *Get ready, she's on a roll.*

Mrs. Bundle found her words first—before Louis could speak.

"Whoo-*hooooo!* Whooooooo-*eeeeeeeeee! Double* dip *fannnnn-*tastical!"

Chapter Thirteen

Damage Control

"Okay," Louis asked, "so where do we go from here?"

She looked skyward, then said assuredly, "Don't worry about a thing, Louis. This is great! Things couldn't be better!" He looked at her skeptically. "No! Really! Trust me. We can make lemonade out of these lemons here, I am sure of it. First off, you go down and finish up your work, just as though nothing unusual had occurred. Then, later this morning, I want you to call all the Board members individually and tell them that you've spoken with me and I've asked for an emergency board meeting for this evening—ummm...let's say 7 p.m. That should give me time...Tell each of them that this meeting could impact the future of the Library and that I would appreciate their presence at the meeting unless they absolutely cannot attend. If Armand gives you a hard time, just tell him it's essential that everyone meet—period. Tell him that I have a plan of action for their review and that I will reveal all tonight. Just say that, Louis."

"'Mrs. Bundle will reveal all tonight.' Do you have a plan?"

"*Well-ll*, not exactly just yet. But believe you me, I will before seven tonight! Just get their commitment to attend. If nothing else, Armand's curiosity will get the better of him." Her eyes were bright, the dark black pupils dilated. "Okay. Secondly, call Carl Andersen. Tell him you've spoken with me and that you need him to do a *very important* task for us. Ask him to come down post haste—this morning—and remove the branch and debris from out back, clean up the area as best he can, and put a tarp over the hole in the roof. And, Louis! Make sure you tell him to keep it on the Q-T for now. He can keep a secret better than anyone I know—make sure you make a point of saying so. If this gets out there too soon, we'll have people going off the deep end before I have time to formulate a plan of positive action."

She closed her tired eyes and sighed deeply, giving her the unusual appearance of a clairvoyant or gypsy soothsayer. She smiled warmly into the hazy sunshine beaming through the one tiny window in the third floor hallway. "*Ye-es-s.* It's coming to me as we speak! I just have to firm up the details." Her eyes snapped wide open which made Louis jump with surprise. "Luckily, I'm meeting Althea later for lunch at noon, and she can help me. We'll put our heads together. I've had my thinking cap on for weeks about this; it's just that now…" she looked around at the mess, "we're in the overdrive mode; things will have to be on a faster track. Look at how lucky we are!"

"Lucky?"

"Yes! With the Library closed today and the damage having occurred in the back of the building, this all should go unnoticed until we can address matters this evening."

She looked intensely into Louis' somewhat bewildered face. "*Don't worry*, Louis! Between now and tonight we will attempt to," she paused, then said firmly, "no, we *will* come up with something great. You can depend on it!"

Louis' concerned look conveyed his disbelief that she would be able to save anything at this juncture.

"I mean it. Don't fret so, Louis!" She smiled, nodding in excitement. "Uh-huh! Just look what wonderful thing we've found *because* the roof caved in! Sometimes, things happen for a reason. Look at the bright side!"

He still looked doubtful, but couldn't help but utter a cynical chuckle at her unbridled enthusiasm. In his best mystical voice he wailed solemnly, "Oh, *Madame Bundle* who sees and knows all, what vision can you uncover in your crystal ball?"

She laughed, *"All will be revealed this evening!"*

They nodded, sealing their pledge to each other.

"You know, Louis, I believe we may need to kick things up a notch now that we've been dealt this hand!" She opened her arms upward and smiled broadly. "The key to solving this whole mess is to get people involved and I think I may know how we can do it!"

Chapter Fourteen

Cracker, Superlative Sleuth, On the Job

"Thank you!" Louis stood at the top of the stairs, admiring her spunk. "Oh, Mrs. Bundle, if I haven't told you…you are a godsend!" She smiled at him and he sighed and nervously rubbed his graceful hands together. "Thank you so much for coming down this morning! I feel better knowing you are in charge." He smiled gratefully. "*Well*, alrighty! I better get right on it. I'll give Carl a call, and then I'll make the calls to the Board members a little later on. Don't worry about a thing. I'll get everything organized for this evening, okay?"

"Yes, that will be fine, Louis. Remember, *'least said, soonest mended.'*" She gave him an encouraging smile.

His steps echoed down the oak stairs as Mrs. Bundle gave the water-damaged low ceiling area one last look. Then, she turned to follow Louis down the hallway but heard a deep *meow* from somewhere along the inside of the kneewall.

"Oh, Cracker, where are you? Come out of there!" Exasperated, she said, "You'll get yourself all dirty, C.C.! Come on now, let's get going. I want a shower—desperately! We've got to get home." He meowed again, louder this time, almost more like a yowl. "Cracker! Come out from there, this is no time to be exploring."

Cracker gave another, more urgent "*Yeeeeoooww!*" and Mrs. Bundle put her ear to the wall, trying to follow his urgent cat-yells.

"What is it, Cracker? Are you stuck? Where are you?"

From his post inside the chamber, he cat-thought, *you're just not going to believe this*, willing her to look inside. He meowed loudly, which was closely followed by an undignified sneeze—what a dusty place this was!

She located his voice in the same general location she had entered twice now. *"Cracker?"*

He yearned for his sleuthing partner to see *his* discovery. This time, his howling sounded like a tomcat in heat.

"I'm coming, Cracker-cat! Hold on!"

Bending down to peer into the hole once more, Mrs. Bundle drew her still-athletic frame into the smallest ball she could. This time, she tried an easier way to enter the space. Hunching her shoulders down and ducking her head under the lip of the eave, she slipped her body backwards into the cubby hole and cautiously scrutinized the area once more. *I feel like Alice in Alice in Wonderland,* she thought, *following the rabbit down the rabbit hole!* This time, she was more cautious as she got her bearings. No rusty nails sticking out, no furry creature's beady eyes staring back at her. She looked around, adjusting her eyes to the dim light and realized she would need proper lighting to explore any further.

Another meow came from the deepest recesses, the corner of the space. Her hand found her bib overall pocket and grabbed what she needed. Turning on her penlight once again, she dragged her knees into the small space and adjusted her eyes to the semi-darkness. The small area was just big enough for her body and possibly one other's, she eyeballed. It felt almost, well…cozy…inside here. *If only I had a magic drink like Alice, I could shrink myself,* she thought, amused at the notion.

"Where the blazes are you, Cracker? Oh! There you are!"

Drawn up into the furthest corner of the space was the faint outline of Cracker's curved body. His topaz eyes shimmered in the artificial pale beam of light. It almost looked as though, from Mrs. Bundle's vantage point, those intense almond-shaped orbs were staring fixedly up at the wall panel before him. He purred loudly.

Look! Look, right there! He urged in crystal-clear cat-thought.

"What have you got there, C.C.?" She maneuvered her torso slowly around, ungracefully but with plenty of head room, moving further into the miniature space, squirming uncomfortably under the closeness of the diagonal rafters, meanwhile, shining the penlight directly on the spot where his cat eyes seemed to be fixated.

It was then that she saw it. There, on the inside panel, barely distinguishable, were the faintest of markings in the wood. Mrs. Bundle brought her face close to the panel, her nose barely inches away from the old beam that framed it. Neatly scripted, as though in longhand blocking, were what appeared to be letters, carved into the rough backside of the beam.

"Oh, Cracker, you are a pip!" she whispered excitedly. "*What* have you found?"

She shone her light on the top of the wide board and began to read slowly, "'M'! *Hmmm*, too fantastical! They're all upper case letters, that's what they are. What would I do without you, Cracker? Okay, let's see — 'M'…yes, the first letter is an M, for sure, and that's a… 'D'! Oh, wait a minute," she cried, exasperated, her bent neck and back aching in this unusual position. If she were shorter than her five-foot-ten frame, more child-sized perhaps, she might certainly have been better able to see this at eye-level.

Hence, she leaned forward as best she could and adjusted her body, then drew in a deep breath, and continued reading the carved letters.

"Double C's! Just like you, Cracker-Cat! 'C. C.'!"

She read the rest of the letters quickly, " Okay…that's an 'L'…and the last one is a 'V'!"

She sighed triumphantly, clearing her throat of the dust and dirt. "A-*hem*! Can you believe that?" she whispered to Cracker and his eyes shone brightly back at her. "Okay, so what have we got? We have to remember these letters, Cracker. Let's see…all of it together is, 'M-D-C-C-L-V'" She said in singsong, "**MDC-CLV!**"

Cracker slid against his mistress' leg, scooching in beside her, straining to see the full inscription on the wall.

Yes, that's right, dear lady, he cat-thought, '*MDCCLV*.' Who knows what it could mean? *Even better, though, don't miss the other thing! There's more—over there—for you to see. There, over there! Look at the bottom of the panel!* He urged her as best he could but his cat-thoughts fell on deaf ears.

She clapped her hands gleefully together, dust flying, and the penlight dropped to the floor. "Imagine that! Look what we've found, C.C.! Secrets! It's just *too* unbelievable. "Curiouser and Curiouser!'"as Alice would say! First, the painting. Now this!" Her eyes began to sting and she made the mistake of rubbing them, unable to adjust to this artificially-challenged lighting. She eyeballed the nearby exit from their mysterious, Lewis Carrol-like rabbit hole.

"C'mon Cracker, let's go. I'm beat! And hot, and tired to boot!" She scooted her feet forward and edged her body out of the opening and then sat back on her heels, gasping for breath. Cracker, right behind her, swept past her quickly, slithering out of the small space between her body and the opening.

Mrs. Bundle smiled broadly at her cat. She was as ecstatic as an archeologist on an ancient dig.

"Goodness, C-Cat! Can you say our favorite word—'*allure*'?"

Chapter Fifteen

No Rest for the Weary…
Except Maybe a Catnap

When Mrs. Bundle got home, she placed the painting in the floor safe located in the front parlor of her farmhouse. The smaller-size safe, hidden under the wooden planking of her 1830's floorboards, had come in handy many times in the past and now she was thankful she had a place for the painting—even if it was just for today, or at least until the Board could decide this evening what to do with it. After removing the fused section of hardwood flooring measuring 1' by 2', she reached in, turned the tumbler to the secret numbers 1-8-3-4 (the year the house had been built), opened the safe and removed the few items in the safe.

One of the items she adjusted belonged to the Corrigans: the fantastic Children of Lir pendant that had been in their Irish family for generations. Once in a blue moon, Jack took the ornate necklace out and admired the jeweled swans, even allowing Erin to wear it on special occasions. Mrs. Bundle carefully lowered the painting inside the larger space below and then placed the Lir pendant beside it. It was a snug fit as she adjusted it gently, then put the remaining bits and pieces back inside. Yes, this would be the perfect place until tonight.

After that, she had renewed her fatigued body, wilted by the heat, with a long, soothingly cool shower and had readied herself for her lunch date with Althea. Now, with a good two-and-a-half hours to spare, she had a chance to reflect.

She sat down in her favorite room in the cozy den rocking chair and ruminated over the morning's events. The wicker rocking chair's rhythmic movement helped her thought process. Cracker lay nearby on his large, poofy floor pillow, drooping in the heat and thoroughly exhausted by their adventure. He had had a good cleaning, too, and was ready for relaxation. He dozed, lulled by the rocking chair's steady motion.

Whew! What a morning! Although she wasn't looking forward to this evening's meeting, Mrs. Bundle couldn't help but be energized by the good things that had come out of this incident. She looked over at her exhausted cat. She had to admit to herself that she, too, was a bit overwhelmed with all the events. *Wait until I tell Althea about the painting,* she thought to herself delightfully. A true mystery! Right here, in *our little world*. Her mind raced as she considered the origin of the painting.

She rocked back and forth, the cadence of the rocking chair matching her invigorated mind. The painting's as-yet-unexplained story intrigued her. *Who* could have painted it, and *what* did it mean? Was it just a simple landscape or a figment of someone's imagination? *Why* was it in the wall, presumably hidden, she surmised... in the *Library*, of all places? And who was Conny? Could they assume that was the artist's name? And signature? Was he famous?

She stopped rocking. What *was* the year the painting had been signed? She tried to remember...yes, it was 1861. Imagine! Over one hundred and forty years before!

"My, my," she sighed aloud. She began to rock again.

And those letters carved into the knee wall!

She had memorized the letters and repeated them aloud, singsong fashion once more, "M-D-C-*(pause)*-C-L-V," then louder, "**M D C C L V...M D C C L V...**"

She rocked faster, intrigued with their rhythmic beat, and then snapped her fingers in triumph. Her feet slammed to the floor, and the rocking chair's runners shuddered with agitation — out of sync — and then stopped.

Cracker bounced, his slack body suddenly shocked by the abrupt, erratic movements beside his furry head.

"That's it! Cracker! Well, it *could* very well be! They're *Roman numerals*! A number, yes. Meaning something… significant, to be sure. Maybe…yes, it could be.." She reflected, quietly thinking what would that be? "'M-D-C-C-L-V…MDC--CLV'." She began rocking again, this time slower, more effortlessly, rhythmically in sync with the sound of the letters, "I'll have to look that up! Yes, that's what we'll do, Cracker." Her breathing became calm and she leaned her tired head back against the rocking chair's headrest. She contemplated the letters, her thoughts slower and more logical, *we'll see what 'MDCCLV' would be in Roman numerals…I know there's some "hundreds" in there..* Sluggishly, she heard her own voice whisper, "Those 'C's'…yes, I'll just think on that…a bit."

Mrs. Bundle closed her eyes and the rocker went still as she became totally lost in thought.

Almost right away, she fell into a dead sleep, giving in to her body's need for a long, undisturbed nap.

Cracker looked up at the still figure beside him, his eyes narrow, sleepy, slits.

I was wondering if you'd come to that same conclusion, he cat-thought to his sleeping mistress. *Yes, my dear girl, it's been quite a morning, all in all. Allure…once again, we've got the makings of a big one here, don't we?* Blinking as he daydreamed (the sleep taking over his body, too) he concluded, *and more that you have yet to discover.* Mouth-wateringly intrigued, he purred triumphantly and drifted back into his catnap.

Chapter Sixteen

A Very Productive Lunch

• HORS D'OEUVRES, ANYONE? •

"Hello, ladies! How's the world treatin' you today?"

Mrs. Bundle and Althea looked up from their Herder's menus. There stood Weezy Bunton with her short, steel-gray, permed curls held firmly in place by a lacy hairnet; she was the picture of health, a strapping, full-bosomed farmer's wife whose ongoing battle with her waistline had been defeated by corpulence many years before.

"Weezy! I had no idea you were working here!" Mrs. Bundle said warmly, fully refreshed from her forty winks.

Here stood her old Pillson friend, known throughout the community, the Wedding Planner for the Combs-Richey affair. Weezy briskly filled their water glasses efficiently and beamed down at them. Her massively round, loveable face matched her figure; conversely, her voice, like her demeanor, was rough around the edges.

"My Lord, Lettie, it's been a month of Sundays since I've seen you! Yup! I started here last week! Kendra said she needed an extra hand for lunch and I offered to help out. Especially now, mind you—said I was a godsend what with everything's that's going on with Tuddy's. There ain't a decent place to eat now between here and West Leb!" She turned to Althea. "Heavens, Althea, when was the last time I seen you? Was it at Cynthia and Hiram's nuptials?" Without waiting for an answer, she turned back to Mrs. Bundle. "Say, by the way, you did a bang-up job figurin' that there mystery out, Lettie. You saved my butt—that's for sure! And that scrawny Harold Snargle? I coulda brained him! Hope his parents have got his number now! How the devil did you ever solve that out? Everyone was real impressed with your detectin'."

As usual, it was hard to get a word in edgewise whenever Weezy was in the conversation. Garrulous and animated, Weczy always had a lot of opinions. "Gabby Weezy" was what Walter Andersen called her. Be that as it may, everyone loved Weezy, her laughter and fun spirit were ever contagious, and it was a wise restaurateur who could snag Weezy as an employee. The fact of the matter was, she also always seemed to be "in the loop" on local news and gossip and knew pretty much everybody in the area (in one way or another).

"Thanks Weezy, thanks for the kudos." Mrs. Bundle lowered her voice. "I was pleased to be able to help Cynthia and Hiram get their marriage off to a good start. And I knew how upsetting it was for you, too! It all worked out well." Mrs. Bundle was uncomfortable with all this praise and changed the subject by asking, "So, you're just here for the lunch crowd?"

She nodded emphatically. "Yup, and back home before the kids get off the bus! I've been busier than a one-armed paper hanger! Course, there's no more Bette's Lunch and Breakfast, not since Bette passed away, God rest her soul. *Gaw!* Didn't we love to watch her slice that ham for each breakfast order! If she liked you, she'd give you a honkin' heavy slice, all that good fat drippin' off! Now, *she* was *the real deal* in home-cookin'!"

When Bette Benois had died the previous winter, Constable Zack Benois, her septuagenarian husband, had tried for a few months to keep the longstanding hole-in-the-wall eating establishment going, but it just wasn't the same without his colorful wife. Ultimately, he had recently decided it was best to shut it down for the foreseeable future. Bette's Lunch and Breakfast had been a fixture in Pillson since 1953, and most of the original regulars had passed away, too. So, Bette's had closed for good, much to all the locals' sadness.

"Yup. And now," Weezy shook her head ruefully, "what with all this trouble at Tuddy's…" She looked around at Herder's four walls, her burly arms gesturing widely, "this is pretty much it!" She gave them both a big wink, "You know what I mean—for a *fine* dinin' experience, since Tuddy's burned down."

Both women nodded emphatically and Mrs. Bundle offered, "We're going over to the fire site to take a look after lunch today."

"That *poor*, poor family!" Weezy leaned forward, placing one hand on her hip and the other on the checkered tablecloth. She lowered her voice to a very loud whisper. "I hear through the grapevine it was torched!" She covered her mouth with her waitressing order book. "And, that's what the paper said in a roundabout way, too, this morning. You read between the lines, too, Althea? Arson! Ain't that awful?"

Althea nodded, "Seems so. They somewhat confirmed that the fire was started 'by unknown causes,' more than likely deliberately set, I think is how they put it, and that the State's forensics lab is looking for evidence of a possible arson. Said they were checking the gas lines. Can you imagine?"

Mrs. Bundle shrugged, "I was too busy today to read the paper."

Weezy sniffed. "Really? Who needs a paper around here, anyway? I heard someone was out to get them. Long time grudge, that's what I heard."

"Really, Weezy! Where on earth do you hear this stuff?" Althea asked.

She threw back her head and laughed with gusto. "Ha! Right place at the right time, that's what I always say. I'll tell you one thing…I'm sure gonna miss them pies! And the hot cocoa! *Hoo-hoo!*" With a girth as ample as Kate Smith's, Weezy's chin fat merrily jiggled in rolling waves of laughter.

"Oh, right! Loved Grammy's cocoa!" Althea agreed; it wasn't too much of a stretch to understand why Weezy Bunton was one of many that were enamored by the signature Tuddy's drink that was thick-as-velvety-mud and a magnificently dark and sweet treat.

Weezy turned her massive frame around and, hearing nearby rumblings, waved amiably to the waiting group at the next table. "Yes, right, *hellooo*! Be there in a jiffy!" She nodded vigorously at a couple just entering the restaurant. "How are ya, Gertie? And you, George?" She waved a friendly hand toward them and another couple waiting on the porch that doubled as a reception area. "Go ahead, seat yourself, your table's all ready. It don't pay to be shy!"

She turned her attention to the couple one table over and flashed a huge smile, "You know I won't forget *you* two lovelies—you just hang in there. Don't worry, it'll be worth it. What's your hurry?" She reached over and placed a basket of piping hot rolls, magically appearing from nowhere, on their table and the previously impatient couple, properly humbled, shrugged good-naturedly and smiled back.

Then, she turned toward the numerous newly-seated and anxiously-waiting diners grouped throughout the cozy dining room.

As though on stage, she raised her voice just a hair and said with complete thespian command, "Okay, *everybody*, listen up!"

The buzz of the room became instantaneously subdued as she took total control. This was Weezy in her prime, her element, and she reveled in the gastronomical limelight. "Hope you're all hungry today!" She laughed a huge guffaw, which was echoed contagiously by the nodding group, along with their rambunctious, "You betchas!", "Uh-huh's!" and "*Mmm-hmms's!*"

Mrs. Bundle watched as she cleared her throat with a sense of importance.

"*Okay!* Here's the deal. I'm gonna give you *all* of the 'Today's Specials' right now so I ain't wastin' your time or mine. Kendra's out in the kitchen just waitin' to get your favorite food on the plate and out here to you! Think about what you want before I come to take your order and we'll get you all fed *lickity-split*! Are you ready?"

More nods as she held their culinary fate in the palm of her hand; they were all with her one-hundred-and-ten percent, their mouths watering, ears keen, their senses on fire—mostly enhanced by the wonderful epicurean smells wafting from the nearby kitchen.

"Here goes!" One could have heard a pin drop as she began her recitations. Like a strict teacher in front of a deeply enthralled class eager to learn, she announced the "Specials of the Day," beginning with the Gazpacho appetizer ("perfect for this dang hot summer weather"). She editorialized on the individual offerings while everyone dared not to listen. By the end, the comfortable assemblage, joined together by their shared love of good food, all appeared to be collectively salivating like starving, thirsty cattle poised to stampede.

Weezy ended dramatically with, "And, if you've got room after all that good chow, you'll have to try the Three-berry Tart Kendra's whipped up—just out of the oven, matter of fact. Can you smell it? Of course, that is if there's any left by the time you're done!"

Everyone laughed, transformed now into a comfortable group of intimate friends and not just diners in a restaurant, all expertly drawn together by the large woman who now made an imperceptibly slight bow. It almost seemed appropriate to applaud such a wonderful performance. A light clap could be heard from the corner table and, as people turned to look, the man's large beefy face turned the color of primrose.

"Bravo." he said somewhat limply, sticking to his guns.

"Much obliged, Sanford!" Weezy said, "I'll make sure yours is an extra big slice! Be with you all in two shakes of a cat's whisker!"

She turned to Althea and Mrs. Bundle and winked again as the room's sounds began to resonate with friendly chatter once again.

"Weezy, you are something else!" Althea said in admiration. "You could keep a group of Marines in line, I daresay!"

"Why, thank you kindly! I'll tell you what, my boys know it; that's for danged sure! Not much gets by Mama!"

They quickly placed their orders. With remarkable and expeditious speed for a woman her size, Weezy nimbly turned on her heel like an elephant on petite ballet shoes, then hustled away to her other waiting fans, pencil poised and ready for the next order.

• SALADS •

Althea fanned her face with a tanned hand and looked around at the peaceful lunch surroundings, "Whew! It's nice to have a break! It's another hot one today. I was out in the garden painting earlier this morning, and it was brutal. Dog days of summer are coming!" Her round, full face was flushed from the heat but she looked her usual lovely self.

"Yes, that's what Cracker and I...funny how that keeps coming up!"

"What?"

"The dog days of summer..." she murmured, then shook her head and said, "I'm sorry I was a bit late, Althea. By the time I woke from my nap, it was time to go! What a morning Cracker and I have had!"

"Napping, L? Before lunch? That's not like you."

Mrs. Bundle leaned forward and whispered excitedly. "Well now, Allie, we've got another mystery on our hands!"

Althea gave her old friend a cautious nudge. "Good grief, L, what have you and Cracker got yourselves mixed up in now?"

"We found a veritable treasure today, at the library, of all places!"

"The library? Our library?"

"Yes! Early this morning! We found a painting! Louis was there—and Cracker, too! It was all quite by accident." Mrs. Bundle's eyes shone with excitement as the information tumbled out bit by bit of the early morning's activities. She concluded with, "And that's when we found the old painting, stuck behind the wall up under the eaves."

Knowing her friend's proclivity for danger and adventure, Althea said, "Really? This is right up your alley! And what's the painting like?"

"It's beautiful. What do you know about oils?"

"Oils?" Althea looked puzzled, and lightly put her fingers to her temples, then pushed the short, light-colored, stray pieces of hair behind her ears. "Hang on, I'm not up to your warp speed on this yet, Okay, I'll bite. It's an oil painting?"

Mrs. Bundle nodded enthusiastically.

"And you want to know what I know about oil painting? Well, I've always been a big fan of the Masters, and they're all pretty much in the oil medium." She stopped and said, "Hang on, L, I need more info first! What kind of painting, how old?"

Mrs. Bundle lowered her voice. "Old, very old. Done in oils—very, very vibrant oils for its age, colorful, a beautiful country scene! And nice technique, too, I'd say, not being a professional. Say, didn't you study art for your Masters degree when you first went to California?"

Althea nodded. "I studied art history for quite awhile. I'm no art critic but I'm pretty knowledgeable about the different eras of painting. You know, 'Renaissance,' 'Romantic,' 'Realism,' 'Baroque,' 'Impressionism,' etcetera, etcetera." She ticked them off on her fingers one by one. "Is that what you mean by knowledgeable? Was the painting dated?"

"Yes—at the bottom corner, as a matter of fact, beneath the signature. *1861.*"

Althea gave a low whistle. "1861. Good grief!" Althea was fairly quivering with excitement. "Tell me everything, L." When they were young girls, Althea's face had been plastered with freckles, and now, decades later, Mrs. Bundle could see the ageless, youthful attractiveness of those remaining freckles peeking through as her friend's face crinkled into a huge smile, mouth open in excitement, bright white teeth ready to bite into every morsel of this newsworthy story.

Mrs. Bundle went over the morning's events in more detail this time with Althea. She ended with the bad news, telling her about the roof damage.

"Oh, Lord! Just what we need—more trouble with the library. How bad is it?"

"Well, it's not as bad as Louis and I first thought."

"That's good. We'll go back to that in a minute, but I'm dying to know more about the painting." Althea was incredulous, her large, green eyes aglow.

"Yes—you should see it. It's so unique; the colors are striking. I brought it home for safe-keeping and I'll bring it with me tonight."

"Tonight? What are we going to do about the water and roof damage?"

"Well, I've asked Louis to call an emergency board meeting for tonight at seven. Did he call you this morning?"

Althea shook her head. "Not sure. Probably. After I finished gardening, I was out and about from 10:00 on doing errands. His message is probably on my machine." She stared at her old friend. "My, my! What a morning you've had! There's something else, though. I can tell. You're *way* too chipper for having been through all this angst this morning." She gently tapped her own broad forehead as though searching for clarity. "*I* know when something's brewing. What have you got up your sleeve?"

Mrs. Bundle laughed aloud. "Ha! Oh, Allie, you know me so well." She leaned in again, keeping her voice low. "Well! Where do I begin? God knows I've been agonizing over this whole library issue, and this morning, when I saw the look on Louis' face-- you know that pathetic look of doom and gloom," (she made a panic-stricken face that looked remarkably like Louis), "well… I was *determined* not to let you-know-who get the best of us!" A disgusted huffing sound escaped from her throat, "*Gaw!* I don't know about you, but I've had enough! He is *not* going to win! We have to save the library; we absolutely must! Moreover, we have to make its financial future safe for our next generation of patrons. We can't have this continual 'lack of finances' issue hanging over our heads for the next few years. It will be the demise of the library."

As Mrs. Bundle's enthusiasm gained steamed, Althea nodded with interest. "I agree with you one-hundred percent! It's a shame what's gone on. So, what have you got?" She was literally on the edge of her seat. "What do we do?"

"Well, I think we need to do something *drastic*, something that will involve the community and get the library back on sound footing. So, this idea has been percolating in my mind and now, after what happened this morning, I think I've got something! It's really the *painting* that gave me the idea and pulled it all together!"

She reached down at her feet, found her purse and retrieved her pocket day timer, then brought up a worn manila folder from the floor marked "Library Foundation" and a separate, carefully folded, piece of paper attached to the front with a large paper clip. She unfolded the single sheet. "I made some notes today apart from what we've already brainstormed. I brought that folder with all our notes, rough drafts of projects, and all the other stuff we've already written previously regarding the formation of a foundation to benefit the Library."

Althea nodded and Mrs. Bundle began, "Okay. We had the basic premise but we needed something *tangible* to work with, something that would allow us to make enough *money* to save the library *and* plan for future years. Everyone always says they want to help, but sometimes it's not money they can give! Maybe it's more people's *time* that is the most valuable *asset* the library can tap into. I think the painting has been the inspiration for..." She paused, slightly breathless in her excitement, and Althea was poised and ready.

"Yeah...I'm with you. What?"

"An Art Festival! On the Village Common! It's the perfect place! This summer!"

Her face was ebullient; Althea's was a blank palette. Mrs. Bundle's words came fast and furious, "You know, with lots of other activities, a weekend of fun and culture! Really, like I said before, it was finding the painting that solidified the idea for me! And I've got a plan already, up here." She lightly tapped her temple. "With the Co-op's help, I think we can pull it off! If each artist from the Art Guild Co-op donated just *one* painting--and we could get other artists from the area to donate, too—we could have a big auction—see this? The antique painting will be a huge draw—it can be our springboard! Think about it—it's historically significant, it's *lovely*--wait 'til you see it, Allie! We can put it on display with a lot of hoopla." Althea was still just listening. "Here, look, I've put some figures on paper... At the very least, we should be able to make plenty to set up a fund that would revitalize the Pillson Public Library. Oh! And here's where the community comes in. We get the villagers involved, volunteering, and the kids, too! We find things for the kids to participate in, like, maybe a talent show…," trailing off, she looked at Althea in anticipation, now wanting feedback or encouragement.

Althea said cynically, "Yuh." She drew in a deep breath. "Okay. And we can get all the planets to line up perfectly…and it's a wonderful world!" She blinked, overwhelmed, and then smiled affectionately. "Your enthusiasm is commendable, L, but…are…you…*crazy*?" She reached out and shook her friend's forearm as though to wake her from her dreaming. "Think about it. Who's going to organize this… *huge* undertaking? Who's going to make sure it all happens?"

Mrs. Bundle looked at her with expectation. "Why…I thought… we…"

Althea stared back at her friend, then gulped deliberately and shook her head. "Oh, no! *No*, no, no! You can't mean us!" She closed her eyes tightly. "You *do* mean us, right?"

"Yes, us! We can do it, Allie! At least for the first year, anyway, to get the ball rolling. And, if you think we can't do it, then think again! C'mon! We know practically everyone in Pillson! And you know the whole artist community in Pillson Falls! We can do this, I know it." Her friend's skeptical look made her forge ahead with another angle. "Better yet, think of the look on old Armand's face if we can pull this off! I know we can do it if we put our combined efforts into it!"

"It's a great idea in theory, L, but *can* we actually get things together? And so quickly, in time for this summer?" She paused, "Which begs the other important question: You really *are* thinking *this* summer, aren't you? So, exactly *when* are you thinking we'd have this grand affair? It's already," she yanked her cell phone from her pocket, squinted at the front face, and cried, "*Good grief*! It's already June 25th!"

"Well, I've had another idea, just this instant. In fact, just now, *you* gave me the idea!"

"Me?" Althea cringed and said, "Go ahead…"

Mrs. Bundle picked up her pocket day timer from the table and opened it to the clear slate of August. "I'm thinking we could have it in August, yes…the weekend of August 15-17—towards the tail end of the summer. That would be…," she paused, clearly for effect, "the last *dog days of summer*—yes, Allie! That phrase keeps popping up, yesterday, today—it's *very* catchy, isn't it? The dog days of summer when it's so hot. That's it! That's *got* to be it!"

"*What's* got to be it?"

"The *Dog Days of Summer*! It works! It's catchy and fun and we can build on it!" She paused, emphasizing her next words, "Wait—even better! The Dog Days of Summer Art Festival! You know, usually the period of summer when it's so hot and everyone complains there's just nothing to do. Well, *here's* something for everyone to do, to get involved, and to have *fun!*"

Althea shook her head in amazement. "How *on earth* did you come up with that? Unbelievable. Oh my Lord!" She blew air past her upper lip and rolled her eyes. "It's really very clever," she acknowledged, "and, of course," she raised two arms in surrender, "I give up. I have to agree, it's a *great* idea!" She smiled warmly at her friend. "Yes, I actually like it! 'The Dog Days of Summer Art Festival,' very catchy, yes! I can't believe it, but…I'm…*in!*"

They picked up their forks and hungrily dug into their house salads.

Their joint enthusiasm was like a rolling ball of heated combustion as they fired idea after idea at each other—

"I'm sure I can get the Guild in line…"

"*And* we can incorporate other things into the Festival, like a kick-off Dog Days of Summer Doggie Parade…"

"Oh! How 'bout a Bake-off? And a sheep-shearing exhibit—and spinning, too! People love that…"

And they were off.

• THE MAIN MEAL •

Weezy Bunton put Althea's plate down squarely in front of her, and the aromatic smells of good, solid home-cooking wafted into their nostrils.

"Here's your breaded tilapia filet, dear, very '*chi-chi*' fish, now, don't you know—do you want some lemon with that?"

"Mmmm, it looks wonderful! If you're watching your cholesterol it's a great low fat meal. I used to have it all the time in California!" Althea shifted her *slightly* full-figured frame in the chair and inspected the steaming plate in front of her with enthusiasm.

Weezy rolled her bug eyes, which spoke volumes about what she thought about California and, using incredible control, kept her opinions to herself. She put a large bowl of succulent steamed mussels in front of Mrs. Bundle.

"And Lettie, hope you like the mussels! Loaded with garlic!" She fanned her face, "The broth is to die for, white wine and the works so I brought you some extra bread." She put the new basket of bread beside the old empty one and stepped back. "Salads stay? I can tell by the way you been yakkin' away that you wanna eat slow. That's okay by me."

She perused the table, making sure they had everything they needed, and then leaned—rather, loomed--over them and asked, "Whatcha working on there, ladies?" She peered at the paperwork on the table.

Mrs. Bundle chuckled. "Oh, just the usual library stuff, Weezy," she said, placing her hand strategically over the notes she had just gone over with Althea.

Weezy tried to whisper (which came out as discreetly as a horse's whinny above the din), "By the way, Lettie, is Ar-*mand* Lim-*pert* still giving you a hard time?" The French pronunciation of Armand's name sounded very strange with Weezy's vernacular, but she said it exactly the way he insisted it be pronounced—with a French accent on the "*mond*" and the "*pare*."

Mrs. Bundle looked around quickly to see if anyone had heard Weezy's question. The neighboring diners appeared oblivious, more occupied with their own dining experience than with the goings on beside them. However, the question's sharp nature and relevance to their table talk startled Mrs. Bundle and, looking up earnestly at the large woman, she queried back, "Why do you ask, Weezy?"

"Oh, you know." She raised a knowing eyebrow, motioning her head towards the Pillsonville town limits. "I seen your old Junie down at the library early, early this morning. I ain't the brightest bulb in the pack, but I'm smart enough to know when somethin's brewin'! You know, your car there--on a day the library's supposed to be closed? And that early in the morning, too?" She waited patiently, but Mrs. Bundle didn't flinch, so she continued fishing, "Figured you and Louis must be workin' out a plan for the library's problems or somethin' of that nature—what other ungodly reason would you have to there at that time?" Her raised, painfully-plucked eyebrows still didn't elicit a response from Mrs. Bundle, so she continued, a bit louder now. "Trying to come up with somethin' ol' 'Ar-mand *Mucky-muck*' will be happy with, am I right? *Gaw!* What a pain! He's been railin' around the village, talking to anyone who'll listen—him and Archie is thicker than the hair on a bear now, don't you know. He's gettin' people all stirred up about the high taxes and the library's upkeep. Seems like he's everywhere, puttin' his nose in. Every time you turn around, there he is!"

Her voice was full-tilt Weezy now and Mrs. Bundle stirred uncomfortably in her chair as the woman went on, bold and brassy as a harlot's finery. "I even heard he was down in Keene t'other day, sculkin' around there…" her huge eyes rolled bug-eyed once again, then stopped as one gave a knowing wink.

"Well, Weezy," Althea inserted quickly before Weezy could go on, "the last I heard, it wasn't a crime to go to Keene! Why, even *I* get to the big city once in a blue moon."

"No, it ain't that, Althea--" Weezy giggled like a schoolgirl, "--it's what I heard that French Casanova was *up* to!" She winked broadly and curled her lip in obvious disgust.

Both Althea and Mrs. Bundle said nothing, so Weezy picked up the empty bread basket from the table, turned it upside down, and shook the residual crumbs onto the large tray beside her, then slipped it under the new basket. "Hey—enough tittle-tattle! That's for the idle few who got time to sit around and tell tales. All I care about is keepin' the library open."

Mrs. Bundle used this opportunity to jump in and attempted to move the topic along. "Well, we're trying to keep ahead of the whole shebang, Weezy. Thanks for your concern—it really means a lot. We've got some ideas we're trying to formulate." Althea and Mrs. Bundle exchanged a knowing gaze, silently acknowledging that when Weezy knew something, the whole world knew about it, too.

Quick to know when she wasn't wanted and not at all fazed by it, Weezy beamed agreeably at them. "*Well, then*, I'll just leave you alone to your formulatin'!" She gave a hard slap to the table and Mrs. Bundle jumped. "I'll tell you *what*! Me and a lot of other folk sure as heck will put up a fight! We ain't gonna lose that Library! That would be a dang shame!"

She sped off back through the kitchen swinging doors, deftly maneuvering her ample backside to narrowly avoid the door's weighty rebound.

• DESSERT, ANYONE? •

"That was the best tilapia I've ever eaten!" Althea put down her fork and wiped her mouth clean, then tried to encircle her waist with her hands. "I'm stuffed! Good grief, I've got to go on a diet!"

By now, she and Mrs. Bundle had finished their preliminary plans for the Festival; Althea took notes profusely (in between bites) while they talked. As they wound down their discussion, they realized they had come up with a very viable plan to save the library, all hinging upon their ability to mobilize the community to participate in the energetic venture. It would require a lot of work on the part of the Library Board; more importantly, it would be essential to get the support of the majority on board, first, to vote in favor of it, and then to pull it off. They both realized they had one shot to put the idea in front of the Board that evening.

Next, they drafted a Mission Statement proposal right there at the table from the notes contained within the "Library Foundation" folder, patching it all together into a rough draft copy (aided greatly by Althea's expertise in grant-writing):

Library Foundation Mission Statement

The foundation is a nonprofit organization created to raise money to maintain and enhance the library's historic and educational qualities.

1) Forming the Pillsonville, Pillson Falls, Pillson Junction, and North Pillson Corners Library Foundation, further described as the **Pillson Library Foundation,** whose goal and mission is to improve services and quality of the Public Library by securing resources to support library programs and capital improvements not met by public funding or supported by the towns using its services. Said Foundation to begin immediately in its first annual appeal for donations and community support.

That said, **The Dog Days of Summer Art Festival** would be the first annual event to kick off the formation of the Foundation and that the weekend of August 15-17 (or, in future years, so designated as the third weekend of August) will be selected for the event called **The Dog Days of Summer Art Festival**

2) That all monies from the first annual event would go toward improving the Pillson Public Library's current condition. Ostensibly, the one area to which money would be applied immediately would be for handicap accessibility, repairs to the roof, and exterior refurbishing and the other structural issues detailed in the most recent building inspection.

3) That the library will need total renovation and ongoing maintenance and so the foundation would create an endowment fund, in addition to the annual charity event, for its future upkeep.

Furthermore, it is the intent and function of the Pillson Library Foundation through its Board to implement its Mission by means of these Guidelines:

To preserve at all times a sense of community in the Pillson Library Foundation, whose purpose is the greater welfare of the Pillson Public Library and to raise, manage, and distribute large contributions and other sums for the long-range benefit of the Pillson Public Library;

To serve as a liaison between the Pillson Public Library and the community; to include the community in active participation in the Foundation to assist the library, its staff, and its board in acquiring volunteer resources and donor support for the future improvements of the Pillson Public Library and to create a website to seek, manage, and allocate annual endowments. Finally, to invest wisely the various acquired capital of the Pillson Public Library.

Mrs. Bundle brushed the sourdough bread crumbs from the table in front of her and shook her weighty head of glossy braids. "Whew! There! Pretty polished for pulling things together helter-skelter, if I do say so myself!"

"I can clean it up and type it before tonight's meeting. I'll make copies."

"Great! Good job! It may be hard to get the Board behind us, especially Armand, but I think we can do it! Don't you?"

"Of course! Piece of cake!" Althea proclaimed. "This evening should be *very* interesting. I'm sure you have a strategy on how to present all this?"

"Of course!"

"Good. It's in your hands—of course, I'll support you 100%! Are you strong enough to handle Armand?"

"As you said, dear friend, piece of cake!"

A perky voice rang out from nowhere. "*Dessert*, girls?"

• FINAL TIDBITS •

Balancing plates like a Russian circus performer, Weezy managed to situate the piece of angel food cake drenched with fresh, sliced strawberries centrally between them. As she placed two empty dessert plates and forks at their fingertips, she inserted herself one final time into the conversation.

"So, ladies, have you met the new bachelor in town?" She fiddled with their utensils, sneaking a peak at Althea from the corner of her eye.

"Not yet!" Mrs. Bundle said brightly.

"No, not really…" Althea snuffled, passing her napkin over her face to disguise her disdain. She drew the corners of her mouth into a thin line as Weezy pushed on.

"I heard he's *quite* the handsome devil—for an old gent. Very snappy dresser, too, from all accounts. I went by last night on my way by from the market. He's moved into the new digs, to be sure; I could see the lights on. Couldn't make out any movements or commotion, though—just lights and lotsa empty boxes set outside the front door. Seems he's got a big dog, too. And his name is Howie."

"The guy?" Althea asked.

"No! The dog!" Weezy threw her head back and laughed, her body shaking as one huge gelatinous figure. "The kids met his pooch—said he's really friendly! In fact, he ate some of their cookies as they came out of Murphy's. He was all by his lonesome—runnin' loose."

Althea gave Mrs. Bundle a "See? I-told-you-so!" look.

Weezy continued smoothly, "Big dog! Huge! German Shepherd, they said." She placed a dishpan finger against her rosy cheek in a quandary. "Not sure what the guy's name is—I ain't heard that yet. Tim Scott was pretty crafty about what stuff he's sharin' with me and everyone else, tryin' to be clever, no doubt. Said it was 'confidential'," she made quote marks with her chubby fingers, "and when I told him I ain't never heard of such a thing, he said since 9-11, the Post Office has to be *very sensitive* about what info they give out. Thinks he's pretty clever, don't he? We all know he ain't, though."

"Well, I really wouldn't know anything about…" Althea coughed lightly and raised her eyes to the ceiling, indicating her interest in the subject fell somewhere between nil and nonexistent. "Might we have our check now, please, Weezy?"

"Sure! Anyways, who knows who you got in your back yard, Althea! Snazzy bachelor, my eye! Could be an axe murderer, for all we know!" With no response, Weezy removed the remaining plates from the table.

Two bright red smudges like brilliant roses had appeared on Althea's round cheeks and she said abruptly, "At any rate, lunch is on me today, L! You deserve it!"

Weezy's expert ears picked up the subtle reference. "What gives? Someone givin' you a hard time, Lettie?"

Mrs. Bundle shuffled, "Weezy, it's really nothing at all." Her eyes took Althea to task.

"Now, Lettie! I can just imagine…" Weezy said, her eyes boring into Mrs. Bundle like lasers, willing her to spill the beans. A split second of silence told Weezy she wasn't going to get anything concrete, so she passed along some sage advice with relish, "Don't let the buzzards get you down, that's what I always say! You know, them big ugly birds circling around for scraps of anything they can get their greedy little claws on? There's always a few of them ready to dive. Get my drift?"

Mrs. Bundle looked at her quizzically, wondering if there was some hidden meaning there that she just wasn't getting…buzzards circling? How much did Weezy know about what was going on with Armand Limpert?

Weezy threw her head back and laughed again. "By the by, I just heard an interesting tidbit! I ain't one to gossip, of course…" Weezy leaned forward, her wide nose crinkled distastefully, giving the impression of a large-beaked puffin passing along morsels to her young. In a surreptitious undertone, she murmured, "but just so's you know, some very strange things are happening *everywhere*. That's what they say, anyway…"

They both looked up intently, biting once more on the proverbial gossip hook. She nodded her huge, cabbage head for emphasis, pushing her reddened work hands through her wiry steel curls and leaned in close. "Uh-huh! Not just *here*, in Pillson, but the next towns over, too! Strange, weird things! For example…you said you're going over to take a look at Tuddy's? Well, you should swing by and take a look at the '*Welcome to Hartland*' sign by the bridge while you're over that way…" her gravelly voice trailed off and she eyeballed them with suspenseful anticipation, watching with avid interest for their reaction.

Mrs. Bundle queried, "*Why?* What about the sign?"

She slapped their check down firmly on the table and deftly gathered up the last few pieces of dirtied napkins and leftover lunch paraphernalia; save for their dessert items and water glasses, the table was now clean as a whistle. Her skilled hands had moved as quickly as the next fleeting comment out of her mouth, "Oh, you'll see…just go on over! You know I ain't one to carry tales that ain't true!"

Her hands full with an overflowing tray of dirty dishes, Weezy expertly backed away from their table, her large hips clearing the table beside them by a half inch. "I don't know about you, but I've got *other* fish to fry!" She laughed. "Literally! Have a good one, ladies!"

As she left them, she called out boisterously to the table of mature women gracefully waving at her from across the room, "Oh, hold onto your hats, girls! We've got all afternoon!" She sent an irreverent, coy grin back to her two friends, winked one last time, and scurried off to her newest audience.

Chapter Seventeen

Tuddy's Ruins

"Oh, mercy!" were the first words out of Mrs. Bundle's mouth.

It was devastating to view the site vacant and empty where their favorite diner had once been. It was as though someone had snapped their fingers and the whole chronicle of thousands of happy dining experiences had been removed. In the place where Tuddy's had always been, there was now nothing except rubble. Nothing, that is, save some bricks, blackened and in ruin, and the burned evidence of a recent disaster. The primary area of the fire was now roped off with yellow hazard tape. As vehicles arrived at the busy four corners, each slowed down, then drove by at a snail's pace, cruising unhurriedly, as if by a bad accident scene, as the vehicle's occupants rubbernecked. Others stopped their vehicles by the side of the road and stood gaping silent. It was a tough scene for anyone to look at; the landscape so different as to appear surreal, the reactions were universal as people solemnly remarked their disbelief at the total disappearance of the restaurant. Althea had left her car at Herder's and had joined Mrs. Bundle. They had parked Junie and were now quietly gathered around the perimeter, sadly viewing the ruins with a handful of other mourners. As each party departed to resume their busy day, they were finally the only ones left.

Walking slowly toward the roped-off rubble, Mrs. Bundle wiped away a single tear from her eye, "How sad! Who would have ever thought?"

"It's very strange, isn't it?"

"In my mind's eye, I can see every detail, every room. Remember how it seemed so small from the outside and then, as you went into it, one room led to another 'til you were way out in that back room? We used to have our own table, Arthur and I. We'd ask for the same one every time we came—they were always so accommodating. I just can't believe it! And, to think about poor Tuddsley!"

Althea clicked her tongue and sighed, "Yes, poor, dear Tuddsley." She sat down at a solitary, ravaged picnic bench, still intact but looking incredibly lonely amidst the burned wreckage. "And all that history, gone in a heartbeat, too!" She shook her head sadly. "Remember all those old photographs and daguerreotypes they had framed on the wall?"

"Yes! And all that old paraphernalia they hung up: old brooms, spoon collections, and the like. All those photos alone must have been worth a fortune. The emotional value to the family must be just as devastating! From what I remember, some of them were from before the turn of the century, I think."

"Oh, yes, even before! I remember Ger saying those soldier photographs were all his relatives. Some of them were pretty creepy-looking, so old and, you know, the way they sat for photographs back then. The way nobody ever smiled. Good grief!"

Their mood was changing as they remembered all the good, fun things at the diner, and Mrs. Bundle managed a smile. "Yes, that one out by the ladies' room especially! Remember?"

"You mean that huge one in the ornate frame, the one on the wall going in, in the Civil War soldier uniform? Oh, yes! Very somber and imposing." She paused, "There was a plaque underneath it, too. I remember the nameplate 'cause it said Tudhope. What was it? Do you remember seeing the name, L?" They got up and began walking toward the back area of rubble.

"Do I? Of course—" Mrs. Bundle closed her eyes and blinked them open just as quickly. "Jememiah! Jeremiah Tudhope, of course! Old Jeremiah's face was so serious and with that huge beard—remember the uniform and hat and all? It used to scare the bezeesus out of the kids when they were young. Matter of fact, we used to play kind of a game with that picture, Karen and I. I remember Karen clinging to me when she was a little girl, she couldn't have been more than three or so. She hid behind me whenever we passed by that particular photograph and say, 'Mommy, please, don't let the bad man get me!' I'd tell her that he wasn't a bad man, that he was a soldier named Jeremiah from a long, long time ago and that soldiers were good because they protected us. She couldn't say his whole name—called him 'Merimiah.' Anyway, it became almost a ritual each time we'd head to the loo. After a while, it turned into a game of sorts. She'd *beg* me to take her to the ladies' room just to go by the painting." She smiled as she remembered, "I'd hold her hand, and she'd say, 'Look, Mom, there's *Merimiah*!' pointing and blissfully scared out of her wits. Later on, it was always a big joke to 'go see Merimiah.' Whenever *any* of us had to *go*, don't you know—Arthur, Leslie, whoever--we'd say, 'Gotta go see '*Merimiah*!'"

They both got a chuckle out of this as they came around the back pile of bricks and debris; they stopped in mid-step.

Althea grabbed her friend's forearm and whispered, "Good grief— look, L! There's Viola!"

Near the blaze's farthest site behind the largest pile of debris was Viola Tudhope, florist extraordinaire, hunched over and looking about as attractive as a forlorn chimney sweep. The soiled condition of her clothes and body indicated she had been sifting through the rubble in the area where her florist shop had once been. She was a little ball of black soot from head to toe. Her hands were stained ugly, variegated hues ranging from rusty brown to coal black. In her hands were what appeared to be the remnants of three red silk begonias with dark green frayed leaves, along with a three inch roll of gold lame' ribbon that had seen better days.

"Gawdy! What is she doing in that mess? Anybody can see it's in total ruins!"

Mrs. Bundle whispered, "Oh dear! The poor thing is crying! Allie...should we leave her...or go over?"

"I think—go over—yes."

At once, Viola looked up and saw them. As they approached her, she froze, looking as frightened as a deer caught in headlights. True to her past behavior of unchecked timidity, she took a step back as if to run away and almost fell into the rubble.

"Viola, hi! Wait! Can we help you, dear?" Mrs. Bundle raised her arm in friendly greeting.

But Viola was already in flight. She gave a sharp cry of anguish as though mortified that she might be forced into conversation. She backed away from the debris and shook her head vehemently at them. Then, with gaining momentum, she turned and ran toward the tall trees behind where the building had once stood.

Her behavior seemed strange to them both as they stood there, openmouthed, and watched her. Rather than run toward the parking lot like most people, she had scurried like a tiny, obstinate badger the few hundred feet between her and the woods. Rushing as though being chased by a thousand demons, she reached the protective cover of trees and privacy.

"Good grief, we've spooked her! Viola, *wait*! We just want to help you!" Althea yelled, but she was gone, the woods gobbling her up like a whale's deep mouth. She turned helplessly to Mrs. Bundle. "Should we go after her?"

"No, no, Allie, I think not. Best to let her be. It's too much for her to handle being here among the ruins, I'm sure." She clicked her tongue in distress. "Gaw! How awful! Think about it--she's lost her shop, her inventory, her livelihood, not to mention the family dog, too. She grew up with the diner. Imagine! Who wouldn't be devastated? And grieving her losses, I suspect. No, it's best to let her go. Poor thing!"

They reached the debris area where Viola had been frantically searching. One solitary brick wall still stood, about eight or nine feet in height and only about fifteen feet wide. Sadly, it was the common wall between the diner and the floral shop. Yellow caution tape surrounded the spot. The whole midsection of the restaurant was gone and now, all that was left was the gaping doorway leading from one space to another.

"Would you look at this, L! Can you believe it?"

Mrs. Bundle looked up to the section where Althea was pointing on the brick wall.

There, miraculously, hanging askance and barely legible over the doorway, was the charred remains of the diner's original ornate brass plaque. Smoky gray, black-stained and streaked, were the still-legible words that read simply,

1875
TUDDY'S EATERY
J. AND M. TUDHO__

The "*p*" and the "*e*" of "Tudhope" had been scorched beyond recognition.

"Oh, *Allie*! How sad!"

"Such a shame. But, they'll rebuild, no doubt. They're a strong family and they'll come out of this stronger."

"Good point! I hope the best for them. It's such a beautiful spot."

They began to walk back to the car and Mrs. Bundle paused and looked around once more. "Allie, wait just a sec. It's so peaceful here. How 'bout we take our hike *here* rather than in Hartland? There's a slew of walking trails out this way."

"Sure—in fact, it's a great idea. It's been a thousand years since I've been exploring over this way. Say! I remember as teenagers, there was a wonderful pond way up over the ridge here, way on the far side of the mountain. Gaw, it's a good couple-mile hike, as I remember it, once you hit Maggie's Stream."

"Past Maggie's Stream? I never knew that!" Mrs. Bundle and Althea had explored many, if not all of, the local haunts together as young girls, spelunking the caves on Tattle Ridge, canoeing and navigating the Big Falls at Hapgood Pond, hiking into the more remote areas of Goochie Pond, but she couldn't recollect a pond in this Hartland Corners area.

"You didn't know about it?" Althea said, "Chaunce took me up there once, it was right before he left for Korea, as I remember."

Althea's face took on a serene, happy expression. "Oh, we went up and up these trails, for miles it seemed! I remember, once we got there, we had a lovely picnic." She shook her dirty blonde mop of hair and laughed at the memory. "Good grief! He could come up with the darndest places for us to explore! He was always so much fun! Seems so fearless now, hiking way into the hinterlands like that."

She raised her arms expansively toward the mountains beyond. "He knew all these woods around here like the back of his hand. He was quite the sportsman, don't you know. Fishing, hunting, whatever–if it had to do with nature, he loved it. Anyway, this place he took me to, way up there in the williwags," she pointed skyward, "was really special. Matter of fact, he and I went up there alone one other time, too," her eyes grew dark, "when he came back on leave that last time. It was really hard to find. Quite a few turns and twists, and it's all uphill." She stopped and shrugged. "Whew, it's hot! I doubt I could even find it, much less get us up there!"

Mrs. Bundle stopped and wiped her brow. "Sounds nice, but extremely challenging for two old birds like us. How 'bout we settle for a leisurely walk on the trail that goes in right over there." In the distance, one could see a small path dividing two sets of bushes. "Not too long…we need to save our strength for that meeting tonight. But we also need to work off some of the extra calories from that superb lunch we just had."

"Right. I'm with you on that, girl!"

"*Good ol' exercise*, right?"

"Right!"

As they picked their way past the dense foliage and followed the trail in, they walked silently along, taking in the pungent woodsy odor and listening to the forest sounds. Their feet made soft thudding sounds as they shushed along, enjoying the combined reverent beauty of their surroundings along with each other's company.

Their reverie was broken when they heard a crashing of underbrush and, lo and behold, Viola appeared from nowhere. The small, pudgy woman merged into the trail like a bull moose in a mad rush, crashing through the brush and almost running into them. She lost then regained her balance, recoiling when she saw them, then stopped in her tracks. It was evident she had been weeping—her eyes were blood red and she spluttered and coughed like a spurting teakettle.

Mrs. Bundle reached out to her with a comforting hand.

"Viola, wait—take a minute and catch your breath, girl! We didn't mean to frighten you back there!"

Althea added quickly, "And we are *so* sorry for all that you've lost."

The troubled girl gave a slight nod to her bowed head, and the tears began to flow like a massive flash flood. Her face looked ravaged, her pain inconsolable, accordingly devastated and debilitated as though she had lost her best and only friend in the whole world.

Althea clucked like a mother hen, "There, there, girl, just let it out." She gave her best friend a look, raising her eyebrows.

Mrs. Bundle's voice was soft. "You *poor* dear! Is there anything, anything at all, we can do for you or your parents?"

The homely girl shook her head violently, looking down at the dark earth. Tears splashed down her jutting chin onto the ground below.

After a time, she looked up at them, and a visible hardening, as solid as steel wool, came over her pained features. She raised her eyes until they were at their level, eyes that burned with repressed anger.

They both reacted in surprise, uttering together, "What—what is it, Viola?"

She grunted, as abrupt as a bulldog's bark. Then, the words all came out in a rush; more consecutive words than, truth be told, either Mrs. Bundle or Althea had ever heard come out of that shy mouth.

"Nope! Nothin' anyone can do. Not now, not ever. It's hopeless!!" She lowered her mournful eyes again and muttered between fresh sobs, "Oh, jeez! Sorry! But… thanks…thanks anyway."

She was listless now, an air of pathetic hopelessness surrounding her.

They tried to reach out to her but it was too late.

She was gone, scurrying away like a frightened jackrabbit.

Chapter Eighteen

Cool Waters

Resuming their hike after all that drama, they came to a stream fifteen minutes later.

"*Oo-eeee!* I need a break!" Mrs. Bundle fanned herself.

"Shall we?" Althea nodded toward the persuasive bubbling brook nearby.

Quickly, they removed their sneakers and sat on the moss at the water's edge, soaking their feet in the cooling waters.

Looking around at the pristine forest, Mrs. Bundle said, "Isn't it amazing to think that all this forest land was once farmland?"

"Sadly, that's the way of a lot of Vermont land. What once was field is now woods. It's so dense now; it's hard to imagine it another way."

They both were quiet, deliberating on their most recent encounter.

Althea traced her fingers lazily in the stream. "Viola was…did you hear what she said? That was truly…bizarre."

Mrs. Bundle moved from the mossy area and stood up, nodding. She repeated Viola's words. "'*Nothin' anyone can do. Not now, not ever. It's hopeless.*' What on earth did she mean, Allie? She seems so…tragic."

"Yes, I agree. It's weird, though. I know she's devastated by the fire, who wouldn't be? But I wonder…there was something very strange, as if…there's something more there. I sensed that. Did you?"

"Right, yes I did. Definitely something more." Mrs. Bundle leaned her sore back gently against a friendly maple tree, gazing into the quiet stream. "And what do you suppose happened to the dog?"

"Tuddsley? What made you think of that, L?"

"Well, I was wondering what has the girl so upset. Here we are in this beautifully quiet area. Not more than a quarter-mile away there's been a terrible fire, a tragedy, and a poor animal somewhere out there that no one seems to be able to find. What could have happened to him?"

Althea shrugged and called out, "Where *are* you, Tuddsley? What happened to you?" The air was still and quiet; the mugginess holding her words in suspended animation.

They pondered that for a minute and then, Althea stood up, brushing off the composting leaves and brush. Mrs. Bundle leaned down and, holding onto the tree trunk for support, put her sneakers back on. She said, "Let's head back to Junie, shall we? We've still got a bunch of work ahead of us."

Althea agreed, "Right. I must admit, it is nice out this way, to be sure." She reached over and brushed some minute chips of bark off Mrs. Bundle's back, lingering pieces from the trunk she had been leaning against. She looked past her, stopped short, and stared at the tree that had left its mark. "Say, L, look over there! Behind you. What is that?"

Mrs. Bundle turned around, looking below her at the ground.

"No! Up here, L, above you, behind your head!"

Mrs. Bundle's eyes locked in on the area Althea was pointing at. Althea said, "See? I'll be darned! Something's been carved into the trunk! Wait, not carved, looks more like burn marks…Ummm…"

They both squinted and Mrs. Bundle exclaimed, "Hey now, it's a symbol! Uh-huh, look at that!"

Althea said, "No! It looks more like a…'W', yes?"

"Yuh! It sure does. But what's all that fancy, squiggly stuff coming off it?"

Burned into the trunk of the tree was something rather resembling the fourth-to-the-last letter of the alphabet or some kind of related symbol. Mrs. Bundle reached out her pointer finger and lightly traced over the rough, dark edges.

It was about 5" x 5", very cleverly and discreetly burned into the tree about five feet above the ground at the level of Mrs. Bundle's chin.

She stared with interest at the depiction. "That's just about the fanciest, weirdest 'W' I've ever seen. Almost like a symbolic representation of something—who knows what!"

"Good grief!" Althea pointed to a lower area of the tree. "Look, L, here, down here! There's something written further down...look!"

Underneath the strange carving was one word, mysterious, somewhat ominous, and burned deeply and with remarkable precision into the timber:

Forever

"*Forever.*" Mrs. Bundle whispered, gasping.

"What do you suppose *that* means?"

"No idea! It's so...professional looking—almost sculpted. Wait! Isn't that peculiar?" She shook her head in disbelief. "Isn't it rather strange to find...these extraordinary carvings...like this...twice in one day?"

"What do you mean?"

"Well, on the heels of the discovery this morning, isn't it ironic that here, deep in the woods, you and I have come across *another*... mysterious...thing? This morning, it was those old letters carved into the back panel. Now, *here's* a letter burned into a tree trunk in the middle of nowhere! It feels like ...*déjà vu.* It's...uncanny."

"Yes! I see!" Althea nodded vigorously. "*Uncanny*! Do you ever wonder, L, how things happen? And *why?*"

"I guess I do. It's all very strange, isn't it?" Mrs. Bundle scrunched up her nose, her intelligent eyes searching the area around them. "Actually, right now, it makes me feel rather…creepy."

Stymied and a little spooked by their discovery, they left the forest with few words between them and hiked back out into the sweltering sun.

As they reentered the parking lot, they first saw the bulbous light atop the official Windsor County vehicle and then spied their old friend leaning casually against the car.

"Well, as I live and breathe. What on earth are *you* two doing here?" called out Sheriff Will O'Malley.

"Hi there to you, too!" Mrs. Bundle waved, smiling.

"God all fishhooks!" The large man stood to his full height and placed his huge hands on his hips, resting them comfortably just above the wide, slung-low, belt holding up khaki pants. "When I saw Junie parked over yonder, I said to myself, 'Why is it that wherever there's a big mess, I can always count on Lettie Bundle showing up?'"

"Oh, well! It's nice to see you, too, Will! How are you?" Mrs. Bundle greeted her old ally with a large grin.

"Fine and don't change the subject. I swear, Lettie, without fail, wherever there's trouble, you're not far from the scene. Don't you know this area is restricted?" He made a sweeping motion with his long arm. "We're still investigating what happened here." He tipped his hat. "Hello, Althea, how goes it?"

"Great, Will, how are you doing?"

"Well, all things considered, can't complain." He turned his attention back to Mrs. Bundle. "So? What are you doing here?"

"Really, Sheriff! Last time I knew, it was okay to take a casual ride through the back country roads of southern Vermont."

He smiled. "You got me on that, Lettie. I guess I'm wondering why you're here, on the fire site and coming out of the woods bold as brass!"

She clicked her tongue. "No ulterior motive, Will, really. We—Althea and I, that is--went for lunch at Herder's, after which we decided to take a ride and we thought well, we'd check out the fire scene just like everybody else is. So, we did. And then, very simply, we decided to take a little hike into the woods while we were here." She pointed toward the forest. "In there. To cool off."

He shook his head in frustration. "Of course you did. Even though you know it's a crime scene, right?"

"Oh, is it? We didn't know it was a *crime* scene." She smiled and held her hands out, palms up. "Do you want to arrest us?"

He had to laugh at the ridiculous thought, and he did. "Ha! Funny! Yes, it's a crime scene. And that's *all* I can say." He leaned back against the car again. "Too bad about Tuddy's, huh?" He had shifted from his official capacity, removing his hat and rubbing his careworn sparse head of hair. Even though Sheriff Will O' was nearing retirement, he hated giving anyone the impression that he was slowing down or worn out.

"Yes, really sad. Viola Tudhope seems really shaken up about it."

"*What?*" He shouted incredulously. "You saw Viola?" His hand came down hard and slapped the metal roof of the cruiser.

"Uh-huh." They both said, surprised.

"I've been looking for her all day! Ger said he thought she might be over here. I need to talk to her—she's the last of the Tudhope family to sit down with me. Been trying to lock in on her for the last two days now. If I didn't know any better, I'd say she's avoiding me. She ducked out this morning, early. I must admit I've never seen anyone so shy in all my days! Lord, how she ever ran that florist business I'll never know. Where'd you see her?"

Both women pointed toward the far end of the rubble.

Mrs. Bundle said, "She was over there when we got here, crying her eyes out and covered with soot. She looked like…she was searching for something."

"Really?"

Althea nodded, "She was picking through the ruins like a bag lady! She ran into the woods when she saw us. And then, we took our hike and ended up over by Maggie's Stream. You know where that is?"

"Yup." He said rather shortly.

"Soaked our feet and came back."

"So, did you see Viola once you were in the woods? On your hike?"

"Yes, as a matter of fact, Will, we did," Mrs. Bundle said. "She was crying her eyes out. Came crashing through off a side path. She seemed pretty distraught."

They recounted their experience to him and he listened with interest.

Mrs. Bundle said, "You don't think she had anything, directly or by chance, to do with the fire, do you Will?"

"Who knows? Seems like she's real cut-up about something from what everyone says, could be more than just the fire," the Sheriff observed.

Mrs. Bundle asked, "Do you suppose it's about Tuddsley?"

"What? The dog? Why do you say that?"

"Yes, well, people *are* really attached to their animals, aren't they? She must have been really attached to that Golden Retriever. He was such a lovely, friendly dog! A lot of people might react that way."

"Hard tellin' not knowin'." He scratched his head and looked up the heavily wooded mountain beyond. "We're still looking for Tuddsley; we've gone way into the woods and beyond. Nary a sign of him, unfortunately. Found his neckerchief—and that's not official so don't go blabbing."

"I already heard that—from Walter, who heard it from Axel Conroy."

"Jees-um crow! There's no keeping a lid on anything around here with all these farmers talkin' up a storm!" the Sheriff said resignedly. "Anyway, we think the dog might be too afraid to come out into the open, at least that's what Ger hopes. They're almost as devastated about the dog as they are about the fire."

"Speaking of that, any ideas on the fire, Will?" Mrs. Bundle asked innocently.

"Lettie," he smiled and said dryly, "you know I can't comment officially…"

Althea chided, waving him off, "Yes, well, we *know* that! But, c'mon, Will…"

He put a finger to his nose in caution and said matter-of-factly, "Unofficially, it's arson, pure and simple. Appears to have been set off in the kitchen—suspicious around the gas line." He raised up his bulky frame to his full six-foot-two height. "We're working on a couple angles right now and need to complete our investigation before this goes out to the public."

Mrs. Bundle leaned closer and patted his arm, "We won't say a word, Will. Girl Scout's honor."

"Sorry, ladies. You know, my hands are tied. Let's see—" he ticked off on his fingers, "—there's my official capacity, and confidentiality—not to mention the rumor mill that runs rampant in this county—"

He was cut off by Mrs. Bundle's gasp. "Oh, wait! What about this, Will? Almost forgot to tell you that we found something very… *interesting* out by the stream. May not have anything to do with anything, but…"

"What'd you find?"

"We—it was the strangest thing. There's a pretty distinctive carving. Well, actually, it's *burned* into the trunk of one of the big maple trees alongside the stream. We'll be glad to show you—another day, mind you, I'm too pooped to go back in now."

His sharp, quick eyes became even sharper, evidence his interest was piqued even though he said evenly, "No, that's okay. *Burned,* you say? On one of the trees?" He shook his head and muttered, "How'd my men miss that? They scoured that area."

"Well, in all fairness, we only saw it by accident. It's barely visible unless you are standing right in that spot and looking at the tree about yea-high." She raised her hand to her neck area. "We just happened to notice it!"

"Of course you did." he said with a shade of doubt in his voice. "On a lark, you say, you found something that my men missed entirely. Uncanny!"

"That's just the word *I* used!" Mrs. Bundle said.

"Well, I'd say best the authorities take a look. You're officially put on notice—keep this under your hat, girls, and I *mean* it! I'll get one of the deputies to go back in today and find it. If we can't, I'll call you to show us where it is. You just never know what may be meaningful in an investigation." He looked at his watch. "Dang! I've got to get my butt in gear and head over to the courthouse. Got a meeting with the DA at three."

"We certainly hope you find out who did this, Will!" Mrs. Bundle said fervently. "People's livelihoods taken out from under them! Not to mention one of our best restaurants burnt to the ground! I *wish* we could do something to help…"

He arranged his sunglasses on the bridge of his ample nose and his voice became stern. "*Nuh*-uh! Oh, no…no! Lettie, you keep your distance from this business, you hear me? No going off on your own, trying to figure things out, you hear? This is serious business and the State and our department are working overtime on it, believe you me. Whoever is involved has committed a crime, there's no doubt about that."

He turned to Althea and raised an eyebrow, motioning toward his old friend Arthur's impulsive spouse. "I'm counting on you, Althea. Keep *her* far away from this."

"Oh, don't worry, Sheriff. We all know L can be…a trifle impetuous, don't we?" She smiled. "I'll keep an eye on her, never you mind. She's already got her hands full with…" she made quote marks with her fingers, "'*other issues*.'"

Mrs. Bundle turned a surprised look toward them. "Are you both ganging up on me? Whatever in the world are the two of you going on about? Me? Impetuous!"

This drew huge guffaws from both her cronies.

She shrugged, smiling, and using Weezy's phrase, said, "Anyway, we've got *other* fish to fry!"

Chapter Nineteen

Smokin'

Back inside the faithful Junebug (after deciding there was time), Mrs. Bundle and Althea couldn't help but take Weezy's recommendation and check out the *Welcome to Hartland* sign. They chatted about nothing important as they made the two-mile trip through the village to the southern outskirts of the Hartland village border.

As they came upon the bridge where the sign was located, they slowed down. The quaint, country sign, handcrafted and colorful, was large enough to read from a good distance when driving by. The well-spaced, hand-painted letters were visible and the sign was intact; however, it was evident the sign had been tampered with. Some of the painted lettering seemed to be obscured by dark black markings the color of carbon which were splodged over the welcoming words. They pulled over to the side of the road and Junie puttered to a stop. Then, they got out so that they could examine the sign up close.

Within fifty feet it was clearer; the damage was more sinister than first observed. They both caught their breath, taken aback by what they saw.

Althea struggled for words. "Good grief! What on earth?"

Mrs. Bundle studied the scene in front of her, peering closely at the overlay markings that had defaced the pleasant sign.

There, seared into the sign with some kind of burning utensil, was a 6" high, somber warning that read:

"Remember! Only YOU can prevent WILD fires!"
"Smokey"

"It's…the old Smokey the Bear saying!" Althea cried, then looked over at Mrs. Bundle and was surprised to see an angry look on her face. "What do you think, L?"

"I think this is someone's attempt at sick humor, no doubt. Not very funny in the light of what has occurred, wouldn't you say? This is really insidious—written almost as a threat, as though to terrorize people."

"I agree wholeheartedly. If this is a joke, it's not very pretty. But, isn't the saying, 'only you can prevent *forest* fires'?" Althea asked, an edge in her voice.

"Yes…but.." Mrs. Bundle ruminated, "I do remember it used to be the catch phrase for kids in the fifties and sixties. Boy Scouts and Girl Scouts, especially. You know, a way to caution them to be safe with their campfires. I think at some point they changed the saying to 'wildfires' instead. In fact, I remember hearing it somewhere recently—on a commercial or something for a National Forest promo. Something like that, I think."

Althea removed her sunglasses and moved in closer. "Well, look at the 'wild', though. It's separated out, larger letters. Look how strangely it's written, like a *nutcase* did it." She shivered in the blazing heat.

"I hope not, Allie. People get really squirrelly when there's someone crazy on the loose. This is pretty eerie, though. I don't like it. Not one bit."

"It's literally burned right into that wooden panel—so much so, it's totally disfigured the sign. They'll have to redo the whole thing, I bet! What kind of tool would someone use to do that, L?"

"Don't know." She paused in serious thought. "Strange, but… it almost looks similar—dare I say? *Gaw!* No wonder Will was interested!" She stared at the handiwork, "He must have already made the connection! It *is* similar to the carving we just saw on the tree by the stream!"

"Good grief!"

"Same dark, indented appearance. Almost the same script, too. Or, is my imagination getting the better of me? This is too bizarre!"

"Could someone have used a blowtorch?"

"Possibly. In fact, very likely." Mrs. Bundle shook her head, the pillbox-braided mass swaying gently. She clicked her tongue in disgust. "My Lord! I ask you, Allie, what kind of sick joke is someone trying to play here?"

"Finding that stuff on the tree was strange enough! But, this '*wild fires*' thing! Was it some kind of warning to people about Tuddy's fire? Or, did someone do this afterward? *That* would put the fear of God in people. Especially with Weezy spreading the news…"

"Yes, Allie—spreading…like wild fire!"

Chapter Twenty

Elvina, Lucy, and Junior

They made one last stop—at Wrinkle's General Store in Brownsville—to pick up a few odds and ends before returning to their respective homes.

Wrinkle's General Store was the hub of Brownsville, a small village known primarily for nesting at the base of the Ascutney Mountain Ski Resort. The general store's successful longevity was virtually guaranteed, between the brisk business from the seasonal skiing community and the local residents, but more importantly, because the closest retail food center was a good eight miles away in Claremont.

However, the Brownsville general store's long run of dissimilar owners over the past five decades was legendary. Most Brownsville natives could remember the store's history from the late 50's onward with amazing accuracy because the store's ownership trail seemed to carry a certain amount of either bad luck or ill will with each transfer.

First, it had been the Petersons—Dale and Sylvia—who, after toiling without one bad word or complaint for five long, seemingly uneventful years, left mysteriously for California one August midnight, leaving all the dairy and fresh meat in the coolers and everything else intact, along with a note tacked to the door that simply said, *Moving on. Carpe Diem!*

It seemed evident to anyone with a keen pecuniary sense that here was an opportunity to step in and make a quantity of money, at which point Homer Alwood, a strict patriarch prone to extreme religious reflection (along with his dismal wife and brood of twelve equally-dismal children), took over the store straight away. He and his family took up noiseless residence in the apartment over the store; it was as though the whole brood moved on cat's paws—swiftly and without sound. Needless to say, Homer's somber, "Thank you, friend," with every ringing of the cash register caused the store's atmosphere to be one of "rush-in, get-what-you-need, give-a-friendly-nod, and get-out,"—not the most upbeat reign, but the efficiency was superb and he ran it successfully into the 1970's.

Still, when Homer died at age 75, there was not a one of the usually-reticent Alwood gang who wanted to stay and run the lucrative store so, after some treacherous infighting, they sold the business to Skeet Starinok, who proceeded to methodically drive it into the ground in the first year of owning it. Ultimately, Skeet "gave" the business to Chase Walter, who won it in a poker game.

Chase ran the business successfully for a decade, then lucked out and sold it for a hefty profit to a large corporation loosely connected with the Mountain; two days later, he died in a snowmobile accident, never able to enjoy his proceeds. After that, the corporation ran into some bad times in the early-eighties and practically gave the business back to the village—this time to a local real estate agent, Stuie Grant, who proceeded to set up his mistress, Sadie Philbrook, in the retail food sales business.

Stuie ran the store "behind the scenes" as they say; that is, before he died from a cardiac infarction in the second floor bedroom directly above the meat counter. Sadly, Sadie didn't have a head for numbers and gave away a lot of freebies (products *and* services), managing the store until there was nothing left to give away.

Her son Roger came back from the Gulf War and took over the tired enterprise, bringing the business back to a successful level for a number of years until he married a Filipino girl and decided to move to Florida where her daughter lived.

Most recently, the newest owners of two years were a husband and wife team named Norbert and Elvina Wrinkle who, immediately upon their arrival, changed the legendary store's name to "Wrinkle's General Store."

After establishing the business once again as a viable enterprise, bad fortune visited the Wrinkle family. Tragically, Norbert, a quiet, unassuming man with a happy-going nature, had taken a critical fall off a ladder the previous February while raking snow off the store's two-and-a-half story roof. He never regained consciousness, dying three days later at Hitchcock Medical Center.

That event had left Elvina to run the store with her grown daughter Lucy.

As they walked into the store, Althea and Mrs. Bundle saw that Elvina was front and center at the register, perched on her trusty stool like a queen bee on a throne.

Elvina could be described as a fading blossom, a rose whose petals were falling in rapid succession off the vine. She was still blonde, eye-catching in a shopworn way, her bleached hair pinned here and there and loosely held in place in the classic style of the "fifties" Marilyn-Monroe coiffure. The long pageboy-like waves were akin to mounds of whipped cream frozen in swirls of hairsprayed loops and curves, defying gravity in their rock solid state. Legend (and her own diffident innuendos) had intimated that she'd won many beauty queen titles in her day. She had an air of casualness about her, her sleepy-eyed expression causing most male heads to turn at least once, then wince slightly with a realization that she was much older than at first glance.

There was a certain aloofness about Elvina, and she took the gentle ribbing of her unusual name gracefully, in self-deprecating fashion. In the short time they had resided in Brownsville, she had gained a reputation for being bawdy and fun-loving; that is, before Norbert's unfortunate demise. Her biggest wellspring of discussion was her hard-working daughter Lucy, whom Elvina mercilessly harangued while she sat there and smoked cigarette after cigarette.

Transplanted from North Carolina or thereabouts, the Wrinkles' speech modulation was distinctly different, slow and smooth as

Southern Comfort and just as refreshing to the Yankee clipped accent common to the area. Elvina's usual ending to most sentences, a guttural *"Tha's raaaah!"* had fallen on virgin Vermont ears, most of whom had never heard phrases without any final consonants.

Natives would remark to one another, "Don't ya know, she's sayin' *'That's right!'*" trying their best to replicate the soft Southern-fried tones as they left the store.

Norbert's strong work ethic and helpful, caring nature had quickly endeared him to everyone who met him, despite the fact that he was from "away." He was also very kind to Lucy, even though word was that he was Elvina's second (or third) husband and that Lucy was only his stepdaughter. Elvina tended to be tightlipped on this subject of past husbands and one other delicate topic, mind you—that of what her exact age *really* was.

With Norbert's demise, this was a fulltime occupation that Elvina (somewhat of a prima donna) had inherited by default, a job she was neither accustomed to nor wanted responsibility of.

Mrs. Bundle was actually surprised to see Elvina in the store at this time of day; everyone knew it was more usual for Elvina to be gone for extended periods as closing time approached, "taking care of errands" or attending Beano or Bingo in one of the surrounding larger towns.

"Hi Elvina." Mrs. Bundle said cheerily.

The woman turned lazily on her perch, eyebrow raised, then smiled in recognition and said, "Hi, Y'all!" and turned back to a waiting customer.

Looking past her, Mrs. Bundle could see poor Lucy slaving away. In previous generations, Elvina's daughter would have been characterized as dull or dimwitted. In today's vernacular, the newest catch phrase for Lucy's aptitude, or lack thereof, was that she probably had A.D.D., the hapless victim of "attention deficit disorder." Lucy was not able to concentrate on more than one task at a time and, if interrupted or questioned, one-syllable answers were all she could handle while her focus remained riveted on each minute detail.

A colorless and plain girl built like an armored tank, Lucy's premature crow's feet crinkled the area around her eyes and mouth as she wrinkled her nose and creased her oily forehead, scowling and squinting through tortoise-rimmed glasses at anyone who gave her the least bit of attention. She was eager to please, trying her best to make each person's order come out perfect. She moved her largeness through life's tedious tasks like a silent and gloomy submarine, barely ever coming up for air or sustenance. When she did resurface, it was usually in the presence of a man, and she tried her best to flirt, her big bovine eyes rolling in their sockets like a moon sick cow in heat, with a goofy smile pasted to her face.

Consequently, her mother watched her like a brooding hawk, often reminding Lucy of her tasks and constantly encouraging her to "keep busy and stop dilly-dallyin.'" As she perpetually plodded along, never stopping for a break, most folk followed her mother's lead and treated Lucy as though she were a young teenager—not the twenty-eight-year-old woman that she was.

Today was no exception. Lucy had her hands full; a hub of activity caused the large, well-lit retail space to buzz like a swarm of happy bees. Chattering away, hands waving delicately to make a point, Elvina Wrinkle was oblivious to any sense of urgency, clearly, as usual, the center of attention. There were people at the six-stooled lunch counter, a number of customers in line at the checkout, while others searched blindly for what they needed.

Lucy, neatly turned out in her crisp, white apron (Elvina prided herself in making sure Lucy always looked presentable) was behind the meat counter methodically pre-slicing luncheon meat between waiting on customers. A handwritten sign taped to the meat case window read, "*Black Angus Special: Choicest rib-eye in the county—$9.99/lb!*" The lifeless girl, ageless in her demeanor and appearance, calmly moved from one task to the next like a hound dog on a hunt with his nose to the ground, simultaneously waiting on the locals at the lunch counter and then running back to the meat counter.

Elvina, the regal Welcoming Committee of One, majestically puffed on a cigarette; as the last patron received their change and left, she gave the two women her full attention. "Why, *hel-lo*, Althea, how goes the painting?" Her wide beauty-queen smile froze in place while her pale, peculiarly blue-and-chartreuse-flecked eyes lazily inspected Althea from head to toe.

"Just great, Elvina. Thanks for asking."

"Ah saw one of your works hanging at the Co-Op—my, oh, *my*! Fab-*ooo*!" Elvina's benevolent smile lingered as she shifted her eyes lazily in Mrs. Bundle's direction. "And Lettie, dear, how *are* you? Ah haven't seen you in a *dog's* age." Her words were as slow and sugary as dripping maple syrup.

Dear Cracker wouldn't appreciate that one at all, Mrs. Bundle thought as she smiled warmly at Elvina. "No complaints, Elvina. How's business?"

"Nevva betta!" Her eyes fluttered, her southern belle image intact as her words came like sugarcane once more, "We've had the *best* week evva, what with all the hoopla over the other side of the mountain at Hartland Corners. It's just *crazy…*" She shook her head ruefully. "Those poor, poor, *poor* people! Ah hope they can get their business goin' again. And, Ah can't even converse about their poor, sad, little *Tudds-ley!*" She drew out the dog's name with feeling, her soft, cool words like a soft breath of fresh spring air.

Althea nodded her head in agreement. "I know. We were just over that way. Sad."

"Any news at all, honey?" she asked in her overly saccharine tone.

Althea nodded, "While we were there.." she began, but was kicked squarely under cover of the front counter by her friend.

Althea blinked, getting the message loud and clear, and modified the most recent news update considerably. "Uh-huh! You know, everything's roped off, all official. Sheriff Will-O was over there checking on things."

"*Reee-ally*?" Drawn out to last an eternity, the word reverberated; avid interest was hard to disguise and Elvina's ears and eyes were riveted, waiting for the next morsel. "Ah just love that man! So…*virile*, and *powerful*. Oh, honey, Ah always did *love* a man in uniform." She gazed dreamily at them. "What did he have to say?"

Mrs. Bundle (finding it hard to envision the Sheriff as anything other than her old friend, "good ol' Will O'Malley") shifted her weight awkwardly at Elvina's twittering and said, "Not much, Elvina. I'm sure someone else will come in with much more interesting info than we have. What with you being right here in the thick of things as you are!"

"You betcha, darlin' lady." She smiled endearingly and leaned against the cash register, gently caressing her molded hair, making sure it was still in the exact same place. "Speaking of *yummy* gossip…. have you met the new tenant at the Elliot place?" Her eyes fluttered again. "*Ah* heard he's positively *dreamy*. That goober Tim Scott says he'll be quite a catch….for some lucky lady! Have you seen him yet?"

Her flirtatious coyness wasn't lost on Mrs. Bundle's observant gaze as she wondered how long the moss would grow under Elvina's feet before she made *her* move.

Althea made a scoffing sound from deep within her throat, "Nope."

"Oh! Tha's *raaaah*, Althea!" She smiled engagingly. "Shut my mouth and hogtie me to a bedpost! Ah forgot—he's *raaaht* in your little ol' back yard," her words were as liquid as sloe gin, "….*isn't* he?"

Althea's face was made of stone. "Yes, he is. However, from my vantage point, it's really much ado about nothing. That's all I've got to say on the subject."

Elvina watched her playfully, sensing she had hit a nerve. Althea reddened as her foot continued to wedge itself deeper into her mouth as she exclaimed, "He's just a *man*, for goodness sake! You'd think the King of England had arrived! Good grief!"

The register gave out a loud *Brnnngggg!* as Elvina hit the total button and silently handed change to another patiently-waiting customer. "Well now, it's always nice to have some *new blood*, if you know what Ah mean, girl." Elvina gave a gentle wink to Mrs. Bundle and then giggled like a schoolgirl. "Ain't Ah right, Lettie? Shakes things up a bit. Ah hear he's an artist, too! And famous!"

Watching the woman with interest, Mrs. Bundle thought, *only four months and…*she stopped herself. Grieving *was* an uncommonly individual thing (she would be the first to admit that). Maybe Elvina's lightheartedness was her way of dealing with grief, but still, it seemed a tad upbeat—what with Norbert just departed four months earlier. Arthur had passed years before and she still missed him every day, but life did go on. *Oh, well,* she reflected, *to each his own.*

And, truth be told, Elvina was known to be a gadabout and flirt even before Norbert's death—often as not, old habits tended to die hard. (Mrs. Bundle had frequently heard Elvina telling anyone willing to listen, "Don't you know, when Ah was smaller 'n a boll weevil, Ah had enough of those godforsaken cotton fields to last me a lifetime, honey! Worked on my daddy's spread like a common field hand! Ah always tell Norbert, 'Darlin', you may like the williwags, but Ah like to be with city folks in West Leb or Keene who like to have fun and play a little bingo—that's where Ah aim to be!' *Tha's raaaah!*'")

Mrs. Bundle coughed delicately. "A *famous* artist? Really? That would be wonderful for the community. I know a couple of our village organizations that would certainly welcome any expertise he might have to offer. Maybe he'd like to volunteer while he's here."

Elvina shrugged lazily and, with little interest in this new subject of civic duty, scanned the face of her watch, then drew one of her Pall Mall 100's from its leather pack and tapped it daintily on the diner counter. "Wonder where that Junior is? He was supposed to be here by now….Ah *nev-aah!*"

With Norbert's death, Elvina had been forced to take on a more active role in the store and it had been a difficult adjustment. The multi-tasking job tired her out; there were clearly some responsibilities she could not, or just would not, perform. And with Lucy was already stretched to the max, Elvina had needed someone to pick up the slack, mostly the heavy lifting and building maintenance-related chores. Consequently, she had hired a part-time handyman (and jack of all trades) named Junior Veakey. Junior was known throughout Pillson as a poor but pleasant fellow who kept to himself; he lived up the road near the Transfer Station with his father. It was a good fit—Junior's multitalented skills and Elvina's loss of her handy husband—and so, they formed a mutually profitable work union. Since mid-March, Junior could often be seen puttering around the store, inside or outside, his old tool box never too far away.

Mrs. Bundle said conversationally, "How is Junior?"

She looked at them both, one eyebrow cocked lazily. "How is he? He's sweet on my Lucy, don't you know! Fool boy! Ah saw them making eyes at each other the other day." She rolled her lethargic eyes skyward. "*Law*, oh law! So, Ah had to set him straight, Hell, yeah, Ah did! Ah told him, 'Ah'll *not* be havin' any of that!' Lucy is *off* limits. Thaaa's *raaah*!"

Elvina's over protectiveness of her daughter seemed somewhat unnecessary. *Maybe Lucy should be so lucky*, Althea's furtive look to her best friend conveyed.

"Junior and Lucy? Really?" Mrs. Bundle eyed the quiet girl behind the lunch counter. "Well, now...he's a very nice young man."

"Well, he ain't gettin' any sugar *here*!" Elvina's voice rang out above the din.

Lucy, hearing her mother's voice, raised her head and cried in embarrassment, "Oh, Mama!"

Elvina said in that slow, southern drawl, "You just hush now, sweetkins! That's what Mamas are for, Lucy darlin'. Thaa's *raaah*! And don't you forget it, now."

Drawing out an elegant, old-fashioned Zippo lighter, Elvina expertly flipped the top open and in one facile move caught the wheel with her thumb. Elvina's habit of smoking was almost ritualistic, and the rasp in her voice was an indication of the habit's intensity. The flint sent a shower of sparks onto the wick into an instant small burst of blue flame. She took a seductive, dry drag on the yet-unscathed cigarette and its end burst into bright red embers. Drawing its pleasure in deeply, she closed the cover with a satisfied *snap*! and placed the fancy mother-of-pearl lighter back into the worn, matching leather and mother-of-pearl cigarette case. Pursing her lips together, she unceremoniously spit out an errant sliver of dry tobacco from the corner of her mouth. Lastly, she blew out the smoke in a satisfied, rush-filled, "Ahhh....!"

Elvina took another waiting customer's items, her Pall Mall dangling from her bright red lips and, while Althea went in search of her staples, Mrs. Bundle's mind wandered as she waited.

She had personally known Junior Veakey all his life and could honestly say she was one of the *very* few people who had cracked his very private, silent exterior. From their first meeting, she had preferred to call him by his given name, Vincent, having taken notice of him at the library. Vincent had experienced what the locals would call "a hard life," living in a one-room cabin (some might call a shack) on TaDaDump Road with his aging and destitute father, Barnabus (known to the locals as Barny). Generations of Veakeys before Vincent had lived in the same section of the village (commonly known as the least desirable area of Pillsonville); their sad plight had been such for as long as she had known of the Veakeys. All that was left of the Veakey clan, as far as she knew, was Barny and his son. They were a private pair, very poor and very proud. Vincent's mother had died of Lou Gehrig's disease right around the same time Vincent had entered adolescence. Mrs. Bundle wasn't sure *why* the Veakeys had always been underprivileged, but she knew they never seemed to be able to dig themselves out of the poverty hole, an entrenched hole dug long before by past generations.

Unassuming, painfully shy, quiet, and nondescript in stature and attitude, Junior's world was one of lonely poverty on the private hillside acre just a few hundred yards before the Town Transfer Station.

Mrs. Bundle had gotten to know Junior well when she had begun volunteering at the Pillsonville Elementary School, long after her own children were grown and gone. Her assignment was helping the children who had a hard time with their reading. Part of her job had been to walk the small group across the street and over to the Pillson Public Library. There, she would show them around the aisles and aisles of books, make them comfortable with the surroundings, and teach them how to find the books that might inspire or interest them. Her memories held a special spot for that young Veakey boy, a small, slight child whose formidable speech impediment had left him virtually frightened to death to utter any words, much less converse with anyone. He often used "quiet speak," a series of grunted responses which did not require forming dreaded consonants. He also was prone to gesturing rather than being forced to verbalize, or often as not, fiercely shaking his head "no" to most advances or questions.

At the time, she sensed that this little guy had a lot to say, but the child's emotions were so dammed up that his lips always formed a solid and firm white line across his impassive face.

On the third occasion that she met with him, he had finally opened up a tiny bit, her kind smile gently drawing him out of his shell. In bits and spurts, he had begun to speak, burping out one painful word slowly, then another, then resting, his face a contorted mess, until he could gain the momentum for the next word. Mrs. Bundle sat patiently, stock-still and intent on listening to only him, as he articulated one difficult word at a time.

Blindly trusting that she might be the *one* person who he knew for sure wouldn't laugh at him or get impatient with him, he painstakingly tried to express himself in short bursts of honesty, his inner thoughts and gentle perspective coming out. She had been very surprised at his astute perceptions and the interesting way he viewed the world through his keenly observant young eyes.

He had loved the Arts section of the library and would sit enthralled, looking through the Painting Masters books, pointing at the photographs of a DaVinci or Van Gogh masterpiece, his eyes bright with newfound interest. She remembered him studying "The Pieta" in the sculpture section of the *Fine Art World Museum* tome for an hour, as though it were the best gift he'd ever opened.

It was as if a whole new world outside TaDaDump Road had opened up to him and, even as young as he was, his eyes moved over the pages with an intellectual, deliberate intent. Mrs. Bundle and he had become fast "friends for life" during this boy's formative years and, to this day, Junior's face lit up whenever his and Mrs. Bundle's paths crossed.

Today was no exception as, just then, the subject of Elvina's ire came slouching through the store's front door. Usually invisible, Junior Veakey's painful shyness precluded open friendliness; he was more the type who tended to blend into the woodwork. Afflicted with a horrible stammer, even now as a grown-up, caused him to suffer from intense fear that he would be called upon to speak in public or, worse yet, to become the center of attention. Short of stature and dressed in simple work overalls and a dingy *"Pabst is King"* T-shirt, Junior's sensitive face glistened from his already busy day of work outside in the blazing heat.

He nodded a curt hello to Elvina, eyes cast down.

"Hey, Junior, there you are, you young buck!" She puffed away on her Pall Mall, drawing in a deep breath and giving him a long, lazy look. "Do *y'all* think you could take care of that outside sprinkler *raaght* away? And bring in those heavy boxes for Lucy to unpack and stock the shelves? There's a lot to be done…"

"Hi Junior!" Lucy interrupted, her face lit up as she waved at him from across the room.

He nodded again, this time in her direction and then, seeing Mrs. Bundle out of the corner of his downcast eyes, his granite countenance changed dramatically and his head came shooting up with interest. He stammered shyly, "H-H-H—Hi, M-M-Miz B-B-Bundle!"

She smiled at him warmly. "Vincent, it's so nice to see you! Mercy, it's been forever since we've had a good chinwag! How goes it?"

"C-C-C-Can't c-c-comp-p-p-plain! Th-Thanks, for d-d-droppin' off th-that c-c-c-crumb c-c-cake." His voice was softly cushioned. "D-D-Dad r-reeeally l-l-liked it." He shuffled and then stopped.

Two strangers had turned to stare at him, then looked away awkwardly. One whispered something to the other; they both nodded and gave Junior a fleeting look of pity.

"Well, I'm pleased that he enjoyed it." Mrs. Bundle said. "How 'bout you? How are you doing?"

He gave her a faint, rueful smile and his eyes clouded over, then cleared. He nodded impassively; he always had a forlorn look about him, but today he seemed particularly cheerless. "I'm d-d-doin' o-k-kay, all th-th-things c-considered." True to form, he had had enough small talk and, as he drew more looks, he anxiously eyed the back door, then said earnestly, "I g-g-gotta go now!"

"Well, you stop over at the farm anytime, Vincent. And give your Dad my regards, won't you?"

He nodded again, then turned abruptly toward the back door, head down, clearly discomfited by the queer looks his lack of clean articulating style were generating from the store's customers.

Elvina puffed on the last vestiges of her cigarette and yelled idly after him, "Oh, *Junior!*"

His shoulders stiffened and he turned around slowly.

"Lucy will give you your dinner later on, after the store shuts down. Ah told her to leave it for you on the picnic table outside. Mind you, now, Ah'll be home by eight, so no funny business, you hear?"

Junior blushed and shut his eyes, gave a quick nod, walked silently past the sign indicating *"Unattended Children Will be Sold"* and scurried out the side door.

"There's a good boy, now…" Elvina called after him. She looked heavenward dramatically, sighed, and then gestured with her crimson-painted thumbnail toward his departing figure and whispered, "See what Ah mean, girls? He's soft on her, you mark my words! Ah'll tell you, there better not be any horsin' around!" She looked at her watch again. "Hell's bells! Ah've gotta get going if Ah'm gonna get my bubble bath in before Ah head out to Bingo!"

Everyone knew Elvina liked a good finger of whiskey (as evidenced by her inclination to freely imbibe at local Grange Hall functions) alongside her menthol-filtered cigarettes and often as not, she just flew the coop, leaving Lucy to handle the load of running the store.

She yelled again, across the store this time, the last smoke escaping from her lips in a haze. *"Lucy?"* The girl looked up from pouring coffee at the far end of the counter. "Ah'm goin', honey! You be good, now. Get that meat done and into the case, and don't forget to take in the sign and the flag at closing now, will you? And take care of these *kind* people here," she said, motioning toward two men heading in her direction.

The busy girl didn't look up from pouring; she just nodded and said blandly, "Yes, Mama."

Elvina flashed a brilliant Miss America smile at Mrs. Bundle and Althea. "Y'all stay cool now, y' hear? Ah gotta beat it or Ah won't get there in time for the first game!"

They said their good-byes and Elvina Wrinkle was out the door in a heartbeat—without so much as a "by your leave" to the waiting customers.

Chapter Twenty-One

Remembering Chauncey

"So, what's *really* going on with you?" Mrs. Bundle's eyes darted sideways at her friend as she navigated the roadway.

They were on their way back to Herder's parking lot where Althea had left her car. Mrs. Bundle had wanted to ask the question all afternoon. After taking note of Althea's behavior change the last few days, Mrs. Bundle was concerned and had decided she was going to ask Althea straight out. The fact of the matter was, Althea's consistently calm amiability seemed to have taken a decided downturn. Lately, Althea's warm and sunny nature seemed to have been invaded by acerbity; her usual unaffected, happy demeanor infected with undue sarcasm and irritation.

Mrs. Bundle waited silently.

Finally, Althea gave a great sigh. She opened her mouth to speak, then stopped, thought, and said gloomily, "Oh, I don't know, L. Things. You know."

"Hmmm?" Mrs. Bundle smiled encouragingly.

"Is it that obvious?" Her friend nodded. "There's no getting anything by you, L, is there?"

"Well, we have been friends now, for…decades! I *know* when something's bothering you. And, truth be told, you seem as though… I'm not sure I can describe it except to say…you're just *not* your usual happy self. You seem…pretty unhappy, in fact. *Are* you unhappy,

Allie? Or…agitated? Something seems to be eating away at you…" She reached over and patted her friend's arm.

She was surprised to see Althea's eyes quickly fill with tears. "Oh, good grief!" She pulled a tissue from her purse. "I'm….not sure! Well, on the surface...my life couldn't be better. By all rights, I should be happy as a clam. It's uncanny, though. Lately, well, I've been thinking about….Chauncey." She heaved a great sigh. "Isn't that strange?"

"Why strange?" Mrs. Bundle asked.

"I mean, to be thinking about him after all these years? A woman of my age, thinking of a past, long-dead sweetheart. The thing is, he's always been there in my thoughts. He truly was the love of my life." This time her sigh held deep sadness.

"And, now?"

"I guess I'd always just resigned myself to the fact that I would never meet anyone that would measure up to him. And now, here I am! My life has whizzed by so fast!" She wiped a tear away. "Oh, it's been fine. I'll be fine. I mean, I've got a happy life, there's no doubt, and very fulfilling, too. No doubt about it." The tightness of her voice belied her earnestness. "But lately, I've been thinking. Emmm…" she hesitated, "I just wonder…is this all there is? I ask myself questions. Like…did I do the right thing to become a nurse and focus on others my whole life? Was I too closed to other possibilities? Should I have focused on meeting a husband, and making a family a priority? Was this…" she raised her arms surrounding the world around them, "you know, was all of the work I did to help others what I was supposed to do in my life? What happened to me? What happened to doing things just for me?" She paused in frustrated silence.

Mrs. Bundle reached over and patted her arm once more. "There, there, friend! Allie, I've never known you to question your goals, your motivation—or your many accomplishments, might I add. Never."

"I don't know….maybe it's just moving back here, to Pillson, to all the memories. It's all come flooding back to me. Good grief, Chaunce and I were so perfect together! I just can't help but wonder how things would have been different, if he hadn't been killed in

Korea. Or, if I had just stayed here and met someone else maybe, and gotten married, you know? Like you did, with Arthur. And had a good *full* life."

Mrs. Bundle winced slightly because her friend had simply forgotten how close to home those words were on this day, of all days. She was silent, trying to control herself, as they drove along, her own eyes involuntarily filling with tears.

Althea saw the emotions Mrs. Bundle's was holding back. "What is it, L?"

"Well," she said, her voice wavering, "it's just so strange that we're talking about this today, of all days." Her eyes glistened and she looked down at her left hand gripping the steering wheel *and* the worn wedding band she still wore after all these many years.

"June 25th!! Oh, Gawdy! L!" Althea sniffled. "Oh, dear, I can't believe it! I'm so sorry. How callous of me not to remember!"

"Oh, no, really. That's okay, luv—one of us feeling bad is enough. *I* should be comforting you. But, it is bittersweet for me. I can't help but remember—with great joy, mind you. June 25th will always be a special day for me, filled with lots of wonderful memories."

"The day you and Arthur were married. I was there."

"Of course you were! You were my maid of honor." She breathed, as though welcoming in spring air. "It was such a gorgeous day! Bright, bright sun, the flowers in the back yard were beautiful! It was the most glorious day of my life." She paused to remember, then shrugged her shoulders in resignation. "And, no one, I can assure you, will *ever* measure up to that man."

"I remember how ecstatic the both of you were that day. He was good to you. And you, to him." They had reached the Herder's parking lot and Althea reached for the passenger door handle, then paused. "I can understand why you say no one will ever measure up to Arthur. You had a wonderful life together. That's rather how I feel…about how it *would* have been with Chauncey."

Mrs. Bundle put a hand out, motioning her friend to stay a moment longer. "Allie, I want to say something to you. I hope you will take it in the spirit of best friend to best friend."

Althea, knowing advice was coming, opened her mouth to protest, then closed it. She nodded. "Shoot! I can take it!"

Mrs. Bundle smiled lovingly and drew in her breath. "Well, dear… just don't burn your bridges! What I mean to say is…you *never* know who might be waiting on the other side of that bridge. And, the other thing I want to say is….it's *never* too late to be happy. *Never* too late. You can still find love." Her friend sniggered and put her hand up in disapproval, rejecting the idea. "Wait! Don't laugh!" Mrs. Bundle said in response to her friend's guffaw. "You know, Chauncey would want to see you happy."

Althea's eyes filled with emotion again; the suppressed feelings rendered her unable to respond.

In the softest of voices, Mrs. Bundle urged, "Just…keep an open mind…in his memory." She paused a moment to let the words sink in. Then her voice brightened and she chuckled to her old mate. "Besides! Think about it. It could be a hoot! And, if it means expanding your horizons at this stage of your life, who's to say it isn't the right thing to do—for you? There just might be the perfect someone out there waiting for the other perfect someone," she pointed, "as special as *you*. You've got to grab onto the surfboard and ride the wave!"

Their eyes locked in understanding.

"And *that's* why I call you my best friend." Althea said; the corners of her mouth slowly turned up and she smiled brilliantly.

They gave each other a quick hug and Mrs. Bundle laughed, "End of sermon, girl! See you in a few hours!"

Chapter Twenty-Two

Prepare for Battle, Mrs. Bundle

"Call to order! This emergency meeting is called to order!" Armand Limpert's odious voice rang out with unnecessary intensity as he put the heavy gavel down and glared at the Board members in front of him. His breath was labored; it was obvious the last half-hour's activities up and down the stairs had seriously taxed his large frame. He stared stonily at the group as they quietly settled in, steadily tap-tapping the gavel with the precise menacing rhythm an overzealous cop might execute with his blackjack.

Mrs. Bundle had an inkling that Armand *might* have partaken of one or two martinis before the evening's meeting; from her view, his brow was sweaty and his heaving chest seemed to be on the verge of erupting. True to form, he was already wrathful and sarcastic in his manner toward the room of Directors. His reading glasses were balanced in a superior way at the end of his nose and, as he looked down the long expanse at the quiet group, he scowled and exclaimed haughtily, "Well, this is a fine *mess* we've got ourselves into!"

The group had adjourned to the second floor conference room after having taken a quick tour of the third floor, where Louis and Mrs. Bundle showed them the roof damage. Together, Mrs. Bundle and Louis summarized all the events occurring that morning, including their collective decision to have Carl Andersen provide the temporary repair work to encapsulate the hole in the roof, a job already completed. Then, Louis sat down at the back of the conference room and unobtrusively took notes for the meeting's minutes.

As though he relished every thunderous sound of his booming voice, Armand continued, "I *can't* for the *life* of me think how we're going to get the town out of this *disaster!*"

Mrs. Bundle fidgeted in her chair like a race horse at the gate, then said coolly, "Armand, please. I frankly don't believe it's as bad a situation as you are trying to portray. Let's look at this calmly."

"Well, my dear woman. Think about this. Look at what we are now faced with. How do you expect this illustrious group of Pillson's finest," his eyes slashed like razors across the faces in front of him, "to come up with a solution for the Library *now?* Now that we're not only in the red financially, but also faced with an *uninhabitable* structure?"

As usual, straitlaced Sarah Church seemed quietly enthralled with Armand's every word. "Here, here!" she meekly exclaimed fervently in her very small voice and gave a pale, dry smile to her fearless leader.

Ellie Waterhouse, thankfully always the voice of reason, asked, "Are things really that bad? I don't think so. I think if we put our heads together, we can solve this without a lot of angst."

Althea said, "I for one don't think things are that bad, really!"

Watson DeVille raised a docile hand. Armand chose to ignore him, looking directly over his bald head at the rest of the Board. "What I can't for the *life* of me understand is, why some of you can't see the writing on the wall here? This building is *doomed*. It's an obsolescent *nightmare*. It's passé and we need to *move on!*"

Watson continued to raise his hand, and a miniature "Yip!" could be heard from below the table.

Armand turned on Watson, who nearly jumped out of his skin. With a grand groan, he complained, "*What is it*, Watson? And, really, must you bring that Bichon *bitch* with you every time you attend a board meeting? It's really *quite* improper."

Hurt (and was that rage, Mrs. Bundle wondered?) flashed over Watson's fragile countenance like a sharp blade, his deportment momentarily shattered, but he courageously pushed on. "Well… now, emm….yes, I really do. Regarding the state of affairs here at the library, Armand, I *do* believe there is some merit in exploring other options. Wouldn't it be prudent to–?"

Armand gave an exasperated moan. "*Really*, Watson. What other options do we have? We have no money. We have no resources. We are charged by our town fathers with finding an inexpensive solution or closing the library. Period. End of story."

Watson sat forward, leaning over his portly abdomen, and reached his meticulous, chubby hands up to straighten an already flawless bowtie. He drew in a deep breath, clearly upset by this colleague's lack of social grace, and gave a soft, "Emmm, *ahem!*" He wanted to object but he was too shy—or intimidated, no doubt. The tubby tweed-suited professor's twin jowls trembled with trepidation. "Oh, never mind," he uttered dejectedly. He looked down at the hardwood table resignedly, then sat back in his chair, defeated. From below, an imperceptible whimper could be heard coming from the quaking Twinkles.

Althea, on the other hand, was not as easy quarry for Armand Limpert. She spoke up, "If the Chairman would be so kind…," she paused, "Mrs. Bundle and I have been brainstorming all day, and I would ask that you give her the floor." She looked inquiringly around the table at the rest of the Board, "And, I would also request, of course, your cooperation and attention, too, at this time so that she can explain our thoughts and her ideas in detail."

Armand opened his mouth to begin another rant but she gave him a fierce look and simply said, "*Parliamentary* procedure. Shall I put my request in motion form? I'll be happy to do that."

He slowly closed his mouth and she gave a confident nod, and all eyes turned toward Mrs. Bundle.

"Well, simply put….Althea and I have come up with a plan of action."

Ellie Waterhouse's eyes sparkled. "A *plan* of *action*! Oh, that sounds lovely."

Mrs. Bundle turned dramatically and pointed to the shrouded object on the easel (covered by a piece of muslin) beside her.

"This," she said expectantly, "this *wonderful* item right here… is going to save the library!"

She removed the muslin with gusto and drama. As if a firecracker went off underneath their seats, they all jumped, then rose up as one from their chairs to get a better look at the richly painted scene. Keen interest was replaced by confusion; they all registered varied reactions.

There was a rush of wind as Armand hurried past Mrs. Bundle to be the first to witness the painting at close hand. "*Where* did you get this?" he asked suspiciously.

Watson toddled behind him, removed his glasses and looked immediately at the lower right hand corner, then stood back and inspected the painting. "It's….quite old!"

Ellie exclaimed, "Why, it's *beautiful*! How wonderful! Can this *really* help us?"

"Oh, my heavens." Sarah Church straightened her prim skirt and sat down, content to wait for an explanation.

Amidst the "ooh's," "aah's," and pointed questions, Mrs. Bundle tried as best she could to continue. "Louis and I found it this morning. In the strangest of places. *Here*, if you can believe it." She pointed upward, "Under the eaves! Upstairs! We discovered it as we were reviewing the damage."

"This is preposterous! Why wasn't I called right away?" Armand asked indignantly.

"Well, Louis and I discussed this, Armand, and we wanted to present it, here tonight, to everyone—at the same time—in an organized, professional fashion. And, in point of fact, you *were* called immediately, along with the rest of the Board. Louis called everyone this morning after its discovery to ask for the special meeting, didn't he? Hence, why we are all here tonight!"

"This," Armand snarled, "is *outrageous*! Not to mention a lot of hooey! What's *really* is going on here?"

Althea cautioned, "Be careful, there, Armand. There's no cloak and dagger here. Why don't you calm down, and I'm sure Mrs. Bundle will tell everyone."

But he would not stop. "It's *all* very interesting, isn't it? And so cozy! We're on the threshold of closing the Library, and all of a sudden, you say you've come up with a *plan*. And, that *this*…" he looked down his nose at the blameless little painting, "worthless piece of *trash*—I, of all people, would know—will somehow 'save the day'?"

Mrs. Bundle stood patiently, waiting for his tirade to end.

He wasn't done yet; his laugh was scornful as he growled, "Tell me. How *do* you propose to make *this*…" he pointed as though to a dishrag, "solve our dilemma?"

"Armand," she looked past him at the rest of the waiting group, "and valued Board members, please hear me out. It's *not* worthless, not by a long shot."

"Well, if anyone would know worthless or otherwise, it would be me." the Chairman said, "Didn't I run an art gallery for two decades before coming here?"

She nodded acquiescently, "That very well may be, Armand, but the jury's still out on the painting's value; historically, intrinsically, or otherwise. Please, Armand, sit down and compose yourself before you burst a vessel, won't you? I will be most happy to explain."

As everyone settled back into their respective seat, Mrs. Bundle continued, "Rather than automatically discount it as worthless, I would prefer to think this painting is a gem of a find. Why, we all are the first to lay eyes on it, I daresay, since the year it was painted! And, that, date, my friends, was the year 1861! If we are lucky, an expert in this particular field may say it's worth a fortune, which will make the enterprise I have yet to share with you even more interesting!"

Although Watson DeVille was battered and bruised by Armand's verbal barbs, he whispered gently, "A fortune, you say? Really, now, that would be…*magnificent!*" His voice articulated the last word with such softness and grace, it was as though an angel had heralded it from heaven. Watson's round head bobbed up and down with renewed eagerness. "Quite…*magnificent!*"

Sarah Church sighed and rolled her plain, pious eyes, then simpered pathetically, "I tend to be realistic about these things. I agree with Armand. What kind of fortune could that old painting bring to us?"

"Who knows? That, dear Board members, has yet to be determined! However, more importantly, when used to address our immediate problem, it can be the *springboard* to a good amount of money—possibly thousands–if we plan things right. It can be the foremost reason we were ultimately successful in returning the Pillson Public Library to its original glory!"

There were murmurs of consideration from the group, and she proceeded to methodically lay out the plan she and Althea had devised.

"If we move quickly, she told them with pure inspiration, "it could be the biggest event Pillsonites has ever seen!"

<hr />

It took some convincing, but Mrs. Bundle and Althea finally got their plan through.

After much discussion, the vote came down to three in favor of the Art Festival Plan (Mrs. Bundle, Althea, and the ever-positive Ellie Waterhouse) and three opposed (Armand Limpert, Sarah Church, and sadly, the wretchedly intimidated Watson DeVille, who had clearly buckled under Armand's tremendous pressure).

Enter the hero of the day: Louis Montembeau, who cast the deciding ballot, putting the vote *just* over the top.

Of course, there had been an outrageous abundance of drama. At the three-three tie, Armand had cried foul when he wasn't able to swing Ellie Waterhouse to his side, declaring a "hung board" with no resolution, thereby ruling with a heavy gavel that the item "would be tabled until further investigation was completed." However, the denouement unfolded in a much different way as Mrs. Bundle (who had the Trustee Rules and Regulations Handbook already opened to the exact page), read clearly (and with shameless enthusiasm) from the Board of Directors rules:

"Yes, here it is." she read distinctly, "'Part 5, Section C, paragraph 4: During an official board meeting containing a quorum of Library Trustees, any vote on the agenda shall be handled as follows: In the event a three-three tie, and proven to be in the interest of harmony and what is *best for the library's operation*," she enunciated, "the current Head Librarian will be responsible for casting the final deciding vote.'"

Armand's face fell as Louis raised his hand in the air, smiling as though possessed by a hyena, and said, "I vote *in favor* of the Art Festival plan."

It was decided to approach the Pillsonville Select Board immediately and request an emergency town meeting to be held within the week to determine if the town would get behind the event, or not. Their decision would be crucial; everyone knew this.

Althea and Mrs. Bundle were elated. As the group slowly disbanded, the two women stood at the beautiful painting on the easel and gibbered quietly back and forth. They moved back to the table and sat down, packing away their folders and other paraphernalia, busily discussing all the things they would need to accomplish prior to the special Town Meeting.

"Now for the hard work ahead of us!" Althea beamed, giving the table area in front of her one last brush, then standing, moving across the room quickly to converse with Ellie Waterhouse before she left.

Mrs. Bundle had begun to rise from her chair, but before she realized it, Armand was at her elbow, and she was forced to sit again.

His heavy breath reeked of alcohol and cloves. She recoiled sharply and asked, "What is it, Armand?"

His smile was pure evil as he snarled under his breath, his voice barely audible, "You think you've won, don't you, *Letitia dear*? There's still the Selectmen's Board, though. They'll *never* go for this. You really can't think you can get your foolish little plan past them, can you? They will *cut you up*," his eyes were menacingly close, his teeth clenched in a grim line, "and *spit you out* like so much dogmeat!"

Another less assertive person might have been unsettled, but she remembered her exchange with him yesterday. *He's a bully*, she thought, *like Hammer Lovelace in my dream*. Realizing only she had been privy his nasty comments, she wasn't surprised at his anger. Chocking it up to his inebriated state, she smiled back at him as disinterestedly as possible and said loudly, "Ex-*cuse* me? Would you be *so kind*, Armand, as to repeat that *lovely* thought for our group?"

All activity stopped as everyone watched her and Armand. He leaned in menacingly above her, violating her personal space, but she didn't back down. Then he laughed, moved deliberately and gallantly to the side, flourishing his hand in mock politeness as though inviting her to rise from her chair and move past him.

Everyone had finished gathering their things together and he addressed the tired group one last time, continuing to complain aloud. "This plan will fail, I promise you that! We're going to be the laughingstock of the village—not to mention the whole bloody county—if we try to do this! We're going to fall flat on our faces and we'll be even deeper in the financial hole. There's too little time, and who's going to want to do all the work! I hope you all know we're going to be met with ridicule! *Ridicule!* I, for one, can't be a part of something destined to fail! I cannot support this—"

"*Mister* Limpert!" Althea's shout from across the room caught him entirely off guard; he was temporarily stunned. Her green eyes were like fiery cabochons; she visually bored two holes into his body as she yelled, "Would you *please*…**knock it off**!"

The usual "friendly-voice-of-reason" had been transformed into a woman not to be messed with—on any level; she looked as surprised as the rest of the group.

Very softly and almost apologetically, she continued, "Excuse me, everyone. I'm very sorry—but I really just can't keep my Yankee temper quiet any longer." She cast her eyes toward heaven and whispered, "Sorry!", then turned and faced Armand directly, her eyes flashing with unrestrained, unmitigated fury as they all looked on. "I have had just about enough! Of *you*!"

He blinked but didn't budge; his lower lip jutted out like a spoiled baby. She walked slowly and deliberately across the room until she was standing directly in front of him.

She continued, "And your threats, too! *You*—are a sanctimonious blowfish! A slithering subterranean!"

She roughly wiped a trace of spittle from her lips as her words hit him like the bristles of a broom: *Fwap!* "Good *grief*! Either jump on board or leave, Armand! You've done everything you can to try to stop any progress with the library, every step of the way. *Why?* Why make everything so difficult? You throw your weight around here like no one I've ever seen! You've alienated everyone." Althea moved in closer and stared him dead in the eyes. "Nonetheless, you have *not* succeeded. Why? Because you haven't seen what can happen when *we* put *our* minds to something! A big overgrown bully, that's what you are!" (*Fwap, fwap!*)

His squinting, bloodshot eyes gave him the appearance of a rabid rodent; his mouth opened, ready to fire back with full battle munitions, but she held up an open hand directly in front of his face with nary a quarter inch to spare. "*Ehhhh*! No! N*ot a word*! I've listened to you all night, complaining, intimidating, and acting like a *know-it-all*! Now *you* let me finish! You just wait and see what really *is* possible when people put their minds to do something good! If you've got one brain cell left in that cabbage head of yours, you will jump on board—either that or *steer clear* of us! We *will* get the job done, one way or another! Despite you, and all your negativity! You just watch out, Mr. *Ar-mand Lim-pert*, because, if you're going to try to screw this up, you're in for one excruciatingly bumpy ride."

His face had turned to ashen, his eyes bright wine-red, like hollow burning anthracite ready to combust; he tried his best to recover. Laughing tensely, he straightened his tie around his bulging neck, moved back a few feet, then leaned over and muttered something conspiratorially to his only friend in the room, Sarah Church. For once, though, she did not support him; she sat stock-still, afraid to move one inch, and coughed lightly, eyes downcast. If embarrassment was a pill, she had swallowed the whole bottle.

Slowly and deliberately, he turned back to Althea, and a ruthless grin materialized on his face. He puffed up his chest in machismo bravado. "Well, if you *think* you can threaten me, Althea Swain, I'll have my attorney—"

"*Ehhhhh!*" She stopped him again; she wasn't done yet. She reached over and tapped him ever-so-lightly on his chest, the lightest feather of a touch that seemed to strangely reverberate like an earthquake throughout the room. "Armand, I would be *very careful* about mentioning anything about attorneys...."

Totally taken aback by her guts, her unadulterated raw nerve, the big man stumbled clumsily backward. "Good God, woman, have you lost your mind? You *dare* to talk to me like a common-—"

Mrs. Bundle, who was in awe, knew there was no stopping her now. *Go for it, girl!* she thought.

Althea's voice was barely a whisper, so quiet, so intense that everyone had to lean in to hear her words. "Be afraid, Armand. You're *lower* than a worm. A mealy-mouthed grub has more class."

He had begun to sputter like a geyser ready to gush, spurts of incoherent words coming out all in a jumble. "Why, I! Ahh—I—I—ah...*errrgggghhhh!*"

Her words were like crystal chandelier prisms shattering on a glass surface. "I want you to hear this *loud* and *clear*." She glared at him, whispering, "You tell your attorney..." she leaned toward him, her nose almost touching his, "..the *next time* your grubby paws come anywhere near my knee..." he held up a shocked hand and shook his head vehemently, unable to speak, "Oh, that's right! My *knee*! The *next time* you grab at me under *this* table or anywhere else near my universe…" she stopped and squeezed her thumb tightly together with her fingers, "you can kiss those pathetic family jewels **good--bye**!"

Sarah Church almost fainted.

An inexorable twitter erupted like loose marbles from Ellie Waterhouse and, with a quick, frenzied wave good-bye, she disappeared in a mad dash out the doorway.

Watson scurried after her without one sound. Twinkles literally scampered behind him like a bouncing cotton ball, puny tail held high and nails clicking on the slippery hardwood floor.

Louis Montembeau, conversely, was captivated, as though watching the most exquisite drama, an ardent and devoted fan of this Sarah Bernhardt-caliber performance. He sat riveted in his chair, hands and feet itching, ready to give a resounding standing ovation.

Equally, Mrs. Bundle had to hold herself back from applauding.

As time stood still, Althea continued to glare at Armand. His face was one huge, dark scowl. His wide mouth twitched like a grouper fish and then, without a word, he simply turned abruptly, wisely choosing to pick his next battle very carefully with this formidable opponent. Without a sound, his round bubblehead swiveled like a beet-red siren and he speedily retreated from the room. He pushed his way past a wide-eyed Louis Montembeau; all that was heard was his heavy feet clattering down the hallway.

Althea sat down, bushed from battle, but followed his exit with one last triumphant glower for good measure.

Sarah Church sniffled, gathered her things hastily, and left the room.

As they listened to her mousy footsteps following his (as he took the steps down two at a time), Mrs. Bundle turned to her friend and gave her a double "thumbs up." With admiration in her voice, she said, "Well done, Allie. I couldn't have done it better myself—other than," she said tongue-in-cheek, "maybe a good kick to the shins!"

Chapter Twenty-Three

Dakota Squibb

"I'm really not sure *what* came over me. I just…blew!" Althea heaved a long sigh as she and Mrs. Bundle walked down the long sidewalk to their cars. "Too much coffee, maybe? And now, all I really want is a nice, hot bath and a good night's sleep!"

Both were worn out but exhilarated at their accomplishment that evening.

"Amen to that! It's been a very, very long day. It's hard to imagine that it was just this morning that Louis called…and this glorious day unfolded!"

Unexpectedly, they came upon a darkly handsome, older gentleman briskly being led by a large, very rambunctious German Shepherd.

Rather than just give a friendly nod and pass by (as was the usual custom while strolling on a summer evening in Pillsonville), this tall stranger boldly came to a stop, then removed a nattily brimmed, beige, "golf bucket" hat, and bowed grandly.

From his lowly position he looked up and gracefully effused, "Good evening, fair ladies!"

Lacking an appropriate response for this throwback to gentlemanly chivalry, both women stood speechless until Althea found her voice and muttered words under her breath, first, low enough for Mrs. Bundle to discern something to the effect of, "That's the silliest looking (*undetectable mumble*) hat!", then sufficiently loud enough for the oddly formal man to hear her exclaim, "For the love of Pete!"

Without missing a beat, the stranger replaced his bucket cap jauntily on his salt-and-pepper (mostly salt) hair, straightened up to his full six-foot two-inch height and pronounced with unconstrained pomp and circumstance, "Dakota Squibb, dear ladies, *at* your service!"

His overall appearance was lanky and lean, his musculature still firm for his age, which Mrs. Bundle guesstimated to be around seventy or so. He wore a plaid button-down, short-sleeved shirt and dark khaki pants, and his casual brown shoes were splattered with teeny tiny bits of colorful spots, clearly resembling paint splatters. He had an artsy, unconventional look about him, fresh, almost *avant-garde* in appearance. *Why,* she thought, *this must be…the new bachelor in town!*

He pointed to his large, happy dog. "This is Howard — Howie for short. We've just moved in — over at the Falls," he waved toward Pillson Falls, "at the Elliot's place." His voice was somewhat affected with a slight accent that was unrecognizable to Mrs. Bundle's ears. *Hmmm,* she thought, *definitely foreign-sounding, but from where?* Foreign to a Pillsonite could be anywhere from Peoria to Poughkeepsie to Peru.

"*Squibb?* That's your name?" Althea sniffed, her nose upturned as though getting a whiff of something odious, and once again, her usually-friendly demeanor stiffened into barely a semblance of a welcome for the comely gentleman. True, the name "Squibb" spoken by anyone wasn't the most attractive ear candy, but the way Althea said it made it resound with a loathsome ring.

Mrs. Bundle gave her friend a slight poke and under her breath, warned, "Althea….," meanwhile smiling broadly at the new resident. In her own usual forthright manner, she stepped boldly forward and offered her hand. "Welcome, Mr. Squibb! Welcome to our fair village!" She laughed as Howie bounded forth and voraciously lapped her hand. "Yes, you, too, Howie! Hey, now! No baths, please!"

As she eyeballed Mr. Squibb with interest, she couldn't help but notice his striking locks: curly wisps of wiry hair that escaped from beneath the natty golf hat. *Rather long by most standards but very well-groomed*, she reasoned, *and certainly, a full mane of hair on a man his age was really quite....hmmm, yes*, she decided pleasantly: *it was really quite handsome.* Tim Scott hadn't been far off the mark! She said warmly, "I'm Lettie Bundle, and this is my friend—and *your* new neighbor—Althea Swain!"

"Al-*theee*-aaaaaahhhh." Mr. Squibb's gaze moved immediately and he said her name as though it were encased in solid gold, the three-syllable utterance imbedded into a beautiful, ornamental jewel. His eyes danced as he took into view the full-figured, attractive woman. His smile was charming. "Please, ladies, call me Dakota."

My, my, thought Mrs. Bundle, *this is interesting, isn't it?* She poked again, discreetly, and gave Althea a pleading look to acknowledge this *very* intriguing man.

Althea's lukewarm attempt to be borderline polite (due only to good upbringing) caused her to reach out a milquetoast-limp hand. Meanwhile, she swiveled her attractive head swiftly back around toward Mrs. Bundle (who found the motion quite reminiscent of that famous *Exorcist* scene), and gave her a good, hard glare. It was a fair warning glare, one that told her friend in bold letters, "You will pay!"

Mrs. Bundle smiled back in the calmest of manner, thinking, *Oh, if looks could kill!*

Mr. Squibb, on the other hand, had not taken his youthful, gleaming eyes off Althea and his look was pure, open friendliness and—what was that—a playful, impish gleam?

He said excitedly, "Ye-*es*, I thought so! That *was* you I saw peeking through the backyard trees and bushes. How *do* you do?"

"Peeking? *Peeking?* Of all the...! I wasn't—I *do not* peek!"

He reached out and patted her hand, his voice refined and smooth. "Althea...I'm just saying it's a *pleasure* to meet you now, *face-to-face*, as they say. And, to hear that *lovely* voice again, too! I believe that *was* you, this morning, wasn't it? Those melodious exclamations that I heard coming straight across from your backyard to mine, *wafting* through the atmosphere like a trumpeting goose?" He trailed his hand through the air, spiraling upward.

Uh-oh, Mrs. Bundle thought, as she watched her friend's face go pale.

Fresh from her unpleasant encounter with Armand, Althea's fuse was undeniably very short. Her round face could have been sculpted from granite, immovable and emotionless, with tiny fissures of annoyance and impatience cracking its foundation.

As though completely blind to her displeasure, he continued, "No? Most remarkably, I could have *sworn* it was you—or someone with an astonishing resemblance to you—that was within such close proximity to my house at first morning's light. In point of fact, I could hear it *all* the way across—about a hundred-odd feet, it was. If, and I say *if*, that was you, fine lady, then I must congratulate you!" Her eyes bulged as he continued, "*Yes*, congratulate! I tell you, what an extraordinarily colorful vocabulary! And *such* a healthy set of lungs you have!" His bright blue eyes twinkled deviously behind the finely creased, tanned face as he genially patted Howie with one hand and pointed directly at her ample chest with the other.

Mrs. Bundle looked on, thinking, *Why, he's trying to be playful with her! Flirting! Very naughty you are, Mr. Dakota Squibb*, she observed, noting she couldn't help but be captivated.

Althea (usually the poster child for affability) had become transformed into a massive time bomb, so thoroughly and obviously annoyed with this Squibb fellow that all she could do was cover her chest with splayed fingers and counter, "Yes, well, *Squibb*, you just leave my lungs out of it!" He chortled, eyes dancing, as she sputtered out of control, "Not that it's any of your business, but *of course* that was me, you nit—" She stopped herself from using a thoroughly unladylike insult, "Furthermore, I'll tell you why I was yell—" (stopped again) "—why I was so upset! Did you know *your dog* got into *my* garbage this morning? And didn't he make a big fine mess, I might add. You might further like to know that it was a mess that *I* had to clean up!" She drew in a large mouthful of air. "*Good* grief!"

Mrs. Bundle patted her friend's arm in hopes that it would calm her down. *Hoo-boy!* she thought, *he's really hit a nerve with her!* For what it was worth (and from her own first impressions), Mrs.

Bundle thought he seemed lovely. *Cultured, articulate, pleasant, and attractive, what one might call "the whole package,"* she observed and, remembering Weezy's comments, she thought, *definitely not an axe murderer.*

Althea persisted, "How he found his way *inside* my shed is really quite peculiar, seeing as I know the door was shut *and* we have a dog ordinance here in Pillson. Has anyone told you you're supposed to keep him on a *leash* at all times? And where, might I also ask," she pointed accusingly at his empty hands, "is your *clean-up bag?*"

Mrs. Bundle squeezed tighter this time; this was not her friend's finest hour and, still trying to warm the frigid air around them, she explained. "Althea's...not herself tonight, Dakota. She's...had a very busy day today. Uh-huh! She's got a lot on her mind...*and* we've just come from a pretty stressful meeting." She pointed toward the Pillson Library and smiled brightly at him.

"I'm fine!" Althea grumbled, "I just don't like stepping in p– –"

Mrs. Bundle interrupted, "Oh, *pshaw!*" She smiled at Dakota, "Really! Don't you mind her—she's usually a barrel of laughs!"

"Really?" Dakota said hopefully, looking for a sign from Althea that all might be forgiven, but her lips were firmly pressed together, her eyes a dead stare.

Covertly, Mrs. Bundle did something she hadn't done since they were schoolgirls—she gave a solid, hard pinch to Althea's backside, the cause and effect of which was a smothered yelp from Althea.

Mrs. Bundle quickly changed the prickly subject of dog mess, asking with wide-eyed innocence, "So-o-o-o, Dakota! How do you like your new digs? I understand you're an *artiste.*"

He smiled. "Yes, *artiste*—how very engaging when you say it, Lettie! To answer your kind question, I *love* it here! This is a journey I've wanted to make for some time and it's absolutely wonderful to finally *be* here. Just marvelous! And," he gave Althea a sidelong glance, "I've met so many *nice* people already."

"Oh, that's wonderful," Mrs. Bundle said. "I'm happy to hear that."

Undeterred, he turned back to Althea. "Oh! *Al-thee-aahhh...,*" he stretched her name again; honey was dripping off every vowel.

Straightening up to fully face her impenetrable, quietly-seething figure, he asked gently, "May I be so bold as to call you Althea, dear lady? It's such a *lovely* name, so very….feminine!" He paused, as she swallowed a ready response, and then skillfully continued pouring on the charm, "*Especially* because we are neighbors and, no doubt, we'll be seeing *a lot* of each other. I...take it there is no *Mister* Swain?"

Althea looked at him as though he had not two but three heads.

Even Mrs. Bundle had to admit she was impressed with this man's perseverance in the face of being proffered such a cold shoulder and she offered willingly, "No, there's no Mister Swain."

Ignoring Althea's shudder and seemingly totally unaffected by her unresponsiveness, Dakota persisted, "Say, Althea, I'll make you a promise! *I,*" he smiled deeply into her flashing green eyes as though she were the only woman on the planet, "will corral this big *lug,*" his craggy face took on the look of an errant school boy and he held back the energetic Shepard, "and *we* will both promise that *he,*" Howie's huge, long tongue spread outward very widely at just the right moment, causing the dog's lips to pull back into a huge, very friendly, doggie smile, "will be a very good boy from now on!" He reached out an elegant hand in truce and said, "Deal?"

Althea sniffed and her shoulders relaxed just a hair. She blew air past her upper lip, causing her bangs to shoot up into the air and then drift slowly back down to her forehead. She said, mostly in resignation and utter weariness, "Oh, *good grief!*"

To her favor, it was a most feeble attempt at cordiality and she muttered, "Um...uhh. Okay, yes!" as she fumbled with her keys, readying her exit. Then, holding her fists at her sides, she said through clenched teeth (her wide lips morphed into paper-thin strips), "Well, I guess, in the interest of being neighborly. Mind you, *Squibb,* I guess it won't hurt to try to forget those past transgressions and start anew."

She gave him a quick warning look. "Of course, time will tell. As they say," she sniffed again, "the proof is in the *pudding.*"

Oh, mercy, Mrs. Bundle thought as she gave her friend one last very discreet jab in the small of her back and smiled affably, "Yes, Dakota, I'm sure it will be fine. Just *fine!*"

"Good! I look forward to mending fences!" His eyes sparkled like brilliant sapphires and he deftly reached over, grabbed Althea's hand before she had a chance to protest and made the expertly formal gesture of kissing it, his lips barely brushing her fingers.

"*Oh!*" Thoroughly appalled, Althea quickly drew her arm back as though she had been stung by a killer bee and protested, "Okay! Really! *Enough* already!"

She held the offended limb away from her side, as though broken and damaged.

He chuckled richly, his friendly face in complete euphoria, and then turned back to Mrs. Bundle. "It's been a *pleasure* meeting you, Lettie."

"Likewise, Dakota!" Mrs. Bundle had all she could do to hold back her glee; the hilarity of the scene had been almost too much for her to handle. *Why, by all appearances it seemed as though he was smitten with Althea!* And Althea, well…it was obvious he had definitely made an impression, although Mrs. Bundle wasn't sure if it was a very *good* one or a very, very *bad* one. *Oh, my Lord*, she thought, *I think my best friend may have met her match, to be sure.*

Mr. Squibb tilted the casual bucket hat jauntily at an angle (a little red feather tucked into the band was pointing cheerfully skyward), ceremoniously saluted the two women and, as he sauntered home in the direction of Niagra Lane (where the florescent green street sign had been altered by a clever prankster—with obviously way too much time on his hands—with a black marker, having crossed out the "N", and scrawled a large "V" over it), he could be heard sweetly whistling a tune with clarity and exactness.

It was "Goodnight, Ladies."

Chapter Twenty-Four

The Library Affair — and Other Goings-on

B efore Mrs. Bundle went to bed that night, she took a blank card out of the tin recipe box and wrote *The Library Affair and other goings-on* at the top of the card. In her fine, detailed penmanship, she jotted down the following list:

1. *Painting—who is Conny? Sweetness?*
2. *MDCCLV What, who, why?*
3. *Tuddy's*
4. *Viola*
5. *"W" burned into the tree*
6. *Hartland Welcome Sign—with big "Wild"*
7. *Strange Coincidences? Fate?*
8. *The Dog Days of Summer—and—The Art Festival!*
9. *Where is poor Tuddsley?*
10. *Armand*

She stopped her writing and rubbed her eyes, swollen and tired from her long fatiguing day. *Was that all?* She reread the list, pausing at #8. *The Festival*, she thought. *Right.* From this moment on, with the Festival plans forming rapidly, she realized she really would not have time for anything but that; the mystery and intrigue would have to go on the back burner for now....

But, it's all so very interesting! She massaged her tired eyes again.

Cracker, who had also put in a very long day, rubbed his silky body gently against her leg. *Leave it for now,* he cat-thought kindheartedly, *for, as you always say, tomorrow is a new day.* His twisting tail wrapped around her ankle, soft fur stroking her drained and fatigued body.

She yawned loudly, "Ahhhhhhhhh!" and raised her arms above her head, stretching, then began to remove the hairpins and unweave the pile of braids atop her head. "You're right, C.C.! It's time for bed! All things considered and being equal, today has been nothing less than…downright *fantastical!*" She pulled the last pin out and the braids cascaded down her back. She shook her head and ran her long fingers through the silvery brown tresses. "And now…," she stifled another yawn, "It's time for bed!"

She picked up the card, then slipped it back into the box with the rest of the collection, placing it under "L," and leaving the top of the card sticking out above the box file just a bit. She resolved to resume her ruminating at a later date when her mind was clearer, promising herself that she would just have to make time…

She smiled. Although it was just the beginning, the kernels and threads of barebone fact were formulating, percolating inside her busy brain, and Mrs. Bundle knew what it meant for her (and her ready and willing assistant): Mystery….Adventure….and *Allure!*

That night, when she went to bed, she slept like a rock. She dreamed vividly, deeply of new and wonderful possibilities, and of hope for the future. She dreamed of success and discovery and surprise—and excitement and intrigue….all handled with ease and remarkable intelligence and aplomb.

Oh, what a dream it was!

Chapter Twenty-five

The Village Listens

Calling in every favor and using every persuasive civic appeal they could muster, Althea and Mrs. Bundle went to work. Mrs. Bundle's urgent call to each Select Board member was successful; it was agreed that, in addition to the monthly Select Board meeting scheduled for the following Monday on June 30th, there would also be an important addition to the agenda. By the end of the following day, the "Events" sandwich board sign had been placed on the Town Hall front lawn. The sign's usual Select Board meeting notice had been amended to include an additional message written in big red letters: "'**Emergency** agenda item. Library Trustees will present a plan of immediate action to SAVE the library from being CLOSED!!! *PLEASE, PLEASE ATTEND!*'"

Then, the two women spent the good part of the next two days on the phone urging people to attend the following Monday evening's Select Board meeting. Word spread fast throughout the little community that all residents should attend the meeting for a special town vote to mobilize for some kind of "special event," the details of which would be discussed at length that night.

By the time the meeting night came, the large upstairs community room at Town Hall was jammed to the rafters, the turnout ranging from concerned citizens to the just downright curious.

The Board of Trustees sat in a straight line of chairs on the stage. It was an eclectic group, to be sure: Watson DeVille sitting erect and proper in his genteel, formal attire; Ellie Waterhouse looking frayed and frazzled from her busy day of mothering and carpooling; the priggish Sarah Church hovering *just* a bit too closely to an impassive, surprisingly quiet Armand Limpet, who himself seemed none too happy to be present. Louis Montembeau, his wiry body as taut and tense as a violin "E" string, sat long-leggedly perched, like a chirping cricket, on the edge of his chair. Althea and Mrs. Bundle sat side by side, quietly conferring while waiting anxiously to begin their presentation after the town business was finished.

The hall was bursting at the seams and the bustle and hum intensified as the wall clock's minute hand ticked closer to 6:30 p.m. As everyone was settling into their seats, Weezy Bunton separated herself from the crowd and scurried up to the stage, face flushed and all aflutter. She motioned feverishly to Mrs. Bundle, who left her seat and knelt down, leaning into the large purple drapes on the side of the stage to hear Weezy's hoarse whispering above the din.

"Oh, Lettie! This is *really* rich! The word's out on the—" (she made quote signs with her fingers) "'—*mysterious painting behind the wall!*' I'm so excited I'm about to pee my pants! How come you didn't tell me? Lord A'mighty, Lettie!" Weezy's chest heaved with anticipation of the melodrama that was about to unfold. "I mean, this just puts the icing on the cake!" Every steel gray curlicue on the top of her head stood on end like a ramrod, and her huge face had a rosy, eager hue. Any attempt for Mrs. Bundle to get a word in edgewise failed miserably, as usual, as Weezy continued on without so much as a hiccup. "Yup! I told Horace, I said, 'I *knew* somethin' was up t'other day when you come into Herder's!' You and Althea with your heads together like two coconuts! I knew! Then, when you called last night to make sure Horace and I'd be at the meeting to do our civic duty and asked if I could help out afterwards….well, this is just *too* special!"

She rubbed her ample beak as though it were a magic lamp, snorted with all the elegance of a dodo bird, and chortled on. "They couldn't keep a lid on it at Town Hall, and now the word's spread like poison ivy. A painting! *Wowzer*! Great turnout, ain't it? I did my part, called everyone I could think of. We're all waiting for the show! Hope you got a good plan up your sleeve." She paused, her lungs heaving from a combination of overuse and exhilaration and then continued, "That painting—I heard from Barbra that it's an antique worth maybe thousands—How much *you* think it's worth?"

Given that this was the first opportunity she had had to speak, Mrs. Bundle rushed in with, "Why—no one knows!"

Weezy jabbed a fat thumb toward the Select Board table where the all-knowing Town Clerk Barbra D'Acunet (the one and the same "Barbra" who had very expediently passed along the scuttlebutt about the found painting), sat at the long table with the rest of the Select Board, her pen and paper ready to take the meeting's minutes.

"*She* said it's the biggest thing that's happened to Pillson, yessiree, since Sylvia Windsong hit the Megabucks. This could be history in the makin', Lettie! Heck, I even brought the kids tonight to see this one!" She pointed and waved a beefy arm in the direction within the crowd where her four cherubs sat waiting with wide-eyed anticipation beside her gigantic husband, Horace. "It's good for 'em to see how government works first hand, in the trenches!"

"Well, that's why we're all here tonight," Mrs. Bundle smiled and said, "Weezy, I really should go…."

Weezy rubbed her large hands together in glee, and whispered "Gaw, look at ol' Archie! He's fit to be tied! He don't know what to make o' this!"

Next to Barbra sat the Head Selectman, Archie Plummer, nervously tapping his pencil, his boyish face housing its perpetual smile. He beamed at the crowd, reaching out to shake hands or wave to others too far away to touch, the consummate schmoozer. His demeanor did seem a bit jumpy tonight, somewhat unsettled, Mrs. Bundle noticed, as she watched his eyes flit from one constituent to another. She looked back at an excited Weezy who asked, "When you gonna let things rip?"

"Just keep your shirt on, Weezy, and all will be revealed later."

The gavel rapped sharply at the head table and Mrs. Bundle said, "I've got to go!"

Weezy waved good-naturedly, "You betcha! Good luck to you, Lettie! We're all behind ya!" She shivered in glee, *"Can't wait for the fireworks!"*

———————•—•—•———————

One hour later, after the town business had been taken care of, Archie Plummer turned the meeting over to the Library Trustees. Tolerant waiting had turned to fidgeting as the air in the filled room became ripe with anticipation.

Mrs. Bundle took the podium and said, "Thank you all for coming out tonight," and then peered out at the huge gathering, smiling. She caught the familiar faces of countless members of the community: young and old; "well-off" to "dirt-poor," neighbors, friends from the well-known to the unassuming, quiet folks that she wagered had never attended a town meeting such as this before. Nevertheless, by the looks of the turnout, every person in front of her had one thing in common; they were all proud citizens of this village–their little world—this place they all called "home."

She nodded to the now-quiet group. "If you don't know me, my name is Lettie Bundle and, on behalf of the Library Board of Trustees, I come to you tonight with a purpose and a goal in mind. Might I start by asking by a simple show of hands, how many people here have used the Library?"

Hands shot up everywhere until finally the whole meeting hall was a sea of raised hands.

She chuckled. "That may seem like a very simple question. 'Of course,' we say, 'we've all used it!' It's a given. If you think about it, you may even recognize that we all rather take our Library for granted. It is a living, essential part of our community. And, it is free."

Murmurs of assent filled the room.

"Whatever your age, your background, your interests, your hobbies, or your life experiences, we all have *one* thing in common—the

Library. You may be a young, new member just visiting the Library for the first time. Or, you may have been coming to the Library for forty years—or more! No matter what, it's a *given* that we've all used the Library services over our lifetimes—or, at least, as long as you've resided here! Even more remarkable, we can also include the lifetimes of our predecessors, to be sure. Your uncle, grandfather, mother, or even an ancestor much farther back, may also have availed themselves of this fine facility. We have *all* needed the Library at one time or another."

She paused, then opened her arms and appealed to the crowd. "Well, now--this is the time that the Library *needs us*."

A slow murmur went through the room like the low hum of electric current. She said, "Please, let's take a look."

The lights went down, and the room became as still as the night air. On cue, Mrs. Bundle gave Althea a nod and so began the slide show, where picture by picture depicted the Pillson Library. First in the presentation was an original, very old photograph that showed the library as a relatively new building; it was magnificent. The sepia-tone image produced *"ooh's"* and *"aah's"* and people began to loosen up. Directly afterward, a present-day photo of the exterior wood trim (sadly in need of paint), much less impressive, to be sure, caused an immediate reaction of surprise from the audience.

What followed was an array of images, all of which caused sundry reactions from the crowd. Throughout the five-minute presentation, there were bursts of comments and exclamations from the audience, some anonymous, some voices recognizable, all reacting with feeling. Amidst the photos of the devastated, ravaged roof, the peeling paint and the old bathroom were other dated photographs of citizens participating in local events, book sales, meetings, and unrelated functions, all by means of the library's facilities.

"Oh, Lord, what a disaster!" were the cries when pictures were shown of the library roof damage.

"There *you* are, Ma, look!" Lonnie Macomber's distinctive voice rang out, as a photo of a much-younger, quite attractive version of Arletta Macomber at the library checkout desk graced the screen.

A couple hoots and cat-whistles followed and she cackled good-naturedly.

With the next slide, another unidentified voice shouted out, "How 'bout that, Joe? That was when you still had hair!" and was followed by lots of laughter.

"*Golly*, ain't those the same chairs and tables as is there now?"

Barbra D'Acunet cried out, "*Ohmigosh!* There's me and my Brownie troop—vintage *1975!*"

"That's our old Granny Kimball, Pops! Right there on the side by the old maple!"

It was a time for people to reminisce as the slides highlighted some of Pillson's most memorable scenes, events, and historical moments. The modern and the old combined fleetingly, joined together inexorably to show what the library had once been, and what it had become. Masterfully portrayed in this silent pictorial, it seemed their Library was like a huge, Ice-Age Mastodon trying to rear its enormous head after centuries of sleep, all without care or sustenance. There—in front of their eyes—played out the compelling impact that their little village Library had had on its community over the many, many decades, along with its current sad condition.

Rich comments continued to permeate the room like lovely lyrical notes in a symphony. It was as though the darkness throughout the room, fused with the colorful images of the slideshow, and gave everyone permission to air their feelings without reserve.

"That's old knob and tube wiring! *Gawd!* That should have been updated long ago!"

"Would you look at that, Maude! Do you remember? We met right there, in that front foyer! July of '44!"

"Mom, is that *you reading* when you were a kid like me?"

In the next slide, an elderly gentleman with fluffy, snow-white hair sat on one of the outside library garden benches, head burrowed deeply in his book, a sunlit streak catching the shine of his bowed head's balding dome.

"Ach! Dat ist my *Manny!*" Mrs. Balshemnik's distinctive voice could be heard. "How he *loves* dis liberry vhen he vas *livink!*"

"Remember that?" rang out a man's voice at the next slide, "The Amtrak wreck! Rain washed out a section of the railroad track north of Pillson—that there is when the Red Cross set up our Library as an emergency disaster center!"

"Gawdy! Ain't it a grand ol' building? Too bad it's gone to pot!"

"I guess it needs more than just a *little* TLC, don't it?"

"Look at those beautiful light fixtures! And the stained glass window! It's a historic treasure!"

Suddenly, total darkness enveloped the room as there was a slight pause. The room became quiet as the last dramatic slide was displayed.

There was a gasp of emotion from the audience.

A final close-up of the Library's massive, mahogany, double front doors framed the photo of two of the most adorable little girls holding a very large, very boldly handwritten sign. They were the Kittredge twins, Kayla and Kila, daughters of longtime residents Kevin and Karen Kittredge and known by most of the community by their remarkably identical looks and distinctive, pale-blonde, waist length braids. The twins were pointing at the sign, their faces bright, youthful, and filled with hope.

The sign simply read, **"Please help save our Library."**

When the lights came on, there wasn't a dry eye in the house.

Mrs. Bundle and Althea gave a solid, concise presentation of their *Dog Days of Summer Festival and Auction* concept, lasting less than fifteen minutes and resolutely asking that the village sanction the concept of a Library Foundation to benefit the reconstruction of the library and help spearhead related charity events.

The crowning glory came when Mrs. Bundle elaborated on the "amazing discovery" that she and Louis Montembeau had happened upon in the library roof's wreckage days before. Louis's enthusiastic, fervent nodding from behind them (without uttering a single word) reinforced her story. At this most strategic juncture, the room was spellbound as the *"Mysterious Painting Behind the Wall"* was dramatically unveiled (courtesy of a helping hand from Ellie Waterhouse and Watson DeVille) for all the villagers to see.

First, "ooh's and aah's" peppered the room and then applause broke out, first in smatters, then in loud, rhythmic smacks (followed by a healthy mix of foot-stomping), as the idea of having an annual Art Festival slowly caught on.

Mrs. Bundle and Althea held their breath in anticipation as their idea took wings and began to unfold...

In the end, even *they* were amazed at how quickly their conceptual idea became a real plan—even without the help or support of Armand Limpert.

Throughout the presentation, Armand had sat with his arms folded on his chest, his face emotionless, only occasionally leaning over to make a quick side comment to Sarah Church or roll his eyes in apparent boredom. Sarah Church, in turn, never failed to nod emphatically, looking like a dashboard bobble toy as she patently agreed with his every whispered comment.

Now, though, it appeared the tide had turned; clearly, the villagers' enthusiasm was a force to be reckoned with and neither of these two library board members chose this opportunity to voice their disfavor for the idea, realizing the battle was lost (at least for now) as people jumped on board the Art Festival wagon.

The Pillson Falls Art Co-Op was represented in full force (having been organized by Althea and occupying the front row of the Hall). Marcus Hotchkiss, the Don of the Guild, stood up at Mrs. Bundle's request and spoke about the mysterious painting's age (which he felt could very well be true to the date of "1861" found on the painting), its condition and superior quality, and finally, validating its authenticity as "a real find!"

The ultimate glorious piece of his presentation was when he told the already-enthralled crowd that the Co-Op had met and decided collectively to support the festival idea one-hundred-percent. To that end, each artist had volunteered to donate one piece of art to be auctioned off at the Festival. Furthermore, as a goodwill gesture, the village's library coffers would reap the total 100% benefit of all the proceeds — in the thousands, he reckoned, all to go directly towards the restoration project.

As he sat down to much applause, the Select Board proceeded to ask their questions, all directed at Mrs. Bundle. Even Archie Plummer's pointedly laborious and flowery questions, asked with cherubic naiveté but meant to break the momentum and the excitement of the moment, were answered good-naturedly. His exhaustive minor objections — all presented with a gigantic, superfluous smile--were overcome with her mature, measured responses, and it seemed the energy in the room remained positive.

After much discussion, it was understood that the focal point of the Festival could be the newly found painting, and that its discovery would be used as a catalyst in promoting the Festival.

Archie asked pointedly, "Mrs. Bundle, how do you propose to get the word out? I'm sure you know advertising is pretty expensive."

"Kevin?" Mrs. Bundle turned to Kevin Trees, Pillson resident and managing editor of the *State Standard* local newspaper, who sprung into action. He assured the town fathers that, if the Festival was "a go," he would be writing a lead story — a front page article in next week's paper, in fact — that would feature the Pillson Library, the discovery of the *"Mysterious Painting Behind the Wall,"* and the fundraiser — *The Dog Days of Summer Art Festival*-to restore the library to its original glory so that it wouldn't have to close its doors.

"It'll be a doozy of a story!" He was as tall as his name implied, with a full head of dark, wild hair that often fought with a comb. He had a quiet, intense demeanor and was known to have a passion for "underdog" causes. He continued in earnest, "Why, this is one of the best human interest stories I've come across in a long time! It has all the key ingredients: secrets, adversity, and fun to boot! The only thing it lacks is S-E-X, which we can't put in our little family newspaper anyway!"

The guffaws could be heard clear to Rutland, and people cheered profusely as Kevin lifted his pad of notepaper in the air, waving genially at the group.

Walter Andersen stood up and yelled, "All I got to say is--Pillson's needed a good kick in the kee-*es*-ter for a long time, and this could be just the ticket!"

More clapping and murmurs of approval followed, even though Archie Plummer's gavel reminded them they were out of order.

"Call to order!!!" He turned to his group of peers. "Does the Select Board have any other questions?" He looked at each member, all of whom shook their heads. He shouted, "I will now open up the meeting to questions and discussion from the audience!"

Most of the questions came in the form of positive statements and reinforcement from the villagers that the Pillson Library was an integral part of their lives, and that complete, unbridled support for an event such as this could put Pillson on the map, if done right.

Many people wondered where the mysterious painting would be kept and where they would be able to view it. This led to much debate, with the Select Board maintaining that, because it was the property of the Library, it belonged to the municipality and so, the responsibility of its safekeeping fell on their shoulders. Barbra D'Acunet, as Town Clerk, insisted it should be kept in the town vault. This suggestion was met with much derision.

Most of the comments from the floor countered that the painting should be enjoyed and used to the Festival's advantage and not be hidden away. Ultimately, it was agreed by all that it should be secured within the Artisan's Co-Op building, with an assurance from Marcus Hotchkiss that it would be stored in their safe after hours. He agreed to take it with him that evening, and so that issue was put to bed.

As the evening's meeting moved toward a climax, Mrs. Bundle crossed her fingers and hoped for the best. In the end, the Town

Selectmen's Board voted unanimously (with Archie begrudgingly, round face flushed, raising his hand in accord while giving a blank look and slight shrug in the direction of Armand) to support the Library Trustee's endeavors — with the only codicil that Mrs. Bundle, who had come up with the original idea, spearhead the event as the "Official Festival Head Coordinator."

She smiled confidently and said, "I will — as long as my dear friend, Althea Swain, agrees to organize it with me."

All eyes were on Althea, who laughed and then said, "Well, if you're crazy enough to take this on, I'm crazy enough to help!"

Armand Limpert sat by in speechless astonishment, recognizing that the project that he never thought would get this far had, indeed, passed without either his sanction or comment. He had been completely, unequivocally bypassed in this venture.

Mrs. Bundle beamed, nodded emphatically, and the gavel was soundly struck!

"The *First Annual Dog Days of Summer Sidewalk Art Festival and Auction* is hereby approved for the third weekend of August!" Archie boomed, "Good luck, ladies!"

They were off!

It seemed the room became instantly galvanized with the large task at hand. Mrs. Bundle stood at the podium and asked for everyone's attention.

At that moment, a wonderfully sweet, yeasty smell had commenced to permeate the Town Hall rafters, timed remarkably well, and just as Mrs. Bundle assured the attendees that, without hesitation, they were ready to get started immediately.

"To that end and without any interruption, I would like to ask that anyone wanting to help us organize the event can stay after this meeting, please, for just a short time — or, as long as you can." She inhaled deeply and pointed to the back of the Hall. "Our wonderful neighbor, Mrs. Balshemnik–you all know her–has been downstairs in the kitchen putting the last touches on her famous *rugalach* — there's plenty for everyone! And to wet your whistle, we've got cold lemonade there, too!"

Pleasurable hungry sounds followed as people filtered out of the community room and headed downstairs to the dining hall. Everyone in Pillsonville knew about Mrs. Balshemnik's delicious hand-rolled delicacies, especially her rugalach, made from the flakiest pastry dough and filled with her own special mixture of cinnamon, walnuts, raisins and secret spices. *Yum!*

And so, the magical night continued. An informal meeting followed the refreshments, with so many great ideas thrown into the mix that it made Mrs. Bundle's job easy. By close to midnight, an Action Plan based upon the original mission statement had come together, addressing all the bullet points on Mrs. Bundle's list. A core group of about seventy very excited citizens volunteered their services to make the Festival a success. It was determined that all the money from donated paintings, philanthropists, vendors, and any other source of donated proceeds would help defray overhead costs to put on the Festival and all monies left over would go directly toward the library refurbishment fund with all proceeds from the volunteer booths (bake sale, trash and treasure, books, jewelry, etc.) and profits from the food kiosks, manned by local residents, benefiting the Library.

Special events throughout the Festival weekend, beginning on the Friday night, would help raise money for the Library, along with a local *Dog Days Talent Show* on Saturday night. The Talent Show would be held upstairs on the stage in the community room. Acts would be open to anyone in the area that wanted to perform for free. A five-dollar donation would be taken at the door.

On Sunday afternoon, there would be an art auction of all the donated displayed art. Included in the art auction would be any other artists who saw fit to donate their works. Marcus Hotchkiss said he would approach the nearby Woodstock art galleries and artists for more donated works to display and auction off.

The officially (and aptly) dubbed *"Mysterious Painting behind the Wall"* would be on display for the next few weeks in the Art Co-Op space, along with information about the upcoming Art Festival.

Committees quickly came together. Scheduled for the weekend of Aug 15-17, the Festival was to be held on the beautiful Village Green where all the paintings would be displayed for two days. Sunday's Art Auction would be the culminating event, the grand finale of the Festival.

Carl Andersen's "big band" dance band, The Pillson Rhythmares, would play a benefit concert Friday night to kick off the Festival.

A Dog Days of Summer Doggie Parade would start the Festival off with a bang on Saturday morning. Kids of all ages would decorate their dogs and enter them into the Parade around the Village Green, and volunteers would decorate floats—all with a "Dog Days of Summer" theme.

Vermont retailers would be solicited. There would be storytellers, street performers, and the like carrying out their craft. A wool-shearing exhibition and other various events would take place Saturday.

All told, it appeared that initial profit estimates could conservatively fall in the $50,000-60,000 range.

As the weary but motivated volunteers filed out of the Festival meeting, their tummies full and their minds challenged, Althea turned to Mrs. Bundle and they hugged each other. In a matter of minutes, everyone was gone and the bustling room had become very empty and very quiet.

The two women were exhausted but exhilarated. They trudged upstairs to the Community room to gather their things.

"Oh, it's too good to be true! Can you believe it, Lettie?"

"I'm amazed! It's....*fantastical!* You know, it just goes to show you—when you set your mind to something, it *can* come together!"

"And people really rise to the occasion, do they not? It's really amazing!"

They picked up their belongings and moved toward the back stairway that led to the parking lot exit.

Althea's lowered voice echoed in the surrounding silence. "Could you believe that sourpuss on Armand's kisser? I think this just about did him in! He didn't even stay for the meeting! He ran like a jackrabbit—couldn't wait to get out of here. I think we're rid of him."

Mrs. Bundle chuckled. "Well, I'm not so sure. We've got a long road ahead of us, and I'm sure he'd love to see us fail. We can't count on any support from him. You know the saying, 'put your money where your mouth is'? Well, we better get busy!"

"I don't care about that old killjoy! I'm so excited—even without his help, I know we can do it!" Althea turned the corner at the bottom of the stairs quickly, but was startled as someone suddenly blocked her way.

"Althea, watch out!" Mrs. Bundle tried to warn her but was too late.

Everything went flying—folders, pocketbook, everything—as Althea ran smack dab into none other than Dakota Squibb.

"Oh! What? *Squibb!* You again!"

"Yes, good evening to you, too!"

"I thought I saw you," she stopped, then added hastily, "*lurking* in the back of the dining hall."

He untangled himself slowly from her as she, thoroughly discombobulated, brushed his helping hands away from the seersucker tunic that accentuated her body's lovely curves.

"Good grief! I can do it!" She bent down to pick up her files, which had gone in every direction. He bent down also; their heads grazing each other as he handed her the pile he had gathered. "Ow!" she cried, grabbing the stack from him. "Why are you still here?"

He looked as jaunty as their first meeting, the bucket-style golf hat tipped rakishly to the side, face tanned. He was dressed comfortably in khakis, the same paint-stained brown loafers, and a faded, but once pricey, golf shirt. He smiled, a flash of white, straight teeth, more inspired than nonplussed by her words, and said amiably, "I was coming back up to see you." He turned his gaze and smiled at Mrs. Bundle. "The *both* of you, that is."

"What on earth for?" Althea stood up and looked at him skeptically.

"Well! To, ah, *congratulate* you and Lettie! Ladies, that was quite a show! I must tell you, I was very impressed!"

"Why, thank you, Dakota." Mrs. Bundle had to admit she, too, was thrilled with the results. "These villagers are truly amazing, aren't they?"

"No, I would say *you*, Lettie—and Althea—are the truly amazing ones--to have been able to organize this event so skillfully and so quickly! Kudos to you both. You've got a lot of work ahead of you." His voice took on a serious tone, "I must admit, though, I couldn't help but overhear, just now…your comments about your nemesis."

"Nemesis?" Althea spat out the word.

"Yes, Mr. Armand Limpert, isn't that his name?" He pronounced it with an impeccable French accent. "I met him yesterday at Crown Point. He, and Archie Plummer, and Terry…uh…Snargle—is that the other gentleman's name? Yes, Terry Snargle. They needed a fourth and asked if I'd like to join them. I agreed, having no partners of my own. This Limpert fellow….he seems quite charming on the surface, doesn't he? But after eighteen holes of golf, I had had enough!" His voice lowered to a raspy whisper. "What a pompous son-of-a-gun!" He chuckled and shook his head, then whispered, "Complain, complain! Meanwhile, I caught him conveniently trying to 'forget' a stroke here and there."

Althea did what she always did when she was tired—brushed her sandy-gold bangs back from her forehead and pushed them behind her ears. She rubbed her eyes and asked wearily, "What's your point?"

Mrs. Bundle was, once again, chagrined at her friend's obvious exasperation with this benignly delightful and attractive man.

His intelligent eyes looked straight into Althea's, "That's why I came tonight. Ironically, his negative comments piqued my interest, you see! It was noticeable—even to an *outsider* such as myself—that he's hardly impressed with your efforts to raise money for the Library. What's his beef, anyway? I couldn't help but hear you say just now…." he left off, asking intently, "well, the question is, *why* does he seem so dead set against it all? Especially if he's on the Board of Trustees? Is it all about small-town politics and one-upmanship—and jealousy? Or, what?" He lowered his voice further to almost a growl, "The fact of the matter is, I really don't get a good feeling about that man!"

"Didn't your mother tell you it's impolite to eavesdrop?" Althea snapped, and Mrs. Bundle gave her a quick, but well-placed, jab in the ribs.

He colored slightly at Althea's harsh words and said glumly, "I'm sorry if I ask too many questions—or, that I happened to overhear your comments, which I have admitted I did hear. Those are both bad traits that have gotten me into a mountain of trouble in the past. Please accept my apology and thank you for setting me straight."

"Oh, don't worry about it, Dakota," Mrs. Bundle tried her best to mend things.

He smiled. "Thank you, Lettie. Might I just say, ladies that I believe in this cause and I want to help. I…didn't want to volunteer until I talked with you both, but…I am available to assist you in whatever area you find my services and skills to be useful."

Mrs. Bundle was touched. "Why, thank you, Dakota that is very kind of you! Do you have something you'd especially like to do? We can use volunteers in almost every area."

"Well, I *could* work with the Art Co-Op. I have a bit of art experience," he smiled, underplaying his vast skills, "and would be glad to help *you*, Althea, with the Guild's contribution to the Festival. I could help you organize--—"

"No! Uh, that is, no, thank you, I don't think so, Squibb." Her words were rushed, "Marcus Hotchkiss—you saw him speak this evening—he was at the meeting afterward, too—I think he's got the Co-Op's part covered. And, he's already volunteered as Chair. You could ask him," she hesitated, "but really, I think we're all set there."

His face visibly fell once again; he was clearly disappointed. His hound dog expression seemed to cause Althea's demeanor to soften just a tad. She mumbled, "Well now…wait a second…let me think." She looked desperately at Mrs. Bundle, who offered no assistance. With a hint of what appeared to be a fraction of a smile, Althea offered, "Look. There *is* the Talent Show. No one's volunteered yet. You know, what with you and your *whistling*! I've noticed you in the backyar....That is, *we* heard you the other night, didn't we, L? It's quite good whistling, Squibb, all things considered."

His face brightened. "Thank you! I did do my fair share of performing in my youth, as a matter of fact! And, if I might boast a bit, others have commented on my whistling ability. I have a bit of dramatic experience also, having supervised a couple of stage productions years ago in the big city. Nothing professional, mind you!" He laughed, "Just amateur productions. Musicals, in fact! Lots of fun. If that's what you'd prefer, Althea, I'd be honored to get involved with the Talent Show."

Mrs. Bundle was thrilled with the idea. "There you go! We definitely could use your help in recruiting and organizing the acts. Why, you could vie for the Master of Ceremonies position, if you like the limelight! And, Althea's right—your whistling is superb, too."

Althea (whose ulterior motive seemed to have been to steer him as far away from her duties as possible), added far too brightly, "Yes, you might even be able to chair that committee, depending on who steps forward."

Dakota was as amiable as a lapdog. "That would suit me *just* fine."

He moved toward the exit, then turned and smiled once again. His handsome face glowed with fun, and his eyebrow arched with just a hint of impish jesting.

"Oh, *Althea*... would you plan on performing at the Talent Show, too? I'm thinking you must have some hidden tal—"

"Good *grief*! No! I can't carry a tune if you gave me a bucket the size of Idaho!"

He threw back his head and laughed. "How wonderful and spirited! Yet, I'll wager you could *outhoot* anyone within a ten-mile radius! Howie and I know that!" His voice matched hers in brightness. "We've heard you, haven't we?" He turned and winked widely at Mrs. Bundle, "Quite *fine* vocal chords on this woman, to be sure!"

Greatly amused, he slipped through the doorway.

Althea's features froze and indignation slowly creased her blazing red face once more. "Wait a minute! Squibb, hold on!" Like a crazed hoot owl, she sputtered under her breath, "Outhoot?"

As the two ladies stepped out into the late night air behind him, a familiar, drawling voice wafted across the near-empty parking lot. "Yooo—hooo! Oh, yooo-hoooooo! Ova here, *Dakota!* Hello, you darlin' man! Ah told you Ah'd wait, now didn't Ah, sugar?"

Elvina Wrinkle reached her long arms into the air and waved. Her willowy body leaned seductively across her metallic blue Thunderbird convertible's front seat. The convertible top was down and, in anticipation of the night ride, her meringue-like waves were stuffed under a gay silk scarf, tied once under her chin, then once again at the nape of her neck "fifties-style."

Oh, mercy, Mrs. Bundle considered, *it looks like Elvina's working overtime to win Mr. Squibb's affections. And, already—just when things were getting so....interesting.*

Althea's stammering remarks at Dakota ceased as she saw Elvina; she sealed her lips tightly.

Mr. Squibb waved sheepishly at Elvina, then turned back to the ladies. "My new friend has kindly offered me a ride to my door," he apologized, and then courteously saluted the two women in the same, familiar way he had done the first night they had met—a goodwill, goodnight wish.

Althea was totally thrown off guard, in considerable angst as she searched for, but could not seem to execute, a proper response.

His dark eyes lingered on her, boring like a drill into the depths of Althea's deep green eyes; he said gently, "Well, as far as performing goes…if you can't carry a tune, Althea, then I shall whistle for the both of us."

He turned and nodded cordially to Mrs. Bundle. "Good night, Lettie! Ladies, I bid you fond adieu."

They watched him cross the parking lot and get into the convertible.

A low rumble, emitted through clenched teeth, burrowed out of Althea. "Arrrggh! That man! There's something very…*unnatural* about him. Nothing seems to ruffle his feathers. Nothing! He's so *charming*…and….*happy!*" She discharged the two descriptive words as though they were expletives. "He makes me feel very…," she searched for the right word in frustration, and then uttered hopelessly, "*uncomfortable.*"

Mrs. Bundle, who had been observing everything with great interest, watched Althea's expression as Elvina threw her head back and laughed gaily at a seemingly very clever and witty remark from the handsome gentleman.

Quietly, Mrs. Bundle offered, "Maybe, Allie…that's a *good* thing?"

"*What?*"

"Maybe that's a good thing….feeling uncomfortable. He seems to like you."

Althea groaned as though having just swallowed a bitter concoction. "Like me? *Squibb?*" she said incredulously. "I don't think so. He gets under my skin like chalk on a blackboard. He's… too dramatic, too artsy for my ta--" she cut herself short.

"Taste? Your taste in men?"

"Yes, if you want to put it that way."

"Yes, well, he *does* seem to like you, even though you're rather… prickly to him."

Althea groaned once more. "I'm tired. It's been a very long day."

"Don't change the subject, dear friend. He really does seem to want *you* to like him, too."

As they watched the car and the couple in it fly out of the parking lot, wheels spinning wildly in the gravel, Althea muttered under her breath, "*Hmph*! From where I'm standing, he seems to like most anybody."

Chapter Twenty-Six

People and Plans
Come Together

The last two days had seemed a blur to Mrs. Bundle. Forming and solidifying committees, delegating—Althea and she deftly orchestrated this large effort to set the Festival up for success. Remarkably, many villagers had already come forward and the volunteers core group was growing in leaps and bounds.

The whole thing seems to be coming together quite nicely, she thought with a smile.

To begin with, Weezy Bunton had volunteered to handle all the kids' events (the hoola hoop contest, face painting booth, pony rides, and other events--all on Saturday and Sunday, along with, as she put it, "a bang-up Strawberry Shortcake Booth" during Friday night's Rhythmares kickoff performance on the Village Green bandstand.

With an assurance to Mrs. Bundle not to "fret 'bout a thing," she'd said, "You know I love bein' in charge! I already got a dozen able bodies lined up to work in shifts through the whole blasted weekend!" Her committee also decided they couldn't leave out the adults in the hoola-hooping category, so there was to be a grown-up version to determine who had the most stamina and skill to win the grueling competition. Bets would be collected, the proceeds of which would be donated, all under the direction of Weezy Bunton.

Lonnie Macomber, their loquacious postman, had volunteered his services and would be offering rides on the back of his antique motorcycle.

His tightfisted older sister, Postmistress Bessie May Macomber-Scott, would be in charge of the Stamping Table. "Mind you," she had clarified, "not 'stampin' like when you post a letter!" In fact, her hobby involved the latest arts and craft craze of stamping individualized designs and letters on note cards, letterhead, T-Shirts, and the like. "Tim and Arletta will spell me when I get too tired of stampin'!"

Dakota Squibb had begun the Talent Show's planning and organizing, having been offered the co-chairing duties with Keith Kittredge, a villager who happened to be a pretty well-known performer in the area and had handled other amateur stage events in the past. Keith was the also the father of the adorable twins, Kayla and Kila, along with three other cuties: Karey, Kenneth, and Kathy Jo, all under the age of ten. Known to the locals as quite an entertaining family, Keith, his five children, and his wife Karen made up "The Colossal Kittredges," a multi-talented amateur touring group—all blonde—that could sing, dance, and perform incredible gymnastics.

Between these two men, Mrs. Bundle was confident the Talent Show's organization and execution would be superb.

The Richeys, Hiram and Cynthia, whose fledgling catering business needed a boost, would be in charge of the food vendors (already lining up in good shape) in exchange for free advertising of their services and specialties in the Festival brochure. Each vendor had agreed upfront to donate their time and contribute a portion of their proceeds to the Foundation.

A sheep shearing demonstration, followed by a spinning and dyeing demonstration, had already been arranged by Walter Andersen, who had asked his farmer friend Axel Conroy to volunteer his expertise in sheep-shearing. Axel had agreed, promising he, his wooly mammals, and his sharpened shears would be good to go for all day Saturday.

Constable Zack Benoit was in charge of public safety and traffic management for the kick-off Dog Days of Summer Dog Parade on Saturday morning, guaranteeing, "That'll begin 9 a.m. sharp!"

The children and their pets would come through downtown, circle the Village Green, and end at the Gazebo for the awards ceremony. A passel of volunteers, thrilled to wear the florescent orange shirts, would help with parking and crowd control. After much discussion, his committee decided that not only dogs but cats also would be allowed in the parade. The finely-attired animals and their owners would be awarded special ribbons for best dressed, most creative, and so forth. "No animal or kid should leave without somethin' and we'll make sure they all do!" Zack stated assuredly.

Ellie Waterhouse would use her freelance writing skills to head the advertising committee. She was thrilled to announce that an "anonymous donor" had contributed two thousand dollars for start-up costs for the festival's promotion, a windfall that most villagers assumed had been contributed by the aged reporter Miss Hattie Underwood.

Marcus Hotchkiss had received twelve donated paintings to date (with more promised by Festival time) along with a Dakota Squibb original. *That kind man is certainly doing his part*, Mrs. Bundle reflected; co-chairing the Talent Show and readily offering one of his larger works was certainly noteworthy.

Kevin Trees, good to his word as Managing Editor of the local weekly, put a rush on the feature article in the *State Standard* so that it would come out in the special Fourth of July edition the following Wednesday. Professor DeVille had provided a helping hand with the Library's history to present day.

Donations of goods had already begun to come in: jewelry, white elephant items, handmade crafts and knitted items, and promises of baked goods. A section of the Town Garage had been cleared out and designated as a holding area for donated boxes of non-perishable items.

Lastly, contributions to the bake-off tables (where natives and their favorite homemade jams and jellies, pies, cakes, pickles recipes would vie for first prize—helping reinforce the Festival as an old-fashioned, down-home, family event. And wonder of wonders, Sarah Church had volunteered to head up the bake-off Judging Committee! *God bless the small miracles*, Mrs. Bundle thought as she remembered how the timid woman had assured her that she would "endeavor, for the benefit of the Library and goodwill towards all men," to get Armand Limpert somehow involved with her committee.

Mrs. Bundle's manila folder was filled to the max with notes and scribbles and plans and numbers and projections and ideas and notes about other notes and, well, she had to admit, she had *oceans* of work ahead of her!

And so, the rest of the week just flew by, everyone in the Village preparing, like worker bees making honey, for their big event in August.

.

Chapter Twenty-Seven

Drought and Distrust Dovetail

Throughout the whole week, the air was muggy and humid and, without one drop of rain, things were drying up quicker than a duck's wink. People all over were beginning to use their well water sparingly, a sure sign that the dreaded word "drought" was beginning to creep into every farmer's mind. Unfortunately, there did not appear to be a drop of rain on the horizon or in the coming forecast, at least not for the next ten days (according to the weather experts). Although the air hung like a dark curtain and it felt as humid and sticky as the underside of a toad, the sky continued to rumble and gurgle as though it wanted desperately to relieve itself.

But no rainwater came forth. The meadows, gardens, backyards, and distant hills and mountains all, as one, became almost as dry as the Sahara Desert, veritable tinder waiting for a wayward spark.

Adding fuel to this burgeoning volatile situation was the word from the State Fire Marshall—the Tuddy's Restaurant fire had officially been deemed arson; his office provided no other details. Everyone in Windsor County was on edge. According to the *Rutland Daily News* (who reported it first), the fire had been started by "persons unknown" and now, the rumor mill was ripe with chitchat.

The task of calming the community fell on the shoulders of the Sheriff's Department; Will O'Malley was the first to admit that he had his hands full. Everywhere he went, people asked him what they should do to prepare for someone trying to burn them down. Although his department tried to assure people that this was probably an isolated case of arson, the villagers didn't believe it. New stories were cropping up every day—all total speculation—about who had burned down Tuddy's and how they had done it. The whole county seemed to be discussing four things: Tuddy's Fire, the Fourth, the Festival, and whether a drought was coming.

The talk on everyone's tongue switched nervously, bouncing back and forth like a boomerang from the arson case to the lack of rain and back. Just in the Pillson Post Office alone, conversations turned from curiosity to fear with each new batch of visitors that gave Tim Scott an audience, often beginning with their first innocent question, "Any idea who torched it?"

"Well," Tim would chitchat, "I been hearin' some pretty strange stuff. Why, I heard it might be organized crime tryin' to get a toehold in Hartland!"

"Lord, no!"

"Well! Did you happen to see that weird message on the *Welcome* sign?"

"Sure did! Who on earth could have *done* that?"

"You know, strange you ask! It's got me thinkin'…we used to call Sam Oakdale 'Smokey' back along in high school—d'ya remember him?"

"He ain't still around, is he?"

More frivolous talk would transpire and then the conversation would move on to the rain issue, which often began with the patron exclaiming, "And they say we got no rain in sight!"

"I ask you, how we gonna handle no rain for *weeks* on end?" Tim would present, eyes gleaming with exaggeration. "It'll get dryer 'n a dinosaur bone around here! And," he would emphasize, eyes wide, "with a *pyromaniac* on the loose!"

"A pyro, you say? Do you really think—?"

Tim would assure them with, "Well, if it ain't an outside job, who is it? Some crazy nut, no doubt, right here among us, waitin' to strike again! Mother and me got our eyes peeled for anything unusual—even though we been right out straight! You'd be surprised what we see in here," (at which point, he would lean in, eyebrows raised, and whisper), "I'm keepin' the shotgun by the back door just for good measure."

"We got family comin' home special for the Fourth!"

"Ditto! Like there's not enough going on! We're *all* busy—and going full boat for this festival, too!"

"Ain't that the truth."

"Well, now, we still got to have fun, don't we? Even if it's hotter 'n a June bride in a feather bed!" Tim would joke. "*Dog Days of Summer*—didn't that liberry committee nail *that* one on the head! Whoo-eee!"

"Hope rain comes soon," the patron would joke nervously, "no telling if we'll need the farm pond—just in case!"

"Wouldn't hurt to update your homeowners insurance," Tim would conclude, with a last warning of, "All's I can say is, better watch your back!"

When Sheriff O'Malley heard some of these rampant rumors with hints of hysteria, he decided it was best to get a statement out to the public. Announcements were put up countywide on every village municipal building, retail establishment, and public notice board urging people *not* to panic, but to keep a watch out for fires or any suspicious behavior—especially in the late night or early morning hours. People were advised to have plenty of water on hand if they were burning (a regular backyard practice in those parts) and to use extra care if they did burn—until further notice.

A church billboard sign that Sunday read: "Prayer is asking for rain. Faith is carrying an umbrella!"

Chapter Twenty-Eight

Erin

Here it was Thursday already! *Mercy!* The day before the Fourth of July.

Mrs. Bundle sat just off her back porch in the comfort of the cushioned white wicker lounger, which was nestled under the shade of the large maple tree's copious, translucent leaves. It was late afternoon, and she sipped at her cool lemonade and sampled another fresh-out-of-the-oven shortbread cookie while she went over her paperwork for the Festival. She wore a light, flowered summer shift and sat shoeless, with her feet up and her head lazily reclining back on the lounger's comfortable pillow.

Ah, peace and quiet!

Beside her lay her latest mystery novel, as yet unread, and alongside it, fresh off the presses, was the weekly edition (with special July 4th insert) of *The Slate Standard*. She was thrilled with Kevin Tree's efforts as she read the front page headline, "**Discovered Painting Sparks Idea for Local Art Festival**," with a sub-caption, "*Local Lady comes up with 'Dog Days of Summer' Plan to Help Save Pillson Library.*"

The article delivered all the stunning details about the Library's "fantastic discovery" and the painting's, as yet, unknown value or history. Also featured were the festival organizers' plans to offer a plethora of activities appealing to everyone of every age, culminating in the Art Auction, all designed to "generate monies for the worthy

Library Foundation cause." Kevin had gone overboard with the presentation (and his praise for Mrs. Bundle, who blushed modestly as she read the article), especially the large color photograph of the painting now known as the "Mysterious Painting Behind the Wall," which was reproduced impeccably in color, quite remarkable for newspaper quality, in fact. The article highlighted the villagers' attempts to retain a piece of yesteryear by restoring their historical Library (rather than tearing it down), emphasizing the massive manpower effort the small village was expending to save their Library. Written just in time for the holiday tourist traffic to Vermont, the article was tremendous free advertising and Mrs. Bundle was elated. She read on:

> The painting will be kept for viewing and safekeeping at the local Art Guild Co-Op while its value and origin are being determined. Ultimately, it will be proudly displayed during the three-day period at the Dog Days of Summer Art Festival. If anyone has any information as to the why's, where's, what's and how's of the painting, they are asked to contact Louis Montembeau, Head Pillsonville Librarian, or Mrs. Lettie Bundle, Dog Days of Summer Art Festival Head Coordinator. *(Their respective phone numbers followed.)*

As she scanned the rest of the paper, there was another notable item which caught Mrs. Bundle's eye. In the bottom corner of page 3 were two paragraphs with a modest headline above: *"Noted Artist Joins Quiet Pillson Falls Art Community."*

Dakota Squibb was described as the "celebrated oil painter, noted for his free form, abstract expressionism style of painting" and "very popular with the more avant-garde collectors" along with a brief description of his more well-known works. According to the article, this world-traveling artist had expressed his interest in spending a quiet, peaceful, and undisturbed summer in the little community of Pillson Falls with as little hype as possible and "with a hope to enjoy its beauty and get some much-needed R & R."

So, it was true! Mrs. Bundle reread the article, then set the paper down. She wondered if Althea would be surprised when she learned that her new neighbor was, by all accounts, a well-known artist. Mrs. Bundle heaved a contented, deep sigh and allowed herself a few minutes of calm reflection.

Cracker lounged nearby, the heat lulling him nicely into his customary late-afternoon slumber. Mrs. Bundle had placed his miniature, whimsical sombrero securely on his head to keep out the beating sun. His sleek, black pointed ears were wedged sideways to accommodate the large brim, making him look like a big-eared, little Mexican soldier—or *soldado*, if one was a Spanish cat. As he catnapped in luxury, his tepid bowl of water within licking reach, he fantasized about his latest adversary, the obnoxious next door hooligan, Chester the Rooster.

Dozing in his exciting dream world, he slung his bandolier holster back and faced the crowing bird, taunting, *I am Don Diego Prego, baddest cat in Mi-hee-co!* He sneered and stroked at his large moustache. *You dare to come eento my leetle world! You will pay, bandito—you scrawny, mees-rable excuse for a cheekin!*

Bawwwwkkkkkk! His nemesis screeched ferociously.

In his dream, *Gallo* and *Soldado* both squared off, swords drawn. With much drama, the battle began, swords clashing and crashing wildly. As *Don Diego Prego* promptly made mincemeat of the interloper (using his swordsmanship skills learned years earlier at *La Destreza*, the famous Spanish fencing school), Cracker's whiskers randomly twitched in delight below his closed eyes. His expert, imaginary strokes sharply zapped the verbose rooster, taking him down a considerable notch in complete silence.

Hasta la bye-bye, Cheester! Regrettably, moments into the Latin duel the fantasy was unceremoniously jarred into reality by a ruckus in the front yard, along with the loathsome, but familiar, distant earsplitting squawking and cackling—interspersed with the slam of the farmhouse's front door.

Cracker jumped up from his nap. As the resultant pounding of petite feet racing through the hallway drew near, there was a deafening, "*Helloo-oo-oo!! Heeeelll--lllooooooooooooo!!!*"

Oh, Dios, Cracker cat-thought, *the cyclone has arrived!*

"Hell-oooo! Mrs. B! *Our Angie's back!* Cracker? Anybody home?" Erin's little voice vibrated like a bullhorn at full volume throughout the house, her excitement unrestrained as she finally exploded through the back shed door and out onto the back porch with her latest news.

She was a sight. Having biked all the way up the hill in the heat, her face was flushed the color of crimson and she was radiating sweat. Her usually curly hair was even curlier, its tight mass a sopping wet mop of disheveled ringlets. A maddening crowing could still be heard from the barnyard down the hill. She opened her mouth widely, took a huge breath and bellowed over her shoulder for all the world and Martha to hear, "*Chester*, lad! Be quiet! SHHUUUSH, NOW!"

Never the shrinking violet, she hollered again, "*Jaysus!* I'll only be a minute, don't you know!"

She bounded down the steps and, reaching Cracker first, bent down to give him a stiflingly brisk hug. "*Mmmm!* Something sure smells grand! Hi, there, Cracker-Cat! Are you keeping cool under your sombrero, now?" Her lips were fairly an inch from his ear. "Did you hear? Our Angie's back!"

He rolled over and played dead.

She giggled and tickled his belly, and he resignedly stretched and reached a welcoming paw up to pat her diminutive arm, as a father might pat a very keyed-up child.

She beamed a generously freckled face and sweaty smile at Mrs. Bundle, who urged, "Lord, child, sit down! You are a mess! You look like you're going to bust a gut, luv."

"I know! I'm *hot*! That's a *long way* up that hill! 'Specially today!" She looked at Mrs. Bundle as though she were spreading a news bulletin. "But, Mrs. B—Angie's home!"

"Well, that's wonderful news, Erin! When did she get in?"

"Last night, late! She's pretty knackered from her trip. She didn't get up until near lunch time, can you believe it? And, she's been over with her friends most of the day, catching up. Oh, mum, it's a grand day!" Her elfin grin reached from ear-to-ear (looking vaguely familiar to Mrs. Bundle), and her strong Irish brogue was amplified by her unbridled excitement.

"Did you ride your bike up the hill? You look pretty 'knackered' yourself!"

Erin pushed the damp hair back and tumbled into the nearby wicker chair, exhausted. "Uh-huh! It's lovely!" she said proudly, convinced that she was the height of two-wheel fashion with her "new" old bike. Gumpy had done her proud, cleaning up and restoring Angie's used bicycle until it shone like a showroom's latest model; bright pink tassels decorated the handlebars, a hot pink banana seat cushioned her and a large pink wicker basket held her traveling essentials in front. A pink polka dot hand-levered enamel bicycle bell sounded a traditional "*dring!*"(which she had a tendency to overuse) and gave fair warning of her arrival.

She looked longingly at the cool pitcher of lemonade. "Emm… can I please have some? I'm famished!"

"*May* I…?" Mrs. Bundle gently chided.

"Oops, sorry, Mrs. B! I'll be forgettin' that forever! *May* I please have some lemonade, mum? And one of those cookies, too?"

"Well of course you can, my dear girl!" Mrs. Bundle smiled, poured her a tall glass and proffered her the cookie tray, from which she selected two pieces of shortbread.

She eagerly took four quick bites of cookie—gone!—and swilled it around with three monstrous gulps from the lemonade. Then, her usual silence period having expired, she breathlessly continued, "Angie said to say 'hey' and tell you she'll be over as soon as she can." She wiped a dusty hand across her mouth. "Can I…*may* I have some more?" Without missing a beat, she continued, "She promised tomorrow we're going to go practice some new lacrosse *tech-neeks*," she pronounced it gingerly and verbatim, then nodded, "Right! From *Sal*-vay-va-*jeee*-na!" She munched again in silence.

"Sounds like she learned a lot at Salve Regina!" Mrs. Bundle chuckled, watching her finish off the final cookie. "After your lacrosse lesson, why don't you both come for tea tomorrow afternoon—before the fireworks? Would you like that, sweetie?"

"Aye, wouldn't I, now? Oh, yes! *Fire*-works!" She said this word new to her vocabulary. "I can't wait for the Fire-works! Gumpy says it's a sight to be seen. All that booming and banging, so loud it might hurt me ears, is what he said! Oh, isn't it just *too* grand?" She clapped her hands, barely able to contain her enthusiasm, then paused mid-air. "Can I bring Chester to tea tomorrow, too? He rides in the bike basket ever-so-nicely now, right in front of me hands. He's not even peckin' at me fingers anymore!"

Oh no, Cracker cat-thought miserably.

"Yes, but you know the rules, dear. He must stay outside and amuse himself. Preferably out by the barn." She leaned over and whispered in Erin's ear, at what she thought was out of Cracker's earshot, "He and Cracker just don't seem to hit it off too well, my dear. Chester rather, uh, rubs his *fur* the wrong way."

Cracker mashed his head into the soft lawn, annoyed that his territory might yet again be invaded by the boastful rooster.

Erin gave Mrs. Bundle an all-knowing, solemn look and put her fingers to her lips. "Shhhhhh," she said, nodding toward Cracker, "I'm *sure* I can keep them apart."

"Good! By the way, Erin, what on earth were you doing out front this morning?" Mrs. Bundle had noticed Erin at the end of the Andersen driveway, industriously working away. "Were you helping Gumpy pile rocks?"

"Yes, Mum! Well, I mean, no! Not for Gumpy." She shook her head. "Surely, and it was me that was piling rocks, but I wasn't helping Gumpy. I'm selling rocks on *me* own, Mrs. B, to make money!"

"Selling rocks?" This sounded familiar to Mrs. Bundle. "Oh! Oh, *ye-es*, Gumpy did mention something about that to me the other day! Why, I've been so busy, I haven't been keeping up with the latest. I remember now. He said you had a plan—how to earn some extra money this summer."

"Uh-huh! Jack always says, '*Gheibheann pingin pingin eile.*'" She beamed and adroitly translated the Celtic phrase before Mrs. Bundle could ask, "'A penny gets another penny!' That's for sure, isn't it, Mrs. B?" She stood up, brushed off the grass and straightened her rumpled outfit. "Watch this!" She put her hands in the air, and in her best circus-barkering voice, yelled full tilt, "Native Rocks for Sale! Aye, get your rocks here!"

Cracker cat-coughed delicately. *No flies on that one*, he reckoned.

Erin's smile dazzled the makeshift stage like a rainbow. Folding her hands together neatly in front of her, she recited with exactitude (not to mention, perfect diction), "'*Authentic* Vermont Wallstones--or just plain rocks for sale! *Take your pick!* Native Vermont Rocks—*Cheap!*" (strong jab to the air), "Buy one, get one free—*any size*—2 for 34 cents! Grown *on* the farm—right here in Ver-mont." (sweeping motion with hand), "'P.S. !! History of your rock for an extra 10 *cents*." She relaxed her stance, and flopped down again. "I started today! Gumpy helps me get 'em down the hill in the wheel barrow and I take it from there. Aye, he helped me make me sign, too!"

"Well! What an enterprising idea!"

She nodded vigorously, "Gumpy said, 'Girl, it's a free *commode-ditty*," (pronouncing it exactly as Walter had said it to her), "so, why not?'"

(A quick consult between her two listeners rendered the following translation of Gumpy's sage advice; rocks *were* a free commodity in Vermont, no argument on that, to be sure.)

Erin's mouth turned downward into a pout and her eyes became fiery. "Those dodgy Clancy twins tried to steal *me* idea, didn't they now? But I told them they better not, or me brother will knock their *bloody*—oops!" She saw Mrs. Bundle's wince, "Sorry, Mrs. B—me brother will knock their blocks *clean* off!"

"Joey and Andrew? The *Terrors*?"

"Yes, mum."

"Where did you run into them?"

"Ach! They stopped by on their bikes." She stomped her foot. "Just because they're one year older they think they're so....lordy! Sure, and don't they get on me last *nerve*!" She gritted her teeth and growled, "Grrrr!"

"Oh, Erin! They're just trying to get your goat. Just ignore them."

She gave this some serious thought, head cocked to one side, and then nodded, her wild wisps of curls flying every which way. "Right! That's *just* what I'm going to do, Mrs. B. Ignore them—*and* kick them right in the *keester* if they—"

"*Erin*....?"

"Right." she nodded. "Aye. I'll just give them a never-you-mind!"

"Good girl. So, did you have any takers today? For your rocks?"

"Ahhh! Aye, I did, to be sure! Doc Jackson was my first customer. She's nice, isn't she now? She says to me," (Erin's imitation of the elderly doctor was near perfect), "'Erin girl, I could use a couple more rocks in my hill garden.' So, I gave her a special deal, didn't I—because she was my first customer and all. Oh! And, some people from New Jersey—grand car they had! They thought me idea for rocks was....," she crooked her little head in thought, "*Ach!* What *was* that word? Yes! Me idea was '*imaginative*'!' So they bought some of the smaller rocks to take back with them to the city. Ahhh! They live in an apartment there and they have *two* Corgis that they left with their sister Rachel while they're here on vacation in Vermont. Friendly, they were, truly!"

"Erin, how do you know all that?"

"Well, they told me, didn't they? Oh!" Her eyes shone with pleasure, "*And* there was a *fine-looking mate* with a funny hat who stopped. Sure, and he said he just came here. He's got a funny name.." she paused in thought, placing her forefinger to her lips, "it's.....what was it, now? It's an American state! I just learned all the fifty United States this year, Mrs. B, don't you know!" She pondered the brainteaser, "Aye! It's... *Dakota!* That's the state. And a silly other name. Squib-bey!" She went into gales of laughter, "No, wait! Not Squibbey. Squibb! Yes, mum, that's it! Isn't it funny?"

"Dakota Squibb stopped by?"

"Aye!"

"Well, I know him too, Erin! And it is a very funny name. Mr. Squibb is new to our village. But, really, Erin, I'm not sure you should be out there talking to just anybody who comes along. Is it okay with Gumpy?"

"Uh-huh. He says anyone daft enough to stop by for rocks is fair for the pickin'! That's *exactly* what he said now, isn't it?" Erin's chest puffed out a bit and she crowed, "Wouldn't *you* be wantin' to buy some of me rocks, too, Mrs. B? I made three dollars and six cents today!"

"No, Erin, dear one, I think I'll pass. I've got *plenty* of rocks of my own right here on the farm for now. Enough to last me a long while, I suspect. I like your idea, though! Very spunky. And, I certainly can help you in *another* way."

"Really?" Her interest was piqued. "How?"

"Well, if you want to offer lemonade, too, while you're down there selling rocks to the Flatlanders and others, I can bring some down! With this heat, you might make a bundle."

"Blimey, Mrs. B, that would be brilliant! Can you make me some of those lovely chocolate chip cookies, too? I get awful famished down there working on me rock pile…"

"Of course, dear girl."

Her attention veered again, and she looked around. "Where's Jack?"

"He's gone with Nick and Chris Clancy fishing, just an hour or so ago. They scooted up there—you know, to their 'secret spot'--after he got through his chores at the garage. Mr. Hudson let him go early. I doubt they'll be back in time for dinner."

Her mischievous look created a dimple in her rosy cheek. "Hmmm! *Someone* will be happy now that Angie's back, won't they now? Are *you* coming down for dinner tonight, Mrs. B?"

"Probably not, honey. I'm going over to Althea's, and then we have another very important meeting with everyone to plan for the big Festival. With Mrs. Bunton, and Mr. Kittredge and all the other people involved—"

"Oh, I can't wait for the Festival! I'm going to be in the talent show! Did you know? I've been practicing with me ukulele. Emm, Mr. Squibb—Dakota…" Erin's voice coaxed persuasively, "he says to call him that, so it's okay….Dakota's in charge, too, isn't he now?

With Mr. Kittredge? He said I must ask first if I can be in it, but—is it okay? Please?"

"That, my dear, is something Gumpy and Jack will have to decide."

"I have just the most special song, now, don't I? Chester and I have been rehearsing and rehearsing!" She stood up and made believe she was strumming, "Say! I could play it for you! I'll bring my instrument over *tomorrow* and show you and Angie. Could I?" She finished with a flourish of her small, forever-motioning hands.

Mrs. Bundle threw back her head and laughed delightfully. "That will be something that Cracker and I will look forward to, luv, of that you can be sure! Of course—bring your ukulele, too."

Erin brushed the crumbs from her tank top and shorts. "Well, I better get back! Good ol' Chester doesn't like me being away too long, does he now! So long, Mrs B! So long, Cracker-cat."

And with that, she was off, with more speed than a sonic boom!

Chapter Twenty-Nine

A Tea Party and A Show, Too

"Oh, mercy." Mrs. Bundle mumbled to herself, "What have I got myself into?" She looked around at the huge mess of paperwork surrounding her and realized she might have bitten off much more than she could chew. There were schedules and festival booth floor plans to be mapped out; there were the advertising logos to be decided upon; there were committees needing to be organized fully so that they could get up and running; there was the growing interest from outside the area (reporters, media) that she would be responsible for managing, and *there*, in front of her were all the bits and pieces of everything that she needed to work on for the next two weeks–non-stop, she recognized now–until everything would inevitably fall into place. "Oh, mercy," she said again.

She said a silent prayer, then nodded confidently and opened her eyes with renewed hope to the jumble in front of her. "Not to worry!" Amidst all this hubbub and planning, Angie and Erin would be coming this afternoon for tea and lemonade. "Fantastical, right C.C.? And then the Fireworks!" she cried out with anticipation. "It's really *too* much fun happening all in one day!"

Cracker gave a very large *me-owww*.

She gathered her Festival papers all together and shuffled them into the large folder, then plopped the bulging folder on top of the *State Standard* and three other books. She gathered up the whole bundle and set everything down in a pile on the open shelf under the wicker table where tea would be served, then sat down again on the wicker lounge chair. "*Books* and *stuff* and *piling* are just the bane of my existence," she said resignedly, thinking about the similar clutter inside. She shrugged, "Oh, well! I'll bet those scones are almost ready!" She pulled herself up from the comfortable wicker chaise and moseyed into the kitchen, Cracker following not far behind.

Deftly working her magic, she found all her provisions; marmalade and boysenberry jam appeared from the top cupboard shelf, along with apple butter, butter and cream from the refrigerator; all the complementary goodies, utensils, and dishes were expertly wedged together on one tray for a wonderful outdoor scone extravaganza.

"Hooeeeee! That oven's hot! Not the best day to be baking, to be sure, Cracker, but they *are* Angie's favorites! *Mmmm*, doesn't that smell scrumptious?" She reached into the hot oven and pulled out the most luscious-looking puffed triangles, neatly arranged in a circle on the cooking sheet and totaling eight in all. "Let's put them in the basket and cover them so they'll be nice and warm when the girls arrive."

Cracker watched with an eager and expert eye, knowing that "treat time" was not too far away as Mrs. Bundle placed two of his very special Liver Lover Cookies on a separate plate. He licked his lips and meowed again. Watching him out of the corner of her eye, she chuckled, "I wouldn't forget you, now would I?"

She drew the large pitcher of lemonade from the refrigerator and set it on the counter. "No tea today, C-cat! Too hot! But 'plenty of *lemonadey*,' as Walter would say. Just have to add the ice," the heavy cubes plunked into the cold mixture, "There! That should be everything!"

Just as she finished, she heard a familiar voice at the back door.

"Mrs. B?"

"There they are, Cracker! Halleluiah!"

"Helloooooo!"

"Here, in the kitchen, Angie girl!"

Angie came through the door, flushed and beautiful, and gave Mrs. Bundle a huge hug. "Hi, Mrs. B! How goes it?" Cracker pranced beside her and Angie reached down and grabbed the cat up into her arms, hugging him to her.

"Oh, Angie!" Mrs. Bundle cried, "We missed you! Does it feel good to be home?" Her eyes shone with happy wetness.

"You bet!" She placed Cracker back on the floor and they hugged again. Angie pointed behind her. "Erin's on her way up the hill. She wanted to ride her bike with," she paused and lowered her voice, "you-know-who."

Catching up in shorthand speak in their usual manner, they were off, chattering away. First, Angie told her just how impressive the college campus was at "Salve" (her newfound experience qualifying her to use the shortened version), then explained excitedly about the latest lacrosse skills and the other athletes she had met.

"Natalie and I had a blast! But, oh, but it's so good to be home!"

Mrs. Bundle caught her up on the latest Pillson events, meanwhile taking in the recent changes in the girl's demeanor and appearance.

Angie looked wonderful, tanned and healthy, her limbs strong and muscled from her strenuous lacrosse workouts. Her hair had taken on more blonde streaks within the chestnut brown layers and was pulled back casually into a scrunched-up knot. She wore a pair of loose workout shorts and a hot pink tank T-shirt with sports bra underneath; on her feet were pink, dog-eared and well-worn, flip-flops. It was evident the love of the color pink had trickled down from Angie and had influenced Erin.

As they both carried everything outside for afternoon tea, stepping off the porch and through the pergola trellis resplendent with bright magenta rugosa roses and then into the back yard patio, a familiar ear-splitting screech could be heard.

They both looked at each other and muttered in sync, "*Chester.*"

Baaaauuuukkkkkkkk! More shrieking, louder and louder still, confirmed the contrary rooster's imminent arrival.

"Oh, Lord!" Mrs. Bundle panicked, remembering, "Where's Cracker?"

Angie looked around her, peering under the chaise and table. "He's not here?"

"Those two are like dynamite and a lit match! We'd better go find him..."

Hurriedly putting their trays down, they rounded the back corner of the house together—just in time to see the unfolding drama.

Erin was a veritable whirlwind of dust as she sped into the yard and slammed on the brakes of her bicycle. She hopped off the bike like a gal on a mission, skipping lightly toward the back garden area. Meanwhile, surfacing out of the wake of the mini-tornado appeared the one and only—Chester.

His shrieking and crowing could be heard light years away as he strutted his stuff like a welterweight champ, proud and brazen, resolutely trying his dandiest to follow his manager and trainer as she raced for the door.

Erin saw Angie and Mrs. Bundle come around the corner; skidding to a stop, she smiled broadly, seemingly unaware of the hullabaloo. Her mouth opened and she cried out a friendly greeting and wave. Unfortunately, the salutation couldn't be heard over the racket.

In another area nearby, all hell was breaking loose as rooster and cat locked eyes.

Cracker, who had concealed his dark body underneath the front porch, crept out slowly, his musculature low and menacing as he stared down his nemesis. His eyes were cold, narrow slits of fire. He stalked the lowly quarry; The Great Warrior Cracker was certainly not impressed with all that noise and blather! In the world of the survival of the fittest, there was a battle to be fought today, for sure. Chester inflated his chest and crowed even louder. Like lightening, Cracker reconnoitered, ready to strike with deadly intent at a moment's notice, cautiously inching his way closer and closer to the menacing noisemaker.

Chester gave a huge, bold and brassy, *"Baauuuuccck!"* The brazen rooster stood his ground, his claws scratching dangerously at the gravel, throwing pebbles this way and that. As they faced off, the rooster's squawks and shrieks were dreadful; his "cock-a-doodling" making the most terrible ruckus as he scolded and taunted

Cracker, egging him on with little concern or regard for the likely consequences of fowl versus feline.

A loud "Ssfftttttt!" erupted from Cracker and he braced his haunches for the charge.

Just in time, Erin bellowed like a drill sergeant. "NO!!! You boys cut it out—*right now*! Surely, and I mean it!" She reached into her pocket and threw some Cheerios at the rooster's feet. It was as if a fairy had sprinkled magic dust.

Disinterested in anything but the delicacy placed before him, Chester stopped his banter immediately, his beak moving as quickly as a darting snake to secure his favorite treat. He pecked away, moving well away from possible combat.

Cracker, wisely knowing when to pick his battles, emitted a guttural and reverberating, "*Spaaaatttt!*" Without further ado, he flicked his tail majestically into the air, and retired with grace to the Garden Tea Party.

———————

"Deee-*lish*!" Angie wiped the last morsel from her lips and pronounced her signature critique of Mrs. Bundle's scones.

With a full-mouthed, "That was yummy!", Erin hopped up from her cool spot under the pear tree. "Well, I'm all done! Can I do my song now?"

"Of course, dear!" Mrs. Bundle said, "We'd love to hear your performance!"

"Aye! I think I might be needin' a spot of help with my stuff."

"Okay, patootie. I can help you." Angie offered.

While Mrs. Bundle tidied the dishes and the tray, Angie and Cracker followed Erin back out to the front yard where she had last left Chester (who was nowhere in sight).

Erin's bike lay on the ground, her ukulele case held firmly in place in the bike basket, wrapped round and round with thin jute twine. To the side of the ukulele, stuck in, was a worn, soft terrycloth towel.

She pointed, "That's where Chester sits." Bits of feathers stuck to the towel like rusty leaves on a vine. On the back of the banana seat, protruding out both sides like a piece of lumber and tied with more twine in the same haphazard way, was a long, skinny, rolled bundle that turned out to be a thin straw mat.

Erin looked around. "Where's my assistant?" She opened her lungs full-boat and yelled, "*Chhhheeeeessssssterrrrr!*"

Through the narrow granite slit under the barn's foundation, a squawk could be heard first, and then the cantankerous cock reappeared, none the worse for wear.

Cracker, resolving to maintain his cool, kept a healthy distance.

Erin insisted that she carry her ukelele and asked Angie to carry the mat as they walked around the house. Chester followed them obediently into the backyard, scratching and squawking, with Cracker taking up the rear of this makeshift parade. They all settled in under the weeping willow tree.

Erin carefully took the instrument out of its worn case. "See? Do you like my new ukulele, Angie?"

"Yes, I do."

Angie and Mrs. Bundle sat down for the show in the big comfortable wicker chairs. Erin deftly set up her "stage," laying down the straw mat on the ground. Then, she put on a brightly-flowered lei that had materialized from inside the mat. Draping it around her neck "just so," she reached over, picked up Chester, and placed him firmly onto the stage surface. She cleared her throat; he stood frozen in place, awaiting his cue.

She strummed a few tentative chords until she found the right beat, and the winsome song began to take shape. It sounded very tropical, the beat soothing and rhythmic, and Mrs. Bundle's foot began to lightly tap to the familiar melody.

Erin whispered, "Here we go, Chester! Are you ready, mate?" He gave a short squawk and her voice, true and strong, sang out,

"I want to go back to my little grass shack
In Kealakekua, Hawaii
I want to be with all the kanes and wahines
That I used to know long ago,"

Meanwhile, she gently swung her hips "hula-style" as Chester suddenly executed a huge hop up from the mat and balanced himself precariously on her swinging backside. It was a minor feat and the audience gasped, but he held on for all the money, his beak soundlessly grabbing at her ukulele, while her next verse rang through:

"I can hear the old guitars playing
On the beach at Honaunau
I can hear the old Hawaiians saying
Komo mai no kaua i ka hale welakahao—"

Erin had a natural gift and her engaging voice expertly executed the Hawaiian native song lyrics. Still swinging, she gave Chester a nod and he gave a quick flap of his wings, carrying out a quick jump up from her backside onto her shoulder! He fluffed his feathers and settled himself in place with remarkable aplomb as Erin wailed loudly,

"It won't be long till my ship will be sailing
Back to Kona, a grand old place
That's always fair to see, you're telling me!"

Erin struck this crescendo peak with such clarity and verve that Chester threw back his cock's head, his fine comb pointed in spires like a majestic crown, his waddle waggling with incredible fury. He puffed out his strong chest as though in acute readiness for the grandest of climaxes.

Erin's clear, strong voice hit the highest notes of the song, quavering a bit as she juggled her hula dancing, the ukulele, and the precariously balanced rooster, all at the same time.

"I'm just a little Hawaiian
A homesick island girl
I want to go back to my fish and pearls…"

With the performance in full swing, the resolute Chester executed his last, most daring move. He hopped, feathers flying, from her shoulder onto her curly head and, hanging on for dear life, opened his beak wide. She continued her swaying motion, her head moving gently while she strummed away.

Bits and spurts of tiny squeaks and squawks could be heard escaping above the clamorous music as Chester prepared his powerful throat muscles to join in with the final chorus. Fluff and dander flew wildly from his body—B-b-bawwk! Aawwk-gwakk, baawwk! The overall appearance was really quite …incredible.

He dug his claws into the wild curly mass at the tip top of her head as Erin smiled widely like a seasoned vaudeville trooper and sang her last chorus full out,

"I want to go back to my little grass shack
In Kealakekua, Hawaii
Where the humuhumunukunukuapua'a
Go swimming by!"

A full cacophony of disharmonic bedlam blasted forth as Chester let loose with a resounding *"Cock-a-doodle-doo!"*

Erin, strangely in sync with his chaotic-sounding accompaniment, raised her voice, strummed the last chords passionately on the ukulele, and sang the grand finale with gusto, "WHERE THE HUMUHUMUNUKUNUKUAPUAA GOES SWIMMING…BY!!" while Chester finished simultaneously with a thunderous,

"Cock-a-doodle-doo!"

There was a spellbound silence.

Exhibiting pure professionalism, Erin took her very deep, dramatic bow and the proud bird slid off her head (just as they'd practiced) and landed with a soft thud on the grassy straw mat. He scratched at the makeshift stage with his rugged rooster claws, proudly throwing back more imaginary barnyard matter in his frenzy and flailing his reddish-brown plumage with wanton unrestraint; it was evident *he* felt a more clever fowl could not, nay, *would not*, be found in all of Windsor County!

Quick as a wink, Erin reached into her pocket and handed her musical partner a Cheerio. He jumped on it like a dog on a bone. "Good job, Chester! You did a grand job, didn't he now?" She bowed once more to her now-furiously clapping audience and threw some more of the addicting treats to her bird. Her eyes shone with pleasure and she gushed, "Gumpy's gonna find me a hula-girl skirt! Sure, and I'm going to be wearing big flowers in my hair, too! What do you think, Angie?" She fluttered her eyelashes. "Won't I look just like a Hawaiian colleen at the Talent Show?"

Chester looked up from his pecking, puffed up his chest and gave one last boisterous, deafening blast! *Bauucccckkkk!*

Cracker turned his back from the duo and lifted his tail skyward, stretching it until the hind section almost left the ground. *All-right-all-ready*, he cat-thought, *the yellow-bellied nincompoop...* He put his bad thoughts aside, his nose aquiver as he sniffed at the dull air.

"Great job!" Angie said and Mrs. Bundle cried out, "Absolutely fan-tastical! I hope Gumpy says it's okay--—"

Erin giggled and she interrupted, "Aye! Mrs. B! I can! And that nice man, Dakota Squibb, he stopped by my rock sale again today, didn't he?" Her words ran together in her excitement. "I told him I have permission! Permission for the Talent Show! Ach, he's *so* blooming funny!" She turned to Angie. "Angie, he wears this funny hat that looks like a bucket turned upside down."

Angie gave her a confused look.

Erin motioned with her hands. "Aye! I think he likes to golf. He said it's a golf hat. And I *can* call him 'Dakota'! 'Cuz *Squibb* is too funny! That's his last name, isn't it funny? Squibb?"

Angie tried to interrupt, "Who?"

Erin stopped long enough for a deep breath, then rushed on, "Oh! And Mrs. *Wrinkles* from the store, she was there, too! All at the same time. Well, really, it was *just* when he was leaving, but up she drove and bought some rocks, too!"

Angie broke in, "Erin! Slow down, girl! Just who is this Squibb guy? Really, girl, how many times have Dad and I told you *not* to be so very friendly to strangers?" She turned and looked at Mrs. Bundle for support. "And Jack tells you the same thing all the time, too! Remember?"

"They're *not* strangers! *Mr.* Squibb lives here now, doesn't he? On *Vi-agra* Lane!" She giggled again. "Everybody always laughs when you say '*Viagra*'! Hah-hah! Sure, and that's what the sign says on his lane now, isn't it?" She screwed her face up into a freckled mess of confusion, "But what does it mean? Something bollocks, isn't it, mum?" she asked Mrs. Bundle, adding, "Tommy Snargle says—"

When she saw the look on Mrs. Bundle's face (who had thrown her hands into the air and was at a loss for words), Erin craftily shifted gears and turned back to Angie, "Besides, Angie, how can I sell me rocks if I can't talk to strangers? Not as many folks from Pillson stops to buy me special rocks, do they now?" She gazed at them logically, "Aye! *They* got plenty already, usually. So, if I didn't talk to strangers I wouldn't get as many customers, would I now, Angie? Mostly, it's Flatlanders, that likes 'em, from what I can see. And I choose 'em special, aye, that I do—just for the Flatlanders!"

"Rocks are rocks. That's what I would say." Angie said with some exasperation. "Don't change the subject. What kind of name is that, *Dakota Squibb*?" She asked suspiciously. "Who is he, and what's he doing around here in our little world?"

"Oh, Angie, I don't think we need to worry about Dakota Squibb." Mrs. Bundle patted her arm affectionately. "Althea and I met him the other day. He came to the special town meeting and volunteered to help with the Festival. Actually, he's staying in the Elliot's place on *Ni-agra* Lane," she raised an eyebrow in Erin's direction, "in the Falls for the summer from what he said. He's an artist of some renown, from what the paper says." She gave a wry smile. "He's *also* quite a whistler—yes, dear, a whistler—and he's volunteered to head up the talent show with Keith Kittredge—it's the Saturday night of the big

Festival weekend. The talent show where Erin wants do," she swayed her hips, "her new act."

Erin piped in, "Yes, mum, that's right. So, today, he says to me, 'look lass, you bring your ukulele and we'll find a spot *just* for you and Chester on the program to be sure.' That's *exactly* what he said, didn't he now? So I told him–I *am!*"

Mrs. Bundle patted her shoulder. "Right. He seems very nice, Angie—I'll admit it's a dite odd that he choose such an off-the-beaten-path place as our dear Pillson, but, frankly, he's quite respectable and *very* charming. The *Standard* said he's in Pillson for some 'R & R' this summer—so I guess Pillson's as good a place as any for that. And," she said with a droll smirk, "he's *also* the newest eligible bachelor in Pillson."

Angie rolled her eyes. "Ugh! An eligible bachelor...just what we need. His name sounds like something out of a smarmy romance novel! I think *we* may need to check this Mr. Squibb out further, Mrs. B." Her eyes glinted. "How *old* is he?"

"I really couldn't say...probably," she coughed delicately, "a bit older than my age, I suspect."

"How old is that?" Erin piped up.

"*Erin!*" Angie moaned.

"Well, never you mind, missy." Mrs. Bundle replied, "Old enough to know better."

"Well," Angie said, "now that I'm home, I'll be bound to check into this—just to see what the scuttlebutt is..."

Erin, undeterred by this exchange, blathered on without a care, "*Ach!* And you should have *seen* Mrs. Wrinkles today! She drove up in her big car, in a right hurry! Aye—and then she took a real reddener when she talked to him, surely she did."

Mrs. Bundle questioned, "A *reddener*? Elvina Wrinkle?"

"Yes, mum, Mrs. *Wrinkles!* A reddener on her puss!"

"Are you saying Mrs. *Wrinkle*...a reddener—you mean she was blushing!"

"Aye, surely, Mrs. B! It's no malarkey! I swear!" Erin's right hand deftly made the imaginary sign of the cross from corner to corner on her chest. "Sure, and she was as red as that there barn over there! And all *googly!*" Erin stood up straight and tall, on stage once again, and batted her long lashes coquettishly. "'*Oooh*, Dakota, *honey* what a fine day! You *know* you really must call me *Elll--veeee—nnaaaaa!*'" Her voice mocked the Southern drawl perfectly.

Mrs. Bundle thought, *oh my*, wondering if Elvina did indeed happen on Erin and her rock sale.

Unable to contain her laughter any longer, Angie's flip flops flew off her feet and into the air as she fell back into the chaise. They landed with a soft thud on the grass. "Erin! *Gaw*, you are funny!"

Erin giggled impishly. "Aye. Angie! She likes him, that's for sure. All *la-dee-dah*! She was making a holy show, wasn't she now, her eyes as big as mince pies!" She batted her own eyelids again. "Chester saw it, too, didn't you, Chester?"

Chester, busy scratching under a nearby peony bush, chose, at this juncture, to ignore his musical mentor in favor of the delicious grub just beyond his reach.

"Erin, honey," Mrs. Bundle said calmly, "first of all, her name is Mrs. *Wrinkle*, not 'Wrinkles'."

"Well, aye, but her face's got lotsa them, doesn't it now? Like that jug there!" She pointed an accusing finger at the finely crackled lines of the porcelain cream pitcher on the tea tray.

Angie chortled again, choosing to ignore the accurate likeness to encourage the girl's story further. "So-o-o….," she wheedled, "Mrs. *Wrinkle* was embarrassed?"

Erin chirped, "Uh-huh, to be sure! Oh, aye! All *blushy* wasn't she, making those googly eyes at poor Mr. Squibb! *Oooooh!* Me stomach!" She made a face, like she'd just swallowed a dose of bitters. "It was *soooo* yucky!" Then she gave an impish smile. "He winked at me when she wasn't looking. Really, Angie, I like *him*, he's funny—and nice! And, *Jaysus*, Mary and Joseph, he sure can whistle! He can even do 'Yankee Doodle Came To Town'! It's grand! *Jaysus!*" she repeated in her enthusiasm.

"Erin!" Mrs. Bundle's gentle warning for Erin's use of language fell on deaf ears.

Finished, Erin now moved without a pause; brushing off the flowery lei, she picked up her ukulele once more and concentrated, plucking at it with renewed interest as she tried to find the chords to "Yankee Doodle."

Angie hooted, "Omigosh!", shook her head and said, "Really, Erin, the things you say!"

The corners of Mrs. Bundle's eyes creased with mirth. "Well, my dear, I must admit you do say the darndest things. Cat's granny! What are we going to do with you?"

Erin looked up from her instrument, a sunbeam of delightful energy. She studied Mrs. Bundle thoughtfully and then reached up to touch the neat pillbox of braids atop her head. "Mrs. B, how do you get all those braids up there to stay up, all neat and the like?"

"How 'bout I show you someday, Erin? We'll braid my hair together." Mrs. Bundle became more serious. "But Erin, could I please tell you something? I want to explain something important to you."

Erin scrunched her face once again until it resembled a rascally chipmunk, concentrating intently as she tried to give Mrs. Bundle her full attention. "Uh-huh, Mrs. B?"

"Well, really, we should….keep some things to ourselves and… *maybe* not say *everything* we're thinking *all* the time. It *could* hurt someone's feelings when we just…blurt things out without thinking first."

"Yes mum! That's what Jack says, too. He says to keep me big gob closed, is what he says, before it gets me in the thick of it!"

"Uh-huh. And you know what Gumpy says about taking the Lord's name in vain."

"Oh, aye, Mrs. B! Yes, mum, I do. You mean saying *Jaysu*—!" she stuttered, "Oops! Right! I'll try, sure, and I will. I promise, mum."

Just then, there came a loud bang from the back screen door and a familiar male voice yelled, "*Oy!* Where is everyone, now?"

Erin squealed and was off at a run. "That's Jack to be sure! *Yoo-hoo!* Jack, we're over here! Having a show!"

He stood on the porch and waited for his sister to reach him. It had been a long day for Jack, and he *was* the worse for wear. Drained and exhausted, he still wore the light-blue plaid, collared, short sleeve shirt he had started the day with at 5:00 a.m. (which he had ironed himself but was now rumpled and messy). The shirt matched the bright sapphire glints in his eyes, and his cropped, glossy hair was a bit of a dark jumble as one wayward, short lock escaped and curled playfully in the middle of his forehead between his eyebrows. His ruddy cheeks blazed red with the heat, his lips more crimson and fuller than usual. He was spent from a full day of working at Royal Hudson's garage (with regular classes cancelled for the holiday). His brawny physique, due to a natural combination of lean musculature and the non-stop schedule of farm work, his part-time job, school, and contact sports like soccer, slouched just a hair.

He looked down at his sister, comic lines forming around his eyes, "What are you up to now, lass? Em, that's quite a necklace you've got on, isn't it?"

She swished her hips and held her ukulele high in the air. "Aye! Jack, see how I hula dance? It's a very swishy dance, isn't it?" She fingered the fake flowers around her neck. "This is my *lei*. Do you like it? Gumpy's getting me a hula-girl skirt. For the talent show. Do you want to see my new act?"

"Yeah, lass, to be sure. Whoa, hold up with the bear hug; you're fair crackin' me ribs! Be a good mate and give me just a minute to catch me breath, won't you now?"

Although fatigued from his busy day, he put a weary, loving arm around his sister and stepped off the porch. He paused as he looked across the pergola to the back lawn–then stalled in his tracks for a second as his cautious demeanor took in the visitor in the sheltered area beside Mrs. Bundle. He instantly lit up when he recognized that it was Angie, lazily reclining in the wicker chair.

"*Dia Duit*!" Surprised, his greeting of hello came out in his native Gaelic.

"Well, look what the cat dragged in!" she shouted back in a charming, easy voice.

Hey, watch those cat sayings, Cracker cat-thought, then meowed as he lay draped over the nearby hassock waiting, to no avail, for a momentary glimmer of an afternoon breeze. *These feline phrases are hopelessly mundane*, he cat-thought, then swatted lazily at a mosquito, determined not to let it sully his day.

Jack flushed deeper, smiling broadly at Angie as he approached her. "Well, now, and who's *this* bonny lass? She's lookin' familiar to me, now, isn't she? Let me think, could it be our fair…*emm*… what's your name again? Aye, yes, now! It would be Angie, right? Just returned from her world travels?"

"The one and only, totally worldly!" Her eyes danced as she greeted her special chum. "Hey, Jack, how are ya? And, what did I miss while I was away?"

His grin was lopsided and he chuckled, "Well now, let's see…. the whole sky has caved in, the sidewalks near folded, and everyone's *foostering* about, what with our fair lass departed for so long!" He flopped down on the grass beside her.

"Right! And I'll bet all you've been doing is lazing around in this heat, fishing and taking it easy with that crazy Nick Clancy!"

They kidded each other relentlessly back and forth, both obviously delighted to see each other. He pulled a stalk of grass from the lawn and chewed absentmindedly on it. Then, he turned toward Mrs. Bundle and raised his eyebrows at her.

"And, don't you know, Angie, Mrs. B is trying to save the world— again." He reached up and placed a caring hand on her shoulder. "She's got herself all involved, hasn't she?" Mrs. Bundle chuckled and bowed her head with no comment. "I've been trying to get her to slow down, but no such luck, am I right? Ach!! She's full into a big *brouhaha* trying to save the Library."

"You mean this festival? Ever since I got back, that's all I've been hearing about."

Mrs. Bundle shushed Jack good-naturedly. "Brouhaha? Never you mind, Jack. I'm fine. And, young man, if anyone should be slowing down, it should be you!" Mrs. Bundle bantered. "You're like a cyclone; I never see you light!"

He shook his head in protest and kidded, "Me? Don't be daft, woman!"

"Yes *you*, who's going from sunup to sundown! *And*, who doesn't barely have time to stop for a decent meal."

A look of feigned bluster crossed Jack's face, "Ach! Didn't you know, now, Mrs. B, that I've these Superman qualities the likes of which our grand village of Pillson—not to mention our fine North Pillson Corners here—hasn't seen? Now, what's that I see on that lovely tray over there? All of a sudden, I'm famished!"

They all broke into laughter, and Mrs. Bundle proceeded to made sure Jack had his fill of lemonade, scones, and plenty of jam and butter.

His mouth full of goodies, Jack turned to Angie, a look between nonchalance and diffidence on his face. "Emm, Angie...," he asked, "You'll be going to the fireworks tonight up at Doc Dot's, wouldn't you now?"

"Of course! Dad said it's probably the last burnin' for awhile, what with no rain in sight! I wouldn't miss it for anything!" She smiled at Mrs. Bundle, then threw her napkin at him playfully. "Here, foolish! You've got butter on your chin!"

He grabbed the napkin, gave her a crooked smile, his blue eyes dancing, and dutifully wiped his face.

She added with a grin, "Isn't everyone going? It's a tradition, right? The Pillson Fireworks—just like Afternoon Tea!"

Chapter Thirty

Friday + Fourth + Fun = Fire

The most spectacular July 4th fireworks were best viewed from any of the numerous high ridges in Pillson or other area villages surrounding the tourist ski town of Ludlow—the base town for the majestic Okemo Mountain Ski Resort who put on the impressive lightshow.

The absolute most fantabulous place in the world, bar none, to experience this magnificently spectacular event was from Doctor Dot Jackson's little hilltop farm, Blue Bird Peak, situated beside Finnard's Brook. Dot Jackson's farmhouse sat perched on a crest of highland that offered a 360-degree vista of the surrounding mountains and villages. The fireworks were ten miles away at Okemo, the southwest view so spectacular from her property that people vied for a spot on her hill.

Imagine three jaggy, lofty mounds rising from the valley and set in a perfect triangle like bumpers on a pinball machine: the first being Okemo Mountain in all its glory as the southwest apex of the triangle; the second lower angular point the smaller, less imposing Ascutney Mountain and, third, about twenty-two miles in the distant northwest, Killington's massive peak.

The bonfire, set to burn alongside Finnard's Brook, was the backdrop for the spectacular fireworks, while everyone socialized nearby in lawn chairs and on blankets.

Angie was right—it was a tradition to trek up to Doc Dot's and watch the fireworks from that lofty roost; most of North Pillson

Corners were there, ready and waiting for the celebration to begin. The bonfire was always lit ceremoniously at 7:00 p.m. sharp—another tradition—and it burned and crackled like mini-fireworks by the brook, carefully being overseen by a handful of attendees.

As the twilight turned into darkness, a hush of anticipation came over the crowd gathered on the gently sloping hill.

"When's it going to start?" Erin asked excitedly, bobbing up and down like a wooden tap dancer on a jump stick.

"Well, now you hold onto your britches," Walter said, "It'll be any minute now, don't you know. What've you got—ants in your *pantalooms*?"

"Erin, come and sit with me." Angie called from her spot beside Mrs. Bundle and Althea. Erin bounded over, herself a veritable firecracker poised to burst with excitement.

"If the lass gives you any nonsense, just give me a holler, Angie!" Jack yelled from his vantage point a few yards away where he sat with his littlest sister in tow on the other side of Walter, Carl, and Clay.

The fireworks began promptly at sunset: 9:15 p.m., on the nose.

With the first loud boom, everyone clapped; the very first stream of sparkling, bright fire jetted into the air.

Little Aineen, wide-eyed and without one iota of sleepiness in sight, stood up and screamed in delight, her gibberish lost amidst all the crowd's cries.

"It's way past your bedtime, *deirfiur*!" Jack chided, hugging his baby sister close to him on the blanket. She wiggled from his grasp and clapped her hands in glee.

"Wook!!!!" She pointed, "*Pitty!* Yay!"

Each display was more spectacular than the last; noisy explosions of chartreuse, sapphire and azure filled the night air! Orange-gold prisms, white, searing circles, a rainbow of designs scattered the star-filled atmosphere with brilliance.

"Boom-boom-boom! *Boom!*" Aineen's newest word crescendoed with each fiery repetition.

More huge explosions ricocheted across the valleys; then even more explosions occurred, riddling the sky with a feast of color.

"*Ooohhh*! Pitty! Pitty fire!" She pointed her chubby finger toward the eastern skyline.

Jack looked on, distracted pleasure on his face as he watched the fireworks while listening to the chatty little girl. "Yes, pretty! Right, it is that!" He pointed toward Okemo. "Look, little one!" He showed her, "Over here!"

"No, no, no! Pitty!" Her hands clutched her bodice, her eyes transfixed. Thrilled, she pointed again, this time with both hands. "See boom?"

He turned from the large firework display and followed her gaze. Toward the east—in the distance—there was a bright orange light, a beacon in an otherwise very-dark scene. "Look, Aineen, look here! The fireworks are over there!" He tried to pick her up and direct her attention toward the fireworks display but she strained, looking over his shoulder at the red-ginger hue.

"No, no, NO!" The "terrible two's" threatened and he sensed a meltdown was imminent.

Erin, who had run over beside him, danced from one foot to the other and pointed, yelling, "Look, *bràthair*! Aye, Jack, can you see it, now? More fireworks!"

More huge explosions followed and impressive distant sparks sprayed like a fountain into the air. More people's attention was drawn to the distant east and the large report of explosive echoes from the valley five or so miles away. From their vantage point, the amazing brightness on that horizon looked like a brilliant rainbow.

"What's goin' on over there?" Angie asked, pointing to the valley below.

"Someone's got their own fireworks!" Althea exclaimed.

"Why, that's clear over to Brownsville," remarked Mrs. Bundle. "There's nothing that I know of going on in Brownsville!"

A greater, more urgent buzz spread through the crowd of onlookers.

"Oh, my Lord!" Doc Dot yelled from her patio. "It's a fire! Someone's got a fire!"

Like a ripple effect, shouts from other onlookers came rapidly now.

"There, over there! Fire!"

"Oh, no!"

"Mercy, me! Another fire!"

Walter Andersen cried out, "If I had to bet my last dollar, I'd say that's Wrinkle's Store! Let's go, boys!"

A flurry of activity ensued.

"Call the dispatch!" Carl cried to Doc Dot.

The men rushed to their vehicles and were off like a flash.

Throughout the night, the facts were gathered piecemeal. By morning, everyone knew of the tragedy. Sadly, a second fire had occurred and Walter was right. This time, it was Wrinkle's General Store.

The tragedy was, there had not been enough resources to adequately fight the blaze. Most all the firepower from Windsor County—Windsor, Springfield, Pillson, Woodstock, Hartland, and Plymouth—had sent their big trucks to Okemo Mountain to participate in the parade preceding the fireworks and then stayed as in past years, as a safety precaution, to oversee the fireworks display. Compounded with the fact that most all of the villages had volunteer firemen only, was the reality that the small villages like Brownsville, Weathersfield, and Cavendish depended to a large extent on their neighbors in a circumstance such as this. The store burned to the ground while a small group looked on helplessly. By the time the trucks had all reached the burning store, the fire was fully engaged and the building was pretty much gone.

But that was not the end of it.

Later that night, there was another fire, this time in an uninhabited hunting camp deep in the Hartland woods. Around midnight, word trickled through the grapevine that there was indeed another fire about ten miles away. The exhausted firefighters, still standing by at Wrinkle's General Store and hosing down the embers, regrouped quickly, sending another crew to the scene. The blaze was extinguished after having razed the camp and surrounding area of about three acres of woodland. Miraculously, no one was hurt and the firemen were able to contain the fire despite the tinder-like dryness of the brush.

The word *"pyromaniac,"* bandied about in the last few days, was full-blown by morning's light, not just by the area fire departments but by the auxiliary volunteers who took the rumors of arson from the fire sites back into their homes throughout the county.

Word quickly spread through the population that there was a very dangerous person in their midst; by all appearances, some madman was trying his best to burn the whole county down.

Chapter Thirty-One

Reality Sets In

"**M**ercy, am I pooped!"

Mrs. Bundle finally had a chance to put her feet up in the cozy den the next evening and cogitate on the previous evening's events.

She took the remote from the side table and switched on the TV, remarking, "Up 'til past midnight, what with all this misfortune, and then early to rise this morning! Cat's granny, the day just flew by, didn't it, C.C.?" Cracker lay on his poofy floor pillow, stroking his shiny fur with his rough tongue and flexing his sore muscles.

I must admit, it has been quite a day, he cat-thought.

She took a sip from her cool, tall glass of iced tea and sighed. This weather was near intolerable! Why, it must still be in the eighties. The television hummed on in the background. Amidst her fatigue, she vaguely realized it was close to 6:00 p.m.

Where had this day gone? She had been so active since early morning, running from here to there, helping out where she was needed, that she hadn't even had a chance to read her trusty *Rutland Daily News* and she reached for it on the table nearby.

Going to presses in the wee morning hours had ensured that the *Rutland Daily News*' lead story Saturday would be the heartbreaking but sensational news of the Wrinkle's General Store fire. On the front page, there was a massive color photo of the huge blaze, courtesy of one of the Johnny-on-the-spot locals, showing the store completely engulfed in fire. The headline read, *"**Brownsville Blaze Whips Wrinkle's!**"* with the disturbing byline, *"'Another Fire Forces Folks into Frenzy. Everyone wants to know: Is a Pyromaniac on the Loose in Windsor County?'"*

For the umpteenth time today, she said, "What a shame!" and shook her head in dismay.

Although the headline itself was imposing, there wasn't much there in the article that Mrs. Bundle hadn't already experienced firsthand or learned from the locals, and her eye traveled downward toward the other front-page feature story.

"Oh, my!" To her surprise, the newspaper had also picked up the story of Pillson's Dog Days of Summer Art Festival and she read the headline aloud. *"'Hidden Painting Discovered at Decaying Pillson Library—Folks Pray It's Worth a Fortune'."* She made her customary huffing sound, "Gaw!"

Featured in the story was the more sensational news surrounding the discovery of the mysterious painting and the library's sad dilemma, obviously included with a primary intention as the "hook" for human interest. There, in less detail than in the *Standard's* version, was the reproduced photograph of the "Mysterious painting behind the wall," along with a shorter, but more provocative, version of *The State Standard's* story.

Capitalizing more on the dramatic aspect of the library's dire situation and controversy, the *Daily News* had chosen for its byline, *"Pillson needs a miracle—this could be it!"* Mrs. Bundle read quickly through the article, *"'Amidst major debate, The Dog Days of Summer Art Festival plans are in the works,'* yes, yes....oh! *'It's true Pillson's in a pickle,'* Archie Plummer, Head Selectman, was quoted, *'but we'll all work together and come out of this winners!' Hmmm...* politicians!" She read on, skimming quickly, "Ah, good! There's the contact phone numbers for donations and help, all accurate, right, great!"

She put the paper on the chair beside her. "Well, it *is* good to see the word getting out about the Festival." The *Daily News's* basic information was indeed accurate, and with a readership much larger than the modest *Standard*, she mused, "I guess free advertising is free advertising. Thank you!"

She closed her eyes and waited for the beginning of the news broadcast; she was sure the fire would be the lead story.

A sad picture loomed in her mind's eye—*Wrinkle's*. All that was left to look at of Wrinkle's General Store now were the charred remains. Mrs. Bundle couldn't seem to shake the image.

Providentially, Elvina and Lucy hadn't been anywhere near the building when it had exploded into flames. The Merrimack County Beano Tournament, a good hour's drive away in Concord, happened to fall on that same night; Elvina and Lucy had gone to celebrate the Fourth in typical Bingo style. But for this reason, they would surely have been killed. With the store closed and their apartment above unoccupied, no one was hurt. Enough people in the area knew Elvina's habits so that it was easy for the State Police to track her down at the tournament. Having been sought out, found, and called back to Brownsville under these circumstances was truly heartbreaking for the mother and her daughter. When Mrs. Bundle had seen them early this morning, they were distressed beyond words, to say the least. She'd tried to comfort them as best she could.

Mrs. Bundle turned up the volume as the evening news began; first was the check-in with the weather which blared, "It's a heat wave, folks! We'll tell you later in the broadcast how this phenomenon and the recent fires are affecting people psychologically. But first," the newscaster's voice urged, "let's get *right* to the big blaze in Brownsville."

The segment narrative opened with powerful images of the fire in full force. Then, there was poor Elvina Wrinkle's ragged face in full-blown image on the screen. Elvina, muddy tracks of dried tears streaking her cheeks, described her feelings of horror to the TV interviewer upon discovering that her livelihood had burned to the ground. She began sobbing anew and cried, "Ah'm ruined now that the store's gone. With no income or inventory, Ah don't know how Ah'll make ends meet!"

When asked if she would rebuild, she sighed, "Ah'm not sure Ah can or will. It's been a struggle since my husband passed away last February. Rebuilding is the last of my worries at this point, what with the little insurance we have on the place....well, Ah just don't know. All Ah can say right now is, it's devastatin', just devastatin'."

The newscaster turned to the camera, "Just a heartbreaking story, all the way around." He turned back to her and asked, "How's your daughter doing?"

Elvina daubed at her eyes as the camera panned to a very lonely Lucy, who stood by the remains of the store with a blank look on her face, while Elvina said, "Why, of course, she's devastated! This store was her life, too. What's she gonna do now? Ah ask you, who, on earth, could do such a terrible thing?" Her drawl petered out into a mournful wail.

The voiceover indicated Mrs. Wrinkle and her daughter were being put up by the American Red Cross at the Pal-o-Mine Motel in Springfield until such time that they could find more permanent housing. For now, the two women would be provided with clothing, necessities, and food and money vouchers to assist in replacing the basic material possessions lost in the fire. "All services by the relief organization are free," the announcer said.

With previously-shot footage showing Elvina and Lucy in the foreground while the building blazed out of control, television viewers across the state could see just how devastating things were for the two victims. Lucy's shoulders were hunched over disconsolately while Elvina stared numbly at the fire in apparent disbelief. The mother had one arm around Lucy while she lit a Pall Mall one-handed with her lighter, the lighter's mother-of-pearl façade glistening against the fire's shadows. Her hand quivered while she still stared at the blaze.

Enter Weezy Bunton, looking larger than life on television, encircling the two girls with her large, protective arms and shielding them from the bright camera lights. A phone number ran at the bottom of the screen for emergency services and donations on behalf of the Wrinkles.

"On to our next big story. Everyone's officially on alert, folks!" The announcer's face was somber, "The Governor's press secretary issued a statement today indicating this summer is shaping up to be the driest one we've had since *1911*. In that historic summer's drought 75 years ago, dry brush and no rain caused a multitude of forest fires, one of which destroyed over 121 homes in West Windsor!" Old black and white images showed acres of charred woodland. "Even with the technology of today, authorities across the county are expressing concern that, because of the lack of rain in our forecast, any more fires could be catastrophic to the area. It's a volatile situation, folks, one that you can be assured our WTMX crew will stay on top of."

Mrs. Bundle wondered, as she watched the TV, if the mushrooming hysteria was being driven, in some manner, by the overzealous media trying to keep ahead of the stories of fire and possible drought in their viewership's small communities. "What do you think, Cracker?"

He stared fixedly at the TV screen, then issued a plaintive "*Meowww!*"

Later in the broadcast, another related spot on the evening news—during the educational portion—focused on an emergency scenario called, "*What to Do if YOU Get caught In a Fire.*" Pictures detailing each step appeared as the reporter's voice boomed forth, "Number 1–*Get out immediately.* Never stay to collect your things. Number 2—*Stay low!* Crawl low to get out of a smoke filled room. The air closer to the floor is easier to breathe. Number 3--Very important, viewers, *Before opening any door, feel it!* If it's hot there could be fire behind and you will need to find another route. And finally, *Once out, stay out!* Never, *ever, ever,* friends, return to a burning building. Remember, it's better to be *safe* than *sorry.* Ellissa Guernet reporting for WTMX. In our next 'Inform the Public' segment, we'll be talking about…."

Mrs. Bundle's tired mind zoned out as the newscast went to commercial. It was all good information, she reasoned. However, the way it's presented surely makes one *quite* uneasy about one's own personal situation.

Cracker settled back into his cushion restlessly.

She picked up the remote and turned off the television, asking, "What's happening to our little world?" In her den, the silence echoed as densely as a thick fog, with no one able to give an uncomplicated answer to her question…

After the local evening news that night, the Sheriff's office received over one hundred calls from outraged citizens, their tempers now as combustible as the fires that had been deliberately set, demanding that something be done to get the perpetrator of these heinous arsons off their fair village streets as soon as possible.

Chapter Thirty-Two

Damage Control

It didn't take long for the Sheriff's Department to make an arrest. On Sunday morning, the news was out that they had someone in custody.

Weezy Bunton stopped by the Andersens that morning on her way to get groceries in West Lebanon and, by the looks of her, she was ready to burst wide open with the latest gossip. She had barely plunked her ample body down into the wooden captain's chair in Walter's comfortable country kitchen before her mouth ran like slippery whiskey down a parched man's gullet.

"Just came from the early breakfast crowd at Herder's! You won't believe it! The whole place is just a-buzzin'. They got someone! Seems they brought Junior Veakey in for questionin' last night. *Junior Veakey*!!!! You know, Barny's son—the one who don't talk too good."

The kids were gone; up at the crack of dawn, Angie and Jack had taken the girls to Goochie Pond for a morning of swimming and would be home by lunchtime.

Mrs. Bundle, who had stopped down for coffee, was sitting at the table with Walter. Mortified at this announcement, she cried out, "What? Oh, no, no. It can't be! Not Vincent. He's not capable of anything malicious like this. I'm sure of that."

Weezy's head bobbed up and down and the antique chair shook violently. "Oh, yessiree! Junior Veakey! That's who they got! I ain't kiddin' ya."

"Junior? That little runt? Skinny as a rail fence, for gory's sake," Walter Andersen exclaimed. "Why, he's 'bout as dangerous as my grandma's petticoat. Always been a harmless fellow, wouldn't hurt," (he put his forefinger and thumb an inch apart), "a flea. Or a tic *or a* mite." He'd made the distance progressively smaller between the two fingers until they finally touched, "For that matter, even a *midgie!*"

"Well, they must know somethin' we don't," Weezy replied, "'cuz he's top on their list of suspects, from what Gladys Pinehope says. She works at the register at Maplefield's and—it being right next door to the Sheriff's digs and the courthouse—all the deputies come in there for their coffee and other doodads morning, noon, and night. Word is, they've got their man."

"Poppycock!" Walter slammed his fist on the table. "I don't believe it, not for an instant. I've known Barny Veakey my whole life—he's tougher 'n a boiled owl but honest as the day is long. Poor as they are, he still taught his boy right. And Junior, why, he's always been a polite boy. Not great in the looks department, I must admit—he's kinda a wiltin' *dandyline.*"

Weezy shook her head vehemently, choking with laughter, and raised her flabby arms in the air, oblivious to the chair's machinations underneath her. "Whoo-*eee!*" She wooped. "That's rare, Walter! '*Wiltin' dandyline*'! Gaw! You mean to say he's a shrinkin' violet, don't ya?" She wiped her eyes gleefully. "I got to remember that one, for sure. All I know is, they've got him in there–in the holdin' tank coolin' his heels—and they ain't letting him go 'til he spills the beans."

"Sounds like a rush to judgment to me," Mrs. Bundle offered. "What with all the hysteria floating around, there's just too much pressure on the authorities right now. Sometimes that can be a problem. I just can't believe–"

Just then Carl Andersen came rushing through the kitchen screen door, his usual reserved manner clearly disturbed. He said tensely, "I just heard some pretty distressing news, Pop."

"Is it about Junior?"

"Yuh, it is. Barny's son. They've arrested him—charged him with setting all three fires!"

"I *told* you!" Weezy cried, smiling like she'd just swallowed the biggest canary on record.

By now, everyone watching her flailing body took a collective breath, unable to ignore the chair. A very distinct "cr-rack!" could be heard from directly underneath of where her round bottom was lodged in place.

Walter shifted uncomfortably, his eyes flinching.

Oblivious, Weezy continued on, "Let's hope they got the right guy—otherwise, we're *all* going to be living at the Pal-O-Mine before this *pyro* is done."

Walter leaned forward, his beady eyes intently watching the lower half of the chair distractedly as she spoke, studying it as though the chair's stamina in holding up the load was a scientific anomaly.

Carl removed his ball cap and motioned outside. "I'm afraid you may be right. Lonnie Macomber just swung by. He heard it from Stevie Bender from the ambulance team who got it straight from Vaughan Kirby who works the night shift cleaning crew at the Sheriff's dispatch. Say, I'd like to give the fellow—Junior, that is—the benefit of the doubt, but from what they're saying, he was seen in both areas of Tuddy's and Wrinkle's the same night of each fire. Lonnie said Steve said Vaughan heard the dispatch say his truck was identified by at least three eyewitnesses."

"Well, that's about as convoluted as it gets," Mrs. Bundle opined.

Carl paused, cogitating a second. "Pretty foolish, though, that he'd take his truck to do a crime, what with that big 'Veakey's Trash and Treasure' sign on the side."

Weezy said, "Not to mention all them dents and paint marks! You can spot that mess of junk a mile away. Gaw! It'd be like puttin' up a marquee!"

"Paint marks and dents—so what!" Walter's eyes snapped with anger. "And, an old truck? Jumpin' jee hozafats, if havin' a danged old dented truck in your driveway was a crime, everybody in these parts would be in the jail! That don't prove *nothin'* no-how to me!"

Weezy leaned in, flushed with all the excitement, and whispered, "I heard he's got some kind of family feud goin' with the Tudhopes!"

Mercy, Mrs. Bundle reflected, *she's certainly brimming over with good thoughts, isn't our fair Weezy?* Aloud, she said, "Really, Weezy, where do you hear these kind of things?"

Carl nodded. "Yup, I gotta say, she's right about that. I heard that one, too—a long time ago. About there being some ongoing vendetta against the Tudhope clan."

Walter held up his hand, as though testifying, and nodded. "And *vicey*-versa! It's true. There ain't no love lost betwixt the Tudhopes and the Veakeys. That's been goin' on forever and a day." The few lone wisps of hair on the top of his head waggled to and fro. "Every *body* knows that."

Weezy Bunton beamed broadly and pointed two plump fingers at no one in particular. "Yuh-*see*?" The chair moaned in agony beneath her, filled to capacity.

"Still, that don't mean he's guilty of a crime," Walter threw back.

Carl continued, "Apparently, they've got something else that they can hang on him over at Elvina's, too. From all accounts, he'd been working on the water line that day, something to do with the well pump at the General Store."

"Yes, we saw him there the other day," Mrs. Bundle said. "Althea and I. He was doing odd chores for her. Since Norbert died, he's been helping out."

Carl nodded, "Well, Lonnie said Hez Woburn says Junior turned *off* the inside sprinkler system—it's required by the state code to be on in public buildings at all times. Word is, Junior's saying he's pretty sure he turned it back on. Sounds flimsy. Anyway, the police think his 'forgetfulness' may have been intentional, because that fire blazed out of control and the system never activated. And that's straight from the Fire Marshal's office where Hez runs the volunteer training program, from what Lonnie says."

Weezy forged full steam ahead. "Not only that! I know for a fact…well, really, ask anybody—everybody knows Junior's sweet on Lucy! Elvina was beside herself trying to keep those two lovebirds apart! Said she's been keepin' a hairy eyeball on them since she first noticed what was goin' on. It even kept her from gallivantin' all over creation from Walpole to Keene--" She stopped short and shifted dangerously in her chair.

It groaned again, resonating with a noise that sounded just like a big, long "No-o-o-o!"

Her face was rosy and she paused, made one more shift to get as comfy as the crunched space would allow, then went on, "Anyway, forget about the gallivantin' comment; it's a fact! She told me so herself! Been goin' on for weeks. Not that Lucy's a looker by any stretch of the imagination, but Elvina, God bless her, thinks she's prime for the pickin'. *And* she also thinks he's not good enough—told him he was 'riff-raff' right to his face! So maybe he' got a...what'd you call it, Carl? A *ven-det-ta* against Elvina Wrinkle, too!"

Mrs. Bundle felt a rush of angry heat entering her body. "What about the fire up at that camp in Hartland? Was he up *there*, too?"

Weezy shrugged her big shoulders dispassionately. "Probly."

Mrs. Bundle said, "So everyone's got him guilty and convicted before he even gets his say in court?"

Walter Andersen patted her arm. "Now, Lettie, don't go gettin' a bee in your *bloomers*. It's only the way country folk talk, don't you know."

But she was firm in her conviction. "Yes, that's right, Walter. It's all talk, *all* conjecture at this point. And look how it spreads! Just like...a fire out of control!"

Weezy hopped up and the empty seat heaved a huge sigh of relief. "Well, enough of this lollygaggin'! I gotta get to West Leb and be back home by noon. Horace'll be needin' some help out in the barn. Gaw! A woman's work ain't never done."

As she passed by, she reached over and tapped Mrs. Bundle's shoulder. "Don't you worry, dearie. If he ain't guilty, he'll get off, for sure. And even if he *is* guilty, why, look at all them big criminals—ax slayers, rapists, serial killers, wife murderers, and such," her eyes were sparkling with the grisly description. "I'm talkin' about them that's *guilty as sin* and go scot-free anyway! All they gotta do is say they're off their rocker—or that they were bonkers when they hacked their loved one to death—or, they got a raw deal growing up and have twenty-odd personalities. And they get off, clean as your mother's whiskers! It's a crazy world! Just watch! Junior'll probably skate, too!'"

Walter stood behind Weezy, discreetly inspecting the weight-challenged chair she had vacated moments before. As he watched the burly woman get into her truck, he tapped the chair's wooden spindle back lightly and whispered softly, *"Good ol' girl..."*

Mrs. Bundle made small clucking noises with her tongue and whispered, "Oh, my Lord, what has he got himself into?" Louder, she exclaimed, "I don't know about you all, but I'm going to keep a good thought for that poor boy."

Chapter Thirty-Three

Barny

When Mrs. Bundle arrived home a half-hour later, her answering machine was blinking rapidly. There were four messages. Pushing the play button, she waited for the first message…but there was complete silence. The second wasn't much different, save for the distinctive *"Click!"* of somebody on the other end hanging up.

On the third message she thought she heard someone (possibly of the male persuasion) sigh deep and long, and then clear his throat. Just as he began his first consonant, the beep sounded long and loud.

On the final message she hit pay dirt. As she listened intently, she was surprised to hear the distinctively high-pitched, shaky voice of Barny Veakey. The proprietor of the local junk haven, *Veakey's Trash and Treasure*, spoke very hesitantly.

"Miz Bundle, ah yuh… it's Barny here, up at the Trash and Tresha. I been tryin' to get ahold of you here at the payphone. Guess you probly heard." Mrs. Bundle heard a huge gulp, followed by a gravelly clearing of his throat. "Uh. My boy's in a right pickle. Yup." He paused and she heard a big gulp. "Well now! He's been askin' for you. I'd be much obliged if you'd come up to the barn. We got plenty of scrap metal I can trade in. The copper alone's worth a fortune. So, don't worry none about gettin' compensated. Yup. I'll be here waitin'. Yup. Okay…" *Beep*!

Barny's inexperienced use of the telephone was evident; more so, the effort of talking to nobody but a machine had left him stressfully tongue-tied.

The last she knew, the Veakeys didn't have a phone—in fact, the last she knew, the local Vermontel phone lines and system didn't go that far up the mountain, which must be why he found himself fighting with a payphone. To be sure, she quickly checked the phone book and found there was no listing for Barnabus Veakey.

She stood silent for a second. Her loyal partner appeared from nowhere.

"C'mon Cracker, let's go."

Mrs. Bundle grabbed her purse as Cracker tripped along quickly—and with fierce energy—behind her. Once they arrived at the "Trash and Tresha," he would courageously face this element of the occupational hazards of detective work. In fact, he would be more than willing to do his part because he knew what they were in for.

Mice! And plenty of them.

She backed Junie out of the barn, and headed for the high country. The ride up the mountain to the Veakey establishment, which was located on TaDaDump Road just before the entrance to the Transfer Station, was always somewhat arduous, partly due to the winding road, but more so, due to the remoteness of the location. There were fewer and fewer inhabitants on the way up as one got closer and closer to the waste facility and, truth be told, not many enjoyed making the trip.

Junebug puttered up the mountain, then made a sharp left and turned onto TaDaDump Road, sailing by the first of only three occupied houses on a road that wended its way slowly around and around the curves and culminating at the Transfer Station, which served all the surrounding small villages including Pillsonville.

The first home they passed was a 1972 rust-colored trailer that Daisy Trumble had retired to "brand new" after her husband Travers had passed away. Although the home was modest and Daisy was now into her 90's, she still kept quite a garden, and her rose bushes (with over twenty different varieties) were already on their first blooming.

"Aren't they spectacular?" Mrs. Bundle asked; Cracker blinked his acknowledgement.

The second house had a huge hand-painted sign on the front lawn: "Experienced House Painters: Inquire Within." The sign had been there, on the front lawn, as long as Mrs. Bundle could remember. On the one hand, it was great advertisement; on the other hand, the multi-hued, (mostly) brilliant-blue house behind the promotional sign, was not. That is to say, the house had *once* been painted a bright shade of blue, almost luminously azure, but the dwelling showed only the remnants of the original color and was more now a rainbow of many other layers of paint. Like the various shades found in the paint wheel at the local hardware store, it appeared almost every color was present and accounted for: chipped white combined with dark gray in some places, yellow-green and red-gold in others. The final shade at the base of the clapboard was the natural gray color of worn, weather-beaten wood. Ironically, the sign's advertisement appeared to have been lost on this house—whose owners, the Conroy Family Painters (in the business for forty-odd years), were evidently much too busy to take care of 4 TaDaDump Road. Truth was, they were known to do a bang-up job on *other* people's property, to be sure.

Traveling on, they passed two long-abandoned, early model trailers, boarded up and with no possibility of resurrection.

The last house was Barny Veakey's combined dwelling and business, located steps away from the big Transfer Station entrance whose bolted gate held an obtrusive sign that read: "Transfer Station hours—Wednesday 8-2 and Saturday 8-4 p.m. **No access any other time!**"

The Veakey family had lived on this mountain for generations. There was a time, decades before, when a lot of the surrounding acreage had been fertile farmland. Over the years, it remained untilled and uncared for; hence, a good amount had now returned to the natural growth of large pines and hardwoods.

During the 1930's, the parcel next door to the Veakeys had been designated as the official Town Dump. It had continued as such until the state tightened up the dumping laws and the same site then became the "Transfer and Recycling Station," with the trash now being transported to another site far, far away from Windsor County.

Trash was the Veakey business; it was where they made the lion's share of their meager earnings, collecting everything and anything of any value. To the undiscerning eye, the Veakey property looked like one solid acre of mounded, pure junk.

Barny and Junior, the father and son team, could be found twice a week at the Transfer Station sifting through the various piles of refuse. They, like other industrious trash entrepreneurs, particularly liked the metal pile: copper piping, tools, old machinery, broken lawn mowers and the like, which could often compute to considerable dollars when sold as scrap metal to the larger scrap metal network (who then sold it on the open and foreign market). As property owners hauled in their "trash" and deposited it in the appropriate pile on "Dump Day," the Veakeys were there lickety-split to kindly take the "treasures" off their hands—consequently, the name of their thriving, next-door business—Veakey's Trash and Treasure.

Mrs. Bundle drove down the long gravel driveway leading into the Veakey empire, which was lined with various metal barrels, cast-off machinery and equipment and other larger paraphernalia, including two early model automobiles: a 1937 Nash Lafayette Coupe missing the front end and a 1970 Cadillac DeVille that had seen much better days. Barny, an expert at vintage anything, also sold used car parts on the side.

The place looked deserted. The modest Veakey home, a small log cabin the size of most affluent people's master bathroom, sat close to the oversized garage or "barn" (as Barny called it), which was chock full of every conceivable household item, doodad, whimsy, thingamabob, gizmo, or overall piece of junk known to mankind—

basically any kind of junk that anyone could ever need or want. Various outbuildings—also chock full—were scattered intermittently throughout the acre or so of property like warts on a blotchy face.

It was a wonder that Barny could ever find anything, but he did.

Folks knew if they needed "it," he was likely to have "it." And, mind you, if you had plenty of time to wait, he'd put his hands on "it" eventually.

A brief description by a potential shopper of any given item most always generated, first, deep thought; then second, a look of recognition from Barny; third, a frantic rummaging around (which could take two minutes or twenty); and finally, a happy, satisfied consumer walking away with *just* that right item.

One thing was for sure; the Veakeys aimed to please, and the customer was always right.

Mrs. Bundle noted that parked out front by the garage-barn was the very recognizable *Trash and Treasures* truck that Junior used in his daily travels to pick up "giveaway" items, do odd jobs, and take care of errands for his father. Barny rarely left the mountain unless it was an emergency and Junior, because of his shyness and speech impediment, wasn't prone to stray much farther than his father did, unless absolutely necessary.

Mrs. Bundle figured Barny had determined that his Junior being ensconced in Springfield Correctional was definitely an emergency—hence, his trip down the mountain to the nearest public phone booth at Gully's Gas-Up-and-Go.

As Mrs. Bundle stepped out of the VW's driver side, she barely avoided hitting the discarded, old sewing machine on its side a few inches away from the car door; meanwhile, she noticed the abandoned toilet in the nearby gully. There was no doubt; it certainly felt a bit like a land mine when you visited Barny. No matter where you stepped, there was a chance you might collide with something.

It was at that moment that Barny Veakey, a crooked little man, came out from behind the building. Everything about him was bent, from his curved, wildly-white eyebrows to his humped, twisted back. His usually-wizened-but-happy face looked menacing today; that is, until he saw it was not a stranger, customer, or Nosy Parker, but his friend, "Miz Bundle." His scowl turned to kindliness, and he smiled broadly, his tongue resting in the large gap between his two incisor teeth (left and right respectively).

He tried to talk, then held up a waiting finger and gummed a mumbled, "Way dust a miniii–," and scuttered, crablike, inside the cabin.

Cracker paced in a small, safe circle, his paws gingerly touching the ground, while Mrs. Bundle looked around in wonder at the myriad of piled stuff. *What didn't he have*, she rhetorically asked herself. *Why, there was even a kitchen sink, right there by that old hand-crank washing machine.*

He was back in a decent time, an upper and lower set of false teeth in his hand, which he quickly popped in place, clicked a couple trial times, and uttered with much greater precision, "Danged teeth!"

Mrs. Bundle extended her hand. "Hi, Barny, how goes the battle?"

He wiped his two gnarled hands on his overalls, then took out an oversized handkerchief, spit into it and wiped them again, before finally extending his own hand and pumping hers enthusiastically. "I *knewed* you'd come! You always been kind to my Junior. Taught him all that art stuff. And patient. I thank ye, Miz Bundle, for all you done. The boy and me always did 'preciate it!"

"I've always thought a lot of Vincent. You know that, Barny."

He motioned to the log hut, and she followed him inside, where her eyes adjusted to the darkened and dank interior.

As they sat in his small kitchen (which doubled as living room and bedroom for the old man and his son), he poured himself a cup of coffee from the ancient percolator coffee pot.

"I likes it cold or hot, makes no matter to me. Sure you don't want some?"

She declined.

He took a long drink, then sat back, deflated, in the rickety chair. "*Gaw!* What a danged, festerin' mess!"

Cracker sat below his feet and feverishly licked at his glossy coat. Looking around, he had to agree with Barny. Meanwhile, he kept his darting cat eyes peeled; the premises seemed ripe for various smaller, more vulnerable creatures than himself, and he didn't want to miss an opportunity.

"The county's got my boy, Miz Bundle! This whole arrest thing's got me thrown for a loop. I'm done in, is all I kin say."

"I know. I was so sorry to hear about Vincent."

"Yuh. Like I was sayin' on the *tellyfun*, he's been askin' for you. They got him down at the new prison."

"How can I help?"

"He says to tell you first, he didn't do it! 'Make sure you say it, Pops,' he says, 'tell her I ain't the one they want!' And, Miz Bundle, I believe my boy. He wouldn't never hurt no one. Not in a lifetime of Sundays! 'Specially, not with what he's been through his whole life."

She nodded sympathetically. "May I ask you some questions?"

"Ask away."

"Why did they arrest him?"

"Don't know. Heck, they don't tell us lowly mountain folk what's goin' on. Came up here, the big brass did, read him his rights," he spat unceremoniously onto the floor, "and took him away in handicuffs. A couple hours later they was back up here once again! Had them papers makin' it legal to look everything over. Only went through the house here but a short time," he looked around at the sparse furnishings, "then the barn, searchin' for Lord only knows—and then *conferscated* all them tools in the truck! Even took his danged blowtorch!" He swore and spat again. "He'll go right off his nut when he finds that out, for sure! Holds great store by them—'specially that blow torch. Gotta have that piece for any of them welding jobs he gets, here and thither."

Strike one, Cracker cat-thought.

Mrs. Bundle shook her head and changed the subject. "What about this thing about the Tudhopes and the Veakeys? Is there any substance in that?" He stared blankly at her. "About you all...not getting along?"

He dug his broken-down heels into the faded linoleum and scowled. "That ain't somethin' I care to be discussin'."

"I'm sorry, Barny, but…is it true what people are saying? That there's some kind of bad feelings between the two families?"

He gave a quick jerk of acknowledgement. "Goes way back," he said tersely. "We Veakeys ain't got no use for the Tudhopes."

"Why?"

"Wee-llll…." he stopped and grunted, "It'd take a month of Sundays to explain, but….well, they's always been tryin' to lord it over on us. Kickin' us when we's down. If you ain't noticed, we're about as poor as Jobe's turkey."

"Who's *they*? Ger and Phoebe?"

"Nope. I ain't got nothin' against them personally, 'ceptin' they's Tudhopes. Mostly, it's that whole Tudhope clan from way back, all of the rest of 'em. They's vicious—murderers and thieves! That's all I'll be sayin'."

Cracker raised a paw of surrender from the dusty floor: *Strike two.*

Realizing this was another definite sore spot, Mrs. Bundle moved on. "What else have they got to hang on Vincent?" She tried to tread lightly. "What kind of questions did they ask you when they were here, Barny?"

He shook his head disgustedly. "Asked me if he'd been '*off balance*' the last few weeks. Was he 'disturbed' about anything particular? Hell's bells! 'Course, he is, I told 'em. I says, 'not any more 'n usual!' Don't he always hang back 'cuz he's *off* a dite–due to his affliction? Ain't he always been a loner? Wasn't we always tryin' to get him some help? Miz Bundle, you and I both know that."

Cracker didn't even bother with the proverbial *three strikes—you're out*! He slapped his mitt ferociously at a wayward cobweb hanging just above him from his vantage point underneath the table. *Poor ol' Junior Veakey*, he cat-thought.

Mrs. Bundle nodded sympathetically and wondered to herself just how much damage had already been done.

Barny leaned back in the wooden chair and went on, "You know, Junior was sickly through most of his youngster years. 'Course, he was born a preemie—tiny pipsqueak of a thing!" He smiled through his thick whiskers. "Fought like the dickens to stay alive, and the little rug rat made it! Been fightin' his way up ever since. I always felt real bad he didn't have no Ma to take care of him through the bad times. I had to be both to him after she passed." He spat. "Well, I done the best I could with what we had." He looked around at their meager surroundings, his eyes finally resting on the nearby cot. He reached over to the bedside and picked up a large black tome, very old and tattered. "Miz Bundle, this is the *only* thing we really got. The Good Book, passed down from Veakey t' Veakey. Used to read it every night when he was a pup. You know," his eyes filled with surprise, "that kid neva, *evva* complained about nothin'. Neva, evva. Best son a father could evva…," he stopped, too choked up to continue.

He took another gulp of the cold dark sludge in the cup in front of him.

"It's okay, Barnabus. If I can help, I will. But I'm not sure how…"

"He wants you to go into that there prison and talk to him. Says he thinks you can hep him. Like I say, I got plenty of scrap metal here. For your compensatin' fee." He looked out the window at his junkyard with a keen eye. "It's worth a fair amount, I believe. Copper's goin' through the roof—Japanese want it so bad they do *what-evva* to get their hands on it! What-evva it takes, I can pay." His face took on a stubborn, proud look. "I can be sellin' the lot of it, if I have to, to get him out of that *pen-tentry*."

"Barny, don't worry about my fee. I'm not even sure I can help."

His eyes fell, and a cloud of defeat came over his face. "Oh, don't say that, Miz Bundle. I ain't got any other…."

She reached out to him and touched his arm. "*But*, of course I will try my best," she reassured him. "We're not giving up on the boy, that's for sure! I'll go right in today and see him. Hopefully, we'll be able to clear this up, one way or another. However, we need to know more to be able to really help him. And, maybe…one final question answered by you, too, before I go."

He looked at her expectantly.

"What do you know about him and Lucy Wrinkle?"

She noted his surprised reaction.

"Lucy *Wrinkle*? You mean, down at the store?"

"Uh-huh. People have said they're sweet on each other."

"Hmm, I wouldn't neva have guesstimated on that. Lucy?" He hesitated, and his eyes studied the dark ceiling. "Well, really now, truth be told, I cain't say. Not that he's never been sweet on nobody. Well, hardly ever; mostly pinin' from afar, if you know'd what I mean. Nevertheless," he leaned his face close to Mrs. Bundle (so close she watched with fascination as his clenched teeth moved jerkily against his gums), "he's been moonin' around here somethin' awful—like a lovesick sparrow—oh, I'd wager for... about the last couple full moons!"

"Really?"

"Yup, I knowed—well, that's to say, I *figured*—he got his heart stolen by someone of the female wiles. Right head over heels, I notioned!" He raised a gnarly hand, "Up and down–happy one day, in the dumps the next—that's exactly how he's been! Off kilter. A father can tell, don't you know..."

"Did you ask him?"

"Huh?"

"Did you ask him *who*? Who he was smitten with?"

He looked at her as though she'd asked him to fetch the moon barehanded. "'*Course* not."

She looked at him quizzically. "Why not?"

He gave her a wise nod. "Why? That's his business, ain't it? A man's gotta have his privacy in this world, even if he ain't got *nothin*' else. Besides, I cain't be askin' him why he's up 'til all hours of the night every night, now can I?" He flicked a grimy finger toward the other cot in the far corner of the room. "Bed ain't even slept in most of the time, comes into this place at dawn looking like a raccoon, his eyes is so dark and tired! And cus-sed *tetchy* on top of everythin'!" He shook his head; his face was a hopeless vision as realization slowly set in. Eyes wide, he moaned, "Good God! Don't look too good for my boy, do it?"

Game over, Cracker cat-thought.

As Mrs. Bundle drove slowly back down the winding TaDaDump Road, she felt her stomach sinking also, bit by bit.

She hoped with all her heart that she would be able to help Vincent in some way because, truth be told, he was going to need all the help he could get. Unfortunately, based upon the naïve statements that his father had shared with her and Cracker in the last half-hour, she didn't think Barny was the best defender of Junior's innocence.

If what Barny had said was true, in all likelihood the authorities may have confiscated what they believed could be the arson weapon used in the fires—and, she wondered, used to deface the Welcome to Hartland sign, too? Based on the little she knew at this point, it also appeared they were easily establishing a case for motive, as well, by the implication that here was the perfect perpetrator: a troubled individual bent on destruction.

And Junior's father, by his own admission, could not or would not be able to substantiate Junior's whereabouts during the times all three fires were set.

"Cat's granny!" she exclaimed, oblivious to the hairpin turns Junie executed with precision as her own distracted mind nervously went over these most daunting obstacles already established in Junior's case. Her eyes roamed the road nervously as she headed for the Correctional Facility, fretting aloud, "Lettie, you're going to have your work cut out for you on this one!"

Amen to that, Cracker cat-thought, as he slid like an oiled duck from side-to-side in this backseat joyride.

Chapter Thirty-Four

Junior

The slight-figured, bony young man sat dejectedly at the stark table, his head in his hands. In terms of looks, the apple didn't fall far from the tree, and there was, indeed, a strong resemblance between Barny and his son. The difference, though, was the youthful spark of fortitude about the lad that Mrs. Bundle usually saw, a certain defiant "stick-to-itiveness," a survivor mentality that he had possessed from the time he was a youngster. It was a trait Mrs. Bundle had always liked, a feature she was convinced showed character and resolve. Trouble was, as she looked at the boy now, she didn't see that spark.

Today, Mrs. Bundle was alarmed at his condition. He looked like he had been run over by a trailer truck, emaciated and done in. His skin was a pale gray, his eyes dull and lifeless. He appeared breathless, as though he had had the wind knocked out of him, and his soft blonde eyelashes had a slight tremor. His hair, usually slicked down and relatively neat, was all askew; sharp peaks of dull, ochre-colored wisps, looking like twisted sticks and twigs, stood up at all angles all over his scrawny head. He was so skinny she could see the silver-blue veins pulsing in his arms.

The first words out of his mouth held the sharp sting of hopelessness.

"Nothin's b-b-been g-g-oin' r-r-right lately. It's all a b-b-big m-m-m-mess."

"It's all right, Vincent. I'm here. If you want me to help you, I will."

He looked up at her, and his eyes were wet with tears. "I…I-I'm a-sh-shamed."

"What? Ashamed? Why?"

"I-I-I've l-l-let my P-P-P-Pops d-d-down…and you, t-t-too."

She leaned into the glass that separated them and gave him a fierce look. "Did you have anything to do with any of those fires, Vincent?"

He glared up at her. "NO! N-n-no!" he shouted, angry eyes disbelieving that she, of all people, would ask him that question. He looked back down at his rough, calloused hands. The nearby guard shifted and his hand moved protectively toward the nightstick on his belt.

Vincent lowered his voice and spoke slowly and as precisely as he could. "I d-d-didn't d-do it! N-N-None of it. R-R-Really!"

"I believe that you didn't do it, Vincent."

His face softened and he heaved a huge sigh. "G-Geez! You d-d-don't know wh-wh-what that m-m-means to m-m-me, Mrs. B." His eyes held the slightest glimmer of hope, and she smiled. He murmured, "You've always…b-b-been th-there for me."

"And you for me, too! Why, when Arthur died, you helped me so much. At the time, just the smallest task seemed so daunting, and you were always there. I've *always* appreciated your help during that time, Vincent."

He nodded. "Wh-When I f-first met you, I w-w-was j-just a scared, unhappy k-kid. You h-h-helped me—n-not just l-learn a whole b-bunch about b-b-books and r-readin', b-b-but m-more. I can c-count on one h-h-hand those that sh-sh-showed me k-kindness gr-growin' up. You—and the Pr-Pr-Professor—th-that's pr-pretty much it. He always done r-r-right by me, ma'am. J-J-Just like you."

"Oh, Vincent, I remember you as a young teenager. How you grew, not just in height, but," she tapped her temple lightly, "here, in your mind, too! And, Professor Watson particularly loved talking to you about history back then."

He nodded and his twisted mouth formed the words slowly. "Y-Yuh! Him g-goin' on and on ab-b-bout ge-ge-ge-genealogy," he paused to catch his breath, "and you t-t-talkin' to m-m-me about m-m-music and p-paintin' and s-s-such."

She smiled softly. "Yes, I remember how you latched onto those Art Masters books especially. You loved those. In fact, if I remember correctly, you were really very artistic yourself. Did you ever pursue that?"

He made a small huffing sound and looked down dejectedly. "Uh-huh. S-S-Sometimes. Anyway—b-besides you and the Pr-Pr-Professor, well…I ain't r-really got n-no one in my c-c-corner." He looked pathetic and swallowed hard. "Mrs. B-B-Bundle, do you th-th-think you can help me?"

"I wish I knew how!" she said helplessly.

"I w-want you to h-help m-me g-g-get off! And f-f-find out who d-d-done these f-f-fires, if you can! It ain't me. And I kn-know it l-l-looks b-bad for m-me."

"Do you have an attorney?"

"Yup." His voice again lacked hopefulness.

"What does he—or she—have to say about all this?"

He gulped and went on, "It's a sh-she. I just m-met with her f-f-for about ten m-m-minutes; then she had to go. Sh-she's a n-n-nice enough l-l-lady, but sh-she's been assigned t-t-to me as a p-p-public def-fender. She's r-r-really b-busy, sh-she said. It kinda f-felt l-l-like she's…goin' thr-through the m-motions."

"Well, that doesn't sound promising." She rubbed her eyes. "Okay. Let's start from square one here. If I'm going to work for you, I need to ask you some questions. And you *must* be as honest and forthright as you can."

He nodded and said, "Sh-Shoot."

"Let me first say everything we discuss, all our conversations, everything--will be kept confidential. Do you understand?"

"Yuh, th-that's what sh-she said, t-too. Mrs. B-Bundle, I n-n-need to get out of h-here!" He glanced around him and it reminded her of a caged cougar. "I c-can e-e-explain most everything if th-they'd g-give me a ch-chance."

"Unfortunately, you've been charged. Now that you're in the system, they have to follow protocol. You have to go through your attorney, and then she will advise what is best for you. However—first things first, Vincent: do you know *why* they think they have a case against you?"

"W-well, they th-think I b-burned that s-s-sign over in Hartland, for st-starters. S-s-said they could t-tell it w-was m-me from my bl-bl-blowtorch in the tr-truck." Worry lines were etched into his forehead. "But, th-there's no w-way th-that can be."

"How so?"

"Well, 'cuz I know I d-d-didn't do it!"

Her tongue clicked in dismay. "Regrettably, that's not a very good defense."

"Yuh. They s-said I g-got it in for the victims of the f-f-fire. I d-don't know wh-what the heck they m-mean by th-that."

"Well, I think they are referring to a feud people are talking about. Between your family and the Tudhopes? I tried, but couldn't get Barny to discuss it with me."

He shrugged and looked disinterested, but there was a cloud behind his eyes. "It's the w-way it's always been. My Pops told me s-somethin' about it."

"What happened?"

He shrugged again. "All I kn-know is the V-V-Veakeys and the Tudhopes have b-b-been b-b-battlin' for d-decades. They all n-n-never l-l-liked each other...n-not one bit. I tr-tried to f-find out m-more, b-but...." The corner of his mouth turned down into a pessimistic scowl, "n-no l-luck."

"Why?"

"D-Dead end. I even asked the Pr-Professor. He s-said he'd try to f-find out, but....n-never d-did. Went way back in my family history—lots of V-V-Veakey relations. P-Pops says the T-T-Tudhopes are why we V-Veakeys are l-l-like we are. They're to bl-blame for everything. Th-that's all I know. Even n-n-now, th-that's why it's bein' p-p-pinned on me, b-b-best I can figure. I'm g-g-gettin' screwed. Probably Ger T-T-Tudhope told the po-police somethin'...lies, more'n likely."

"So, you think that he—or someone—has evidence linking you to Tuddy's that night?"

"Well, I *w-was* over th-that way....but I d-didn't have n-n-nothin' to d-do with it."

"What were you doing?"

Suddenly, his face took on an evasive, troubled look.

She sat back in her chair, startled.

"N-n-n-nothin'!" His stammer was pronounced.

"But, Vincent, if I'm to help you, I need to know."

"I w-was...dr-drivin'. J-J-Just dr-dr-drivin' ar-r-round."

"I'm trying to get to the bottom of this. If the police can place you there, in that location, it strengthens their case against you."

He sat back in his chair, his lips two grim lines.

"You said the Tudhopes are to blame for why you, a Veakey, are the way you are now, today. I don't understand what you mean. How can they be to blame?"

"Mrs. B-B, look around! L-L-Look at wh-where we live. We g-g-got nothin', P-Pops and I, 'cept each other! We're p-p-poor as can be, if you h-h-haven't n-noticed. Somethin' b-b-bad h-happened. Th-that's all I kn-know." He stopped. "And n-now, I *really* got n-nothin'." He looked around at the four walls. "Nothin' and no-body."

"I know this is uncomfortable, Vincent. We can discuss that issue later." She, herself, was getting tired out from all the dead ends, but she pressed on. "What about the fire in the camp up in Hartland?"

"Well, it's tr-true I was up in H-Hartland th-that n-n-night." He shook his weary head. 'B-but, I d-d-don't even know wh-where exactly they're t-t-talking about! Everything's d-d-dry as a b-b-bone n-now, anyway!" His lower lip jutted out defensively. "H-How do they kn-know it wasn't j-j-just a br-brush f-fire, st-started on its own?"

"You *were* up in Hartland—after midnight?"

Again, she discerned a slightly evasive look. He grumbled, "Well, I b-b-been havin' tr-trouble l-l-lately sl-sl-sleeping." His speech was difficult and labored. He threw his hands into the air in frustration. "Th-th-that's *it* in a n-n-nutshell! I dr-drive all over cr-cr-creation, s-s-s-s-sometimes!"

Mrs. Bundle had to admit Vincent's story must sound very weak to someone who didn't know him or believe he was innocent.

"Your father says you've been upset lately."

His head jerked up. "N-No!"

"He said he thought there might be someone you cared for?" She offered this idea gently. "Maybe, you've been upset about a girl?"

His face closed, emotionless as a porcelain owl; he sat there, looking down at the hairline cracks in the table. "N-N-Nope."

"Vincent, how can I be any help to you if you won't be honest with me?"

He looked at her, and his face held a desperate, pain-filled intensity. "Mrs. B-B-Bundle, I w-w-want to be. B-B-But...I'm... There's j-j-just some things...I c'can't...s-s-say."

"What about Lucy Wrinkle?"

He blinked impassively. "What ab-b-bout her?"

"Some say you're sweet on her. And that she likes you, too."

"Gaw!" He sighed with disgust. "No way. Sh-she's okay...we're j-just fr-friends, th-though. I f-f-feel b-bad for her s-s-sometimes."

"It's possible the police may think you were out for revenge on the Wrinkle store, for some reason—maybe because of Lucy."

He looked at her, uncomprehending. "You m-mean, they th-think th-that's why I'd st-st-start a f-fire there?"

"Yes."

He looked puzzled, then guffawed sardonically. "I th-thought it was ab-bout the spr-sprinkler s-s-system! Th-That's wh-what they s-s-said. And, I'm s-sure I d-did turn it b-b-back on before I l-left th-that night! I d-don't get why th-they're tr-tryin' to p-pin that on m-me!"

"Elvina Wrinkle is convinced you're after her daughter."

He looked sideways at the guard and leaned forward. "Well, I g-got no f-feelings whatsoever for L-L-Lucy Wrinkle. Or her m-m-mother, for th-that m-matter. You c-can take that to the b-b-bank."

"I don't mean to pry, Vincent, but I have to ask. Is there...something else going on...in your life? Or...a person who...might hurt you?"

"No." He shivered, and Mrs. Bundle could see the goose bumps on his skinny arms.

"Are you sure?"

He kept his eyes downcast. "I…I c-can't be sayin'. It's p-p-personal."

Mrs. Bundle's hand came down hard on the table—*whap!* "*Vincent!*"

He looked up, startled by the fire in her dark brown eyes.

She wanted to shake him, she was so frustrated. She drew in a deep breath and said, "Look here! I believe in you! Even though you won't give yourself a fighting chance! Please, Vincent. How do you think I can help you if you won't help yourself?"

"I kn-know, Mrs. B-bundle. It's p-pathetic, ain't it?" His face was as long and unhappy as a floppy-eared hound.

He looked so woeful she couldn't help it; the corners of her mouth turned slightly upward into a tense smile, despairingly hopeful.

"I'll do whatever I can to help you, even if you're too…" she tried to read his mind, "…is it *stubborn*? Or, cautious, or scared? *Whatever* the reason is, whyever you're holding back, even if you won't help yourself! However," she looked at him sternly, "I want you to do me one favor while you're here."

She looked around at the stark white walls and steel-reinforced windows of the Southern State Correctional Facility meeting room.

"Wh-what's that?" He leaned forward, his gaunt features and untidy thorn-like mane giving him a strange, buzzard-like appearance.

"I want you to promise me you will keep yourself healthy while you are here. You *must* eat something! Mercy, you look like you could be blown away with a feather!"

He looked at his own scrawny body as if he was examining it for the first time in weeks.

"Will you promise me you'll start taking care of yourself while you're here?" she asked. "Eat right? And get some sleep?"

He nodded.

"Now, let's talk about where we go from this point on."

.

Chapter Thirty-Five

Help From Angie

"I'm not sure when I'll find the time, but I must do my best to get him out of there! He looks terrible! It's the most desolate place, and he is beside himself."

Mrs. Bundle was taking a much-needed break from her Festival paperwork, which she had begun work on immediately upon her return from visiting with Vincent. Angie had stopped over to say hi and visit and, as the sun went from late afternoon into evening, she provided a welcome ear for the frustration Mrs. Bundle was feeling after having met with her new client.

"So, you're convinced he didn't do it?"

"Absolutely!"

"I saw him on the news at noon today when we got back from swimming. They showed the Sheriff's deputies bringing him in. He's at Southern State now, right?"

Mrs. Bundle nodded glumly.

"He was pretty pathetic-looking. Honestly, Mrs. B, he looks really…," she searched for the right word, "furtive! And that hair! Makes him look like a crazed wildman. I can't help but say, he *looks*….guilty. To the general public, I mean—if you don't know him at all. All gloomy and everything."

"Well, I daresay you'd look pretty gloomy, too, if you'd been accused of something you didn't do."

"That's true!" She chuckled, then saw how worried her dear friend was. "Sorry! But, honestly, he just looks a little too creepy, like he's got some secrets, you know, something to hide."

"Yes, he is a challenge, that is for sure. But remember, just because someone may look guilty doesn't mean he is."

"Right." She thought about this for a minute, then said, "Well, all I can say is, you've sure got your hands full. I wish I could help you."

She picked up yesterday's *Rutland Daily News* lying on the settee and perused the front page article highlighting the painting and the Dog Days of Summer Art Festival. "Pretty good publicity, huh? Them picking up this story? So, how are things going with the Festival? That'll be coming up here…well, in about a month, right?"

"Don't remind me! Althea's up to her eyeballs in paperwork, planning all the committees, crossing my 'T's' and dotting my 'I's' like nobody's business. I don't know what I'd do without her. We're both right out straight. It's unbelievable how much work is involved! Posters to be ordered, overseeing the advertising, food, organizing the art auction with Mr. Hotchkiss, you know, just getting everyone on board so they all know what they're doing." She leaned her head back on the comfy chair and drew in a deep, unsettled breath. "And this heat!" She fanned herself, closing her eyes.

"Boy, you can say that again! Another scorcher today! Swimming felt great this morning, but once you get home, whew! When do you think we'll get a break?"

"According to the weathermen, no relief in sight."

Angie continued to review the article, commenting, "This is really pretty interesting. About the painting and everything." She looked up and asked, "So, what are you going to do? About Junior?"

Mrs. Bundle opened her eyes, shrugged her shoulders, then smiled. "Good question. All this planning doesn't leave me much time for Vincent, but I'll make time. I know he's innocent! And, all the other stuff I wanted to work on, like finding out more about the mystery painting, will have to fall by the wayside." She chuckled. "Oh, wasn't I looking forward to getting my teeth into *that* puzzle! I'm dying to explore the circumstances of just how it could have come to be placed inside the wall. Not just because of the Art Festival, although it would have been great if we could have discovered the painting's 'story' in time. You know, really explore the history of the painting, find out more about that magical, private location under the eaves." Her eyes looked away toward the mountain horizon in deep thought, "you know, the *allure* of the discovery, right?" She slapped her knees with determination. "But! *If* I'm going to get ready for the Festival and try to find something to get Junior off from this ridiculous charge of arson, I know my limits. I'll never have time!"

Angie's head jerked up from the newspaper.

"Hey! I want to help! Let *me* explore the painting!"

"What?"

"I can help!"

"Oh, Angie, no, no, no! I never thought of involving you. It's summer, for goodness sake! It would be a lot of work and you should be out enjoying the weather, having fun."

A serious, determined look spread over Angie's face. "Mrs. B, I can do it!"

"Oh, my dear! It's not that I don't think you can do it. Heaven knows how capable you are! There's just so much going on—related to the Library…" she hesitated, unsure of how much she should share. "It's not been pretty, believe you me. You know, there are people that were dead-set against this festival idea. Or, even saving the Library, for that matter. Some tempers really flared."

"I know. I know all about that *Lim-pare* guy. Talk about creepy!"

Choosing not to outwardly agree with Angie's description, Mrs. Bundle said, "Truth be told, Armand Limpert has attempted to put a wrench in anything to do with the Library. Now, he seems to be keeping a very low profile, which somehow doesn't give me much comfort. And there are others, too, that would like to see the town let the building go. People have been on edge, *especially* with this terrible heat—and with no rain in sight. We've got so many crisis's on our hands right now—and I've got an…uneasy feeling." She gave her young friend an awkward look. "I'm afraid someone…might get hurt! And I could never forgive myself if my doing got you in trouble again."

Angie reached over and took her mentor's hand. "Mrs. B. You've been…like a mother to me my whole life. You've been to my games; you've helped me with schoolwork; you came to my school performances. You…..always made me feel so welcome here at the farm, with our tea parties, and well…everything. I'd…I'd do anything I could to help you out. Remember, I'm not a little girl anymore. Geez Louise, I'll be *eighteen* in January! I'm pretty much a grown-up at this point, and I'd like to help you out." She smiled engagingly. "And, I could make it really fun, you know, get some friends involved, make it a serious venture, kind of, *and* all the while, keep it on the 'Q-T'. That would be so much fun! I know Natalie would love to help, and I'll bet Jack would, too! It might take a little convincing with him, but… I've already got a couple others in mind that I could ask, too."

Mrs. Bundle pondered the girl's proposal carefully, not wanting to hurt her feelings. "Well, Angie, all I can say is, *if*, and that is a big if — *if* you were going to help, and mind you, this is *only* if your Dad approved, you would have to absolutely promise me that you would be careful and use discretion. And, if anyone ever gave you any resistance at all, or one iota of trouble, I would want to know about it immediately."

Angie nodded, her pony tail bouncing up and down. She asked excitedly, "You're going to let me do it?"

"Not so fast! I haven't said yes yet." The expression on her face was doubtful. "I wouldn't want you or your friends to get in any trouble because of all this controversy."

"Oh, don't worry about that! Nobody pays much attention to kids, you know — a lot of times they're never taken as seriously as they should be." She grinned, coaxing, "I'm thinking we'll form a club of sorts. Maybe a *secret* club — Yeah! A secret society! You know, something that will make it really *fun*." Angie was already fully engaged now, talking with the speed of lightening. "And, I promise, I will be careful *and* I will keep you in the loop at all times. What can possibly happen? We're just looking into a piece of art that was painted over a hundred-forty years ago! It will be fun!"

"As long as you know, before you do anything on this, you *must* ask your Dad. And get his permission—no if's, and's, or but's!"

Angie pointed with both hands toward herself and, with raised eyebrows, cried, "Remember? Almost eighteen? I promise—I'll ask him tonight! He'll be fine with it." She reached over and gave Mrs. Bundle a hug. "There, now you can tell me everything you know so far about the painting!" She folded the newspaper carefully and snapped it lightly in the palm of her hand. "Everything, please!"

Mrs. Bundle proceeded to brief Angie in detail about everything she knew thus far about the painting. Then, they moseyed into the kitchen (where Cracker was relaxing on the old rocking chair), and she opened the tin canister and pulled out *"The Library Affair and other goings on"* card, which referenced the two issues relative to the "Mysterious painting behind the wall" and all the details she knew to date.

"Yes, here it is, # 1 and #2." She read her handwritten notes from the card, "*'Painting—Who is Conny? Sweetness?'* See, I wondered, is it a first name, last name, nickname, what is it? And look here, *'MDCCLV What, who, why?'* That means, what exactly do those letters mean, is it Roman numerals equaling a number?? And who wrote it there?" She looked up at Angie, "The Roman numeral carved clue is really quite interesting, isn't it? Well, I say Roman numeral, but really, I haven't had time yet to fully research what this *'MDCCLV'* clue actually could mean."

Angie pointed toward the den. "Do you mind if I use your computer for a minute?"

A quick nod from Mrs. Bundle and Angie moved lickety-split. She was already on the computer by the time Mrs. Bundle and Cracker joined her, going to a search engine and inputting the letters in a quick question format: "Roman Numerals MDCCLV—numbers?"

Sure enough, the Roman numerals appeared to have a significant numeric meaning.

"Look, Mrs. B! '1755'! Could it be the *year* 1755?"

"Mercy! That was quick." She looked over Angie's shoulder but appeared puzzled. "It could, but somehow that doesn't seem to fit with some of the information so far, especially the date on the painting. Remember, that date is 1861. So, I'm in a quandary about that." She shook her head, then pointed ruefully to her brain. "It's all in a jumble up here, to be sure. It needs time and organization."

"Well, you leave that to me. I know I can help you sort this out. I was wondering, though. About the signature on the painting. What are your thoughts on that?"

"Yes, that is a big part of the mystery. What does 'Conny' mean? Or, a better question is, who could 'Conny' be? If we could find that out…"

"You mean we need to find out as much as we can about him—or her! We really don't know if it's a woman or a man."

"Yes, true! And, we have to find out if that's the artist's real name. Or, if it's a *nom de plume*."

"Right. Like, sometimes artists sign their work different from their real name. Sure! It could just be his—or her—last name, or a nickname."

Cracker stretched his long limbs and jumped down from the den ottoman, intrigued with all the rapidly increasing excitement.

"Exactly. Or, even a first name, possibly," Mrs. Bundle said.

"But it's not likely it's a girl's name, because if it was, it would probably be signed with an 'i-e'—you know, C-o-n-n-i-e, not C-o-n-n-y."

"Yes, right!"

Angie snapped her fingers. "Couldn't Conny could be short for Conrad? Or Conner? Or, even Conway?"

"Heavens! Very good, Angie! See, brainstorming is always so beneficial. It gets the juices going."

Angie was enthralled and asked more questions until she felt she was pretty thoroughly briefed with all the information. Meanwhile, Cracker followed their conversation, his head swiveling from one to the other as though watching a tennis match.

Just as they were finishing up, Jack came loping through the back door, returning from a long afternoon of pumping gas at Hudson's.

He stood in the den doorway. "Ach! *You* again? Saw your old junker outside and knew trouble with a capital 'T' was here, didn't I now?"

She flicked her head and her pony tail swished from side to side. "Oh, be quiet, you old pooh-face. I love the Chocolate Monster," (her nickname for the old chocolate-brown panel truck), "I thought maybe you missed me."

"Did you, now?" His bright teeth flashed, and he smiled warmly. There was no one like Angie to loosen up his toughened exterior; the two women shared a smile with each other.

He saw the look and, sensing some bit of conspiracy, his forehead wrinkled. "Aye. So. What's going on?"

"Well, for starters, I've volunteered to help Mrs. B."

"Oy! You don't say, now." He turned to Mrs. Bundle. "Did you really want this bird helping you, mum? Right, a bit dodgy, isn't she?"

"Say what you want. You'll be sorry." Angie threw back.

"Right lass, and just exactly *how* would you be helping this grand lady?" He put a friendly arm around Mrs. Bundle. "Something to do with the Festival, eh?"

"Well, not exactly, no. It's something…much more mysterious." She sighed long and rolled her eyes. "I'm not sure I can say…," she taunted him and he moved quickly, grabbing her arm playfully.

"Give it up, lass! Stop twistin' hay and tell me what hair-brained scheme you've come up with now."

"All right, all right! Stop it! If you must know, I'm going to help Mrs. Bundle with her detective work."

"Oh, no!" Jack's head shook vehemently. "No way. Ach, what are you thinking? Do you not have a memory of all that happened not less than eight months ago? What'll your Da have to say about this?"

Mrs. Bundle said, "I've already tried, Jack. She's determined to help out in some way."

"That's right, I'm determined."

"Are you daft, girl?"

"Jack, I'm serious. Stop yelling and listen to me. Can't you see how worn out Mrs. B is?"

"Well, aye, of course I can, but the detecting, that's another story, isn't it now? Dangerous it is, in a word!"

"No, it's not. Not this time. It's just a little bit of helping out. And Mrs. B needs me. Actually, she needs *us*! Which is why you and I–"

Mrs. Bundle interrupted their lively interchange. "Really, you two, you're talking about me like I'm not even here—"

Angie jabbed at Jack with a pointed finger to get his full attention, "Which is why *you* and *I* need to pick up some of the slack here, *mate*."

"Blimey! You can be a foolish wench when you want, can't you now? Might I be so bold as to ask, why *me*?"

Frustrated, Angie cried, "Wait just a minute," and disappeared from the room. When she returned, she had the newspaper in hand, having retrieved it from where she had left it on the kitchen table.

She shoved the paper's full front page view into Jack's face. "Here! Look! Look at this!"

Jack eyed her quizzically, then adjusted his eyes downward at the print. "Ach! What are you blatherin' on about, lass? You mean the big fire? I already know all about it!"

"No, not the fire, you big dope! Look! The other story!"

"What the bloody….Angie, would you kindly tell me what you're playing at here?"

"Silly! Look here! It's the article about the mystery painting. *That's* how we can help her. Right here. Would you please take a look at it?"

He took the *Daily News* from her and looked where she had pointed. His eyes focused as he took in the article, "*Hidden Painting Discovered at Decaying Pillson Library*." After a few seconds, he looked up at her, inquiringly. "Eh?"

"We're going to help Mrs. Bundle in another way. No danger involved. Just research." She pointed above the article and said, "See this photo? It's the painting they found—the '*Mysterious painting behind the wall*.'"

"Right!" He glanced quickly at the accompanying color photo of the painting, and then looked back up at her, still confused. "*Emm…

hold on! Aye, is that what *we're* going to do now, eh? Help her with the mystery of the *Leabharlann* painting?"

"The Library!"

"Right, that's what I said, lass! The *Leabharlann*! Aye. Now I see!" He relaxed a smidge, then looked with quick disinterest at the photograph once again. "So that's the mystery painting, is it now, lass?"

"Yeah. It is. I've offered to help Mrs. B find out more about the painting. It'll be fun. You know, *we*—you and I--can help her out—but without all the danger." Angie was on a roll; her perkiness was usually infectious but Jack still seemed dubious.

"Uh-huh." He raised his eyebrows, and his ruddy cheeks turned abit brighter red. "Emmm, you offered me, too, didn't you now?"

She nodded.

His long sigh could have been heard in Pittsburgh. "To do research."

She nodded again and his hand went into the air with a strong "halt" signal. He turned to Mrs. Bundle. "This whole Library thing's more serious than she thinks, I'll wager. It's giving me the heebie-jeebs!"

"You mean the heebie-jeebies?" Angie broke up in laugher. "The '*heebie-jeebs*'—omigosh!"

Jack gave her a lop-sided grin. "I'm so delighted, lass, to give you a laugh, aren't I now?"

Angie's eyes never left Jack. He continued to stew over the idea.

He shook his head, gave a pleading glance to Mrs, Bundle, who shrugged her shoulders. He looked back at Angie who smiled and wrinkled her nose; a hint of a smile formed on his face.

Both Cracker and Mrs. Bundle were thoroughly amused by this interplay.

"You'll help me, Jack, right?" Angie wheedled, "Think about what we might discover! And, how it could help so much with the Library."

On his last legs of skepticism, he asked, "How?"

"Well," Angie scrunched her forehead in exasperation, "it's a part of its history, isn't it? Pillson's, too. Maybe, uhh…" she organized her thought, "maybe finding out about the painting will show how much the Library is a part of everyone's life. Maybe, just maybe, we'll discover something really....fantastical!" Her eyes sparkled at Mrs. Bundle. "Something intriguing, and...*romantic!*" Her eyes flashed and he choked on a chuckle. "We'll form a…" she lowered her voice furtively, coaxingly, "a secret society."

He laughed outright.

"Oh, c'mon Jack, be a sport! Let's have some fun with this!"

"Emm..aye, it's fun that you're after. And something *intriguing* and *romantic*, too. Right! Bloody hard to turn down all that excitement!" He scratched his head and teased, "Wait now, lass, let me think on it, would you?"

"No! There's no time for that, Jack! I want to get started right away. Tomorrow, in fact." Angie planted her fingertips together and tapped impatiently, formulating her plan. "At the library. Yes! Louis will help us, I know he will. And, I know *just* who we'd get to help us with research, too."

"And who would you be thinking that would be?"

"Anthony Clancy."

"*Anthony* Clancy? Aye, to be sure, all he cares about is reading. His noggin's in a book every time Nick and I try to get him to go fishing with us."

"That's right. One, he works at the library. Two, he's smart. He knows a lot about 'stuff.' Ask him anything and he's read about it."

"Oy! Stuff, yeah. Well, I'm not so sure he or anyone else, for that matter, will go along with your *secret society* blather." He gazed distractedly at the picture. "And, we can't be going all over creation looking for God knows what…" his voice trailed off as he stared at the newspaper once again.

"Oh, I give up!" Angie flopped down onto the loveseat. "I'm not going to try to convince you anymo–"

Out of the clear blue, he yelped, "What the *divil?*"

Angie threatened, "I'm serious, Jack—"

He held up a hand to silence the girl, focusing his gaze intently on the representation of the painting.

He brought the paper closer to his face, perusing, as best he could, the fuzzy color image. He studied it as though it was the most intricate puzzle to be solved. Finally, he looked up and stammered, "W-well, right! I'll be *gobsmacked*!" He pointed, "This is it?"

Angie leaned over disinterestedly. "Yeah, Jack, *this*," she pointed, "is the painting that Louis and Mrs. Bundle found. Behind the wall."

He looked at her as though disbelieving her words, mouth open.

She spoke as though to a child, calmly accentuating each word. "That's what I've been trying to tell you about for the last five minutes. This..is...*it*."

He snorted and shook his head wryly.

"What?" Angie asked. "You saw the real painting, didn't you?" She turned to Mrs. Bundle. "I thought you said it was here at the house for awhile."

"Well, it was," Mrs. Bundle said. "But then I brought it, let's see… I brought it first to the board meeting and then to the special town meeting. And now, it's at the Co-Op."

"You never saw it?" Angie asked Jack.

He shook his head, staring intently at her, then back again at the photo image.

Somewhat taken aback, Mrs. Bundle said, "Why, I guess you never *did* see it while it was here, Jack. Between your schedule and mine. It was in the safe, and….What *is* it, Jack?"

He was silent.

"Ohh! Jack! I mean it, you are making me crazy!" Angie shook his arm impatiently, "Gaw! Speak, would you? What's the matter?"

Jack looked back at them both. Finally, his lips parted into a huge, exceedingly comical grin, an uncommon occurrence for this young man more prone to seriousness than triviality. "Huh! That's *brilliant*, isn't it!"

They both smiled back, waiting in anticipation.

"*What?*" Angie was saturated with interest. "Jack! Tell us, what's brilliant?"

"Well now. I'd lay down a thousand quid—not that I have it, mind you," he chuckled, "but—I would, wouldn't I? I'd lay down a thousand quid right this moment. *That*," he pointed, "—your '*Mysterious Painting behind the Wall*'—that would be our secret fishing spot, wouldn't it now?"

Both women gave him a dumbfounded stare.

"Bloody Hell!" he exclaimed, "It is, I tell you!"

Chapter Thirty-Six

Strange Coincidences....

Mrs. Bundle rummaged like a squirrel looking for acorns through the nearby magazine rack until she finally found what she was looking for. She pulled out the crumpled version of last week's *State Standard*. She rifled through the disorganized pages and finally found the front page, where there was a similar, but much better representation, of the same painting.

"Here it is! I knew I still had it. Look at this one, Jack! Tell us what you think! There! It's a much clearer, bigger photo of the painting."

He grabbed it hungrily from her hands and studied it intently.

"*Jaysus*!" He swore again, this time under his breath. "It is!"

"Where is it? The fishing hole!" Angie asked impatiently.

He slowly shook his head. "Emmm....Sorry, missy, but... I'm sworn to secrecy on that."

She huffed loudly and promptly stomped her sneakered foot on his.

"*Oww!* Angie! What the *divil*?"

"Are you kidding? You can't tell us where it is?"

He rubbed his sore foot gingerly. "Well, now that would be telling a grave secret, wouldn't it, lass? I'd have to clear it with me mates, Nick and Chris, wouldn't I? You see, now, I made a promise. When the Clancys first brought me up there, they made me swear an oath not to tell a bloody soul where their favorite fishing spot was..."

"Oh, for the love of Pete, Jack!"

His face broke into a wide grin. "Wait!! Let me finish. C'mere, lass and listen, will you? I can't be sure, now, can I? About this bloody painting scene. Aye, all I'll say is, it's the spitting image of our fishing spot." He lowered his voice, "And—all I'll say here and now is... emmm...where we go fishing is *not* around here in Pillson anywhere. Not in these parts, to be sure. It's...further away—but in Windsor County, to be sure."

Angie blew air past her top lip, totally discombobulated. "Well, that helps, seeing as it's safe to say that would cover over a few hundred square miles, most of which are backwoods and country roads, Jack. Thanks, thanks a lot!"

Both Mrs. Bundle and Cracker could see he was getting Angie back for the throbbing foot he was massaging, not to mention any teasing she had ever subjected him to.

"Sorry, luv, but you'll not get it out of me!" he said. "I'll not say another word 'til I talk to me lads, Nick and Chris Clancy!"

Mrs. Bundle nodded. "Quite right, Jack. Check with the boys and make sure it's okay to tell. Meanwhile, maybe it would do for you to see the original painting."

"Well, to be sure. I'll go into the Co-op and take a look right off!" He nudged his mute friend, who was borderline sulking at this point. "I can promise you one thing, Angie."

She looked skeptical but muttered, "What's that?"

"I'm in."

"Huh?"

"Well, sure and you'll be needin' me more than ever now, won't you? Me, and Nick, too." His eyes crinkled with mirth, "You know, for your," he made quote marks with his fingers and gave her a dry look, " '*secret society*'?"

"Jeesum crowbars! What a pain in the 'you-know-what' you are, Jack O'Rahilly Corrigan!"

Part III:
J U L Y

Chapter One

A Secret Society

Angie was stunning; her comely face was flushed with nervous excitement, her golden-olive complexion further tanned from the summer sun. Without doubt, she was the quintessential picture of youth and vitality as she stood before them, in charge and ready to begin their private meeting. She cleared her throat, a sense of melodrama and suspense unmistakable behind her brightly shining doe eyes.

"Ahem!" In her best "mature" voice, she repeated, "Ahem!" All eyes were on her.

They were meeting privately this first time, owing not only to the sensitivity of the subject matter but moreover, because somehow, it made the subject matter much more intriguing, more exciting, to come together in a clandestine fashion.

She had decided it seemed most beneficial and most enlightening for the group to gather at the scene of the discovery of the painting: the third floor of the Pillsonville Library, and had obtained permission from Louis Montembeau to use the Library that Monday afternoon, explaining that it was for a special meeting to help Mrs. Bundle do some research.

Utilizing the library space as a meeting place was not an unusual request, in itself, as it was used often by various small group assemblages, such as, the seasonally-active Dueling Daisies (the local garden club), the Peanuckle Sisterhood (a women's support group), the American Society of Dowser's Guild, or the Coon Club, (who held their quarterly business meeting there). All of these groups, whether civic or private, usually met in the second floor conference room during the Library's regular business hours or, if during the evening hours, were sometimes entrusted with the private location of the library key in Louis's absence. Because today, Monday, wasn't a normal library business day and Angie's group was of the younger generation, Louis, accommodating as ever, had agreed to grant their request, telling Angie he would meet them at the Library entrance to let them in. He said he would be able to stay approximately one hour, indicating that he could get his assistant to cover for him in Chester (his usual Monday day job) and that the large quantity of unfinished work on his desk would keep him quite occupied while they met upstairs.

Angie had given a lot of thought to whom exactly she would choose to expedite her goal of helping Mrs. Bundle. She had lots of friends, lots of acquaintances, too, for that matter, but this mission boiled down to one thing—moving quickly, discreetly, and making good choices. She had asked everyone to come together precisely at three o'clock.

As promised, Louis opened the door when Angie arrived first, and gave her a mildly amused look. He made a grand sweeping motion with his hand.

"Enter, fair lady!"

She smiled and stepped discreetly inside the empty, darkened foyer.

"Hi Louis!" Her voice, low and husky, echoed eerily in the space.

"Hi there, Ms. Andersen!" He rubbed his hands together. "The room's all unlocked, but it's still pretty messy, so I've set you up in the first room—on the left—for your little 'chat.'"

The air was rife with collusion and she whispered, "Thanks *so much* for letting us meet upstairs! I appreciate it."

He nodded and whispered back, "I suspect it's best just not to ask…"

She nodded quickly. "Yuh-huh. It's a meeting for—" her shoulders lifted in a hesitant shrug, "—actually, we're just trying to help out Mrs. B and the Library without causing too much hoopla."

He held up a hand, "I know, it's okay. I was happy to oblige! Not a problem!" He placed graceful fingers delicately over his animated eyes. "*I see nothing!*"

"Thanks...thanks so much."

"I'll wait for the others. You go on up, all right?"

She gave him a quick nod and ran up the two flights of stairs, taking the steps two at a time as she quickly passed by the "*Third Floor Off Limits! Employees only, please*" sign. Her heart beat fast as she entered the first room in the long, third-floor hallway.

The room was sparsely furnished with only three metal folding chairs and an ancient library table pushed up against the wall (underneath of which was a myriad of boxes) in the confined space. As each arrived, they found a place to light. Now, she stood in front of the small group, confident and capable.

In the end, she had settled on just the four: Jack Corrigan, Nick Clancy, his younger, erudite brother Anthony, and Angie's best friend and fellow lacrosse player, Natalie Hufferman.

"Thanks...I appreciate you all showing up." Angie said. "First of all, before I begin, I really need everyone to understand that what is said in this room stays in this room."

Nick Clancy, a strapping young man with an engaging personality, shrugged and asked, "Sure, no problem. But why all the cloak and dagger?" His sandy curls were trimmed into a short and neat haircut; his light eyebrows were naturally refined, shaped perfectly to frame pale azure eyes, a Red Sox baseball cap at a jaunty angle backwards on his head. A square-cut jaw and dimpled chin complimented his high cheekbones, and his handsome, enthusiastic features promised a good-natured interior. He had a brawny build; like his father, Jesse, his shoulders were broad and strong and he held himself with calm assurance.

"I'll get to that," Angie promised.

"You *know* I can keep a secret." Natalie said.

"Absolutely! It all stays here. "Anthony Clancy said seriously.

Everyone looked at Jack expectantly.

Jack smiled and gave Angie a quick nod of endorsement.

Nick looked at his watch. "Okay, I've got less than an hour here—took a late lunch so I could come," (referring to his full-time job at Harper's Feed Store), "What the heck's going on, Angie? I'm totally clueless. I heard something about a painting that was discovered here at the Library, and something from Jack, here, that the painting may have something to do with our fishing spot. Which, I'll tell you right now, couldn't possibly be, because I can count on one hand the people that know about that spot." He looked around the musty, hot room. "And why are we meeting way the heck up here?"

Natalie said, "I don't think I've ever even been up to this floor. It being," Natalie crooked her fingers into quotes, "'*off limits*.'"

"Well, here's the deal," Angie said. "Jack is already pretty much up to speed on this, but let me start at the beginning and I'll tell you everything I know." Holding a graceful, poised hand in the air, she touched one index finger to the other, and began, "First of all, Mrs. B—Mrs. Bundle, that is—consented to giving me this job and I'm bound and determined to do what needs to be done to get it taken care of for her."

She tapped her next finger lightly but with emphasis, "Second, in doing this job, I had to think about who could help me. That part was hard because I had to think more about, *who can I trust?* You know, who can really be *trusted*, who can I really depend on to get things done? That's why you four are here. To help me help Mrs. Bundle—and Althea Swain, too. You all know her. She's Mrs. Bundle's best friend."

Nick nodded, "Right. I know that. Okay, so you need us to help you. But why so much secrecy? I don't get it." He rubbed his chin. "Of course, you know that you can count on me. Hey, I love a challenge. Anthony's in, too—right, punk?" He jabbed his brother in the ribs.

His brother Anthony nodded profusely, thrilled that he had been asked to attend this meeting. As usual, he looked randomly put together, oversized T-shirt and huge khaki cargo pants dwarfing his slender, gangly frame. He couldn't help but stare at Angie. *She*, the object of his juvenile affection, had chosen him! Quirky, more a bookworm than a social butterfly and always cerebral, his whole body was ajitter with adolescent anxiety. Right now, he was about as puffed up as a pubescent peacock. His freckled face was attempting to convey the usual, plastered "teenage nonchalance" that hid the thrill of having been asked by an older pretty girl—one whom he happened to secretly adore.

He cleared his throat and stammered, "Definitely! I-I'm in!" He smoothed down his dark, rumpled hair and straightened the crooked eyeglasses that seemed to perpetually slide down his nose, his brave effort to present a better overall picture.

Angie looked at Jack, who still hadn't yet said a word, just intently watched; his piercing eyes seemed to soften whenever he and Angie bantered back and forth. *Ach!* Truth be told, she meant the world to him. Those same piercing, beautifully azure-blue eyes flashed, and he winked shrewdly at her. "Go ahead, lass. You're doin' a grand job. Keep tellin' your tale, will you now?"

Raising a good-humored eyebrow at him, she went on, "Like I said, Jack already knows most of this."

"Aye, lass, aren't I a glutton for punishment?"

Natalie Hufferman, always gregarious and fun-loving, whose countenance showed emotions as plainly as a neon sign in the middle of the desert, nodded cheerfully. Her big-boned, athletic figure was dressed casually, a newly-acquired Salve Regina lacrosse shirt over running shorts. "I'm in, for sure. So far it sounds like it will be fun." Natalie was a "not-a lot-of-fluff-but-plenty-of-substance" individual, honest and straightforward. "But what do you want us to do? To help, I mean."

As Angie began to explain, a deep crease meandered its way across her forehead. "Well, here's what I'm talking about. You may or may not know there's been a lot of controversy over this library issue. Whether or not to close, who's calling the shots, and now, a lot hinges on whether or not this Festival will be a success. Something very strange is going on. Some people have been stirring up a lot of trouble." She raised her eyebrows in consternation and took a deep breath. "And through it all, Mrs. Bundle has been trying to make things better for the Library."

Natalie's limitless energy was like an overeager Labrador puppy. She bounced upright in her seat. "My parents are *way* for this whole Festival idea. They've already volunteered to do one of the booths. They said it's a huge effort! And I think most everybody feels the same way. Who would want to see the Pillson Library close? I don't. Wow! So, we're going to help her with this library thing? The Festival, and all that?"

"Well, not exactly. We're going to work behind the scenes to find out what we can about the painting. The 'Mysterious Painting Behind the Wall.'" The crease reappeared again in her forehead. "But, there's a bit of trouble."

Everyone sat forward in anticipation, and Jack said, "Trouble?" He brushed the dark curl from his forehead and looked intensely at her.

She smiled at him. "Relax. It's not really that serious, Jack. Things are just...weird around here. These bizarre fires have happened, and now, the likelihood of a drought makes things even more...weird. People are afraid."

"Well, they've got the guy that did the fires behind bars, haven't they?" Nick made more of a statement than a question.

"Nuh-uh." Angie shook her head. "Don't be too sure of that. Mrs. Bundle doesn't think so. Do you know old Barny Veakey, the father of the guy they arrested?"

"That old coot? The guy up at the dump?"

"Nick!" Natalie shot him a look that said she was ready to throttle him.

Angie proceeded, "Uh-huh. He's hired Mrs. B to help prove his son is innocent."

"No way!"

"Yup. So, she's going to be up to her neck with that, too. If she's right and Junior's not the one, then someone else is out there starting fires. So, because of that possibility and everyone being so keyed up about this drought, too, the bottom line is, she's got her hands full."

"You're right about how squirrelly everyone is," Nick said. "People are getting really squeamish about a drought and fires. You should see the people comin' into Harper's! We've had a run on fire extinguishers—sold more of those this past week than Carter's got pills. And dowsers! Dad said the Dowser's Guild is really busy, what with people's wells goin' dry. And the way people are carryin' on! Everybody's all up in arms. Farmers are concerned about whether they'll lose their early summer crop, whether their farm ponds will go dry. We sold out of rain diverters, ordered six dozen more! You know, just in case we get a downpour, these old guys want to save every drop rain they can."

"Yuh," Angie nodded, "my grandfather has rain barrels all over his property—he hates to use the well water for the garden in times like this."

"Well, look, we haven't had a really good rain for over a week," Nick said, "If the winds pick up here, it could be disastrous, what with brush fires and the like. I joined the fire department last summer—after I graduated—and we've been having special training for wind-fueled brush fires. It'll only take a really good wind and there goes hundreds of acres—just like that!" he snapped his fingers. "So...," he imitated the old-time farmers who frequented Harper's, lowering his voice an octave, "'Yessa, don't you know, it don't look too good.'"

Anthony added shyly, "The only thing that's keeping anybody's garden going at this point is the natural high water table. That, and the farmers that have got their overflow ponds from their wells. I've been reading a lot lately about global warming, and its impact on the weather patterns."

"There might be something in that, mate." Jack said.

Angie waved a hand, "Okay. Sorry to get off track, but it all does kind have something to do with why we're here. If you add in fires that have been set *and* the fact that there's no rain in sight *and* all the stress those things bring into the mix with the Festival planning and Junior's arrest, you can see why we're here. Basically, Mrs. B is right out straight!"

Anthony's freckled face blushed red as a brick as he raised a questioning finger.

She nodded in his direction.

"Will it be at all dangerous? What we're going to do?"

Angie's comely face became earnest and her dark brown eyes came alive, their green-gold flecks dancing with enthusiasm. "No, I don't think so, Anthony. Not that I can imagine anyway. More...*exciting*, I think. My idea is, well, to form a group, a *committee*—I guess if you wanted to give it a formal name—a committee to work behind the scenes—fly under the radar—to help Mrs. Bundle discover more about this old painting they found here, in the Library. And to try to get as much info as we can before the Festival, so that we might be able to use what we've found out to promote it. To help make it a success! Right now it's just a mystery waiting to be solved. And whoever solves it first...well, I think it could be fun."

As their interest was piqued, Natalie and Anthony broke in with questions while Nick seemed to be editorializing about how much he hated "committees."

She held up a hand above the din and said, "Hold on, wait a minute. Let me finish. Chill, everyone!" They all went quiet, and she said, "Okay, here's my idea."

She pulled a list out of her jeans pocket. "I've written down all these notes, things we know about the painting so far, you know, and things Mrs. B and I went over."

She read off the first item. "Okay. First of all, the reason we're up here in this room is because the painting was discovered just down the hall. In the last room, under the eaves, in a knee wall. Very mysterious. All wrapped up and safe. So, I thought we should look that area over, after we get done here."

She looked around and they all nodded. "Second, we know the painting was signed by someone called 'Conny.' So, he—or she—is the artist we need to find out more about. It's a funny name. We're not sure if it's a guy or a girl. Mrs. B has a hunch it's probably a guy because of what was written on the *back* of the painting."

"What did it say?" asked Natalie.

She referred to her notes. "It said, *'To my sweetness. May our love endure forever. C.'* That's it. Signed just, 'C.'"

"Ooohh! Pretty mushy stuff!" Nick said; ignoring him, she went on.

"So, we know what it said on the back of the painting, how it was signed, that is. And we know the year it was painted: 1861, or so it reads beside the signature. Okay, now we come to what the painting is. Jack is pretty sure it's a scene of your secret fishing hole, Nick. Right?" she asked Jack, "Can you say one-hundred-percent it's the exact scene where it was painted?"

"Well, I can't say 100%, but it's bloody close. I can pretty much guarantee it's the same place where me mate Nick, here, and I go fishing. I went into the Co-Op, didn't I now, just before I came here, to take a look." He gave a very interested Nick Clancy a quick nod. "Surely, it's what I thought, though the trees in the painting have changed a lot. Aye, that makes sense, though. Some of the trees are gone, others are much bigger now." He unfolded the *State Standard* newspaper and held up the photo to everyone. "Right, Nick! I was gobsmacked, couldn't believe it!"

Nick piped up. "Let me see it, dude. I can tell you for sure, if I can see the painting."

Jack handed him the photo.

"Hmmm…" Nick stared at it more closely. "Get out of town! That's unbelievable!" He scrutinized it further. "It looks very similar…but *there*….that tree is different." He pointed, then, more to himself, said, "Well, of course, now it *would* be different, all these years later. But, wait! Those rocks there, they're *exactly* the same, aren't they, Jack?"

"Aye, they are."

"And, there's the pool at the end of the waterfall…." Nick nodded at Jack. "Exactly. Well, except that back forest line is kinda different— it's a lot more…yeah, a lot more dense now. But there's no denying that stream, big in the middle, right there, the *same* huge boulder there, the *same* deep pool at the end." He studied it one last time. "Uh-huh!" He traced a rough forefinger over the photo's background. "Wow! Look! There's that big field down there, and there, *that's* the old farmhouse way down the hill!"

"Bloody right, mate. Sure, and that's exactly what I thought, too. We'd have to get back up there and really compare things, to be sure."

"Yeah, that would be the right thing to do, get back up there, compare it in detail… maybe you'd like to go, too, Angie?"

Nick's smile was engaging and warm as he looked up at her, his eyes big and round like an excited little boy, and she nodded back, "Of course!" (Rumor had it that Nick cared more than just a little for Angie; she, on the other hand, seemed oblivious to his attention.)

Jack interruped, "Aye, mate. It's our fishing hole, to be sure. Imagine! So far out there, in the middle of nowhere! Who would think? It was the boulders and the waterfall that made me take notice. But what really clinched it for meself was," he pointed, "that huge crooked tree limb. Maple, I reckon, hanging out over the stream. Right, it's much, much higher now, but it still hangs over like a long, twisted finger, out over the water." He turned to the girls and smiled. "Right, surely, it's a beautiful spot. Nary anyone goes up that far, that's the beauty of it. It's virtually untouched. Blimey, Nick, how many blokes have we ever seen up that way?"

Nick held up his thumb and forefinger together, the universal signal for zero.

Natalie asked, "Exactly where is it?"

Jack winked at Nick, who said, "Should we tell them *exactly* where it is?"

Jack shrugged his shoulders and joked, "Should we, now? I'm not so sure…"

"Well, maybe we should make them sign in blood that they won't divulge it…"

Angie laughed. "Boy, you guys really know how to make a meal of it, don't you? Just say where it is, will you?"

"Right, then." Jack said, humor behind his eyes, "It's near Hartland Four Corners, but past there, off Mace Hill Road."

Nick said, "You know where we're talking, up in behind that old farm. There's a break in the wild brush, an old, overgrown, trail going in. Pretty hard to see, even harder to follow unless you know the way in. It's way up the mountain pretty far—way up from where the stream runs along the road there. And then, you have to go about a *mile* upstream from there, pretty much following it the whole way."

Jack nodded. "Right! It's a fair hike."

"When we go, we backpack our gear. It's quite a trek, but it's the best trout fishing around, and that's no lie. And, well worth it in the end." Nick turned to Angie and asked, "So, what do you think about that?"

"That's great! There's even more to this story, though."

Natalie asked, "What?"

"Well, here's the rest of the mystery." Angie proceeded to tell them about the candy wrappers and the carved letters inside the hidden knee wall space, then further, about the "MDCCLV Roman numeral" theory—that is, the possibility that the letters signified something having to do with the number or year 1755.

"So," she concluded, "as you can see, there's a lot more to it than just having found an old painting. What we'll need to do is solve the mystery of who painted it, why it was painted, maybe for whom was it painted—because of the message on the back— and most of all," she brushed back golden brown wisps of hair, her hands smoothing down the long strands, "how it came to be in behind the wall? How did it get there? And *when* it was put there—we're still on the fence about that or a timeline of sorts."

Nick said eagerly, "Yeah, yeah, okay, now I get it." He glanced through the article, reading quickly. "This is really pretty interesting. Geez, so it really is a bona fide mystery."

"Right! And, I think we have the ability and the resources to figure it out. I think we can do it. Anthony, you're really good at research and history—*and* you work here at the library, too. I'll bet you'd know how to go about finding out more about the historical side to this."

He smiled somewhat bashfully, "Thanks! Well, yeah, I know how to search archives, and do microfiche, etcetera. But, we'd need to be really organized if we're going to get anywhere."

Angie nodded, "That's why I want you to handle that piece if you think you can."

He said breathlessly, "Definitely! I can go to the Pillson Historical Society, too, and see what was going on in that era. I already can tell you one thing that I know for sure! If the painting was done sometime during the year of 1861—that was right around Civil War, or thereabouts, and there was a lot going on. It was a really volatile era and so much was happening in this part of the world with manufacturing, factories coming in. The nation was really starting to become industrialized to a large degree." He snapped his fingers. "Wait a minute! I just thought of something that might help us. Well, actually two things. First of all, you know old Professor Watson?"

They all nodded.

"Well, he comes into the library all the time. He was a history professor at Dartmouth and he's a wealth of historical knowledge, especially of this vicinity. I could talk to him, just generally, you know, about that era the next time I see him and see what he might know, or where he could send me to research that year."

"Good idea. Keeping it general is the *operative* word," Angie advised, "I've promised Mrs. Bundle we'll keep things very low key."

"Right. Also," he held up the newspaper photo, "*The State Standard* just celebrated their sesquicentennial anniversary! Did you see it? The paper did a special edition, when was it, last month?"

His brother looked stumped. "So what?"

"That means that they've been around for *one-hundred-and-fifty* years! So, that would mean they've been in business since…" he calculated quickly, "1853. And, if they've been around since 1853, that's way before the date on the painting."

"Right!" Angie said, "Good thinking! There'd surely be information, news, and such on those years surrounding that time period if they've kept an archive."

Anthony said, "And I know the Library *here* has some archival data like historical maps, all kinds of stuff." He stopped abruptly, concerned that his enthusiasm might be misconstrued as not very "cool," then slumped casually back into the hollowed-out part in his ancient folding chair.

Clearly, everyone was impressed with his knowledge. Nick gave an approving slap to his brother's back. "Not bad."

"Wow, that's great information!" Angie said. "I can help with that piece. And we can also look into variations on that name 'Conny.' You know, anything that begins with C-o-n. Maybe we'll be able to find some kind of link with the name and the artist."

"What would you be wantin' *us* to do?" Jack queried, motioning an extended thumb at Nick and himself.

"Well, here's the thing. We may need you and Nick to run interference for us, especially if...well, if anyone tries to hinder or stop our research. I'm not saying anyone's going to...I'm just not sure if we're going to meet with any resistance—if there's any hint of trouble, we regroup and let Mrs. Bundle decide what we do next. Anyway, it's great that you guys are pretty sure about the actual site of the painting. That's fantastic. That's the piece you can concentrate on. Maybe there's other older generations who have fished there, or who know something we don't—you could 'fish around' for info!" They all laughed. "Who knows? If you could revisit the site, confirm that it is, in fact, the same as the painting, for starters. Maybe there's more to see up there, something we might be missing in the painting that would help us."

She looked around at the earnest group. "So, are we all in?"

Their eager faces assured her—was there any doubt?

"Great!" She sat down on the lip of the table and pulled a pencil from her shirt pocket. "Next! I think we need a name for our group, you know, something we can talk about with each other, to call and leave messages, whatever, without having to mention the painting or the library."

"You're kidding. You don't mean," Nick rolled his eyes, "something corny like the *Pillson Pirates*, or something like that? Nuh-uh. Nope. No way."

Natalie slapped his arm. "No, you twit, she doesn't mean something like that."

"*Ow!*" He feigned pain and laughed good-naturedly. "Forget it, you guys. I'm just not into a lot of hoopla. You know," he put his fingers in quotes, "'secret fraternity' stuff. Come *on!*"

Angie nudged him playfully, "Well, get over it. Because we're forming a secret society and we're going to name it something clever!"

He melted and said begrudgingly, "Well…if it's not really lame…" then turned to his brother and grabbed him roughly by the shoulder. "I just better not hear *anyone* say *anything* about this queer stuff outside of this room. I have a reputation to live up to, you know."

"Oh, *puuuullleeesssse!* Get over yourself!" Natalie cried.

Anthony yelped. "Uh-yuh, ouch! Okay, don't worry, I'm not going to be blabbing to anyone. Anyway, we're supposed to keep this *confidential.* Didn't you hear Angie say that in the beginning?"

"Well, yeah, okay. Confidential. All right."

"Good. Glad we have things back on track. Now, does anyone have any ideas for a name?" Angie asked. "Anthony, how about you?"

He nodded tentatively. "I was thinking…how 'bout taking the first letters of key words to form the group's name?"

"Gaw! What, you mean like a secret code?" his brother asked, revolted.

Anthony said. "No, not a secret code. An abbreviation. You know, something like 'The Library Sleuthing Team.' Take the first three letters of the words?"

"Hmm. Yeah, the '*LST*'s, that's not bad….," Angie said, deep in thought.

"LST?" Jack shrugged indifferently.

"No—I don't like it," Natalie said. "It's not…catchy enough. Sorry, Anthony."

Anthony slunk back into his seat.

"Em, wait a minute, mates." Jack offered, "How about if we take the first two letters of Library—that would be *L-I-* then add, *something, something*…, you know, to form a word."

"I get it! Like—how's this?" Natalie said quickly, "'Library Country Kids'! Let's see, that would be *L-I-*" Natalie raised her eyes to the ceiling in thought, then shuddered and hooted as she choked out the words, "*C-K!*"

The guffaws were loud and long.

"No way!" laughed Nick. "That sounds gross—forget about it! Why not something *really* lame like Library Mystery Patrol?"

Angie yelped, "Are you sure? That would be...*LiMP!* How pathetic is that?"

They all howled.

"I think I've got it!" They all looked in surprise at Anthony, who had shot up like a jack-in-the-box. They all gave a nod of encouragement and he humbly offered, "How about—Library Mystery Buffs?"

"L-i-M-B!" One and all tried the letters on for size. "*LiMB?*"

Silence.

"You know," Anthony said, "because of the tree limb crashing through the library roof...and well, you know, like what's in the painting?"

Jack added, "C'mere, now! You may have something there! Aye, yeah, mate, like that long tree limb over the pool of water, d'ya mean?"

Anthony nodded earnestly.

Angie jumped in. "Well, one of the things I really like about *that* name is that *LiMB* really doesn't sound like much of anything important...LiMB...you can say it anywhere, around anyone, and who would notice or care?"

"LiMB." They all tried it on for size in varying degrees of vocal renditions.

She looked around at the group expectantly, her eyes resting finally on the biggest critic. "What do you think, Nick?"

Nick made an offhand gesture. "Yeah, sure, I guess so." He eyed his brother, admiration behind his playful eyes. "Sounds pretty good to me...Library Mystery Buffs...I can't say I love it, but...." He ruffled his brother's already-mussed head of hair, "Better '*buffs*'—" the usual kidding lacing his voice, "than buf*foons*."

As they all groaned in agony, he smiled and said, "I guess I can put up with you girls, too, for a little while, if I have to, just to get this job done right!"

Natalie gave him another good-natured whack and Angie just grinned back at the big lug.

"Aye, so shut your gob, mate and let's get started!" Jack kidded him.

Natalie said exuberantly, "Let's go look at the secret hiding place!"

Angie beamed at the group and asked, "Is that it, then? Are you all happy with the name?"

They all nodded in complete agreement.

And so, **The LiMB Society** was born.

Chapter Two

A New Discovery

"I'm dying to see the scene of the crime. Well, not a crime, really, but where they found the painting." Natalie bounced up from her seat. "And the other stuff, too?"

Angie rubbed her hands together in delight. "Let's go see what we can find under the eaves."

She led them down the hallway, past the boxes, desks, and long table lining the wall, and into the last small room to the exact place where the "mysterious painting behind the wall" was discovered.

Thanks to Angie's Uncle Carl, the back roof damage had been temporarily covered over with tarping, and the only natural light in the room, albeit limited, entered through the small attic window.

Angie's eyes traveled to this third floor half-moon-shaped window and she gazed out, her eyes drawn down the lengthy, quiet Main Street. She looked past Murphy's General Store and further up the road still, toward Pillson's Village Green and then, further in the distance, the Town Hall. She shook her gaze free from the lofty sight and pointed to the wooden wall panel as everyone piled into the small room together. "Yuh, here it is, right here under the hole in the roof, just as Mrs. Bundle said."

Natalie said, pointing "It really *looks* like a secret space."

"That's where the painting was found, back behind this knee wall," Angie said and, under her direction, Nick and Jack pulled on the now-flimsy, old oak panel that was leaning haphazardly on its side.

Tugging, they worked it free to fully reveal the small, hidden area under the eaves.

"You've gotta be kidding. Mrs. Bundle was actually inside here?" Anthony asked.

"Yup." Angie said, "She said she went in there three times."

Nick said, "She's a pistol, that's for sure." They all laughed as he knelt down in front of the opening. "Cool!" he said, pulling a small flashlight from his Harper's golf shirt pocket. "Have flashlight, will travel!" His buoyant nature was catching.

Jack stooped down, joining him, both on their haunches, carefully surveying the perimeter first.

Nick said, "Seems pretty safe." Over his shoulder, he said, "Dude, I'll go first," and crawled carefully inside with Jack close on his heels.

Those left behind could hear them rustling around in the tiny space, their muffled voices kidding back and forth.

"Jaysus! Watch where you put your big boats, would you now?"

"Who's got big feet?"

"Ouch! Clear off, mate! Get your foot out of me backside—are you loopers?"

"Watch out yourself, you big Irish bum!"

Bangs and clattering could be heard as they attempted to adjust their bodies in the small space—really only big enough to accommodate a much smaller framed person or two.

"Here we go, mates, right!" Jack's dirty hand emerged with a stack of the old candy wrappers; Angie and Natalie grabbed them from him.

The girls laid them out on the nearby stacked boxes as he backed out gingerly. Straightening up from exiting the space, Jack joined the girls and Anthony to take a look.

"Whew! Sure, and it's bloody hotter 'n an oven in there!"

"And grubby to boot!" Natalie said, pulling a face at his appearance.

His hands were filthy from a combination of old floorboards and residual roof damage, but Jack gingerly picked up one of the wrappers and read the fine lettering. "Aye, they're fancy, aren't they now!"

Meanwhile, Anthony leaned down, calling to his brother, "What's going on in there, Nick?"

Rummaging around could be heard and then, all of a sudden, two big boots came out first followed by two long legs and groping hands, flashlight still beaming. Nick wiped a sticky gossamer cobweb from his curly towhead, passing his rough hands down his shirt. Angie reached over and nonchalantly brushed off more silvery strands from his back; his handsomely flushed face turned a bit rosier. He spoke quickly, clearing his throat of the dust. "Man, what a blast! It's just as Mrs. Bundle said. There's those carved letters in the wall, for sure. I saw them plain as day, all neat and right in a row." He flipped the flashlight button to the off position.

"Did they look like Roman numerals to you?" Angie asked.

He was out of breath, but managed to declare, "Well, they're all strung together in one long, straight line, if that's what you mean!" He leaned back, exhausted from the heat, and took in a deep breath of fresh air. "And..." he got another blast of energy, 'they're all capital letters, plain as the nose on my face! What did you say those numerals mean?"

"1755."

He spoke in bits and spurts. "That's *very* interesting—1755. Especially—because there's *another* carving in there."

"Another carving?" Angie and Anthony said in unison.

"You found something else?" Natalie asked.

He nodded, inhaling deeply. "Uh-huh."

"You mean, something *else* that Mrs. B missed?" Angie asked.

"Yup. Sure did."

"What is it?"

"Well, it was way down below the other letters, at the very bottom of that inside panel." His breath still came in spurts. "Whew! I can see why she would have missed it. It's pretty faint—" he caught his breath, "—looks old, like the first carving."

"Well? Are you going to tell us what it is?" Natalie urged, frustrated.

"*Gawd!* Give me a minute to breathe, wouldn't you?" He blew out air and paused, took a nice long breath, exhaled, and then said distinctly, "It's a number. 1855. For real. You know, like the date! Like someone wrote Roman numerals above it and then wrote 1855 below."

Anthony's scientific mind kicked in; he looked puzzled. "Huh? That doesn't jive with the Roman numerals 1755."

"I've got to see!" Angie cried out as she grabbed the flashlight and entered the space.

Natalie followed closely behind her.

Anthony, left behind, scratched his nose in bewilderment. "Wait a minute, this is confusing me. How come another date? We know the year of the *painting* is 1861. We've got…the Roman numeral 1755—if that is a date—" he mumbled to himself, "—but long before the date the Library was even built! Let's see, I'm remembering something I just heard…," he paused, the finely-membraned lids and lashes closed over his eyes and creased into little rows, "Yeah—that's it! 1849! That's when the Library was built, I'm pretty sure! That's what Louis Montembeau said—just the other day I overheard him telling Mrs. Bundle." He stopped and looked up, slightly embarrassed. His brother, noting his discomfort, afforded him marginal attention and interest. Anthony blushed. "Well, it's not like I was eavesdropping or anything! Really, I wasn't listening on purpose; I was just nearby where they were talking. I don't know what about, except I heard Louis say the Library's been open since 1849."

Nick added, tapping his temple, "Yeah, bro, ever notice above the entrance, plain as day? I've seen it a million times! 'Established 1849'!"

Anthony slapped the palm of his hand to his forehead. "That's right!"

Muffled squeals burst forth from the space below, "Omigosh! See it, Natalie?"

"Yes!"

Returning none the worse for wear except for dust on their knees and dark smudges on Angie's nose and cheek, the girls emerged from the space.

"Would you look at you, now! It's a raving beauty we have here!" Jack smiled and winked mischievously at Angie. "C'mere," he reached over and attempted to wipe the smudges from her face, but his dirty hands made it worse. "Comin' out and lookin' like a street urchin straight from Dublin!"

She laughed, ignoring him, "I *saw* it! It's there! We've got another clue! Oh, boy!"

"Guys, this is kinda weird," Anthony said.

Natalie scrunched her perky nose, the little freckles forming mini connect-the-dots on her face. "I bet you want to know the same thing I do, Anthony. How come there are so many dates? Gaw! It's too confusing! I can't keep track of them all." She dusted herself off like a frisky cat, then paused. "Hey! What about this idea? What if…" she scrunched her nose even more, "the Roman numeral letters *aren't really* Roman numerals? What if…they're like our *Li.M.B.* letters? You know, could they stand for words, too?"

Anthony said, "Yeah! What you're saying is, could they mean something entirely different?"

This sparked an animated discussion of various theories; they all spent the next few minutes poring over the candy wrappers and comparing opinions of the different scenarios: who might have stowed the painting in the tiny space, what the dates could mean, where they should go next with their investigation.

Angie interjected, "Okay, we may be getting ahead of ourselves. I think we need to organize each part of this mystery." She turned to her friend. "Natalie, can you be in charge of researching the candy wrappers? You know, finding out as much as you can about the candy company and, maybe, when the candy was made, where, etcetera?"

Natalie nodded enthusiastically.

"And Anthony, you're going to explore the year 1861 and check on the Pillson history, right? What was going on then, right?"

"Absolutely. There's a lot of history to look into."

Jack added, "Right, mate. It seems we should be focusing on the timeframe *between* 1855—now that we have that date carved on the wall—and 1861. Would we, now?"

"Yes! Excellent point, Jack. We'll make sure that's covered." Angie said. "Nick and Jack, we've already discussed your end. You're going back over to your *secret fishing hole*—"she grinned, "— *not* just to fish, mind you! You're got to verify that it definitely is the same spot as the painting. Maybe take a snapshot of the painting with you and look for detail, noting the likenesses of the site now and the *differences*, too. We need to be sure about this."

Nick said, "Yeah, we're on it. No problem."

"Remember," Angie said, "every detail may just be the key that unlocks this mystery. Right?"

"Right!" They all approved.

"But what about those dang Roman numerals?" Angie asked. "They don't fit in. I'll take that piece and explore that."

Anthony said, "Remember what Natalie suggested. They may *not* be Roman numerals! I think we have to keep an open mind…it's something totally unknown to us but meaningful to somebody."

"I'll let Mrs. B know about that idea. And the new clue! She'll be thrilled we've found even more to research." Angie's excitement was infectious. "This *is* kind of like doing a research project, isn't it? Anthony, if you'd like, we can go together to the Pillson Historical Society and the *State Standard*."

He nodded emphatically.

"Geez, look at the time!" Nick exclaimed. "I gotta get back to work or they'll fire me, for sure." He brushed his hands over his shirt. "They're gonna think I've been rolling around in the dirt!"

"Well, you have!" Natalie pushed him.

Angie's face was aglow as she looked around the room. "Right! I think we got a lot accomplished today. We've all got our assignments."

As they began to move toward the doorway, she cautioned, "Oh! One last thing. I agree with what Anthony said; let's all keep an open mind!" She raised her hands up high, "The sky's the limit! We'll have our next meeting with Mrs. B at her house. She said to plan on it." She looked at the date on her watch. "We're already heading into the second week of July. How about the 1st of August? That's a

Friday and a good two weeks before the Festival. Plan on an evening meeting so we all can be there. Does that work for everyone? Okay, then! The first meeting of The LiMB Society is *hereby adjourned!*"

———————•◆•———————

Thus began the secret society's research, which would continue through the rest of July.

Their intense work would not be in vain.

Ultimately, their incredible findings would prove to coincide in bizarre happenstance with the other powerful events in those pivotal summer months.

The forces of good and evil were destined to collide in the oddest of ways—which, Mrs. Bundle always believed, was often how things tended to naturally happen, curiously intertwined like groping tentacles amongst the unfolding events of the unfortunate hay baler tragedy.

Part IV:

JULY
INTO
AUGUST

Chapter One

The Hay Baler Tragedy

Mrs. Bundle was frozen in space (or so it seemed), sitting here alone, contemplating the day's sordid events and the circumstances that had, in due course, lead her tangentially round and round to finally rest beside the ominous hay baler on this last day of July. Mere minutes had passed, but the last few weeks' events had passed before her in lightening quickness.

Surrounding her was the open and gradually sloping field, two long rows of baling on the east edge of the field having been completed, the second row heading south down the long slope. Bales in a row, like ducks in a row...

In these last few minutes, she'd had time to think about the bold, but naïve, plan for the Dog Days of Summer Art Festival. And the three horrific blazes and their impact on the community—and the longest drought since 1911, taking hold of the whole county like a rattlesnake's fangs, literally, putting everyone into a state of panic and confusion. People were uneasy about the possibility of more fires, even though the politically correct statements issued ongoing assurances that the State had arrested "the right man" for the arson crimes.

There, in the Southern State Correctional Facility, still sat Junior. Poor Vincent who, she was still convinced, was totally innocent of the crimes that had been committed.

Her promise to help him lay like a dead, cumbersome weight in her stomach.

Til now, she had not had a minute to reflect, to just…think about the challenges she had chosen to take on, consuming her every day. She'd not been able to take the time, even an hour, to stop and just meditate. The Festival, coupled with Junior's arrest, had overwhelmed her: both huge projects, both thrown together into her world through coincidence. Truth be told, it was utterly intimidating at times.

One of those tasks seemed headed toward success; the other seemed destined to fail. The Festival had taken on a life of its own, gaining momentum with each week that went by. Why, it seemed the whole of Pillson had jumped on board. Conversely, the investigation to free Vincent had led only to dead ends.

Right now, she had the weirdest feeling that the world surrounding her was moving at a tediously deliberate, awkwardly-lumbering pace, as though in slow motion. She leaned over and picked up her battered straw hat that had fallen to the ground when she had collapsed in shock.

Where on earth was the Sheriff?

She reached impatiently for the comfort of Cracker's warm, sleek body but he had meandered off, snuffling the low ground. He nosed his way along, delicately past the baler's base and then up its hard steel side, straining to get a better look inside.

"Cracker-Cat, come over here, would you?"

From her seated position on the ground, she looked past Cracker, under the baler, and noticed a bulky, lone piece of lumber; she guesstimated its length to be about four feet. What on earth was *that* doing there?

She looked up once more at the woefully chubby, dead body and felt a wave of extreme sadness…and regret.

Oh, poor Watson!

She had not seen the urgency of meeting with Watson DeVille. He was always so meek, always so unassumingly, so unpretentiously *interminably* mild-mannered.

It was his ultimate downfall, she thought ruefully.

Unfortunately, she had missed the signs. She had been too busy, diminishing the importance of his woeful request: his need to see her.

What had he called it? She reached into her memory—seemingly a lifetime ago—not just this morning. Yes, he had alluded to..."a very important meeting."

She went over things carefully, reconstructing as best she could. What exactly had he said when he had phoned her early this Thursday morning?

"Uh, good day, dear woman. Salutations! It's Watson…Watson DeVille."

(Of course, Mrs. Bundle had known it was the professor. For one thing, there was only one "Watson." She smiled sadly, remembering that was *always* how the gentle man had identified himself to her for the thirty-odd years she had known him.)

"Hello, Watson!"

He had continued in his typically formal manner."Uh, er, ahem! How *are* you?"

"Good n'you?"

"Oh, fine. Thank you for asking. Lovely day today."

His voice had held its usual tentative quality. In retrospect, Mrs. Bundle now realized there was something else. It had seemed throughout their conversation that he was waiting for *just* the right timing, trying to find *just* the right words to venture into the dangerously tedious territory of what *exactly* his point was to be. She gave a huge sigh of frustration. *Was* there another reason he had called?

She remembered looking at the clock, noting the time as her mind wandered to the many things she must accomplish today."Yes, we've got another hot one, Watson. Paper says it's the twenty-ninth day in a row now." She had paused, waiting expectantly, but he had hesitated. *He* had been the one to call her, hadn't he?

"Yes, that's for certain. *Ahem*…Lettie, I was wondering…"

"Yes, Watson?"

"Ah, yes…uhhh…right! Would you permit me to be so bold as to ask...well, I understand you've been hired by Master Barnabus to help out our friend, Vincent. A fine young man. That is, I understand you're working to get the poor boy out of jail and home where he belongs..."

"Yes, that's right, Watson. Quite informally, really. I've been working on his case—in between the Festival."

"Wonderful, wonderful. I'm pleased to know someone is in his court." He repeated, "He's a fine young man, a really fine boy." She had waited while he drew in a very long breath and then continued, "Well, then. Mind you, normally, as a rule, Twinkles and I would never get involved. Well, that is…" he paused, "as a rule. However, I really had no idea, until now, you see…that things had become…so diabolical!"

"Diabolical?" The word was a strong one for Watson. "Really? What do you mean?"

There was a sneeze at the other end of the line. Mrs. Bundle waited while she heard a long honking and serious nose-blowing. *Watson's nerve allergies must be kicking in*, she had thought.

Finally, with a sigh, he continued, "So, so sorry, Lettie." He cleared his throat. "See here, Twinkles and I would never want to start any trouble. No, we wouldn't, not at all, would we?"

She heard the peeps and yaps of the pip-squeaked Bichon in the background.

Getting what she wanted of Watson was like pulling candy away from a starving child and she said, "Yes, Watson…I understand what you mean. Nobody likes to get involved in anything unpleasant. However, if you think you have something that could possibly help Vincent, well, I would appreciate you sharing it with me."

"Well, as you say, getting involved could be…stressful—and we certainly don't want to be a bother to you, either. Yet again, it would be a travesty if that young man went to jail for a crime he did not commit."

"You are so right! So, what's on your mind?"

"Well, yes, you see, as I say, there's the conundrum." His logic was maddeningly methodical. "On the one hand, we certainly don't want to get into the fray. On the other hand," he paused, ticking his tongue against his teeth, "*Tch, tch*, oh bother! Not to put too fine a point on it, I *think* there *might* be a *remote* possibility," his long pause prompted a long, expectant sigh from Mrs. Bundle; finally, he had exploded with, "that we may be of some help, however remote a possibility it might be."

"Watson, really, however insignificant you may think it is, if you have something that would help Vincent, you're no bother at all. I'm all ears! Certainly *anything* you have to share could be very helpful."

"Well, there are *things* to be considered."

Although attempts to cut to the chase had yet to be fruitful, Mrs. Bundle had tried again, asking, "So, what have you heard?"

"You see, well, it's not exactly what we *heard*. It's quite a dilemma. It's my research, well, and, what we saw...in *conjunction* with what we heard, too."

There was an excruciating silence as she waited. She had thought at the time, *just be patient with him, Lettie. It's coming, slowly but surely.* She had known Watson long enough to know that, as always, his well-thought-out point would come out eventually. "Yes, well okay, Watson. So, it's *not* so much what you heard but it has to do with your research and what you saw..."

Dead silence on the other end—she'd continued waiting, lightly drumming her fingers against the table, her eyes moving to the stack of Festival paperwork.

Finally, his tentative words came and he said, "Well I must first qualify that my visual observations are suspect— I'll be the first to admit that my eyes have gone poorly the last few years; thank goodness for my Twinkles! I've made an appointment for new glasses with Doctor Mastraccioni in Woodstock. Consequently, with that clarification, I think it's best to state it's what we *think* I saw. I should say, yes, it is *definitely* what *we think* I saw—"

"Professor, please!" Mrs. Bundle's eyes were glazing over at that point, and she had rubbed her forehead. Admittedly, her patience had been worn to a nub. Holding herself in check, though, she had urged, "Okay, Watson, let's start at the beginning." Using his exact words, she had said with deliberation, "Not to put *too* fine a point on it, what *exactly* do you think you may have seen or heard, or know or think, and how does it relate to your research?"

"Well-stated, Lettie! And, therein lies the problem."

Thankfully, his own deep sigh had masked her huge gulp of aggravation.

Cracker, listening from his soft hideaway nearby, had snuffled deeply into the upholstery pillow, temporarily cutting off the air passage to his lungs. *Arg-gg-hhhh*, he had cat-thought, *please somebody, put me out of this misery!*

But, sadly, Watson's revelation was not to be. Somehow spooked, he had lowered his voice. His voice trembled and the whispered words came even more cautiously, gently,"Ahem! Well, you see, I have a theory, a hypothesis, that is to say, which I have yet to finalize. I have one more piece…which could be noteworthy. I'm of the mind that well, owing to the private nature of this...ah, insidious situation... that it would be best for you and I to discuss it…face to face—later today. I mean to say...could we, possibly, meet this afternoon? If you were available, that is? Then *you* could tell *me* if what I perceive to know is *really* important or just the silly, cerebral meanderings of an old professor."

"Surely, I would be glad to meet you Watson! When and where? I've got to run the final draft—the news release proof—to the printer once Ellie Waterhouse drops it off, but yes, of course. And Watson, whatever it is, it will go no further, I can assure you."

"Oh, wonderful, wonderful!"

He had sounded relieved, almost lighthearted, as she remembered it.

Covering the phone's mouthpiece, he spoke aside. Mrs. Bundle had heard his muffled words,"Twinkles, dear, everything is going to be fine!" at which point a series of high-pitched, very shrill barks had come through the phone. He had come back, almost cheerily, telling Mrs. Bundle,"Oh! She's so excited! Yes, yes, dear little one, I'm coming,"(he spoke to the little Bichon, whose yapping escalated in the background)"You are a godsend, Lettie, truly you are! Not like others who think we're just Nervous Nellies!"

The piercing yelps continued and she could barely hear Watson over the din...

At this instant, as she stared at his lifeless body and recalled his blissful change, it was as though his melodious, carefree words came back to haunt her from within this deathtrap beside her.

"Who thinks you're just a Nervous Nellie?" she had asked.

"Oh! God bless her! A 'worry wart' was what she said. Well, no matter!" A nervous laugh had erupted and he had whispered, "You see, the thing is, people should be held accountable. If someone is at fault, or is found to be, *ahh*, deceitful, then...Twinkles and I think justice should prevail." The squeals and yelps were now at a level so uncomfortable that Mrs. Bundle had held the phone away from her ear.

In retrospect, she now realized Watson's confused ramblings were an indication of his anxiety level; however, during their conversation, his inability to focus had only exasperated her.

Why, oh why, hadn't she followed through?

She closed her eyes, trying to focus on the remainder of their conversation that morning.

Focus!

He had said...yes, that's right, he *had* said, "Twinkles and I think justice should prevail."

As she was about to reply, Watson had interrupted with, "*Twinkles*, no, my dear little one! Oh, no, *not* again! No, dearest, *not* on the couch, *please!* Have I upset you? Mercy me!" His voice had come frantically through the receiver, the emergency with Twinkles seemingly spurring on Watson's sense of urgency. "This is all much too disruptive for my sweet Twinkles. Yes, a *very* important meeting today, to be sure! I look forward to putting all this to an end."

"Fine, Watson. What time? Would you like me to come up there? To North Puckerbrush?"

"Oh, no, no! Don't trouble yourself. I'll come down to you. After I take Twinkles for her afternoon constitutionals, we'll be over straight away. Say, at two o'clock?"

"Yes, Watson, that would be fine. I'll be waiting right here." She had paused for a brief second, and then, compelled for some strange reason, she made one last attempt, calling out, "Professor?"

"Yes?"

"Are you sure you wouldn't want to tell me *a bit* of what this is about, before you come?

He had lowered his voice again, barely to a whisper as he comforted his best little friend. "There, there, calm down, dear." Then, to Mrs. Bundle, "Oh, Lettie, no. No, I think not. It's best to discuss this in person, in *complete* privacy."

What final irony, Mrs. Bundle noted now, that he decided against sharing. She couldn't help but wonder; would it have made any difference?

Chapter Two

Poor, Departed, Watson

And that, sadly, had been the last time she had communicated with Professor Watson DeVille.

So much for putting things off.

She couldn't help but believe that what he had wanted to discuss with her might possibly have contributed to, his death.

Who was it, she wondered, *that he had talked to?* He had said '*she*'; *She* had called him a "Nervous Nellie."

Such a gruesome, diabolical way to die! *Oh!* She started. That was the same word he had used, wasn't it? *Diabolical.* A meeting with her—or someone else, too?

Mrs. Bundle shuddered, making small clicking sounds with her tongue. Her instinct was strong on one matter. Whatever he had wanted to tell her was the ultimate result of his demise. Yes, she nodded. He had erred in keeping his secret to the point that, now, his dead body lay beside her, stuffed into the baler like sausage into a meat grinder.

His allergy reaction and Twinkles' interminable yapping, her little "mistake" on the couch; it all boiled down to…fear.

Suddenly, the dog's miniature face came into her mind. *Where*, she thought as she looked around her with growing alarm, *could Twinkles be?*

There was no sign anywhere, at all, of the spooked pooch.

Sniffling to herself, she hesitated and then wrinkled her nose in distaste as she drew in a faintly acrid, smoky odor.

"What's burning?" she said aloud, looking around with fear.

Cracker had jumped past the baler and, clearly agitated, was circling an area nearby. He snuffled suspiciously at the ground, paws treading lightly around the small area's perimeter. His head shot into the air, and he meowed loudly; she watched with interest.

There, not thirty feet away, like a huge blotch of darkness on the saffron-colored meadow, was an irregularly-shaped, scorched area of land about the size of a pool table. Framing the area was the surrounding, freshly cut pasture, a bright ochre against the mottled, dark brown and black of the charred area.

Fire! She scanned the area quickly in panic and, noticing no smoke or evidence of flames, sat back in relief. No need for immediate worry—but fire, up here? Most alarming was her realization that this was the very recent remnants of a burning. Here, in the middle of the meadow! *Why,* she thought, *if this had caught on, it would have been a catastrophe for the whole vicinity.* Somebody had intentionally tried to start a fire, possibly to cover their tracks.

She was devastated—the murderers!"My Lord, it can't be! This is really too unbelievable!" She studied the burned area."A case of intentional destruction. What kind of lunatic does this? First, murdering poor Watson, and then a fire, too! Why, C.C., why?"

Cracker's meows grew louder. His cat-thought came through loud and clear: *Yet again, arson rears its ugly head!*

"Thank goodness whoever lit off this grass failed. It didn't take. Lord knows why!" Her hands covered her heart."And, in this terrible drought, too! It would have spread quickly. Everyone around would be dead."

You bet, came Cracker's response, *us included!*

She tried in vain to get a clear thought.

Cat's Granny! A murderer....and a firestarter.

Without trouble, she called up that ongoing mental image of the lonely, troubled man sitting dejectedly in the jail cell. But now, rather than feel a large knot in her stomach, she felt a strange sense of affirmation. She plopped her straw hat back on her head and tied the ribbon securely under her chin.

"*Hallelulia!*" Her voice echoed throughout the large expanse of field. She yelled again, releasing weeks of frustration."*Hallelulia, Horatio!*"

Chapter Three

Murder Most Foul

The field was a blur of activity. The cumbersome State forensic trailer had only been able to drive up the cow path about fifty yards into the pasture. A whole acre of the north field surrounding the murder scene had been roped off with official yellow emergency tape and the perimeter was dotted with all the officials bent on assembling information. The Vermont State Police monitored the cordoned-off area, their faces grim and serious, their eyes searching the gathering crowd for anything unusual.

The victim was pronounced dead at the scene.

Word had traveled fast. *Did you hear about Professor Watson? Up in the Andersen field! He's been murdered! And, there was another fire! A big one, they say, could have burned up the whole of North Pillson Corners and beyond! Yessuh, up in the field—right near the dead body!*

Neighbors, passer-bys, and concerned citizens had begun to congregate in and around the Andersen farmhouse. The fire department, in its haste to contain any fire, had dispatched two trucks after having been notified there was the possibility of an intentionally-set field fire in progress. Both trucks sat there now, its members waiting like everyone else.

Sheriff Will O'Malley and the state's forensic detective had sequestered Mrs. Bundle off to the shelter and shade of the nearby Andersen barn. After giving her plenty of cranberry juice and a package of crackers, she felt somewhat revived, although the overall experience had left her drained.

She wanted to tell them about the morning's conversation, but they said that could wait until a bit later.

The Sheriff conferred with the State Police detective and then dispatched his two deputies to whereabouts unknown. When Mrs. Bundle asked, he would only say they were actively pursuing information relative to the case and then asked Clay Andersen to drive her and Cracker home. She protested that she could certainly walk the short distance over the hill, but he insisted. He was also adamant that she not talk to anyone about what had transpired, and that he would be over when he finished up at the murder scene. With that, he turned and asked to see Angie Andersen.

Once home, she was grateful she had taken him up on the ride. Cracker purred and flexed his body close to her and they shared more sustenance together in the form of reheated meatloaf washed down with a large glass of lemonade (for her), and his favorite liver cookies and milk (for him).

Later, in the early evening, the Sheriff arrived at her house with the State's forensic detective in hand. "Sorry, Lettie, but we've got to do our job."

"It's all right, Will. I know."

They proceeded to question her at length about her own possible interest or motivation in seeing pitiful Watson dead. The detective interjected his own questions every so often.

Did she kill Watson DeVille?

Had she had a disagreement with him?

"No!" she had assured them. "In fact, he was coming over to discuss something very important, he said, something that had to do with Junior Veakey's arrest, which he knew I was working on."

What had he wanted to discuss with her?

As succinctly as she could remember, she told them of her morning conversation with Watson and of their scheduled meeting and his consequent no-show. The questions continued, which she answered each in turn.

Was he at all agitated with her?

Did she have any idea what specifically he wanted to tell her?

Did she know whether it was common practice for him to come through the backland, through the woods, rather than drive over from North Puckerbrush?

Had she moved anything at the murder site?

What about the fire? How had it started?

Did she see the wooden stud under the baler?

Had she touched it or moved it?

Did she see anything or anyone unusual at all in the distance, by the stand of trees, or nearby?

And so it went.

After two hours of intense questioning, the general consensus between the two men was that Mrs. Bundle's (and Angie's) coming upon the murder scene was pure happenstance.

The two men conferred privately in her parlor while she and Cracker sat in the kitchen. When they returned, their manner was less interrogative and much gentler as they asked if she would be willing to help them further with their investigation.

The detective, a large man with an official, resonant voice said, "What we need you to do is to try in the next few days to remember any detail, however insignificant, of your conversation with Professor Watson. We believe it may be crucial. You can meet with the Sheriff in the next week or so."

She readily agreed and, with his examination of her finished for now, he hustled away.

She was left alone with Sheriff O'Malley; she walked outside with him, neither of them speaking. He stood on the front steps of her farmhouse and scratched his balding head. Then, he stretched and leaned his huge frame unofficially on the porch frame.

"It's a strange world, isn't it, Lettie? Bizarre, to say the least."

"Yes, Will. It surely is when something as nasty as this can happen right here in our little world." She made her little clicking sounds.

"Murder! Not your typical garden variety, either—with all due respect. Plus, a failed attempt at arson—luckily."

"Yes…" She hesitated, wishing to make a point, but decided to wait."Do you have any idea who might be involved?"

"Nope." He touched the side of his nose and lowered his voice."We've got one, maybe two sets of tracks—very light, hardly distinguishable in the crushed hay. Footprints don't seem to match Professor DeVille's shoes—mind you, we've got to check the Andersen men's boots, too. Hard to tell in this dry weather, but forensics is working on it." He stared at her intently."Do you realize it's very possible *you* scared them off, Lettie? With Angie? Did you think about that?"

"Yes, that thought did occur to me, Will."

"A fire in these parts—it's unthinkable! With the ground as dry as it is, the whole area would have gone quickly. I daresay Pillson's resources would never have been able to contain the fire."

"It's incredible, Will, really mind-boggling. I can't believe it."

He sat down in the nearby porch rocker, his body spent, and rubbed his tired eyes. He looked up at his old friend."Not to put too fine a point on it…here's the facts as we know them. We know he was supposed to meet you at two, and that he was usually a very punctual individual. Did he come through the woods on his own? It seems he may have started that way, through the woods from his place on North Puckerbrush with his intention to get to your house the back way. Based upon our initial discovery and the coroner's cursory exam, it appears the murder occurred within that window of time—between approximately 1:35 and say, 3:15 p.m. The coroner will be able to further determine and tighten that window, for sure, once he does his full autopsy."

"I'm thinking—maybe you've already determined this—that he *must* have brought Twinkles with him, as he said he would."

"The dog? Yup. Looks that way. But the mutt can't be found anywhere. Either she got spooked and ran into the woods or the killer—or killers—did her in, too. No sign of her anywhere—as we speak."

She clicked her tongue in disgust and muttered to herself."Just like old Tuddsley."

"What's that?"

"Tuddsley, the Tudhope's dog! You know—Tuddy's?"

"By God, *Tuddsley*! Lettie, you're right!"

"Do you think there's a connection? It seems outrageous that they could be related in some way."

"Something to think about…although I'll be dangblasted how they could be."

They both chewed on the idea, and then Will said,"By the way, I've got something here for you to take a look at."

He reached into his pocket."Ever seen this?"

He opened his large hand, palm up, and revealed a small zip-lock plastic bag. He held it out for her, and she took the baggie from him."Better yet, does it remind you of anything? Anything at all?"

She examined it, asking,"What the heck is it?"

"Take a good look." He watched her carefully.

She scrutinized the little object secured in the plastic bag: hard metal, shiny, round with a 1/4-inch extension off a rounded top, screw-like but flat-ended on the end that should have been pointed, threaded to the end and steel-colored.

"Never seen it." She handed it back to him."What is it? Is it some sort of a nail? Or a tack of some kind?"

"No…we think it's more like a miniature fastener, a screw or a rivet of some sort."

"Uh-huh. A screw of some sort." She shook her head, looking quizzical."No idea. Why show it to me, Will?"

"More than anything, process of elimination. When we showed it to the three Andersen men earlier, not one could tell me anything about it."

She reached out and took the item from him once more, looked again with closer scrutiny this time, and muttered,"It's very tiny, isn't it? Almost miniature." She scrunched her forehead in deep thought,"Common sense would tell us it must go into—or, I guess, screw into—something rather small."

"Good 'seat of your pants' deducing. Same thing we thought."

"Do *you* have any idea what it goes to?"

"Nope, not yet. I thought we might get lucky and you or the Andersens might have an idea where it came from. That would be the easy answer."

"You found it in the field, didn't you?"

He hesitated, then gave her a crooked smile."Yup, we did. Talk about needle in a haystack. But...here's what's interesting. We found it *inside* the perimeter of the burned area."

"Really?" Mrs. Bundle gave that some thought."*Hmmm.* What do you suppose?"

His big shoulders shrugged."Not a clue as yet, but we'll see what our analysis can come up with. We may have to send it away to a more sophisticated facility than we have here in our area."

"Do you think it has something to do with the murder?"

"Well, we can't rule it out. We're just not sure. It could have been in that field for years—decades, maybe—but, between you and me, I think not. It's too shiny, isn't it? No rust to speak of." He hunched his body over and stared intently at the item in her hands."But, who knows?"

She handed the bag back to him and wearily followed him to his cruiser, watching him as he carefully placed the bag into a brown paper bag and sealed it tightly.

The sun was setting on the westerly hill and, as she watched him, a bright tinge of reddish light shone like an aura around his large form. He turned toward her and she covered her eyes.

"Sheriff, before you leave, I must say this...please bear with me—it's about...Vincent Veakey."

He frowned at her and reached for the door handle."The wheels of justice, Lettie! You know I can't talk about Junior or anything to do with that case. Don't put me on the spot. He's in jail and you work for him."

"Well, Will, I know that! But, I had some time while I waited alone in that field—you know, just before you and your men arrived. And, a very clear thought came to me. I'll bet you already know what I'm going to say…" She paused as he passed an enormous hand over his sweating wide brow.

"Oh, geez, Lettie, there you go, putting me between a rock and a hard place. Case in point: you *know* there haven't been any cases of arson since he was incarcerated."

"Will, that's exactly right! No cases of arson *until now*, that is. A fire intentionally set in a big field where a murder has also been committed." She waited. "Common sense, Will. Think about it and you'll realize this is attempted arson, which could have been much worse, to be sure. *Once again*, Will."

He got inside the car. "Don't preach to the choir, Lettie. I think you should trust in the fact that we may know more than you do!"

She pushed on. "Another deliberate act of arson in an area that hasn't seen this type of crime wave in decades—if ever, to my knowledge. It means, dear friend, that you and the State Attorney's office have even less of a case—very little reason, in fact—for keeping Vincent in custody any longer." She placed a hand on the open window. "Really, wouldn't you have to agree?"

"Well, what I will agree with is that you're like a dog with a bone, Lettie—that's for dang sure! You just don't give up, do you? Even after the day you've had, you still can think about that boy?"

"I can, Will, and I must. He's still in jail. I made a promise to that boy, and I mean to keep it."

Donning his Sheriff's hat, he said, "I wish I could say more, but I can't. All I can say right now is...we'll have to see what the DA's position is—now that this event has taken place, that is." His pudgy fingers shaped quotation marks, "'They' don't like to backtrack, as a rule, don't you know? Nobody wants egg on their face, and sometimes people have to suffer because of that. But, that said—and don't hold me to it—I believe you may, *just may*, mind you, be on the right track, Lettie." He held up a hand. "And that's all. We'll see. Well, I gotta go!"

"Thank you, Will! For everything."

"Get some sleep, would you? You're going to need it. You're our key witness right now to maybe the grisliest murder this county has ever seen."

She gave a wan smile and a light wave as he tipped his hat and drove off down the road.

———————•—•—•———————

The petite dog shivered, not from the twilight air, which was very hot and dry, but from the horrible display she had been forced to view earlier in the day, not comprehending what was happening until it was too late.

Evil! Evil!

She had run, as fast as her squat, stubby legs would carry her, scampering wildly, blindly...until somehow she had ended up here, miles away on this mossy mound, hiding underneath a multitude of protective ground ferns. Fatigued and dehydrated, she had collapsed, her sore sides bursting, her panting breaths coming in short, quick gasps.

She had never been lost before, but the terror drove her to run away from that ghastly scene with all the strength she possessed.

After some lapse of time, she recovered her breathing, still an unnatural panting as she lay deep, deep in the woods, protected by the oncoming darkness. Her dog mind raced, severely traumatized by the images.

Oh, her poor, dear Master!

That evil, evil person...

She squeezed her little pooch eyes very tightly in an attempt to wipe the mental picture away. She began to whimper, unaccustomed to not being pampered and protected now.

The sad yapping continued with abandon through the night, the dog completely inconsolable as the early morning light began to peek through the heavy green foliage.

Hours later, she raised herself delicately on unsteady paws. Trancelike and more by instinct, she sought out a water source. She reeled unsteadily as she edged her way haphazardly through the forest, flopping down and resting when she was too overcome with either grief, dehydration, or both.

Finally, dementia set in from too little water and too much distress; she could go no further. Weaving in slow motion, she buckled, and then fell softly, like a cotton puff, to the ground. Her curly, apricot-hued head rested plaintively on a nearby fallen branch and the wretched whimpering sounds began again, fainter this time.

The staccato last images of her Master were too gruesome to bear and her mournful cries could be heard ricocheting eerily deep, deep into the wood and then back, ping-ponging from tree to tree. Her tired voice modulated to only the hoarse remains of intermittent, pathetic croaks.

At last, her heart gave out and she lost consciousness, but not before she felt the final horror of someone's hands around her sad, little neck.

Chapter Four

Joining Forces

O ne week later, Mrs. Bundle sat with Sheriff Will O' in his office. At his urging, she had come to Woodstock to meet "unofficially" with him at the new County Sheriff Department digs on Pleasant Street (previously the site of the historic Woodstock County Jail).

He passed a document across the table to her entitled "Sheriff's Report: Watson DeVille Case." He swiped a hand in the air and said, "Go ahead, Lettie. Read it. Can't do any harm at this point."

The report was wide-ranging, beginning with the decedent's profile, his physical stats, and the cause of death: "massive head injury by entanglement within the hay baler's rotating secondary drivelines and large feed opening."

The second section detailed the hay baler specifics: an early John Deere round hay baler (1972, model 300), and a very lengthy version of the inner workings of the baler, along with its capacity. A special note was made: *"Cause of death is believed to have happened by intentional failure to set the support bar, causing the heavy gate to release and close down on the victim, pinning him in place."* In addition, there was Walter Andersen's testimony indicating the compressor rods that control the hay pickup radius had been altered since their own use of the baler that morning, the report further noting that *"the compressor rack had been adjusted to a different operating height, thereby intensifying the volume of material that could be fed into the baler."* Walter also indicated that the baler's tying mechanism had been troublesome this season and had been recently repaired.

Next, Mrs. Bundle was somewhat unsettled to read through her own testimony, along with a specific timeline of her actions from that morning's call from Watson until the arrival of the authorities. She moved quickly over this section. As she read through the last quarter of the report, she stopped, exclaiming, "They *used* the two-by-four?"

"Uh-huh. Whoever killed him knocked him out first. The Andersens think it came from a pile of scrap used for fencing nearby." He looked over her shoulder and pointed out the section. "See? 'A *3' 10," 2 x 4 wooden stud was found underneath the hay baler and is being analyzed for evidence. Early indications are that two human white hairs consistent with the deceased's hair texture and length have been discovered on one end of the wood. Slight indentation in the wood in the same area also indicates trace samples of human DNA and some blood. No fingerprints were found on the stud. It is believed the victim was then propelled headfirst and unconscious into the balling mechanism of the baler.'"*

She continued, reading aloud. "'*A statement has been taken from the local U.S. Postman, Lonnie Macomber. He states that on the morning of the incident and again on his way back through North Pillson Corners and surrounding area route, he sighted the tractor and baler in the distant field from the main road. In his interview with Sheriff Deputy Sikes, he confirmed that he first saw the Andersen men in the field working with the hay baler before 11:30 a.m. and subsequently, the baler and tractor equipment had been moved from the earlier sighting to the baler's present location observed around 2 p.m., upon finishing his mail route. His remembrance was that he saw no one in the field at that time, just the equipment.'"* She stopped, mystified, "So nobody saw nothing!"

"That's the long and short of it. Not the Andersens, you, or even the postman!"

The last section of the report, entitled "**PART V. PHYSICAL DOCUMENTATION/TIME LINE**" was as follows:

1. The temperature at the time of the incident was approximately 92°F and the wind that day was out of the north-northeast at an average speed of 20 mph with gusts up to 36 mph.

2. There has been no measurable precipitation for at least three weeks, so the ground was dry. Forensics is continuing to work on two possible tracks found near the site.

3. It has been determined the decedent was murdered by an unknown suspect or suspects at or around 2:00 p.m. and no later than 3:15 p.m.

4. It is hypothesized that the murderers must have had knowledge of how to operate a tractor and the connecting large round hay baler's mechanism and hypothesized, at this point, that at least one strong person, in all probability male, (and more than likely two), would have had to accomplish the action of throwing the victim to his death.

The following scenario likely occurred:

9:00 a.m.-12:30 p.m.: The Andersen father and two sons baled approximately 15 bales, leaving a partial bale in the baler. The vacant machine is left turned off in the field with the intention that they would finish baling later in the afternoon.

2:00 p.m.-3:00 p.m.: The perpetrators knock out the victim with the 2x4, start the tractor (the key was found in the "on" position), and leave the vehicle's motor running. The baler's power take-off control (also known as the PTO), is engaged, and the hydraulically operated hay baler's rear gate rises into the "open" or "up" position. The murderer(s) purposefully does not set the manual support bar in place, ejecting the partial bale of hay. Then, the position of the compressor rods for the hay pickup radius and compressor racks is changed to a higher level of intake. Two requirements are necessary to accomplish the above steps: expertise in heavy equipment and a certain level of strength and stamina.

Next, the unconscious victim is lifted up and then propelled beneath the elevated gate. The gate lets go, descending and thus crushing him between the belt rollers (which are connected to the gate on each end by stabilizer bars), the closely spaced pickup teeth, and the floor of the baler.

After some time, the baler's engine burns out by the continuous jamming effect of the feed opening's inability to accommodate the density of the victim's body. The tractor runs out of fuel and is not running at the time the victim's body is discovered.(Walter Andersen indicated there was very little gasoline left in either the baler or the tractor fuel tank. He had taken the two 5-gallon gas cans from the tractor back down to the farm with him when he and his boys left the field at lunchtime, with the intention of bringing the full cans back when they returned to finish their work.)

2:45-3:15 p.m. The murderer(s) attempt to start a fire in the dry brush nearby. This attempt fails for unknown reasons, possibly due to the arrival of Mrs. Bundle, who the criminal(s) may have thought could observe them from a distance. The fire fails to burn sufficiently; the murderer(s) then flee(s) the scene.

The fire, which burned a small area of approximately four feet by eight feet, dies out in a matter of minutes, no evidence that there was any attempt to rekindle the fire.

Final Evidence: The tractor, baler, and surrounding area have been dusted for fingerprints, and have been sent to the crime lab for testing. The surrounding ground area's footprint impressions found in the packed-down hay and grass are being analyzed. Very little other evidence is apparent at this time other than *One Item of Possible Evidence:* Found at the scene inside the scorched area was a very small screw, rivet, or fastener of some sort (see attached photograph to scale; identified as Evidence Photo C-1). Item has been sent to the crime lab and is being researched to determine its origin and possible significance to the homicide.

No arrest or arrests have been made to date.

Respectfully submitted,
WILLIAM J. O'MALLEY
County of Windsor Sheriff

Mrs. Bundle shook her head, looked up at him."So strange, so very strange."

"You betcha! This one will go down as the strangest. Murder in the middle of a hayfield inside a baler...they don't come any stranger."

"So no word yet on that little screw thing your men found?"

"Nope, the jury's still out on that. They want to do some more research. Seems like it may fit on a small mechanism of some sort—something that would hold one minute object within another—a universal rivet or fastener,"(he made swiveling motions with his fingers),"and still allow movement."

"What about the fingerprints you found? Anything?"

"Still going through the process, Lettie. Nothing of significance—yet."

"And the fire—what about that?"

"Hoo*ee*, you're sure full of questions, aren't you!"

She gave him a sober look."Well, Sheriff, I've got a lot on the line. Let's see... Number one: Watson's been murdered and, unfortunately, I was the one who found him. Two: Vincent Veakey's in prison for a crime I believe he didn't commit. Three: everyone's afraid of their own shadow what with murder on top of arson on top of, yes, that would be number four: the biggest drought this area has seen in almost one hundred years! Last but not least, add in the small detail that, in only seven days, I have to put on a 'little' Festival that will draw thousands people during its three-day run. Need I go on?"

"Like I said the other day, you don't need to preach to the choir, Lettie. This is hardly a barrel of laughs for me. I got enough on my plate right now to last me from now til I retire next fall, that's for dang sure. That's one of the reasons I called you in here. I need your help."

"Well, now you're talking. What can I do?"

"Officially," he sat back in his big swivel chair,"Nothin'!"

"Wait a minute, Sheriff, you just said—"

"Let me finish! Hang on! By all rights, I should just let you be. You just said you've got enough on your plate already running that Festival!" He was agitated."Gaw! You always were so gosh darned impetuous, Lettie—Arthur used to remark on that all the time." He frowned at her, his hulking body swaying precariously in the same old leather swivel chair he had used his whole career. "And I don't need to remind you it got you into a heap of trouble last year."

She frowned good-naturedly back at him, then sat back, heaved a big sigh, and waited as patiently as she could.

After a few more moments, he began, "Now, to finish my thought... I think you can be of help....*unofficially*, that is—" he repeated.

"Yes, Sheriff, *unofficially*."

"Well, first off, we need to look at *everything* surrounding Watson's death. No one else has come forward; you were the last person to talk to him, by all accounts. I need you to go over everything in your mind, once again."

"Will, I've thought about that afternoon over and over and nothing else—"

"I *know* you've done this already, but I think there's something there that we've missed. The day of your meeting, he wanted to tell you something. Anything, any detail could be the key here, Lettie. We already know it was of grave importance to him—we just don't know what that was. A search of his property has revealed nothing of significance that we can determine, certainly nothing improper." He scoffed, "Gaw! The man had more books and files than you can shake a stick at! Every room was chock full! It'll take a month of Sundays to go through it all. However, we *did* find a copy of his will in his roll top desk. Leaves everything to a charity called *The Dogs Without Boundaries Foundation*. It's an animal charity formed to help dogs in crisis situations throughout the United States. You know, all those retired greyhounds, abandoned dogs, et cetera."

Mrs. Bundle clicked her tongue. "Yes. That would be just like Watson." She winced slightly, "Any word on Twinkles?"

"Not a sign. Poor thing was probably scared out of her wits. We suspect she probably ran back into the woods. God knows where she might be now."

"Did you ever see her, Will?" He shook his head. "Cute as a button, but she was afraid of her own shadow. If she was with Watson at the time he was murdered, I don't think her little heart would have survived the shock of seeing him in danger."

"I know we went round and round on this already, Lettie, but I need to ask you again. Did Watson have any enemies that you know of?"

"Not anyone, I daresay. He was such a gentle old soul. There wasn't a single person he ever could have harmed, or insulted, or done wrong to, and vice versa, I'm sure. Everybody loved him. Mind you, his indecisive nature could be maddening…but not enough to cause someone to take his life!" She clicked her tongue in revulsion."Cold-blooded murder! In *our little world*, Will! I still can't believe it. Who could have done it? He was just a pleasant, retired history professor for goodness sake—and excuse me for saying it, but how much more *boring* could he have been? Every time I ever talked to him, he was working on some research, or someone's genealogy chart. Historical minutia was his forte; he loved talking about history to anyone who would listen."

"Right." He urged,"Keep going."

"Well," she placed her pointer finger to her head,"of course, other than that, there was the Board. As a trustee, he was diligent to a 'T.' Never, ever missed a board meeting in all the years he served. Other than that, he tutored the local kids after he retired—mostly the needy ones who couldn't afford to pay for extra help. Let's see, that was for about the last ten years."

"It's a bizarre situation to say the least, Lettie. A gentle soul, no enemies to speak of, brutally murdered. And," he leaned in closer and looked at her intently,"*that*'s the second reason I brought you in here today. Now listen to me carefully. Of course, you are aware we've got a full blown investigation going which I cannot compromise, but…I want you to know…speaking as a friend—and your Sheriff—*you* need to use caution!"

"*Me*? Why me?"

"We're thinking…we're exploring the possibilities that this might somehow have something to do with the Pillson Library."

"*What*? That's ridiculous! Not a chance." The mountain of silver-brown braids atop her head shook vehemently.

Her protestations caused him to hold up a beefy hand. "Now, don't shake your head at me, Lettie. We have to explore *every* possibility. And it may sound ridiculous to you, but we have our reasons. There's been too much going on with all the Pillson Library hoopla to deny there might be some connection between Professor DeVille's death and all this controversy within the Board with the Festival. We want you to take this seriously and you need to know we will be interviewing all the other Board members, too."

"Why, on earth?"

"Mind you now, Lettie, this is all confidential what we're talking about here."

"My lips are sealed, Will."

"You said you and the Professor both served on the board for all those years and nothing ever happened out of the ordinary. Life was simple, commonplace, the way our world usually is in these parts. Right?"

"Right enough."

"Then along comes all this hullabaloo with the Library problems — which bred controversy — and the whole village is turned upside down. People are unhappy. And, when people are unhappy, odd things can happen. And, there seems to have been a lot of pressure on and surrounding the Library Board, even at this point! What do you think about Louis Montembeau?"

Her head jerked and she said abruptly, "Just about one of the nicest individuals you ever could meet."

"Wouldn't you say he's a bit high-strung, a bit…over the top?"

"Well, he's…*Louis*. He would never do anything to harm anything or anyone, especially anything to do with the Library. He's very loyal. He likes everyone." She paused, "Well, that is…except…there is one person…"

"Go ahead…"

"I shouldn't say…but, there is one thing, although quite small. Not just about Louis, mind you, but related to Watson. Of course, now that you ask, it seems to jump out at me." She nodded. "Armand Limpert. The Board Chair."

"Yes. We know who he is."

"He was relentless with…most everyone on the board, Louis included. But he tended to goad Watson mercilessly about… I know it sounds silly, but…about Twinkles. Moreover, that goading carried over into our meetings. Armand was very harsh, hated that little dog with a passion. But, of course, that's not a premise for murdering someone."

"Our initial findings have led us to that 'gentleman' a couple times already. Let's be honest. This Armand Limpert has been making a name for himself ever since he moved here, rumpling a lot of egos with, from what I hear, some very pretentious and annoying airs. His name popped up in our investigation as a *very* unpleasant person to deal with—if you cross him, that is."

"I guess you could say he has made being on the Board of Library Trustees very disagreeable for the lot of us—of that you can be sure."

"Tell me more."

"Well, he's from 'away,'"(they gave each other a knowing glance),"and he's had a lot of ideas that really don't seem to suit the way things have been done here forever. He's abrupt and pushy about the way he goes about it. I'd be the first to say change is good if done at the proper time, but he has tried his best to thwart any kind of program to improve the chances of the Library being saved. He's made some of the board madder than a hive of hornets at times—especially when he tries to throw his weight around." She paused in thought."However, since we have started the Festival plans, he has pretty much disappeared off the face of the earth—willing to volunteer on a cursory level, mind you, but most always unavailable whenever I call upon him. He's working with Sarah Church on the Judges Committee for the Bake-off tables, and such. Passive resistance, I think they call it. Althea and I are still convinced that he would love to see it fail. I can't say I've had much to do with him since, oh, the middle of July, other than an occasional five minute's passing conversation. When he calls, it's usually for picayune stuff, mostly just to rattle my cage, which, truth be told, has been a blessing, if you really want to know. I can handle that, no problem. I've pretty much written him off. Of course, he's off playing golf or tennis with Archie a good part of the time."

"Archie Plummer?"

"Yup. And, whenever I see or talk to Archie, the honey's dripping off him, he couldn't be nicer. I think he's happy we're solving the town's problem of the Library and he appears to have jumped on the bandwagon. So, maybe his being friends with Armand has helped and Armand's seen the light. Mind you, with what all I've got going on heading up the Festival, trying to help Vincent's case, and everything else, it's been a welcome relief not to have Armand climbing down my back about every little library issue."

"Anything else that strikes you funny about him?"

She sat up straight in her chair, her large brown eyes flashing. "Well, this will sound *really* silly, I know, but his reputation as a...um, well..."

"What about his reputation? You mean...romantically?"

She turned a shade of pink and nodded. "He's got roving hands!"

"Roving...?" Will sputtered, then held his emotions in check and asked, "Did you say '*roving hands*'?"

"Yes! Yes, he tried to...well...grab my knee. Under the table," she squirmed uncomfortably, and then laughed, "hard to believe, I know, at my age, Will, to be sure, but it's true!" Her tongue clicked away. "And I had to put him in his place. So did Althea, for that matter." She turned her attractive head to the side and then looked back at him and shrugged, somewhat sheepishly.

"Good God, why didn't you say something to me? Arthur would turn over in his grave! So...this Armand is quite the Don Juan, eh? Or, so he thinks? Must be that rich, romantic French blood coursing through his veins, right?"

"I'll use your words, Will—you betcha—or so he thinks! Not to worry, neither one of us is intimidated by him in the least. Especially Althea!"

"Yes, he met his match with you two, that's for certain." He looked at his watch, twisted his body and then leaned his forearms on the desk; he gave her a quick nod. "Well, we've got his number. We brought him in already, informally, mind you, to ask him a few questions."

"You brought him in? Oh, that must have been quite a meeting. What's his take on things?"

"He's a slippery one. Can't seem to pin him down. Pleasant, courteous, acts real refined—you know, real *city-fied*. Of course, that's not at all consistent with what we've been *hearing*, though." He tapped his nose and smiled at his old friend. "We know different, don't we, Lettie? The fact of the matter is, a lot of the library problems seem to be fueled by your current Head Director, who I'm getting to know pretty well at this juncture. Everything problematic with the library controversy always seems to lead back to him. I'm fast coming to the conclusion that, until he arrived here in Pillsonville, nobody seemed to *ever* have had as many issues with the library."

"Well, in all fairness to him, his arrival may have just been coincidentally timed with the fact that the library needed restoration and updating. And then there's the State's requirements that have to be met, too. Some of his ideas might have worked if he had approached things differently. But, you're right. He has fueled a lot of the angst and dissension about the Library."

"And now, it's the focus of a huge festival that he was not in favor of in the least. Wouldn't you agree?"

"Right."

"I'm not saying Armand Limpert had any kind of hand in this murder, but you're not the first to tell me about his feud with the professor. *Everyone* seems to know about this ongoing dispute with his next-door neighbor."

"Evidently, he has a prize horse that he spent a fortune on. Brags about it all the time. And, like I said before, he hated Twinkles, mostly because of his horse, I think. Watson's little dog tended to stir him up, from what I hear." She squinted, "They have a terrible bark, some of those Bichons, more like a high-pitched squeal, you know. Can raise the shackles on your neck like nothing you've ever heard."

"So we've learned. You know how neighbors talk. But it's more the abrasiveness of the newcomer than the annoying bark of the dog, according to them. Not too many up that way have too much good to say about the 'New Yorker Flatlander.' Cripes, from what we hear, his own bellowing in the early morning hours could be heard for miles around! Seems the people up on North Puckerbrush are able to put up with dogs howling—more so than they are with Limpert's." He laughed and the rolls in his chin vibrated. "He seems to be viewed by the folk up there as a puffed-up invader, an interloper in their small community. Throwing his weight around everywhere—not just at the library—making his importance known. And, that breeds enemies."

"Well, in regard to the Professor and him, certainly there was no love lost there, especially on Armand's side. He made it clear to the Board he barely tolerated the poor man and he hated his dog, to be sure. Gave Watson such a hard time about it, bordered on verbally abusing him, if you want my opinion. Watson was such a gentle soul and it really took a toll on him. He had these terrible stress attacks, kind of like allergy attacks where he'd start sneezing like no tomorrow. Poor Watson would have never hurt a flea, but I have to say, he was often distraught because of Armand. And, push come to shove, his dear Twinkles was like a baby to him and I have no doubt that he would have protected her to the enth degree if Armand had ever come near her."

"Right. Well, it may seem trite, but we have to look at everything. So, we know Armand has ruffled a lot of feathers; even yours, more so now that I know about his...inappropriate behavior towards you. Not to mention, Althea's feathers, too."

"Uh-huh. True enough. He's been, well, incredibly hard to deal with."

"Right. So, I just ask that *you* use caution. Try to stay out of the line of fire, here, until we finish this investigation. And stay away from Limpert."

"Well, Will, I can't do that! I have to work with the fellow!"

"Look, Lettie. I'm just saying... I don't have anything to nail him on, but I don't trust him. He has a very dicey look about him."

"Yes, I agree. I was just wondering. Does he have an alibi for during the time Watson was...?"

"Airtight, yes. Seems he was in Keene for the whole afternoon with his buddy Archie, playing golf at Bretwood. We've checked it out. Their stories matched. That's confidential, too, by the way." He looked at his watch again. "Well, we've got his number and we may bring him in for questioning again. Instinct tells me he knows something, that's for danged sure, maybe not related to this. There's something about him that's a bit too slick, too superficial."

"That murder scene was gruesome—malicious to kill someone that way. Wouldn't you agree this is someone definitely with a really bad grudge?"

"That's an understatement." He rubbed his palms together. "So, we look at the whole picture, and we can't exclude anyone. It's a huge mess, especially when you add in the elements of the attempted arson; that scorched area nearby the baler and tractor is a mystery to us. But we know one thing. That was *no* coincidence. The two incidents go hand-in-hand. Someone's out there trying to start fires."

"Not at all like the peaceful world we're used to, is it?"

"Our phones are ringing off the hook. I don't need to tell you the public is scared. And no rain in sight! Everything's dryin' up to the point that all the fire departments in the county are chasing brush fires every day! And when the winds kick up, it's brutal—everyone gets even more jittery! The whole county's worried sick. Who's going to be next—arson? Murder? Choose your poison, it's not very pretty. There's so much focus on this case right now, I feel like people are ready to explode. I don't like it one bit. Add in all this festival stuff and we've got the makings of some pretty serious impact if anyone else gets hurt, what with the huge turnout expected. So, be aware. And careful."

"I can take care of myself, Will."

"Well, now, Lettie..."

"Well, I thank you for your concern, Will, but I also need to do my job. Don't worry. I know enough not to be foolish. And, getting Vincent off and finding the real criminal or criminals who set the fires will make me and everyone else feel a *whole* lot better."

He shook his head in resignation and sat back, preferring, rather, to pick his battles."Let's move on. One other thing. Good news for you, I think. The last reason I had you come over today—I thought you'd like to be the first to know…"

She looked at him expectantly,"Yes, Will?"

"The DA has reviewed everything and will be asking the district court judge to release Junior—due to insufficient evidence—and the fact that there has been another case of arson."

"Oh, are you serious? Will, that's wonderful! When will he be released?"

"Well, probably not 'til after the weekend, possibly late Monday or early Tuesday, by the time they get all the paperwork done and figure out how the bigwigs are going to eat crow and come out looking okay. You know how politicians are—they don't like to get left holding the bag. But, I thought you'd like to know before the press gets ahold of it and has a field day. I'll give you a 'heads up' when it happens."

"I can't believe it! Barny will be so happy!"

"Well, we really couldn't keep Junior any longer—all circumstantial."

"It was the right thing to do, Will, and I thank you for your influence in getting him out of jail. Your opinions must have been instrumental, if not crucial."

"I wouldn't have recommended it if I didn't believe in it. And, you've got enough on your hands. With Junior out, maybe you'll be able to concentrate more on the other stuff."

"By the way, Will, for what it's worth, Vincent has sworn from day one that he had nothing to do with this."

"Well, at this point, it really doesn't matter, does it?"

"Right you are. The good news is Vincent will be freed." She stood up to go."Well, I'd love to stick around and chat…" he rolled his eyes and she smiled good-naturedly,"but I've got another *very* important meeting to get to. And, a big batch of fried chicken to cook up on top of that!"

Chapter Five

Angie and Anthony

Across town, Angie and Anthony sat together, alone, deep in the belly of the *State Standard Newspaper* building, totally immersed in their computer research. The archive area of the newspaper was located in two basement rooms, insulated and carefully climate-controlled to maintain the integrity of the hard copy versions of the vintage newspapers in nearby wall containers. Although the original issues were safeguarded and unavailable to the public, all the issues had been put on microfiche.

The long wall in the newspaper's archival room was lined with cabinets organized by year, of which each drawer contained the films of several newspapers issues going back more than a hundred and fifty years. Two weeks before, Kevin Trees, the Managing Editor, had helped them find all the weekly issues printed between the paper's budding years beginning in 1854 (the first year the newspaper began) and continuing through 1861 (the date on the painting).

Today, all that could be heard was the whirring of the microfiche pages as they each pushed their respective machine's rotary control "forward" switch, reviewing each issue page by page, then zooming in on any specific item of interest. Although the process was arduous, they persevered, working silently side-by-side.

The LiMB meeting with Mrs. Bundle that had been scheduled for August 1st had been cancelled, the murder of Watson DeVille having taken its toll on everyone. Anthony was particularly devastated by Watson's passing, having seen the kind man on almost a daily basis at the library. Just days before his death, the Professor had promised Anthony he would bring in the genealogical information that he had in his files on anyone whose name was a derivative of "Conny"; notwithstanding that his passing meant the loss of possible valuable information, the boy's obvious affection for the elderly scholar made his death hard to comprehend.

A few days after Watson's death, as things settled down, Angie had rescheduled the meeting with Mrs. Bundle for this evening, where everyone would be congregating at Mrs. Bundle's house for supper first. Angie's and Anthony's competitive spirits made them feel the pinch to come up with something, anything, before tonight's meeting.

During the last three weeks, Nick and Jack had revisited their fishing hole site a number of times (both indicating, tongue-in-cheek, that they needed to do a lot of research) and were prepared, at tonight's meeting, to verify that the isolated location and the scene depicted in the mystery painting were one and the same. In fact, this afternoon they were going to go back up to the site once again, following Maggie's Stream and hiking a mile up the mountainside, with the intention to bring back digital photographs from the area so that they all could compare the similarities.

Natalie had done an excellent job researching the chocolate candy wrappers. She had already passed her report along to Angie, which she and Anthony had gone over before they began their work today.

To date, Angie and Anthony's research at the Pillsonville Historical Society had been a bust; neither had been able to identify the painting, the artist, or shed any light on the "MDCCLV" clue. Somewhat disheartened, they were still determined to thoroughly search the *State Standard* archives. That job had been harder than they anticipated; their four previous visits perusing the beginning years of the *Standard's* issues had been a disappointment to them both.

So, today, they plodded on, working together, silently reading page after page on microfiche. They had been there for two hours, sifting through each newspaper issue's stories, advertisements, and editorials, looking through every bit of minutia, searching for something, anything, that would link their key dates and the artist.

Anthony picked up Natalie's report from his lap, and read through it again for the hundredth time, scanning it quickly and silently so as not to disturb his research partner. The report read as follows:

Bonbons Chocolatier Timeline

In **1795**, the first chocolate factory was established in the U.S. primarily for "chocolate drinking" not chocolate as candy.

Around **1847**, Fry & Sons created a "Chocolat Delicieux a Manger" in Bristol, England. This is thought to be the first company that manufactured a solid chocolate for eating. Their chocolate factory molded this first chocolate bar, using a new invention, the **cocoa press**. No one had yet perfected chocolate in bar form: prior to that, people only used chocolate in beverage form because the process of separating the cocoa butter from the roasted cocoa bean was so laborious and technology had not reached a stage suitable for doing this effectively.

1849 - Joseph Fry & Son and Cadbury Brothers, sons of Richard Cadbury, join forces and display chocolates for eating at an exhibition in Bingley Hall, Birmingham, England.

1851 - Prince Albert's Exposition in London was the <u>first time</u> that **American tourists** were introduced to bonbons, chocolate creams, hand candies (called "boiled sweets"), and caramels called **Bon Bons Chocolatier**, created in England, but given a foreign, exotic twist by giving them a **French** name. Fry and Sons had a table at the Exposition featuring their **Chocolat Delicieux a Manger.**

1853— Heavy Import Duties Are Reduced: At first, English duties made Chocolate a luxury only for the wealthy, but that changed in 1853, allowing more cocoa and drinking chocolate manufacturers to get into the business. Still predominantly an English delicacy, the heavy import duties which had made chocolate a luxury that only the wealthy could enjoy were reduced, **allowing more exporting of chocolates as a confection**, so that chocolate and cocoa became less costly and within the reach of the wider population; with the Industrial Revolution came the mass production of chocolate.

(Natalie's notation: The trail ends here in regard to the chocolate confections wrapped in the waxed wrappers found in the library wall—**Chocolat Delicieux a Manger**. No other research was found regarding whether the chocolates were imported from England or manufactured in a sister factory here in America—or whether they were sold anywhere in Vermont.)

Conclusions and Discussion Questions for the LiMB Society:

1. The candy was made during the 1850's through the 1900's. The fact that the wrappers found refer to the Prince Albert Exposition (1851) signifies a tighter time frame between **1853** (after duties lifted and solid chocolate candy was created) and 1865 (Industrial Revolution and mass production in full force) when such luxury items had become more accessible to the general public.

2. Could someone have brought these back from England? Or, were they imported sometime after the fact from England to an America business and then sold?

3. Hypothesis: Because they were considered delicacies, could someone possibly have been hiding them in the third floor knee wall area because chocolate was so hard to come by? Or, were they being secretly enjoyed by someone in the little cubby hole under the eaves? Or, were the wrappers just discarded there or gathered together from some other source by mice or other nesting animal?

*Report respectfully submitted on July 25ᵗʰ
by Natalie Hufferman, LiMB Society*

Anthony pushed his errant glasses back up to the bridge of his nose, muttering under his breath,"*Hmmm.* Chocolates *after* 1851. Uh-huh, right, these years *have* to be the correct time period, the exact years. The library was built in 1849, the chocolates could only be there since during the 1850's. What, if anything, does that have to do with the date on the painting—1855? Someone could have left the candy there. The *State Standard* was started in 1854. Painting in 1861…the dates are all coming together…" frustrated, he slammed the report down on the table and rubbed his tired eyes,"in a big mish-mash!"

Angie looked up from searching, her own eyes somewhat glazed over, and pushed back the wisps of golden hair that had escaped from her pony tail."Whew! Who knew it would be this hard?"

"I know! I'm trying to figure out what dates we should key in on, and what we should be looking for in trying to find some evidence that this mystery artist existed."

"We'll find something. I'm sure of it. We're definitely on the right track. We've got the time period, for sure. Windsor County's population is small *now*, and it was a lot smaller back then—we'll find the artist."

"It would help if we knew *what* we were looking for. Other than the dates, and the artist 'Conny,' what else should we be researching?"

"Maybe we should review each other's information and notes."

"Great idea." He gave her a sideways glance. "Let's work a little bit longer. I'm actually having...fun."

She gave him a crooked smile and huffed, "Fun? Down here? Anthony, I'm sorry to tell you this, but—if you're having fun, that would fall in the 'get a life' category."

He stared into her lovely eyes and then looked away. From anyone else that statement, in his eyes, would have been construed as criticism and his sensitive feelings would have been hurt. But, coming from Angie, for some reason, the words were playful, and he guffawed loudly, and then uttered, "Uh...geez."

She crinkled her nose at him and smiled.

He went back to his searching, happier now, and they were both peacefully silent for another thirty minutes.

Previous to today, they had exhausted every *Standard* issue between 1854 and June of 1857. Today, they had started with the issues beginning with July of 1857. The laborious process continued as they now both reviewed the publications for the month of August of 1859.

"*Building of the Suez Canal Begins*" one headline read; another, "*The Latest Paris Fashions*" displayed women in colorful bonnets and plumed hats, and bustled long, full, and, presumably, very cumbersome gowns. There was an advertisement for steamship cruise tours on nearby Lake Winnepesaukee in New Hampshire, then, the local County news, followed by the Arts section ("*Miss Sarah Heath Performs as Juliet*") and on to the Births, Marriages (with photographs of very stiff-looking brides and grooms), and the Deaths section...and on, and on, and on, one page at a time.

Anthony's scanning eyes suddenly lit on something. He cried out, "Hey! Angie! Look at this!"

He magnified the lower quarter section of the page and sat back so she could see.

In front of them on the screen was an advertisement:

TENTH ANNIVERSARY 10% OFF EVERYTHING SALE
MISS SELMA'S
SIMPLY SWEET CANDY SHOPPE
As always, offering the newest confections and sweet sensations—

Hand-made by Miss Selma!! Also, imported favorites, too, like Bons Bons Chocolatier, and Fry and Sons' boiled sweets.

STOP IN AND SEE MISS SELMA AT
MISS SELMA'S SIMPLY SWEET CANDY SHOPPPE
LOCATED AT 15 ELM ST., WOODSTOCK
DAILY HOURS 11 A.M. TO 3 P.M. OR BY APPOINTMENT
(COME TO THE BACK DOOR)

"All right!" Angie whooped."There's where they bought them!"

"We're getting there...." he muttered excitedly, reactivating a new page of microfiche."Let's keep going."

Renewed, she also went back to her machine.

Push button, *whirr.* Push, *whirr.* Push, *whirr.*

The sounds continued in twin, monotonous rhythm.

Push, *whirr*…….and then….silence from Angie's side.

A low whistle came from the girl and she stared at the microfiche screen."Got something."

Anthony leaned over and looked as she focused the machine on one single item.

Unable to speak, she stared at the screen, entirely engrossed in the article in front of her. She pointed at what appeared to be an editorial accompanied by a pen and ink political cartoon picture.

The editorial was entitled: *America Needs More Labor Force*; he skimmed through it quickly. The gist of the article urged the acceptance and incorporation of immigrants, who were carrying the lion's share of the heavy labor in the country, into American society. The views expressed advocated granting citizenship and voting rights to these immigrants, particularly the Chinese, which would lead to successful assimilation into the work force and would help, from the Editor's point of view, contribute to industrialism and a stronger United States. Further dismissing arguments that these immigrants would harm the labor force, the author encouraged the acceptance of the Chinese, often labeled "poor Barbarians" and subjects "who couldn't understand civilized form of government."

Eyebrow raised, he looked at her. "What does this all mean to you?" he asked, stymied.

"Not just the article, Anthony. Look—look at the drawing."

The drawing, a political cartoon, depicted powerful pen and ink etchings of a very ethnic Chinese laborer carrying the weight of a heavy load ten times larger than his small frame. The heavy load portrayed was a "3-D" cut-out of the United States of America, solidly balanced on his back. Firmly planted in the American soil were factories with smokestacks spewing dollar signs. The laborer's face strained, sweat pouring down, his oriental eyes squeezed tight, and a long braid flailed out from under his cap like a wild snake behind his back. It was a professional and detailed representation by an obviously very talented artist, far superior to what they had reviewed previously in the provincial newspaper.

At the bottom of the illustration, the cartoonist had written in quotes, as though the laborer was speaking, "*Rights and Freedom—except for ME!*"

The representation was stirring, rousing emotion even now in the two 21st-century teenagers viewing the insinuation of a lack of human rights and freedom. What was quite remarkable, though, were the letters in the very farthest right hand lower corner—a signature.

Angie pointed, her hand slightly trembling in excitement. "What does that say? Can you read it?"

"It looks like C-O, with a squiggle—is it C-O?"

"Yes! And, I think that's an 'N', and then another hump, and—"

"Yup—it's a 'Y.' No doubt."

"'C-O-N-*blank*-Y'. Is that what you think, too? Do you see it?"

"Oh my gosh. We found it!"

"It's him. *Conny.*"

"We did it." He leaned back and grinned from ear to ear. "*You* did it!"

"We both did!"

They beamed at each other, then, spontaneously, gave each other a spirited high-five.

Anthony hooted, "Yaa!"

"Let's see if we can find some more!" Angie said.

Just then, a silver-haired, pleasant woman stuck her head in the door. "Sorry, kids, we're closing up now. You'll have to come back in another time."

They both looked up disappointedly at the clock on the wall. Angie sighed, "Dang! Oh, thanks, Mrs. Morin. We'll just print this one item off, if that's okay."

She peered, with marginal interest, over their shoulders. "Sure, no problem."

"We'll be back tomorrow."

She shook her head. "Can't. Sorry, guys, but we're closed on the weekend."

"Oh, that's right! Darn it!" Angie said, "That's okay. First thing Monday, then."

"Let's go. I'm starving!" Anthony said.

Exuberant, they printed off their findings, and then headed back to Mrs. Bundle's house to attend their meeting and enjoy a fine fried chicken supper.

Chapter Six

Amazing

"Have another piece of chicken, please, everyone, help yourself. And more potato salad, too! There's plenty more out in the kitchen." She looked around at the young faces. "You must be hungry after all your work today."

"Don't mind if I do, Mrs. B. I'm starved after everything that's happened." Nick Clancy reached over and refilled his plate to capacity, chewing with contentment.

They all were there: Nick, Jack, Angie, Anthony, Natalie—LiMB Society *en masse*—along with Mrs. Bundle and Althea. Cracker sat nearby on his large burgundy velvet pillow, licking his chops after having shared in the buffet-style dinner Mrs. Bundle had laid out for them all. After gallons of lemonade had been consumed by the thirsty crowd (along with sumptuous crunchy fried chicken and new red potato salad) the early evening's heat seemed to dissipate a smidge and they settled down to business.

Nick wiped his hands on his paper napkin and opened one of the two manila envelopes he had placed beside him. Marked "Pictures of the painting," he pulled out a number of heavy sheets of soft-gloss picture paper. One by one, he positioned the photographs on the table in from of them. "Hot off the printer. My Dad got this new digital camera and let us borrow it to take up there to get the photos. Really slick. We went up for one reason, but you're not going to believe what *else* we found while we were up there. We just got back and printed everything off before we came over. Took only about ten minutes!"

Jack, who stood beside him, nodded, his face lacking expression. He said softly, "Hang on, mate. One thing at a time. Right, first off, let's take a look at these."

They all leaned in and examined the photographs, all high-quality, shiny, extremely colorful renditions—close-ups of the stream and pool, distant shots of the mountain and field below, and finally, a replication of the exact angle and spot represented in the painting.

Beside their photos, Althea laid an 11" x 17" digitally-exact photograph of the painting, taken days earlier at the Co-Op where the painting was still on display.

"My, my!" Mrs. Bundle clicked her tongue and smiled. "Amazing! The wonders of technology are truly wonderful!"

"It's just like it, isn't it?" Natalie said. "It's the same spot, to be sure!"

"Exactly!" said Nick.

Mrs. Bundle's parlor filled with excitement; the LiMB Society was bursting at the seams.

"So it really *is* the same place as the painting!" Natalie repeated.

"Wow, I really wondered if it could possibly be the same area," Angie marveled.

"Now we know for sure," Anthony said.

Angie added, "Right there, at your secret fishing..." She stopped, concerned. "Why so glum, Jack?"

"Emm, unfortunately, after today," Jack said grimly, "it won't be a secret anymore, right Nick?"

Nick nodded, motioning to Jack to continue.

Jack said, "We...found something this afternoon, Mrs. B, something else, not related to the painting, while we were up there."

She heard the concern in his voice and asked cautiously, "Something else?"

He took the other manila envelope, opened it slowly, and, before placing what looked like another large photograph on the table, said, "It's pretty gruesome, mind now. You girls may not want to look at it. Aye, before you see it, Mrs. B, I want you to know we already called the Sheriff to let him know."

Angie cried out,"The Sheriff? Jack, what?"

Cracker, tail swishing nervously, had moved quickly from his plush floor cushion to his place beside Mrs. Bundle.

"Jack, dear, what is it?" Mrs. Bundle leaned over and laid the photo on the table so she could see.

His voice was gentle."It's the remains of a dead animal, Mrs. B. A large animal." She and Althea pored over the photograph as he continued."It's the body of a....dog. Emm...a large one, with a reddish-gold coat of fur." He couldn't bear to see her upset; his cerulean blue eyes flashed with anger.

"Oh, no! What a shame!" Mrs. Bundle's perceptive mind was ahead of the rest of the naïve group; her eyes traveled from the photo to Jack.

He looked back and nodded to her grimly."Aye. A Golden Retriever."

As they all crowded around to look, a number of gasps precluded him from continuing. What they saw was the muddy, decomposed body of a large dog. Jack waited until they all had had a chance to absorb the facts.

Poor, friendly mutt, Cracker cat-thought, *just as we had suspected…*

"Tuddsley!" Angie cried.

"It's the Tudhope's dog?" Natalie asked.

Jack continued, his voice sober,"Aye, we discovered him way up there at the top, buried in that hole," he pointed,"there on Maggie's Stream. It's a shallow grave they dug, didn't they, on the banking. And, just nearby where we took the other photos, in fact, wasn't it, now?"

Mrs. Bundle asked,"You could tell, from seeing it, that it was… *him?*"

Jack nodded."Well, *emm*, aye, mum. Actually, it's…what Nick and I deduced, surely, when we saw the reddish gold coat and realized it was a Golden Retriever."

Nick said, "We figured it had to be Tuddsley. So near Four Corners and the diner."

"Good grief!" Althea said.

Nick wiped his face with his napkin, his brow perspiring slightly, and said, "Uh-huh! It was weird. We noticed it while we were standing on the big rocks taking pictures. I says to Jack, 'What the heck is that over there?' It was in the deeper pool area, see, over near the high banking. Jack says to me, 'Oy! Do you see it, too, mate?' So, over we go across the stream, and at first we're not sure what it is, but the closer we get, the more we can see it's an outline of something kinda half buried. Kinda hump-like, it was, and we realized it was pretty suspicious-looking. I've been out hunting with my Dad enough to know when animals have been left in traps to die, or their carcasses are buried after their fur's been taken sometimes, but this was different. I don't know; it just looked weird—a half-buried animal, so we climbed closer to take a look. Then Jack, here, took his foot and moved some of the leaves and debris out of the way."

"Right!" Jack continued the account, "It was all branches, and ferns and the like, all laid one on top of another. We could tell the poor blighter had been buried, then covered over, right there under the banking. The banking has given way a bit over the last few weeks as the water level has subsided along that ridge, there." He pointed to a line of what appeared to be clay-like dirt along the stream bank. "Sure, and not by accident was he laid there, either."

"As soon as we realized what it was," Nick said, "we took this picture—along with a whole bunch more," he patted the thick manila envelope, "and then we left the poor animal and the site undisturbed—as best we could. We called the Sheriff on our way out of the woods when we finally could get a signal. He was real keen to get his men up there to take a look this evening. We gave him directions—which was pretty difficult, so he wants us to take him up there tomorrow morning, first thing. Meanwhile, he said he'd call Ger and Phoebe and let them know."

Jack said, "Then we came back, printed off the pictures at Nick's, and came here straightaway. Aye, after we're through with our meeting here, Nick and I are going back up to Woodstock and drop these off for the Sheriff to see."

Althea shook her head in dismay. "The Tudhopes—and Viola, too—will be heartbroken. What a terrible shame!"

"Who could do such a thing?" Natalie asked, near tears.

Angie was pensive. "So, does this mean that whoever started the fire at Tuddy's also *killed* that poor dog?"

Jack nodded grimly. "Seems likely, eh?"

"What kind of monster does that?"

Anthony had been very quiet. He asked, "How'd they get that dog way up there? I mean, physically, he's way too heavy, isn't he? That puny Junior Veakey couldn't have done that alone, for sure. So, how'd someone get him up there? From what you guys have said, it's a good mile uphill…"

"Maybe someone led him up there, then killed him," Angie said.

Jack nodded, "Right, lass, that's what we were thinking, weren't we now, mate?"

Nick raised an eyebrow in speculation and nodded silently.

"Terrible! That really stinks!" Angie said, outraged.

"Now, now…it really is very upsetting," was all Mrs. Bundle could say.

The group continued to discuss the poor dog's fate for another few minutes, venting and speculating.

After a bit, Angie suggested half-heartedly that they get their meeting back on track, sighing," We still have our job to do here."

Nick reached for a cookie and mumbled through his first large bite, "I guess. What can beat this, though? Jack and I got the mystery painting location confirmed, and to top it all off, we find the dog missing in a large arson case, too. Well, I mean…"

Natalie cut him off, "Nick, really! Do you have to be so…" she searched for the right word, "*tactless?* Everyone's been working really hard, including me, and we *all* have a report to give, or something to contribute, no matter—"

Nick's face turned crimson. "No, geez, I'm just saying…," he paused, and then said apologetically, "Hey, Nat, I'm sorry. Really. It's been kinda an adrenalin rush today, finding something so important like that. Sorry." He smiled at her engagingly.

She rolled her eyes, then smiled back, "You're forgiven."

Trying to further win her favor, he said, "By the way, your report on the chocolate was great. I read the whole thing." He put an arm around her and turned to Angie and Anthony. "So! Did you guys find out anything? Really, we want to know."

Jack added, "Aye, what did you find in your research?"

Anthony pulled out the black pen-and-ink cartoon representation. "This." He spread out the corners of the rolled-up paper and carefully placed four empty glasses on each corner to hold it in place.

They all leaned in and looked at the editorial cartoon.

Natalie said, "Wow, that looks old! Where'd you find it?"

Angie said, "In the *State Standard* archives section. August 15, 1859. Anthony and I have been in there for days looking through all their old newspapers on microfiche. Really tiresome work, I'll have you know."

Natalie nodded with enthusiasm. "Yeah, I know. Better you two than me!" She focused on the photocopy. "That's one of those political cartoons, right?"

"Yes. And, look at the signature."

"Is that—?" Natalie placed her hand over her mouth.

"Yup." Angie's face was triumphant. "*Conny.*"

Nick said, "You *found* the artist?"

"We think so," Anthony said tentatively.

"And that date of 1859 fits in pretty good with the '1855' carved clue we found, doesn't it?" Nick asked.

Anthony nodded an emphatic "yes" to his brother. "And, the later date of 1861 signed on the painting, too!"

"Well, I'll be!" Nick clapped his brother soundly on the back.

Angie beamed. "We're going back in on Monday to find out if there's more of the same drawings by him—we think it's a *him*, anyway—and maybe, if we find out his real name, we can find out more about him and the painting. And, I figured, if we find anything really important, we'll call a special meeting of LiMB. What do you think?"

Nick said, "Wow, that's really great! Good work!" He rubbed his younger brother's head roughly, and Anthony pushed him away, a bashful smile plastered on his face.

"Oh!" Mrs. Bundle snapped her fingers. "I've got wonderful news, too! I came from meeting with Sheriff O'Malley this afternoon, and he tells they're going to release Vincent!"

"NO!" Spontaneous hand-clapping broke out. "All right!"

"That's wonderful!" Althea said.

"When?" Angie asked.

"He says after the weekend, definitely within the next few days, but probably at the latest, by Monday or Tuesday." Her face was flushed with excitement. "Basically, the authorities have admitted that they don't feel they could keep him any longer, especially after the latest fire that was started…" she hesitated, her head motioning outside, in the Andersen farm direction, "…up in the field. Our poor Professor…" she was at a loss for words, and tears came to her eyes, unexpectedly, even to her.

Jack reached over and patted her arm. "It's been a tough summer, Mrs. B, to be sure."

She looked around the collection of eager, concerned faces and smiled kindly. "He was a good friend, and a sweet man. His death has hit me hard, I must admit."

Angie nodded, that same look of shock and pain reappearing on her face as the day of the murder.

Mrs. Bundle took her napkin, blew her nose soundly, and smiled. "That said, I want to tell you how completely buoyant I am at your progress. You all have done *great work*! I couldn't have done it better myself, could I Allie?" Althea shook her head. "You've all been so diligent about getting your piece of the puzzle solved. I'm very proud of you—each and every one. I'm *very* grateful. Let's keep going."

Angie said softly, "Hey! How 'bout if we make a toast?" She raised her glass. "I'll do it!"

Everyone nodded silently and they all raised their lemonade-filled glasses.

She said soberly, "Here's to the memory of our Professor Watson," and then, with a confident smile, said, "and here's to the LiMB Society! And to all our hard work paying off!"

"Cheers!"

———————

Much later that evening, Jack arrived home from Woodstock exhausted, but pleased that he and Nick had been instrumental in helping the Sheriff with his very difficult case. Mrs. Bundle and Cracker were waiting up as usual. They had a cold glass of milk and homemade chocolate chip cookies, and sat talking before going to bed.

"The Sheriff said his deputies would bring the dog's body down the mountain first thing in the morning, after they investigate the site. Aye, he said they would do an autopsy post haste to see if the dog's death could shed any light on the fire at the diner. Sure, and I was wondering if there was anything else Nick and I need to do, Mrs. B—do you know?"

"I'm positive the authorities can take it from here, Jack. Kudos to you and Nick for a job well done."

"By the way," Jack's handsome ruddy features became more serious, "I'd like to have your ear on another subject, if you don't mind, mum."

"Of course, Jack, what is it?"

"Well now, it's about Erin, isn't it? Well, really, about the lass and this Dakota Squibb bloke. Aye, I've met the fellow on a couple occasions. Once down at the Pub, the other time at the Post Office. Seems very nice—bloody charming, in fact, isn't he? Quite the talker, chews your ear off, right? Wanted to know all about Ireland, how we got here, you know. Em, if you must know, Mrs. B...I'm just not sure how to take the fellow."

"Yes, I understand. He seems to have charmed most of Pillson. But, you mentioned Erin, Jack. I can tell, there's something on your mind. You seem concerned."

"Well now, Mrs. B, here it is. This bloke seems to have taken quite a shine to our Erin, hasn't he? And she to him, too? C'mere now, she's been over there every day working on that talent show, or helping him with his painting—with permission, of course. Aye, he calls her his 'little right hand helper.' Says she's a very talented little girl."

"Yes, it seems he has made quite a lot of her. But, she *is* very special, isn't she? And, as far as the Talent Show goes, he's doing quite a job with it. He's planned every detail, gotten some fantastic local talent to volunteer. Why, they've already sold a large number of advance tickets. Between you and me, I think it's going to be a huge success. But you seem troubled about Erin. Why?"

"Well, I'm a trifle worried. People usually...think me wee sister is a bit...," he searched for the right words,"too *bubbly*! Emm, truth is, she comes on like a whirling dervish, doesn't she now?" He scratched his chin."You don't think it's unusual, him taking such a shine to her?"

She sat back in her chair and reflected."Actually, no, Jack. It's almost the opposite, in fact. *She* rather took *him* under her wing from his first days in Pillson." She chuckled."Sold him some rocks and their friendship developed from there. I think he finds our little girl Erin's umm...," she chose her words,"shall we say, overzealous enthusiasm? I think he finds it somewhat a challenge and probably very refreshing compared to his usual busy, urban world. He likes nurturing her natural artistic ability, I daresay. He thinks she has talent. *Loves* her singing voice, too—well, we all do. And, I don't think we need to worry about *her* skills in being ready, willing, and able to tell someone where to get off. She's got lungs the size of Canada. There are no flies on that girl!"

They both chuckled and Jack acknowledged,"Right you are on that one, mum. She seems to really like the bloke, too."

"I think he's harmless, Jack. Everyone seems to like him. That said, I think we should be watchful, as ever."

"Well, em, older brother that I am, I'll be keepin' an eye on him. Not that I want to mollycoddle her, mind you." He leaned back and relaxed."Strange, isn't it now, though, how he strikes up a conversation at the drop of a hat? Aye, goes out of his way…not sure I'm used to someone that *chatty*. Do you trust him, now, Mrs. Bundle?"

"Honestly, I think he's just a friendly man. Very knowledgeable about lots of subjects. And, between you and me," she leaned closer, lowering her voice,"I think he's sweet on Althea."

"*Hmmm!*" Jack's head jerked back."Oy! Would he be now? And what does the colleen Swain think of his advances?"

"Well, the jury's still out on that. They seem to clash with each other at the drop of a hat, more so good-naturedly now, than when they first met. They banter back and forth and have had some pretty lively debates. She keeps him on his toes, that's for sure. And, Althea would never admit it, but I think she finds him interesting…and very challenging to her strong, independent nature."

"Emm...well, that *would* be quite a match, I reckon." He deliberated a second, then, with some hesitancy, said,"Not that it matters, probably, but the last time I was at the Post Office, it looked like that Elvina Wrinkle—the General Store lady—had him pretty captivated," he smiled sheepishly,"more *captive*, I'll wager."

Mrs. Bundle laughed,"Yes, Erin told us the same thing back along—Elvina stopped by to buy rocks the same day Dakota did.'Mrs. *Wrinkles*,' that's what she calls her. Said she was 'all googly' over him. Quite comical, the way she described it."

"Huh, right, now? Just *happens* by when the new bachelor first arrives in town. Sounds a bit queer to me. If you'd be asking me my opinion, that Wrinkle bird is…," he hesitated again, innate respect for his elders holding him back somewhat,"well now, she's rather like a vulture, isn't she, Mrs. B? Sorry to say so, especially with all her hard luck from losing her business in the fire and everything—but she reminds me a bit of a sleeveen, you know?"

"A *sleeveen?*"

"You know, a *sleeveen*. Irish, it is. A bit dodgy at times, do you think? With men?"

"You've a keen eye, Jack. I suspect Elvina knows her wily way around the 'man department,' to be sure. And I suppose, well…now that Norbert's gone a fairly decent time, she might be lonely and looking for a replacement." She clucked knowingly, and said, "Did that sound harsh, Jack? I do believe the older I get, the more truth I see in that darker, more real side of human nature." She said ruefully, "At any rate, it's much more interesting and *exciting* to look at things that way at my age, dear boy. And, as far as romance goes, Mr. Squibb might find Elvina Wrinkle a bit more mysterious and alluring than our Yankee straight-shooter, Althea Swain. You know," she flitted her lashes coquettishly and slowed her voice, "that *Southern drawl* of Elvina Wrinkle's and that sultry way she acts might just intrigue him."

He scrunched his nose and and his lips curled as he had a hard time envisioning Elvina as sultry. "Right, if you say so, Mrs. B."

"And, of course, she's from away—like he is—so they would have *that* in common, too. Plus, she's got a certain way about her. When she wants something, she's got *chutzpah*, that's for dang sure! Why, even after losing the store and all her belongings, it hasn't slowed that woman down. She still goes to Bingo all around the county, don't you know—in between batting those Southern eyelashes at Dakota Squibb. By all appearances, she seems to be *moving on*, as they say."

"No, Mrs. B, if it were me choice to pick, I'd prefer Miz Swain in a heartbeat. She's a plucky one if ever I saw it, isn't she now? Aye, I suspect if *she* wanted something bad enough, she'd win the battle hands down, to be sure."

Mrs. Bundle laughed heartily. "You know, I'd put my money on her, too, any day of the week. Allie's word is good as gold, that's for sure! I guess on the other side of the coin, I daresay I wouldn't hang my hat on the bulk of what Elvina Wrinkle has to say. She's been known to exaggerate just a shade."

"We Irish have a bit of a saying, '*Chomh cabach le giofóg*'!" Let's see…translated, it means 'gabby as a magpie.'" He cocked a smile sideways at Mrs. Bundle.

"Uh-huh. That hits the nail on the head."

"Right! I suspect she's told a few tall tales—especially after a pint or two of ale over at the Grange in Claremont. That's the word anyway, isn't it now, down at the local, after she gets going with her bingo and her tipping a few." He motioned drinking with his hand. "Course, I wouldn't be one to know firsthand, mind you…" his slow smile spread, "but there's quite a few fish tales that get told over a cold brew, aren't there now?"

"Yes, I suspect you're right on that one, Jack."

He cocked his head and a snigger escaped his lips as he stood up to his full height, stretching his longs arms toward the ceiling. "Well, enough gossiping for one night, mum! Ach! We're shameless magpies, too, aren't we now?"

"I'm afraid I'd have to agree. Shameless."

"Gotta get up early. *O íche mhhaith*, Mrs. B."

"Good night to you, too, my dear. See you in the morning. Sleep well."

She turned off the lights after him and Cracker followed her (his long tail swishing) up to bed.

As she lay in the dark, she thought about the daunting tasks that lay ahead. Would the Festival be a success? Would the community come together, as she trusted, amidst all this past adversity and would they rise to the challenge?

She hoped so with all her heart.

Strangely, her mind shifted from worrying about the Festival to poor Tuddsley and the fire at Tuddy's Diner. It all had started there with that fire, it seemed. *Why*, she asked herself? Why would someone want to burn that beautiful old Diner to the ground? And who on earth could have killed that poor, friendly animal? What were the reasons, the motivation? Was it revenge, or just a crazed pyromaniac on the loose? She searched her mind for answers, but her questions lay like a huge, aching puzzle.

She shifted gears. And Watson, too? That was the most painful puzzle to her. That someone had taken that poor man's life—but more than that, she was so just so vexed by the manner in which his life had been taken. Just a cruel, cruel way to die. Almost as though someone had thumbed their nose, tauntingly, at the absurdity of such a scheme.

She rearranged her pillow, then breathed a huge sigh. She hated to admit it, but the stress was beginning to show on her and tonight she was feeling very vulnerable. Her mind had handled a lot in the last couple months. Truth be told, the trauma of finding Watson a week ago had been almost debilitating, but as always, she had assumed she could just push through.

Looking back now, she realized that it would be a lot for anyone to handle. Cat's granny! She just felt so bad about Watson. She felt… *guilty*.

Shoulda, woulda, coulda.

If only things had been different, *maybe* if she had been more patient with the poor man…She squeezed her eyelids together tightly. Oh, it was awful to think about, but she felt compelled to ask herself the question.

Would he…*would he still be alive today?*

She was so tired. She had to acknowledge, or at least face and explore, her own responsibility in his death. Could she have changed poor Watson's fate?

Maybe she should have gone right up then, that morning, and met with him.

Maybe she missed something important, something she neglected to hear during their conversation that might have helped him. Or, might help him now, *something* that would help find his killers. He had seemed so…disjointed. If she had been less stressed, would she have been more patient? Still, she had to confess, he had been very tentative, very unsure. She admitted now, she wasn't sure that someone else might have just disregarded his concerns as the meandering thoughts of a befuddled old man. She lay there and surprised herself as a couple small sniffles escaped involuntarily.

Stop it, Lettie! She chided herself. *Stop feeling sorry for yourself, for heaven's sake. People are depending on you*. And things *are* getting done, she sighed. She was proud of everyone's efforts.

She drew in a deep breath. *Focus.* Focus on the good things. She turned her tired mind to more pleasant thoughts.

For starters, Vincent Veakey was going to be released. That was a wonderful thing. She would go down to Springfield to the Southern State Correctional Facility where he was being held as soon as they agreed to his release, and she would pick him up for Barny, and bring him back to their house. That was the least she could do. So, that piece was going to be complete. She sighed, and closed her eyes.

And there were other good things to focus on. *The LiMB Society.* Oh, what a gift they were to her! She was so proud of that group of remarkable young people. They had solved a good part of the painting mystery all on their own, and wasn't it all so very interesting and exciting?

She tried to clear her mind, her eyes getting heavier. Tomorrow was another day. Yes. She had a lot of work ahead of her. At this point, all that was left for her to do—to *focus on*—was to make sure the Festival turned out to be a huge success. That was what she needed to concentrate on, and that was what she would do. Hard to believe, next Friday night was the opening night of the Festival—one week away!

Beside her bed, the phone rang shrilly and she jumped, grabbing it on the first ring. "Hello?" Cracker stirred at the bottom of the bed, then sidled up beside her shoulder to listen.

"Letitia?" It was Armand.

Oh, now what? she thought to herself, bracing for another problem or issue.

"I tried you earlier today, but all I got was your machine."

"Why didn't you leave a message?"

"Because I wanted to talk to *you*—not a machine." As usual, his persistent nature knew no boundaries.

"It's late." Tired beyond reason, she asked, "What *is* it, Armand?"

"Well, I've been thinking." His voice was slippery, almost slurring, as he articulated slowly, "I know we've had our differences. However, I'd like to put that behind us."

"Really." She was amazed at his contriteness. "Armand, I'd like nothing better."

"And not just for the good of the festival, either. I've had a heart-to-heart with Sarah Church and have decided to take her advice. I've agreed to not only *help* with the judging, but to take on the Head Judge position."

"That's…wonderful." *Why this change of heart, she wondered?*

"We both decided she's too wishy-washy to make those types of decisions."(Mrs. Bundle and Cracker couldn't help but be amazed at his sheer pomposity.)"But I have a small favor, Letitia."

Here it comes, Cracker cat-thought, *he wants something…*

"And that is?"

"Dinner. I'd like to have you join me for dinner some evening."

"Dinner?" *Was he serious?*

"Yes. Up here, at my place. Soon."

Mrs. Bundle had never been to Armand's, never invited, as a matter of fact.

"Armand, I'm not sure that works for me…"

"No pressure. Just a friendly dinner. To mend fences, let's say."

"I'm so busy with the festival, I doubt there would be—"

"Look, just think on it. I won't pressure you. But, I'd like you to know I've always…admired you. I'd like to bury the hatchet if we could."

Yeah, maybe in a million years, Cracker cat-thought.

Mrs. Bundle was silent.

He cajoled sweetly,"Is it a deal? Can I plan on having you as my guest—sometime in the near future? If not before, then after the—"

"We'll see, Armand. After the festival when we have a breather, let's talk."

"Great. I'll very much look forward to that. Have a nice evening."

She hung up. The saying,"Hold your friends close and your enemies closer" came into her mind.

Aloud, she said,"What are you up to now, Armand?"

I don't believe him either, Cracker cat-thought, *not for one minute.*

Mrs. Bundle lay back on the pillow, trying to put the troublesome call on the back burner.

Sleep well, she had said to Jack. Taking her own advice, she breathed in deeply and thought calming, pleasant thoughts.

Slowly, but finally, she fell off to sleep.

Yet, Mrs. Bundle's thoughts would come back to haunt her as she tossed and turned all night, slumbering fitfull, dreaming.

It's right there, a stentorian voice was telling her over and over.
What?

It's right there! The three words repeated, over and over.
Where?

She stood at a crossroads, unsure which way to go. In her dream state, the trees, the houses, *everything* looked vaguely familiar. She had been there before, at this crossroad. She stood in the middle of the road, looking up one way, then down the other.

Right there. It's right there.

Confused, she turned round and round, spinning like a top at the intersection, dodging speeding cars like the "beep-beep" roadrunner, asking the same questions over and over. *Which way do I go? Which direction? Where is it? Where should I go?*

She woke up the next morning with a faint remembrance, wondering sleepily what it all could mean.

Chapter Seven

Happy Monday

Will O'Malley's voice boomed over the telephone. "Well, it's as we suspected!"

Mrs. Bundle had just finished breakfast and was balancing a cup and saucer in one hand as she held the phone to her ear with the other. "Will? You're at it early!"

"Yuh. Right at it." His voice sounded exhausted. "Happy Monday."

"You sound tired."

"Haven't gotten much sleep, but that's not why I called."

"So, what's going on? Do you know what killed Tuddsley?"

"Yep, sure do. We're getting closer to solving this whole mess, Lettie, that's for certain. We got the toxicology report back. The autopsy on the dog is all done. It confirms that he was drugged. That dog's friendliness was more than likely his downfall, I suspect. So used to meeting and greeting everyone at the diner door. Probably followed the guys right up the mountain after they got the blaze going, at which point they killed him by giving him the narcotic."

"That's terrible."

"Official autopsy found the remnants of a pretty hefty steak laced with barbiturates in his stomach."

"Really. What kind of barbiturate?"

"Pentobarb."

"Pentobarb? Sounds somewhat familiar."

"Yeah, pretty common drug. Doctors use it to sedate. Sometimes vets do, too, on animals they need to put down. We're searching doctors' offices now to see who else might have had access to this drug, and we're also reviewing any of the recent pharmacy thefts in the area. It's not a hard drug to come by so we'll either get lucky and make some connection or we'll hit a dead end."

"What can I do?"

"Nothin'. Like I said, just sit tight. We're trying to put all the pieces together."

"Well, thank you for keeping me in the loop, Will. I appreciate it."

"Right. Also—just got word from the DA and thought you'd like to know. Junior's out later this afternoon. Should be sprung by three at the latest."

"Three o'clock? Wonderful! I'll be there to pick him up."

"I thought you would. I'll let them know. They'll probably let you leave the back way—by the service entrance—so as to avoid the press. I'm sure they'll all be there waiting for a statement from him. Do you want me to arrange that?"

"Thanks, Will, yes. Thanks very much."

She got off the phone and sat down at the computer to research Pentobarb.

After a few hits, she found a pharmaceutical website that gave a detailed description of the drug. She skimmed though the information quickly. *Actual name, pentobarbital. Available as free acid or sodium salt. Popular short-acting barbiturate used primarily as a sedative. Also used to reduce pressure...*she silently read on, completely absorbed.

"Fascinating!" She looked up at the clock, realizing there were things to do. Before she went down to pick up Vincent, she would scoot up to Woodstock and pick up the Festival brochures to be handed out to each fairgoer, detailing the scheduled events, handicraft booths and the like, along with particulars of the artwork being auctioned off. If there was time, she might even be able to fit in a hike, too.

"We can't be dilly-dallying here, C-Cat! It's another busy day in our little world!"

The immaculate feline purred loudly and hopped off his large, comfortably elegant cushion. *Ready I am!*

She hit the "print" command and printed off the rest of the pentobarb information, committing to read through it thoroughly when she could find the time.

Chapter Eight
The Lovers...

"Well, what shall we do now, C-Cat?" She looked in the rearview mirror and saw that her admirable companion was dead to the world.

They had picked up the brochures in Woodstock and now, wonder of wonders, she had a good two hours to kill before heading south to the jail to pick up Vincent. *What*, she marveled, *can we do, just for fun?* As her mind wandered, Junebug's pug nose and tenacious motor (also with a mind of her own) headed naturally in a southern direction; they put-putted along in contented silence. Minutes later, Hartland Corners came into view, a naturally pleasant ride that was her usual back route to Pillson.

Crossroads. Like her dream.

Without knowing why, she parked the emerald-colored VW at the original Tuddy's Diner site and sat, mildly perplexed, in the deserted parking lot, looking around at the now-vacant land. Demolition had been completed, and the site was now a clean slate, ready for reconstruction.

She stared at the empty land. *This is where it all started*, she thought. The first fire, back in late June. And where, she acknowledged, everything seems to keep coming back to—the Hartland Four Corners.

Cracker's tummy rumbled as he slept at his quiet post in the back seat.

The stentorian voice came through again. *It's right there. Right there.*

"*What is it?*" She asked herself aloud, though it was barely a whisper. "What do I need to figure out here?"

Cracker stirred and looked up with lazy almond eyes. *I'm hungry,* he cat-thought, *what's going on?*

"We're here...and we need to find out....what happened." She looked at her watch. "It won't take long…"

His sleek, black head jerked up. *Wait a minute,* he cat-thought, *you can't mean we're getting out...*

Mrs. Bundle opened the driver side door and reached for her sneakers in the back seat. Cracker was at her side in a heartbeat and, as she put on her sneakers, he quickly evaluated the scene. *You want to hike over to Maggie's Stream again,* he cat-thought, purring wildly.

"Right, CC! Let's go. I'm not sure why, but something is drawing me to this area." She buckled her fanny pack around her waist and grabbed the full bottle of water from the cup holder. "There's something here. That day we ran into Viola in the woods I could… feel it. It's here, I know it."

He tripped along behind her as they crossed the parking lot and walked into the cool comfort of the forest. Hiking silently, as was their custom, they reached the stream and searched up and down in the same area where she and Althea had been before. She knew it was here somewhere. She looked at the line of trees dotting the stream at various sections.

What are you looking for? Cracker's common sense told him something was up; his keen cat intuitiveness was on edge.

"Here it is! Got it! Finally!" She stared, pointing, and Cracker saw the strange symbol, the curious "W" carving that had been burned onto the tree's rough trunk.

So that's what you saw that day with Althea, he cat-thought.

Her breath came quickly and they both studied the symbol on the tree.

Below it, was that one eerie word, just as before: *Forever.*

She sat down, exhausted, beside the tree and took off her shoes, placing her feet in the cool stream water.

After a time, she turned back to the tree and they studied it together from every vantage point.

Who could have burned that queer symbol into the tree trunk like that? What type of wood-burning instrument was used? Mrs. Bundle stared at the curious 'W' carving, and then at the cryptic words below. "*Forever,*" she said aloud.

Cracker purred loudly, concentrating with his uncanny ability. '*Forever' is infinite, a word meaning through eternity and endless ages*, he cat-thought, asking rhetorically, *what is the **one true object** that defies an ending and lives on '**forever**'? Think, dear lady, about life's one undying, forever experience: it is……*

"Love! *Love* is forever. Yes, Cracker-Cat, yes. I see. It's a puzzle, isn't it? *Forever.* True love *is* forever, isn't it? Lovers? For each other? Is that who carved this?"

She spent the next thirty minutes deep in thought, staring with great intensity at the symbol carving. She was vaguely reminded of something long ago in an art class. She cleared her mind and placed herself there, in that time and space. Slowly, a memory came to her. There she was, in junior high art class, and the instructor, Mr. Manahan, a great artist in his own right, was giving them a lesson. She could see him at the front of the room, hands in pocket, casually talking about....

The word that she popped into her mind was '*pyrography.*' He had taught them the word, and then she remembered, as a young girl, she had repeated it over and over to herself until she had it memorized. Pyrography. He had said it combined two Greek words: writing (graphy) and fire (pyro). Then, he had shown them what it meant—the art of burning patterns into wood. It had been fun learning how to use the pyrography tool to burn designs into the grain of the wood plank—she stopped in mid-thought.

Burned...pyrography? Was the burned "Welcome to Hartland" sign related to this tree, deep in the woods? Or, just a weird coincidence? She wondered.

Her forehead wrinkled as she remembered those art classes. There was something else too—something that, years ago, Mr. Manahan had taught her and her classmates how to do. Not with the wood-burning, but during another art class.

What was it?

It's right there...right there!

She stared at the "W" again, scrunching her eyebrows together and closing her eyes tightly, then opening them slowly, only to see the vexingly fancy, weirdly-configured letter square in her face.

Even now, as she closed her eyes in frustration, she could still see the W, the W, the W...

It's right there, Mr. Manahan's voice was saying. *Right there, look, Lettie, see it right there*, his big finger pointing on her art station. He slowly traced the image at the bottom of the painting in front of her on her desk.

What had it been? She searched her child memory. Yes, it was coming. Something to do with...how artists...sign their work.

It hit her like a ton of bricks.

"*Monogram!*" She shouted aloud, staring."It's a *monogram!*" It all came back to her in a rush, as she remembered Mr. Manahan showing their group how to take their initials and turn them into a personalized, more artistic version of one's signature. One need only take the initials of one's name and create a design of one or more letters to decorate or identify an object. She remembered how she and Althea had spent hours afterward, taking the initials of their own names, playing with them, attaching them at odd angles, upside down, sideways, embellishing the letters in dramatic or funny ways.

To this day, when Mrs. Bundle daydreamed and doodled, she would play with her initials and create new monograms.

She stared with new insight at the monogram in front of her.

Yes, there it was. The curlicue at the beginning of the "W," what was that? Some kind of design, no doubt, to personalize the author's monogram. Moving on, she scrutinized the next section; the second interior extension of the "W" that looked like the head of an arrow pointing skyward. Wait, she contemplated, could that be...it *could* be an upside-down "V," couldn't it? Continuing, she looked at the second "V" section of the "W". There was a straight line at the top... got it! She thought. *That's a 'T'!* So far, the letters "W,""V," and "T" had revealed themselves. She sat back and pondered. Who did she know with the initials WVT in that order or shuffled around?

She spent the next half-hour looking intently at the monogram, turning it upside down in her mind, breaking it down, considering all the options of the conundrum.

Cracker had wandered off, in search of playful hiding spots and a snack for his hungry tummy.

Finally, Mrs. Bundle murmured,"Wait a minute." She spoke softly to herself, and her voice echoed in the quiet air."What if...?" She continued to study it, considering her next hypothesis."The word *'forever.'* Could that mean two people forever linked? Love's one undying experience. Could it be...What if it was two sets of monograms? Yes, *two* sets fused together as one."

Excited, she studied the symbols with new energy."Two 'V's—no three, counting the upside-down arrow, which was really an upside-down 'V' and a 'T' as the last letter."V-V-V-T."

She sat back against the tree and closed her eyes. *V. V. V. T.*

All of a sudden she sat bolt upright. "Oh, what a fool I have been." She threw back her massive head of silver-brown braids and guffawed loudly. "That's *it*! Fantastical!"

It explained so much.

She heard a twig snap and looked around, then relaxed. Nothing. More than likely a rabbit or some other tiny forest creature, she thought with distraction. Cracker returned, prancing up and down as though he was possessed. He swatted at a mosquito buzzing around his head.

She sat back again, totally and utterly exhausted. As she contemplated her next move, she wondered if she should say anything to *either* of them, then put that thought aside quickly. *Of course, she must*. It would have to be discussed today, as soon as possible, at the very least.

Whew! She closed her eyes once again, this time totally at peace

Cracker settled in beside her, his body curled into a sleek, black "O." *Good work*, he cat-thought.

She knew it all now. And it felt good to have put it all together.

Her body relaxed against the tree and her mind drifted.

She heard another crackle, closer now, a much more solid crackling of twigs under someone's heavy foot atop the dry, forest floor.

She looked up, focusing her eyes from their momentary darkness. There, in front of her, was a very disturbed-looking Viola Tudhope. Her eyes were wild with emotion.

In her hand, tightly clenched, was a small, but very deadly-looking, hand hatchet.

Chapter Nine

Viola

Mrs. Bundle's eyes moved up from the menacing ax, seemingly and strangely undaunted by the dangerous weapon held so precariously close to her exposed head.

She smiled at the imposing, intense woman above her who had appeared from out of nowhere.

"*It's you.*" Mrs. Bundle's words, uttered simply, were spoken as though she was Alice in Wonderland and fully expecting this strange creature's arrival at her tea party.

Viola stood solidly, the heavy black rubber handle of the hatchet clasped firmly in her hand, staring down at Mrs. Bundle. She was very close, so close Mrs. Bundle could see the carotid artery in her neck throbbing wildly.

"I know everything, Viola. You don't have to hide anything anymore."

Viola gawked at her, plain eyes bugging out like two fried eggs, and then slowly relaxed the white, taut, fingers encircling the tool. The heavy hatchet dropped to the ground with a thud and she burst into tears. "Oh, Mrs. Bundle!"

"I know, dear, I know. What a mess." She stood up and put an arm around the wretched, homely-looking girl.

"I'm so…*unhappy*!" Her voice was hoarse and husky.

"Well, of course you are! There, there, don't cry! You've been trying very hard to protect him, haven't you dear?"

She nodded and another burst of tears ruptured forth and traveled down her cheeks like water leaking from a split hose.

"You love Vincent Veakey very much, don't you?"

"Yes. But…how did you know?"

"I figured it out. Here." She pointed."Your monograms. You're V-T. Viola Tudhope. He's V-V. Vincent Veakey."

Viola nodded grimly."I *knew* someone would decipher it. I've been so…afraid."

Mrs. Bundle encouraged her to sit down, and they both settled into the soft green moss bordering the stream. They were silent for awhile as the stream water trickled softly nearby.

When she was ready, Viola began to speak, haltingly, at first."We met…for the very first time…right here. Both of us were…lonely."

"As I thought. Yes."

"And, I know people don't believe in it, but…it's true. It *can* happen." The words came in bits and spurts as though she was putting her words together aloud for the very first time. Her rough voice softened as she spoke."Love…at first sight. It happened, to us. He…Vinny…was sitting right here, by the stream. I came upon him. He looked so lonely, so forlorn and I…well, we just started talking. I had never, ever done that…before. It was…the most natural thing in the world."

Understanding that this was a most unusual occurrence for both of these two very shy people, Mrs. Bundle gave a gentle nod and smiled encouragingly.

"Of course, we had no idea who each other was." Viola said,"And, we just…didn't say. We'd never ever met, never had even seen each other—that we could remember, anyway. I think…our paths had never crossed. Nevertheless, it happened that day. We sat here, by the stream and talked, for hours it seemed. It was…magical. Not about everyday stuff, but philosophy, and our own beliefs, and things that I'd never shared with anyone before. When it was time to go, we decided to meet at the same place and time the next day. It was so simple… and lovely. Just to talk to a stranger, and not feel…embarrassed, or shy…or on guard. That *first* day he called me his muse, his Mona

Lisa. *Me!* I couldn't believe it. He told me…" she gave a sideways glance to gauge Mrs. Bundle's reaction,"I was beautiful…and when he said it, I…believed it." The plain girl wiped a wayward tear from her cheek."I know what I am, Mrs. Bundle. I get all tongue-tied with people. And self-conscious. I've never been pretty. Never even attractive. A plain Jane. A wallflower." She smiled wistfully."But, not that day. Not to him! To him, I was...everything. And in my eyes, he is *perfect*. He has no flaws, no faults. From that first day…I was his." She threw her unadorned head back and laughed lightly."I called him…" her voice dropped off and she looked into the eyes of the older woman, unsure of herself.

"It's okay, Viola, I won't laugh."

"Well, it sounds foolish when I say it aloud. But it was kind of a funny, playful thing. And it fit him. I called him…Nature Boy. You know, from the Nat King Cole song." Her eyes took on a dreamy, faraway look and she spoke the lyrics softly, rhythmically, as though she had said them a million times before.*"There was a boy, A very strange enchanted boy, They say he wandered very far, very far, Over land and sea, A little shy and sad of eye, But very wise was he, And then one day, A magic day, he passed my way, And while we spoke of many things, Fools and kings, This he said to me,"The greatest thing you'll ever learn, Is just to love and be loved in return.""* She repeated the words wistfully,"The greatest thing you'll ever learn, is just to love and be loved in return." Her poor, homely face was so melancholy, so hopeless; ironically, it was a mirror image of the memory Mrs. Bundle had of Vincent's face at the jail that first time.

"That's all I ever wanted in life. And I knew, Mrs. Bundle, I had been waiting for Vincent my whole life. I truly loved him from the first day." She stopped, her eyes clear and true as she looked questioningly at Mrs. Bundle."Can you understand?"

"Of course. It's a beautiful story, Viola. Just beautiful."

"We met here at the stream three more times and it was lovely…the first time he ever kissed me..." Words failed her and she swallowed hard, then continued,"He told me he had never felt that way about anyone. We were so happy, and then…I know it's not the way things usually happen, but…he asked me to spend the rest of my life with him, knowing nothing about me, nor I about him! Of course I said 'yes' without hesitation. We were *so* happy! I remember we laughed and cried, and hugged each other, and he said, 'My Mona Lisa, if we're going to be married, I suppose I should know your given name!"

She put her head in her hands and moaned, too distressed to go on.

Mrs. Bundle touched her shoulder. "I know, Viola. When you found out who he was, you—"

She nodded. "It was as though the sky had fallen in on our world. We knew it would be a tremendous uphill battle. Of all the people you could meet and fall in love with! The Veakeys and the Tudhopes. We knew no one from either side of our families would ever want us, or allow us, to be together. We knew it would never work."

"And so, you continued to see each other. You met secretly?"

Viola's mouth turned downward; her wan face was dully emotionless. "Yes, once we knew it would be a problem, we did. For a good amount of time we continued on, meeting here or…up on the mountain nearby his property. It was… so awful. He told me over and over not to worry, that we would work it out, but I could tell he was affected by the change, too. He said it was a silly ridiculous curse, a feud that didn't affect us at all. And he tried to prove it by doing that." She pointed to the wood-burned carving. "He carved that, just for us, is what he said."

Her hands traced over the monogram, then the word "*forever*." "But, we both knew it couldn't be." The sigh she gave came from the bottom of her insides, a hopeless, resigned exhalation. "Right before I ended things, I just, in passing, mentioned the Veakey name to my father. It was as if I had said the worst swear word in the world." She shuddered. "All hell broke loose! Said they were a bunch of useless bums, and dirt-poor to boot. He also said it would be a cold day in hell before *he* ever talked to, or had anything to do with, any Veakey. My father refused to talk about the feud so, later, I asked my mother. She said she had heard the story when she first came into the Tudhope clan. She said they all hated each other because of a love affair gone terribly bad—some love triangle that ended badly and caused a huge rift. She said after that, each generation hated the other more and more. And she said the Veakeys have been cursed with bad luck for years! It all seems true enough. I asked my father why he couldn't just put the feud behind him. He told me it would be impossible. When I saw my father's face, I knew. I've even tried to find out on my own why the families hate each other so much, but... After that, it was all I thought about. I…gave up without trying. I failed. It was such a big mess!"

"Yes, sometimes we get overwhelmed and give up before we should."

"I know, I just couldn't get past it. It all seemed so hopeless. So, I told Vinnie that night that we could never, ever be together."

"Yes. Let me guess. That was Sunday, June 22rd."

She gave Mrs. Bundle a puzzled look."Yes! How do you know th—?"

"The day before the Tuddy's Diner fire. The fire was on June 23rd. You've been trying to protect him. I remember reading about it in the *Rutland Daily News* on the 24th. When I put it together now it makes perfect sense. That's why, when we saw you that day, you were so upset."

Viola's eyes grew troubled once again.

"You know, two days after the fire—on the 25th—it's my wedding anniversary, dear, that's how I remember the date so clearly." Viola nodded, and Mrs. Bundle went on,"That's when Althea and I saw you. Do you remember? You said,'It's hopeless.' That there was 'nothing anyone could do.'"

"Yes! I was beside myself! I thought…it was the curse again. I thought…I had to protect him from himself. That he had gone crazy…after I cut things off."

"You assumed…,"

"Yes. Can you believe how I've failed him? I thought…it *was* he who had set the fire. In retaliation. I was so heartbroken! Honestly, I really don't think I was thinking straight after breaking things off." She hung her head disconsolately and said very quietly."And I haven't seen him since that awful night. I heard that Barny Veakey hired you to help Vinnie."

"Yes, he did."

"I was happy someone was on his side."

"So, you've been conflicted. You've probably been worried sick about him."

"Yes! I should have gone to him right away! But the feud, the families' curse! I was…so confused. But now I *know*, Mrs. Bundle. I know he *couldn't* have done those fires. And the things people are saying! It's so cruel. He's *not* a pyromaniac. He's kind, and very gentle, and he's special…in many ways. You have no idea! I know… his heart is broken. And so is mine."

Mrs. Bundle pointed to the hatchet on the ground,"You came here today to use that, didn't you?"

"I was going to cut out the letters on the tree—destroy our two monograms as best I could. I'd seen the authorities up this way looking for our dog, Tuddsley, and anything that would shed any light on who started the fire. I've been avoiding the Sheriff, hoping he wouldn't ask me about Vinnie. I'm…a terrible liar. This could incriminate Vinnie if anyone figured it out. You know, that he would burn down the diner because of the old family vendetta and because I had broken off our…love affair. I'm frantic to help him in any way I can."

"Oh, Viola, you've expended so much energy trying to keep things secret. It's such a shame."

Viola's face was bright and her speech was hurried."Yes, but now I know we can work this out between our two families. You see, I found some old sweetheart letters in the antique family trunk up in the attic at the farm. They've…helped me understand what true love really means. They're unsigned, but obviously written by someone very much in love with my great-great-great grandmother. There was an old diary, too, in the same box with the letters—hers. In reading her diary, I felt I…knew her. She was a wonderful woman. And, because of her, I don't care about the past now! I know our love can be, if Vinnie and I work together."

"Really, Viola. How remarkable!"

"And I'm going to tell Vinnie I'll be his. That is, if they'll let me see him. I must get into the jail and talk to him. Do you think they'll let me see him?"

"Oh, Viola! Don't you know?"

Viola's face was blank.

Mrs. Bundle grabbed her hands. "That Vincent's being released? Well, of course, how would you know? In fact, I'm head—"

"What?" Viola's transformed face held pure joy intermixed with disbelief. "When?"

"Today! He's being released today. They are freeing him and dropping all charges."

"Today? This afternoon? Oh, thank you, Lord! Mrs. Bundle, I—I need to go to him! Now!"

"Yes, I understand, of course you do." She reached for the girl. "In fact, I was planning on picking him up at the jail myself, *today*— and bringing him home to Barny." She looked at her watch. "Oh, gosh, I've got to get going! Viola, the media will probably be there at Southern Correctional Facility, waiting. It may be a circus."

"Oh!" A look of consternation clouded her happy face. "I...don't do well with crowds and I'm scared to death of the media. You know...I get all tongue-tied if I have to talk to...just about anyone. But, I need to speak to Vinnie...alone."

Her eyes filled with tears, and she cried out, "What shall I *do*, Mrs. Bundle?"

"I understand." She put a comforting arm around the poor girl and then paused, "Why not..? How 'bout this, Viola? I'll pick him up and bring him to you, if you'd like."

She clasped her hands together. "Would you do that?"

"Of course! I'm pleased as punch for you—and him, and I hope you can work things out. I hope the best for you both, I really do!"

"Thank-you, Mrs. Bundle."

She gave the odd girl a huge hug and then reached for her fanny pack.

Carefully, Mrs. Bundle tore a piece of blank paper from the back of her day timer and wrote a quick note.

And then they made their plan.

It was a beautiful sight to see. Mrs. Bundle and her trusty Junebug (a most inconspicuous vehicle and very willing accomplice), slipped into the Correctional Facility service entrance parking lot, bypassing the TV station vans situated out front who were like ravenous vultures waiting to pounce on the scrawny man, so intent were they on getting his picture and maybe a story. After spiriting Vincent away from the jail and the waiting media, she flew up the mountain and into the Veakey's Trash and Treasure junk yard as though the feisty emerald-green Beetle was on wings, not rubber tires. Vincent's neck craned, excited to see if his father was there to greet his homecoming. Sure enough, as the crusty Barny stepped out the front door, the glee on the old man's knarly face was evident. *His boy was home!* Mrs. Bundle watched a moving reunion between the two.

Even more poignant, though, was the young man's first sight of Viola, who stood shyly inside the doorway. She greeted her sweetheart with a huge smile, then timidly opened her arms. Disbelief, followed by pure joy, radiated from Vincent's being. Every part of his body seemed to emanate serenity as he reached for his love—this simple, uncomplicated, unadorned girl. As soon as his father saw his son's unmitigated bliss, he stepped aside, and the note he had been clutching in his weather-beaten hand fell to the floor. It read, *Barny—please accept this girl into your home. She is a friend of mine, and all will be explained when I arrive back with Vincent this afternoon. Thank you for understanding. Your friend, Mrs. Bundle.*

No explanation was necessary as the tears flowed and Barny was introduced to his son's beloved.

Chapter Ten

LiMB's Final Piece

It wasn't until around six p.m. that she arrived home that day, exhausted and exuberant, following Vincent and Viola's poignant reunion. As she drove into the yard, she saw Nick Clancy's new Chevy pickup parked in the yard, along with a sporty red Nissan, which she remembered was Natalie Hufferman's car.

She drove slowly past the two empty vehicles. "What on earth is going on?"

Pulling Junie up into the open barn and shutting off the car engine, she quickly exited, almost running into a breathless Angie and Jack, who met her and Cracker outside the door.

She cried out, "Did I forget we had a meeting? I'm so sorry! It's been...quite a day."

"No!" Jack said, "It's all right, Mrs. B. We—"

Angie interrupted excitedly, "We had to call an emergency meeting! We've solved it!"

The both of them were near exploding. Cracker jumped up and down excitedly beside the peony bushes. *What*, he cat-asked, *what?*

Angie cried, "We've solved the painting mystery! And, you're not going to believe it!"

Mrs. Bundle started to ask, "What—?" but Jack held up a calm hand. "We'll be wanting you to sit down and take a load off, won't we, Mrs. B? You look fairly beat! Aye, we don't want to steal any of the LiMB Society's thunder, so let's let them all tell you about it.

Nick, Natalie, and Anthony, too! It's too bloody remarkable, that it is. Right, and they're all on the back porch waiting for you."

"Well, let's go see, then!" She beamed, and they walked around the side of the big farmhouse.

Gathered in all their glory, the LiMB Society waited for her arrival. Nick Clancy was lazing on the porch swing, Natalie was pacing, while Anthony sat on the edge of the granite stoop, obviously restless. When they saw Mrs. Bundle rounding the corner with Angie and Jack, they all began to talk all at once.

Jack held up his hand and silenced them.

"Sit down, mates! Mrs. B looks totally knackered, doesn't she now? Give her that chair, there, Nick! Now sit here, mum, and put your feet up on that hassock. It's going to take a bit of time. Would you be wantin' a cold drink, now?"

"No, no, I'm fine. Tell me what's—" She reached as Natalie handed her a frosty glass and she took a large mouthful.

They heard a car's wheels spin on the gravel driveway.

Angie said, "Oh! That would be Althea! We called her."

"I'll go fetch her." Natalie offered, and she was off like a shot. In a matter of seconds, Althea Swain, looking somewhat confused, came through the screen door and onto the back porch with the energetic girl.

"What's going on?" She asked. "There's enough cars out there in the yard for a party!"

Mrs. Bundle smiled, albeit wearily, "The kids have called an emergency LiMB Society meeting—something important has happened and it seems they've got a lot to tell us!" She turned towards an eager Angie. "The floor's all yours, Madame Chairwoman."

Angie smiled broadly and took a large, calming breath. "Okay! Well! Where to begin?"

She looked at Jack and he nodded and said softly, "Go on, lass. Start at the beginning."

"Okay. First of all, everyone knows we've spent the last month researching every nook and cranny of the Pillson Library, the Historical Society, and the *State Standard* archives to see if we could find out the history or background of the 'Conny' mystery painting. And last Friday we hit pay dirt. Well," she shook her head impatiently,"we already all know about what happened last Friday."

Jack agreed,"Right! We were *all* feeling just about as useful as a lighthouse on a bog, that is, until last Friday, weren't we now? But today was even better."

Nick motioned toward his brother,"Anthony here came up with something pretty special today."

Angie urged,"Go ahead, tell, Anthony, you tell."

Anthony cleared his throat."Well, it's about this book I was reading last year for school. It was about the Civil War and General George Stannard, who commanded the Vermont troops at Bull Run and Harper's Ferry, and Gettysburg, too. Anyway, I kinda remembered something. I remembered all the pictures. I thought I remembered that there were some of these same kind of etchings, you know, black and white political cartoons and such, throughout the book. So, I went and got it out again this weekend—from the library, that is, and last night, as I was flipping through it, there it was." He scratched his full head of dark hair, pushing it back from his freckled forehead."I couldn't believe it! Actually, well, here it is." He stood up from the stoop, removing a thick and very large book from underneath him. There was also a manila folder that he left there. He opened the book to a bookmarked page."There!"

Mrs. Bundle took the book and remarked,"Hmmm…It *is* the same style of political cartoon etching as the one you found in the *Standard* and from the same era, too."

Anthony said proudly,"Not only that—it's the same artist!"

Nick was beside him, pointing,"See? It says right there."

There, scrawled, was the now-familiar signature "*Conny*." The rough, black, pen-and-ink etching was a caricature of Abraham Lincoln being portrayed as the carriage driver of a large stable of six powerful Morgan horses, whose heads were not horses' heads, but the superimposed heads of very proud and austere Union Army Generals. Each General's name was branded on their respective horse's backside: "William Wells," "Lewis Addison Grant," "John

Wolcott Phelps," "George Jerrison Stannard," "Edward Henry Stoughton," and "George Crockett Strong"; notably, it was a fair likeness of each, compared to the stark individual photographs featured on the opposite page.

"Good grief! Vermont Morgan horses!" Althea said.

"Right. And all Vermont Generals," replied Anthony. The man-horses, steam blustering from flared nostrils, were making a mad gallop toward a large, distinct sign that was surrounded by huge magnolia bushes and hanging wisteria. The sign read,*"The South."* He continued,"All it says under the photo here, is,*'unknown commentary on the War, found in General Stannard's war effects after his death.'"*

"My goodness. This is very interesting," Mrs. Bundle said, studying the political cartoon and the photographs on the opposite page.

Angie continued,"So, that got us thinking. The one we found Friday was from August of 1859. But, remember, the mysterious painting was dated 1861. And that's the same time period when the Civil War began, too."

"Right!" Anthony said,"April of 1861. The Confederates took over Fort Sumter in Charleston, South Carolina."

Angie nodded,"So, we thought, we'll concentrate on the Civil War period. And first thing this morning, Anthony and I went back to the *Standard* and started back through all those old issues from 1861-on."

She gave Anthony a nod."Anthony?"

Anthony picked up the flattened manila folder that he had been sitting on. He grinned, pushed his sliding glasses back up the bridge of his nose, and opened the file high above Mrs. Bundle. He let the contents fall softly into her lap—a good dozen or so pieces of sheet paper. He couldn't contain himself, whooping gleefully,"*We hit the jackpot!*"

As they all spent the next few minutes enjoying the discovery, consisting of a number of political cartoons all authored and drawn by their mysterious artist, they became familiar with the artist's recurring theme. Each cartoon was a commentary on the Civil War in one way or another and all were dated.

"That is *really* remarkable!" Mrs. Bundle said.

Angie gathered the cartoons up and put them in chronological order."See? It's pretty weird when you analyze them. They start out being pretty upbeat and gung-ho about the war effort, but then, well, they get kinda dark and sad."

Nick offered,"Yeah. I noticed that too. Like, look at the etchings from these battles. This one's called,'*The Men Who Are Fighting*', and this one,'*A Quiet Place to Reflect After Battle*.'"

Jack pointed,"And then there's this last one called,'*Death and Destruction*.' Ach! They're pretty gruesome, especially in black and white."

"Really kind of scary, too." Natalie said. True enough, the artist's etchings were a detailed chronicle of war at its most devastating.

"Good grief! I know! I've *been* there." Althea's face was grim."Nursing in Vietnam. War is never glamorous like they portray it in the movies."

"Yes, that's so true," Mrs. Bundle agreed."I must say, you have done an incredible job to find these!"

Althea agreed,"When you give them a job, they certainly know how to take the bull by the horns!"

Angie said,"Wait a minute! That's not all! In fact, it's just the beginning!"

"Just—the beginning? You mean, there's more?" Mrs. Bundle asked.

Jack, usually reserved, was downright talkative tonight."Aye, there's more! Much more! Wait 'til you hear what else they found!"

"So, we figured," Anthony said,"well, we concluded, he must have gone to war with the Union Army. And we realized we needed to keep looking."

Angie jumped in, "So, anyway, we broke for lunch and called Natalie. She came over and helped us out, too, on the microfiche. There we were, the three of us, and, all of a sudden, we found the best—" she stopped, and shook her head, "no, well, actually, the *worst*—part, however way you look at it."

Natalie took over. "Yeah, the worst for sure. It's really pretty sad."

Mrs. Bundle looked bewildered, "Worst? What?"

Angie said, "Okay. The good news is, we now know who the artist is!"

Natalie added, "The bad news is, he died a very tragic death."

Mrs. Bundle said, "I'm beside myself! Tell me!"

Anthony said, "Okay, I'll tell. Like we said, we figured out he, the artist, must have gone away to be in the War, because of all the battlefield etchings of the war. So, when we came to August of 1863, we saw the front page story—all dedicated to the Battle of Gettysburg, which had occurred in early July. It was like a memorial; the whole page was about Gettysburg, because so many people died there. And, along with the story was a slew of Conny's etchings, all featured on the front page—a lot of the same ones we had found before in the newspaper. Underneath them, it read, '*In memoriam.*' So, we went to the Obituary section of that issue, and..."

Solemnly, Angie placed a last piece of paper in front of Mrs. Bundle. They all were quiet as she read aloud:

STATE STANDARD
Obituary: *August 25, 1863*

Standard Mourns Loss of Local Artist
Cornelius Lorenzo Veakey

She stopped, in awe, and they all nodded. Then, she continued reading:

GETTYSBURG, Pennsylvania—Cornelius Lorenzo Veakey, 20, of Pillsonville died July 3, 1863 at the battle of Gettysburg, Gettysburg, Pennsylvania.

Sargent Corporal Veakey was born on June 4, 1843 in Pillsonville. He was the son of Charles and Eunice Barstow Veakey. He is a graduate of Pillsonville Normal School and was known in the area as an up and coming artist. He was employed at the *State Standard* as its newspaper artist prior to being drafted into the 13th Vermont Regiment in service for the War. His pen and ink etchings have been featured numerous times in area publications; his talent was widely recognized.

Marching in the Second Vermont Brigade, 13th Vermont Regiment commanded by Thirteenth Regiment Vermont Infantry Colonel Francis V. Randall under Brig. Gen. George J. Stannard, Sergeant Corporal Veakey died on the front lines at Cemetery Hill, according to his longtime friend and fellow soldier, 1st Sgt. Jeremiah Tudhope.

This paper received notice of Sgt. Cpl. Veakey's untimely death via correspondence two days hence from Tudhope, whose detailed account indicates the Brigade marched to Gettysburg, arriving on the first day of battle, July 1st. He writes of the infantry's valiant battle on July 2nd, overtaking guns on Emmitsburg Road and capturing rebel prisoners. It was on the third day of battle on July 3rd that the 13th Vermont Infantry was placed in the front line of battle to the left of Cemetery Hill. In this position they remained, sustaining heavy assaults during heavy artillery fire, according to Tudhope's chronicle. A heavy rebel column bore down steadily upon the Thirteenth and Fourteenth Vermont, and it was at this time that Veakey was mortally wounded. His friend, Jeremiah Tudhope, stood fighting by his side and was there to comfort him as he lay mortally wounded after battle.

The Union Army eventually overcame the rebels and succeeded in capturing many prisoners. Total casualties in the regiment were 8 killed and over 150 men wounded or missing.

Also enclosed in Tudhope's correspondence were Veakey's effects, including his last drawings prepared for The *Standard* publication, detailing the Battle of Gettysburg from Veakey's perspective from Cemetery Ridge. Particularly poignant is the etching titled, "War's Toll" which depicts a tired soldier's grief after battle as he kneels over a fallen comrade.

The *Standard* publishes this and the other depictions on the front page of today's issue in honor of our fallen soldier and friend.

He is survived by his parents, his brothers Horace and Samuel, and his sister Eunice and her husband Todd, and niece Lorene. He has also left behind his beloved fiancée of Hartland, Margaret Dorothy Collins.

The deceased was esteemed for his gracious manners and gentlemanly deportment, but his virtues are better known to those who were intimately acquainted with him. A Christian, a kind and affectionate son and brother, and a sincere friend, he leaves a large number of friends and a village to mourn his death.

A memorial plaque will be placed in his memory at the Pillsonville Cemetery family gravesite in honor of his service in the Army along with his superlative service to *The State Standard* with these moving depictions of war since the beginning of 1862 through July 3, 1863.

"He is gone—gone to the bourne from whence no traveller ever returns, where sickness, sorrows, pain and death, are felt and feared no more."

Our loss is his gain. Requiescat in pace.

Mrs. Bundle looked up from the article, her eyes moist.

"Absolutely fantastical," she murmured softly. She reached up and took Anthony's arm and squeezed it. "Really good work."

Emotion showed on his young face, and she looked around at the silent group. Angie nodded somberly, reaching down to pick up a small, long twig nearby; she tapped it between her fingers. Then, in the patch of dirt next to Mrs. Bundle's chair, she wrote in large, bold lines, forming three capital letters:

C-L-V

She handed the twig to Jack, and he continued silently writing the last three mysterious letters:

M-D-C

Mrs. Bundle whispered, "Cornelius…Lorenzo…Veakey." She looked at the obituary again. "The fiancée? Mercy, you're right! *Margaret…Dorothy…Collins.*"

Nick said, "Pretty clever, huh?"

Mrs. Bundle nodded, her eyes shining. "The answer we've been looking for! To the mystery of…the Roman numerals."

Natalie said, "Not Roman numerals—their initials! Two people's initials!"

Mrs. Bundle said simply, "M-D-C , C-L-V."

"Yes." Angie said softly, "Their initials, carved into a wooden beam in the dark eaves of an old library's knee wall."

Chapter Eleven

The Library Commemorative

Now, it was Natalie's turn to shine. She drew one of the old chocolate candy wrappers out of her pocket and said,"*Sweetness.*"

The light went on immediately for Mrs. Bundle."Yes! How he addressed the back of the painting:'To My Sweetness'!"

"Uh-huh!" Natalie's exuberance was barely contained."I'll bet Cornelius Veakey called her that because she loved chocolates, and…they were sweethearts! Somehow, they must have been there, in or near that room upstairs, together. That's what I think, anyway. It's all very romantic."

"Yes, that is possible, Natalie, very possible."

Althea asked,"L, do you suppose.. Cornelius *Veakey*…could be related…?"

Mrs. Bundle finished her sentence," to Barnabus and Vincent?"

Angie nodded effusively and snapped her fingers."That's what we've already thought of! This Cornelius is probably an ancestor of their's! Wouldn't that be really weird? You know, that *you* know them, and that you've been working to get Junior out of—"

"Oh! Oh!" Mrs. Bundle cried."I've got to tell you all! I've just come from Barnabus' house!" She took a deep breath. "Sheriff O'Malley called me this morning." Her proud face looked majestic in the evening's soft light."Vincent Veakey, I am very pleased to say, was set free this afternoon and all charges against him have been dropped!"

"Are you kidding?" Nick whistled.

"That's great!" Angie said.

"Yes, it's wonderful to say the least. And, yes Angie, it's very strange indeed that here, in front of us, is the obituary of, very likely, one of the Veakeys' early Pillson relatives."

"That's bizarre!" Natalie said.

"An amazing coincidence, isn't it now?" Jack agreed.

"Hmm...yes, amazing." Mrs. Bundle considered this and then cried out, "*Tudhope!*"

She grabbed the obituary and scanned through it once more. "Yes, here it is! It does say...*Jeremiah Tudhope!*" She looked at the group and repeated as though they all should know, "Jeremiah Tudhope!"

"Jeremiah Tudhope? What?" said Althea.

"Yes!" Mrs. Bundle threw back her full head of silver-brown braids and laughed with gusto, " Gaw!'*Merimiah*,'Merimiah!"

Althea started laughing, too, catching on immediately. "'Merimiah! Karen's saying! The diner restroom!"

"Yes!"

While the others looked on doubtfully, Mrs. Bundle explained her and Althea's mirth, telling them the story of the somber picture in Tuddy's that one had to walk past to get to the restroom. "That Jeremiah—is the *one* and the same! The Civil War soldier. He's...a relative of Ger and Phoebe Tudhope! And Viola Tudhope, too!" She clucked her tongue, putting the pieces together quickly in her mind.

Nick stirred, chuckling, "Yeah, dude, right! I remember that painting. It gave me the creeps when I was a kid. Real stern face."

Jack agreed, "Aye, and it says right here that he was this Cornelius bloke's 'longtime friend.' They were mates, then, weren't they?"

"Exactly! That...is *remarkable*, to say the least!" Mrs. Bundle said.

They all looked at her blankly, and she muttered to herself, "Yes, the Tudhopes and the Veakeys." She raised her eyes at them, her expression was veiled with uncertainty, then said, "Silly thought— never mind...something I'll explore, for sure, another time." Shifting in her seat awkwardly, she reached for Jack and he gave her a hand up. She smiled at the group and said,"For right now, let's focus on your discovery!" She placed a thoughtful index finger to her chin."I *think* we need to see if we can reach Louis Montembeau. Let's see, today's Monday, and he's not around, probably. This would have been a Chester Library day for him…but," she looked at her watch,"maybe…let's hope he's home by now. C'mon, let's go give him a call!"

They were all crammed into the farmhouse's front hallway where Mrs. Bundle sat at her telephone table. She dialed Louis' home number and waited, then smiled broadly into the receiver."Ah, Louis!" she paused, listening,"Good,'n you? Thank goodness I caught you!" Pause."Is this a bad time? I know you probably just got home and you're exhausted…well, I wouldn't be calling you after hours but this is *important*."

She waited, listening, and then said,"Are you sure it's not a bother?"

Cracker sat at her feet, his black tail swishing from side to side. Silence again, and then she said,"Good! Thank you so much. You see, the kids have made a great discovery. Yes, the LiMB Society! Can you, would you, meet us at the library?"

A quick response from him, then she continued,"Yes, right now! I think you'll be very surprised and thoroughly delighted." She laughed at his response."Oh, Louis, thank-you! You're a peach. You can meet us there in ten minutes?" The group all nodded in excitement."Great, we'll be right down! See you there in afew."

She turned to the waiting group."Let's go!"

The rush of adrenalin was evident as they hurried, *en masse*, into the gravel driveway.

Althea cried,"I'll drive!" and Mrs. Bundle, the two girls, and Cracker piled into her car.

Nick shouted,"We'll take the truck!"

Nick, Anthony, and Jack followed behind Althea's car, and, barely within the speed limit, they all traveled down the long, winding hill from North Pillson Corners to Pillsonville and the Pillson Public Library.

When they arrived, Mrs. Bundle asked Althea to "just pull up front," and they all piled out from the two vehicles and walked, together, up the front walkway to the main entrance of the Pillson Library. It was still light out, although twilight was setting in.

"Yes, look everybody! First, I want to show you all something." They gathered round her."See the plaques on each side of the doors?" They peered closely."Look at this one here!"

She pointed to the long brass plaque on the right hand side of the large doors."It should be right here, under 13th Vermont Regiment... Company A...Yes!"

They all stared. She said,"Can you see their names?"

There, in front of them, where she pointed, was the name:

VEAKEY, CORNELIUS L. SGT. CORP. A

And directly above his name was the name of his friend:

TUDHOPE, JEREMIAH 1ST SGT. A

Cracker wove his way between the stationary feet of the group that was so absorbed in seeing the real names of real people who had lived over one-hundred-and-forty years before.

Nick gave a low whistle."Dude!" Quietly, he confessed,"You know, I *never* woulda thought I'd buy into this LiMB thing, secret society and all...but," his voice trailed off.

Angie whispered,"Yeah, it's really pretty cool, isn't it?"

Louis arrived as they were remarking on their discovery.

Greeting him excitedly, the group, taking turns, gave him the exciting news about the painting's origin and the local artist who painted it.

"Unbelievable!" he kept saying, "That is absolutely…unbelievable. What a crew you are!"

Mrs. Bundle said, "Louis, thank you so much for coming."

"Anything for you, Mrs. B. If you hadn't found the painting, we'd never be here, less than a week away from our glorious Festival."

"One of the reasons, though, Louis, that I dragged you down here after hours was because I remembered what you told me — something about the Library having been closed only once in its history."

"Yuh. It was early, sometime near when it first opened, I think." His brow furrowed in thought. "If I remember correctly, it was something about the use of the operating funds in exchange for a war effort. Some kind of state mandate."

She asked, "Do you think we could…?" She motioned toward the big doors.

He interrupted her, excited, "—look in the records inside?" He fumbled for the key in his pocket, and cried, "Yes! Of course! Come inside, and let's look it up."

They followed him inside, and he sat down at the large oak desk behind the front counter. As he rifled through the bottom drawer, he chattered on, breathlessly, "I think it was the Spanish-American War, or maybe earlier, could have been the Civil War."

He pulled out a very old, thin black ledger book. On the cover, in finely handwritten and detailed penmanship, was written:

𝔏𝔦𝔟𝔯𝔞𝔯𝔶 𝔯𝔢𝔠𝔬𝔯𝔡𝔰 1849-1870

He turned on the reading lamp on his desk. "Give me a minute…"

They all looked eagerly over his shoulder as he put on his reading glasses and flipped through the beginning section of the ledger. "It was in the first few years…I remember seeing it. Yes, here it is!" He read aloud, "'Library services terminated. December 14, 1861.'" He flipped to the next page, perusing it with interest, "And then—the library reopens in…late May, 1865 because of the end of—"

"*The Civil War!* I knew it!" Anthony yelled.

"Right! That would be the right time frame, wouldn't it?" Louis read through the data. "In any event, the town's funds to operate the Library went directly toward an effort to cut municipal costs and thereby, raise war revenues."

Angie said, "He—Cornelius—must have left the painting at the Library—for some reason—*before* he left for the war."

Natalie added, "And he didn't ever retrieve it…"

Nick said, "—because he was gone those two years—1861-1863!"

Anthony, beside himself, jiggled from foot to foot. "And then—he died before—"

"—he could get it back." Jack said solemnly.

"He died, leaving it there. Yes." Mrs. Bundle agreed.

Natalie said, "That is *so* sad—he never came back."

Jack said, "Em, and the library was closed up, wasn't it, until after the Civil War? Aye, it must have just stayed there, in the wall, forgotten."

Mrs. Bundle clapped her hands gleefully. "You've *done* it! You've got it figured out! The candy wrappers, the painting and probably, why it was left there! Fantastical! You all have done some very powerful work here, and I congratulate you—each of you."

The five young adults were delighted with their discovery.

Mrs. Bundle said, "Now, we *may* have one piece left to find out. So, I *may* need your services to complete something else for me."

They all asked eagerly, "What is it?"

"Really, it can wait for now," she chuckled. "For the present, enjoy! Great job!"

"Yes, absolutely, positively, unequivocally—great job!" Louis repeated.

"Ditto!" Althea said.

The group looked as though they had been all been awarded the Olympic gold.

Mrs. Bundle beamed at them. "Let's go home and celebrate! How about burgers on the grill? With all the fixings? I'm *starved*!"

Nick said, "Yeah? I'm so hungry I could eat the north end of a southbound skunk!"

"Oh, Nick! Geez!" Natalie cried out painfully, and they all laughed.

Chapter Twelve

Holes Can Be a Good Thing

The next day was Tuesday, the 11th of August, and, although there was Festival work to be completed, Mrs. Bundle's first item on her "to-do" list was to pay a visit to the Veakeys. She had two objectives: one was to make sure Vincent had settled in comfortably after his ordeal in jail, the other was to tell his father and him about the newest discovery: their antecedent's artwork.

There was an overly large sign posted at the entrance to the long, winding driveway. Painted in blaze orange in fat, roughly-drawn script was:

Keep Out!! XSpechily Repotters!!! T & T is temproly CLOSED! —THE Mgt.

The property looked deserted.

From inside the car, Mrs. Bundle eyeballed the shack, looking for signs of life. *Oh, I do hope they're home*, she thought.

Two figures stepped out warily from the hovel's doorway. It was, she realized, Vincent and Viola. Although their combined age bordered on sixty-five, they both looked all of fourteen, hands linked together, two small heads on petite bodies, hers round, his slight. When they saw it was the familiar emerald-green Volkswagon Bug and not an interloper, they waved and ran to meet her, arriving just as Mrs. Bundle opened her car door.

Viola spoke first, cautiously. "Nobody knows I'm here! And, I haven't told Dad or Mom yet—about us."

Vincent said firmly, "I'm g-going over th-there with Viola t-t-t-tonight. We're g-g-going to t-t-tell them w-w-we're in l-love. And that's th-th-the end of it!"

The conviction in his voice was evident; there was no deterring either one of this pair now, she was happy to see.

All of a sudden, Barny stepped nimbly out of the large garage, shotgun raised, long stringy hair escaping from the hat pulled down to his bushy eyebrows. The fierce, protective look on his face dissipated. "Goldarn, Miz Bundle!" He lowered the gun. "You almost got in my line of fire! Thought you was one of them pesky re*pot*termen! They're been like gnats, buzzin' around here, trying to get an interview with Junior."

"I'm sorry, Barny. I guess Vincent is somewhat of a celebrity, especially now that he's been released. Everyone wants to talk to him."

"Well, it ain't no use them comin' around where they ain't wanted. Where was they when the poor boy was in the *hoozcow*?" He clacked his teeth together sharply.

Vincent said soothingly, "It's okay, P-P-Pops. Everything's okay, n-n-now that Viola and I are b-b-back t-t-together."

Barny leaned forward and whispered hoarsely to Mrs. Bundle. "Right nice girl. I like her. A lot. She fried up a mean hash this mornin' with the leftover venison." He winked, then tipped his battered, colorless Red Sox baseball hat at the quiet girl standing nearby, who proceeded to blush and then, grinned shyly.

Mrs. Bundle said, "I *knew* you'd like her! By the way, Barny, I've come with some pretty exciting news."

"Oh?" He pushed the cap back on his head and wiped his brow.

"I'm not sure you've been aware of all the hubbub going on this summer. What I mean is, about next week's Dog Days of Summer Art Festival in Pillson?"

"Nope, can't say as I paid it much mind. Sorry, Miz Bundle, pretty much everything I been doin's been mindin' the premises right here, keepin' this place goin' while Junior was in the lock-up."

"Yes, as I thought. Well, let me tell you a little bit about what's been going on."

She proceeded to tell the three of them about the beginning momentum for the Festival, keeping it short and to the point, and concluding with, "…so, you see, we found this old painting in behind the wall of the library, and from that came the idea of the Dog Days of Summer Art Festival. It so happens that the painting we found is over one-hundred-and-forty years old. Painted in 1861."

"Right-o." Barny squinted at her, waiting with all the patience he could muster.

"Yes, you see, the interesting thing is, I believe it may have been painted by one of your ancestors."

"What you say?" He scratched his head with the intensity of a dog with fleas. "Our kin? You mean, a *Veakey?*"

"Yes, that's right."

"That *cain't* be right. Ain't likely, anyway."

Vincent, on the other hand, became very animated, "W-W-Wow, th-that's exciting."

Viola nodded, grabbing Vincent's hand.

"You see," Mrs. Bundle continued, "some of my young friends formed a group this summer specifically to research the painting's origin. They worked all this last month piecing together what they could about the painting. Yesterday, they discovered the final pieces, and it all fit into place. The artist's name is Cornelius Lorenzo *Veakey*. They discovered that, during his time, he was quite well known in the area for his pen and ink etchings. Political cartoons and commentary, and the like. The kids found a bunch of these drawings in the *State Standard Newspaper* archives. Turns out, the artist, Cornelius Veakey, went off to fight in the Civil War—but never came back. He died during the Battle of Gettysburg on July 3, 1863."

"Well, now, that's right interestin', truth be told. Cor-nee-lee-us, you say! I'd like to see a paintin' done by a relative of our'n. Found behind the library wall down Pillson, you say?" His back hunched and he cackled, "Don't that beat all!"

Vincent asked, "D-D-Do you kn-know *w-w-why* it was th-there? B-b-behind the w-wall?"

"Well, no…we haven't fully figured that piece out yet, but we're working on it."

Barny smiled crookedly and straightened up, as best he could, to his full height, all of five-feet-three inches. "When can we take a look-see at this here paintin'?"

"Anytime, really. Right now it's at the Art Co-Op, there until this weekend. Then, the painting will be on display at the Festival, throughout the weekend, in fact. It's really quite lovely. He was quite an artist. You should be very proud of your relative."

"*Hmmmph!*" Barny gave her a derisive grin, the full set of false teeth in their rightful place. "'Proud don't get you money, mister.' That's what my pappy always told me." His shoulders, which had been almost straight, went back to their hunched, crooked look. "Well, see here, I gotta get back to the barn. Got a load of junk to untangle. Thank ye, again, Miz Bundle. For gettin' my boy back to me."

He walled toward the barn with purpose, body bent, interested in nothing other than his world of junk.

Vincent said, "Th-That g-g-goes for m-me, too. W-W-With all the h-h-hassle yesterday, I n-n-never did say, 'Th-thank-you.'"

As Barny exited the out-of-doors and disappeared into the barn, Vincent squeaked, "Odd w-w-w-orld! G-G-Gaw! You're n-n-n-not going to b-b-believe, this, but…"

He stopped and Viola placed a calming hand on his arm. He began again, slower and more deliberate this time. "You kn-know that C-C-Cornelius? A while back, the P-P-Professor told m-m-me s-somethin' about that g-g-guy you're talking about — my relative, C-C-Cornelius Veakey. I r-r-remember his name because, w-well, I think I was n-n-named for him — d-d-down the line some, of course."

"You were named after him?"

He swallowed hard and continued, "M-M-My middle name. C-C-Cornelius. Just l-l-like th-that g-guy! 'V-V-Vincent *Cornelius* Veakey'," he said proudly. "M-M-Matter of fact, now I r-reckon, P-P-Pop's name is Barnabus *Lawrence* V-V-Veakey."

"Lawrence…" Mrs. Bundle pondered, then cried out, "*Yes!*"

Vincent smiled, "I'm r-right? Isn't L-L-Lorenzo *I*-talian for Lawrence?"

"Why, yes it is! And certainly indicates another connection to the artist, one would think. What else do you remember Professor Watson telling you?"

"Well, t-t-truth be told, I c-come to Professor W-W-W-Watson a while back l-l-looking for historical information on the V-V-Veakey clan, you know, like I t-told you before, at the j-j-jail. He was really n-n-nice, like I t-t-told you. M-Mostly, h-he was a f-f-friend." His eyes moistened and he said softly, "He sure l-l-loved all that ge-ge-genealogy stuff. I f-f-found it p-p-p-pretty interesting, too."

Mrs. Bundle tread on the next subject gingerly, "Actually, Vincent—and Viola—there's more to this story that I think, in a roundabout way, may indirectly involve the *both* of you."

He instinctively moved closer to Viola, protectively, and Mrs. Bundle continued, "Nothing bad, mind you, quite the contrary, in fact. Knowing how your father feels about the Tudhopes, though, and," she turned to Viola, "vice versa, how your dad feels about the Veakey name, Viola, I didn't want to spring this on Barny just yet, until we—you, Viola, and I—had a chance to discuss things."

They both looked at her expectantly, eyes hopeful.

"You might want to sit down."

Nearby, a broken down and rusted settee with vinyl cushions silently begged to be used after all these years. Vincent and Viola took a seat.

She handed the obituary notice from 1863 to the couple. They took their time and, together, read through it, silently and carefully.

Viola gasped when she came to the part about Jeremiah Tudhope.

"*Tudhope?*"

Mrs. Bundle nodded, "That's right. A Tudhope." She went back, and when she was finished reading, Mrs. Bundle said, "Viola, I was wondering…would it be possible for me to take a look at your letters and diary that you found upstairs? I have a bit of a hunch…"

She nodded.

"It may have to wait a few days until after the Festival. What I'd like to do, when I have time—is to take a look at those old letters of yours before I make any conclusions. As far as talking to your parents tonight…that is your choice, Vincent. My suggestion, though, would be that you both sit tight and keep a lid on things—that is to say, I think we can work things out peaceably between Barny and your parents. I really do believe we can. We just need a little time."

Vincent was dubious. "How l-l-long do w-we have to k-k-keep things under wr-wraps? I w-w-want to tell the w-w-world about us t-t-two. I l-love her!"

His sweetheart gave his hand a slight tug. "Vinnie, dear, I trust Mrs. Bundle. If she says wait…"

They looked at each other and gave a mutual slight nod of their heads.

Mrs. Bundle smiled broadly. "Good! It won't be long, I can assure you. One way or another, I promise you both that we're going to straighten things out between the Tudhopes and the Veakeys. Deal?"

They both nodded again, more hopeful.

Viola's face glowed, her smile clear of all angst as she gazed at Vincent, and the two lovebirds gave each other a quick peck. Mrs. Bundle thought it was the sweetest thing she had seen in a very long time.

Viola tugged on his sleeve once again. He gazed at her lovingly. "What is it, dear?"

She pointed to the ground. They all looked down.

She gave him a knowing look and pointed again to the ground, mouthing words that looked like "*the hole*" to him.

Mrs. Bundle saw the gesture but had no idea what Viola meant, so she waited for an explanation.

It was the first time Mrs. Bundle had ever heard Vincent Veakey laugh. He threw his head back and the sound was like a melodious but very wild jungle bird. It echoed through the junkyard, bouncing off the tin and metal like nobody's business.

Finally, he wiped his eyes and said apologetically to Mrs. Bundle, "My dear V-V-Viola h-h-here,…well…she w-w-wants me to sh-show you s-s-something…" he cleared his throat and said very boldly, "Actually, *I* was w-w-wonderin', if you'd take a look at s-s-something I've b-b-been workin' on."

Game as ever, Mrs. Bundle said, "Of course!"

"C-c-come on," he waved gleefully for her to follow him, "this way."

He led her out behind the barn, Viola bringing up the rear. They trudged through tiny, tight, winding paths surrounded by mountains of rubble, red-rusted unidentifiable wreckage and unknown debris, until they finally came to a large piece of rusted, corrugated tin roofing strewn haphazardly on the stacked ground.

By all appearances, it looked like just another pile of junk.

Vincent pulled it aside slowly, and another magical journey began for Mrs. Bundle.

Chapter Thirteen

Down the Rabbit Hole...
Again

*"The rabbit-hole went straight on like a tunnel for some way,
and then dipped suddenly down, so suddenly that Alice had
not a moment to think about stopping herself before she found
herself falling down what seemed to be a very deep well."*
—*Alice in Wonderland*

And so, it was with total abandon and a queer sense of freedom (mixed with a dose of sheer expectation) that she followed blindly behind the strange being known as Vincent Veakey. He turned and looked at her, smiled intensely, and then his head disappeared below.

Just as before, when entering the library knee wall portal to find Cracker, Mrs. Bundle was reminded once again of Alice following the rabbit down the rabbit hole. Today's events were reminiscent of the classic's continuous twists and turns, the mad characters, the never-ending excitement—right now, she knew *just* exactly how Alice felt. She lowered herself gently, step by step, into a secret inner sanctum of total darkness.

Without one iota of fear, filled with anticipation, and totally without sight, she followed behind Junior, holding onto the back of his shirt as they wended their way down five, and then a sixth, barely discernible, roughly-hewn steps until she finally landed at the bottom, both their sets of feet making a "*kerplop*" sound on the cold dirt floor. She moved one step forward, and Viola reached the bottom landing directly behind her. They were all so close to each other that she could feel Viola's breath on her neck. She was sure Vincent could feel the slight tremble of excitement of her hand through his shirt.

Junior lit a match and the cavernous hole came ablaze briefly. All she could see was directly in front of her nose as she was blinded by the immediate beam of a sharp, close light—a flashlight—shone directly into her eyes.

Mrs. Bundle's *sotto voce* whisper burst forth, "'*Dear, dear! How queer everything is to-day!*'" She giggled as Alice's prophetic words came to her lips. The stars and squiggles dissipated slowly in front of her eyes, finally adjusting to the semi-darkness.

"D-D-Don't be a-f-f-fraid, M-M-M-Miz B-B-Bundle! I c-call this place—*m-my pl-place*—'Th-The *Hole*!'"

"Well, of course you do!" she laughed.

He reached down with one hand and picked up the thick orange twine of an extra heavy duty extension cord. When he plugged it into another end, the room became ablaze with a soft, beautiful, golden shaft of light.

Mrs. Bundle was mesmerized by the extent of Vincent Veakey's personal magical transformation. His face, like the room, was lit up like a Christmas tree; he looked like a small boy with his first toy.

Describing the "rooms" in this magical underground world—the world of Vincent Veakey, created, owned completely, and imagined by him—was like describing a delightful new planet. He had completed the subterranean space with ultimate privacy and serene freedom in mind—an area where he was open to think and create without the negative influences of the outside world above. It was cool, calming, and very quiet; one almost forgot where they actually were—which was, eight feet below the ground.

First, he had created a hallway measuring approximately 10' in width, 5' long, and about 6' in height. Sturdy uprights braced the underground room, which had then been covered with plywood and soft dirt. One small, discreetly-placed, makeshift skylight was visible, allowing in a small amount of natural light during the daytime. Doubling as a second exit to be used only in an emergency, it presented itself outside as an old storm window cleverly embedded sideways into the pile of rubble with a haphazard heap of dirt strewn around and over it.

A single light powered by a buried electrical cable from Barny's house several hundred feet away lit the interior of this space. Vincent pointed and said, "I ran a 400-foot long extension cable to the house and then attached a surge protector!" The underground space was further lit with clip lights.

Astro turf covered the floor like a natural, soft rug.

He led her slowly, deeper into the space; Mrs. Bundle was awed to see two additional underground rooms. He explained how he had shoveled everything by hand. It had taken Vincent a long while but he had used the excess dirt to build walls and then dumped the rest to create bunkers to camouflage his secret den. Eight-foot-long rafter beams had been stretched over the top and were supported by wall branches, similar to a mineshaft, and then a layer of plywood, which was then covered in dirt.

The first large room measured approximately 12' by 12'.

"This is my therapy room." Vincent chortled.

To Mrs. Bundle, it looked more like an anteroom for working or laboring. It was primarily empty, save for a wooden worktable with safety glasses and various tools, a metal folding chair, and some odd-looking paraphernalia (generally described by anyone as junk) which was located in small piles throughout the room.

He picked up a blowtorch from the floor. In his exquisite, finely-shaped hands, the tool seemed to take on a more advanced role. He did not light the torch off, but held it briefly, and then lovingly put it down.

"Here." He pointed to where there was a large opening (devoid of a door) directly off this room. With a wild smile, he motioned her ahead of him and whispered, "W-W-Welcome to my G-G-Gallery!"

He flicked on another makeshift floor switch and, suddenly, the room was transformed into a thousand little pin-pricks of light. This, clearly, was Vincent's inner sanctum, the end of the road, the last space in his underworld of privacy, and Mrs. Bundle stepped inside a wonderland of imagination.

She could barely believe what she saw.

Astonishingly, this main room, measuring 15' long, 14' wide, and about 7½' in height, was filled to the max with incredibly large, wildly inventive, metal sculptures in varying degrees of completion.

As Mrs. Bundle looked around in awe, she saw that this area was, really, a gallery filled to the gills with amazing metalwork, underground art that he had created using the junk his father had collected from the dump next door.

"I b-b-been m-making art p-p-p-pieces out of all the j-junk! B-B-Been doing it f-f-for years. All on m-my own."

Silently leading the way, Vincent Veakey, metal artist, took Mrs. Bundle's arm and drew her from one sculpture, then to another. Each piece was more beautiful, more fanciful than the next. It was a wonderful odyssey the likes of which Mrs. Bundle had really never seen or experienced.

One word kept passing her lips: "*Fantastical!*"

"Look, Mrs. Bundle." Viola pointed to the welded signature on one piece.

Vincent had signed his artwork with the same monogram on the tree by the stream: one "V" with a curlicue along with an attached, upside-down arrow to represent the other "V" in his name.

"Isn't it all...so beautiful?" The pride on Viola's face gave her the appearance of a child enjoying a sweet, gooey cookie and she beamed first at Vinnie, then at Mrs. Bundle.

And, as his Muse, she had bragging rights to be sure. How ironic that, from the piles of debris up above, had come these magical creations below. Looking above her, Mrs. Bundle realized the blowtorch sculptures were just the beginning. Metal mobiles, hung from the ceiling and again, composed primarily of odd pieces of junk, had been transformed into beautiful, ethereal pieces of suspended art.

"I'm absolutely awestruck!" Mrs. Bundle said. "*How* do you do this?"

"I use the welder and a blowtorch, of course, and bending t-tools and fasteners of all types, to cr-create all my w-works." He seemed so calm, so together; his usually-nervous, stuttering voice had been transformed into a new "quiet speak" voice, strangely calmer, significantly more articulate in this subterranean space. "I try to use all the old s-s-scrap metal, the ugliest, the least desirable stuff that comes in. I like to turn it into something else...more beautiful."

Mrs. Bundle looked at the steel sculptures where Vincent had notched and knocked out perforated holes, giving the piece a lacy, fragile appearance. A certified welder, he wielded his industrial blowtorch as if it were a crochet hook, burning dainty, intricate designs into the heavy, flat, scrap metal pieces. Some of the artist's hanging wall sculptures looked like large steel doilies and massive crocheted beams of steel, gracefully perforated with a masculine, artistic flair.

There was a huge twisted form of a fish on the wall directly in front of her, massively constructed in sheets of bent, rusty, weather-beaten metal. Shaped haphazardly into wonderful waves of moving scales and fins, the fish's whole body appeared to be in perpetual motion, ending with a whimsically active, flipped tail fin.

As they moved on, he demonstrated one of his metal sculptures, called "Motion In Progress." "This is my n-newest stuff," he said shyly.

The piece ingeniously utilized a series of old cog-wheels set into a large frame, with large metal tube pieces passing through the middle of each cog-wheel. He pointed to the first cog-wheel, the largest of them all, at the bottom of the piece and smiled, then laughed gleefully, "*Go ahead*! T-Turn it!'

She reached over and turned the first wheel. Instantly, there was motion as the cog-wheel's inside tube, set in and through the wheel as a connector, allowed the wheel to turn easily; its motion started a series of other progressive motions throughout the work of art. Gradually, other connecting wheels turned, moving slowly upward toward the top of the piece.

At one point, a lever came to life and pumped up and down, then a spiraling metal pinwheel whirled and whirled, creating an illusion that its coiled metal was one solid, swirling piece. As each smaller cog turned, the first wheel continued to create a reaction to the motion. Finally, a wrought iron, beveled-glass lantern located at the pinnacle of the sculpture seemed to radiate sparks as its wick was touched off, and then burst into flames!

"*How* did you do that?" Mrs. Bundle asked, awestruck.

"Easy." His face shone with exhilaration and he spoke freely, "The wheel creates m-motion, which creates m-more motion through the other moving parts, thus creating friction—then action! I c-call it *Active Art*." He picked up a lighter from the nearby table. "See? I g-got the idea from this!"

He flicked the lighter's wheel and the flame burst forth. "S-Same concept, only on a gr-grander scale."

He showed her four other Active Art pieces, each one more extraordinary than the last. Motion and junk had been intricately combined to create spectacular pieces of art in action. Not only cleverly conceived, they were beautiful to look at; Mrs. Bundle was impressed.

"I really think you need to display these for the world to see. I think you have a wonderful talent, Vincent. Really, I do!" She pointed upward. "You know?" She could tell convincing him of that fact would be somewhat difficult. She looked intensely into his deep-set eyes. "You have expressed yourself here, in a very difficult venue, and I think it's absolutely *fantastical* to look at. You have what's called… *allure*." She smiled mischievously, thinking how much Cracker would love to be here and hear her say that word. "These should be on display where people can enjoy them!" She tried to appeal to his pecuniary sense. "And maybe purchase them, too?"

"That's *exactly* what I told him!" Viola said.

Joining forces, Mrs. Bundle said, "Well, I agree! I think I know *just* the spot to introduce your talent to the world."

His face took on a doubtful look.

Viola said excitedly, "I know, too!"

Mrs. Bundle gained steam, "That's right! The Dog Days of Summer Art Festival! You've got plenty of time! All of four days! You just need to get organized and set up, of course."

Viola nodded passionately. "Yes, that's what I thought, too! You can do it, Vinnie, I'm sure!"

Mrs. Bundle asked, "How 'bout it?"

At first he looked like he was going to discard the idea. Used to being rebuffed, he was inclined to be the first to discourage rejection rather than face any possibility of more. Then, he looked at Viola, who nodded again and took his hand.

He turned to Mrs. Bundle and, with inspired confidence, said passionately, "Sure, why not?"

Part V:
AUGUST

Chapter One

Chaos Turns Into…
All is Ready

The room wasn't just abuzz, it was downright noisy. Each person, intent on making their point, was descending on Mrs. Bundle with equal intensity.

Most vocal was Weezy Bunton, whose voice was booming directly over Lonnie Macomber's oblong head while Elvina Wrinkle chattered away in her Southern drawl directly behind her. Lonnie, seated in front of Mrs. Bundle and being, thereby, shoved in tight as a sardine at the long table underneath Weezy's massive chest, seemingly took no notice of the chaos as he gazed up at Mrs. Bundle and continued on affably with his comments and questions for the Head of the Festival.

Althea was taxi-ing throughout the room, trying to organize the volunteers into some semblance of order, but no one seemed to be listening. Dakota Squibb followed blithely behind her, whistling a cheery, warbling rendition of "Meet Me in St. Louis, Meet Me at the Fair," at which point he accidentally bumped into her and she shooed him away. Not at all discouraged by her rebuff, he moved on, chatting amiably to each new arrivee.

Hazel Balshemnik's strong German accent drifted across the room as she discussed the finer points of baking pastry with the Pie Booth chair, Barbra D'Acunet. "Ve *dun't* vant to mix too much, do ve? The crust, it must be so crumbling it melts right in your *mout*! You agree?

Oh, *yoohooo*, Lettie, ve must axe you —" Her question was lost in the hustle and bustle.

Mary Clancy (Nick and Anthony's mother) was attempting, over Weezy's voice and without much success, to tell Mrs. Bundle that there was just no more room anywhere for all the donated household items to be sold on the "Odds and Ends" table, while the Dueling Daisies Gardening Chair, Mrs. Snargle (the delinquent Harold's mother), wanted to know how much she should charge per pot for the annuals in full bloom at the Plant table.

Louis Montembeau, usually panic-stricken in these emergency scenarios, seemed totally calm as he reviewed his "to-do" list and sat ready and waiting for the meeting to begin; waving to her from afar, he pointed to his watch, and made a forward rolling motion with his hand.

To complicate matters further, Mrs. Bundle's biggest festival protester was also in attendance and he was already complaining and causing trouble. Since his late-night call to Mrs. Bundle, he had been making a big show of his so-called rebirth as a compliant advocate of the Festival. Old habits die hard, though, and the self-designated "Head Judge of all the Homemade Food Contests" was, at this moment, fighting with the head organizer of the Preserves table about exactly where her entry's prized jams and jellies would be located on the Village Green. Looking down his perpetually-tanned, thin, long nose, his sunglasses perched atop his large mane of dark black hair, Armand stated contentiously, "I'm sorry, Clara Jean, but this is where the Judges have decided your table should go. To that end, *our* word is final. Don't buck the system, please."

His imperious voice grated on Mrs. Bundle, and she had immediately called over the introverted, countrified woman. Amidst the commotion, the poor homemaker was beside herself, beseeching Mrs. Bundle to move her closer to the other food table entries and not to leave her over by the sheep-shearing and miniature pony ride sites, which had no tree cover and would melt all the jellies in their parrifin-covered jars (not to mention would stink of manure from the neighboring penned areas).

Meanwhile, Walter Andersen was embroiled in a heated discussion with Constable Benois about where all the cars would and should be parked so as not to create a traffic jam in downtown Pillsonville.

Finally, with a gentle raised arm, Mrs. Bundle was able to obtain order where there was previously pandemonium.

In her quiet, steady voice she said, "Please, please, everyone, take a seat. I promise we'll get to each committee and address all these last minute details and concerns. And we'll try to move things along as quickly as possible so we get out of here at a reasonable time."

Speedily, one and all found seating at the long tables in the Town Hall first floor dining hall and the meeting began.

Mrs. Bundle stood in front of the large group of committee chairs, assistants, volunteers, and vendors. As she looked out at the crowd and smiled broadly, she reckoned it was natural that people would be on edge, this being Thursday, the night before "THE BIG WEEKEND." It was all coming together, bit by bit, but with a pinch of chaos thrown in for good measure.

Althea joined Mrs. Bundle and started handing out sheets of paper to all in attendance, a group of about fifty-odd energetic and spirited volunteers.

Mrs. Bundle began. "Welcome, everyone! I am so excited to say we are *finally* here! I must say, without the help of all of you, we just could not be here, where we are right now, on the threshold of what appears to be a pretty big *wingding*!"

Everyone laughed, and she went on. "Take a look at what Althea is handing out to you. It's an agenda for this evening's meeting—mostly to make sure I've got everything included and in order from the beginning, that is, from the events planned beginning tomorrow night 'til the big finale Sunday afternoon—the Auction! As I said before, I promise we will get to you and the important part you are playing in this weekend's events. I know you have questions and concerns and I want to address them in an orderly, timely fashion."

Tim Scott, who sat beside his lanky brother-in-law Lonnie, raised his hand.

"Yes, Tim?"

He stood up, a full five-foot-five in height, round-faced, and bald. In his high-pitched voice he said,"I see you got me *way* down here on this agenda at Item number 11. And, well, Bessie May's not feeling too chipper—nothin' serious, mind you, just getting' over a cold or the flu or something, really ugly it is." He shook his head in dismay."And in this blasted heat, too! She's been right thorny to deal with, I want to tell you! Sneezin' and fussin' all week!"

Weezy Bunton interrupted, yelling from behind,"Gaw! Don't I know it! She's a mess! Sneezin' all over that package I picked up yesterday! Hope I don't get what she's got."

Elvina Wrinkle, who sat demurely beside her, gulped and tried, without success, to keep a straight face.

Tim Scott's face blanched as he tried to disregard Weezy's comments."Well, it's not like we got extra staff to run things at the P.O. when someone gets sick. There's just Arletta, when she feels up to it, that is. She *is* seventy-five, you know. And Lonnie here, but he's out on the postal run most all the day."

Lonnie Macomber turned round and nodded agreeably at the group, his large Adam's apple wobbling like crazy with every nod, and raised his index finger to make a point of his own, but was cut off by Weezy's guffaw.

"*Ha!*" Startled that Tim's nose might be out of joint due to her comments, Weezy hollered across the large room,"*Jeeeez* Louise! Hold on to your britches, Timmy! I wasn't complainin'! Just statin' the facts as I see em! And, don't think I ain't appreciative of all you and your family does to run the Postal."

Her recant seemed to appease him, and he continued on, addressing his comments to a very patient Mrs. Bundle."Like I was sayin', she's been down with the flu or some such all week. Now, it's her sinuses that's backed up real bad. Wicked, from the way she keeps honkin', trying to get some relief! Might be an abscess. Arletta's with her now, but *she* goes to bed at 7:30 sharp—right after 'Jeopardy.' So, anyway, I was wonderin'— I gotta get to the pharmacy afore it closes, seein' as how she's run out of her antihistamine, and I'd appreciate it if you could move me up a notch on this schedule so's I can get home to her."

"No problem, Tim. Why don't you go first with your report?" Hushed but resigned grumbling could be heard throughout the room, which Mrs. Bundle appropriately ignored, asking, "So, are you all set with the Stamping Booth?"

"Yup. Got all the supplies, and we'll be set up first thing Saturday mornin' as planned and get a good start right out of the gate. Arletta'll be running the P.O. 'til noon when it closes, then it'll be the three of us there, stampin' away." He jerked his thumb and said, "Course, Lonnie here will be doin' his own thing over across the way with the Antique Motorbike ride."

Lonnie beamed innocently at the group. "That's right!" Rising to his feet excitedly, the large Adam's apple working overtime, he promoted his service in his best barker voice, "Stop by and get a ride on the '45 for the time of your life! Only two bucks a pop!" People twittered politely and he grinned widely. He went on to guarantee that the trike bike would be specially adorned with ribbons and old college banners. (He didn't mention that he would also provide, free of charge, his long-winded but good-humored views on everything from how to hold a coffee cup and drive at the same time to which state in the Union had the most mail during the holiday season.)

Tim watched with a bored look that said he'd seen the spiel before, "Oh, sit down, Lonnie, and take a load off."

Obeying his brother-in-law, Lonnie sat down meekly, demonstrating what everyone already knew: that poor Lonnie was the last bird in line in the postal family pecking order.

Tim puffed his chest and intoned, "Back to the Stampin' Booth! We figure we'll get about four or five hundred, easily, toward the Library Fund."

Polite clapping from the group followed this statement, and he added, puffing up his chest just a smidge larger, "And that's not takin' into account the special orders we sign up, which we figure should bring in another four or five hundred, if we're lucky."

Louder, still-polite clapping, and he concluded his report with, "Which should give us, the Stamping Booth *all* on its own, a grand total of close to a thousand big ones!" He nodded genially, his face flushed and round, at the final smattering of claps and he sat down.

Mrs. Bundle thanked him, and the henpecked husband left the hall immediately to minister to his wife in her hour of need while the ever-amiable Lonnie stayed for the rest of the meeting.

From that point on, the agenda was followed to a 'T' and the first hour was quickly eaten up as each committee person gave their report.

Zack Benois, the octogenarian village Constable, was all set with public safety and mentioned he had plenty of orange cones left over from the Horse Pull last Memorial Day. His primary job,(apart from organizing the parking situation) was the *Dog Days of Summer Doggie (and Cat) Parade*, which would start the Festival off with a bang on Saturday morning.

He reported about thirty youngsters had officially registered their animals; the decorated dogs and cats were sure to be a big hit. His account drew chuckles when he said Samantha Sevigny's mother had asked if her four-year-old daughter could walk in the parade with Honey, her pet rabbit, and Zack had made an emergency executive decision to let the girl and her animal in.

"Hope it won't cause any undue controversy," he intoned officially, "seein' as we'd already decided to let the cats in." He finished by saying the parade would circle around the Village Green, that the Parade committee volunteers had decorated his cruiser with a *Dog Days of Summer* banner, and his son Mort would lead the parade in his vehicle while Zack monitored the activity from the sidelines, making sure all went without a hitch.

Next, Carl Andersen reported that his band, The Pillson Rhythmares, were all set to provide the best Big Band dance music possible for the Friday night concert at the Gazebo on the Village Green. The musicians' spouses were all set to pass the Library Fund hat at various times throughout the evening during their performance.

It was at that point that Armand Limpert added his two cents with a fairly positive comment, "The whole town will be at the concert Friday night—it's a *great* way to kick off the Festival. And, it will keep people occupied while *we* do our important work—judging. The judging committee is going to have a *very* tight schedule that evening, organizing and reviewing all the food entries in all the different categories in able for us to give out awards on Saturday."

Walter Andersen added, "Gaw, with everyone on the Village Green, the rest of Pillson will be like a ghost town!"

"Item 5?" Mrs. Bundle looked up from her sheet, intent on keeping things on track. "Marcus?"

Marcus Hotchkiss, Don of the Guild, rose to give his Art Auction report, adding that there was a late, but exceptional entry; that of Vincent Veakey, who the Guild, he said, was very proud to have chosen to showcase one of his unusual metal Active Art pieces. This comment drew considerable murmurs of surprise and speculation from the Peanut Gallery as he quickly moved on to describe the other donated art works, none of lesser quality than the other, all obtained from the surrounding art galleries, including some pricier pieces from Woodstock.

He reported that he and his committee expected many interested dealers from outside the area to come and bid during the Grand Finale Art Auction, indicating the final tally of donated monies might far exceed their initial projection. This drew a huge round of applause from the group of volunteers.

And so it went, each committee head giving their report. After another half-hour, they were about halfway through the agenda, and Mrs. Bundle suggested they all take a ten-minute break to wet their whistle. "Ten minutes only, mind you!" she said good-naturedly. "There are cold drinks in the kitchen for you all."

The group moved quickly from the dining hall to the kitchen, and Mrs. Bundle waved toward Dakota. "Dakota? Could I grab you and Keith for just a sec? I'd like to go over some minor details with the Talent Show Committee!"

Dakota Squibb and Keith Kittredge stepped up to the front table and Mrs. Bundle quickly went over the list of acts for Saturday night's show, discussing the queue of performances.

"Is everything all set upstairs?" she asked, referring to the large Community Room where the Talent Show was being held.

"Seems to be!" Dakota said brightly, and added, "I've been really amazed at all the local talent."

Keith nodded enthusiastically. "I gotta tell you, it's going to be a bang-up show. Really top-notch, if I do say so myself! If we pack the hall upstairs—which it appears very likely—I figure we'll bring in about two thousand dollars in donations."

"I think we *may* need extra seating." Dakota added.

"How 'bout if we bring over additional folding chairs from the elementary school?" Mrs. Bundle suggested.

Dakota nodded. "Good idea! I'll take care of that tomorrow before dress rehearsal."

"Is the dress rehearsal still scheduled for three o'clock?"

"That it is! Everyone is very excited, especially the kids acts. Why, our little Erin Corrigan is beside herself! She can't wait!"

Thrilled with their concerted effort, she thanked them profusely, "Really, thank you, Dakota, for taking this on. You too, Keith! You're both troopers! You've made my job easy!"

"No problem. It's been a real hoot!" Keith said.

As they moved toward the kitchen, Mrs. Bundle touched Dakota's arm. "Dakota, I want to thank you, too, for being so kind to Erin. She has loved being your 'right-hand girl' for the talent show. It's kept her occupied this summer, that's for certain."

"Kind? Me? Why, I really like the little monkey!" He smiled. "She makes me laugh."

"Yes, me too!"

"Like I just said before, she's very excited. I talked to Jack, and he has given her permission to stay for the whole dress rehearsal tomorrow. I promised him I would bring her to him at the bandstand for the concert." He glanced over his shoulder and his eyes brightened.

Althea, face flushed and looking particularly fetching this evening, had appeared from nowhere and joined their conversation. "Good grief, L! Someone said the Talent Show will probably be a sell-out! I'm worried about capacity. Do you think we need to get more—"

Dakota raised his palm and tried to soothe her jittery nerves. "Already taken care of, Althea. I'll go over to the school with the truck tomorrow and pick them up before the dress rehearsal."

She opened her rosebud mouth and then closed it, eyeing him somewhat peevishly. She asked with exasperation, "How is it you always seem to know what I'm going to say? You are continually finishing my sentences. Frankly, it's rather…annoying."

He smiled, teeth sparkling white, eyes full of delight, and tapped his salty-gray-haired temple. "One day you will realize what a rocket scientist I truly am. I'm always one step ahead of you, and don't you forget it!"

Althea rolled her eyes at Mrs. Bundle, who couldn't help but notice the uncontrollable smile her best friend was having a hard time hiding.

He added, "Besides, I enjoy seeing you act quirky."

"Quirky?" She flushed and the smile faded as she tried to find an appropriate answer.

He overlooked her obvious disapproval and changed the subject. "By the way, I may need your help tomorrow," he cajoled gently, "that is, if you're going to be around."

She huffed uncomfortably and said, "Of course, I'll be around. Good grief! You're not going to ask me to fill in for someone and play the spoons or anything, are you?"

He laughed, "No, no, no. See? That's just *exactly* what I mean. Heavens, woman, you just never fail to crack me up." He controlled his expression and said seriously, "No, it's just that, if I get tied up helping," he patted Mrs. Bundle's arm, "and our Head Organizer, here, will have her hands full, so I cannot prevail upon her, I may need you to wait with Erin Corrigan over at the Bandstand after the dress rehearsal until Jack arrives. He has to work late at Hudson's and may not be able to get away to pick her up until a bit after seven."

"Is that all? Of course, I can help with that, Squibb."

He rubbed his hands together."Good, I'll plan on meeting you..."

Thoroughly convinced Dakota's request was a lame excuse to spend Friday evening with Althea, Mrs. Bundle excused herself, smiling, and left them to joust back and forth. *Those two!* She stepped outside quietly for a quick breath of fresh air before restarting the meeting.

Most all of the group had trailed back into the room, but there were a few stragglers left outside. Lonnie Macomber was talking to, of all people, Sarah Church, who seemed, strangely, more animated in his presence. Snippets of their conversation could be heard, and it surprised Mrs. Bundle when she heard Sarah laugh outright. Lonnie was patiently (and with much detail) describing the inner workings of his vintage motorcycle engine, and Sarah seemed quite intrigued by the diatribe. Skirting their position softly, Mrs. Bundle stood just outside the door, in the darkening light, and drew in a deep breath.

Whew! She thought, *it's still hot, even at this time of night!* She stood silently for a few seconds, enjoying the chirping crickets.

She noticed Elvina Wrinkle, down at the end of the building, who appeared to be smoking one last cigarette before reentering the meeting. The flash of Elvina's long, thin lighter burst forth, and she leaned against the building wall.

Observing her with keen interest was the dandified Armand Limpert who, by all appearances, was doing his usual "invasion of personal space" thing. Elvina was almost as tall as he, and she blew the smoke out slowly, almost with deliberation, directly into his face.

Mrs. Bundle laughed to herself. *That'll show you*, Armand, she thought as she watched the casual interplay. If anyone could put him in his place, the experienced Elvina could. *Why*, Mrs. Bundle wondered plaintively, *does he do that?* She knew from her own experience just how uncomfortable it was to have him lean in that way, and she gave an involuntary shiver.

From her elbow, she heard Dakota Squibb whisper, "*Interesting, isn't it?*"

She turned and chuckled as he nonchalantly jerked his head toward Elvina and Armand.

"Yes, *very*," she said playfully. "Aren't you jealous?"

He chuckled in return. "Personally, Lettie, I like a more spirited chase."

Concentrating on Armand's interaction with Elvina, Mrs. Bundle observed his wide mouth moving seductively, talking to Elvina as he moved in closer. *Doesn't he ever learn?* She watched, intrigued by the wiles of Elvina. The bleach blonde took in one last drag, quickly stubbed out the cigarette, and then turned languidly, unperturbed by his closeness and clearly disinterested in his advances, her face impassive as she moved lazily past him.

He was left standing there, the theatrically-strong features of his face bemused and, yes, she thought, almost confounded.

Good for you, Elvina! Armand strikes out again.

Elvina, like a radar device honing in on its subject, spied Dakota in the shadows behind Mrs. Bundle and her whole demeanor changed.

Her chartreuse eyes became hazy and her voice took on its soothing lilt as she said with a small titter, "*Darlin'* man! You've been avoiding me! Do you have time for a drink after the meeting, honey? Lucy's at home watching TV. We could go ova—"

He stopped her abruptly. "No, not tonight, Elvina. I've had quite a day today, and I've got a big day tomorrow."

She shrugged and shifted her attention to Mrs. Bundle. "Hey, Lettie. Great job in there. You and Althea should be congratulated for pulling this together. How'd you eva do it? Who would have eva thought it would really happen? Why, Ah was tellin' Weezy just the other day—"

At that moment, Weezy Bunton's large head, surrounded by the expanse of tight, steel-gray curls, poked through the doorway with a vengeance and she barked unceremoniously, "Hey, Lettie! Let's get this show on the road, how 'bout it?"

Mrs. Bundle rolled her eyes graciously at the two of them and, per Weezy's directive, resumed the meeting promptly.

***

The rest of the meeting flew by: Bake-off and Bake Sale tables (Barbra D'Acunet, Chairperson); Canning Committee (pickles, jams, and preserves competition, Clara Jean Barker, Chair, whose was relieved to learn her booth could, in fact, be squeezed in neatly between the home-made pies and cookies tables under cover of the large maple trees); Judging Committee (whose judging protocol was read imperiously and very thoroughly to all by Chair Armand Limpert and who also informed the group that his crony, Archie Plummer had been recruited, along with Terry Snargle, to be judges); Sheep-Shearing Pen (organized by Chair Walter Andersen who assured the group that Axel Conroy said he had five sheep "ready for a snippin" and he was "good to go"); Catering and Volunteer Food Booths (Cynthia and Hiram Richey); Advertising Committee,(headed by Ellie Waterhouse), followed by Kevin Trees (Chair for Final media and print promotion), Used Book Sale Table (Head Louis Montembeau, as usual on top of everything, indicating there would be a "Closed for the day—gone to the Dog Days of Summer Art Festival" sign—with an arrow pointing eastward toward the Village Green—on the Library front door all day Saturday, *just* in case anyone happened to stop by), the Jewelry Table (Hazel Balshemnik, Chair, who also added with a great amount of pride that she had donated five German "Bleck Forest" pies, and four "Apfelstrudels" for the Pie Table), the Plant table (Mrs. Snargle and Doc Dot Jackson)—and so on, down the long list, until an hour later, they had finally reached the very last item of the agenda.

Weezy Bunton, surrounded by a crew of volunteers, spoke up."Agenda Item *Number 20*—last but not least—that'd be us! Me and my assistant, Elvina…"(Elvina smiled graciously),"…we got our report right here!"

The large, efficient woman raised her heavy frame and stood, instantly taking command of the room."In a nutshell…we're all set! Lettie, you don't even need to spend more than a minute here on this!"

Elvina sat smugly beside Weezy, smiling a cloudy, lethargic simper of utter boredom and, unable to hide her feelings, covered an obvious yawn and nodded,"*Tha's rha-a…*"

I'm sure, Mrs. Bundle thought benevolently, *Elvina would much rather be at her Bingo game at this time of night, rather than here.*"Thank you for being so patient, ladies. I appreciate it. I'm sorry you had to be last on the agenda."

Drawing her large body to full height, Weezy boomed,"Hey, no matter! Somebody's gotta be last, don't they? Okay. Here's the deal." Weezy ticked through her list."*Kid's Events*—Number One—Face-painting Table.' *Done!* Lizzy Turcotte," she turned and pointed to a very young-looking, very freckled, bright-red-haired, teenage girl sitting three seats down from Elvina,"is going to handle it all day Saturday with a couple of her teen friends who like to paint designs and such. Give a wave, Lizzie!"

Lizzie gave a shy smile and waved limply to the group.

Weezy continued on."Sunday, I'll be sittin' there with my Aunt Doris from Charlestown. She's a real artist—does that tole paintin' and everything— the kids will love it." With no comments from the tired group, she moved on quickly."Let's see," she looked down at her list,"*Football Throw, Frisbee Toss, Three-legged Race.* Done, done, *done!* Next—-*Egg and Spoon Run, Midget Horse Rides*—courtesy of Horace—my husband, you all know him! This'll be run by my two older boys…*all set!* Oh yes, and there's the *Cake Walk*—all cakes courtesy of that Peanuckle Sisterhood—you know, that women's group—they've been terrific! They've got *sixteen* cakes for the kids to do musical chairs to, which'll be done throughout the two days on the hour, as time permits." Looking around, she drove her point home with the sharp end of her pencil on her tablet."*Done, Done, done!*" Ending this part with a flourish, she took a deep breath, chest heaving and, almost bleating with excitement, exclaimed loudly,"*Gaw*! What a day it's gonna be, folks! That's it for the kids,'cept for the candy and fun food vendors, which ain't my department. That's for Hiram and Cynthia to handle, which seems, from their report, they got that covered."

She deftly turned her pad of paper over."Okay! *Number Two*— Hoola hoop contest. *Done*! That will occur at 3 o'clock Saturday on the Village Green. One contest for the kids, another for the adults. People can bet on who'll twirl the longest. We searched all over creation for enough hoola-hoops to go around. Final tally—the kids got *forty-four* hoola hoops brought in for the event! Can you believe it? Lucy Wrinkle'll be helping out with that, right, Elvina?"

The indifferent woman looked up and nodded."*Tha's rh-aa.*"

Weezy steamrolled ahead."Grand prize? Listen to this, folks! A free season ski pass—*donated*, mind you, we didn't have to pay one red cent—from Ascutney Mountain. One adult, one child!"

Looking up from her tattered list, she went on with an out-and-out rush of adrenalin."*Number Three*—Strawberry Shortcake Booth— *done*! This is *only* for Friday night, mind you, I got enough on my plate! Me and Elvina will run the show on that! Besides ourselves, we got a number of able bodies here,"(the rest of her crew sat solemnly by, looking like prisoners on a work release program),"who *will* all show up during the evening to help out! Ain't too much to puttin' together the fixin's for shortcake, so that should go off without a hitch. At three dollars and fifty cents a servin', we'll do a couple hundred servin's and make some good cash that night. All supplies—strawberries, whipped cream, paper bowls, and everything—the whole kit and caboodle, donated by DeMoulis's Market.'Cept the biscuits—those are being hand made by my mother-in-law, Daisy. *Number 4*—"

As she listened, a sense of jubilation spread over Mrs. Bundle, who, after hearing this final detailed report by Weezy, was certain they had found their all-around Chief Cook, Bottle Washer *and* new Art Festival Head Coordinator for *next* year.

Thank the Lord!!

Chapter Two

Friday at the Festival

She wasn't supposed to be here. She had broken a promise; but by the time she remembered that she had made that promise, she was already halfway across the Village Green. Resolutely, she had decided she would run as fast as she could, grab her prized instrument and be back in time, hopefully, without too many consequences.

She found it right where she had left it and knelt down beside it. Oh,(she planned with naïve cunning), if she could just move speedily, she would run *right* down the stairs, pick up her best friend (who was waiting patiently by the door), and hurry back to the bandstand. Her petite fingers moved quickly.

Just then, her ears picked up voices from somewhere close by. Low, reserved voices, to be sure. Whoever it was sounded as though they, like her, were being quite sneaky. She could hear their voices in undertones (*two of them*, she thought), and her inquisitive nature got the better of her. With great care not to make a sound, she peeked out from behind the heavy velvet, dark purple curtains.

She gulped as she saw them, arms wrapped passionately around each other, communicating in conspiratorial, intimate tones. Taken aback, she could barely make out their words; most of it came to her in sporadic bits and starts. She knew one thing for certain; she did not want to be here, or caught *anywhere* near here — that was for sure! However, when she tried to move, her feet stuck there, as though the soles of her thong sandals were covered with sticky bubble gum.

She overheard one person whisper, "Tonight...most excellent timing...do it while...busy...music."

The other said in muffled tones, "...better get going...should be loaded... timing is... library."

It was then that they kissed, a long, lingering, exceedingly ardent kiss.

"Yuck!" she said under her breath, thoroughly disgusted. She hated when grown-ups did that. Her stomach was queasy. She had seen enough.

Not bearing to watch any further, she turned and knelt down, clumsily closed the hard cover case, latching it as quietly as possible, and tiptoed softly across the large expanse of wooden stage.

Whew! If she could just get to those back stairs, no one would be the wiser, would they now?

She stopped dead in her tracks when she heard the loud, raucous screech. *Baauucckk!*

Uh-oh! Trouble with a capital "T"!

She panicked. *Oh, no! Better run, quick! Run!*

She scrabbled down the stairs as fast as she could.

As she turned the corner after the bottom step, a dark, menacing hand reached out from nowhere and grabbed her collar, jerking her back savagely. She strained in terror under the vice-like grip, craning her neck just in time to see another's hands held tightly around the neck of a rasping, hysterical Chester.

Then, like a tremendous thunderbolt, everything went black, fading into nothingness.

"Well then, where is she?" Althea stood, arms akimbo, watching Dakota Squibb.

"I told you! The talent show dress rehearsal finished, and we came right here per our agreement last night. Well, that is, we got sidetracked for a few minutes over there," he pointed, "at the midget horses paddock, and then Erin said she was *famished* so we bought a hotdog, and well, then *we* were looking all over for you and couldn't find you!"

"I told you I would be right here by the bandstand! When you didn't arrive on time," she pointed to her watch, "I went searching for you." She pointed accusingly, "You've got mustard on your shirt!"

He wiped the ochre-colored splotch on his golf shirt emblem, making it even worse, then scanned the area around them, which was quickly becoming congested with people.

"We must have missed each other in passing. We arrived here and as I said, we were looking all around for you. All of a sudden, the little imp got very upset, hollering like a banshee that she'd left her ukulele over at Town Hall! Uncle Carl, it seems, had promised her this morning that she could sit in with the band and play in the background. I told her to wait and that we *must* find you first. I turned around and saw you coming across the Green and waved to you, and then, when I turned back, Erin was gone! That must have been when the little monkey scooted off—before I knew it—before I could catch her!"

"Oh, good grief! With so much going on, who knows where she is now? I swear, Squibb…"

The Rhythmares were tuning up, their scales and tones becoming louder.

He raised his voice a hair to be heard over the instruments. "Right, there's no need to worry. She's back over there, I'm sure." He waved his hand toward Town Hall in the distance. "I would suggest we just go find her and give her what for. She's scared me to death!"

She looked anxiously through the crowd. "Well, let's find Jack so we can let him know we're going to look for her."

"He's not going to be here for a while." He looked at his watch, hesitated, then implored, "Please, Althea, no. He will certainly be furious she's gone off once again without letting anyone know or getting permission." He shook his head in frustration. "She's so bloody independent and impulsive! We don't need to get the little urchin in more trouble than she's already in. For that matter, *I'll* take the heat for it if she gets in trouble. It's *my* fault I didn't keep her in my sights."

She gave him a lopsided smile and said resignedly, "Oh, c'mon. Let's go find her."

They crossed the Village Green together, a fair distance, and headed down Main Street, rounding the corner. As they neared Town Hall, they passed by a breathless Armand Limpert, high-and-mighty as ever, who tried to breeze past them without acknowledgment.

Althea yelled across the street, "Hey, Armand! Have you seen the little girl, Erin Corrigan, over this way?"

His robust body still in motion, with breaths coming in huffs and puffs, he glared at them. "Erin *who*? That Corrigan brat?" They crossed the street, momentarily blocking his way.

"Well, have you seen her?"

He shook his head, disgusted. "Why would *I* have time to notice little girls, or anyone's kid for that matter, right now? I'm a very busy person, Althea. I'm trying to do my job. They need me over at the judges' table post haste—they can't start without me, in fact." He held out large hands bedecked with flashy gold jewelry and scrunched his shoulders in an "I don't know" motion and said with exasperation, "It's a *Fair*. She's a *child*, for God's sake, common sense would tell you she's probably over there stuffing her dirty little face at the cotton candy table or some other—"

"*Enough!*" The shout rang out. Dakota's usually amiable face was darkened with ire. "The *lady* asked you a simple question, sir. She does not need to hear a dissertation."

Armand, looking flushed and rather caught off guard by this confrontation, opened his big mouth. His huge lips wobbled and trembled slightly but nothing of substance came out.

"*Hell-ooo!*" A woman's voice shouted out from afar. "Armand? Oh, Armand!" The colorless Sarah Church stood waving her arms wildly from afar, calling from outside one of the fair tents. "Armand! Over here! We need you—over here!"

"You see? Now, may I go?" Briskly, he placed his ever-ready sunglasses over his angry eyes, turned on his heel, and left them standing there.

"He really is a *very* unpleasant fellow, isn't he?" Dakota spoke under his breath glaring after him. "If I had my way, I'd give him a thrashing he wouldn't forget anytime soon!"

"Well, we have other fish to fry. Just leave him be." Althea gave an irreverent chortle under her breath. "I must admit, though, it was nice to see someone *else* make verbal mincemeat of that buffoon. Well done, Squibb."

Just before reaching their destination, they ran into Archie Plummer, who was locking up the small building that housed his business—Picket Fence Realty—next door to Town Hall.

The sign above the storefront window said it all, "*Where all roads lead to your best real estate buy!*" In the large picture window, there were color photographs of this month's "Featured Properties."

He fiddled with the lock, turning round at the sound of their voices. "Hey, you two!" His cherubic face held its usual plastic smile.

Althea said, "Hi, Archie, working late?"

He looked a bit awkward as he placed the key in his pocket. "Uh-*huh*! Supposed to meet Armand over at the judges' station fifteen minutes ago, but I got hung up here. Putting together the last 'John Hancocks' on a big land deal. Really big." Verbose as usual, he couldn't help but toot his own horn. "But, I'm heading over to the festivities right now. Where are you guys bound?"

Dakota pointed to Town Hall. "Next door. Looking for our little friend, Erin Corrigan. Think she might be upstairs in the community room looking for her ukulele. You haven't seen her, have you?"

"The little girl with the rooster? *Gaw!* She's a real kick, isn't she! Thought I saw her go by a while back—I was with clients in the conference room." He jerked his head toward the closed, darkened office.

"Thanks!" Dakota sighed with relief. "I'm sure we'll find her." They moved away, intent on their mission. Dakota turned back, amiably, and asked, "See you at the concert?"

"I'll be there! In between judging the best strawberry jam or apple crumble pie and other goodies!" He patted his oversized belly and laughed.

They went their way and Archie Plummer scurried away, his fat little legs moving quickly toward the Judges' tent.

Moments later, Althea and Dakota entered the empty town hall building through the back door, knowing the front door would be locked during the hours the town hall was officially closed (although everyone in Pillson knew the back door to town hall was open most all the time).

"No need to use the front stairs," Dakota said.

"Right, we'll go up the back way."

They came through the back entry, circumventing the kitchen, and into the hallway heading round toward the back stairs entrance and leading up to the community room.

"More than likely, she left it behind the stage. That's where we've designated all the props to be left." He grumbled good-naturedly, "She has to bring that blasted ukulele with her everywhere she goes!"

"That and Chester!"

They both chuckled, and Dakota said, "Right! Good ol' Ches—"

Rounding the corner, they happened upon Elvina Wrinkle coming from the opposite direction, all in a dither.

Dakota held out his hands to stop her. "Whoa, hey there, Elvina! We almost had a collision! Why does everyone have to be in such a rush? What's so important?"

Flushed and breathless, Elvina brushed her hands over her long, immobile blonde tresses and her words came quickly, for her. "Well, colliding with you is pleasant anytime, Dakota, dear man! But Ah'm in a hurry, that's for sure, sugar! Weezy sent me over here on a last-minute food emergency. Ah'm just headed to the kitchen now—we're running out of strawberries for the shortcake *already*. We'll need even more…for after the concert, too. She says there'll be more in the icebox. Strawberries, that is…," She batted her eyes, gave Althea a sly, sidelong look, and turned back to Dakota. "What about *you*, darlin'? What brings you here?"

"Well, we're looking for someone. You haven't seen little Erin anywhere around, have you?"

"Erin? That little Corrigan imp, *raaght*? The one who was sells the rocks?" She chuckled. Her usual slow drawl returned. "Yes! Just did. Ah did see that *darling* child."

She smiled and waited while Althea did a slow burn; Althea asked, "Well? Where did you see her, Elvina?"

Dakota explained, "We need to find her. She was over at the bandstand just a few minutes ago, and then when I turned around, she was gone. I'm afraid it was my job to keep an eye on her. I seem to have lost her."

Elvina gazed at him for a split-second and then drawled, "You just missed her. Ah *just* saw her run down there," she pointed down the hallway toward the building's front entrance, "Lord! Ah think she went into the basement. Ah heard the door slam—scared me half to death! *Raaght* over there..." She gestured, clucking her tongue, "Ah wondered *what* on earth she was doing here alone. Ah hollered to her, and she said something about that annoying puny rooster having gotten away from her!"

"Oh, no!" Althea wailed. "Good grief! Chester? In the basement?"

"Ah would have offered to help her but Ah'm on a mission of my own and you know how Weezy can be. She was gone in a heartbeat, the little rascal. Should Ah have tackled her, grabbed her up like a sack of potatoes, and kept her here, with me?"

"Oh, no," Dakota said, "that's fine. We'll go get her. Don't worry."

Elvina followed them down the long, wide hallway, still somewhat breathless, and pointed at the large basement door. "This is where Ah saw her go, oh...not more than a few minutes ago."

Althea gave her studied look. "Are you all right, Elvina?" As she surveyed the woman's face, she noted her pale eyes were brighter, almost feverish.

Elvina drew a hand across her brow, took in a deep breath, and smiled. "*Hot*! It's this dang heat. Lord! Just you neva mind me. Ah'll be fine. Tha's *raaah*." She laughed her slow, husky laugh. "Ah'm just not used to hoofin' it like this, in this infernal heat!"

"Right." Dakota opened the solid oak door basement door and, gentleman that he was, moved aside for Althea to pass through first.

"Erin?" Althea yelled and peered down the long stairway. She said over her shoulder, "Where's the light switch?" Even with plenty of daylight left, it was pretty dark as she took her first step down the stairs. Skeptically, she said, "I doubt Erin would last a minute going down here." She turned to Dakota, then Elvina. "Elvina, are you *sure* you saw her over here? I'm…getting worried."

"As sure as that little button nose on your face, honey! Yes, she was down the stairs faster than a flipped flapjack. Look here. Here's a light switch, *raaght* there." She pointed to the hallway wall outside the entrance door and Dakota flipped the switch.

"Ah, that's better!" Althea started down the stairs. "Erin?" she called. Her voice echoed in the cavernous space. "Erin, are you down here, love?"

There was no answer. The quiet, musty air was interrupted by the musical sounds of "Moonlight in Vermont" coming across the Village Green.

Elvina's voice traveled down the stairs from the hallway. "Oh, drat! Ah've got to get back…the music's starting. And Weezy wants those strawberries…"

Althea, worried now, called out, "Erin! Where are you?"

Elvina grabbed Dakota's arm. "Look, if Ah don't get back, Weezy'll tan my hide. Dakota, sugar, Ah'm really not one for basements. They're so….creepy, don't you think?" Elvina quickly reached into her pocket and took out her cigarette case along with a shiny orange lighter, nervously taking a smoke from the pack.

Dakota, who had been quietly viewing the situation from the top of the landing, nodded absentmindedly. "You go ahead, get back to your strawberries and Weezy, Elvina. We'll find her, I'm sure she's around here somewhere. If not down here, upstairs, no doubt."

Elvina took a step back, lit her cigarette with steady deliberation, and smiled demurely, "Well, you stop back at the shortcake table after you've found her, y'hear?"

"Erin! *Erin?*" Althea's voice was becoming more urgent as she descended the first few steps into the mausoleum of a basement.

"Wait for me, Althea!" Dakota took the few stairs between him and Althea, then reached for the woman and grabbed her arm, quickly slipping past her, now, more than ever, intent on finding the little girl. With a sense of urgency, he yelled, "Erin, this isn't funny. *Where are you?*"

Over his shoulder, he said distractedly, "Elvina, thank you. Just leave that door ajar, would you?"

"Sure, honey, no problem. Good luck, you two!"

"*Erin?* Yes, thank you, Elvina."

He hadn't gotten to the sixth tread when the light bulb above him went out.

Althea and he both yelled together, "*Hey!*"

Almost instantaneously, they heard the heavy oak door shut with a solid *Bang!* followed by a dreadfully dead-sounding *Thunk!* as the door latched solidly behind them.

They automatically grabbed for each other in the darkness.

Chapter Three
Nervous Nellie

Weezy Bunton had her capable, hefty hands very full across town on the Village Green. Under the bright red Strawberry Shortcake tent, she barked orders like a commando to her three underlings as the line of hungry customers grew longer. Decked out in an old-fashioned long, white shift worn under a festively decorated strawberries apron and a white, fluffy bonnet encircling her steel gray curls, she looked as though she had just stepped out of a fantasy strawberry patch. Across her vast chest, haphazardly inscribed on the oversized apron bib was **Mother of All Who Love Strawberries.**

"No, honey, you need to cut the biscuits three ways!" She showed the young volunteer how to make the dessert, flabby arms flailing, her wide face flushed with the heat as she demonstrated with the precision of a gourmet chef. "Use that ladle, and glop it on. There, you got the hang of it! First, a layer of strawberries, then another atop t'other, that's good! Then plenty of whipped cream. Slather it right on, we gotta give 'em their money's worth--they ain't here to get just a taste!" She wiped her hands on her large apron, everything about her in ideal order and as impressive as her crew. She spun around to find Mrs. Bundle at her arm and didn't even flinch.

"Lettie. What's shakin'?"

"Weezy, have you seen Althea? I can't find her. Or Dakota Squibb?"

"Nope! Sure they ain't off spoonin' together? They got a thing goin' on. Anyone with two eyes blinded can see it!"

"Weezy, I'm serious. We can't find Erin Corrigan either."

"Her, too? That little one's gone missin' again? Don't she ever stay put? Gaw, I just never could get how come some people can't keep an eye on their kid!" She huffed disparagingly, hands busier than the slicer-dicer man. "At any rate….nope! Haven't seen any of the three! Not for awhile, anyway. I do recollect I seen Althea earlier, over there." She waved toward the parking lot. Heavy beads of sweat teetered on her broad brow, and she took a nearby paper towel and wiped her forehead. She threw the used article into a bucket under the table.

"Lettie, not to put you off, but…I kinda got my hands pretty occupied here right now. Gaw!" She handed an empty bowl to the timid volunteer beside her, nodding toward the waiting crowd, and shook her head in disgust. "Can't anyone stay put? Seems like everyone's gone missing now that it's busy!" She motioned to the long line and then to her skeletal crew, who were working like little ants, quickly, silently, and with precision. "Don't you know that gadabout Elvina left me high and dry a good ten-fifteen minutes ago. Said she had to go tinkle," she harrumphed disparagingly, "refused to use the Porta-Potty over yonder—and I haven't seen hide nor hair of her since."

It had been a busy day already for Mrs. Bundle, and her tired eyes searched the growing crowd for her right-hand organizer and best friend. "Oh, I'm sure she'll be back."

Where on earth were they?

Minutes before, Mrs. Bundle had left Louis, along with Cracker, at the Library Book Sale Table, where the head librarian was setting up for tomorrow's big opening day. Promising them both she would be right back as soon as she located Althea, she began her search of the busy festival grounds.

As she had come across the Green, she'd run into Walter Andersen, who had told her Jack was looking for Erin and Dakota Squibb, and did she know where they were? He said Jack was pretty upset, having made arrangements to meet him to pick up Erin when he got out of work. It was then that she told him she couldn't seem to find Althea, either, and that it was possible they might all be together, reminding herself of the plan she had heard Dakota and Althea formulating the night before. Accordingly, she and Walter had decided to split up and make the rounds separately and this was why she had ended up here, lastly, at Weezy's colorful booth.

By now, Mrs. Bundle was a trifle anxious. "Well, if you happen to catch sight of any of them, Weezy, send them over to the Gazebo, over where the band is going to be playing shortly. That's where Jack Corrigan and the Andersens should be."

"Will do!" Weezy's hands moved like Edward Scissorhands, producing a large portion of shortcake for the next customer, a lanky drink of water decked out in farmer's attire. "All righty, Axel, there you go! Hey, she's a cutie, looks just like ya! You say it's your granddaughter? What's her name?"

A chunky little girl had grabbed the outstretched bowl and spoon with gusto and proceeded to take a huge bite of the sweet mixture.

The tall, elderly man tapped the little girl on the head, "That's Georgia. She's my Georgia peach, ain't you, punkin'? Say thank-you to the nice Strawberry Lady."

Mouth full, Georgia managed to say, "Mm-mm! Mank— ooooh!"

"You're welcome! Next!" Not wasting time with pleasantries, Weezy moved on and the gentleman and his granddaughter turned to leave.

Mrs. Bundle, having watched this exchange from behind the table, came to the aged man's side and asked congenially, "You're Axel Conroy, aren't you?"

"Yup! Been my name my whole life." He eyed her, squinting in concentration, as though he thought he recognized her, too.

She smiled. "You don't remember me. I met you years ago at the Agricultural Fair when my husband Arthur was still alive. I'm Walter Andersen's next-door neighbor, Lettie Bundle."

"Arthur Bundle? From North Pillson Corners? Yes, yes, I remember. Sure!"

"And you live over in Hartland Corners way, right?"

"Yup, we do! How d'you do?" They shook hands. He pulled a nicked, very worn tobacco pipe from his blue jeans bib pocket and firmly clenched the grooved bit with his teeth, both teeth and bit fitting together like a seat to a saddle from the pipe's many years of use. "So," he leaned back on his heels, rocking, "You're the big honcho here, ain't you? Walter's told me all about you. Quite a 'to-do' you're putting on. Lot of work, I reckon. We think it's great, don't we, punkin'?"

His granddaughter smiled, vacillating between slurping and chomping as she nodded, thoroughly enjoying her dessert.

"Well, I thank you for the kind words, and for your volunteering, too! I think the sheep-shearing will be a huge draw, especially for the kids. We hope all the hard work will pay off for the library."

Smiling crookedly, teeth firmly clamped on his pipe, he said, "Hard tellin', not knowin'—but from the looks of it, sure appears that way. I'll be doin' my part tomorrow afternoon, anyway. Over yonder." He pointed across the way to the makeshift pen area. He pulled a lighter from his flannel shirt pocket and held it up to his pipe.

He skillfully flipped open the lid of the plain, steel Zippo lighter, and then ran his thumb quickly along the flint wheel and a bright flame burst forth.

It was as though time stood still. The small action was like an electric shock to Mrs. Bundle's brain as she watched with intense interest.

His mouth moved, forming slow-motion words around the dark wooden pipe, but she didn't hear a thing as she concentrated on the flame.

At some point in her suspended moment, she interrupted whatever he was saying with an urgent, "Axel, would you mind…could I take a look at that?" She pointed to the lighter that was now being slipped back into the plaid shirt pocket.

His hand paused and he handed it over to her. He eyeballed her quizzically as she studied it carefully, turning it over, peering at the inner workings, scrutinizing the item for about a half a minute.

Finally, he offered, face stoic with Yankee common sense, "Jist a plain ol' Zippo. Works dang good, though, I guarantee. Had it forever."

She handed it back to him and said with a quick smile, "Thank you, Axel! I appreciate it! Sorry, but…I've got to run! Nice to see you!"

She scurried back around the table to the other side, grabbing Weezy by the arm. The busy woman reeled backward in surprise.

"Lettie, what on earth has got into you? First, you go on about—"

"Weezy, this is important! Was it you that told Watson he was overreacting?"

"Watson? The Professor? Whatever are you on about? When?"

"Watson! Sometime before he died. You had a conversation with him, didn't you? What did he tell you, Weezy? Think!"

Weezy scrunched her forehead in thought, distractedly wiping her large hands on her apron.

Mrs. Bundle continued urgently, "He told me he'd told someone something that was really bothering him. Was it you he confided in?"

She recoiled, then offered blandly, "You mean about seeing them in Keene? And all that gene pool stuff? Gaw!"

"You mean genealogy? Who? Who did he see in Keene?"

Weezy put her hand over her mouth and, not wanting to blabber this delicate tidbit of information to the world, carefully whispered in Mrs. Bundle's ear. Then, stepping back, she exclaimed loudly, "Gaw! I told him he was worrying about nothin', and just to let things be! Jeezum crow! He could go on and on, couldn't he? As I recall, he was all in a tither, and heavens to Betsy! Don't we all know what a Nervous Nellie the old professor was! You know I ain't one to tell tales out of school. I just thought it best, all things considered." Her hands went back to working their magic, absorbed with strawberries—not this urgent matter.

Mrs. Bundle didn't panic, although she was beside herself with worry now.

She knew she needed to move quickly. Others could be in danger.

From the deep recesses of her mind, she heard the kind, deep voice of her darling Arthur, patiently speaking to her as he often did. *Think like a criminal, Letitia. Think what it is they want, what it is they could be up to—and, why?* Plain as day, she heard him say, *Consider the timing…*she concentrated, drawn to that one thought.

Timing. Her voice, barely audible, asked no one in particular, "It would have to be before…? Someone who's totally out of control and bent on destruction? Better yet, where would someone with an uncontrollable urge to burn get the best bang for their buck—right now, tonight?"

In a split-second, she raised her eyes to the sky, issuing a silent, *Thank you, dearest.* She had it, she was pretty sure. However, warring with what she should do, she reasoned that if she was wrong about this, it would cause havoc here. *No, not tonight,* she thought, looking around, *not after all this work!* Better to go check things out discreetly—on her own, first.

She got Weezy's attention once more, "Weezy!" The woman looked up sharply, "Weezy! Listen to me. I've got to go check something out—right this minute. If Elvina comes back…" she paused, thinking, and then said, "…no, wait—I need to have you do something for me." Weezy nodded at Mrs. Bundle's earnest face. "I need you to send one of your boys over to Louis Montembeau at the Book Sale tent right now and tell him that if I'm not back in twenty minutes…" she backed away from the table and started half-walking-half-running toward the parking lot; Weezy watched, perplexed. Over her shoulder, Mrs. Bundle yelled, "This is important, Weezy. If I'm not back in twenty minutes," she paused, reaching in her pocket, "tell him to call the Sheriff and come find me!"

"Where's he supposed to find you?" Weezy barked, finally aware something big was up.

"The Library!"

Weezy nodded again and, opening her large mouth, hollered at the top of her lungs, "Scooter!"

A scruffy, mustard-haired boy of about seven appeared from nowhere. "Yeah, Ma?"

"Git over here! I need you to run me an errand!"

Mrs. Bundle was off like a shot headed toward the parking lot—already halfway to where she'd left Junie.

Chapter Four

The Truth Comes Out...
Like Molasses

They were locked in the dark, dank basement of the building. Quickly, they let go of each other.

"What's going on? What happened?" Althea turned around on the stairway.

Dakota ran up the stairs and struggled with the heavy door. "Elvina? Elvina! Are you daft? Let us out, would you now?" He pounded and yelled, "Elvina, open the door, please!"

Althea was behind him in a flash, repeating, "What's going on? Did she turn off the light?"

"Elvina! I--She's locked us in, Althea! What a fool I am! I left her there, right at the top of the stairs, never thinking—" He shook his head disgustedly.

Althea shoved him aside and tried to push on the handle. It wouldn't budge.

"It's no use, Althea. We're locked in."

"That—hussy! Are you saying she's deliberately trapped us down here?"

"It appears…yes."

"Why? What is going on here?"

"I'm not sure. Something, though," his eyes were flashing with fury, "is terribly wrong."

There was barely enough natural light in the cellar for them to see each other's face.

As realization set in that they'd been hoodwinked, both their countenances took on identical looks of horror.

Althea spat, "The witch!"

Dakota nodded derisively. "Ahhh! How could I be so stupid? Something seemed off, didn't it? I smell a rat. A big one! Southern-style, with bleached blonde hair."

"Good grief. She's set us up, hasn't she? Why? She's mixed up in something. And it's evil. My gut is always right! I felt uneasy, just now when we were standing there talking to her."

Dakota stiffened in the cramped section of stairway, his ears picking up a peculiar sound. He rasped, "Shhh! Listen! Do you hear that?"

They both stood very still on the stairway, listening intently.

The odd sound came again.

He whispered, "What is that?"

There was a muffled fluttering and then, a rush of queer, garbled clatter came to their ears, forming into a dry, hoarse croak, then followed by a series of distinctive, but weak, squawks.

B-aaauwwwkkkk! Squawk! Squawkk!

Althea grabbed Dakota's arm and dug her nails into his skin.

"Ow-ww!"

She exclaimed, "That's Chester! He's…down there!"

"Right! I'd know that screech anywhere!"

They both knew without saying—wherever Chester was, Erin couldn't be, *mustn't be,* too far away!

"Erin! Erin, we're coming!" Althea was fumbling with the railing now, trying to hurry down the basement stairs. Dakota moved quickly, passing her. He bounded down the steps.

"Behind that door down there, on the left, Squibb!"

He bolted down to the bottom faster than a man of his years should, ran across the empty expanse, and pulled open the heavy boiler room door with Althea at his heels.

Daylight from the upper brick foundation cracks and metal venting seeped in like thin laser beams and lit the floor in front of them. In the dusky, dusty atmosphere, he could see a small and barely discernible lump before him. He reached down in horror into the darkness and his hands found Erin in a pathetic, abandoned heap. She was unconscious. He could see the faint outline of her impish waxen face; her little hands lay limply by her sides.

Chester was cowering in the dark corner, flapping his wings, distraught, looking as though he was on his last legs. He attempted to make a fuss, but it was evident he had been severely manhandled to the extent that not much came out of him except a sporadic, weak croak. His neck was almost devoid of feathers, and his head jerked spasmodically from side to side.

Erin's ukulele case laid dejectedly upside-down beside her, abandoned, as though thrown haphazardly to the concrete floor.

"She's hurt. Oh my God, little one!" Dakota's voice was bereft. "Who did this to you? I'll bloody kill them! Is she--dead? Oh, God, Althea, help me get her up--"

"Don't move her! Squibb! Let me in!" Fearing the worst, she pushed him roughly aside in her haste to help the poor, forsaken urchin.

Dakota was distraught. "What's wrong with her? Oh, the sweet, dear thing! Erin, my darlin' wee one, what has happened to you?"

"Calm yourself down now, man," she soothed him. "Let me see her." Althea knelt down and looked Erin over thoroughly, nurse-like, then gingerly moved the dark curls away from her forehead.

"Good grief! She's got a huge bump on her head." She placed her trained ear by the little girl's open mouth, then placed her fingers on the small wrist and took her pulse. "Her breathing is strong but somewhat irregular. Could be from the trauma of the blow, or," she speculated, "she may have been drugged." She opened one eyelid and stared at the girl's dilated pupils. "I'm not sure! I'm just not sure what has happened. Who did this to you, luv?" She looked up at Dakota, who was a puddle of emotion. She said quietly, gritting her teeth, "God, Squibb! Elvina! I'll kill that woman! That—smooth-talking hag is involved somehow!"

"I fear you're right."

"We've got to get Erin to a doctor."

"Will...will she be all right, Althea?"

"I'm not sure—we need to get her looked at immediately. I'd rather not move her...here, help me cover her." She unbuttoned and then removed the summer jersey she was wearing, revealing a light shell underneath. They draped the jersey over Erin's body.

Dakota reached over and stroked the girl's hand, his face shrouded in deep emotion. "If it is Elvina who has done this to Erin, I'll throttle her myself! And..." he realized at once, "be sure of the fact that we're in danger now, too. My God! Attempted murder." He shook off the thoughts forming in his mind. "For now, we've got to concentrate on getting the wee one some medical aid!"

"Right. First things first. Are there any other exits?" Her eyes searched desperately. "And what about the windows?"

They both looked around helplessly, assessing the situation as best they could in the failing light, swiftly moving around and touching the perimeter of the thickly-walled cellar. They stood under the darkened basement windows, and then both started yelling for help at the top of their lungs.

"Is anybody out there? Help! We're trapped down here! Help!"

They both could hear the boisterous music in the distance, successfully drowning out their attempts. At this point, everyone would be over across the way watching the concert, to be sure. The Pillson Rhythmares had started the benefit concert, thoroughly blotting out their cries. After their brief attempts, they stopped, realizing it was hopeless.

Dakota looked at her helplessly and said, "We may just have to wait until the concert lets out."

Althea sat down on the cold, damp floor and ran a feathery, soothing hand very lightly over Erin's pale face.

The little girl stirred and gave a groan.

"There's a good girl, Erin." Althea said, "That's a good sign...she's coming to."

Dakota jumped and said, "It's okay, we're here, little one." His voice was soft and soothing as he knelt down beside her and patted her delicate arm. "It's all right, we're going to take care of you. Shushh, now…don't you worry, lass."

Althea's heart softened a bit as she observed the tenderness he exhibited toward Erin, even using the term "lass" with the little Irish girl. She rather wondered, in fact, at the degree of his caring. It seemed there was something very endearing, almost paternal, in his manner. Without regard, she felt compelled to say, "Squibb, you were so worried about Erin, almost beside yourself. And look at you now! You're a wreck, man."

"Yes, well, I care about this little girl very much."

"Well…it seems rather…odd to me. You're more than just attached, she's obviously very dear to you."

His eyes became suddenly misty as he continued to stare down at the child. Then, he gave a deep sigh.

"You know…you're right, she is very dear to me. She, Aineen, and Jack, too, for that matter." He looked up at her, opened his mouth to speak, then hesitated. With a look of resolve and a burst of boldness, he said, "I've wanted to share this with you, to tell you more than anyone about them, since the day I met you."

"What on earth are you talking about?"

"Honestly, Althea, I've been trying to decide the best way…to find the wherewithal to come clean so that no one is hurt."

She looked at him sharply. "Come clean?" He nodded. She snapped her fingers. "I knew it! I've known all along you were hiding…covering up…something! I could feel it. So, what is it?"

"This is…difficult. Things came so easily when I first arrived in Pillson. I met everyone I needed—and wanted—to meet, right away. It was as though God was guiding me, helping me. Everything seemed, well, it all just fell into place, here in this lovely, untouched world. I've been biding my time…waiting to tell Jack, and Lettie, and, especially, you!" He struggled with his words.

"Me? And Jack? What on earth has Jack Corrigan got to do with this?" He cast his eyes downward and took a huge breath in. She urged, "Well, get it out, man! It can't be all that bad!"

"In a way, it is. However, I think my own dishonesty has been for the best."

She clenched her fists together and ground her teeth, "I'm going to scream! Good grief! Just spill it, would you, Squibb? We haven't got all day!"

"Oh, that name! Squibb! That's the worst of it, how I hate that name, how I hate to hear you, of all people, call me that! Listen to me!" He grabbed her by the arm, his eyes flashing, "My name isn't Dakota Squibb! That's a name I've...well, appropriated, for lack of a better way of saying, when the PRA--" She stared at him as though he were speaking Greek, "--yes, Althea, an Irish group, a splinter of the Sinn Fein--" he was fumbling in his haste to explain himself, waving off these details as though they were insignificant, "--an earlier version of the Irish Republican Army. I know it sounds fantastic, but they sent me away to America in 1947, after I was a witness to something... horrible—that happened in Ireland. I—needn't go into it all. It was all very long ago, almost a lifetime, in fact." His voice stammered with frustration, and she stared at him silently. "You see, I began a new life—with a new name. I became an American, a free spirit. I studied my art and started painting. I'd abandoned my Irish heritage. I had no family here, no ties. And I knew I'd never see anyone there, in Ireland, ever, ever again." He felt her body stiffen beside him as he stared down at his hands in disgrace and utter misery.

When she spoke, her voice came barely above a whisper. "What, pray tell, is your real name?"

"Please, Althea, love. I'm hoping you, of all people, will understand."

She was startled by his term of endearment; "Love," he had called her.

He drew in a deep breath and then sighed, as though in tremendous relief. "My name. It's Ian...Ian Kelley. It feels wonderful to say it aloud. Ian Kelley!!! And, wonder of wonders, I found my family—or what's left of it—here, in Pillson! I'm the Corrigan kids' great uncle. Their grandfather, Aengus Kelley, was my brother. He and the rest of the Kelley clan are long gone. That is, except for my dear grandnieces and grandnephew." Frustration filled his voice as he explained, "When I found them, I couldn't believe it! I tried, three times in fact, to make contact with Jack through legal channels but he wouldn't respond. I don't know why! Oh, bloody Hell! I am their mother's Uncle Ian from Ballyhaise, Ireland, Althea—of that you can be sure."

"Good grief! I…" she said slowly, "don't know who you are. You've been lying…all along about—who you are. You're…a fake."

Ian raised his voice, "No! I'm not a fake. I've had to…" He looked into her eyes. "Oh God, give me strength!" He coughed lightly, the reflex exacerbated by the air, which seemed to have become staler, hazier. "I don't know why I'm explaining this to you now, except… we're in a jam here…I need you to know the truth—you…are important to me, dear."

He looked intently into her deep, lovely eyes.

Abruptly, Althea pushed him away from her and stood up, crinkling her nose in obvious distaste, cutting off any further explanation. She whispered suspiciously, "What's that?"

"Won't you please let me explain?"

"Shush!" She sniffed the air suspiciously. "Do you smell it? Something…burning? Something…is burning!"

He inhaled deeply, then coughed and spat out, "Bloody Hell!"

They looked in horror at each other.

"Good grief!" Althea yelled, "She's set the place on fire!"

———————•-•-•———————

Althea got up and frantically started searching for another way, any way out, as smoke seeped through the ceiling above. "Squibb—Ian—! We've got to find a way out--before it's too late for us!"

Dakota jumped to his feet, indecisive about which way to go. To be sure, that was smoke they both smelled—and saw!

The Town Hall was on fire.

Frantically, they investigated every cranny, looking for any possible way out. Skirting his way around the basement circumference, Ian checked again for any egress.

He studied his surroundings, looking through the shafts of fading light that emerged through the cracks and chinks in the brick foundation. "We're on borrowed time here. Windows are way too high and all closed in, boarded up from the outside from what I can see. Hammered shut, no doubt, to discourage any break-ins." He eyeballed the eight-foot height. "If I could climb up there, I might be able to push—"

Althea, on her own mission, rushed into the back recesses of the boiler room, frenetically probing the walls. "On the outside of the building, in the back, I seem to remember a bulkhead in this area, maybe we—" she fumbled, "Got it!" Althea yelled as she pulled, then pushed on the dull, heavy metal door leading to the outside bulkhead. There was a huge rusty padlock hanging from the connecting latch. "Oh, no!"

He joined her quickly. "Hold on. We've got to break the padlock. Let me find something to use to crush the latch and dislodge it!"

He hurriedly searched, once again, this time looking for any type of tool to use but the basement was clean as a whistle. "Nothing! The basement's empty. It's no use."

"Then our only hope is back up the stairs," she cried. "Maybe we can jimmy the lock on the door."

They groped their way through the darkness together now, as a team, reaching the top step in a jiffy. As they struggled with the door, pushing and straining, their hands shook with desperation. At this level, the smell of smoke was more prevalent, and Althea choked back a cough.

"You hold the latch down, while I jimmy it....." she whispered, intent on the work at hand.

Precious seconds passed as they attempted to release the lock.

"Wait! I think..I have something that might work." Ian searched in his pocket until he removed a flat, metal, double-pronged pick used to remove dirt and grass from the bottom of golf shoes. He held it up for her to see and said simply, "Golf shoe pick!" Gently probing, he inserted the pick from every angle into the lock, initially with no success. Finally, he pushed the slim pick in between the door and the door jamb near the locking mechanism, sliding it carefully along the ridge until, finally, they heard a slight click. He shouted, "Got it!"

Althea turned the knob simultaneously. Miraculously, the door let loose without further struggle.

As they opened the door, a blast of heat, along with dangerously curling, dark smoke, met them. Ian stepped out, quickly assessing the situation, then rushed back onto the basement landing and, making sure to turn the bolt on the outside into the "unlocked" position; he closed the door.

Althea hissed, "What are you doing?"

He held up a hand of caution. "Listen to me. There's smoke everywhere out there! Not sure where the fire is exactly, but it must be here on the first floor." His face was inches from hers. "You go now. I'll go get Erin and follow along."

To his shock, she said, simply, "Nope."

"What do you mean, 'nope'?"

"I'll wait right here. You go get Erin."

His voice was stern. "Absolutely not. You will go now, if I have to throw you out there myself."

Althea insisted "No, I won't!"

"What's wrong with you, woman?" He looked at her incredulously.

"We must go together! I can't leave--"

The man's patience was wearing very thin. "Listen to me, dearest Althea, now is not the time for us to disagree. I promise you, by all that's good on this earth, that I will make things right--" His words came quickly and he covered his face and coughed. "But, for now, dearest, you must go! I will carry her out!"

They could both feel the heat on the other side of the door pressing in on them. She stood her ground. A huge crash was heard and he opened the door a slight crack, pushing her forward. "I'll not stand for this malarkey! I told you, you daft woman! Go! Go now!" Barely able to see around the corner and down the hallway about twenty-odd feet, his worst fear was realized. Through the haze, he could see flames reaching out like orange fingers.

Time was of the essence, calling for desperate measures.

"God help me," he muttered under his breath, suddenly seizing her by the shoulders and kissing her roughly, full on the mouth.

That split-second in time seemed an eternity as she struggled, sputtering. Then, just as quickly, with a fervor that surprised even her, she kissed him back.

From this brief moment, they separated their lips and stared with disbelief at one another.

"Good grief!" she gasped.

Only one other man had ever kissed her like that. Chauncey. Her eyes welled up and one tear fell, hit her cheek, and dribbled indelicately down her quivering chin.

Nodding simultaneously, they gave each other an unexpected look of knowing.

He reached over, quickly wiping her drippy chin. "I promise," he nodded encouragingly, "we'll be right behind you."

She smiled tersely, then quickly turned, covering her mouth and sheltering her eyes. She hurried through the heat and smoke, down the hallway, past the kitchen door, toward the fresh, open air.

Never looking back, more tears begged to escape from her eyes, but she bravely defied them as best she could.

Chapter Five

Rescue

She was crawling on her hands and knees through the last few feet at the back passageway rear entrance. The smoke and heat were almost unendurable. Althea reached the back wooden landing outside and felt, rather than saw, the three steps below her. With some agility, she rolled her body into the walkway, landing in the gravel parking lot, gasping for air.

It was surreal; she could hear shouting but couldn't see anyone. Her eyes stung, and her throat felt as rough as sandpaper. There were people gathering from many directions.

She yelled hoarsely in desperation, "Please! Save them! They're… inside!"

A pair of strong hands found her shoulders and roughly pulled her up to a sitting position. She reached up and grabbed for someone, anyone, to help. "They're in the basement! Get the firemen in there!"

"Who, Althea? Would you tell me now, who's in there?"

It was Jack Corrigan's voice she heard.

"Oh, Jack, quick! Sound the alarm, get the firemen! It's Erin, and—,"she paused, searching for words, "Dakota! Dakota Squibb! He's gone back down there—to the basement—to get to her!" She squinted up at him through her bloodshot, streaming eyes.

Jack's face went completely stiff; his countenance froze in despair. He ran past her toward the back entrance she had just exited.

"No, Jack! Stop! Don't go in. Everything's blazing hot! It's too dangerous!"

The fire truck's siren rang out. It was a madhouse as people began running from every direction. The distant music stopped suddenly, and it was a melee as word spread, "Fire at Town Hall!"

Jack, beating back the smoke, changed direction and ran the few extra feet toward the large bulkhead door that Althea had tried, unsuccessfully, to open from the inside. Recklessly and with total abandon, he pulled on it. It didn't budge.

Nick Clancy appeared from nowhere, half-dressed in his volunteer fireman chaps and gear. He yelled, "Jack! Over here. We need you!"

Jack grabbed him desperately. "Nick, man! Little Erin's in there! With Dakota Squibb! Jaysus! They may be trapped down in the basement! D'you have a crowbar? Can you get this bulkhead open, mate? We've got to get in there! I'll go around to the front!" He backed away from him, frenzied, prepared to run around to the front of the building.

Nick nodded just as the volunteer fire truck, which had been resting and set up on the nearby Village Green in preparation for the festival crowd, came screaming into the parking lot. In less than ninety seconds the crew had sprung into action, beginning to run their lines and cordon off the building.

Right behind the fire trucks were the village's two ambulances, also just a football field away set up for tomorrow's festivities. The water hoses gushed and began their work on the back of the building, directed toward the flames originating from the kitchen area.

Jack left Althea and ran around to the front of the building. He was desperate, driven to do anything to save his sister. As he cleared the building's corner, he ran smack into all three Andersen men, ready for action.

Carl, dressed in his blue Rhythmares outfit, grabbed Jack's arm and yelled, "What's going on?"

Jack wrestled his way free and yelled, "Erin! She's inside!"

He tried to bound up the front steps, but Carl's strong arms prevented him, seeing he was in no condition to do anything, frantic as he was.

Clay latched on, too, and they held him back, restraining him as best they could until Walter grabbed him, too.

Jack yelled in agony. "Let me go! Hump off! Bloody hell, she's in there, d'you understand! Let me go, would you?"

"We cain't!" Walter puffed, pulling on his shirt. "Hell's bells, let them firemen do their job! You'll perish for sure in there, if you go in!"

Jack squirmed and pushed the limits of his strength until he left his torn shirt behind in their hands as he broke loose and ran up the front steps. He reached for the door and pulled, but it was locked.

"God in heaven," he screamed to anyone, "They're in there!"

He looked around for something, anything that he could use to break the windows beside the door.

Instantly, he lost his balance as the force of the heavy door, bursting open from within, pushed him back in a rush. Jack grabbed for the large door, pulling it toward him, and catching his balance just in time.

Ian Kelley, desperately clutching tiny Erin closely to him, both of them covered with smoke and grime, fell into Jack's body.

Ian's face was badly singed and mottled, his features strangely distorted, as though stuck like clumps of play-dough on his face. Jack was horrified to see that the man's hands were raw-red, already-blistering clubs that looked like uncooked steak, and he grabbed for his sister like a man possessed.

Erin was protected within Ian's sturdy but straining arms, and he croaked, barely able to speak, "Don't move her head, Jack! Her head is hurt!"

With great care, he handed Erin over to her brother, then stumbled and collapsed on the granite steps, tumbling roughly like a rag doll downward and, finally, coming to rest at the mid-point section of steps.

Speedily, the Andersen men picked him up and carried him over to the Pillsonville Rescue Squad's triage unit set up nearby on the grassy area. Meanwhile, others guided a very defensive Jack (carrying his sister as though she was a precious, breakable doll) to the same area, thus sequestering both of the injured parties, Ian and Erin, far away from the building as they began to administer first aid.

By now, Althea had regained her sight enough to come around from the other side of the building just in time to see Ian burst forth through the front door with Erin. She hesitated, torn between which one to go to first. She could hear Ian groaning in pain and so, reaching Erin's side, she bent over the team working on the semi-conscious child. She cautioned them, recognizing one of the EMT's. "Patrick, watch the girl! She's sustained a head wound, and was possibly drugged! I think she may have a concussion. How's her breathing? Her pulse was irregular. Please, be easy!"

Jack watched in agony, touching the only part of her body he felt was safe to hold onto, her little sandaled foot, which he was shaking very gently, as if to wake her. "I'm here, luv. *Brathair* is here." He looked over with out-of-control scorn to the prone man who had brought her from the burning building. "What in the bloody hell happened, Squibb? How could you—?"

Althea looked up, startled, "Jack, stop! He saved her life! Listen to me!"

Erin's little body stirred and she coughed, first a sputter, then a series of hacking, smoke-filled attempts to clear her windpipe. Subsequently, her eyes fluttered open momentarily, and she whispered hoarsely, her throat dry and caked with soot.

"Arrgghhhh….Ach, it hurts so! Owww! Ouch!"

She grimaced in pain as they checked her vital signs, urging her to lie still, but she continued her attempts to talk.

"*Owwwwww!!!* Oh….Wrinkles!" Her words came through, labored and broken, but the little imp persisted, even as Althea tried to calm her. "Wrinkles!"

Althea soothed her, "Shush, yes, love, we know!"

Erin whispered hoarsely as she stared into Althea's eyes, "Ach! Mrs. Wrinkles, it was." Her pleading eyes held a very scared look. "So…so awful, mum!"

The Pillson Rescue Squad techs worked deftly, gently placing a neck brace around her head.

Patrick, the EMT, said gently, "Lay still, little girl. Lay still and let us help you, now."

Erin moaned, immobilized, but still trying to talk, "She's...owww! *Ohhhhh*—me head...hurts so much! She made me..." She began to cry in pain and anger. "She's a very bad lady, she is." Her eyes opened wide and she yelled, "Jack! I want Jack!"

His voice boomed from her ankles, "It's all right, luv. Brother is right here with you, lass, isn't he now?" He moved and knelt down beside her, taking her little hand in his. His cerulean blue eyes were moist and he tried to smile. "You're going to be fine, *a chailin mo chroí*, don't you be worryin' now."

The look of relief on her face at seeing her brother was very telling, but it changed again quickly; her face contorted grotesquely, replaced with horror. "Ach! Jack! She was so mean! Me bird! Where's Chester? Where's me...oy!"

Althea, fighting back tears, didn't have the heart to tell Erin about Chester's demise in the smoky blaze. *Sadly*, she thought, *she will learn of that soon enough.*

Erin continued, confused and dazed, "Chester! I saw them, didn't I now? Aye, they were kissing. Oh, Chester...!" She moaned, "Ach... *tá sé nimhneach*—it hurts, brother, *oww-ouchhh!*"

His eyes pleaded with the EMT. "Can you give her something, now, for the pain?" Patrick shook his head, putting the last touches on the brace. Jack smoothed her hand, trying desperately to comfort her, and looked up at Althea helplessly.

She reached across Erin and touched his shoulder. His face was dark with anger.

Discreetly, he mouthed the words silently, with quiet determination, asking, "Who did this to her?"

She whispered, "Later, Jack. Let's get her to the hospital first."

He soothed his sister, "No one will hurt you now, my lass. You're with me—of that you can be sure."

Althea, refocusing her attention, concentrated on soothing the girl, "Erin, my luv, you've had a nasty bump on your head. These nice men are going to take care of everything."

"I...want...Chester!" She began to cry and could not be comforted.

Althea looked up, "Are you almost ready to take her?"

Patrick nodded, "Hush now, girl, you just lay there and rest. No more talking."

But she was bawling uncontrollably now, and asked, pitifully, "Where's me rooster? And Dakota—I heard him talking to me, too, didn't I? Where is Dakota?"

Meanwhile, a ruckus had been developing nearby.

A distraught Ian Kelley had raised himself on his elbows and could be heard yelling, "Let me up, man! I mean it! Let me up!" Somehow, he had gotten to his knees, keeping all at a distance, blindly punching the air while others tried to calm him. He seemed unaware of his serious injuries. Like a pile of faulty, misshapen building blocks, he lost his balance once again as he'd attempted to hoist himself to his feet, then shook off the scrappy EMT desperately trying to break his fall.

The emergency medic yelled, "Hey, man! Stop! Get back here! Those burns on your hands and face are bad!"

Over his shoulder, the other tech had yelled, "Somebody, quick! We need help over here!"

The Andersen men quickly lent a hand and, with the other men's support, tried to calm him as he was plunked down like a wet, wobbly noodle. They lowered him until his backside was firmly planted on the grassy earth.

A lone feather drifted to the ground beside the stricken man and there was a very distinct *Squawk!*

Strangely, another faint, feeble sound emanated from inside of Ian's tattered, soiled shirt, somewhere in the vicinity near his ribs and under his armpit—*Squawk!*

Walter Andersen grabbed at him, reaching adroitly into the depths of the charred shirt, and nimbly removed a much-deflated, scrawny looking—but alive—rooster.

Chester (or, a barely recognizable facsimile of the poor thing) gasped for air. Most all of the pulverized poultry's feathers had been singed from his backside, making him look like he was halfway headed toward the main course on a dinner platter.

"Baau--cccccckk..." he sputtered weakly, releasing a puff of smoke through his beak.

Walter Andersen cried out, "Well, I'll be jiggered! If that don't beat all, Dakota! Lookee here! You saved that danged, cock-eyed, foul bird for our Erin! Jeesum crowbars!"

***

As Erin was asking for him, Ian had gasped above the din around him, "How is she? God, man, is she alive?"

Althea was by his side in a heartbeat. She whispered under her breath, "Lay back. Calm down, Ian."

His lungs heaved and he gasped for clean air, "Is she going to be all right?"

He was exhibiting all the symptoms of shock now: glassy eyes, a face that had turned a pale gray amidst the blotches of beet red, his breathing rapid and shallow.

Althea soothed him, saying, "Yes, yes, she's fine. She fully regained consciousness, she's fine! Let the men help you."

He shivered, and one of the EMT's covered him with a blanket. Althea nodded at the paramedic as Ian gazed blankly into her eyes.

"Erin?" he bleated.

The EMT said urgently, "He's going out...pulse is weak...let's get him stabilized."

Ian fainted dead away.

Meanwhile, as Erin was being loaded onto the gurney, she had heard the familiar squawking, and hollered, "Chester!!!" Then she coughed and moaned and whispered, "Dakota! Oh, thank you, thank you. Chester, lad, I hear you!"

Out of the corner of her eye, she spied first her rooster, and then her injured friend, and faintly smiled through her tears, unaware that her friend was gravely injured. As she was being loaded into the ambulance with Jack at her side, her little hand raised itself in a feeble wave.

The ambulance radio crackled orders from the hospital base, "Hold your position at the fire. Wait for instructions; we may need you to bring other casualties in with the child."

Ian Kelley opened his eyes, glassy and disoriented. He tried to communicate, but it all came out in unintelligible gibberish. "Althea? The ceiling…we got turned around…the smoke blinded…couldn't get out, fire too hot… *Evil*! Elvina…bloody woman! We're fine, now…we're going to be…..Althea! Sorry! You must tell Jack—"

"It's all right…shush now! You did it, just as you said. You got them both out. I can't believe it, but you did it." Althea leaned over him, trying to calm him.

"Althea, you must…stay with Erin…and Jack! Tell Jack… everything! You must…make sure you tell him why—why I'm—tell him everything, you hear?"

"I will, I will, I promise! I'll stay with them."

The tech nudged her, then leaned in close to her ear, "Ma'am, we're ready to take him. He needs to go, stat. His hands…"

"Oh, good Lord!" Pulpy and bright as the inside of persimmons, his hands were difficult for Althea to look at and she winced. She said lifelessly, "He's…an artist."

They quickly loaded him into the other waiting ambulance. She learned that, because of the severity of his wounds, it had already been determined he would need airlifting. Instructions could be heard from the radio inside, indicating the helicopter pad at Dartmouth-Hitchcock Hospital was being readied, with plans in progress for him to be flown within the hour to Massachusetts General Hospital's premier burn facility at the Sumner Redstone Burn Center in Boston.

As the ambulance containing Ian Kelley rushed away, Sheriff Will O'Malley's cruiser came roaring up. He sprinted toward the smoldering building and one of his deputies met him halfway, filling him in and pointing toward Althea, who stood waiting outside the remaining ambulance.

Althea yelled to him, "Will! Will! Over here!"

He crossed the space of fifty paces in record time and peered into the ambulance.

"Is that the girl inside, Althea? You were with her?"

"Yes! It's all too ghastly. We were trapped in the fire."

"Why were you in there?"

Clinically and rapidly, she gave the salient details relative to their search for Erin. She ended with, "It's Erin Corrigan, Jack's sister… you know Jack."

Jack nodded grimly at the big man from his perch beside Erin within the ambulance.

"She may have a concussion, I think, Will, but she's conscious, seems to be okay. However, I need to tell you! About Elvina Wrinkle!"

"What about her? She's involved in this, too? Was she—or anyone else--inside?" He peered at the now-smoking structure.

"No, Sheriff, but please, listen! It's Elvina Wrinkle that caused of all this! First, she locked us inside! Locked us in the basement, me and…and…," she paused for a second, "Dakota….Squibb. And, she tried to murder poor Erin."

Jack snarled from inside the ambulance, "Jaysus! I'll kill that woman."

Will barked, "You hang onto your shirt, son. We're going to handle this, don't you worry!"

Althea continued, "She must be out of her mind. She started the fire, too. It must be her! You've got to find her, Will!"

"We'll take care of it, Althea." He called over one of his men, spoke to him in low tones, at which point the officer nodded and quickly sped off. Going back to his vehicle, he barked a question into his radio, waited a second for a response, and then spoke again.

Precise and to the point, Will O'Malley came back to the waiting EMT, then turned back to Jack, ordering him in no uncertain terms that he was to stay with his sister and not leave her side.

He told them, "The building's all clear, no other casualties. Althea, you go with them, too. I'll send a deputy along to meet you at the hospital. We'll want a detailed statement from you and one from Erin Corrigan once she's stabilized and lucid enough to talk to us. And we'll put a guard at the little one's hospital room door, just in case."

Althea nodded grimly and jumped into the back of the waiting ambulance; the Sheriff slammed the ambulance door shut and it sped off quickly.

At that point, he walked over to Ralph Woodsum, the Pillsonville Fire Chief, who briefed him quickly on the fire situation. A crowd had gathered, solemnly watching.

Wiping a grimy glove across his sweating brow, Ralph said, "We've got it under control. Not that bad a fire, really, not a huge amount of damage overall. Mostly smoke damage. Got a couple firemen dealing with minor heat exhaustion, but other than that, I think we're okay. We caught it in time—were able to contain it pretty quickly, Sheriff. Mostly, just by luck we got the alarm so fast and were already right over there." He pointed toward the Village Green. "The fire was isolated to the first floor back section of the building— started in the kitchen, we're pretty sure, spread to the hallway and we caught it just before it was headed toward the back stairway. A small section of the floor in the kitchen in the back collapsed into the basement. Intentionally set, by the looks of it. Like I said, mostly smoke damage throughout the first floor front and basement—the back kitchen section's another matter. Funny thing, sprinkler system never kicked on! Smoke damage will take a few days to mop up, and it'll need a new kitchen, to be sure. Structurally, most everything seems intact except that section of kitchen floor and back hallway area. We'll get the structural engineer in right away. Fire Marshall can do up his report—another case of arson, Will. Caught this one in time, though."

People were milling around, necks craning, as the Chief issued quick orders. "Pete, let's get that truck out of the way! Clear this area, move those people back. Let's try to get things back to normal here."

The Sheriff spoke to Carl Andersen, then looked past the officers confining the crowd and boomed to the group, "It's all right, folks, fire's over—nothin' major, and all is well. You all go back to the concert." He repeated, "Like I said, all is well. Just a little excitement to interrupt your fun time—but the Rhythmares are ready to get the music going again. Right, Carl?"

Carl Andersen, looking very official in his traditional blue band uniform with its shiny brass buttons and bright gold epaulettes, nodded, speaking up, "That's right, Will. We'll be starting right back up in a jiffy!"

Soothed and sensing that most of the excitement was over, the crowd started moving back toward the Village Green gazebo. He moved his hands as though herding sheep, "Go ahead, now. The bandleader's heading back over to the bandstand. Yuh--it's all right! Go on. Go ahead now."

Slowly, people moved along, talking and laughing amongst themselves, murmuring and generally in good humor as they walked back.

He called his deputy over and articulated under his breath, "Cyrus, call the dispatch and put out an APB for Elvina Wrinkle. Owner of Wrinkle's General Store." The deputy asked a question and Will rubbed his eyes. "Yes, one and the same. White female, height five-ten or so, blonde, longish hair, age fiftyish, drives a light blue early model Thunderbird—convertible, if I remember correctly—considered possibly armed and very dangerous. Serious business. Notify the State Police, too, just in case she's hot-footin' it out of the state. She may not be aware her victims here survived." Cyrus nodded and moved hastily toward his waiting vehicle. Sheriff O'Malley barked, "Oh! Hang on!" He said in hushed tones, "It won't take long for the news of the fire to reach the media and get on the radio and TV, and then we've lost the upper hand if she finds out. Describe her only as 'a person of interest.'" He snapped his fingers. "Dang--that's right! She's got a grown daughter—name is...Lucy, I'm pretty sure—find her, too, Cyrus—and take her into custody for the time being until we can find the mother. This Wrinkle woman may still be nearby, maybe even still here, at the festival, hiding somewhere, for all we know. Get every available officer on this—do a house-to-house search if you have to! I want her found!"

"You got it, sir!"

Sheriff Will O'Malley first looked up at the sky, which had begun to cloud over slightly, then over at the mess of hoses, water, and disorder, all caused allegedly by one woman who had wreaked havoc at the Pillson Town Hall, all transpiring within minutes. He muttered under his breath to no one in particular, "At least no one was killed. Thank Christmas!"

As Will turned back toward his car, the lanky figure of Louis Montembeau could be seen sprinting like greased lightning, arms flailing wildly, as he ran like blazes toward him and the Town Hall.

Zipping along swiftly and silently beside him was a tiny creature on all fours closely resembling a cat, elegantly attired in a rainbow-colored, very festive bow tie.

Chapter Six

Murder and Arson Go Hand in Hand

Mrs. Bundle, intent on her mission to prevent yet another crime from taking place, drove through the Village Square and over the bridge to the other side of Pillsonville, meanwhile going over the "light bulb" moment that had occurred just minutes before with Axel Conroy. When he had opened the Zippo lighter and spun the wheel, it had first brought to mind, in slow motion, Vincent Veakey's metal art work, specifically the Cog-wheel Active Art piece that had fascinated her so much. It was the bigger version of the same concept.

In that moment with Axel, it had all clicked into place for her. A cog! Turning round and round….and then, a flame! Connected by….a little, insignificant…*rivet.*

How could she have been so blind? The realization had caused an explosive chain reaction in her mind, simulating a step-by-step process of the art piece's action. *Heavens*, she remembered, *Vincent had even picked up a lighter at the time to show how the process worked on a smaller scale!*

She thought about the small screw, or rivet, that had been found at the murder site, meanwhile, in her mind's eye, opening and closing the Zippo lighter's mechanism. Then, she envisioned the top of a very special and ornate lighter; again, a Zippo, being deftly flipped opened, the "cog" of the wheel being turned by the murderer's dainty thumb and finally, she imagined the skilled lighting of the brush fire.

That must be it! She realized, with growing horror, that there was a murderer in their midst—right from the beginning.

Another image from last evening came clearly into her mind's eye—the seductive leaning in, the quick, intimate exchange of conversation—*Armand!*

The second of two names Weezy has whispered in her ear. Of course! Elvina didn't flinch at his invasion of her personal space last night because….*yes,* it all made sense! Because Elvina was *used* to it, familiar with it, and yes…she *liked* it!

The three arsons, the lighter, framing Junior, and…murder!

It all fit.

She gasped, grasping the final piece. "Oh, my word! And, the pentobarb!" That, too? It all kicked in, her mind in high gear as she realized she must somehow corral Elvina Wrinkle—at least for the next few precious minutes—until she did any more damage—to property, or to anyone.

———— • — • ————

The irony was, she *was* there, just as Mrs. Bundle had supposed she might be—at the Library. She sped into the Library parking lot, Junebug's chassis tipped precariously on two wheels. There was Elvina's metallic blue Thunderbird, carefully hidden out behind the library, far from the main road's view; it was empty.

With horror, Mrs. Bundle realized that undoubtedly, her hunch was dead-on right. There could only be one reason Elvina was here; this was the firestarter's next casualty—the stately, old, very dry and brittle Pillson Public Library.

And then, at the back library entrance, there was just a flash of a woman's backside, an apron fluttering, then disappearing.

Elvina!

She vanished through the back door, unaware of Mrs. Bundle's arrival. Mrs. Bundle jumped out of Junie, hearing a small clatter as she closed the door behind her, too distracted to see what it was.

I've got to stop her at all costs, Mrs. Bundle thought, and sprinted across the parking lot with lightning speed. She pulled on the back door—and it opened!

She came face-to-face with Elvina Wrinkle.

The other woman looked somewhat surprised but held her emotions in check, a washed-out smile on her countenance. "Lettie, dear! What brings you here?" Her words came slow and drippy as usual, but they had lost that sugary tone and were now just soft and somewhat cautious. Caught by surprise as she was, she appeared faintly off balance. One hand went casually into her "**Strawberries**" apron pocket; the other was hidden behind her.

"Don't do it, Elvina."

She stared at Mrs. Bundle, a blank look on her face. "Honey, what on earth are you talkin' about?"

"I mean it. I know everything."

"Everything?"

"For starters, about the pentobarb."

There was a small beat, a millisecond of silence, and then Elvina said with a chuckle, "Have you lost your mind? What in the heck is pentobarb?"

"Pentobarb, Elvina, also known as Pentobarbitol. Used by doctors in the treatment of self-induced or chemically-induced comas."

The willowy blonde woman blinked but didn't move an inch.

Mrs. Bundle shook her head, refusing to let fear take a hold of her. "Elvina! The concussion drug they used on Norbert was Pentobarb—that's it, isn't it? His doctors will confirm it. When the authorities open that can of worms, they'll ask all the questions—the same ones I'm asking you now. He hit his head when he fell off the roof but he didn't die. How did you do it, Elvina, without them knowing? Did you give him a little extra, just to send him off for good? And then, afterwards, you saved more of the dose somehow, knowing you might just be able to use it in the future. That's what did you in, Elvina. I know we'll be able to prove it! You never thought they'd find the dog, but they did. You put pentobarb in the steak and fed it to that poor dog! The game's up, Elvina."

"Ah don't know what you're talking about."

"Elvina, stop pretending!"

She paused, and Mrs. Bundle reasoned, "Would you answer me this one question?"

"What?"

"Whatever happened to that beautiful vintage Zippo lighter you used to have? The one that goes with that leather cigarette case you always carry?"

"My lighter? Everyone knows Ah lost everything in the fire."

"No, you didn't. You carried that lighter with you everywhere! I remember seeing the lighter on TV—after the General Store fire, when you were being interviewed by the television reporter."

"Fiddle-faddle! Whatever, Lettie! Honestly, why does it matter?"

"Well, I think your lighter broke. Much later on, in fact. And, frankly, at a very inconvenient time for you, wasn't it? Elvina?"

She shrugged, "You know, now that you ask, Ah can't rightly remember what happened to it."

"Last night at our meeting, I noticed you were using another lighter. It was orange, newer, very modern, in fact. Not like the antique Zippo you always carry." Mrs. Bundle's hand reached discreetly into her sundress pocket to retrieve her cell phone; it wasn't there. *Drat!* Trying not to panic, she said, "In fact, I bet if we search your things at the hotel, we'll probably find it. Minus a couple key parts. Am I right?"

Elvina threw back her head and a gruff, low chuckle exploded. "Ha! You're just too damn clever for your own good, aren't you Lettie? Ah can't imagine where ya'll come up with all this drivel."

"Your lighter broke on your second attempt to torch the field—the rivet popped out and you couldn't get the grass fire going again."

Elvina was silent, staring her down.

"Let's clear things up right now, Elvina. I say we go back and find the Sheriff."

"Are you that stupid, honey? If Ah'm what you claim—a murderer, for heaven's sake—why would you evva think Ah'd go along with that? Oh, Ah think not, Lettie." Elvina's slim, long hand came out of her apron pocket. "Ah think not!"

As if by magic, a gun appeared and Mrs. Bundle stared down the pistol's slim barrel. Elvina brought her other hand from behind her back; in it was a box, red and white with a thin blue stripe, rectangular, with familiar lettering on its side.

Wooden stick matches.

Elvina chuckled again. "You're so trusting, Lettie. So willing to give people the benefit of the doubt. That's your downfall, honey." She spoke low, as though she were scolding a naughty little girl. "Really, Lettie," Elvina snarled, hatred in her voice.

Mrs. Bundle stood there, frozen.

Outside, abandoned on the ground beside Junie, there was a tinny, light-hearted ringing, the musical sound of Mrs. Bundle's cell phone, ringing and ringing.

.

Chapter Seven

Elvina's Explanation
(For What It's Worth)

They were facing each other, the gun gripped tightly in Elvina's hand; she shook her head in disgust, and the immovable blonde waves framed her hard face like a comic mask. "That stupid little screw. Flintwheel fell off in my hand but Ah couldn't find the dang screw! Why, Ah had that lighter twenty years—first nice thing Ah ever bought for myself—and the dang thing chose that time to break! Knew it was somewhere in that field, but Ah didn't have time to look once Ah saw you coming over the hill."

"Rivet."

"What?"

"It's a rivet. The rivet is the flint wheel screw that holds the flintwheel in place; it's used to spark the flame of a Zippo lighter. You've stopped using your signature lighter because it broke that day. All the pieces started fitting together."

"Whatever, honey—that's so lame, Ah can't believe they'll ever be able to link that to me." She placed the box of matches on the table beside her, still aiming the gun squarely.

Mrs. Bundle's keys jiggled nervously in her hand. "You know, it defies logic how you lifted that poor man into the baler. The police were of the mind that only a large man, or men, could have lifted an unconscious Watson. They assumed he would have been too heavy for a woman! But, it came to me. I remember what you said about working on your father's cotton farm. What was it you told me, Elvina? 'Ah worked on my daddy's spread like a common field hand!' I bet you still have muscles most women never acquire, working the way you did as a kid."

Elvina tightened her vice-like grip on the gun, replying in surprisingly good spirits for someone confessing to such a heinous crime, "Oooh, you're good Lettie." She placed her other hand on her willowy frame's thigh. "Ah may not look it, but Ah'm a hardy farm girl." She laughed, almost gloating, proud of herself. "Heck, Ah'm used to lifting bales of cotton twice the size of that puny Professor. Why, on my Daddy's farm, you either worked in the field or you didn't eat."

She shrugged. "Poor Watson. He didn't stand a chance." She spoke casually, as though having a conversation with a neighbor over the back fence, "Why, do you know, we walked the whole way together through the woods, nice as pie. He thought it was…" she caught herself, "another person…he should be afraid of." She guffawed. "He never even considered Ah might harm him! Ah knew he was headed over to your house to spill the beans. What a silly old worrywart he was!"

She looked nonchalantly at her manicured nails and shrugged, "After Ah smacked him on the back of the head with that piece of stray fencing, lifting that triflin' ol' man was a piece of cake, darlin'! Then, Ah scooted back through that old Class 3 tote road slick as can be—by the back way behind Goochie Pond—got my car, and headed back to the Pal-O-Mine where Lucy was waiting for me."

"But Elvina, why Watson? What could he possibly know?"

She scoffed, "Too much for his own good."

"He knew about your…indiscretion? When Norbert was still alive?"

"Huh! That old Professor was too bright for his little tweed knickers. You're right again, Lettie. He and that miserable little mutt saw me and….my lover….in Keene."

"No need to hide it, Elvina, I've already figured it out. The fact of the matter is, it's Armand that you've been…Armand's your 'lover.'"

It all fit together when I remembered last night…how he looked at you. It's hard to hide…that type of intimacy."

"Last night?"

"During the break, at our meeting. Outside, in the twilight. The way he leaned into your personal space and you didn't move or even flinch. It's just something…two people who are close can't hide."

She hooted, flailing the gun in a circular motion. "We-ll-ll! Raaght you are again, Lettie. Our little Professor didn't know when to mind his own p's and q's. On top of that, he had the nerve to do research on his own. The egghead! Why, Ah neva! He told Armand that he'd done a genealogical study on the Limpert family and there were some…inconsistencies, as he put it, that he wanted to discuss with him. Armand was incensed, whoo-eee wasn't he! But he played along to buy some time. Ah think the Professor knew it was the only pull he had against Armand! That silly little dog. Watson was so darned attached to it! Ah guess Armand's constant needling about that little bitch must have eaten away at him. Drove him to the point of trying to find out some dirt on my darlin' man!" She sighed. "Nevertheless, Ah think he'd put it together and knew Armand wasn't really…all he'd said he was. You see, Lettie," she explained conversationally, "Armand came to Pillson as this big New York City gallery owner, and he'd said—always the one to make things bigger than life, my lover is— he told everyone he was distantly related to the founding father—George Pillson!" She smiled coyly, "My land! Well, it was a bit of an exaggeration."

"Uh-huh."

"Well, we couldn't let that come out, could we? It was just a matter of time before Watson would squeal like a pig—about the other things, too." She giggled like a school girl gossiping about the latest news. "Oh, la-de-dah!" She waved the gun in the air, distracted. "That's the way it goes. Ah think the old coot may have overheard us one night out on Armand's patio…we got to drinkin' just a few too many martinis, and got maybe a wee bit too loud, talkin' about… things to come. Anyhoo, Ah saw him peeking through the shrubbery. Like a dang pervert, he was! Heck, Ah think he was researching me, too! Askin' all kinds of questions! Ah figured he was puttin' it all together." She concluded, chortling, "So. Like Ah said, he was just a bit too curious for his own good. Ah just couldn't take the chance."

"So you had to kill him? And in such a brutal way?"

"Well, you know, darlin', you make do with what you have. That day, Armand picked me up out in the boonies and brought me to his place." She went on matter-of-factly, "Yuh, we'd planned to leave my convertible in the williwags up by Goochie, like Ah said--and then he made sure he was long gone long from the house on his way to Keene before Ah 'ran into' Watson as he left for your place. We knew his habits; it was like clockwork the way that little man lived. He always took Twinkles for her walk, usually through the trails out behind his house, and always around one or two o'clock—always within that time frame. Ah just told Armand, 'you leave it to me, darlin'.' He knew Ah could take care of everything. In fact, he delighted in it. And, to answer your question, well, a hay baler is such an….efficient way to take someone out, wouldn't you agree?" The woman's cold chartreuse-flecked blue eyes were like pieces of steel machete, glinting.

She is mad—a raving maniac, in fact, Mrs. Bundle realized. *And Limpert, too!* Forcing a look of interest and discovery on her face, Mrs. Bundle asked, "And the 'Welcome to Hartland' sign? That was you, too?"

Elvina nodded with glee.

"Who exactly burned in the warning: 'Only you can prevent…'?"

Elvina slapped her thigh with the gun, guffawing, "That was a nice touch, wasn't it? Bit over the top for my style! That was… Armand's idea—so dramatic, my lover man is. He thought it would be a nice opportunity to further lay the blame on that ol' goober Junior. Actually stole Junior's blowtorch from the back bed of the Trash and Treasure truck the night after the Tuddy's fire and did his handiwork. Uh-huh! And then, he returned it later that same night. Piece of cake!" She smiled slyly. "It worked, didn't it? Helped scare the whole county, dare Ah say? Law, oh law!" She laughed wickedly.

Mrs. Bundle thought, *I must keep her talking*, as the minutes ticked by with interminable slowness. Already knowing the answer, she asked, "How could you frame Vincent?"

"Junior? That lovesick sucker? Ah knew he was sweet on that Viola Tudhope. Imagine! Why, she's ugly as sin—not near as pretty as my Lucy. He and Viola were skulking around meeting each other secretly and Ah knew it. Ah spied on those two knuckleheads when Ah was casing Tuddy's. It was perfect. Sublime, really. He doesn't ever talk to anyone, afraid of his own shadow, right? The jughead! All Ah had to do was get him on our property, set him up, and we were golden. That was a piece of cake, too. Ah needed a worker, he needed work...*Thaa's raaah...!* After that, it was so easy to just let the rumors float about him and Lucy. You know how folks just love gossip, especially that ol' Weezy! Just give her a thread and she runs with it, that's for dang sure. Adding in that Ah was deadset against their little patticakin' was perfect, just perfect." She sighed again, almost in pleasure, and relaxed, her hand shifting the gun slightly. "Listen, Lettie! Oh, just listen to that music!"

The Rhythmares Band could be heard playing in the distant twilight air, playing a rousing rendition of "Take the 'A' Train" by Duke Ellington.

She giggled and tapped her side playfully with the gun, "Don't you just feel like dancin'?" Lightheartedly, her foot began tapping to the rhythm.

Oh, mercy! There went her chances for being heard by any passersby, Mrs. Bundle thought in despair, knowing that shouting, even the report of a gun, would more than likely fall on deaf ears. *Oh, Louis*, she thought desperately, *I'm counting on you!* "Did you ever think about your actions might affect Lucy? What about her?"

Elvina's mood changed instantly and she snarled and raised the gun. For the first time, Mrs. Bundle noticed concern on Elvina's countenance as the gun pointed ominously at her. "You leave my baby out of this! She doesn't know a thing! All Ah have is Lucy; she's all Ah've ever had that was mine and mine alone. She's just a pure, innocent soul, my little girl is. If Ah evva did one thing right in my life, it was having that daughter. Ah've protected her all her life. Just like Ah wish someone had protected me." She swallowed, looked skyward, her eyes dead flat. "Little Elvina May Leary. You don't know…you have no idea what it's like to feel totally alone in this world. It was my Daddy who beat me first, that son of a biscuit! Ah saw what he did to my Mama, but that was nothin' compared to him layin' that strap on me. Ah went from him to Wilfred, my first husband, who was far, far worse. Ah was sixteen. Sixteen! Married to a…nobody, goin' nowhere. He beat me harder 'n my daddy ever did. Why, he punched me square in the stomach when Ah was seven months pregnant with Lucy. Can you imagine?"

Melancholy shaded her face for a second and then was replaced with something resembling revulsion. "After that, Lucy was born preemie. Ah knew something was terribly wrong with her. Right from the beginning. Oh, Ah knew it was his fault." She was unraveling before Mrs. Bundle's eyes. That glint of hard steel reentered her eyes and her narration continued in dull tones. "Ah counted the days. Ah planned it, wishing every day Ah could destroy him the way he did me and Lucy. He was going to pay, someday, for sure. Ah waited, made everything so nice for him. The perfect little wife, perfect in every way. Just to get that sweet, sweet revenge."

Her lips curled into a slow, spite-filled smile. "And Ah did."

Her colorless face twisted into pure evil, hauntingly intense. "Ah fixed that ol' firing pin on his gun, and the next time he went target shooting….Boom! Gun backfired. Blew his whole face off. That was that." She smiled again, and her playful, wicked nature was back. "*Tha-a's raaah!* He was gone. Toast. The insurance money was enough to get Lucy and me out of that hellhole. Ah'll never regret that, not in a million years. The rest was… well, pretty easy."

"Easy?"

She brandished the gun, her laugh sarcastic. "What do you know about anything? Talk about easy! You've had your easy life here in your perfect little world, perfect in every way from the looks of you. It's so simple, isn't it? Playin' by the rules always works in your world, Lettie. But not in mine. In my world, you make your own rules.

And," she grinned mockingly, "y'all really can't imagine how easy it is to get what you need, if you really want it."

Mrs. Bundle didn't miss a beat. "And what about Norbert, Elvina? Didn't he give you what you needed?"

"Norbert. Hmpph!" Her eyes were blank, as though she was watching a tiresome movie. "Well, truthfully, he came along just at the right time, didn't he? And, he loved Lucy like his own, even adopted her. Ah'll give him that. He was a gentle soul, but number 'n a pounded thumb, poor old houndawg. And, Lawd, boring! Ah have never been as bored as the years Ah spent with Norbert! But, he got us out of trouble—" she laughed, "—me and my little gambling thing, again, Lettie—and he brought us here."

"Let me guess. And then there was…Armand."

"How did you know? Here Ah was, bored to tears with Norbert out here in the williwags, and along comes Armand Limpert. Handsome, and strong! He was…dangerous—and fun, too. The whole package! More my speed, if you know what Ah mean, darlin'." She touched her solid golden locks of hair, the pageboy style curling under meticulously just at shoulder-length. "And what a boy he was! Ah knew Ah had met my match in more ways than one. If ever Ah was cunnin', he's ten times better at it 'n me. Once Ah met Armand…well, Ah knew he was my soul mate." She giggled and whispered with delight, "The waitin' to see him, meetin' secretly like two crazed kids—it was more than Ah could bear at times. Of course, Ah never loved Norbert, and after a time, well," she sighed tediously, "he had to go, too."

"Elvina! You killed him for Armand? Do you really think Armand cares a hoot for you?"

"Hush yo' mouth, Lettie! Of course he does. Me and only me! There's no doubt in my mind. We're so close, Armand and Ah. No one could understand but us…." Her eyes took on a dreamy, faraway look. She heaved a tremendous sigh and looked intensely at Mrs. Bundle. She repeated, "There's no doubt in my mind. As Ah said, we're soul mates. We think alike. And, everything can still work out for us. As long as we keep our heads."

That despicable man's got her believing him, Mrs. Bundle thought, *he's gotten a ready, willing and able accomplice to take the bull by the horns every step of the way!* In no way did she feel sorry for Elvina, but she was thoroughly disgusted, thinking about the Svengali-like hold he had on some women; she asked, "What about Sarah Church?"

Elvina waved a hand as though batting lazily at a pesky fly. "Her? Wrapped around his little finger. Four words." She ticked them off dispassionately, "Pathetic. Lonely. Shriveled up."

"And Dakota?"

"Oh, him? Yes! Wasn't that delicious? Such a handsome specimen! Oh honey, that was so much fun! Ah knew everyone was watching him. He was available! It was perfect. Ah couldn't help but cause a little trouble there and stir things up a bit." She winked. "A great distraction, wasn't it? And, so much fun to see that lemon sucker Althea Swain's nose so out of joint. Even our inquisitive little Erin Corrigan thought Ah was hot for him. Ah made such a nice show of it. Anyway, all that cooin' and fawnin' over him was just pure entertainment for the masses. Of course, we don't need to worry about them now."

"You seem so confident, Elvina, that no one will ever catch up with you and Armand. Again, it almost defies logic."

She pointed to the large leather chair beside the round oak library table. "No one will, you can count on that. Have a seat why don't you, Lettie?"

When Mrs. Bundle didn't move, Elvina pushed the hard metal nose of the gun roughly into her chest. Mrs. Bundle unwillingly sunk into the library wing chair and Elvina quickly moved behind her.

Mrs. Bundle felt the cold barrel of the gun on her neck and Elvina's other hand gripped Mrs. Bundle's bad shoulder—the one that had suffered a bullet wound less than a year before. She winced, holding back a yelp of pain and cried out, "Are you going to kill me, too, Elvina? Like you did the Professor?"

Elvina looked at the clock on the wall and clicked her tongue. "Tsk, tsk! Would you look at the time? Almost half past seven!" She sniggered and said, "Sorry to say, yes, Lettie, time is running out for you, my dear."

"Are you…expecting Armand?"

"No! Ah just don't want to be gone too long. That fat ol' Weezy may get suspicious. Of course, my precious Armand is covering for me. Like he always does." Mrs. Bundle could hear the sadistic smile in her tone.

An ambulance's keening could be heard in the distance.

Mrs. Bundle asked, "What's going on?"

"Sounds like there's big doin's up the road!" She threw her blonde head back and laughed. The chortle was evil personified.

Realization hit Mrs. Bundle. "What have you done, Elvina?"

"Never you mind, Lettie. If Ah were you, Ah'd be worryin' more about what's gonna happen here at the Library, not up the road." The woman's voice held a bit of calm madness in it.

Keep her talking, keep going, Mrs. Bundle told herself, *it's your only chance.* "But I have so many questions…"

Elvina came around the large chair and looked down at her, the gun held squarely in Mrs. Bundle's face, so close she could smell the gun metal. "Ah guess Ah can indulge you two more minutes, Lettie, them all bein' so busy over at the Town Hall. For old time's sake? So? Go ahead—ask!"

Mrs. Bundle swallowed hard. "How…how did you get the fire to start in Brownsville with you away?"

"That's easy. Same thing we did at Tuddy's. Both were on a timer, under the floor boards beside where the propane gas line comes into the store. Set to ignite and then burn really good. And, of course, no way to trace it back to us. Armand and Ah figured out how long we would need. In my case at the store, plenty of time for me to get to Concord, get settled in and then be," she feigned wide-eyed innocence, "'oh-so-surprised-and-shocked' when the police came to find me to tell me my precious business had burned to the ground. Timed to detonate at the same time as the fireworks. Wasn't that clever? And, plenty of reason for poor, stupid Junior to take the blame for turning off the sprinkler system, which Armand made sure was off before he left for the fireworks display at Okemo. And, just as we thought, the Fire Marshall ruled it as intentionally set, with those burn marks indicating the gas lines may have been tampered with. Pretty brainy, wasn't it?"

"And the camp?"

"Same thing. Hunting camp only used in the fall: gas line, timer, detonator, boom!" She blew on her fingernails in mock ease. "All the same. Piece of cake, honey."

"Was it just for the insurance money again? Setting the other two fires as a decoy just so you could do your own arson and not be suspected?"

She nodded with amiable good nature. "Pretty much, yes, *tha's raaah!* Had to make mine look like it was one of a series of crazy pyromaniac crimes. Not sayin' that's what Ah am, mind you, sugar…"

"Why kill the dog?"

"Ol' Tuddsley? That's easy. We knew the dog might be a problem, might bark or cause a ruckus, so we planned it. Took days. Brought along a nice big steak for him—rib-eye, as Ah recall—right from my little ol' meat case. Darlin' dog. He followed us right up that mountain, reached the top, and the fire was a-blazin' like crazy below—so romantic to watch it from afar like that. Tuddsley never looked back. Don't worry 'bout him, Lettie. He didn't feel a thing—went right to sleep after havin' the best meal of his life! Of course, who'd have thought they'd ever find the mutt?"

Mrs. Bundle lowered her head, as though in deep despair. "And all for insurance money." She made her familiar clicking noises with her tongue, meanwhile, trying to think quickly.

"Well, Ah'd be lyin' if Ah said that was the only reason. Truth is, sugar, Ah like livin' on the edge. And, Ah've found out something very interesting about myself."

She grinned and slapped the gun on her thigh for emphasis. "Don't Ah just love a good fire! Bright orange! Red flames, high, reaching up to the sky! There's somethin' about the way it burns, the intensity, the heat…it's exhilarating! Why, it makes me feel so alive!"

Her breath had quickened and her voice was passionate. "Alive! *Tha's raaah!*" She paused, "But of course, the main goal was to get the money—pure and simple. We knew the insurance company would pay up big; it was just a matter of time. So, Ah kill two birds with one stone. Ah get rid of that damn store—someone else can build there for all Ah care--and Ah pay off my gambling debts and start fresh! After that, we figured, there'd still be plenty left over for the condo project."

"Condo project?" Mrs. Bundle asked incredulously, Where?"

"Well, now, just look around you! Oh, yes, honey, condominiums! Didn't Ah tell you? Archie Plummer and Armand have been planning it behind closed doors for months, that's why Armand went on the Library Board! They want to tear down this mausoleum and put up expensive condos. Sell them for oodles of money! *Raaht* there on the river, with the view of the Falls! It would have been easy as pie. But, you and your interfering, triflin' ways really put a wrench in that plan. Armand wanted to throttle you! Ah told him to just bide his time, that there was just no way you'd ever be able to pull off the Festival, especially with such a short time to get it all together." Her nature changed markedly; she was snarling like a Vermont fisher cat now. "But you have, haven't you? You're just too clever, Lettie. You screwed up his plans; you made him mad. Armand doesn't like to be disappointed. So, now, you're gonna pay…too."

"What makes you think others haven't figured out your scheme?"

"Like who?"

"The Sheriff, for one. He already suspects Armand."

"That big bodunk, Will O'Malley? He couldn't find his way out of a paper bag!"

In an instant, Mrs. Bundle caught herself, and asked sharply, "What did you say earlier about Dakota, and Althea, and Erin?"

"Oh, now you want to know about your dear friend Althea? And your precious little Erin?"

"What, Elvina? You said 'we don't need to worry about them now.' Right?"

"Righty-o."

With waning hope, Mrs. Bundle asked, "You didn't mean….you couldn't...? Elvina….what have you done?"

Elvina's voice heightened and she snarled, "Don't be foolish! Of course, Ah meant it. Ah figured, what's one more burnin'? It'll keep 'em busy while we take care of this one last piece here! And, now it's even sweeter, what with you here and all, too."

"So," she was afraid to ask, "Althea…and Erin — and Dakota?"

Elvina Wrinkle stared with evil purpose into Mrs. Bundle's eyes, relishing the moment. "They're gone, Lettie. Dead."

That one word hung in the air like a suspended shell on the verge of exploding as Elvina said, "*Tha's raaah!* Ah made sure of it. Just like you're gonna b—"

The rush in her ears made it impossible for Mrs. Bundle to hear much past the terrible word "dead."

As Elvina raised her gun and aimed, Mrs. Bundle roared with anger and, with an intense purpose and unmitigated vengeance the likes of which she didn't know she possessed, lunged upward at her foe.

"No-o-o!" she cried out in anguish.

Chapter Eight

Rage

Mrs. Bundle still had her keys gripped in her hand and their sharp points raked deeply into Elvina's bare arm as she rose in a rage, like a crazed demon, from her chair.

Caught off guard, Elvina screamed in pain and tried to re-aim the pistol. Mrs. Bundle was too quick for her, however, as she knocked Elvina backward; simultaneously, the gun flew out of her hand.

Although she had never fought like a possessed boxer before, Mrs. Bundle's fury at discovering three of those dearest to her had been victimized and murdered in cold blood caused her to go to another level, an echelon of retaliation she had never accessed before.

Wild and raw as Elvina was, the woman had now met her match in Mrs. Bundle.

Elvina was a tomcat, clawing and snarling with abandon. Mrs. Bundle moved quickly, a battling dynamo, as she fought off each of the desperate woman's blows. Elvina's chest was heaving with the struggle, her nails ragged and broken, her molded hairdo a wreck now, her smeared make-up turned ghoulish in the twilight's shadows. Elvina screeched between blows, "Not you…," she grunted, "…not anyone." She snarled, "Nobody's gonna stop me from gettin' what Ah want!"

They fought like two primal cavewomen vying for survival. Books and magazines flew off the shelves, propelled by the wayward hits and misses of the mêlée. Expertly, Elvina, fully engaged, grabbed

Mrs. Bundle's exposed arms and, with the strength of a wrestler, pushed her back.

Mrs. Bundle lost her balance and slammed into the mahogany wall, slipping a bit lower than her usual height. Elvina had strong man hands—dangerous, strangling hands that reached down and grabbed her around the neck.

Argghhh! Their grunts and screams were guttural, emanating from a visceral, primitive place within the both of them. Mrs. Bundle's hands pushed and pushed at Elvina's, straining for some leverage.

Finally, desperately, she freed herself from the deadly clasp but freedom was fleeting as she slammed to the floor on her knees.

Both women screamed again: one in rage, the other in sheer madness. Elvina clutched desperately at Mrs. Bundle, straining for anything to grab onto; she finally made contact and grabbed the pillbox head of silver-brown braids. She pulled, simultaneously reaching a long thumb downward, grinding it into Mrs. Bundle's eye.

The pain was excruciating, but Mrs. Bundle was in it for the long haul. *Just give me one good shot*, she thought in relative calmness, ignoring the throbbing pain as best she could. She reached out blindly, flailing at the air as her one good eye searched like a roving beacon for Elvina's weakest spot. Slowly, she was able to raise herself up, edging her back up the wall, using it for support.

Elvina was growling like a crazed dog, her throaty voice rumbling and her long, sharp fingernails digging in. A smile spread across her face as her nails sunk into their mark, deadly as a mountain lion's claws. She could see victory.

Spots and colorful prisms appeared before her eyes, but Mrs. Bundle clenched her fingers tightly and drew her fist backward, scarcely thinking of her stinging scalp beneath the weighty head of hair. She concentrated on one thing—winning this deadly battle! The severe pain under those lethal hands was a far-off annoyance.

With all her might and remaining strength she could muster, she willed her fist every ounce of strength she had and punched Elvina Wrinkle square on the chin.

The force of her knuckles hitting flesh and bone shot a blast of pain up Mrs. Bundle's arm, but strangely, it felt good—because she *knew*, she was *positive*, in fact, that she had made a direct hit.

Paradoxically, the impact from her fist was amplified by the lovely gift that had graced her right hand ring finger for two decades, lovingly presented to her by her children: her Mother's ring. *What irony*, she mused in a dreamlike haze. The two half-carat gems--an amethyst for February (Karen) and a sapphire for September (Leslie), round cut, center stone, and deeply set into a bezel setting, carried a pretty good wallop.

Elvina's eyes rolled back into her head and she was knocked out cold, as dead to the world as the momentous occasion when Ali knocked Foreman out in the eighth round in what some considered the biggest upset in boxing history.

The tall, brawny woman slowly slumped to the floor in a lifeless weight, finally coming to rest flat on her back, arms outstretched in total unconscious surrender.

Just at that moment, the back door burst wide open and Sheriff Will O'Malley rushed inside, gun drawn.

He took it all in quickly. "Lettie!" He spied her, flush against the wall, gasping as she bent over Elvina. "Lettie, are you all right? Goldarn it, I told you—!"

Completely out of breath, she looked up at him and heaved weakly, "She—she did it, Will! All of it!"

Louis Montembeau, eyes wild, hurried in behind the Sheriff with her dear Cracker-cat, himself possessed with speed, not far behind.

Louis dashed up to Mrs. Bundle and placed his arms around her, helping her right herself and settling her in the wing chair. She shook her head, the tremendous pain momentarily giving her pause, then hung her head in an attempt to avoid hyperventilating.

"Sit down here." he urged her. Cracker meowed loudly, his dark ebony body electrified as he checked to see if his favorite person in all the world was all right.

Louis Montembeau cried, "Thank God! Are you all right? Oh, heavens! I was so worried when you hadn't returned; I said I didn't care who thought I was crazy! Twenty minutes and I knew something was terribly wrong! Especially when I couldn't reach you on your cell phone! I ran over and got the Sheriff at Town Hall, just like you said to do, and I—I," in his haste for words he fumbled, "I-I told him we had to find you post haste."

She lifted her head up. She was astonished to see Armand Limpert coming cautiously through the door, white as a ghost. His face was grim as he quickly assessed the situation. He surveyed the scene, books and periodicals strewn everywhere, the library's usual order totally destroyed, and his eyes finally came to rest on Elvina lying on the floor, unmoving.

Armand stammered, "I volunteered to come along, as soon as I heard!"

Mrs. Bundle struggled for air. Her throat felt as though she had a huge, spindly chestnut burr stuck inside. Her eyes locked with the Sheriff. "Elvina—she—she burned down her own store—"

The Sheriff nodded, reaching down to pick up the gun from the floor. "We know. She tried to burn down Town Hall tonight. Evidently," he looked around at the chaos and said dryly, "she's been on a burning rampage." He scratched his head in amazement. "Did you actually knock her out?"

She nodded, then realized in horror—the ambulance! "No, it's not true! Will! I can't bear it! I heard the ambulance….Althea, and Erin! Elvina said they're—are they really…?" She couldn't finish the sentence, beside herself with anguish, and grabbed for Cracker. She held him closely to her.

Will patted her shoulder, trying to calm her. "Gaw! No, no, they're fine, and safe. Don't worry! They all got out of the building just in time. Thanks to Dakota Squibb."

She looked fiercely at Armand, who shrank slightly from her

glare. Then, she cocked her head toward the supine figure of Elvina. "She confessed everything to me, Sheriff. The murder, the arson, everything. I know how she did it. The rivet, Will!"

He blinked, then nodded in vague comprehension. "The rivet. Right."

"It's from her cigarette lighter! You'll be able to find her own—vintage, mother of pearl—it's at her place, I'm sure. It holds sentimental value for her. She—"

"Stop! Lettie, please. Slow down." Will O'Malley shook his head. "You know, I'm getting kind of tired of trying to read your mind, woman."

"Wait!" She took a gulp of air and pointed an accusing finger at Armand. "Arrest him, Will!" She couldn't get the words out fast enough. "They're...lovers! In cahoots! Elvina and him! They're both in on this together. Oh, mercy! And poor, defenseless Norbert! Oh, don't you be shaking your head, Armand! Yes, it's true—and Archie Plummer, too, he's involved somehow. Something about a condo development, here, at the Library site. That is, with the Pillson Library burned to the ground, they'd have their way, to be sure. You've got to arrest him, Will!"

Armand stepped back, shrinking, and turned for the door. "Arrest me? I've got to get back."

A silent deputy in the doorway blocked his exit.

Limpert tried in vain to push past him. "You can't arrest me! I—I want my attorney. Let me pass!"

"Shut up, Limpert!" The Sheriff's stone demeanor said it all. "Don't say another word." Taking a pair of handcuffs from his belt and without further comment, he began, "'You have the right to remain silent...'"

The large, vain man shut his eyes in bleak withdrawal, reconciled to surrender, at least for now. He clamped his mouth tighter than a steel trap, remaining totally silent.

When the Sheriff finished, he asked Armand, "Do you understand, Mr. Limpert?"

A long, low groan could be heard from the floor. Elvina was just coming to. She asked hazily, "Ar-mand, *darlin'*? Is...that....*you*?

Armand turned his face away from her in disgust and nodded at Will.

"I can't hear you," Will said.

He blanched. "Yes. I understand."

Mrs Bundle cleared her throat and, rising from the chair, walked painfully over toward him. She leaned in very close, closer than comfortable, into his personal space, and said in a hoarse undertone, "If I were you, I'd cut a deal, Armand. Otherwise, you'll be going away for a very long time—without that clever, sinister, very ill woman who's coming to on the floor, mind you. I suspect she'll have her story worked out quicker than three shakes of a lamb's tail once she's fully awake and sees you really don't care about her and the game is over. Oh, yes," she whispered, "I wonder who'll leave *who* in the dust to take all the blame."

He closed his eyes tightly, and when he reopened them, Mrs. Bundle thought she could discern the slightest tremor in his overly-large mouth. Just above his upper lip, minute beads of sweat shone like little pinheads in the fading light.

Chapter Nine

At the Hospital

L ater that evening, close to ten o'clock, a weary but very determined Mrs. Bundle arrived at Hitchcock Medical Center to check on the condition of Erin Corrigan.

Her own disheveled appearance was, in no way, assisted by her present hairdo; the pillbox of silver-brown braids, usually piled high, tightly woven, and neatly coiffed, was barely held together now, long strands escaping willy-nilly, creating rather a look of lunacy about the woman as they framed her exhausted face.

Her head still smarted and stung from the severe pulling it had received. Mrs. Bundle's previously neat, stylish summer dress was ripped at the shoulder and was mottled with blood; the earlier wrestling match with Elvina had taken its toll. She had huge bruises on her bare arms and knees, and deep, rapidly burgeoning, purple finger marks embedded into her long neck. And by this time tomorrow, her left eye's soreness indicated she would have quite a shiner, she surmised, touching it gingerly to see if the puffiness had gone down at all. Her right hand felt numb, her knuckles grazed. Catching a look at herself in the reflection of window glass, she realized she looked as though she had been run over by a football squad. *Well,* she mused to herself, *this will certainly all make for great conversation this weekend at the Festival.*

Against everyone's advice, she had insisted on coming here this evening, not wanting to wait until the morrow. Louis had agreed to take Cracker home, and the Sheriff had made her promise she would only stay for a short time before getting herself home safely and soundly. She assured them that she might look as though she'd been run through the mill, but she was a *very* hardy individual — just as hardy as Elvina, never you mind. She had to admit, though, as she walked alone down the corridor, she was pretty sore from head to toe.

Nevertheless, the smile on Mrs. Bundle's face told an entirely different story as she turned the corner toward Erin's room after talking to the nurse on duty, who had also ministered to her bruises.

Althea was alive; Erin was going to be fine; that was all that mattered. The condition of Dakota was unknown to her.

She was met at the darkened hospital room door by Jack, who first put his fingers to his lips, then threw his arms around her and hugged her tightly, gripping her as though he hadn't seen her in a month of Sundays.

"She's all right," he mumbled, a sob escaping from his throat. *"Buíochas le Dia!"*

"Thank God!" she repeated back to him.

They clung to each other and then went into the hushed room.

Erin, almost angelic in appearance, lay sleeping soundly, a huge bandage circling her little head, the dark brown wisps of unruly hair escaping from beneath.

Althea sat at her bedside, her round cheeks flushed with the excitement of the day. She smiled when she saw her best friend and reached up, squeezing her friend's outstretched hand, and whispered, "Hi, L! They just got her down. It took the whole floor of nurses to convince her it was time to go to sleep. She's all right, minor concussion with a hairline skull fracture, no evidence at all of any intracranial bleeding — they're watching her very closely for the next few hours but think she's going to be just fine. Seems she'd been drugged, too. A very lucky little girl. She's all worried about..." Althea's voice cracked slightly, "Dakota."

Jack added softly, "Aye, him and that bloody Chester, too! Right, even though we've tried our best to reassure her about a dozen times that he's home with Gumpy, safe and sound. She wants to see the daft bird! She was wanting to know if we could go and fetch him for her, of all things! And she's already begging to be allowed to be in the Talent Show tomorrow night, isn't she? Won't take no for an answer. Right, we'll have to see about that one."

They kept their voices low as they continued their conversation.

Althea looked squarely at her friend midst the low lighting, finally taking in her disheveled, bruised appearance. "Where on earth have *you* been?" She looked at her suspiciously. "What's happened?"

Mrs. Bundle shifted from one foot to the other, reluctant to tell everything that had transpired since she had last seen them. In her raspy voice, she whispered, "Oh, it's nothing. It's all over; everybody's fine."

"What's over?" Althea asked, "Who's everybody? What do you mean, everybody's fine?"

Mrs. Bundle looked over at Jack, not wanting to upset the boy further, and then shot a pleading look at Althea. "I think it can wait until tomorrow," she said.

Jack put his arm around his mentor. "It's okay, mum. Don't fuss about me, I already know. Everybody knows. You'll be wanting to say something about that dodgy Elvina Wrinkle, to be sure. She's an evil wench, isn't she now? Did they get her?"

Mrs. Bundle nodded, biting her upper lip lightly. "Yes, Jack, but she hurt a lot of people in the process, including Erin, and Dakota Squibb. Poor Dakota! I understand he's been airlifted to the burn center at Mass General."

Althea nodded grimly. "Yes, last word was that he could lose the use of both hands if there is permanent nerve damage. We've been waiting to hear about him; the nurses said they'd let us know as soon as they heard. He saved Erin, and even brought that ornery rooster out of the blaze, too. I've never seen anyone so selfless." She paused and her voice softened. "And stubborn, too. One thing for sure, that woman is pure evil reincarnated."

Mrs. Bundle said, "Right, it's diabolical, to say the least. There's more evil there, too, to tell you about. Brace yourself," she paused. "She set all the other fires. And, she murdered Watson, too."

They both looked at her skeptically.

Althea blinked and rubbed her forehead, pushing back the dark blonde bangs. "She killed the Professor? Good grief! Whatever for? And how?"

"Bloody Hell!" Jack spit the words, reacting sharply. Drawing in a long breath, he lowered his voice to barely a whisper and growled, "Jaysus! And she set the fire at Tuddy's Diner, too?"

Mrs. Bundle nodded.

"*Gránna diabhal!* That ugly *divil*! And that camp up in Hartland?"

"Uh-huh."

He looked confused. "Why—her own store?"

"She burned down the General Store, ostensibly to get the insurance money, from what she confessed." Mrs. Bundle looked a bit reticent as she added, "Actually, I spent a very unpleasant session with her this evening, during which she confessed everything to me."

"To you? When?"

"Right after she tried to burn down Town Hall. It's a long story, but…well, I found her at the Library. She was ready to burn that down, too."

"Good grief!"

"Ach! The Library?" Jack asked.

"Uh-huh. She's in debt up to her eyeballs. Set up this elaborate plan. She and Armand Limpert. Why, he's just as bad as she is. Evidently, that's why they tried to do away with Erin tonight– because Erin saw them kissing each other and overheard their plans at Town Hall that they were going to burn the Library this evening. They knew their secret wouldn't be long for the keeping. The jig would be up."

"So she drugs her," Jack asked, astounded, "coshes her on the head and leaves a little girl for dead? That's bollocks!"

"And then tries to kill us, too, when we come upon her deed!" Althea said angrily, "Unbelievable. She must be out of her mind."

"I think she is…unbalanced, to say the least. I saw it in her eyes tonight. It was…very daunting, to be sure." Mrs. Bundle's words came in a rush, her dark brown eyes flashing. "And poor Watson! He wasn't just an innocent bystander—call it being in the wrong place at the wrong time. He happened to see them in Keene when they were meeting secretly before Norberts's death; they were in the process of making their plans. Seems Watson may have seen them at the insurance office and later, may have put two and two together about the insurance scam to collect money on the store. Anyway, he took it upon himself to research Armand's genealogical claims that he was a descendant to George Pillson. Bit off more than he could chew; I'm not sure what exactly he did know, but whatever it was, it will forever remain a mystery. The fact of the matter is, she was convinced that he knew what they were up to. It may have just been all up here...," she tapped her temple, "but...she said she knew he 'had to go,' as she put it when she saw him peering at them through the bushes near Armand's back patio. And..." she stopped for a breath, gulped, then finished. "What's really horrible is that she admitted to me that she murdered Norbert. First, by 'helping' his fall from the roof, and then later, when he was in the hospital, by giving him an overdose. See, I figured out she was the one that killed poor Tuddsley, using the same drug the doctors used during Norbert's hospitalization—when he was in a coma." Her eyes went directly to Althea, knowing, as a nurse, she would understand. "It was pentobarb."

"Pentobarb! For concussions. And for inducing comas to aid in recovery."

"Right. But she made sure he had just a bit more....and then, after his death, kept the balance of it in her private stash for good measure, just in case."

Jack's ruddy cheeks were ablaze and his eyes sharpened. "Poor bloke! Why the blue *divil* that witch did all this is just sick! I can't get my mind around it, surely I can't! Gaw! It makes the hairs come up on me neck all prickly. She's been a very busy bird, hasn't she now?"

Althea was disgusted. "So sweet— the honey always dripping off her! Meanwhile, she's doing all these wicked deeds. Dastardly!"

Mrs. Bundle gave them a lopsided smile. "Not to worry. She's out of commission now, as they say. They've got her in custody. And

Armand, too—such a wimp! He confessed everything, folded like a house of cheap cards. Turned on her in the end; he's trying to cut a deal for himself. The jury's still out on what will happen to them. You can be sure jail is in their future. Let's hope for a very long time."

Althea gave her a studied look. "Are you all right? You're not telling us everything."

Mrs. Bundle stifled a yawn and nodded lazily. "Allie, my story will have to wait for another day. You know what? I'm just happy to see you safe and this little one in one piece. Look at the smile on that diminutive imp's face!" She wiped her moist eyes. "Let's all go home and get a good night's sleep. I'll tell you all about it tomorrow, after we've all had some rest. Enough, for now. One thing is for certain. We don't have to worry about Elvina Wrinkle ever again!"

Jack shifted in the doorway. "I'm thinking maybe I should stay here. Right, and I was ready to rip Mr. Squibb's head off, thinking he was the criminal—'til I realized he's the one who saved our Erin. Ach!" He rubbed his tired eyes. "Blimey! Sure, and I'm afraid I haven't treated that bloke very well. Not very well at all."

Althea started and then covered her mouth in alarm, as though she'd been hit with a bolt from the blue. "Oh! Jack, with this entire crisis, I haven't had a chance to…tell you. We need to talk."

She turned toward her best friend and shivered. "Oh, L, I'm so glad you're here…I need you for support. I have something important to tell Jack that he may or may not want to hear…about Dakota Squibb."

"What now?" Jack asked suspiciously.

Mrs. Bundle looked at her quizzically. "What is it?"

Althea looked earnestly into Jack's eyes. She began slowly, "Dakota Squibb. He's—That's not his real name. He wanted me to tell you everything."

"Emmm…well, then—go ahead."

"For starters, his real name is Ian Kelley. His brother's name was…. Aengus Kelley."

The young man's eyes flinched. "Kelley, you say? Aengus Kelley? Right, now, that would be very strange, wouldn't it?"

Disbelief slowly registered on the boy's striking face. He said dully, "My grandfather's name was…Aengus Kelley. From Ballyhaise. My Mum's Da."

"Yes, I know."

"But…surely, that would be…impossible."

"No! I mean, yes! Yes, it is possible. It is the same Aengus Kelley. That's what I'm trying to tell you. Dakota Squibb….real name, Ian Kelley… is, in fact, your great-uncle. From Ireland. Well, originally, from Ireland, but he's been here in the U.S. most of his life. Left Ireland decades ago."

Jack seemed to process this information with difficulty. His fingers rubbed at his temples, then rippled nervously through his thick, dark locks.

He muttered, "C'mere, that's bollocks!"

"No, Jack. It's the truth. He told me. Tonight, down in the Town Hall basement before we knew whether we'd get out of that mess alive. He wanted to…come clean. I…I haven't been very…nice to him, either. You're not the only one who's treated him badly." Her face clouded over and she looked at Mrs. Bundle. "I have, too. And he's been nothing short of a gentleman towards me since the first day we met. When we were trapped tonight, he wanted me to know the truth about him and his past. We were in the cellar…and he said he had been wanting to tell the truth for a very long time. He said he had been wanting to especially tell you, but he didn't know how."

"Bloody Hell! Sure, and this is the uncle me Ma said was shipped off to America? Because of the underground? Something to do with the Sinn Fein?"

"The very same--well, an offshoot group called the PRA, is what he said."

"Me Ma thought he was dead, for sure. There was never any mention of him, she said, after he left Ireland. No one knew what happened to him!" He looked confused, tapping his creased forehead as if to enhance his memory.

Althea nodded. "He says he took on a new identity, knowing he could never return to Ireland. He swears he was an innocent witness to…something that he says put him in terrible jeopardy. That's what he told me and I'm sure he wants to tell you everything, even more. He said as much. And, that's why he's here, in Pillsonville, too. He wanted desperately to see you, meet you, to connect with you and the girls--"

His face darkened. "Ach, what a gom I've been! I should have known this, shouldn't I? I knew he reminded me….always made me think of me native soil, didn't he now? Always asking me about Ireland and the like."

Mrs. Bundle had been listening intently and exclaimed, "Oh! The correspondence, Jack! The letters from that New York law firm — the one that came last month!"

He stood up, his body electrified, as though ready for combat.

"I've got to go. Now."

"Jack, wait! Where — where are you going?"

"Mrs. B! *Blimey!*" His eyes softened and suddenly, misted over. "He's me great-uncle, isn't he now? Me only blood relative left, for all I know. And he's sufferin' and God knows, he could die. We don't really know anything, do we? If he loses the use of his hands, it would be a tragedy, and all because of watchin' over the lass like he did, am I right? I've got to go to him, to help him if I can. Right off."

Althea stood up, as determined as he was. "Jack, I'll go with you. I need… to see him, too. To make sure he's all right. He and I have…unfinished business." Her voice was soft and very vulnerable. The lump in her throat caused her to pause. "But, wait… Let's think this through with more logic and less emotion. Wouldn't it be best to leave first thing in the morning? After a few hour's sleep? That's reasonable, isn't it?"

"Yes, Jack, that does makes better sense," Mrs. Bundle added.

"Good grief!" Althea put her palm to her forehead in frustration, realizing what she was saying. "Oh, L," she looked at her friend, "I can't go to Boston! What about the Festival? I've got responsibilities tomorrow and Sunday. Especially, now that Dakota…I mean, Ian, won't be there. We've got to make sure it all goes off without a hitch!"

Mrs. Bundle knew Althea needed to go. It was already clear to her how her best friend felt about Ian Kelley.

She gave Althea a hug. "I think we can manage. It'll be fine. You need to go."

"Are you sure?"

"Are you kidding? With all the help we've got, everything should go like clockwork. At this point, everyone is so pumped and ready, the Festival should almost run itself, for mercy's sake."

"Thank you, L. You're the best."

Mrs. Bundle motioned toward the door. "Well, we better get going if we're going to get some sleep. And, you can leave early on the morrow."

Jack leaned over and gave his sleeping sister a light kiss. "The nurses will take good care of our wee one. And Gumpy and the boys have already said they'll be in here first thing in the morning when Erin awakes. Angie's going to take good care of Chester and Aineen."

He turned to both women and a tired smile appeared. "Let's go home."

Mrs. Bundle stood up and gave the sleeping child a light kiss on her cheek. There was a slightly mischievous look to the little imp, even in repose. Yes, she realized with accomplishment, that was the *same* look, vaguely familiar to her, that she had noticed on Dakota's playful face the first time they had met!

As the trio walked into the corridor, she said, "Ah, sleep! I'm going to sleep better tonight than I have in weeks. Don't you know? I've got a Festival to run in the morning!"

As they walked outside, wonder of wonders! A gentle rain was falling, a steady night shower washing everything clean.

Rain!

Mrs. Bundle put one arm through Althea's and hooked the other through Jack's.

The three of them stood together, without words, feeling the rain gently splash on their bare heads and arms.

It was heavenly.

Mrs. Bundle looked up at the wet sky and smiled as the rain spattered her face, taking it all in with the unbridled delight of a child.

"Isn't life …*fantastical*?"

Chapter Ten

Bedside with Ian

"Yes, I'll say it again–it all went great! The Talent Show was a huge success!"

It was Sunday evening and Angie was at Ian's bedside, along with Jack and Althea. Angie had just arrived from the three-hour drive from their little southern Vermont village, bringing them the latest news of the Talent Show, in addition to the Festival's last hours.

"They moved it over to the gym's stage at the elementary school. The place was packed to the gills. The Colossal Kittredges took over and ran everything, including your duties. From beginning to end, they did a real bang-up job. Keith, especially! He was great. Of course, the program was already printed with your name as Master of Ceremonies, along with your whistling act, so Keith Kittredge made a short announcement that you'd had a medical emergency and that he hoped all would be well with you."

He winced and asked feebly, "Was Erin able—"

"Yup! The firemen fetched her ukulele from the Town Hall basement, which, unbelievably, was none the worse for wear—smoke damage and everything-- and brought it over to Gumpy's for her. After that, there was nothing to stop her! Boy, you should have seen her on that stage! Started out a little shaky, what with Chester being manhandled and everything, but all of a sudden it kicked in, in full gear. What a hoot! She and Chester were a huge hit! They brought the whole house to their feet on the final chorus. It was—amazing!"

Ian leaned back and sighed, the excruciating pain temporarily forgotten as he smiled.

"That's wonderful. She's not hurt—"

"Nope! Pretty much fully recovered. Big bump on her head but rambunctious as ever. She was in rare form, as usual. Asking when she can see her 'Uncle Ian.' She's very worried about you. Wants to know if you can still whistle after all this."

He smiled and laid his head wearily back on the pillow.

She continued on, filling everyone in on the details of the Festival, as they all listened with great interest. It was winding down but still going strong when she'd left for Boston; both days had been sunny, described by many as the best weather ever. Remarkably, during last night's late evening hours, it had rained another inch again as it had the night before. Consequently, the county-wide fire alert had been downgraded to "stand-by," and a weather pattern indicated a heavy rain was headed up the Eastern Seaboard and would reach the Northeast sometime Tuesday. As a result, all was well in the rain department; there would be no more drought for Windsor County, she assured them.

Record numbers had attended throughout the two days, and that afternoon had been the finale: the Art Festival Auction. People had come from all over to bid on all the wonderful pieces. She made special reference to the fact that Vincent Veakey's metal Active Art had been a smash hit, too.

She looked at her watch. "Vincent's stuff was really cool. I suspect the Auction is over now, and the crowds are heading home."

She told them the final toll for the Festival would be tallied in the next few days, but Mrs. Bundle was confident they had more than accomplished their goal.

"And, that's pretty much it. Oh, she sends her love to all of you." She looked Ian over with concerned eyes and asked, "But enough about the Festival and the Talent Show. How are you doing?"

He opened his glassy eyes halfway; he was heavily sedated, but it was evident that all this information had given him pleasure. Dreamily, he said, "Me? Oh, I'm fine. I'm so happy…Jack…" He reached out, closing his sleepy eyes.

Jack said gently, "Yes, Uncle, I'm here. There's no need to worry. *Codladh sámh, Uncail.*"

"'Sleep well,' yes, I remember. Jack..." he whispered, "do you believe that little Erin? Ach! What a lass!" He smiled through his pain, succumbing to another lapse of exhaustion.

The day before, Ian had awoken with Jack on one side of his hospital bed, and Althea on the other. He was feverish, his wounds severe, and the Sumner Redstone Burn Center nurses had cautioned that he should not become stressed or upset in any way. His last evening's condition of "critical" had been upgraded to "stable" and he smiled wanly when he saw Althea. She reached over and lightly touched his shoulder. He tried to speak, but Jack hushed him as a huge tear drifted down from the corner of his eye.

The rest of Ian's upper torso, naked to the waist, was either bandaged or covered with a gel-like, zinc-sulphate-based substance that helped his burned, blistered body retain liquids and fight infection—in addition to the intravenous tube, which channeled antibiotics and sedative directly into his traumatized body. Below his waist, he was covered by a thin white sheet as starkly pallid as the whites of his eyes and in deep contrast to his bright red upper body. He looked like a terrible caricature of himself, beet-red, hairless body, and all.

Early indication from his doctors was that their patient's outlook was "promising," although skin-grafting was a likelihood. They would not commit to anything more, and Ian, for whatever reason, had not yet asked about the functioning of his scorched hands.

Ian was so overjoyed at seeing Jack, he had insisted, in painful bits and starts, on telling him and Althea the whole story of how he came to be in the United States.

"I came to America as a petrified teenager—almost fifteen I was, and I had to make my own way from the get-go. I had a knack for drawing and painting, and was so amazed by the city skylines I was soon painting on the streets of New York. Over time, I was taken in… by a family and I went to college to study art, honed my skills and went out into the world. I knew I could never contact my brother, for fear that I would be discovered." He motioned toward the table and Althea daubed his dry lips with ice chips.

"Are you sure you want to — ?"

He waved her good intentions aside and continued, "I saw… something very disturbing back when I was only fourteen. I was a rebellious chap, a hothead who knew everything, to be sure. I'd joined a group without knowing the consequences of my foolish decision at such a young age. I was sworn to a life of secrecy, barely two weeks after I left the little village of Ballyhaise--the only home I had ever known. Before I knew it, I was up to my elbows in trouble."

He lifted his sorely bandaged arms up scarcely an inch and chuckled derisively through the severe pain.

When Jack tried to silence him, he said through clenched teeth, "No, no! You deserve…I must tell you the whole truth. D'ya see this marking on my back?" With incredible strength, he pulled his head forward so that they could see the area between his left shoulder blade and the nape of his neck.

A small circular tattoo, much like a garland, was evident. Albeit faded with time, they could see it measured about two inches in diameter and portrayed intertwined red roses and green shamrocks. Most striking, though, was what was in the center of the wreath: a black dagger dripping with two drops of blood.

"The Wild Irish rose and dagger is what that is, mate. Their mark, one that branded you as one of them. They called themselves the Progressive Real Activists, or the PRA. You see, after that, for a young bloke of fourteen, there was no turning back, was there? I had made my bed. I was too afraid to back out and run home, which is what I wanted to do. And then, they sent me on a 'mission,' they said, to prove myself and my loyalty — this cost me dearly. So dear, in fact, that I was never to see Ireland again." He struggled with his words, and his voice broke with emotion. He swallowed, and his eyes hardened.

"I saw three men—English soldiers they were—brutally murdered by this splinter group of the Sinn Fein. I was so traumatized by what I saw, they thought hard about murdering me, too. In the end, I was blindfolded, drugged, and thrown into the hold of a freighter ship as a stowaway, bound for America. The last I remember is being told never, never to return to Dublin, or even my dear home, Ballyhaise. They said they would murder my family and hunt me down if I ever repeated anything I saw or heard."

His eyes were moist, and he drew in quick breaths. "One of the ship's hands, a Brazilian laborer named Tiago, found me, starving and near-dead I was, and befriended me, thank God. So you see, when I arrived in this country, I left the ship in the dead of night, was spirited away to El Barrio, or Spanish East Harlem, by friends of Tiago's. Without them, I would have been left alone, abandoned, to fend for myself. Time went by, and God knows how, but I survived by sheer miracle and determination. Later, when I'd been in America awhile, I read something in a dated, older issue of *The Irish Times* that shocked me—my name was there in black and white for all to see—Ian Kelley, it said. It linked me to the murders, although I had nothing to do with them. Nothing, I tell you. Of course, I had to change my name. The risk was too great. And so, I made a good life here in America—I've never been in trouble with the law."

He leaned back, shifted uncomfortably, and Jack adjusted the sheet for him. "Thank you, lad. I was so lonely and afraid in the beginning. The first few years I often actually imagined I was being followed. It's a terrible thing to feel the eyes of someone evil on your back. Time went on, and I kept my nose low to the ground. I worked hard. I fell in love with the rich Barrio art, and began to paint murals. After that, as I became involved in my art, my work, my life, I put the thoughts of terror out of my daily existence. I never saw or heard from the PRA again. Of course, it was all a very long time ago; most, thank God, if not all, of them are probably dead now, and the group is dissolved, of that I am fairly certain." His voice was rusty, barely above a whisper. "And that, dear boy, is my story."

"Shush, now Uncle." Jack's voice had a raw, but light twist to it. "Sleep and we can talk more about all your exploits as a young chancer tomorrow. Aye, we all make mistakes in our youth, to be sure. Right, and I'm not going anywhere, don't you know?"

———•—•—•———

Later Sunday evening, when Ian awoke, Althea was sitting alone by his side. She jumped when she saw his eyes open.

He asked sleepily, but with some concern. "Where's...Jack?"

She hushed him and said, "Jack and Angie went down to the cafeteria for a bite to eat. They'll be back shortly."

He smiled weakly. "He's a grand young man."

"He was very worried about you, Ian." She paused, "It seems...odd. To call you by your real name."

"I'm glad you're here, Althea, dear."

She reached over and put her hand very near his bandaged one. "You'll be all right, if you listen to the doctors, that is. And do everything they say you must do, to recover fully."

He looked down at his swathed hand. "Do you...have they told you...about my hands?"

She shook her head. "No...not yet."

He sighed and said, "I'm not sure...it will be hard going, I tell you, if I can't do what I've done my whole life. If I can't...create."

"You'll always be able to create. It might not be...the same way. Only time will tell. Just remember that saying, Ian. 'Where there's a will...'"

He winced, "Oh, yeah—'there's a big problem!'"

They both chuckled. He sighed, "I know, I know. You want me to remain positive."

"Well, it would help."

"I will try. And, really, I'm not that worried. Frankly, after all that's happened, all I care about is that the people I love are well and happy. And with me."

She blushed and gently drew back her hand.

Ian reached out and rested his bandaged hand delicately on hers.

He said softly, "You do like me, just a little, don't you?"

Her expression was veiled, but her eyes, which were welling over with emotion, told a different story. "You...could grow on a person if that person wasn't very careful, Ian Kelley."

"On that you can depend, dear one. Can I...depend on that, Althea?" His injured wrist brushed her wayward bangs away from her eyes.

She turned her face away, too moved to speak, and he put his lips together and tried to whistle to her, but nothing came out.

As she turned back to him, he said with a playful, yet tired, smile, "I'm a damaged man, woman. Why, I can't seem to even whistle anymore..."

She reached over and, trying to keep things light-hearted, tapped his raised knees through the sheets. "Oh, go on! Good grief, you'll be whistling again before you know it."

He smiled and stared into her large, opalescent-green eyes, the only sound the distant hum of the hospital's air filtration system.

She leaned in slightly, and whispered, "Give it time, Ian. Give it all time, and it will all work out."

He cleared his throat and his voice, raspy and low, said gently, teasingly, "Maybe you'll help me practice getting my lips back into condition..."

She sighed and rolled her eyes. "You, Ian, are relentless! Well, Mr. Kelley, I guess you're going to just have to get better first, and then we'll see whether I'm willing--"

But her sentence was abruptly interrupted by Ian gently nudging her down to him; their lips came together as one.

Later, his tired eyes closed gradually, yearning to memorize every facet of her lovely, comfortable features. She had stroked his forehead softly for a few moments more, and finally, his heavy eyelids closed completely, and he fell into the deepest and most restful sleep he had had in the last two days.

Part VI:

FINAL DAYS OF SUMMER

Chapter One

Tying Up Loose Ends

It was Sunday, a week after the Festival; pleased to say, the event was now a happy memory in just about everyone's minds. Gone, too, was the interminable heat—at least for now, replaced by a mildly pleasant, cooler temperature.

This afternoon, Mrs. Bundle's large front parlor was chock full of guests, some seated, some standing, but all listening with great interest to her every word. She was positioned by the fireplace in front of her secretary desk, surrounded by the assemblage. Outside, a gentle, fresh rain fell, providing a calming effect in the highly-charged, crowded room.

Yes, The Dog Days of Summer Art Festival was a memory now, albeit a good one for most. The Library Foundation coffers had netted well over $100,000 when all the bills had been settled up. However, most amazing to all was that the community had come together in a short time and, quite miraculously, had put on an event so successful that plans were already in the works for the "2nd Annual" Dog Days of Summer Art Festival.

The day before, the library trustees had been thrilled to announce that there was now plenty of money to not only add the necessary state-mandated requirements of the handicapped-accessible ramp, but also to repair the most urgent of items (the roof) and begin scheduling a long-term plan for complete restoration, to be sustained by the income from the future monies from the annual

Festival, along with private donations. Needless to say, the new Board Chairman of the Pillson Public Library, Mrs. Bundle, (having been placed back into the position of highest authority with the downfall of Armand Limpert), was overjoyed with the outcome from every vantage point.

The existing Library Board of Trustees' first order of business had been to vote on and then welcome two new board members. The Board was now restructured to include Karen Kittredge (mother to the five Colossal Kittredge kids and wife to Keith) and the quiet spoken Carl Andersen (multi-talented instrumentalist and erudite farmer). These newest board members seemed to be natural replacements for the deceased professor and the disgraced Limpert and, upon their acceptance, had been welcomed by the Library Board.

No one needed to, or wanted to, talk about Armand Limpert— especially today.

Sitting at the secretary desk beside Mrs. Bundle was a glowing Althea, who had been eagerly nodding in accord at various intervals, often adding a word or two as necessary, as Mrs. Bundle's story slowly unfolded.

Two of the twenty or so in attendance were Viola Tudhope and Vincent Veakey, who sat as close as two peas in a pod on the formal robin's-egg blue loveseat, with Barnabus Veakey standing defensively behind them, uncomfortably shifting from one foot to another, obviously very unaccustomed to this formal and graceful setting.

At regular intervals, he cocked a bushy, suspicious eyebrow at his nemesis, Ger Tudhope and his wife Phoebe, who sat, stiff-backed, far across the room, on the piano bench. Their pained demeanor clearly indicated they were still estranged from their only daughter, as they stared straight ahead at Mrs. Bundle, blatantly disregarding both Viola and Vincent. Needless to say, it had taken some coaxing on Mrs. Bundle's part to get both the Tudhopes and Barny to attend this important meeting, but luckily, curiosity had won out, and both Vincent's father and Viola's parents had acquiesced to be present.

The Andersen men (Walter, Clay, and Carl) stood like sentinels at the double french door opening behind the Tudhopes.

Angie and three of her clever LiMB Society members (Natalie, Anthony and Nicholas Clancy) all sat on the braided rug on the floor in front of Mrs. Bundle. In contrast, Weezy Bunton had helped herself to the largest (and most comfortable) Queen Anne chair in the parlor, and presided nearby, preening with pride. Weezy's acceptance and newfound status as Head Organizer of the 2nd Annual Dog Days of Summer Art Festival was just the ticket for the woman who had almost single-handedly performed miracles at the first Dog Days of Summer Art Festival, setting a precedent few could match. Her acceptance in the coveted role had been (more than anything) a welcome relief to Mrs. Bundle.

Also in attendance and sitting in a united row along the large bay window seat at the back of the room were the other trustees of the Library Board: a smiling Sarah Church (who seemed quite changed for the better after discovering the magnitude of her former champion Armand's deception); Ellie Waterhouse (harried and pleasantly cooperative as ever); the soft-spoken but articulate new member, Karen Kittredge; and, last but not least, swing-vote Head Librarian Louis Montembeau (beaming and as sprightly as ever).

A very wan-looking Ian Kelley had arrived back in Pillson Falls two days before from Boston to convalesce at home. Insisting on being present at the meeting, he sat quietly tucked out of the way in the comfortably upholstered corner chair. Looking like a victim of recent warfare, his left hand was bandaged clear up to his elbow; two fingers on his right hand were loosely swathed, and the rest held visible signs of his recent injury. Large, slow-healing blisters and severe redness still lingered on his long, graceful digits, his bare forearms smattered like a cotton field with sterile, trauma-burn bandages. The only other remnant of the conflagration's fury was evidenced on his face, which was beet red and as smooth as if he had just had a chemical peel. He was completely devoid of eyebrows (which gave him a perpetually startled look); his lips were still puffy and blistered, and his forehead was peeling; the tufts of hair at the top of his head, usually copious amounts of wavy salt-and-pepper locks, still held singed-brown ends, having been burned to shorter than a half-inch in places.

Jack Corrigan stood silently at his great-uncle's side, as usual, a quiet, unobtrusive observer. He had an air of protectiveness about him as he watched patiently, proudly, while Mrs. Bundle talked.

The inimitable Cracker preened at his feet, his ebony neck adorned with a formal black bowtie chosen specially for this occasion. Occasionally, he emitted well-placed *"meows"* of support for his mistress. *She's done herself proud on this one*, he cat-thought regally.

Last but not least, there was Sheriff Will O'Malley, hat in hand, observing from the room's fringes near the front hall doorway. He leaned his large frame against the door jamb listening intently, took in a deep breath, exhaled slowly—and relaxed.

Man, does that feel good, he thought. He was here today more as a spectator and friend to Mrs. Bundle than in any official capacity, having, for now, put all the county's crises to bed. The drought was over and rain was plentiful, the most heinous murder of many decades had been solved, the arson cases were a thing of the past, and things seemed to be back to normal in Windsor County, for which he was entirely grateful.

Mrs. Bundle had been expounding in detail for these first few minutes, filling in the gaps of a very intriguing—and unbelievably true—story: her version of the events involving two young people of a bygone era.

She sighed, smiling at the group as she continued. "And so, that's why we believe what happened, what we all," (she motioned to include the young people in front of her) "as a group, can pretty much substantiate—and which I'll try to do as I explain the rest and why we're all here."

She clasped her hands together and continued. "As I was saying, the library was shut down and locked up directly after Cornelius Lorenzo Veakey left for the war in late 1861. You see, the State of Vermont mandated that all towns close," she looked down through her glasses and read from her notes, "'*any and all municipal buildings not essential in the town's daily activities until further notice.*' Those unused dedicated municipal funds then went directly toward the War effort. Consequently, with the library locked and boarded up until after the War, we think his sweetheart—the girl, Margaret, for whom he painted the picture—was not able retrieve the painting from behind the wall. The fact of the matter is, she *never* returned to the Library. Tragically, after receiving word that he had perished in the Gettysburg battle in 1863, she couldn't ever bring herself to retrieve the painting."

Mrs. Bundle stopped as she saw Weezy raise a pudgy hand in the air. This was a move much more formal than Weezy usually employed and spoke volumes to her newfound pride at having been invited to attend this special gathering in such a formal setting.

"'Uh, yuh. Scuse me for interruptin', Lettie, it's all a tragic story to be sure—just like a movie, ain't it? So, how do you know it's not a lotta baloney?"

Mrs. Bundle turned toward Viola Tudhope, who turned crimson but gave a quick and solid nod to go ahead.

Mrs. Bundle reached behind her and picked up an item from the fireplace mantelpiece. Very carefully, she held up a stack of aged-looking, brown-tinted, frayed letters tied neatly with a tattered, dull, sky-blue silk ribbon. The ribbon had lost its original rich luster, and spoke to a bygone era of formality; its use signified it held what was, at one time, very dear to someone. She placed the packet beside her on the open secretary desk, then reached back once again. Beside the stack she laid a small, but very thick, russet-colored book whose pages were once locked in an old-fashioned clasp, now unfastened. She opened the book's front flap; inside, the pages revealed curious, fancily scribed words.

Weezy whistled below her breath. "Glory be! Those look ancient!"

Mrs. Bundle nodded and pointed to the antique letters.

"First things first. These are the love letters that Cornelias Veakey sent to his fiancée, Margaret Dorothy Collins, over the course of the year-and-a-half he was away during the Civil War—where his life was ultimately ended as a Union soldier in the 13th Regiment of Vermont Volunteers. Cornelius and his best friend, 'Tuddy' Tudhope," she nodded toward Ger and Phoebe, "yes! Yes, Ger and

Phoebe, *Jeremiah* Tudhope was his full name. From what we've gathered, he and Cornelius stood side-by-side at that battle. Sadly, only one of them survived the battle and came home."

Phoebe was the first to speak. Confused, she said, "I think I've seen…those letters before."

Ger Tudhope swallowed hard and asked, "You mean, my great-great grandfather, Jeremiah? Who fought in the Civil War?"

Mrs. Bundle nodded and he swelled with pride, opening up for the first time. "I'm proud to say he was in the Vermont Brigade under the command of Brigadier General George Stannard, who helped to turn Picket's Charge, don't you know. That was the last gasp of the Confederate attack at Gettysburg, and he was right there in the thick of it!"

"That's right, Ger. One and the same. Your relative." Mrs. Bundle chuckled, "*And*, the one in the photograph, stern face in his Union regalia, that once graced the wall in the Diner outside the ladies room."

She nodded toward Anthony Clancy, who sat below her on the floor, his back rigid with excitement. "After we got the initial information, I asked Anthony Clancy, who's a history buff, mind you, and especially knowledgeable about the Civil War, to research this further and so, he will continue on with this part of the narrative."

Anthony couldn't hold back his enthusiasm and sprung to his feet, facing the group. "You're right, Mr. Tudhope. He was there at Gettysburg! And so was Cornelius Veakey. Actually, it was Colonel Francis Randall who commanded the Thirteenth Vermont Infantry under General Stannard. Randall—and the boys from this area— were all soldiers from Vermont who fought together on the morning of the third day of battle at Gettysburg. All of them—Cornelius's and Jeremiah's regiment, that is—were placed in the front line to the left of Cemetery Hill. They remained there, sustaining heavy assaults and heavy artillery fire. Colonel Randall said…" Anthony held up a sheet of paper and turned to Mrs. Bundle, "May I read from the end of his original report, Mrs. B? The one taken from the *Gettysburg Order of Battles?*"

"Of course, Anthony. Please do!"

He cleared his throat and shifted his glasses on the bridge of his nose, then said apologetically, "Sorry! Hmm, let's see. I guess I'll just read from the important parts." Thus, he began to read aloud from the Colonel's official report, " *'From the report filed by Francis V. Randall, Colonel Thirteenth Regiment Vermont Volunteers for the period of July 1,2, and 3…,'*" he moved his finger down the report and read, "*'As our front became uncovered, I moved my regiment a little by the flank.….General Stannard sent orders to me to bring my regiment back to the main line, and he sent a portion of the Fourteenth Regiment to support Colonel Veazey. This rebel column, however, about that time commenced to diverge in the opposite direction, and entered the woods to the south of us, where they were pursued by the Sixteenth and Fourteenth Regiments. This substantially ended our part in the battle. General Hancock was wounded while sitting on his horse giving me some directions. I was standing very near him, and assisted him from his horse. General Stannard was also wounded soon after, and compelled reluctantly to leave the field, since which time I have been in command of the brigade. The casualties in my regiment, as near as I can now ascertain, were 8 killed,'*" he paused, "*'89 wounded, and 26 missing. As we know none were captured, probably many of the 26 may prove to have been killed, or severely wounded, and cared for in some private house.'*"

Anthony looked up from his reading. "One of those killed was Cornelius Veakey. All reports say the Vermonters back then had a reputation for not running from the fight. They were very brave and very fit, being country boys from Vermont. They were considered the best marchers in the Sixth Corps at Gettysburg, some say because they were used to taking long, loping steps—like Vermont boys did when walking long distances. Anyway, they fought fiercely and played a very key role in helping to win the battle that last day of fighting in Gettysburg. Later, in the *State Standard's* obituary of Cornelius Veakey," he paused, "which we discovered in the archives—it was stated that," he scrunched his forehead as he quoted from memory, "*'his friend, Jeremiah Tudhope, stood fighting by his side and was there to comfort him as he lay mortally wounded after the third day's battle.'"*

"Friends? You ain't tellin' me they was bestest friends?" Barny raised his fist in protest; his face was incredulous. "A Veakey and a Tudhope? Nope. Neva. *Neva eva.*" He shook his head, disbelieving this portion of the tale.

"J-J-Just l-listen, P-P-Pops." Vincent Veakey murmured as he calmed his father.

Angie piped in earnestly, "It's true! They fought side by side and were together from the day they left Vermont. And—you can see—if you go right down and look—their names are engraved as Soldiers in the 13ᵗʰ Regiment on the big brass plaques hanging beside each of the Pillson Library front double doors."

Nick added knowledgably, "You know, we've all seen 'em but probably never took time time to read 'em…" He shrugged, "they're plaques that were put up in 1868 by the town fathers to commemorate the men from Southern Vermont who fought in the War Between the States."

Angie said, "We made copies of the obituary notice. Here you go."

Angie first handed the Tudhopes and Barny Veakey each a copy of the obituary, then handed around more copies to the group who weren't already familiar with the particulars of Cornelius Veakey's demise.

Seconds passed as they all read silently.

Finally, Ger Tudhope looked up and said, "So, this Margaret Collins—Veakey's fiancée—well, she has to be, if it's one and the same Margaret Dorothy Collins—"

"Yes! She would be—" Mrs. Bundle agreed.

Ger interrupted, "—my great-great Grandmother Tudhope! I'll be a monkey's uncle!" He scratched his head in thought. "I know it must be—because it was her family came from the old Collins Farmstead, where we Tudhopes still live to this day. She lived to be over one hundred years old! Spry as all get-out, by all accounts! I remember as a young child, everyone always talked about what a ticket ol' Grammy Maggie was."

Mrs. Bundle confirmed, "Uh-huh! Your direct ancestors, Ger—whose father, your great-great-great grandfather on Margaret's side—left his daughter 'Maggie' and her husband, *Jeremiah Tudhope*, the Collins farm—from which they started the farmstand at the Four Corners," she looked around at the group, "and then became a modest eatery, which eventually became Tudhope's Diner!"

"And don't forget—there's Maggie's Stream, too!" Althea added, "On the mountain acreage behind. That must have been named for her."

"Right, it was! I'll be doggoned." Ger stared at the paper in front of him and shook his head. "That's unreal about her and Veakey, though. Unreal."

Walter slapped his knee. "Jumpin' Jehozafats, Lettie! That's quite a yarn you're spinnin' there!"

Angie nodded excitedly and, rising from the floor, turned and faced the group. "Yes, and there's more. The *State Standard*, which was a relatively new paper at the time and was considered quite progressive, originated a few years *before* the Civil War in 1853. At the time, it was the only newspaper in these three counties until long after that War. Cornelius sent all these letters to Maggie through their mutual friend, who was the Editor of the *State Standard*. His name was Samuel Forrester, who, at the same time, would also receive and print Conny's pen and ink renderings of the Civil War scenes, along with his artistic commentary and political cartoons about the War. Those ink renderings from Cornelius Veakey were published on a regular basis by *The Standard*, which provided a firsthand view of the war for the people in this area."

Mrs. Bundle added, "But it's here in these love letters to 'his darling Maggie,' signed only as 'C,' though, that tell a wonderful story of love and longing for the two to be back together, one day. They were Maggie's and 'Conny's'—her name for him, and also, the way he signed his artwork—these were their lifeline to each other, and are a wonderful testament to their undying commitment to each other. It's true that Maggie eventually moved on through her grief, married, and had a large brood of children with none other than Jeremiah

Tudhope," she smiled at Ger and Phoebe, "although, fortunately, Maggie kept the love letters from her first fiancé, Cornelius, for the rest of her life, safely stowed away, and then, probably later in life, totally forgotten, in an old trunk." She sighed, "And so, these letters were instrumental in helping us complete the mystery of the painting behind the wall."

Phoebe exclaimed, "*That's* where I've seen them! In that old trunk upstairs! I remember, as a young newlywed living at the farm, years ago, exploring up there. I even remember there was an old Union soldier's uniform in the same trunk and pictures and such. Why, I never gave it any mind, really. Just a lot of old junk in the attic! 'Course, then we decided it would be a great idea to take all of those old ancestral photographs and paraphernalia and put them in the restaurant! God, that was in the '60's, wasn't it Ger? We took it all down from the attic and put it up in the Diner. Some of those old Tuddy's photographs even showed the farm in its original glory. And, there was one that showed the first farm stand, too."

"Yes, I remember!" Mrs. Bundle smiled.

Ger added, gaining excitement, "The actual history is that the farm came to Maggie, but as farming fell by the wayside—like many farms of those earlier generations—their small food business was booming. My parents always said Grammy Maggie single-handedly made Tuddy's what it was, because she was renowned for her simple home-cooking. All those pictures we had on the wall told the story." He sat back in his chair. "Of course, now that Tuddy's is gone…well, it's sad to say, all the memorabilia is gone, too. One of a kind, that's what it was. Gaw! There's not enough insurance money in the world to replace all those memories and photographs."

Phoebe nodded, "At the very least, it was kinda a novelty—really homey, and the customers just loved all that junk, don't you know!"

Viola Tudhope spoke for the first time. "Oh, *Mother*. It's not junk," she said fervently, "it was someone's real life!"

Vincent patted her hand.

Mrs. Bundle turned toward Viola Tudhope and smiled. "Lucky for us that Viola had gone through the rest of all that '*junk*'—your words, Phoebe—because she rediscovered the letters and the diary, too. And, in these letters, she recognized…the power of love."

Viola sat quietly, her hand and Junior's scarcely touching, but whose connection clearly created a spark which caused a glow on her face. They both snuck a gentle, supporting smile, lost in each other's gaze. It was at that moment that everyone else could see, in this simple couple's smiles, how love can change two people. With that one look Viola, considered a wallflower by many, was transformed into a most beauteous maiden and Vincent Veakey could only be her charming prince.

Mrs. Bundle continued. "Viola found her great-great-great grandmother's letters in the bottom of that old trunk upstairs in the attic in her family's farm. Maggie Collins lived on that farm all her life—her father was a large landowner and agriculturalist in Hartland throughout the mid-to-late 1800's."

Anthony added, "Right. That is, until the industrial era, when business and manufacturing kicked in and the farmland started being used more for production plants, industry and the like."

"Thank you, Anthony, that's right. And the Tudhopes, by then, had a successful eatery to run." Mrs. Bundle held up a small, yellowed recipe card. "Remarkably, Viola also found this item, which had been used as a bookmark in the diary."

Craning her neck, Weezy said, "We're all spellbound, Lettie! What is it?"

Mrs. Bundle motioned to Viola who first shook her head, and then, after being nudged by Vincent, blurted out a string of words in a hurry, "It's the original copy of the recipe for *Maggie's Special Hot Cocoa Drink*!" Her face, through this torrent, had turned three shades of red and settled on crimson, but she persevered through her timidity, "Yuh-see…she *really* loved chocolate."

"You don't *say*!" Weezy cried.

Natalie further explained, "Yes, we do! She loved chocolate bonbons—from England! We found all kinds of wax candy papers under the library eaves where the painting was found. You see, we think she and Conny must have used it as a secret meeting place before the War. And, that's why Cornelius called her his 'Sweetness'! Matter of fact, that's *exactly* what it says on the back of the painting, 'To My Sweetness.'"

Viola spoke with more self-assurance than ever, *"Yuh*!! She did—love chocolate to no end! And, once they started the Diner, her cocoa was always a favorite."

Ger, forgetting his estrangement with his daughter in the excitement of the moment, offered, "You betcha!! Right up to today!" Then, his face fell, "Well, that is…maybe once we get it up and running again."

"Don't you worry 'bout that, Ger! It'll happen!" Carl Andersen said.

An appreciative murmur spread through the group.

"Ya see? Just when a body thinks you *know'd* everything, you go and *learnt* more than you knew!" Walter cried, "Tuddy's *Cocoa!*"

Mrs. Bundle nodded enthusiastically. "Yes! And there's more. Viola has been a very brave girl, trying to keep secrets, trying to not tempt fate, knowing how terrible the feelings were between her family and the Veakeys. That is, until about a week or so ago, when she and Vincent finally decided it was a much better thing to try to *repair* the confusion that happened so long ago. It would be a better world if everyone could just remember: for every problem there is a solution—no matter how big or insurmountable the problem seems." Her knowing eyes sought out Viola's; the shy woman's eyes locked with Mrs. Bundle and they shared an understanding smile. "Thank you so much, Viola. You have helped us all immeasurably. Everything fell into place after that. It all fit together, everything about the Tudhopes and the Veakeys, and why they feuded with each other over these many decades. The irony is, it seems it was all based on a *misunderstanding.*"

Viola nodded silently and looked over at her father beseechingly.

Mrs. Bundle's eyes gazed directly at Barnabus and the Tudhopes. "Viola, Vincent and I agree that it's time to heal old wounds. We hope that today, with this story coming to light, it will do good for the families involved. That it might help heal their differences now."

Weezy snorted loudly. "Ha! I don't get how this heals nothing much! That was all *eons* ago. My own people have lived here forever, and they and everybody else know Veakeys and Tudhopes have always hated each other! Why, that'd be like putting a family of badgers alongside ornery horned toads all together in one room." She stopped short and looked around, realizing that's exactly what could be occurring at this moment.

Mrs. Bundle raised an eyebrow. "Well now! Here's *why* it's time. Let me start at the beginning. The true facts are that, before the War, what *everyone* knew was that Jeremiah Tudhope, (or 'Tuddy', as he was called) and Conny were the best of friends. They left for the war together, one to return, and sadly, one not to return. Conny's and Maggie's happiness was not to be—they were never to marry, never to have children and never to live a happy long life together. The diary says it all. True to his promise to take care of Maggie if something happened to Cornelias, Jeremiah, (who had always carried a secret torch for Maggie), came home from the war and was horrified to find her in such poor health. She was nearly dead from grief and had contracted the deadly influenza. Selflessly, Tuddy spent countless hours with the failing girl, reading to her, and talking much about the common bond they had: *Cornelius*. The fact of the matter was, Tuddy was the *one* person she knew understood her beloved Conny as she had. Tuddy's amiable and open disposition—by all accounts as fine a man as Cornelius, and a very kind one, to boot—was what healed her slowly, and their kindred friendship deepened into respect, and then love." Mrs. Bundle's voice was soft, and very calming to the group.

"Ultimately, this all led to Jeremiah asking for her hand in marriage. Jeremiah Tudhope was a good husband, hardworking and honest, and their combined union brought forth five Tudhope children, all of whom first worked in the family's growing roadside farmstand, and then as the years passed, the eatery."

Weezy, slow on the uptake, asked, "Yeah…so what about the Veakeys?"

Cracker meowed and stretched his body, reaching long, sharp claws out lazily in the Queen Anne chair's direction.

"Yes, exactly, the Veakeys! Unfortunately, the Veakey family, sadly misinformed about the circumstances of Jeremiah's intention, never forgave Jeremiah. Not just for marrying Maggie, but really, truth be told, for coming back from the War." She made her familiar clucking sounds. "Uh-huh. To lose a child is a terrible thing. Even worse is to lose the oldest son in a tragic war. That was...devastating. Their grief was so profound, their loss of Cornelius so great, that they just couldn't bring themselves to forgive Jeremiah's safe return. Stories began circulating. And so, their hatred of the Tudhopes festered. And then, it turned into blame and regret and disillusionment. Unfortunately, like many families who lost loved ones to the Civil War, they never recovered, burying their grief in hatred and mistrust."

Barny Veakey snorted and wiped his gnarly face with a much worn bandanna. "You ain't tellin' me *nothin'* I don't already know. That there Cornelius fellow was brothers to my great-great grandpappy Barnabus—yup, name's just like mine. I looked it all up when you was tellin' us about that artist back along, Miz Bundle. It was written down in that odd scrawly handwriting in God's Good Book, you see. Matter of fact, I got the whole Veakey family tree in that old Bible at home, right y'ar by my bed—passed down from one Veakey kin to the next. Used to read all them names, over and over, the family and me. What you was sayin' the other day, Miz Bundle got me to thinkin'. The more I thunk on it, the more I recollected. Yessir! And, I got kind of a mem'ry of this here what you're talkin' about—a Veakey who'd made a name for himself as a real famous artist, with that there name 'Lor-en-zo' being right in the Good Book. I always remembered that swanky foreign name, and now Vinnie tells me—I'll be darned if it don't mean Lawrence in *I-talian*, just like my own middle name. Makes me feel kinda connected to the fellow. Y'see, this relation was way, way back along—the kin all talked about him—said he'd died too young. Consequently, and so forth, we heerd about this here feud you're goin' on about the whole time I was growin' up, don't you know? Passed down, right, one Veakey to t'next one, just like that there bible. My Pop and his Pop before him all know'd it too, truth be told. That for sure's what we was always told—'*don't you never trust a Tudhope, neva, ever!*' It were just the way things was to be!"

He peered over through thin-slit, bushy-browed eyes at Ger and Phoebe.

They stared back, stoic Yankee expressions on both their countenances.

Barny pointed a crooked finger at them. "Those Tudhopes—they was *always* lordin' it over on us! They *all* thought they was too good for us. 'Course, us bein' just poor folk from the mountain and all. And don't you deny it, Ger, neither! Wasn't that the way?"

Ger Tudhope looked as helpless as a firefly on a sunlit day and shrugged without a comment.

Mrs. Bundle shook her head sadly at Barny. "Excuse me, dear friend, but I must say with all due respect that not being able to forgive and forget is a terrible thing—as evidenced in this situation."

He turned and glared at her. "Forgive and forget? What d'ya mean?"

"Well, all these vendettas that followed each and every Tudhope and Veakey generation. Really, now, Barny." The old man was silent.

Ger Tudhope's forehead creased, and he cleared his throat to speak. "I...honestly, I'm not sure exactly what triggered all this feuding, as you call it. Personally, I just tried to steer clear of them all, 'specially as a kid. The Veakeys..." He motioned toward Barny, as though case in point, "Well, they were always a bunch of ornery son-of-a-guns, every one of 'em! Leastways, that's what it always seemed." He held up his hand as Barny's chin jutted out and he began to protest. "Sorry, Barny, but that's what my father always told me, too. 'Never happy with what they got, that lot! Always got a chip on their shoulder' he'd say. They hated us, so...we hated them back."

Mrs. Bundle's tongue clicked with agitation. "Such a terrible shame! You see how things can snowball? Over the years, the feuding intensified and the Veakeys and the Tudhopes became first, bitter enemies and then, coincidentally, rivals—mostly due to this misconception—specifically, the ill-formed rumors that Jeremiah had *stolen* Maggie's affections and had been in love with her *long before* Cornelius died at Gettysburg. Of course, this was all totally untrue, but the ubiquitous village rumor mill takes on a life of its own—especially in these parts, *and* because Maggie refused to ever speak publicly of Cornelius again after his sad death. The rumors went unchallenged, however," she held up a cautioning finger, "very interestingly, Maggie writes very eloquently about her feelings on this matter." She flipped through the pages of the diary and stopped. "She writes, '*I am deeply troubled by the way people talk. I wish we could put this behind us, Tuddy and I, this terrible burden of the love we shared for dear Conny.*' She goes on to articulate that the feuding between the two families is '*intolerably painful*' to both her and Tuddy, and she has sworn him to '*silence and prayer*' in an effort to squelch the deepening bad feelings."

She flipped through the diary again, stopping at another page, "In a later diary entry she believes the feud is exacerbated by the continued idle gossip throughout the community, saying '*I cannot bear to discuss the subject, so I will let the rumors die an ugly death. Why must people continue to feed this sorry fire?*' She hoped things would get better, but that was not to be. Other issues were laid on top of the original rift as the offspring of the two families clashed, and she writes, '*I pray these two families will put their differences aside. My husband and I will not be deterred; nor shall we condone that our children participate in hating or harming any Veakey. It is over; he is gone.*'"

Mrs. Bundle closed the diary. "Cornelius was gone, that was true. But the bad blood was not. And so, this intense feud based upon falsehoods was allowed to proliferate over and over through many generations."

A shocked Weezy threw her hands in the air and cried, "Gaw! *Do tell!*"

Barny Veakey motioned resignedly and started to speak, his face tired and old, then nodded silently, acknowledging Mrs. Bundle's facts.

He asked, "So that's it? That's what she says in that there diary?"
She nodded.

He looked over at Ger Tudhope, who silently nodded back at him, displaying a faint, grim smile.

Mrs. Bundle continued, holding up the small, worn diary once more. "Maggie's journal tells a different story, to be sure. She speaks glowingly of her devotion to Cornelias' memory, and her respectful admiration for her husband's true commitment to her, a commitment based upon the foundation of Tuddy's complete loyalty and devotion to his best friend Conny. It was a subject she says they both rarely ever discussed again, quietly putting it behind them once they were married and committed to each other."

Mrs. Bundle held the diary aloft.

"In fact, from what she writes, the two of them did their best to bring the community together with their modest eatery—despite the rivalry and hatred that had grown between the Tudhope and the Veakey families."

Mrs. Bundle let the impact of her words sink in to the group.

"In conclusion, (and not to put too fine a point on it), this gossip was insidious—as hearsay always is—and over time, contributed to the destruction of the Veakeys, who were viewed as poor folk who kept to themselves up on the mountain. The Veakey family suffered one catastrophe after another, more bad luck than you can shake a stick at! Worst was losing their farmland to the county after a few years of severe weather and unproductive crops. It seemed as the Tudhopes flourished, the Veakeys suffered, spiraling downward through each generation."

"That's what I'm talkin' about!" Barny cried.

"Frankly," Mrs. Bundle continued, "the prejudice against the destitute Veakeys deepened throughout the community. It became common knowledge that the Tudhopes and the Veakeys were enemies, the cause of the rift having something to do with a Tudhope 'running off and marrying one of the Veakey boy's sweethearts.'"

Althea shook her head ruefully, adding, "And there's even more to this story. It's actually substantiated that one Tudhope descendent, who was the head foreman in the 1930's at the old Pearson Sawmill on Twenty Mile Stream, had a tragic connection with another Veakey.

The foreman, one Silas Tudhope, was by all reports ruthless in his dealings with his workers. These reports indicate he was accused of tormenting and harassing his already-overworked employees. An unfortunate incident involving substandard conditions occurred where a worker ended up dying. That employee was a Veakey who had worked as a laborer at the Mill for thirty years. It seems he died of 'undetermined causes' on the job. The doctor's report stated that the inconclusive, but likely, cause was *'a cerebrovascular accident (i.e., stroke) brought on by undue stresses'."*

"A stroke?" Walter Andersen said. "Y'mean he just keeled over on the job?"

"Uh-huh, but more than just by accident. Seems it was peak season and the man was forced to stay on the job until the job was done. He had complained of an excruciating headache but was not allowed to leave—Silas Tudhope was the man in charge who insisted he stay. Elmer Veakey ended up working three full, continuous shifts without a break, and collapsed at the end of the last shift."

Barny cried out, "That's the truth! That would be Uncle Elmer, my great-uncle! My pappy told me all about this. Said those dang Tudhopes had done it again! How'd you eva find—"

Angie broke in, "Anthony and I found out at the Pillson Historical Society records just the other day—and Althea helped us, too. Of course, the old sawmill is long gone now, but there's a lot there on record about Pearson's Sawmill, including the weekly reports by all the foremen. There were also injury records, somewhat vague, indicating there was a pretty high incidence of injury on the job back then. It wasn't often a doctor was ever called in, though, so this was must have been a pretty big event. There were even some statements taken from the workers, too. There's a log of everything that transpired, all submitted in longhand to that foreman's superiors."

Althea concluded, "Seems after this Veakey was killed on the job, there was an investigation and, even though the foreman stayed on, some kind of small insurance settlement was given to Elmer Veakey's wife. Things were hushed up even though there was no question it all happened under this foreman's watch—very tragic, it was."

Mrs. Bundle closed the diary and placed it carefully on the table. "Sadly, this is a story that teaches us that this feud should be put to bed now, in this generation, with a much more hopeful ending if all can be resolved peacefully."

"Whew! That's rough!" said Ger Tudhope. "From my perspective, there seems to be a pretty big dose of fault and blame on both sides. So, where do we go from here?"

Barny's chin jutted out even further. "Well now, hold on! I got one question. I thought we was here to discuss that there paintin'—the one my kin Cornelius Lorenzo painted. Ain't that right? Ain't that why we're here?"

"Yes," Mrs. Bundle nodded, "that is *one* of the main reasons we're here. To discuss the painting's ownership. And hopefully, to clear up some misunderstanding."

"Well, that's what I'm askin' about—this here painting. So, if what you say is true, would you be sayin' that painting belongs to the Veakey family? Or does it belong to the Tudhopes?"

"Well, that's a good question, Barny," Mrs. Bundle said. "And yes, by all rights, it does."

As both patriarchs looked at each other with confusion, she laughed lightly. "Wait. Let me be clearer. By all rights, Cornelius Veakey gave the painting to Maggie, would you both agree?"

Together, they nodded.

She continued, "However, Maggie then never went back to claim her painting, correct?"

Ger shifted in his seat, "Well, wait a minute, now…"

Barny said bluntly, "Let's jist cut to the chase here. So, who owns it? Legal-like, I mean."

Walter Andersen hooted. "Jeez, *Loo-eeezz*, Barny! You're more nervous than a long-tailed cat betwixt tap dancers! Calm down! She's gettin' to it!"

Cracker placed his paws over his pointed ears.

Junior and Viola stole a frustrated looked at each other and shook their heads.

Junior said, "P-Pops, Mrs. B-B-Bundle is trying to help things here! L-Let's see what she h-h-has to say."

His father's knobby hands rubbed impatiently at his scrubby face, but he nodded in resignation. "You're right, boy. I got that streak in me that makes a conclusion way too quick. Sorry, ma'am. Go on, now. I ain't gonna interrupt agin."

Mrs. Bundle gave both father and son a patient smile and said, "The Library Board—we're all present and accounted for here today—I'm happy to say, is unanimous in our support of this decision. The Library Board has determined that the Veakeys and the Tudhopes—because Cornelius painted it, but also because the Tudhopes are the heirs to Maggie and Jeremiah Tudhope's union—are both directly predisposed to ownership of the painting. *Together.*"

"Well, I'll be jiggered!" Barny Veakey yelped.

Ger Tudhope looked baffled.

Weezy, ever impatient, interrupted once more. "So, what're you goin' to do? You can't be tearin' the danged thing in half, now, can you?"

Althea choked and Mrs. Bundle laughed aloud. "Oh, Weezy! No, we can't tear it in half. We feel—the Board, that is—we feel that this story makes everything about this painting even grander, even more intriguing! Look here, the LiMB Society has solved the mystery! This painting that intertwined two families forever has survived for almost one-hundred-and-fifty years! The fact of the matter is—the whole story will make for a great yarn to tell your grandchildren, won't it?"

Phoebe Tudhope harrumphed loudly.

Walter piped up, "But who's goin' to decide who's goin' to get to keep the dang thing? We sure don't want another feud over this. It ain't worth it."

Mrs. Bundle first looked at Barny, then passed her gaze on to the Tudhopes. She sighed dramatically. "Well, I guess that's for you all to decide. Like adults."

"Golly, that's a tough one!" Ger Tudhope wiped his brow. "I don't want any part of any feud any more, that's for sure. That painting's been at the library hid away, all these years. I almost wish it hadn't been found. 'Cause now, the way I see it, we got a whole new problem."

Barnabus Veakey scratched his knobby head. "Well, it don't seem right to me that the library ain't gonna get anything out of this, seeing as you all are the ones who found it. Could have stayed behind that wall for another hundred years, by all rights!"

The two men eyed each other like two very wary, tough-skinned rhinoceroses while no one moved an inch.

It was Ger who broke the ice first.

He said, gingerly, "I must admit I agree with you, Barnabus. But— now, don't get your horns out—let's just admit it. You and your boy sure could use the money if the painting was sold."

Barny raised his proud, but very poor, head high in the air. "Well, now, listen to *you* go on! You ain't sittin' so pretty yerself! Ain't like you even got a pot to pee in anymore, since you lost the eatery!"

Ger Tudhope bristled in his seat. "Ah, heck! Well, Barny, don't you worry about us! We got the insurance, which'll cover a fair amount. So…it's all taken care of!"

Phoebe Tudhope began to protest and he hushed her.

Barny raised his voice and his, pointy, belligerent chin reached out with further defiance. "Well now, Mister, I'll tell you what! It ain't somethin' you and I are gonna bicker and wrangle on about, that's for dang sure. Let's make a decision and be done with it! Let's put this to bed once and for all…and move on!"

"Hey, don't preach to the choir!" Ger's voice rose, "Enough fighting. I can tell you right now, no matter how ornery you get, as I live and breathe, we're not taking one red cent if that painting is sold!" Ger argued back, eyes glowing like hot embers.

This interesting display of machismo was viewed by the entire room of silent spectators; all sat by, electrified and with hope against hope that all would be resolved, as the two men from opposing families squared off.

Vincent Veakey stood up, cleared his throat, and then, at a loss for words, looked at Mrs. Bundle as though begging her to come up with a viable solution.

At that moment, a scratchy, deep voice was raised from the parlor onlookers.

"Might I…add a thought?"

All eyes turned toward Ian Kelley, who sat up weakly in the corner chair. Slowly, he said, "I think I might have a solution."

Both patriarchs eyed him warily, both unsure of exactly who he was, or what role he played here today.

Weezy, totally enthralled with the drama, urged excitedly, "Geez, go on! We're on the edge of our seats! What do *you* have to do with all of this, Dakota?"

He cleared his throat, still raspy, his voice still hoarse from his ordeal. "Very simply….I would suggest keeping the painting on display at the Pillson Library. Let people see the wonderful work and legacy of this young man."

The two men looked unconvinced at his simple resolution, and he held up a bandaged hand. "Oh, I know it's worth a fair amount, and so, I think I have a solution for that, too, but first I *must* explain my own motivation in coming to this conclusion."

He moved his body slowly, and then sat up straighter in his chair, his eyes intense as he addressed the group.

"I have worked very hard all my life, as I'm sure both of you men have in your respective fields of endeavor. Now, luckily, I am reaping the monetary benefits of my once meagerly-financed painting career. You see, in recent years, my artwork has become quite collectible, even prized in some venues, for which I have been very satisfied—primarily, because it has allowed me to become…ahh, shall we say…comfortable? However, recently, I've had a bit of a windfall! Quite a large one, in fact."

The group waited as he explained. "It seems my artwork—especially now, since my, ah, recent unfortunate accident—has increased tenfold in the larger venues, specifically, in the New York and London art world." He waved his hand airily, then winced, "My recent misadventure and subsequent injuries have made the prices even dearer! There are some European critics that have already reported me near-dying, or even," he chuckled, "I was told, dead." He smiled sardonically at them. "Of course, as I sit here, breathing and very much alive, we all know different."

Titters cascaded throughout the room.

"Be that as it may, the figures my agent has called me with—the newest quotes from this morning—are unbelievably generous! Far, far more money than even I ever imagined. Word on the street, apparently, is that I will *never* paint again."

He smiled diffidently at the group as some of their faces took on a look of pity.

"Please. Don't be alarmed at the way I look—the doctors tell me I'll be back painting in no time, to be sure. I have suffered only the slightest nerve damage in my left hand, and my painting hand," (he held up his right hand for all to see), "is, or will be, fine. So, there are more Dakota Squibb originals to be painted." His grin deepened. "However, there are other things to consider, too."

He stopped briefly, gazing across the room at Althea, whose cheeks took on the slightest tinge of fuschia.

"I have an announcement. From this day forth, although I will continue to be known to the art world as 'Dakota Squibb'—actually a pseudonym, or pen name, as it were. However, to my friends and family here in Pillsonville, my given name of Ian Kelley—" he cleared his throat and raised his voice as though in proclamation, "—Ahem! *My given name* that I was born into—is the name that I will proudly answer to!"

Ian stole a look at Jack and winked, who returned one of the biggest smiles Mrs. Bundle had ever seen the boy conjure up.

Ian continued, "You may ask, 'What on earth does all this have to do with the Cornelius Veakey painting and the Library?' Bear with me; I am getting to that." He shook his head. "Truthfully, I must admit I had a fair amount of time this summer to reflect on what is important in life. Bear in mind, my fellow artist, Cornelius Veakey, did not have that luxury in his time. His life was tragically cut in half through the circumstances of fate. I, on the other hand, have lived my share of life. Yet, I have regrets. I have *not* loved as he loved. I am sad to admit that I have existed, but not *lived*. What I mean is, I have not *lived* life to its fullest, that is for certain. Nevertheless, I am at a stage of my life *now* where I think I can make amends for that, where

I think it is fair and appropriate to reap the benefits of all my hard work; where settling down with someone special and spending time with family are the *most* important things to me. Family. Nothing—I repeat, nothing—will ever stand in the way of that again for me. I think you gentlemen would agree on that one statement for certain. That *family is everything?*"

Both Barny and Ger nodded their accord to this question.

Ian reached for Jack's strong arm, and the young man helped him to his feet.

"Thank you, dear nephew. You see, I have finally found my family, notwithstanding, the last of it—there's no one left from the Kelley clan but me and my Corrigan nephew and nieces. Aye! I am ecstatic that they are willing to accept me into their lives, too. Pillson is where I want to be, and where I'm going to stay and paint 'til I'm too old to lift a brush. That said—well, it's time for me to give something back. Back to the community, to participate, to put down roots, and make *other* people happy. Those are my goals." He looked around at the group. "And so, having the means and the wherewithal to make that happen, nothing, I repeat, *nothing*, is going to deter me. I want to make the best of all the years I have left. With the people that I love."

He smiled directly and with great warmth at Althea, who reflected radiance back in his direction. Continuing, he said, "I think this feud thing can be put to bed once and for all by implementing the plan I'm about to suggest."

Everyone sat, quiet as church mice, waiting for his resolution.

"Right...As I said earlier, I would suggest placing the painting at the Pillson Library entrance, inside that large, impressive foyer. Of course, that does not address the painting's worth, intrinsically or monetarily, to the respective families: the Veakeys," he lowered his head respectively toward Barny, "and the Tudhopes. To that end, I am prepared to donate a $10,000 endowment toward the Library Fund, with the understanding that the painting is to remain in the Library's keeping and stay on perpetual display in the refurbished library's foyer, in the memory of *both* Cornelius Lawrence Veakey and Margaret Dorothy Collins Tudhope." Hushed murmurs of approval filled the room. "In addition, I will match that amount in grant form, to begin a library scholarship fund dedicated in the name and memory of Professor Watson DeVille, devoted past Director of the Library Board of Trustees and beloved member of the Pillson community."

The commotion that followed bordered on pandemonium.

"Ten *thousand* dollars? Times *two*?" Walter cried.

"Holy Mackrel-Andy!" cried out Weezy.

"*Wow!*", "Yeah!", and "All right, dude!" came from Anthony, Natalie, and Nick.

"*Great*, great, great idea!" Angie said.

Althea sat in silence, delightedly looking like the cat that swallowed the canary.

Ian shifted awkwardly from one foot to the other, somewhat uncomfortable with his newfound benefactor status, but smiling widely. "Really, it's the least I can do. I think it's a simple solution that accomplishes everything and should, if executed through the Board's capable hands, make everyone happy!"

Ger Tudhope stood up, and the room quieted down. Acquiescently, he said, "Well, I know Phoebe and I would go along with that plan."

Phoebe added, "Yes, of course we would! In memory of the two who were meant to enjoy the painting together but didn't get an opportunity to do so. If things had been different at Gettysburg...who knows what would have happened, who would have come home, or for that matter, where our family would all be now!"

All eyes turned toward Barnabus. He chewed on his lip, his upper dentures clattering away like an agitated washing machine. Then, he shrugged his bony shoulders and said with resignation, "Never had no money, us Veakeys, and we was plenty happy without it, was we not, Junior?" A hint of a grin could be seen transforming his grizzled face. "And this kin of our'n, Cornelius Lorenzo Veakey, he sounds like he was a gentle soul. He wouldn't never have wanted anyone combating, that's for dang sure."

Junior and Viola both nodded emphatically.

Barny nodded back. "So there, I'd be going along with that there proposal in a heartbeat!" He turned to his son. "Then, it's a done deal! And I know he—Cornelius—would want you kids—Viola and Vinny here—to be happy, just like he and Maggie was supposed to be!"

Viola and Vinny moved even closer together. Vinny found her hand and kissed it tenderly in front of all the world to see as she looked lovingly into his eyes. "Pops, d-d-don't you worry about that. Specially now."

Weezy Bunton eyeballed the lovebirds and asked, "Do *we* have something *we'd* like to share with everybody?"

Vincent Veakey looked at the group shyly, then stood up and looked straight into the faces of Ger and Phoebe Tudhope. "I h-h-ope, sir, we can forget—"

Ger Tudhope cut him off. "Never you mind, son! I think the feuding between the Tudhopes and the Veakeys can be put to rest for good. So, you go ahead, now. Time's awastin'—" he motioned excitedly from Vincent to his daughter, who sat holding her breath, her eyes big as flying saucers.

Vinnie looked deeply into her eyes.

She smiled sweetly back at him, her face aglow. He spoke without a stammer, without hesitation. "We've already decided our first step is to get married—as soon as possible!"

Transfixed with joy, they both broke out into uncontrollable gales of laughter, as happy as two crazed kookaburras, and then hugged each other tightly.

"Hallelujah Horatio, Barny!" Walter Andersen cried out. Jumping up like a comic jack-in-the-box, he pumped the prospective father-in-law's worn hand, who exclaimed proudly, "All righty, now! Don't that just beat all? A Tudhope and a Veakey, marrying! All *righty!*"

Between her tears of joy, Viola's words were unleashed and fluid as she exclaimed elatedly to all within earshot, "Vinnie's going to do his artwork! And I'm going to do my floral arranging! We're going to have a studio—together!"

Her parents moved quickly across the room and then stood on the brink of an arm's length of their daughter, hesitating for an instant. She reached out her arms, hugged her father, then her mother; all were unmistakably ecstatic with the union.

As the group relaxed, there was a hearty round of handshakes between Vincent, Ger, and Barny, culminating in cheerful "man-talk" and banter back and forth. As the hemming, hawing, and jaw-boning ensued, Weezy Bunton jumped to her feet and whooped, "Just *wait* till everyone hears about this!"

Mrs. Bundle turned away from the happy assemblage and gave Althea a perceptive smile, who nodded and smiled back at her. *Yes, just wait. Good ol' Weezy.*

Like a swarm of happy bees, the couple was surrounded by congratulatory folk.

Hugging and backslapping followed the couple's happy announcement and before long, a gay party was in full gear.

Chapter Two

Love in Another Era
December, 1861

THE YOUNG GIRL RAN UP THE SECOND FLIGHT of stairs swiftly and silently, trying with all her might not to let her foot sounds alert the stalwart, ironfisted Miss Bromley, who sat like a prison guard at the large front desk below. Her kidskin boots, laced up along the inside of the ankle, made sharp, tiny pinging sounds against the shiny, hard, oak treads, the slight weight of her toes barely imperceptible in the cavernous hallway.

When she reached the top landing, she loosened the worsted wool shawl that hung heavily on her slight shoulders and gently smoothed her long dress and petticoats. She tried without success to tame her windblown curly long tresses, straightening the large silk blue bow atop her head, its long double ribbon cascading loosely down her back. Then she promptly pinched her already-flushed cheeks just for good measure.

She looked at her image in the massive, dust-covered, ornate mirror leaning dejectedly nearby against the plaster wall.

Yes, she assured herself unwaveringly, ready or not!

Slipping between the long, heavy tables shoved up against the hallway wall as tight as jammed river logs, she squeaked through the small opening left between the tables, then scooted past the wooden crates piled one atop the other, crates that held new, richly bound books as yet unread, stored along the dark corridor walls. She peeked around the corner of the doorway of the last room.

This was "their room." Her's and Conny's. Her heart quickened as she saw him standing there, alone, waiting patiently. He stepped out from behind the lone table in the small chamber. Yes, she sighed with contentment, this was their secret place, a private sanctuary within a public building. They had made it their own, their personal spot for so many, many times before it was hard to count.

Oh, he was so beautiful! The dark-haired young man was dressed in an unbendingly-new, dark blue Union uniform, the brass buttons sparkling like fine Christmas ornaments. A military hat rested on the nearby table, its brim starched and as-yet undamaged by battle, and a pair of light tan leather gloves lay side-by-side like diligent hounds awaiting the feverish hunt.

At first sight of her, the corners of his mouth curved slightly upward and he placed his hand gingerly on the saber sword hanging neatly in the scabbard at his side. The hilt of the sword glistened and sparkled as the sun's brilliant rays streamed in through the small window and hit it just right. It was shiny, brand-new, ready for service; just like him. Clean-shaven, save for a neat moustache, his forehead was free of worry lines. He brushed a couple wavy, chestnut locks of hair back behind his ears and his dark brown eyes fairly danced as she fully came into his view. A smile lit up his fine, delicate features.

"Oh, Cornelius! You look so handsome in your uniform!" she said admiringly.

He made a sweeping motion with his arm, bowing low with great exaggeration. "I am at your service, ma'am."

They both laughed and she nimbly rushed the last few feet to him with complete abandon. When she reached him, he took all of her in his arms, cradling her protectively, as though he was the mighty fortress that would forever safeguard her. His gentle, elegant artisan hands reached around her slight figure, enveloping her tightly. They looked intensely into each other's eyes, words backed up like a surging dam. They both knew their time together was short.

"I wasn't sure if you would be able to come! Are you all right?" He gently caressed her shoulders and the shawl slipped down and fell to the floor. He gazed down with concern at the beautiful, dewy eyes, which looked adoringly back up at him. She nodded her youthful head, long ringlets flying, her eager face so very close to his. He could feel her quick breath rushing, pushing through the fine hairs on his upper lip as she spoke.

"Father had to go up to Northfield this morning! He took the wagon and the horses but left the buggy, so I hitched up Moonshine and—" she gasped for a breath—"here I am!" She knew her father would be furious if he found out, but nothing mattered now except seeing *him*. She had driven all the way from their huge farm over at Hartland Four Corners. It was a good eight miles, and not the easiest of trips, to be sure. But she had to see him, today of all days.

Her brow furrowed, the machinations of what it had taken for her to get here today etched there. Then, she smiled broadly, looked deeply into his eyes, and all was right with the world.

"Oh, Maggie, can you believe *today* is the day?" He looked longingly into her face, his own becoming a confused roadmap of varying degrees of emotion. His look of pure love was intermingled with unadulterated distress. So much to say in such a short time! His young forthright face spoke volumes to her as she looked back at him, his male eyes full of young, hopeful love overshadowed by stress and trepidation, for what was to come.

He kissed her fingers. "We march today. All of us, eleven in total from the 13th. We're a small group, but we're strong, to be sure. Gaw, Tuddy is so excited he can barely contain himself! They've not told us our destination, but we believe it to be Pennsylvania and then, on to West Virginia." He smiled as she winced slightly, drawing her small hand up to her mouth.

She said breathlessly, "So far away, it's farther than one can imagine…how will I—"

"Now, now, don't fret." He took her chin in his hand and looked deeply into her eyes. "You must believe that I'll be fine. And you know you'll hear from me regularly. I'll be sending my etchings back to the newspaper weekly, God willing. And, I'll include correspondence to you, my sweetness, just as I said I would. You know I will. And, Sam promised me that he will get the letters to you."

"Sam" was Samuel Forrester, his employer and the Managing Editor of the *State Standard*; that is, he *had* been his employer up until one week ago. Forthwith, his fulltime position as the newspaper's resident political artist had been curtailed by his induction into the United States of America Union Army's 13th Vermont Regiment, Company A.

She squeezed her eyelids shut very tight and drew in a deep breath of resolve. She knew that she must accept the fact; he would no longer be here in Pillson. He would be in danger and she had no control over it. Her only contact in the many months ahead would be his precious letters.

Now that he had been drafted into military service, part of Cornelias' side job would be to report back to their little community—through his moving artwork—on the progress of the War Between the States. His pen and ink renderings of any war events would very likely be received many days, if not weeks, after their occurrence.

Her eyes pooled over and she tried to hold the floodgates back, the wetness welling up and over her lids like silky water across smooth sea glass. "Oh, Cornelius..." Her voice trailed off hopelessly as she was unable to put words to the escalating emotions.

He took her heart-shaped face in his hands, his long, elegant fingers caressing her quivering chin. "Do not worry, my sweetness," he said with firm resolve. "I will think of nothing else save my darling Maggie, every hour that I am away."

As the next few minutes that passed reaffirmed their passion, their poignant murmurings and whispers of hopeful love fell on the deaf ears of the third floor library walls.

The two had been together most of their lives and had been sweet on each other as long as they could remember. The Pillsonville Normal School, located just a few hundred yards down the road, had been their playground, drawing pupils from the area villages of Pillson, Brownsville, Ascutney, and Hartland.

When the brand new Public Library had been built in 1849 to serve the surrounding communities, it had become their meeting spot in a time when boys and girls never mixed unless chaperoned. They had always enjoyed each other's company and reciprocated creativity: Cornelius for his artistic talents, Maggie for her quest for knowledge, not to mention her growing proficiency in culinary skills.

Now that they were older, they had found true love together, he at the age of 18, she, still a very young 16.

Maggie's mother had passed two years ago. Her father was a hardworking farmer who expected Maggie to carry the lion's share of the household duties. Everyone knew Cornelius Veakey and Margaret Collins were sweet on each other. Even her father had seen the signs, and his own strict upbringing demanded the right rituals take place at the proper time. He had been adamant that there would be no impropriety between his headstrong only daughter and "that older Veakey boy." And so, their clandestine meetings had proven to be the best they could come up with such strict rules imposed.

Nevertheless, there was no doubt in either of their minds that they were to be matched forever; this was something they both had always known.

After a blissful period whilst time had no meaning or consequence, she leaned back peacefully and, straightening her bodice coquettishly, she sighed, and looked around at the quiet walls surrounding them. "Do you remember what we would do here when we were young? Remember?" She giggled and ran behind the table, pulling at a corner of the wall. "C'mon! Conny, let's see if it's still here!"

They both knew which wooden panel to loosen. They deftly slid it back a foot, barely revealing a small knee wall area under the eaves of about five feet by three feet in size. Deftly, she pulled the panel aside further to reveal the covert space behind. Before he knew it, she was on her knees like a school child, exploring, her neck craning to see if everything remained intact.

He couldn't help but chuckle. It was here that Cornelius has first found Maggie. As a shy, young girl, she would sneak upstairs to the remote third floor attic, stealing away from the rest of the youngsters (at great risk of reprisal), flying like a little wren up the two flights of stairs to this private space. There, her innocent, mundane world would turn to fantasy as she lost herself in her reading. Other worlds, more majestic, more daring, filled her thoughts as she daydreamed in total solitude. During those formative years in the 1850's, most girls weren't allowed the basic right of a library card, and so she reveled in the world that had opened up to her, here in the modest village of Pillsonville's grand Library, gobbling up stories in monstrous, voracious bites.

Maggie had cherished her right, no, her privilege to borrow books from the Library; it was like a magical adventure to journey from her remote country home to the shiny, bright library building and up to her private, magical space. Making believe it was for her use only, she had moved that wooden panel back and crawled deep inside, where she would spend many hours reading, her imagination soaring as she ravenously read every book she could put her hands on. No one seemed to miss her, quiet as she was. Only the darkening sky above would warn her that her private time was expiring, and she would hastily gather up her books and join the others downstairs.

When Cornelius had come upon her that first time, it was quite by accident. He also had been drawn to that private, remote room for its peace and seclusion, bringing with him his pen and paper as he searched for a tranquil place to draw, unconstrained. Noticing the gaping opening in that same farthest wall, behind the crates and tables, he had bent his lanky body down and peeked inside. Surprised, he had quickly jumped back. There, alone and deep in her private flight of the imagination, was a young girl reading. Totally absorbed, she beguilingly munched on a chocolate confection, her mouth covered in the dark brown luscious cream.

He tapped, and her body jumped, banging her head on the eaves.

"Ow!" She looked up, her face screwed into an unhappy glare of pain and surprise.

She had been overwhelmed at first sight of him, a young man with tousled hair and long, elegant hands. Then, fearful that this interloper, discovering her secret spot, would tattle on her, she hissed, "What do you want?"

He had put his fingers to his lips, and then smiled shyly. "*Shhush!*"

He quickly assured her he would keep her private space a secret—with the understanding that he would be able to draw quietly nearby. In truth, they were somewhat familiar with each other: Cornelius knew of her from a distance as "the Collins child from Skunk Hollow over in Hartland." She only knew him as that tall, older boy (all of eleven, mind you!) who didn't talk much but liked to draw.

As time went on throughout the year, they came upon each other in the quiet room, then found their meetings coincided weekly on the designated school visits to the library. Stealing an hour away from their own separate worlds, they entered their private haven with respect for each other's privacy and quiet. It was here, over time, that they became fast friends, sharing ideas and thoughts. Their innocent pastime would often turn to fantasy, where their combined imaginations knew no boundaries. Here, he could draw the rich stories she could conjure up. Here, they could make believe they were pirates stashing their treasure on a deserted island or pioneers using this hidden area as a sanctuary against wild Indians. Often as not, though, their time together was dominated by collectively peaceful, safe moments where she would read quietly while he would draw, their silent endeavors strangely comforting to each other.

Now, years later, Cornelius bent down and reached for something on the inside kneewall floor. He held out his hand, smiling. She took the remnants of a chocolate-stained square paper, one which had previously covered a sweet confection. The outside wrapper read, "*Fry and Fils Chocolatiers.*" "*Chocolat Delicieux a Manger*" was elegantly written underneath. Their nostrils were filled with a sweet smell of chocolate within the closed space, still evident even after time. She laughed, pointing to the other wayward wrappers that dotted the floor of the small space, the remnants of the bonbons and chocolate creams, the boiled sweets she loved so much!

He gave her hand a squeeze, covering the wrapper, which made faint crinkling sounds. "My, my, missy, you and your chocolate! Such a sweets lover—you are shameful! My terrible little *sweetness*," he chided her, using the special name he had created just for her. He remembered Maggie's little girl body curled up in the small space, reading her books and lost in her fantasy literary world. As they grew older, how her face would light up when she was torn from her book to look up and see him looking down at her. She would scoot over, and he would sit beside her in the dim light, drawing her as she read. Yes, they shared each other's secrets, hopes, and dreams.

She smiled, and said softly, "Uh, huh. *Your* 'Sweetness,' Conny."

They both smiled at their private joke. She poked her head further into the space, straining to see into the dimness. Her voice echoed in the empty space and she exclaimed, "Oh, look, Conny! It's still here! Where you carved our initials! How very dear that was!"

Inside, in the far corner, were the finely etched carvings of CLV, linked directly beside the initials MDC, conjoined so closely that all the letters melded together into a jumble: MDCCLV.

"Yes, sweetness, of course it is!" Underneath the script, at the very bottom of the panel, he had also roughly carved the numbers "1855."

He had been all of thirteen years old; she had been ten when he had carved this date on the panel. Even then, their intermingled oneness was apparent as they had shared and discussed their quixotic ideas and hopes, the best of friends.

She traced their initials, now longingly wishing for those unhampered days and whispered, "Margaret Dorothy Collins, Cornelius Lorenzo Veakey….." once, and then again, in singsong, *"Margaret Dorothy Collins, Cornelius Lorenzo Veakey."*

She stood up and turned toward him; they kissed ardently once more, the memories of their young intertwined lives now coming full force into view with the new reality that they would not be together again for a very long time.

Finally, he broke away and said with resignation. "You must go soon, sweetness. But before you go, I have so much to say. So little time…"

She protested, and he smiled gently. "Now, now, my darling girl, look here! I've brought you a present…just for you." He reached behind him on the table, bringing forth a mid-sized square package whose approximate measurement was 17" by 19". It was wrapped in an oilcloth stained with the bright colors of his oil brushes and tied off with frayed, jute-like twine roughly cut with a scoring knife.

"Oh, Conny! What… have you done?"

"Well, open it, silly one!"

She untied the string, carefully storing it in her dress pocket, and then slowly unwrapped the thick oilskin from the hard surface beneath. She peeled back the thick covering slowly, then gasped. Poignant, huge tears were stinging her eyes once more. She held up the oil painting and looked at it closely.

"Oh! Oh, my! I can't believe it! It's…our special place! You painted our secret picnic spot, up on the far hill! Oh, my darling man!"

She viewed the colorful landscape of the remote, hidden area, precious to her and Conny, located at the furthest boundaries, the "williwags," of her father's farm. Most of the 100 acres of rough farmland was worked alone by her father, in this area of Hartland untouched by industry. And yes, there in the distance, far below, was the huge pasture with their farmhouse, the Collins homestead, barely visible. There was the large stream that meandered down the far, remote mountainside, beautifully interpreted.

However, the focal point — and most important part of the image in front of her — was the most special place she had brought Conny that first summer day long ago. It was the gentle swirling, cool pools of a private swimming hole. Since that first time, it had been their spot to meet privately. Truth be told, traveling all the way from Pillsonville had been a trial for him, but worth it, and when they spent their secret time together, it was as if all time stood still.

"I just — well, I can't believe it!" She threw her arms around him, and they hugged each other with intensity, fully realizing the sense of urgency, and the innocence they were leaving behind today for good.

How on earth could she let him go?

"It's so beautiful! Thank you." She turned back to admire and fully study the wonderful gift he had painted just for her.

The oil painting's beautiful vibrant nature scene was a study in color and intensity. He had captured the essence of this quiet water sanctuary, their private meeting spot where all was right with the world. The natural beauty of the still pools and small reservoirs was interspersed with the intense whiteness of the bubbling water, which cascaded with abandon down the tiers of progressively larger, unusually formed rocks. The darker pool at the end of the rapids had the intensity of purple velvet, a private lagoon rich with fish, turtles and frogs. It was a remarkably peaceful and serene setting, captured with the artist's expertise of coloration and hue.

The trees along the creek seemed to beckon the viewer to come and sit, to reflect. It was a scene that intrigued one's imagination with a sense of privacy, a respite to the weary or tired in the heat of the summer.

He had signed the painting simply, *Conny, 1861.*

"I just finished it yesterday!" He smiled and a faraway look came into his eyes. "Gosh, remember how interminably hot it was last summer? So much fun! Hottest summer on record, so they say. Especially in August!"

"*Hoo*! I guess!"

"Those scorching dog days of summer! So much fun, swimming in the cool water, and diving off the rocks—right there!" He pointed, "—into the deep end? And the fishing, gaw! It'll always be *Maggie's Stream* to me…that's what we'll call it now, after you! And it's our memory, forever—no one else's, but our's. Oh, Maggie…" His words trailed off.

He sighed and gave her a lopsided grin. "At any rate, my dear, we've had the most wonderful times there, and I wanted you to remember, you know, to always remember it all…while I am gone." He looked at her, adoring her, his artist mind retaining every line, every expression, every beautiful piece of her face so that he dare remember it all.

"It's beautiful, just beautiful! Maggie's Stream, yes…our special place." Her eyes brimmed over, and she swallowed back tears. She smiled up at him, longingly. "It's where we…." Her words halted and she blushed, her long lashes low, and he filled in the words.

"I know. It's where we pledged our love forever, sweetness."

She nodded, "Oh, Cornelius, I will miss you so!" Holding the painting close to her breast, she declared resolutely, "Every time I look at this, I'll think about all our fun, swimming together, and, oh! The picnics! And catching frogs!" They laughed lightly and her voice became wistful. "And that hot, hot summer sun trying to capture us in its grip from the cool shade! So much to remember! But especially," her eyes gazed at him, transfixed, "I'll think about how dear you are to me."

"And will you remember the first kiss I gave you, right there?" He pointed to a section of the scene where a small, half-grown maple tree and its funny crooked lower limb hung with determined impudence, extending out and over the rushing water, a dainty, twisted bough gently brushing the current below.

She gasped, eyes fluttering, and blushed deeply. "Sir, you embarrass me!" Then, they both giggled like two schoolchildren. "And where you carved our initials, too, just like you did here, behind the wall!"

He turned the painting over in her hands, nodding. Then, turning solemn, he whispered, "Read the inscription. Here, sweetness, on the back."

Written in fine penmanship with a rough artist's pencil, were the words: "'*To my Sweetness. May our love endure forever. 'C.'*'"

One forlorn tear dropped from her long lash, splashing onto the painting's rough brown paper backing. She placed the painting solemnly on the nearby library table.

Cornelius took her small hands in his as his face, too, became very serious. "I have something else, Maggie, something I want to ask you."

"What is it, darling?" His serious look worried her.

Cornelius slowly went down on one knee. His saber sword clattered unceremoniously as the pointed end of the sword's steel scabbard hit the floor. He brushed the scabbard back and looked up at her from his kneeling position.

Taking a deep breath, he stuttered, "I—I know I should have gone to your father first, but….there was no time. I promise I will write him, and ask him formally, but...dearest Maggie, will you… wait for me?"

She looked down at him.

He cleared his throat bravely in anticipation. "Margaret Dorothy Collins, will you be my wife upon my return?" His hands still clutched hers; his dark eyes reached deeply into hers, intense orbs filled with the passion of the moment.

She leaned down and kissed his upturned face, her own face buoyant and overflowing with concentrated, unchecked, happiness.

She whispered intensely, "Oh, my darling man. Don't you know how much I love you?" Hands still held tightly in his, a tear slipped unchecked down her cheek, then toppled off her chin and landed on her breast, splashing with total abandon. "My dear, *dearest* man. Of course I will wait for you....forever! I love you! And I *will* marry you! You'll see," she assured him earnestly. "Father will come around. I know he will! He already knows, though he doesn't want to admit it. It will all work out!"

As they sealed their promise to each other with a kiss, a sharp voice rang out, shattering their private world. "You say somebody is in the restricted area?" A pause as feet scurried, voices murmured. Then, a loud booming voice rang out, *"Who's up there?"*

Oh, no! Miss Bromley! Her words were as cold as icy water to the face, and they both went into action as they heard the Librarian's heavy footsteps marching to the second level, then pausing in the hallway. Since the strict librarian had arrived a year ago, her constant attention to the Library's policies had been circumspect, in particular, to the "off limits" third floor rule, sometimes compromising their secret meeting spot.

"Oh! Cornelius!" Maggie whispered desperately. "She's coming all the way up here!"

Cornelius picked up the painting and quickly wrapped it back into the oilskin sheathing. She drew the string out of her pocket and he tied off the painting, and then looked at Maggie in desperation. Determined footsteps at the second level moved quickly and, with strong foreboding, began the ascent to the third floor.

Flustered, Maggie pointed to their secret hiding place. He reached behind him and quickly wedged the painting deeply inside the open knee wall chamber. Quietly, together, they neatly slid the wooden panel back into place. The slight scraping noise betrayed their location.

"I say! Who's up here? I know you're here." Louder, closer, the voice echoed from the third floor landing.

He whispered to Maggie, "You go! I'll come down later. She mustn't find us together. Go!" She reached desperately, without words, toward the closed panel. Her eyes pleaded, saying, *what about the painting*? He whispered hoarsely, "You can come back and get it another time! Go, go, now!"

In a split second she had raised her mouth to his and kissed him quickly, her lips warm and soft as they brushed his, and then, after one longing last look, she turned and ran out of the room, squeezing between the long tables lining the hallway.

She lightly called out, "It's only me, Miss Bromley! Lord, how you fuss!"

"What on earth? Is that you, Margaret? I thought I saw you come in ages ago. Child, what are you doing up here? You know this area is off limits to patrons!"

Maggie curtsied to Miss Bromley, bowing her head as though she knew her only response should be total regret and apology.

"I...I'm sorry, Miss Bromley. It won't happen again."

Somewhat appeased, Miss Bromley said curtly, "Honestly! With all that I have to do! Mercy! Come down with me, straight away!"

"Yes, Miss Bromley."

Miss Bromley shook her head in exasperation, revolving back around in one swift movement. She moved rapidly down the stairs, clucking impatiently. Why, she was much too busy to deal with wayward patrons!

Maggie turned quickly back to the entryway. Conny's head peeked around the doorway and he winked.

Maggie gave him one last smile, bold and valiant, as though committed to providing him with this last remembrance of her as happy, not sad. She quickly wiped away the tears that had spilled onto her blushing cheeks. It was the last smile he would ever see on her beautiful face. He gave her a slight, quick wave and she disappeared down the stairway.

He waited, standing perfectly still as he stood watching from the third floor half-moon window. Moments later, he recognized her slight figure racing out through the big front door, then down the brick walkway to the waiting horse and buggy.

As it rumbled down the gravel lane, spitting a cloud of powdery snow, dust, and grime behind it, he gave a gentle sigh. *Good-bye, my Sweetness...*

The buggy wended its way up the snow-dusted country road about twenty-odd rods, past the distant General Store, then much further along, passing by the Village Green, becoming a slow-moving, infinitesimal, black dot as it rounded the corner toward Town Hall, until she was forever gone from his sight.

———————•◆•———————

And so, the Library had closed within a week, and the money saved by its closing was designated by the State of Vermont to be sent over the remaining years to the war effort's brutal conflict. Maggie had intended to retrieve the painting in those next few days after her bittersweet final meeting with Conny, but she could not get into the building in time before it closed. Large padlocks were put on the massive front doors, the windows were boarded up, and a huge sign stated starkly: "CLOSED FOR THE WAR EFFORT." Consequently, Maggie's intention had been to return and rescue her dear fiancé's gift when the library reopened; and so, it sat behind the wall, irretrievable for that space of time, but not forgotten, throughout the next nineteen months. Then tragedy struck and the painting was brutally forced out of her mind, replaced with grief and despair. Sadly, Cornelius was just one of the 51,000 total Gettysburg casualties in the three-day campaign that ended so wretchedly, its brutal battle finalizing, with heartrending reality for many mothers and fathers, the fate of their brave sons.

Chapter Three

Another Mother's Son Returns

The merriment was in full force. Amidst the resulting hubbub, the phone's shrill '*Brinngg!*' rang out, and Mrs. Bundle motioned from across the room to Jack to grab it.

Jack spoke briefly, then raised the phone in the air, "You'll want to take this, mum!"

She made her way toward the phone, asking, "Who is it?"

Jack just smiled, his friendly, lopsided, Irish grin, and handed her the phone.

Her interest piqued as she said, "Hello?"

"Mom? Mom, how are you?"

"Leslie? Oh, Leslie, dear! How are you? Is everything okay?" Remarkably, their connection was clear as a bell as she conversed with her son over five thousand miles away in Japan.

"Mom, everyone's fine—what the heck's going on there? It sounds like you're inside a train station!"

"Oh, we're having a little celebration. The Festival, you know, last week? The Dog Days of Summer Art Festival? We've had a grand time with it! I've got *quite* a lot to tell you, Leslie. It was a huge success, and we've had a *wonderful* mystery—and, oh, yes! The murder is solved, Leslie! Did I tell you?"

"Mom, you promised me—"

"Oh! Let's not waste the minutes, Leslie. You go first. Tell me about what's been happening with you!"

"Well, I've got some great news! No!" He covered the phone, then returned, "Wait just a sec, Mom."

Mrs. Bundle could hear other voices and rustling in the background. She waited patiently, barely making out her son's muffled words to someone nearby him, "Please, yes...you're excited, I know! All right, here you go...*you* tell your Grandmother."

Mrs. Bundle said excitedly, "Leslie, is that Les with you?"

A boy's voice came onto the line, older, more mature than the voice from last month's conversation. "*Gram*? Hi Gram! Hey!"

"Oh, Les, it's just wonderful to hear your voice! How are you? How's the baseball going?"

"Gram, listen! We're coming home!" There was silence on the other end, and he asked, "Gram, are you happy?"

"You're...coming *here*? For a visit? Oh, Les, really, dear? That's... *fantastical*!"

"Yuh, right! But, Gram! We're coming home....for good! To the States!"

Mrs. Bundle held the phone a good distance away and couldn't contain herself. "*Hoo-hooo!*" She waved the handset with unbridled delight and yelled, "*Yippee!*" just for good measure while the many friendly faces in the room stood gawking at the usually-mild-mannered lady.

"It's my grandson! From Japan!" She cradled the handset, "Hang on just a sec, Les!" She motioned to a nearby Jack to come close and she grabbed him with her free hand. "Jack! They're coming home! To be with us!" He put his arm around her, his eyes dancing, reflecting her happiness, while Cracker jumped up in delight.

She yelled breathlessly, "Walter!"

"Yuh-huh?"

"Can you find that champagne? Over there?"

"You betcha! Carl?" A wave across the room from Carl indicated he was on the task, and Walter whooped, "Open that bubbly quick, would you, son? Let's get this *swarry* goin'!"

Oh, happy day!

Final Footnote

Chapter Four

Au Revoir, Armand

From *The Rutland Daily News* late Friday afternoon edition, September 12, 2003

Con Artist/Arsonist Confesses— Blames All on Love

Founding Father George Pillson is probably turning in his grave after hearing of a man claiming to be his direct descendant who was, in reality, a con artist, arsonist, and whose lineage appear to be far less notable.

Pedigree may be the least of his worries as a North Pillson Corners man, confessing he conspired with his lover, has admitted responsibility for three acts of arson that occurred earlier this summer; he will go to prison for a 5-to-12-year term, with no chance of parole earlier than 2010, beginning immediately at Southern State Correctional Facility.

Waiving his rights to a preliminary hearing, Armand Limpert, 55, of North Puckerbrush Road, was sentenced Friday in White River Junction's Vermont District Court.

He pleaded guilty to three counts of first-degree arson along with one count of unlawful mischief. The first-degree arson charges involved separate fires at the following buildings: the popular local eatery, Tuddy's Diner; the Wrinkle's General Store in Brownsville; and a North Hartland hunting camp. The misdemeanor "unlawful mischief" charge was for defiling the *Welcome to Hartland* municipal sign in June.

Asking, through his attorney, that he be sentenced quickly so that he could begin serving his prison term immediately, Limpert acknowledged that he helped his then-girlfriend, Mrs. Elvina Wrinkle, set the fires. Mrs. Wrinkle is the same alleged felon that weeks ago was arrested and charged with the premeditated first degree murder of Watson DeVille, a local well-respected, retired professor.

In related cases, Mrs. Wrinkle has also been charged with four counts of attempted second-degree murder, three counts of arson, two counts of attempted arson, and one count of property insurance fraud. The District Attorney's office has also begun an investigation (per court-filed documents) alleging that Mrs. Wrinkle "deliberately and with premeditation" carried out the murder of her husband, Norbert Andrew Wrinkle, who died in February of 2003 at Dartmouth-Hitchcock Medical Center. The medical records and death certificate state that he died after suffering "severe head trauma from a fall off a snow-covered roof."

At the special hearing, Limpert apologized for his actions and begged the court for mercy, indicating he was, as he stated, "overcome by the wiles of my paramour and forced into doing things I would normally never have done."

Breaking down and sobbing a number of times, he made the following statement: "I would like to say how sorry I am for what I have done, and for what I have put everyone through, especially the cherished people of Pillson who put their trust in me. I really don't know what I was thinking and hope they can forgive me. I am humbled and shamed by this experience. Passion and lust can do strange things to people, and I rue the day I ever got involved with Mrs. Wrinkle." A number of his victims sat stone-faced in the courtroom, clearly unimpressed with his display of emotion.

As part of his sentence, Limpert will also have to pay restitution to victims for any uninsured losses of up to $200,000, payment to begin six months after he leaves prison. On a related matter, Mr. Limpert's attorney also verified reports that all of his client's real estate, personal property (including an extensive art collection), and all valuables have been seized by the government for unpaid taxes. Having passed himself off as a descendant of George Pillson, the apparent phony blueblood had no comment on this matter directly, only stating through his attorney that he would work out the details related to restitution and back taxes in accordance with the court's determinations.

Although the State brought only these four charges against him, investigators have allegedly linked Limpert to all the other related misdeeds but chose, in a plea-bargain, to allow him to turn state's evidence and cooperate with prosecutors to reduce his sentence in exchange for his future testimony against Mrs. Wrinkle, who at this time is being held without bail in the Women's Southeast State Facility in Windsor, and whose trial date has not yet been set.

The End

AUTHOR'S FINAL NOTES
&
BBLIOGRAPHY

1. Page 7, Browning, Robert; Pippa's Song, "All's Right With the World."

2. Page 413, Natalie's history of chocolate taken from various combined internet sites and sources.

3. Page 477, Carroll, Lewis; Alice in Wonderland quote

4. Pages 478, Carroll, Lewis; Alice in Wonderland quotes

5. Page 589, Captain Randall's written report of Gettysburg's Cemetery Hill Battle was taken from his original accounting and direct quotes from the *Gettysburg Order of Battles*.

6. Page 633-635, After the author's joyful "hands-on" research of various delectable recipe combinations (to accommodate the tale, mind you), all recipes were modified or embellished as has been done for centuries by cooks throughout the world.

RECIPES

Mrs. Bundle kindly offers this section
(usually designated for her own recipes)
to the following three very special women:

WEEZY'S
STRAWBERRY SHORTCAKE RECIPE

The **Biscuits**:

> 425° preheated oven. 2 cups all-purpose flour, 1 tablespoon baking powder, ½ teaspoon salt, 2 tablespoons sugar, 1 stick butter cut into 8 pieces, chilled, ²/₃ to ³/₄ cup milk or cream.

Cut butter into dry ingredients and mix lightly, stir in cream until mixed—do not overmix! Roll out and cut into 8 nice thick rounds. Cook in buttered, foil-lined cookie sheet. Bake for 10-15 minutes until golden brown.

> 1 quart fresh strawberries, hulled and cut in quarters
> A bowl filled with gobs of fresh whipped cream

Cut the biscuits horizontally in three sections. Put lower piece into a dessert bowl. Add a layer of strawberries. Put the next top on and slather on a good amount more of strawberries. Put the top on, add more strawberries and mountains of whipped cream. Serves 8.

(Weezy's notation: *Multiply this recipe by 20 if you need to feed an army—or put on a Festival.*)

Mrs. Balshemnik's
Rugulach or "Schnecken"

To make the Dough:

1 (8 oz) package cream cheese
2 sticks (1/2 lb) sweet salted butter
2 cups pre-sifted flour

Filling:

White sugar, cinnamon, finely chopped walnuts, sweet shredded coconut, finely diced maraschino cherries or dried cranberries—or raisins, if you prefer.

Let cream cheese and butter stand in mixing bowl until room temperature (or can be easily blended). Cut the two together with a fork. Add 2 cups of pre-sifted flour, a little at a time, using your hands and kneading together until all flour is absorbed and a ball can be formed. Chill in refrigerator or freeze for later use. When ready, take half of the dough and roll it out on a floured board with a floured rolling pin, rolling lightly into a round. Repeat with the other half so you have two rounds.

Sprinkle filling ingredients: white sugar, cinnamon, finely chopped walnuts, sweet shredded coconut and maraschino cherries or dried cranberries. Slice the sprinkled circle into halves, then quarters. Working with one quarter at a time, cut slices, like you would a pizza: 3 pieces each. Roll up each slice widest to the center point and tucking the point underneath like a pinroll—pinch this so it will stay in place.

Place on floured cookie sheet and brush each one lightly with slightly beaten egg. Bake at 350 degrees for about 10-12 minutes, or until toasty. Makes 24 rugulach.

(Mrs. Balshemnik's note: *Ess gezunterhait*—Eat in good health!)

Maggie Tudhope's
Famous Old-Fashioned Hot Cocoa Recipe

1 cup scalded milk
1 cup boiling water
1 ½ tablespoon sugar
2 tablespoons cocoa

Mix cocoa and sugar. Add boiling water, boil for a few minutes, then pour in scalded milk. Beat well and serve. serves 2. Recipe can be combined tenfold to serve twenty-odd eatery customers.

(Maggie Tudhope's note: *Chocolate brings solace to our deepest sorrows.*)

About the Author

ALLISON CESARIO PATON, author of the Mrs. Bundle Mystery Books, grew up in Vermont and has deep respect and love for Vermont, its rich history, and its people. She enjoys their unique views on life and the rest of the world.

Allison and her husband, John, a native Vermonter, divide their time between Scarborough, Maine and southern Vermont, where they thoroughly enjoyed the unique experience of rehabbing an 1830s brick cottage. They also love to ski, take long rides through back country roads, and try new wines.

Her sojourn into the creative genre of mystery fiction began in early 2001 when she first created the "little world" of Mrs. Bundle and North Pillson Corners, a place that intertwines two families and their exploits and is rich with strong female protagonists, tradition, danger, local color, and intrigue. She wanted her stories to be universal in appeal; her readers include every age group from young women to those people "of a mature age." She also uses real towns, landmarks, buildings, stores, topography and events to tell each story, all set in a village modeled after the real Vermont villages that inspired her.

Both the author and Mrs. Bundle agree that, "Really LIVING every day to its fullest means going from complete certainty to complete discovery."